MW00813921

THE KNIGHTS OF ERADOR

THE ECHOES SAGA: BOOK SEVEN

PHILIP C. QUAINTRELL

This is a work of fiction. Names, characters, places, and incidents either are the product of the author's imagination or are used fictitiously. Any resemblance to actual persons, living or dead, events, or locales is entirely coincidental.

Copyright © 2020 by Philip C. Quaintrell
First edition published 2020.

All rights reserved. No part of this book may be reproduced or used in any manner without written permission of the copyright owner except for the use of quotations in a book review.

Cover Illustration by Chris McGrath
Book design by BodiDog Design
Edited by David Bradley

ISBN: 978-1-916610-15-6 (hardback)
ASIN: B0851JCZYV (ebook)

Published by Quaintrell Publishings

For Paul and James - thank you for falling in love with this world...

ALSO BY PHILIP C. QUAINTRELL

THE
NIGHT
SEA

THE DREAD WOOD

SILVYR HALL

HYNDAERN

NIMDUHN

STORM'S REACH

THE BROKEN MOUNTAINS

KH.

SNOWPE.

THE RUINS OF TOR VALAN

THE WAVETOWER OF ARQUNSUIN

DRAKANAN

DRAYMON

THE RED FIELDS OF DURMAR

FREYGARD

SUNHOLD

CARSTANE

THE VENG.

THE DEEP

THE CITY OF NAETH

MOUNT KALISTA

THE RUINS OF VALANDAR

THE TOWER OF JAIN

VANGALA

ERADOR

RIVERWATCH

ELDERHALL

THE HOX

FARNFOSS

THEDARIA

TORINN

CARTHAM

WARTH

LAKE TALON

HEMON

THE RED HOLD

HARAN'S TOWN

ALLISANDER

BROADCASTLE

QALANGATH

OLD DRIFT

DRAMATIS PERSONAE

Adilandra Sevari

The elven queen of Elandril and mother of Reyna Galfrey

Alijah Galfrey

Half-elf and King of Erador

Asher

Human ranger

Athis

Red dragon, bonded with Inara

Doran Heavybelly

A Dwarven Ranger/Prince of Clan Heavybelly

Ellöria Sevari

The Lady of Ilythyra

Faylen Haldör

DRAMATIS PERSONAE

An elf and High Guardian of Elandril

Galanör Reveeri
An elven ranger

Gideon Thorn
Master Dragorn

Ilargo
Green dragon, bonded with Gideon

Inara Galfrey
Half-elf Dragorn

Kassian Kantaris
A Keeper of Valatos

Lady Gracen
The governess of Felgarn and lady of Lirian

Nathaniel Galfrey
An ambassador and previous knight of the Graycoats

Reyna Galfrey
Elven princess of Elandril and Illian ambassador

Sir Ruban Dardaris
Captain of the King's Guard

The Crow (Sarkas)
Late Leader of The Black Hand

Vighon Draqaro
King of Illian

PROLOGUE

For more miles than he cared to consider, Glamren Stormshield had heard nothing but the sound of the wind, its howl whipping through his hair and whistling past his ears. Now, standing before the tallest trees the dwarf had ever seen, the wind fell away as if snatched by the forest itself.

The towering pines stretched north and south, disappearing into the mist in both directions. It was dark inside, a place where even the sun dared not venture. Glamren had never seen the trees of The Dread Wood before, but he had heard enough legends to stay out of them. In fact, he had heard enough tales to keep well away from the place.

In that eerie silence, Glamren could only hear the laboured breaths of his companions. The company of four said not a word in the shadow of the pines.

Then there came a sound...

A long exhalation blew out from The Dread Wood, washing over the dwarves, before it was then inhaled by those same trees.

"*Is it just me,*" Orin posed in their dwarven tongue, "*or is the forest... breathing?*"

None of the Stormshields answered. Glamren's eyes shifted anxiously, searching between the trees for any threats. With nearly a century to his name, the dwarf reminded himself that he was experienced enough to handle any monster that a forest could produce; after all, he had faced the real beasts of the world, creatures that lurked beneath The Whispering Mountains...

A twig snapped somewhere beyond the tree line. Glamren gripped his spear. A shadow darted through the wood.

It was unsettling.

For the first time in many years, the dwarf could feel the cold touch of fear taking a hold of his bones. The company of dwarves kept their eyes fixed on those trees, too anxious to look away.

Ferek shook his head, his large axe hefted in both hands. "*We shouldn't be here,*" he warned. "*I told you we were going too far west!*"

Dovum crunched forward through the snow, his head tilted to the side. "*Nothing,*" he said. "*No sound at all. No birds... No anything.*"

"*There's something right unnatural about it,*" Orin added, his crossbow levelled.

"*Of course it ain't natural!*" Ferek snapped. "*It's the bloody Dread Wood! We've all heard the stories. We're not supposed to come this far west. We've got no business leaving the mountains.*"

"*Easy fellas,*" Glamren croaked, his voice out of practice. "*They're just trees. Never has a dwarf feared the likes of a wood, especially Stormshields,*" he added, wondering why his words sounded so hollow.

Dovum gave a sympathetic shrug. "*Ferek's got a point though, Glamren. Why* are *we here?*"

Tearing his eyes from The Dread Wood, Glamren looked over his shoulder to take in the jagged line of mountains behind them. "*Because orders are orders - you know that as well as I.*"

Orin huffed. "*The king can shove his orders up Grarfath's—*"

"*Stow it!*" Glamren barked, pushing his own fear down in the hope of burying it under aggression. "*The Hammerkegs have been getting sneakier of late. Remember their attack on the southern outpost?*

2

The king's fearing for Hyndaern's flank. If their clan were to find a way north on this side of the mountains, the city might be vulnerable. That's why we're here."

Ferek looked north and south along the stretch of snow that separated the woods from the mountains. *"Well, I don't see no Hammerkegs!"*

"Aye," Orin chipped in. *"Back to Hyndaern I say!"*

Glamren shook his head in despair. *"I never thought I'd see the day you two lost your nerve because of some trees..."* The dwarf trailed off, his attention caught by Dovum or, more specifically, Dovum's wide eyes. *"What is it?"* he demanded, following his companion's gaze into The Dread Wood.

"There's something in there," Dovum whispered.

Orin and Ferek braced themselves with weapons raised. Glamren didn't miss Ferek's quick look to check that the passage back into the mountains was still clear.

Another twig snapped from within the wood and two shadows dashed through the trees before vanishing. The urge to fight had long been a trait associated with those of Glamren's bloodline, but something about The Dread Wood made him want to turn and run as fast as he could.

Glamren huffed and pointed his spear at the trees: he had orders. It took some effort to convince his legs to take action but, one after the other, his feet ploughed through the thick snow, taking him closer to the trees.

"What are you doing?" Ferek hissed.

Glamren paused to reply over his shoulder. *"If there's something out there, we need to make sure it ain't no Hammerkegs."* The dwarf flicked his head. *"Now spread out."*

Ferek and Orin appeared to be on the verge of insubordination until Dovum pulled free his sword and went south of Glamren. The other two reluctantly fanned out to the north.

Passing through the trees was an experience unlike any other Glamren could recall. The air was thick and oppressive, a contrast to the crisp chill that threatened to steal one's breath in the clearing. Overhead, there was nothing but pines and shadow...

Looking to his left, he could just make out Dovum between the branches and trunks. To Glamren's right, Ferek and Orin were sticking closer together than he would have preferred, concerned that the net they were casting wouldn't be wide enough to catch the Hammerkegs.

"*Pss!*" Glamren waited for Ferek to find him before encouraging the dwarf to advance.

The Stormshields pushed on as one, their silvyr armour dulled by the natural darkness of The Dread Wood. Glamren was the first to find evidence of intelligent life creeping between the trees. The stout warrior crouched down and examined what were clearly boot prints in the snow. They were far apart, suggesting that the one who created the prints was either moving fast or tall in stature.

"*Pss!*"

Turning south, Glamren discovered Dovum had come across similar prints, though whether they belonged to the same individual remained to be seen. The other dwarf held up his boot and motioned for Glamren to place his own inside one of the tracks. Obliging, he side-stepped to bring himself in line with the running prints.

The tracks were narrower than his own, but certainly longer.

There were a few creatures who could claim to possess such a foot, but the first, and most obvious one, that came to Glamren's mind was a human...

"*Impossible,*" he mumbled.

Dovum's heavy footfalls gave away his advance and it became clear that the dwarf was following the tracks towards Glamren. "*They're going north,*" he observed quietly.

"*Aye,*" Glamren agreed, "*but who are they?*"

Dovum nodded along. "*They don't belong to no dwarf,*" he stated confidently. "*I'd say they're human if I had to guess.*"

Glamren was shaking his head before his companion had finished speaking. "*There ain't no humans north of Vengora, never mind* west of *The Whispering Mountains. I'd bet me place in Grarfath's Hall no human has ever even* seen *The Dread Wood. It just can't be...*"

"*Look!*" Dovum pointed his sword between the trees. "*There's more of them!*"

Glamren looked up from the boot prints with a growing pit in his stomach. Dovum was right; the disturbed snow farther into the wood was undoubtedly more tracks - tracks without apparent owners. The two dwarves explored beyond the nearest trees and attempted to guess at the number of the opposing party. There were too many, however, and the piled snow made it even harder.

"*They outnumber us,*" Dovum surmised.

Glamren agreed, though he countered, "*We don't* know *that they pose a threat. These are just tracks.*"

Dovum arched a frozen copper eyebrow. "*We're in The Dread Wood, Glamren - everything is a threat. Especially humans who aren't supposed to be here.*"

"*True enough,*" Glamren conceded, hoping, more than anything, that he hadn't walked his companions into a trap. "*Alright, we've seen enough to know that something ain't right. Let's get back to Hyndaern and report our findings. I'm going to suggest that we post a battalion on this side of the mountains - do a proper sweep of the tree line.*"

Dovum was in happy agreement as his eyes scanned the gaps between the trees. "*Let's tell them two the good news and get back to the mountains.*"

Glamren's spear led the way north, along the tracks, as they searched for Ferek and Orin. "*How far did those idiots go?*"

Weaving between the trees, the dwarves searched frantically, their concern growing with every crunch of snow beneath their boots. They quickly found their companions' tracks but they went on and on, leading, seemingly, nowhere but deeper into the forest.

Coming across a small rise of dark rocks, Glamren stepped up and climbed over them using one hand on the stone for support. Reaching the other side, he gripped his spear in both hands again to continue the hunt for his companions.

Red...

It was an easy colour to spot in a landscape of browns, greens, and white snow. The haft of his spear was stained with what could only be blood. Glamren stopped in his tracks and looked from the spear, to his hand, and back to the rocks. That pit in his stomach was becoming cavernous.

"*Blood...*" Dovum whispered absently, his eyes darting across what little they could see of the forest.

Glamren spun on his heel to face one way then another, his rage churning. "*Ferek!*" he cried. "*Orin!*"

A voice of warning told Glamren that shouting was a foolish thing to do in a place such as this, but he feared for his companions, both counted as friends long before they became soldiers in King Gandalir's army.

They pushed on a little farther until they came across a scene that robbed both dwarves of their breath.

"*Ferek...*" Glamren let his spear fall to the snow as he approached the blood-soaked tree.

Pinned to the trunk, several feet in the air, Ferek's lifeless body hung limply, his torso impaled by a spear too long to be wielded by any dwarf. Whoever had killed him struck swiftly and with great efficiency to have speared Ferek through the narrow gaps in his silvyr armour, not to mention the strength required to pin him so high.

At eye line, Glamren gripped the boot of his old friend, which was dripping wet with blood. Looking up, Ferek's chin rested against his breastplate, but his eyes were wide open, still filled with shock.

"*Who could have done this?*" Dovum questioned, holding back his grief. "*To have killed him without a sound, and with such brutality!*"

Glamren was asking himself that same question. The length of the spear suited a human, but he didn't recognise its make nor the red cloth that hung from the end.

"*Humans couldn't have done this,*" he concluded, sure in his heart that they were dealing with something far more monstrous. "*Where's Orin?*" he demanded, searching the bloody scene.

There was no sign of the youngest among their party. If they had been attacked, and by a larger force, it stood to reason that he would have retreated to the mountains for more advantageous surroundings.

Glamren growled, picked up his spear, and charged through The Dread Wood. He could hear nothing but the crunch of snow and the blood pounding in his ears. He wanted to shout out to Orin, but he kept his mouth shut and continued his run back to the tree line.

As glimpses of the clearing shone white through the trees, Glamren had the spark of hope in his heart. He had come across no enemies nor their tracks, but he was sure he had caught sight of Orin between the trees, standing in the snow...

Finally breaking through the trees, Orin was indeed standing in the clearing. No, he wasn't standing, the young dwarf was staggering towards the mountain pass. One hand clung to his throat while the other hung by his side, absent his crossbow.

"*Orin?*" he called, his hope slowly being sucked down into that bottomless pit.

Orin stopped and turned around. His blond beard was stained red and his face was similarly splattered. Bloodshot eyes focused on Glamren, though there was little recognition in them, only fear. Fresh, rich blood pulsed between his fingers, steadily drenching him. It was a mortal wound if ever Glamren had seen one.

First he dropped to his knees. His eyes glazed over and lost their life. Then, he fell face first into the snow, dead. Glamren almost choked on his shock and grief, but a righteous anger rose up in him, demanding his full attention and instant action. He spun around to face Dovum with a command to battle...

Dovum wasn't there.

Glamren's orders died on his lips. The Stormshield levelled his spear at the forest and scanned everything in sight. The only tracks were his own.

"*Dovum?*" he hissed.

The forest wasn't quiet, it was devoid of all sound, a vacuum that consumed any sign of life. Glamren swallowed hard, determined to let his anger drown out his mounting fear. He would find Dovum and avenge his fallen companions. After a quick prayer to Yamnomora and Grarfath, the Mother and Father of dwarf-kind, the Stormshield trekked back into The Dread Wood with the point of his spear raised.

He called quietly to Dovum here and there, but his oldest friend never replied. He had to be alive. Dovum was a veteran of many battles, a capable warrior. Glamren struggled to convince himself that he was still alive, however, having seen so much brutality and death in the last few minutes.

Rounding the next tree, his teeth gritted with resolve, Glamren tripped over something and landed in the snow. He rose to his hands and knees, careful to keep the spear in his grip, and came face to face with Dovum. An extra moment confirmed Glamren's worst fears.

Retrieving his gaze from Dovum's face, he looked back to see that it had been his friend's body that had tripped him up, several feet away from his head...

Glamren gasped and rushed up to his feet. Blood was everywhere. Dovum had been decapitated with what appeared to be a single clean swipe - no easy feat. The Stormshield fell back to his knees as the death toll hit him all at once. Ferek, Orin, and Dovum were gone, just like that. He had known them for decades and fought beside them time and time again.

How could they all be dead?

The silent snow behind him gave way to fresh foot falls, snapping Glamren out of his deep sadness and into a state of battle rage. With his spear in hand, he jumped to his feet and turned on his enemy with fire in his veins.

There was nothing before him but more trees. It did nothing to dampen the fight in him. He turned on the spot, desperate to find something to spear. Then, the distinct sound of a sword being drawn from its scabbard filled the silent air. Then another, and another.

"Show yourselves!" Glamren blurted.

And so they did...

From between the trees, The Dread Wood revealed the enemy that had stalked the Stormshields. Encased in black armour, not a hint of life to see within, they strode towards Glamren with their drawn swords. Dark cloaks flowed over their backs, dragging in the snow behind them. They walked like humans and certainly possessed the height of one, but there was something about them that made the dwarf feel cold, as if his body knew that death itself was coming for him.

The four that advanced on him were soon backed up by dozens more, their sleek black helmets filling the gaps between the trees in every direction. How could there be so many of them?

A war cry on his lips, Glamren did the only thing left to him: he charged. Spear first, he impaled the closest of the dark soldiers through the gut, lifting him off his feet. Driving his foe to the ground, Glamren twisted his spear in a fashion that would ensure death.

Still, the others continued their steady strides showing no reaction to the death of their comrade. It was an odd sight, but Glamren wasn't going to let it distract him - he would kill them all for what they had done to his friends.

Startling the Stormshield, the soldier on the end of his spear gripped the haft, preventing Glamren from removing it. For the second time this day, the dwarf decided that what he was seeing was impossible. The soldier, without so much as a groan, reached up and gripped the spear with his other hand and began to pull himself up the haft, towards Glamren.

"*What foul thing* are *you?*" The words left his lips as he slowly backed away from his own spear.

The armoured soldier found his feet and freed himself of the spear altogether. Not a sound...

Glamren staggered backwards. Death really had been sent to claim him. He tried to form a prayer but the words wouldn't seem to align in his mind.

The soldier who should be dead crouched down and retrieved his sword while his comrades flanked the Stormshield. Fear had finally won out, robbing Glamren of any fight to be had. He looked to Dovum, his friend's fate soon to be his own.

"I'll see you soon, brother..." he whispered, ashamed of the tears that welled in his eyes.

The cold steel that slid through his back, between his ribs, and out through his torso took Glamren's breath away. He barely registered the other three, all of which found gaps in his armour and plunged into his body. In his last moments, he could only hope that Yamnomora would take pity on him and convince Grarfath to give him a place in His hall.

Down on his knees now, he could only watch as a fifth spectre approached. Though clad in the darkest armour and tattered cloak, like the others, this fiend of The Dread Wood wore a helmet that rose into five tall spikes. There were two black slits in the mask, but there was no sign of life looking back at the world.

The dwarf coughed up blood and observed the new soldier pull free his jagged blade. The swing of that blade was the last thing Glamren Stormshield ever saw...

PART ONE

CHAPTER 1
GATHERING SHADOWS

*S*ix months later

Vighon Draqaro looked up at the summer sky, a stretch of wonderful blue that knew no end. Without a cloud in sight, it was a glorious day for basking in the warmth and enjoying the finer things in life.

Except he was bloody freezing.

In The Ice Vales, Illian's western province, the land hadn't known the touch of summer for over a thousand years. The history attributed to the region was well known to the king, who had taken a greater interest in the past since being crowned, and he knew the province had been cursed long ago, during the elven civil war.

It certainly wasn't the best place to call home but, for those who did, they dwelt within the fortress-like city of Grey Stone. Built into the sheer cliffs of Vengora's southern tip, the city itself was hidden behind the rock and more akin to a maze inside, its walls that of the mountain stone.

PHILIP C. QUAINTRELL

Scrutinising the cliff face, Vighon could only see one way in and one way out - a single fissure where the cliff had been broken in two. Fifteen years ago, he and a few brave others had stood their ground in that chasm and kept the hordes of orcs at bay. Those had been simpler times, before he wore a crown...

Now, he was on the other side, wondering how best to take the city when that narrow entrance would reduce his vast army to thirty men abreast as they pushed through. Inside, the high walls would provide the inhabitants with plenty of vantages from which to rain down all manner of assault.

How had it come to this?

Peace. That had always been his goal, the only thing worth wearing the crown for and shouldering all that he did. Now, it was all starting to slip away from the king. Instead of continuing with his life-long task of rebuilding the country, Vighon had marched the majority of his army south from Namdhor to confront Thedomir Longshadow, an old friend.

General Garrett's familiar voice boomed across the landscape as he ordered the soldiers into formation. He had multiple captains under his command, all of whom were more than able to relay his orders, but Garrett was a man who believed in generals being seen doing their job rather than sitting quietly on a horse growing ever larger, as his predecessors had.

Mounted on his own horse, Vighon waited patiently for his general's steed to sidle up beside him. When they had first met, fifteen years ago, Garrett, son of Graynor, was a grizzled warrior, his battles easy to see on his weathered face and in his cool, blue eyes. Now, he was akin to a piece of old leather, though that old leather was still bound to a strong frame that refused to adopt any fat.

Garrett was also the only reason Vighon had yet to give in to the comfortable lifestyle that accompanied royalty and lose his own chiselled frame. At forty-four years of age, the king knew he only had so many good years left with which to apply his body to the tasks of the kingdom. Illian needed a strong and able king and

14

Garrett, one of his closest friends, always ensured Vighon was in shape.

"I told you it would come to this," the general grizzled, adjusting his helmet.

Vighon sighed. "You also told me you wouldn't say that..."

"Well, here we are. And I did tell you. Thedomir Longshadow is a greedy son of a—"

"*Easy*, Garrett," Vighon bade, eyeing his closest subjects around them. "Thedomir is still a *lord* of these lands."

The leather between Garrett's armour creaked as he turned to look at his king. "Are you telling me, even if this doesn't come to bloodshed, that after all this, he's going to keep that title? You *gave* it to him."

Vighon craned his neck to look up at the plateau over Grey Stone. Up there, above the rabble of the city, the high borns and Thedomir himself enjoyed their extravagant halls and elevated lives. Was it that different to the way he lived, in The Dragon Keep at the top of Namdhor's mountainous rise?

"He isn't greedy, Garrett. In fact, we're not that different. He's threatening separatism because he thinks that's what's best for his people."

Garrett shook his head. "He wants a crown on his head. He's always wanted this, even before the end of The Ash War. Thedomir just wants to hear his name come after *king*."

Vighon wasn't foolish enough to believe that didn't play its part, but he had known Thedomir for too long to believe it was his only source of motivation. In fact, it was the source of that motivation that had robbed the king of sleep in recent days.

"Then why wait fifteen years?" Vighon mused, and not for the first time. "Thedomir has been more than comfortable as lord of The Ice Vales and steward of Grey Stone. We both know the timing of this is more than suspicious."

"True enough," Garrett conceded.

Rather than continue to fall down the rabbit hole with Garrett, as he often did and late into the night, the king turned away and inspected his army's surroundings. There was nothing but plains of snow to the north and south. Directly behind them, to the east, sat a small but dense forest.

Of course, he wasn't really scrutinising the environment - he had already approved of their position. He was searching for any sign of *her*...

"You spoke with her?" Garrett probed, missing nothing about his king. His own eyes roamed over the sky and cliffs and discovered about as much as Vighon did.

"Inara knows we are here."

Vighon didn't miss Garrett's attention flit to Sir Ruban Dardaris before fixing back on himself. "I heard she didn't... *approve*."

The northman, as he would always be, similarly shifted his eyes from the captain of the king's guard before settling back on his general. "Inara holds the title of Guardian of the Realm and she takes it seriously. She and Athis wish to protect the people, *all* the people. She said that choosing a side would mean choosing to kill half the people. She believes this can be resolved through diplomacy."

"I'm sure it could," Garrett agreed far too readily. "*If* it wasn't Thedomir *bloody* Longshadow residing over Grey Stone. He's never been a man of words. He's a fighter to his bones."

Ruban brought his horse closer. "Do you think she will come, your Grace?"

No amount of years would prevent Ruban Dardaris from addressing Vighon with all formality. Just as violence was in Thedomir's bones and loyalty in Garrett's, there was nothing but respect in Ruban's. Approaching forty, the captain of the king's guard was in excellent shape, the perfect companion to his shining armour and flowing cloak of navy blue - which was somehow always cleaner than everyone else's.

Vighon glanced at the skies again. "She's already here; I can guarantee it."

Ruban searched the nearby cliffs. "I cannot fathom a world in which Inara Galfrey simply observes."

"Dragon's breath would certainly move this along," Garrett opined. "Athis's presence alone could stop this from turning into all-out civil war."

Vighon almost winced hearing it said aloud. They were only fifteen years into the Fourth Age; they couldn't possibly endure a war so early, especially one sparked from *within* his kingdom.

"We should proceed as if she means not to help," he concluded.

Garrett gestured to Grey Stone's entrance. "I've got every archer ready to rain arrows down on that ravine."

Vighon didn't want any of them to release their arrows if it could be helped, but he appreciated his general's readiness. Looking around, the spearmen were lining the front of his considerable forces, followed by row after row of swords and shields. Closing them in, the archers took up the wings - every one of them having already nocked an arrow.

Beside Vighon and his guard were the Riders of Namdhor, a fierce battalion of knights on horseback who would smash through the frontlines of any enemy. In their wake would be death and chaos, the best environment for his spearmen to sweep in.

The king hated thinking like this, but the crown on his head made it a necessity. If he could get Grey Stone swiftly back under his control before any further rebellion was sparked in the kingdom, he just might be able to maintain peace and find those responsible for starting all of this.

"That entrance isn't going to be easy to breach," Ruban pointed out.

Vighon subtly raised his fingers from the reins in his hand. "We might not have to breach anything."

General Garrett surveyed the riders and the soldiers around them. "Then why did we bring all of them, your Grace?"

Vighon gave his old friend an exasperated look. "Just in case..."

In truth, the king had only wanted to bring a small company of knights with him, in the hope that he would be well received and they could talk this through. But knowing Thedomir as he did, he knew the man would only respond to a show of great force. Vighon felt he had delivered on that...

"Are the men comfortable with the new shields?" he asked the general.

"I've been overseeing their drills myself," Garrett replied proudly. "The dwarves of Grimwhal might drive a hard bargain, but they certainly know a thing or two about sieges."

Vighon nodded along, looking back at the spearmen. They all possessed a rounded shield, forged by the Heavybellys, that possessed a hook and a latch, allowing one shield to lock into place beside the other. The king had witnessed a few of their drills himself and knew the strategy involved locking the shields over their heads as well as their flanks. It was a great invasion manoeuvre that made a hundred men appear as one giant shielded beast.

"I'll be sure to thank Grarfath in my prayers," Vighon jested, his own faith reserved solely for the strength in his arm.

In the silence that followed, there was only the peaceful tranquillity of The Ice Vales. Grey Stone remained as quiet as a tomb, but for the flags that flapped in the breeze, revealing snippets of the bear, the ancient sigil of Grey Stone. Thedomir had likely been wanting to replace Vighon's sigil of the flaming sword for some time.

Garrett leaned in. "Your Grace, we should consider attacking soon. We've been here a whole day and night. The last thing we want is for the men to grow tired or worse... *hungry*."

The king offered no reply. He kept his eyes on that ravine, where rows of torches betrayed the sentinels of Grey Stone - soldiers loyal to Thedomir.

"Wait here," he commanded, directing his horse towards the city.

"Your Grace?" Ruban's voice was laden with concern.

Vighon had long taught the man that he wouldn't give his command twice and continued towards the city, a lone rider in the snow. His advance was slow, speaking of his peaceful intent. Of course, Thedomir was of such a character that he could easily be inclined to release a volley of arrows and kill the king of Illian in one stroke. Vighon was counting on their history to avoid such a death.

A little over halfway, he brought his mount to a halt and addressed Grey Stone. "As the king of Illian, I demand Lord Thedomir Longshadow come forth!"

The soldiers filling the ravine didn't budge. These were hard men all, products of their harsh terrain. It wasn't long ago that Vighon felt these people were among his own, subjects of his kingdom. Now, they felt apart from the rest of the country, looking at him as if he were some foreign invader.

"Thedomir!" he bellowed.

Still the men of Grey Stone didn't budge. Above them, filling the haphazard bridges that connected the two sides of the ravine, archers took aim in the king's direction.

Vighon held his nerve. "Thedomir!" he shouted again. "Speak with me and perhaps no one has to die today!"

The king waited a few more minutes, eager to catch a glimpse of Thedomir. If there truly was a way to end this peacefully, he was sure to find it.

On the verge of turning back to his own men, Vighon cried one last time, "Thedomir!"

Finally, the soldiers of Grey Stone parted down the middle and the lord of The Ice Vales was revealed. Even older than Garrett, Thedomir should have had the appearance of a man in his final years, his body and face wracked by wars. The man who approached Vighon on foot, however, was anything but fragile.

Though his once burly physique was reduced to a wiry frame, Thedomir still looked every part the warrior. Scaled armour, the colour of bronze, protected his chest and the top of his arms, but his helm was covered with the pelt of a large brown bear, its furry hide running down his back in the fashion of a cloak. Over that, he had slung a shield that he could never wield due to the two-handed hammer he carried. It looked damned heavy, especially in the hands of a man who had seen more than seventy winters.

Vighon wasn't intimidated, but he was most definitely impressed.

"I'm afraid the demands of house Draqaro fall on deaf ears in The Ice Vales!" Thedomir explained on his approach. "The banner of the flaming sword no longer flies in the western winds!"

The king of Illian called on all of Reyna Galfrey's lessons in diplomacy and jumped down from his horse, removing the perceived intimidation of his superior height. "What are you doing, Lord Thedomir?"

"Didn't you read my missive? It's *King* Thedomir now. Everything you see falls under my rule."

"*King* Thedomir," Vighon mused, chewing over the sound of it. "You will be known as the *fool* Thedomir if you continue to court war with the realm. You must see this is folly."

"Why? Because you brought an army to my door? Grey Stone won't be brought down by northerners."

Vighon flicked his head over his shoulder. "We both know I command more men than you see before you," he corrected, hoping his words would sober the older man. "And I told you fifteen years ago: there is no more *us* and *them*. Illian is one people now. Why would you jeopardise the peace? Have I not been generous? I gave the lordship of The Ice Vales to you, just as you wanted. I haven't interfered, I haven't called on your forces to go to war! I only raise the taxes to continue the rebuilding of the realm!"

"You couldn't understand, boy!" Thedomir spat.

As refreshing as it was still to be considered young by someone, Vighon didn't care for his lord's tone. "Then make me understand, Thedomir! I ordered thousands of men away from their families and homes and I would very much like to see them all returned."

"Oh, I know who you brought," Thedomir replied with an air of arrogance. "I see thousands of Namdhorians, northerners for sure.

But I can also see thousands of bannermen who answer to Lady Gracen..."

Thedomir shouldn't have known that. Disturbing as it was, Vighon simply adjusted his stance and maintained his composure. Those that had been rallied was known only to the king and his closest allies and, of late, Grey Stone could not be counted among them. It also meant that Thedomir knew Namdhor was coming to his gate before they even arrived. Gathering shadows indeed...

"House Penrose has long spoken of its deep loyalty to you," Thedomir continued. "You could call upon Lady Gracen and all of Lirian to fight by your side. But The Ice Vales are not the only people who seek independence. Your list of allies diminishes with each passing day. How long will it be before Velia raises the banner of the wolf again? And the people of Tregaran, a kingdom so far away you couldn't possibly hope to keep your grip on them."

Vighon clenched his jaw and looked past Thedomir to the soldiers in the ravine. "We are living in a time of peace. I'm trying to forge a new kingdom, one which sees equality between the provinces for the first time in centuries, if ever." The king was beginning to seethe. "I have worked tirelessly for over a decade to rebuild the realm! And now what? You would plunge us into civil war so you can wear a crown?"

Thedomir looked at him with pity. "You could never under—"

"I understand!" Vighon cut in. "Everyone tells me you're greedy, but I know that isn't the truth. I know you truly believe the province should be under the rule of one who has *ice* in their veins, like all those kings who sat in The Black Fort before yourself. I know you only want what's best for your people." Vighon took a breath. "And that's why I can't allow you to retain your power in these lands. I need lords who can see the bigger picture. There's more to the realm than *your* people. I *need* you to see that your decisions affect everyone, everywhere."

Thedomir sniffed and licked his top lip, an air of aggression growing around him. "You must be blinded by your lofty view from

The Dragon Keep. You talk of peace and equality and *good* taxes, as if there is such a thing. There have been rumblings of rebellion for years, violent protests against laws and traditions thrust upon people who have never known them. Illian was doing just fine with separate kingdoms. I see no reason why it shouldn't finally return to that."

Vighon could see where this was leading, but he would be damned if he wasn't going to try and save as many lives as possible. "Individual kingdoms breed wars, feuds over lands and power. I accept that the realm isn't all that it could be, but it never will be if the provinces don't cooperate with each other. If you force my hand this day, how many will die? And for what? I have the superior force, our victory is inevitable, and Grey Stone will still remain in the fold."

Thedomir smirked. "You're not troubled by the death toll. You're concerned about what happens *after* today. Thanks to the mages of Valatos, Velia teeters on the edge of drawing its own lines on the map. If we go to battle, right here and right now, they will know that King Vighon kills those he considers his own people just to keep his power. Civil war will be the end of your reign..."

"Civil war will be the end of us all," Vighon replied absently, his eyes lost in the snow as his hand came to rest on the hilt of his enchanted sword. Thedomir had mentioned the mages of Valatos, the heart of the king's suspicions where this rebellion was concerned.

"Have they spoken with you?" the northman asked directly. "The mages of Valatos?" Vighon already knew the answer since the report came in from his spies that an envoy had recently visited Grey Stone.

"Why are you talking to me about mages?" Thedomir replied. "Look around you. Today has bigger issues..."

"Did they promise you something?" Vighon dug a little deeper. "Are they behind your sudden change in allegiance?"

"My allegiance is to the vales!" Thedomir snapped. "And after today, the mages of Valatos will be of no concern to you."

"Oh? And why's that?"

Thedomir tightened his grip on his hammer. "Because we're going to resolve this in the old ways, much like the way you yourself found that crown on your head."

Any spark of hope that Vighon might have felt was drowned out by everything that he knew about Thedomir. "That won't work," he said, well aware of Grey Stone's older traditions.

Thedomir raised a bushy eyebrow. "You know of our ways after all. It's the only chance your men have of returning to their families."

The king stole a glance at the hammer, noting the notches etched into the flat side. "That tradition died the moment the crown touched my head. In fact, it isn't even needed when the whole realm resides under one banner."

"We're past that now," Thedomir shrugged. "Fight me, here and now. If I win, your army heads north and never returns. The Ice Vales has its independence. If you win, Grey Stone will submit to your rule and everything will continue as it has."

Vighon had to laugh. "We both know what will happen if I kill you. Your son, Thaddeus, will pick up that great cleaver of his and march the army of Grey Stone into mine. You can guarantee nothing in death, Thedomir. Besides Thaddeus, the governors of these lands have been poisoned by your words for too many years to leave this be. And I warn you, if your son leads the army, he will fall with the rest of them. My actions here will be swift. I cannot allow civil war to ruin all that I've worked for."

Thedomir had a faraway look in his eyes. "You spoke of my children the last time you convinced me to fight for the realm, against the orcs. It worked then. It won't this time. But, I give you my word: kill me and Grey Stone will submit. Can you give me the same assurance that your men will leave?"

Even killing just Thedomir was more bloodshed than Vighon wanted, but it was a price worth paying if it avoided a war that could divide the realm. "I give you my word," he said reluctantly.

"Very good. I suggest you return to General Garrett and inform him so."

The king hesitated. "I believe your traditions allow for a champion to fight in your stead..."

The look of a man insulted flashed across Thedomir's old face. "It does, aye. Would you have me fight someone else, King Vighon? Sir Ruban Dardaris perhaps? I hear he's good with a sword."

Vighon bowed his head by way of apology. "I will return shortly."

"See that you do. I've got a kingdom to run..."

Ignoring Thedomir's last comment, Vighon mounted his horse and galloped back to his forces. His brief explanation wasn't met with welcome ears.

"I can't let you fight," Ruban protested, letting his manners slip momentarily. "No king's guard in history has stood aside and *watched* his liege fight."

"I say let him fight," Garrett chimed in from astride his war horse.

Vighon paused before handing his fur cloak to a squire. "No one is *letting* me do anything," he clarified.

Apparently ignoring the statement, Garrett continued, "I'm an old man, which makes Thedomir an ancient man; this'll be over in seconds."

Vighon looked back at Thedomir, a solitary figure in the snow. "Killing him won't fix everything. First of all, there's the image of me slaying an old man to contend with. Secondly, he isn't wrong about the other provinces. Dissent is like a disease, and I fear those that conspire against us have spread it far and wide."

"We can replace them all," Garrett pointed out as if it was a simple matter. "The governors of The Ice Vales, Thedomir, the lot!"

"And *there's* another image that will spread dissent," Vighon countered, adjusting the collar of his silvyr breastplate, a gift from Dakmund, the dwarven king of Grimwhal.

He started forward when Ruban held his hand out. "You're missing at least four pieces of armour, your Grace."

Vighon stopped himself from rolling his eyes. "You know I'm not fighting in armour." He couldn't count how many times they had had this debate.

"You already are," Ruban said, gesturing to the breastplate. "I only ask that you consider wearing a little more, your Grace."

"I'm only wearing this because its damned light," Vighon argued. "We both know how strong it is," he reminded the knight.

Deciding that he would hear no further argument, the king strode off into the snow and made his way back to Thedomir.

"I didn't want it to come to this," Vighon said honestly.

"And yet we were always destined to come to this," Thedomir lamented. "For what it's worth, I've always considered you to be a *good* man. But we fight for more than ourselves now..."

Vighon took a deep breath and withdrew the sword of the north. The very moment it was lifted free of the scabbard, the silvyr blade was set ablaze with licking flames - a gift from the elves of Ayda. That weapon alone should have been enough to make Thedomir reconsider the fight, but the man was nothing if not stubborn.

Thinking ahead, to Thedomir's inevitable funeral pyre, Vighon decided to give the man a promise. "I'll run you through," he said, his tone even and absent of any malice.

"Thank you," Thedomir replied, hefting his hammer. "I'm afraid I can make you no such promise."

Vighon raised his sword in both hands but kept the blade to the side to ensure the flames didn't blind him. Like his breastplate, the sword was light yet undeniably strong, its edge capable of cutting through steel given enough force behind it. The blade's unique weight, combined with a younger body, would give him the advantage in this particular fight, and it wasn't every day that his age played in his favour.

Proving that one should never underestimate the enemy, Thedomir lunged forward and raised his hammer with a swiftness rarely seen in a man of his years. Vighon jumped back and evaded the edge of the hammer by a hair's breadth. Judging by the heavy *thud* it made in the ground, the northman had just avoided having his skull caved in.

Thedomir was quick to bring his weapon up again, ready for another swing. This wasn't the first time the king had faced an opponent wielding a hammer and, like then, he knew it was an inferior weapon when fighting someone with a sword. Thedomir couldn't thrust, the hammer being blunt on all sides, and he was always forced to put a mighty swing behind his attacks - an effort that often gave away his intentions.

The self-proclaimed king of The Ice Vales heaved his hammer again and again, swinging it through naught but air and hitting naught but snow and mud. Vighon had but to lash out and Thedomir would lose something he couldn't afford to live without. It was tempting. Ending the fight as soon as possible would move everything along, just as Vighon wanted, but to kill the man so quickly would be an insult to the people of Grey Stone. And especially Thaddeus. The king had met the young man a handful of times and knew him to be a brute in size and manner; he could do without fighting him as well...

The hammer went up and the hammer came down, only now the northman could see that Thedomir was tiring, his swing lacking his previous vigour. Raising the sword of the north with both hands, Vighon intercepted the haft of the hammer and kept it aloft, over their heads. He intended to swing his blade in a circle, taking the hammer with it, and then fling the larger weapon aside, disarming his foe.

Thedomir, however, was nothing if not still that wily warrior who had found victory in his every battle. One of his hands abandoned its grip on the hammer and tugged hard on the handle fixed to the bottom of the haft. A nimble short-sword, forged to hide perfectly inside the hammer's length, came free, catching the morning sun across the steel. It flashed across Vighon's midriff, a mortal blow to anyone, be they man, elf, or dwarf.

In this instance, the short-sword came off worse. The edge of the blade was immediately dulled by the silvyr breastplate that had been ready to meet it. Thedomir dropped the hammer and came again with a slash of his new weapon; dulled or not it would still kill a man if it was put in the right place.

Vighon, of course, had no intention of letting him put it in the right place. The flaming sword of the north deflected the next attack, intercepted the second, and batted away the third. Thedomir's momentum saw him rush past the king, who shoved an elbow into the back of his head. Tumbling into the snow, Thedomir came up on all fours with a wet face and an air of exhaustion: he had overestimated himself.

A low growl rumbled out of his throat and he found his shortsword on his way back up. The blade had three significant indentations in the steel; it simply hadn't been designed for extensive fighting, never mind fighting against a sword forged from silvyr. His eyes flashed to the hammer, now lying on the ground behind Vighon.

"Don't try it," the king warned.

Thedomir roared in defiance and came at him with his damaged blade. Vighon stepped towards him, one hand primed to grip Thedomir's sword hand by the wrist and the other to plunge his flaming sword through the old man's chest.

The tip pierced through armour and flesh and even the shield strapped to his back. Death collected him on swift wings, taking the light from his eyes and the breath from his lips. The king caught him and lowered his body to the ground while sliding his sword free.

It was quiet in the clearing between the city and the army of Namdhor. Only the sound of dancing flames reached Vighon's ears and he was thankful for it. Thedomir had risked so much with his bold claim, but his past deeds, deeds of heroism, should not be forgotten. He deserved a moment of silence to mark his passing.

The moment didn't last.

A call to battle echoed out from the ravine of Grey Stone's entrance. It was a booming voice belonging to a large and very angry man. His call was soon followed by a chorus of roars and chants from the men of The Ice Vales.

Vighon cursed under his breath as several hundred men poured out of the ravine and charged across the snow. They were led by Thaddeus, son of Thedomir, and his cleaver. The king chastised himself for being so naive. Thedomir hadn't made the same arrangements as Vighon - in fact, there was a very good chance he had intended to die in combat and pave the way for his son, a younger warrior, to lead The Ice Vales into the future. War had been unavoidable...

It also seemed, right now, that Vighon's death was unavoidable. He was a good fighter and had fought off an ambush of enemies many times in his life, but he couldn't survive the wave of raging soldiers running at him. From the east, his own forces charged out, led by General Garrett, Sir Ruban, and the Riders of Namdhor. As close as they were, however, the king was exposed and, potentially, moments away from being caught in the middle of a violent collision.

Vighon braced himself.

A blinding light and a scorching heat cut a line from north to south, separating Vighon from the advancing soldiers. The king protected his eyes and turned away to see that the Riders of Namdhor were bringing their mounts to a sudden halt. Over the sound of the roaring flames that now divided the white ground, there was but one sound that pierced the air.

The roar of a dragon!

Athis the ironheart, his scales a blood red against the blue sky, glided through the air on his way back around. Situated on his back, her red cloak billowing in the wind behind her, Inara Galfrey raised her Vi'tari scimitar. Illian's most powerful guardian had just joined the fray.

Or at least that's what Vighon thought. It soon became apparent that Inara and Athis had no intention of fighting anyone. The dragon came to land on the Namdhorian side of the fire, though his significant bulk could easily be seen by the men of Grey Stone. He proceeded to exhale a long breath of ice across a short strip of the fire, extinguishing the flames and revealing Thaddeus and his men.

No one moved.

Inara jumped down and made for the smoking strip between the two forces. As always, the half-elf Dragorn looked just as she had fifteen years ago. And, as always, her anger did little to diffuse her beauty or detract from her warrior's visage. The enchanted sword in her hand, however, often proved very distracting. Besides the legendary tales that accompanied Vi'tari blades, Inara's bore a crystal for a pommel. The magic stored within lent the crystal a twinkling glimmer when it caught the light, as well as the power it housed.

"Return to your homes, men of Grey Stone!" Inara's voice carried across the plain, enhanced perhaps by a touch of magic.

Adding to her command, Athis let out a sharp huff from his nostrils, an audible reminder that his breath was enough to end any violence. Thaddeus tore his eyes from the dragon and looked past Inara to settle on Vighon. There was fury in those eyes.

"Will you hide behind them?" Thaddeus provoked. "The Ice Vales *will* have its independence!"

"Not today," Inara replied boldly, her blue eyes locked on the new ruler of Grey Stone. "Return to your homes," she repeated.

Thaddeus's rounded chest heaved under his furs and he clenched his jaw. There was no fight to be had as long as Athis cast his shadow on the ground, but such a foolhardy attack wasn't beyond Thaddeus.

"We will have our war," the young man assured Vighon. Following his lead, the men of Grey Stone turned to trail Thaddeus back to the ravine where they could disappear from sight.

"Wait!" Vighon requested, sheathing his sword and extin-guishing the flames. The king instructed two of his knights to pick up and carry Thedomir's body across the smoking threshold. "He deserves a great ceremony," Vighon added.

Thaddeus had no reply but to pick up his father's body and return to his home, beyond the cliff.

A few orders had the Namdhorians and the Lirians return to their camp. A few more orders from General Garrett had them taking up defensive positions. There was no avoiding Inara though. Her inevitable look of scorn came Vighon's way and he did his best to stand up to it. This wasn't the first time they had disagreed on something in the last fifteen years, but it was perhaps the most pressing issue they had ever dealt with.

Leaving Ruban and the rest of the king's guard outside his tent, Vighon entered behind Inara and waited for the barbed words that were destined to find him. The Dragorn, surprisingly, held her tongue and focused on the table in the middle of the tent, her eyes scouring the map and the pieces placed strategically on top.

"I know what you're thinking," he said.

Inara kept her eyes down. "And what am I thinking?"

"That the map is starting to look like we're already at war."

Vighon knew that's what she was thinking because he had entertained the same thing. The map showed where he had recently stationed new garrisons of soldiers and the parchment had been scribed with numbers, showing how many potentially opposing soldiers each province possessed. To anyone who didn't know Vighon personally, it would appear he was closing his grip around the realm with a show of force.

The Dragorn nodded along. "So you do know what I'm thinking. You just *choose* to ignore my counsel then..."

Vighon sighed and moved to pour them both a cup of water. "I have always listened to you—"

"I told you not to bring half the army to Grey Stone!" Inara interrupted; one of her many privileges. "You said you didn't want war, and I told you there could be nothing *but* war if you arrived at their home prepared for one."

"You're not my only advisor, Inara—"

"Well maybe I'm the only one you should be listening to!" she countered.

The king held out her cup with a patience his predecessors wouldn't have shown her. Inara eventually accepted it but decided on taking a breath before a sip. Her next words were of a more civilised volume.

"I'm sorry," she began again. "You just had to kill Thedomir Longshadow. I know that couldn't have been easy."

Vighon didn't actually touch the water in his cup before he placed it beside the map and let the details therein consume his vision. "Killing him was easy. We shall see how I fair living with it... We also have to see how we all fair living in a world in which The Ice Vales seek independence."

Inara walked around the table. "I'm assuming you have already been counselled on the replacement of the governors, as well as Thaddeus."

"Everybody says replacement, but that's not what *I* hear." Vighon pinched the bridge of his nose. "The last thing the province needs right now is multiple executions, but I fear that conclusion is as inevitable now as Thedomir's death."

Inara stopped opposite the king. "This *cannot* be allowed to turn into civil war, Vighon."

"Look at the map," Vighon directed with notable despair. "Look at the reports," he added, gesturing to the parchments beside the map. "There are days I wonder if it hasn't already begun and we're just burying our heads in the snow."

Inara disagreed. "We have both seen war and this is not it. The realm is in a state of unbalance right now, but it's nothing we cannot fix. Though, marching thousands of soldiers around the land won't help our cause..."

"There's only so much diplomacy before something stronger becomes necessary," Vighon reasoned. "And I fear those that work against us wish for just such a thing."

Inara didn't roll her eyes, but she had clearly been close to doing so. "*I* fear that you have begun to look for enemies where there are none."

"You still don't believe me?" he asked, sweeping his arm across the map.

"Believe what? That a few *supposedly* powerful individuals conspire against the kingdom? You told me of your concerns before you left Namdhor and I had hoped a trek across the plains would clear your head."

The king jabbed his finger over the city of Velia, on the east coast. "Valatos," he said accusingly.

Inara nodded but allowed some of her disbelief to shine through. "The mages," she replied dryly. "You still believe these conspirators are mages?"

"Fifteen years ago it was just a school for magic. Since then, they've purchased more and more land within Velia's walls, always expanding."

"That's no bad thing, Vighon." Inara shrugged. "They've been recruiting and discovered a lot of magic users."

"It's more than that," Vighon pushed. "My spies tell me they have set up secret trading contracts around the realm. They grow ever larger and yet pay the same amount of taxes every year. The first whispers of sedition started in Valatos, Inara - talk of independence, as if they could have their own kingdom inside a city of a larger kingdom." He threw his hands up. "I have done nothing but support the mages of Valatos - I was there when they opened the gates for the first time!"

"Their numbers and resources have grown significantly in recent years, I'll admit," Inara replied. "But I fail to see how a few mages seeking independence have led to today's tragic events."

"Perhaps they are cunning," he suggested. "They know independence is beyond their reach, but if they can persuade the lords and provinces to rebel, I will be weakened..." Even Vighon could hear the desperate tone he had adopted, as if he were grasping at straws.

"Is this why you've sent my parents to Valatos?" Inara enquired, her eyes narrowing on the king.

"Reyna and Nathaniel Galfrey have an uncanny skill when it comes to discovering things that wish to remain hidden." Vighon suddenly felt like he was defending his decisions.

An immaculate eyebrow arched over Inara's right eye. "But you believe that Valatos is currently harbouring a nefarious group of powerful mages who wish to harm the realm?"

Hearing it put like that did give Vighon pause. "Your parents are arriving under the guise of ambassadors, which they *are* by the way. I'm having them enter talks with the Archon again about this private army they've amassed: another strike against Valatos I might add."

"The Keepers are not an army," Inara told him firmly. "They're more like... knights. They're just mages tasked with protecting the school, nothing more. They're rarely seen outside their own walls, Vighon."

The king shook his head. "I don't have all the answers but I know Valatos is where it started. Whoever *they* are, they have spread these wild ideas to the lords on purpose and now my hands are stained with the blood of an old friend. They're already winning. I'm of a mind to march every soldier still loyal to me to the gates of Valatos and question them all..."

"I would counsel caution," Inara said, looking down at Velia on the map. "You're starting to sound paranoid."

"I'm trying to prevent all-out war!" Vighon swiped his cup of water, sending it careering across the ground.

"I'm sorry," he said eventually, his voice quiet. "I feel like I'm starting to lose control. I can't just take my army from one province to another. I need to find the source of this rebellion and quash it before it spreads any farther."

Inara made her way back around the table and placed a soothing hand on his shoulder. "Hopefully my parents will find the truth in Valatos, perhaps even make them see the sense in remaining part of the kingdom."

Her words did little to alter his mood. "I find my hope fading in days of late," he admitted. "I have given everything to the realm. Every day I'm pestered to find a wife and make princes, as if I have time for any of it. From the moment the crown was placed on my head, I've done nothing but rebuild what the orcs brought down. It might have taken fifteen years, but something sinister has risen to challenge us, I am sure of it."

"One problem at a time," Inara coached softly. "I don't believe our troubles in The Ice Vales have abated just yet."

"*Our* troubles?" Vighon questioned. "I wasn't so sure I could count you among those loyal to me."

Inara replied with a look of hurt. "We will ever be great friends, Vighon Draqaro, and I will never see you come to harm in my presence. But my loyalty is to the realm and the people. No man will tell me, nor Athis, who is good and who is bad so that we might scorch the ground beneath their feet. I will take no sides in a civil war that isn't fuelled by evil."

"Haven't you been listening?" Vighon shot back. "I have no doubt that Thedomir only wanted the best for his people, but what of those that planted this idea of independence? Whoever *they* are, they care nothing for The Ice Vales. There is a plot underway to undo all of our work, to undo the kingdom itself. Their motivation can only be one of evil."

"Focus," Inara said gently. "Velia, Valatos, they're on the other side of the country and all we've heard are naught but rumours and the whispers of spy masters. What we do know, is that Grey Stone just witnessed its long-time steward executed by the king. Thaddeus just lost his father and he has the loyalty of the soldiers. We need to fix the situation here before we go looking for shadows elsewhere."

As always, the Dragorn spoke the kind of sense only a fool would ignore. "We will allow them to burn Thedomir first; let them grieve. After which, we will attempt to open talks again. But," he added quickly, "I have thousands of men sitting in the coldest place in Verda. We cannot stay here for long."

"As ever then," Inara quipped, "time is against us..."

34

CHAPTER 2
THE MAGES OF VALATOS

Under the midday sun, the coastal city of Velia was pulsing with activity. As always, the cityscape was busy with scaffolding and workers as they went about reconstructing ancient spires and putting the towering kings of old back together. Even fifteen years on from The Ash War, there was still plenty to be done to return the province of Alborn to the way it once was.

Of course, any splendour to be admired was lost on Kassian Kantaris. As always, his wild green eyes were drawn to the interior of Valatos, his home. Thanks to the magic at their disposal, the architecture within their high walls was superior to the city that encompassed them, not to mention of better design.

The buildings dotted between the gardens were unique and individual, the stonework a level of craftsmanship that no mason could dream of attaining without magic. From atop the parapet that ringed the central hall, Kassian looked to the south, as he always did when reaching the end of his morning patrol. From up here, the Keeper could see his home, nestled neatly within the comfort of Valatos's walls.

Looking down at the gravelled paths that criss-crossed the

grounds, Kassian searched for Clara, his wife. As the students took their lunch, Clara, a creature of habit, would leave her classroom and make her way to the dining hall on the other side of the campus. It had become something of a game for them both. He would look for her among the throng of mages that filled the grounds and she would try and move unseen.

Clara had long been able to outsmart him and pass from one building to the next without him spotting her. He had been half tempted to accuse her of using magic, but he knew better than to question her methods.

Searching now, he hunted for a glimpse of her auburn hair. He had left their home first, at dawn, and couldn't begin to guess what she would be wearing today.

"Keeper!" came the call of a young man.

Kassian was loath to take his eyes off the grounds below, but the young man had the sound of urgency in his tone. Turning away, he discovered one of the prefects, often tasked with a variety of duties within the grounds. Judging by his unusually close proximity to the domed top of the central hall, Kassian presumed this particular prefect wasn't so fond of heights.

"Keeper Kassian!" he called again before coming to a stop in front of the warrior-mage.

"Catch your breath, boy."

After a nervous glance and a much-needed breath, the prefect stood up straight. "I was sent to find you..."

"Is *that* why you're calling out my name?" Kassian replied sarcastically.

Unsure how to respond, the prefect could do nothing but report his message. "The ambassadors have arrived, Sir. They're at the gate."

Kassian looked to the west, where the looming black gates stood securely locked by every manner of warding magic. "Run ahead and tell them to open the gates on my command."

The prefect didn't look at all happy about the prospect of having to retrace his steps at the pace of a run. There were none but the Archon themselves, however, who would challenge the order of a Keeper, and so the young man began his journey to the gates.

Kassian hadn't been looking forward to this particular mandate, but the Archon had tasked him specifically for the duty of escorting and protecting their imminent guests. Being charged by the Archon was an honour and so he decided to see it as such, even if he didn't want to welcome the famous ambassadors.

He spared one last look over the lip of the parapet for Clara. No sign of her. It was another defeat to add to his growing list, but he enjoyed nothing more than the victorious smile on his wife's face when he returned home.

By the time he reached the black gates, they were already being closed again, the burden of their weight seen to by the wands of the Keepers on duty. The ambassadors walked up the middle of the path side by side. Married or not, Kassian would have to be blind to miss Reyna Galfrey's striking beauty. Her blonde hair flowed like silk over her travelling leathers, revealing just the tips of her pointed ears. Emerald eyes looked back at the Keeper, a shade brighter than his own.

The warrior in him took note of the acclaimed bow slung over her back. There were tales of Reyna's heroism in The Ash War as well as The War for the Realm, all of which included the powerful bow, enchanted long ago by the wicked Valanis. Kassian had heard it said that any arrow fired from the bow would never falter in its flight until it struck true.

To assess her age was an impossible task. Elves maintained their beauty for eternity and he didn't know enough about Reyna Galfrey personally to say when she had been born. Were she a human, Kassian would have assumed the ambassador to be in her late twenties, only a handful of years younger than himself.

Walking confidently beside her was Nathaniel Galfrey, the almost-fabled knight of the old Graycoats. The histories of The War for the Realm, against Valanis and the Darkakin, described him as a great warrior. The later stories, from The Ash War, named him as the immortal man. Seeing him now, a man in his seventies with the face and body of a thirty-year old, it was a title well deserved.

The ambassador wore a tightly-fitted long coat, much in the style of the ancient Graycoats, with a one-handed sword on his belt. His chestnut hair was razored short like a soldier's, and he certainly carried himself in that same manner. Together they appeared a very pleasant couple and easy on the eye. It was hard to believe that these two people were among the deadliest in the realm.

Seeing them up close made the Keeper assess his own attire. Kassian wore the floor-length coat of his order, made from the hide of a basilisk. The material was lined with ancient glyphs, though anyone but a Keeper would struggle to find them within the pattern. Serving as more than fashion, the glyphs offered protection against a variety of spells and elements.

Strapped to his thigh was a leather holster, the resting place of his wand. The slender length of oak was varnished with dwarven oil, inlaid with the ashes of a griffin, and infused with a core of Demetrium, the key ingredient for any human wielding magic.

Being one of Valatos's protectors, no Keeper could rely solely on their wand or even just the protection of their coats. Kassian's person was laden with weapons both magical and traditional, though his sword came under both.

Deciding that he embodied the image of the perfect Keeper, Kassian chose not to dwell on his appearance, or the fact that his sandy hair was in need of a trim. He had, having been prompted by Clara, taken some scissors to his beard and moustache and shaved his cheeks. She had reminded him that while he was escorting the Galfreys around Valatos, he would be in the company of the Archon, and they wanted everything and everyone to look their best.

The renowned couple were often celebrated wherever they travelled and Valatos would be no different, despite the reason for their arrival. The Archon had been preparing for the ambassadors for days, from exotic food being imported to the hiring of Velia's best musicians.

They approached the Keeper with disarming smiles, but Kassian knew they would need a lot more than that if they were going to persuade the Archon to desist in their campaign for independence. He wanted to tell them not to bother, but that wasn't his place.

Instead he offered a welcoming smile and bowed his head. "Ambassadors, welcome to Valatos."

Both Galfreys bowed in return. "Thank you, Keeper," Reyna said pleasantly. "Though this is a return visit for us."

"Of course," Kassian replied apologetically. "You must have seen Valatos in its earliest days, before my time."

Nathaniel took in the grounds. "I remember when all of this was a smoking pile of rubble, courtesy of the orcs."

"Yes, well, we have tried to make a few improvements since then. Do you have any bags? I could have them taken to your room."

"We have all we need, thank you." Reyna patted one of the matching satchels they each wore. Kassian had items such as those himself, bags and chests enchanted to hold a pocket dimension.

"Very good. If you would follow me, I will show you to your room. The Archon will be ready to receive you at dusk."

The ambassadors followed him without protest, happy to be patient. Kassian was aware that their every expression, movement, and word was all part of the role they were required to play by the king of Illian. He had no doubt that the real Galfreys were hidden beneath many layers of facade.

"Are we to call you Keeper?" Reyna enquired as they crossed the yard to the steps of the central hall.

"My name is Kassian Kantaris," he answered, though he was happy to be referred to as Keeper.

"Well met, Kassian," the elf replied with a flash of her flawless teeth. "How long have you been trained as a Keeper?"

Kassian hadn't been expecting any personal questions, but he was adaptable enough to keep up. "Eight years this winter, though I took up residence in Valatos ten years ago. Almost to the day in fact," he added, the timing only just occurring to him.

"Have you found Valatos agreeable?" she probed, absent any prying tone.

"Most agreeable." Kassian motioned the Keepers to open the doors ahead of them.

"What about living in the heart of Velia?" Nathaniel asked. "This is like a city within a city. Do you get any complaints from the people?"

Kassian could think of multiple occasions over the years when the Keepers had been forced to deal with protestors. "Rarely," he lied. "And those who complain are often ignorant to magic, believing us to be some kind of cult. We do nothing but good here, forging something even better than anything ever achieved in Korkanath."

Reyna nodded along. "And Lord Carrington has shown you nothing but kindness."

Kassian felt there was more behind that statement, an accusation perhaps. "Yes, Lord Carrington has been very patient with us. He has even set patrols around our perimeter for protection."

"From you or for you?" Nathaniel quipped a little louder than was polite. Kassian didn't miss his wife's hand knock against his own.

"No one has anything to fear from within these walls, Ambassador, I assure you."

The Galfreys absorbed the information without reply and Kassian was more than happy to escort them to their room without further discussion. He had wanted to return home and see Clara before the ambassadors met with the Archon, but he felt their guests to be unpredictable, and so he remained close by, awaiting their departure.

Other Keepers passed by and he held brief conversations with them. There wasn't a soul in Valatos, however, who didn't know the Galfreys were visiting nor the purpose of their visit. For Kassian, unfortunately, that included an awful amount of time standing around doing nothing...

～

As the sun kissed the horizon, the Galfreys emerged in finer clothes and absent their famous weapons. That saved him one job, Kassian thought.

Showing them to the grand library, where the Archon had prepared to meet them, proved to be a much slower journey than Kassian had ever known. Reyna in particular often paused along their route to admire the relics on display and the ruined portraits hanging on the walls.

"Are they all from Korkanath?" she questioned with genuine curiosity.

Kassian obliged her interest and turned to face a long display case that housed one of the foundation stones from the ancient school. "Most are, yes. This particular stone was taken from the island so that we might never forget."

Nathaniel cocked an eyebrow. "Never forget what?"

"That for all the promises in the realm, no one but ourselves can protect us." Judging by the tension that filled the space between them, Kassian had stepped over the line and brought up the awkward topic the ambassadors were actually here to discuss.

"Did you ever see Korkanath?" Reyna looked back at the stone. "Before it fell?"

"I did. I was born and raised in Velia, Ambassador. On a clear day, anyone could see the island from the harbour." Kassian recalled the night it fell. "I also watched it burn, just before the orcs attacked the city."

"Both attacks were a surprise," Nathaniel pointed out.

"And both were under the protection of the Dragorn," Kassian countered, careful to keep his tone even and free of the anger that simmered under the surface.

"You were in the city when the orcs attacked?" Reyna changed the direction of the discussion.

"I was barely a man then." Kassian didn't want to go into the details and so he offered a piece of information that was sure to kill their conversation. "The orcs killed my parents and my sister. If it wasn't for Valatos in the following years, I would have been left to wander the realm as a man with no skills, destined for a life of begging or crime."

Both ambassadors swallowed and nodded with sympathy that Kassian didn't care for. Having no reply, the Keeper motioned for them to follow him to the library. It wasn't much farther and he was thankful for it; dwelling on the fate of his family stirred the worst in him.

The hall outside the library was lined with fellow Keepers, their increased presence a result of the Archon's gathering. They only came together once a week for a day of meetings, but when they did, their personal guard came together.

The tall doors were opened for them and Kassian stepped aside to allow the ambassadors their grand entrance. The library was situated inside the dome that topped the central hall but, as grand in size as it was, the vast space was hardly notable when compared to the spectacle that swirled above. Twenty feet up, thousands of books, new and old, flew around the dome. It always conjured images of fish to Kassian, as they glided through the open water in magnificent shoals.

Always in motion, the books filled the library with the faint rustle of ancient pages. It was a peaceful atmosphere that gave one a moment of tranquillity while also instilling a sense of awe and reverence for the history contained therein. The Keeper had visited the library quite recently to learn more about the very guests he had just escorted through Valatos.

The ambassadors, both of whom had witnessed more wonders in the world than most, craned their necks and marvelled at the vortex.

Kassian wanted to draw his wand and show them how the books could be landed, but the Archon approached.

In simple robes of grey and white, and a single chain of gold around their necks, the seven mages of the Archon would always stand apart from the world or, more specifically, high society. Their basic attire was one of many characteristics that demonstrated their focus to things that truly mattered, such as the betterment of Valatos. Of course, their unique characteristic was the all-encompassing masks they wore.

Apart from their difference in height and gender, all seven masters of the Archon looked the same, their features hidden behind the strange fabric of reflective masks. How they could see, hear or even breathe through them was beyond Kassian. Without names - given up in service to their role - they were identified by title alone.

Kassian respected them all the more for their devotion to his people and his home, unsure if he could make equal sacrifices. He certainly couldn't imagine life without Clara... or a name.

Of the four men and three women, one mage broke free of the Archon and bowed his head to the ambassadors. The master was at least in his seventies judging by the liver spots and pronounced veins on his hands, a contrast to Nathaniel Galfrey - a man of similar age - who shook the master's hand with all the appearance of youth.

Like all of the Archon, this particular master had survived Korkanath's downfall during The Ash War. It was said that the Archon had even known the legendary Gideon Thorn when they were only students at the school.

"We know why you are here," the master said bluntly, taking the smile from Reyna's face. "I fear you have travelled a long way for nothing, Ambassadors."

Reyna retrieved her smile, though it appeared somewhat hollow to Kassian. "You can see Velia from our home, Master. I assure you the journey was no effort at all."

Kassian hadn't been expecting this kind of tension nor this kind of reception. Where was the banquet table and the expensive food he had heard talk of? Where were the musicians and their gentle melodies? His confusion was clearly apparent for the master nodded his head at the far wall, signalling the Keeper to take himself aside.

"It is an honour to be welcomed in this place," Reyna forged ahead. "King Vighon sends his apologies, for he would have come himself were he not required in The Ice Vales."

"You mean," the master corrected, "the king would have thrust himself upon us, regardless of the lack of any invitation. Indeed, you yourselves were not invited to Valatos. We received a missive from Namdhor *telling* us you were to be expected."

"We are all subjects of the king, are we not?" Reyna quickly replied with a tone as disarming as her smile. "We serve at his leisure."

The master tilted his featureless head. "I thought the king was supposed to serve his people..."

Reyna maintained her composure. "It is the king's concern for the people that has seen us to your gates."

From observation, it appeared to Kassian that Reyna was the dominant force of the couple, always ready to respond and make an appropriate comment. Nathaniel was quieter, his countenance that of a soldier accompanying his general into meetings he would rather not be a part of. The Keeper could empathise.

Another master, a tall and wiry man, stepped away from the rest of the Archon and began to circle the ambassadors. "You have come to Valatos in the hope of persuading us against the prospect of independence."

"That's not true," Nathaniel finally spoke. "We're here to *remind* you there is no independence from the kingdom. The realm sits under one banner, a banner that has long been absent inside the walls of Valatos."

The old Graycoat was blunt, a characteristic that Kassian had long enjoyed in his companions, but he was quickly growing to dislike Nathaniel Galfrey. Where Reyna appeared the diplomat, he appeared as the bully, like some hammer of the king.

"Our separation is inevitable," the tall master purred. "The ability to wield magic gives one a different perspective. We have grown a community within these walls, a community that does not associate nor relate to the people outside, including King Vighon. We do not seek war, simply the independence to govern ourselves and, more importantly, protect ourselves."

"Against what, Master?" Reyna took back control with her innocent tone. "Valatos has nothing to fear. The steward of Velia, Lord Carrington, has shown you no ill will. And the greatest benefit of the realm sitting under one banner is the absence of war. Were Velia, and therefore Valatos, to be threatened by another province, the king would intercede."

"Most of us," the first master said, "yourselves included, Ambassadors, have been around long enough to know that not all threats come from other provinces. We simply wish to make preparations to see our students and residents protected. We feel this can be achieved with better results if the king of Illian doesn't place any more *restrictions* on our practices."

Reyna was quick to reply, "Those restrictions have been put in place for a reason, Master. The last two wars that wracked these lands were started by people who abused their power over magic. That cannot be allowed to happen again."

"I can assure you, Ambassador, there are no *evil* mages within our walls."

"Nobody is born evil," Nathaniel said. "It festers and grows in the shadows, always hiding. Trust us, we've met enough tyrants to know they didn't start out that way."

The tall master came to a stop. "You have a point, Ambassador Galfrey?"

"You don't *know* of any dark mages in Valatos," Nathaniel articulated. "And even if there aren't, it could simply be a matter of time. The king saw fit to place the restrictions over you to ensure any such person could never gain too much power."

The smallest of the masters stepped forward with concern

creasing her silvery mask. "I fear we are to continue in circles on the matter. Ambassadors, the Archon *is* going forward with a strong campaign for independence. Perhaps we would be better discussing how Valatos and the kingdom of Illian can coexist?"

Nathaniel almost snorted with laughter. "Coexist? Valatos is situated inside Velia, a city that counts itself as part of the kingdom."

"For how long?" the tall master drawled. "Lord Carrington is sure to entertain the idea of becoming a king rather than a steward."

"And I wonder who put that idea in his head..." Nathaniel's snide remark only worked to rile Kassian up - it was an insult to the Archon!

Reyna shot her husband a look and he clenched his jaw before he could speak any more on the couple's suspicions. To Kassian, the old Graycoat was deluded. The Archon would never turn the other provinces against the king; their interests lay solely with Valatos.

The smallest master continued her efforts to steer their debate along the path of reason. "What of Lady Ellöria and the elves of Ilythyra?"

The topic wasn't what Kassian had expected, but he quickly came to see the wisdom in bringing the elves up.

"Their independence is a little more complicated than our current situation," Reyna countered.

"They reside *outside* of the kingdom," the first master pointed out.

"Yes," another master croaked eagerly, his mask shining under the torch light. "They live on Illian soil, yet they remain *independent.*"

Reyna glanced at her husband, revealing to Kassian the smallest of cracks in their efforts. "Lady Ellöria and those of my kin who have journeyed from Ayda call The Moonlit Plains their home - land long given over to the centaurs and avoided by human settlements. As long as they are content to allow the elves of Ilythyra to expand on the plains, King Vighon will not get in their way."

"Your argument suggests our only problem is one of location," the first master reasoned.

Nathaniel replied before his wife could. "The elves adhere to the laws of the realm. And besides that, Lady Ellöria serves as an ambassador for Queen Adilandra, as do all of the elves under the lady's authority. Their presence in Illian is to strengthen the alliance between ourselves and Ayda, not to mention their continued help with the Drakes."

"Their reason for being here aside," the first master continued as if Nathaniel's answer meant nothing, "the elves of Ilythyra are proof that existence outside of King Vighon's kingdom is possible."

Reyna expressed a look of sympathy. "I am sorry, Master, but that simply isn't the same for Valatos."

"There's one kingdom and one banner," Nathaniel reiterated. "Anything else will disrupt the peace."

The tall master took his staff in both hands and leaned in to it. "The news that has reached these halls speaks of unrest countrywide. Too many cultures in the same pot. This is simply an echo, history repeating itself. Gal Tion failed to hold the realm together a thousand years ago and the same can be said of Vighon Draqaro."

"*King* Vighon Draqaro," Nathaniel emphasised.

The tall master's mask stretched over his jaw but the first master held up his hand, assuming control. "I think we know what the other wants," he said. "I suggest we take the night and rest, so that we might dwell on tomorrow's proceedings. Hopefully, rather than debate, we shall find solutions to make this work." The master gave Kassian the nod to see the ambassadors out before either of them could protest.

The Keeper opened the doors and gestured for them to make their leave. There was an air of deflation to Reyna, quite different to the irritation and frustration that clung to her husband.

"Kassian?" the first master called.

Kassian signalled one of the other Keepers to escort the ambassadors back to their room. It wasn't every day a member of the Archon wished to speak with him. Kassian tugged on the lining of his coat before turning around to approach the councillor.

47

The master gave him a friendly pat on the shoulder as if they had long been friends. "You are among our most distinguished Keepers, Kassian. I hear regularly of your skill with both the wand *and* sword."

"Thank you, Master," Kassian replied, walking in step with the councillor.

"I also hear you've read more than a few books you shouldn't have..."

Kassian swallowed. "Well, I just like to be prepared, Master. I find it's always better to know more than your opponent."

"Indeed," the master agreed. "And speaking of our opponents, I hear you are a fine judge of character. I would know what you make of our new *guests*."

Kassian hadn't spent nearly enough time with the ambassadors to judge them in any detailed capacity. "Of their character I can hardly say, Master. But I understand their motives in being here, as well as their tenacity. I can't see them leaving Valatos until we agree to remain under the king's banner."

"I couldn't agree more," the master replied with a broad grin stretching the unusual fabric of his mask. "You have been tasked with escorting them around the grounds, a task that sees to both our protection and their own."

"It was indeed an honour to be asked by the Archon," he replied, though the orders found him via the echelons that existed between himself and the masters.

"Indeed," the master intoned. "As a Keeper, you have the most important job in all of Valatos: keeping us safe. I trust you understand the seriousness of these talks?"

"Of course," Kassian was quick to answer. "Our independence is the only way Valatos will continue to grow."

"Very good. But do you also understand the consequences of these talks? With the ambassadors? They speak on behalf of the king, their words his own. There is a very good chance, and I *dread* to think of it, that this will all come to violence."

That shocked Kassian and it clearly showed on his face.

"As we speak," the master continued, "violence is already sparking across the realm. We stand on the cusp of rebellion. Can the Archon count on you, Kassian Kantaris, to keep us safe by the edge of your sword and the point of your wand?"

The Keeper replaced his concern with conviction. "Until my dying breath, Master."

"And would you kill to keep Valatos safe?" the master probed.

Kassian had been ready to answer positively and swiftly to the next question, but that one caught him off guard. "I would see any threats to Valatos dealt with severely," he finally answered, unable to say that he would kill.

"Then the Archon can rely on you as it so believed." The master sounded satisfied as he gestured to the library door.

Kassian made to leave, noticing the rest of the Archon watching him expectantly from afar. The Keeper paused on his way, a burning question bringing his feet to a stop.

"Yes, Kassian?" the master enquired.

"Forgive me, Master." Kassian turned sheepishly. "If this was always to be the ambassadors' reception, why did we order so much exotic food and... hire musicians?"

The master almost shrugged. "They're for the *king*."

That answer only confused Kassian all the more. "The *king* is coming to Valatos?"

"Oh yes!" the master replied rather happily considering the company he was talking of. "We're going to have quite the celebration when he finally arrives..."

Kassian could see the Archon had said all they were going to, leaving the Keeper with nothing to do but bow his head and leave the library. He had entered that grand chamber sure of mind and left with a degree of uncertainty, an unfamiliar feeling to the Keeper. One thing was for certain; sleep would elude him...

CHAPTER 3
PLAYING THE GAME

As it ever had been, The Pick-Axe was a hub of activity and constant noise. However, and rather more unusually, the source of the raucousness was not the tavern's patrons nor the travelling band from Palios. In fact, the patrons had run from the tavern screaming, abandoning their drinks, and the band had ceased their playing and cowered in the far corner, hugging their instruments.

"HEAVYBELLY!" came the recurring, angry call from The Pick-Axe's owner, Russell Maybury. "Why is there a Gobber in my tavern?"

The Gobber in question was an alpha among its species and therefore slightly larger and more aggressive than the majority. It was also very upset about being captured and dragged from its dwelling by one Doran Heavybelly.

"I didn' think it was goin' to wake up, did I!" the dwarf yelled over the Gobber's shrieks.

"Why did you even bring it in here?" Russell shot back, leaping over the bar to reach his famous monster-killing pick-axe.

"I was thirsty!" the son of Dorain shouted, hefting his double-sided axe.

"You couldn't have delivered the Gobber to the employer first?" Russell swung his pick-axe horizontally but the monster leaped over it and through the hatch to the kitchen, taking most of the framework and some of the wall with it.

"I told ye!" Doran snapped. "I-was-thirsty!"

"So were my customers!" Russell argued, kicking the door through to the kitchen and disappearing beyond.

"Bah!" The son of Dorain waved the old wolf's problem away. "They'll be back! This jus' makes it all the more excitin'!"

A loud kerfuffle exploded from the kitchen. Glass shattered, plates broke against the walls, cutlery fell to the floor, and heavy pans bounced around. Then Russell came flying through the hatch, splintering what was left of the wooden frame with his broad shoulders. The tavern owner smashed into the front door covered in food and fresh cuts.

Finally, Doran turned his attention on the only patron still sitting at his table in one of the cosy booths. "Are ye goin' to help or are ye jus' goin' to sit there drinkin' ye Galoshan tea?"

Asher had found the whole scene rather amusing, right up until one of his oldest friends had been hurled from his own kitchen. The ranger put his tea down and got to his feet, his warrior's mind already working through the scenario that was about to play out. Given the cramped quarters inside the kitchen, he left his two-handed broadsword resting against the table and drew the short-sword from his back.

Despite his decades of drawing blades from their scabbards, the sound never grew tiresome. The *ring* filled his ears and immediately sent his heart rate up, tensing his muscles, and focusing his senses. The silvyr blade caught a ray of light piercing the window, exaggerating the runes that ran up the middle. It was as deadly as it was beautiful.

The kitchen door swung on its hinges after Doran stepped

through. "Ye should o' stayed asleep, beastie!" The Gobber screeched and their battle was renewed.

Asher paused on his way to check that Russell was conscious. The old wolf was sitting up, rubbing his bruised head and dusting himself down, sprinkling the floor with pieces of glass. He had taken harder hits than that in his time, but the curse of the werewolf was finally starting to take its toll, ageing Russell with every full moon until he found his end.

"I'm fine," he groaned. "Do me a favour and get rid of that thing..."

Judging by the crashing sounds that boomed out of the kitchen, Doran wasn't winning. Asher swept his green cloak behind him and strode beyond the bar as the terrified band made their hasty escape.

What greeted him was a sight only Doran Heavybelly could have achieved. The dwarf was without his axe and his sword still rested on his hip. Instead, the son of Dorain wielded a pair of iron pans...

"Come an' get it ye ugly—"

The Gobber shot forward and robbed Doran of his words. The two fell over in a tumble of limbs, claws, and gnashing teeth. The dwarf swung an arm free from their tussle and came down with the bottom of a pan. It collided with a satisfying *bong* followed by a pained grunt from the Gobber - which was now furious. Cornered as it was, the beast lashed out with its claws, raking at Doran's chest-plate. Being an alpha, it had the clout to throw the dwarf about, slamming him into the counters and shelves.

A shelf of hard cheeses dropped onto the Gobber's head, disori-entating it long enough for Doran to bring both of his pans to bear.

The dwarf chuckled. "Now ye're goin' to get it..."

The son of Dorain used the pans like hammers, pounding the Gobber relentlessly with one then the other. Fangs were knocked loose and the beast fell back, its limbs wild.

Asher saw his opening and knew a swift flick of his wrist would bring a definitive end to the fight, but Doran looked to be enjoying himself. The ranger remained close, watching the dwarf beat the Gobber back towards the hatch, one pan flying in after another.

Something of the monster's feral nature kicked in and it fought through the pain and the beating to attack again.

Claws of bone lunged forward with exceptional speed and attempted to open Doran's throat. Asher had no choice but to intercede with his short-sword. A flash of silvyr chopped down through the Gobber's wrist like butter and the second, horizontal, swipe passed through its reptilian neck and sprayed hot blood across the walls. Its lizard-like head slowly slipped away and fell to the ground absent its body.

Doran froze and his jaw dropped. "What did ye do that for ye dolt?" The dwarf kicked the lifeless body. "What am I supposed to do with that now? The contract was very specific about it bein' alive!"

Asher picked up a cloth and wiped the blood from his sword. "You're welcome."

"Oh no," Doran began, shaking his head. "Don' ye make out that ye jus' saved me life! I had that under control!"

"Doran, you're holding a couple of *pans*. You're lucky it didn't rip your head off; you know that's an alpha."

"I was usin' pans on purpose!" Doran threw his arms up. "Ye can' kill anythin' with pans, which was all part o' me plan ye damned idiot!"

Asher recalled a fight from many years ago and knew well how easy it was to kill with a sturdy pan, but that had been another life. In this life, he had to contend with a haughty dwarf and old bones...

The ranger turned on his heel and left the kitchen behind, already feeling sorry for Russell and the mess that had been made. Doran threw the pans down and retrieved his axe, sure to follow after Asher with more name-calling.

The rangers came to a stop when they noted the pair from the city watch, standing in the doorway. Attired in hauberks of yellow and green, the colours of house Penrose, the two soldiers surveyed the chaos that had erupted when the Gobber arose from its dwarf-induced slumber. Russell was sitting on a stool off to the side where he was still nursing his head.

"It's a'right fellas," Doran assured with his large axe in both hands, "we took care o' it. Jus' a Gobber that didn' know when to quit."

The taller of the two soldiers frowned. "We're not here about some Gobber. We've come on the orders of Lady Gracen of house Penrose."

"Oh..." Doran looked around at the disaster. "Ye're not 'ere about the monster that was on the loose?"

"No," the soldier replied bluntly. "Lady Gracen wishes to speak with the ranger known as Asher." The soldier had three people to choose from and naturally landed on the man himself. "Would that be you, Ranger?"

Asher considered his answer. These men had never seen him before and he was a master in the art of lying; he could convince them he was their father given enough time. But, anyone who held a title before their name often had plenty of coin to spare, coin a ranger could rightly do with when there were so few jobs available. Of course, there was every chance the lady of Lirian wanted him in irons. It was so hard to say with the life he had led...

"That's me," he answered gruffly.

"You are to come with us," the taller soldier demanded, his tone suggesting it was to be irons then.

"Hold on fellas!" Doran protested. "On what charge do ye arrest 'im?"

Again, the soldier frowned. "There's no charge. Lady Gracen requests the ranger's time, nothing more. We have been instructed to tell you there is coin to be made."

Asher held onto his smile. "I'll get my things."

"Coin?" Doran echoed, licking his lips. "This is abou' a job? Does Lady Gracen know that Doran, son o' Dorain, o' clan Heavy-belly is in Lirian? Perhaps she is in need o' my particular set of skills also?"

Asher heard *delicacy*, but he knew she meant *discretion*. "Something you can't rely on your own men for?" he pried.

"My position is a complicated one, much like yourself, Ranger. I have advisors and such, all powerful men and women who vie for my station. Manoeuvring around them is all part of the game."

Asher glanced at the door over his shoulder. "I fail to see how I or a fellow ranger can help you to play this game."

"Oh, I think you see a lot more than you let on, Asher." Lady Gracen finished her wine and walked over to a large square table.

Asher followed her and laid eyes on a map of Felgarn, the province that housed The Evermoore and all the land Lady Gracen was to steward. It was a vast piece of land and had long been known as the heart of Illian.

"What do you know of the Drakes?" the lady asked.

Asher looked from his host to the map, specifically a patch of The Evermoore just north of Lirian. It was there, written between the trees, that the ranger found Ikirith, home of the Drakes.

"I know they're a very private people."

Lady Gracen pouted. "Come now, you know more than that. I may have only been a child when you fought in The Ash War, but I have since read all there is to know. For instance, I know of your presence on the battlefield when the Drakes came into being. There are some references that even state you are responsible for their existence..."

"It seems you already know a lot about them, my Lady."

"Not nearly enough considering they live within my domain."

Asher didn't know what the lady had in mind for the Drakes, but he knew he didn't want them to come to any harm. "They're very peaceful," he said finally. "Passive almost. They like living among the trees and have little care for the things humans consider essential."

"Essentials such as walls or weapons," Lady Gracen verified, further demonstrating her knowledge of the Drakes.

"Among others," Asher continued. "They have no memory of

their lives before the transformation. Their years living as orcs is lost on them, though they understand what happened to them."

The lady nodded along. "Yes, the elves have been most generous with their time and aid. What do you know of the magic they are said to wield?" she added casually.

Some of the larger pieces of the puzzle fell into place for Asher. "If it's an alliance you seek with the Drakes, my Lady, I fear you are overreaching. Unlike the elves, they are far less inclined to share their knowledge of magic."

"You believe I seek their friendship as some kind of power play? I am offended, Ranger. The Drakes live under the rule of King Vighon and are therefore members of this kingdom. Living inside The Evermoore makes them *my* responsibility, something my late father was happy to forget."

Asher frowned, struggling to peel back the layers of Lady Gracen. "Then you wish to bring them to Lirian?"

"The Drakes are welcome in any town or city in Felgarn," the lady replied confidently. "We both know, however, that they would never accept such an invitation. No, my concerns lie with those of our own kind. Those powerful people I mentioned? Not all of them agree that the Drakes are subjects of the king, nay even a being of intelligence."

Asher had seen and heard that kind of attitude before. "They still see them as orcs," he said.

"Quite. And, as such, hunting parties are gathered regularly. I put a stop to most of them, but Governor Hatwell of Wood Vale is as stubborn as he is influential. Word has reached me that a new party has been dispatched into The Evermoore to hunt down as many Drakes as possible."

Revelation crossed Asher's face. "And you cannot be seen to be opposing the governor."

"Now you're grasping the game," Lady Gracen smiled. "I need someone of great skill to see that these hunters never claim their prey. Someone who doesn't wear my colours."

Asher looked back down at the map, his thoughts dwelling on Ikirith. He had never been into the Drakes' woodland home and had made a point of steering clear of the land around it.

"And you're doing this because you just want to save the Drakes?" Asher clarified with obvious disbelief.

"Do my reasons have an impact on your accepting the job?"

Asher narrowed his eyes. "Maybe..."

The lady offered a coy smile. "I like you, Ranger. You need the coin, there's no arguing that. But you have a code now, a set of morals where once I would bet you didn't. It's honourable. But your questions have just lowered your reward," she added sharply. "I want you to intercept these hunters and disrupt their hunt because their *prey* deserve to be called people."

Asher heard it all, as well as what she wasn't saying. "But it wouldn't hurt if Lady Gracen, of house Penrose, was the one to finally bring the Drakes into the fold..."

The lady pursed her lips and corrected her composure. "You're losing coin by the word. The ludicrous reward I was offering is starting to look handsome at best."

The ranger turned away, considering his options. This wasn't how he normally haggled his contracts, but the contract in question was suspect when the person with all the coin was damn near royalty. They were a hard breed to trust.

"I realise I'm asking you to take the lives of men rather than beasts," the lady remarked, pouring herself a new glass of wine. "I've been led to believe this is outside the norm for your line of work."

Asher had seen men commit the kind of atrocities that blurred the lines between humans and monsters. He himself had blurred those lines on numerous occasions. Still, if the lady was willing to pay handsomely he wasn't going to bring up the contracted rates he usually worked with. Or that he would hunt down these men for free...

"I'm not an assassin," he stated firmly. "I won't kill any of them unless I'm forced to."

"Very well," she agreed. "I'm certain a man of your talents has many ways to dissuade them from continuing their hunt. Twelve hundred coins, Ranger; shiny new ones. I will see that you receive half now and half upon your return."

Asher was forced to call upon his Nightfall training in order to keep his face straight. Twelve hundred coins would see him through to the next summer! He turned back to face the stewardess of Lirian and found her hand waiting to grasp his own. Why was he finding her so hard to read? That was the problem with her kind; they were too experienced at wearing multiple faces.

Ultimately, he could do nothing but look at the job for what it was: simple. It was also well within his abilities and he didn't want to see any Drakes hunted down like animals.

Despite his unease, Asher shook her hand. He really needed the coin...

CHAPTER 4
FLAMES IN THE DARK

The flames of Lord Thedomir's pyre burned bright in their reach for the heavens. Black smoke billowed up into the twilight sky, preceding the dark of approaching night. The people of Grey Stone gathered with candles and torches in the narrow streets below, filling the winding steps that rose up to the icy plateau.

Inara Galfrey stood by the very edge of the high plateau, the flames drowning out the blue of her eyes. The Dragorn had received more than a few derisive looks from the high borns that circled Thedomir's pyre. She was clearly seen as being on the king's side of their divide, but as a Dragorn, the Guardian of the Realm, Inara was afforded a level of respect.

In truth, she suspected the only reason action hadn't been taken against her was because Athis stood beside the slab-like doors of The Black Fort, not far from the funeral.

How many of these will we witness? she asked her eternal companion. *How many lords and ladies will we watch burn on the pyre over the centuries? How many kings?*

That last thought stung Inara deeper than she would like to admit, but Vighon's mortality was a fact that could never be changed.

I fear the world will pass us by, Athis. The cycle of life and death will stretch on forever as we stand by and watch, unchanging.

Regardless of the few hundred yards that separated them, Athis's voice was crystal clear in her mind. *True enough,* he replied. *Our resolve will be held steady by our perspective, wingless one. We cannot see the world as a cycle of birth and decay, for such a thing can only bring madness. Always remember; we are not watchers. We do not stand by and observe the world around us. It is our duty to always be a part of the realm, if not the pillar that keeps it up. As Vighon Draqaro's light fades from Illian, we will be there to carry it forward, to the next ruler, and the next.*

Inara turned away from the pyre and looked down on the clearing below, where the Namdhorian forces were camped in a thick line. *I've never known a world without Vighon...*

And you still don't, Athis reminded her, raising her spirits. *You can't allow your immortality to cloud your view of what's in front of you. Live in the present, Inara. Our life is too long to always be looking to the future...*

Of course, Athis was right. He was always right and annoyingly wise: the boast of all his kind. Inara dragged herself back to the moment and paid her respects to Lord Thedomir. His past actions had kept Namdhor from falling against the orcs and he deserved to be honoured.

The funeral carried on until the last light of dusk disappeared behind the mountains. The high borns scattered to their grand homes and the people of Grey Stone returned to their lives below. *King* Thaddeus, as he had named himself, fell into the huddle of his men and made for The Black Fort, built into the next cliff face that rose even higher than the plateau.

Considering he believes himself a king, Athis observed, *Thaddeus has only a handful of men accompanying him. I see very few soldiers here.*

The dragon was indeed correct; Inara had seen very few soldiers of Grey Stone at all. **They must be down in the city, in case Vighon attacks.**

The king would never do that, Athis protested in the defence of Vighon.

We know that. I fear the people of The Ice Vales have been led to see him as something more akin to a tyrant...

Then we shall inform them otherwise, the dragon replied, eyeing Thaddeus.

Having been extended an invitation into The Black Fort, prior to the funeral, Inara was of a mind to do just such a thing. There had been violence and death thus far, but she was determined to find a conclusion with words alone. She marched across the plateau thinking of everything she was going to say to Thaddeus, making sure her argument was well laid out in her mind.

If my parents were here, they could probably convince Thaddeus to submit to Vighon in minutes.

And they taught you everything they know, Athis reassured.

Inara passed the dragon by, offering him an affectionate look, as she journeyed beyond the massive doors of The Black Fort. The soldiers stepped aside and uncrossed their overlapping spears to allow her entry into the ancient throne room of Grey Stone. Thaddeus was already lounging on the dark throne that had belonged to his father for the last fifteen years.

The son of Thedomir was unnaturally comfortable on the throne, as if he belonged on it. Such a responsibility should be harrowing in Inara's opinion. He was certainly more brutish in appearance than his father ever was. His clean-shaven head was contrasted by a thick, black beard and the furs draped across his back only added to the width of his considerable shoulders. Perhaps the most obvious feature to the man, however, was the golden chain around his neck. It was the only piece of jewellery he wore and it clashed with his rugged look.

A great hearth stood in the centre of the chamber, its flames an ever-present blaze in The Black Fort, and said to have been ignited a thousand years ago. There were shadows lining the throne room, soldiers hovering behind and between the pillars.

Inara bowed her head before the throne. "Thaddeus, son of Thedomir, I thank you for your invitation. I hope to find a peaceful resolution that ensures your father will be the only casualty in this debate."

Thaddeus's left eye twitched. "Debate? Is that what this is? How civilised! I thought when one king killed another it was *war*..."

"If that were truly the case, I believe the people of the dead king would, in fact, submit to the victor. As that is not the case, we must examine the simple facts: the king has killed one of his subjects in legal combat, initiated by the deceased no less. The matter of independence should now be laid to rest with your father, Thaddeus." Inara regretted her choice of words for a moment, wondering if she should have taken a softer approach.

Athis disagreed. *Thaddeus is not the sort to have his mind changed by a soft approach.*

"You think this ends with my father?" Thaddeus laughed, filling the chamber with his booming voice. "The people wish for things to return to the old ways, Guardian. *Our* ways."

"Do they?" Inara questioned, doubting the young man. "Do they want their husbands, brothers, and sons to go to war so that you might be crowned a king? How many would die? And for what? How would The Ice Vales be any different to the way it is now?"

Thaddeus stood up. "The people, my people, will not accept the laws of a foreigner any longer. It's time to remember the past."

The timing of all this was beginning to gnaw at Inara, whether it be Thaddeus's words or Vighon's. "They have not only accepted the rule of a foreign king for fifteen years, but they have also thrived in a world ravaged by orcs." The Dragorn chewed over her next question until Athis encouraged her, his own curiosity growing by the minute.

"Why now? Why after so long would your father risk everything for independence?"

Thaddeus clenched his fists and the knuckles *cracked* over the sound of the hearth. "You think my father was mad to do such a thing," he stated, wearing his anger like armour. "He knew what was going to happen," he continued, surprising Inara. "He knew the northman would be the end of him. He had no other choi—" Thaddeus let go of his anger, replacing it with a flash of brief amusement before a hint of fear crossed his face. "You have no idea what's coming, Guardian."

Inara tilted her head and narrowed her eyes as a sinking feeling pressed down in her stomach. The Dragorn hadn't expected this...

"What are you talking about?" she asked gravely.

Thaddeus blinked hard and focused his distant stare. "The best any of us can hope for is a place in the new world," he whispered.

"Thaddeus?" Inara urged. "Tell me what—"

"It's already begun," he interrupted, nodding at one of the shadows.

A call rang out and was relayed through the halls until it reached the men on The Black Fort's doors.

Inara! Athis warned. *They're closing the doors!*

That wasn't all the men of Grey Stone were doing. Through her bond with Athis, Inara could see the weighted nets being dropped over his head by men hiding above the doors. His head was dragged down and spearmen advanced on him immediately. Walking towards the dragon was another, hooded and robed in black. Athis could feel the magic that cocooned the mage and knew a destructive spell was being cast.

Inara had problems of her own. As Thaddeus picked up his two-handed cleaver, the shadows of the throne room came to life, revealing the hardened soldiers of Grey Stone.

Furious that she had walked into an ambush, Inara drew her Vi'tari blade and fell into the aggressive fifth form of the Mag'dereth. Thaddeus leapt from his elevated throne and came down on the

Dragorn with his cleaver in both hands. Thanks to half of her heritage, Inara was a lot stronger than she appeared and met the incoming cleaver with a solid defence.

Face to face, Thaddeus hissed, "Who will protect your king now?"

That sinking feeling in her stomach became an abyss. She wasn't the only one who was being ambushed...

With his black cloak and dark furs wrapped around him, Vighon enjoyed the best pipe weed in the realm under the icy reign of the starry sky. Smoke diffused into the air around him, partially masking his view of Grey Stone. The towering entrance to the city was illuminated with a soft, warm glow from the night's events. The people would share a drink in remembrance of Thedomir.

The same could not be said around the Namdhorian camp. The men had sought sleep as soon as it was available, preferring the warm shelter of their tents. Here and there the king could see patrols pacing up and down, some on horseback, some on foot weaving between the camps.

It was quiet, a precious commodity in a king's life.

Yet, right now, he didn't want quiet. He wanted distraction. Balanced precariously between peace and war, the king's mind was swimming with strategies and contingencies for both scenarios. He trusted Inara to make progress, but he wasn't about to underestimate Thaddeus's violent nature.

It was all giving him a headache. Thankfully, the peaceful atmosphere was soon disrupted by a collective laughter a few tents over. The king could see the glow from a fire and was drawn to it, as well as the merriment.

Rounding the tents, he immediately recognised the captain of his guard, Sir Ruban Dardaris. It was good to see him enjoying a drink with the other men, rather than advancing his diligent training. The king had often told him there was only so much training a man could do, and the knight always told him there was more. Of course, he was still in full armour. He had replaced his helmet, however, with a thick scarf which sat comfortably in front of his mouth.

Unfortunately, upon sighting their king, the men grew quiet and even attempted to stand in his presence. Vighon bade them to stay seated and even asked if he could join them. Sitting beside Ruban, he happily accepted a tankard from one of the soldiers and encouraged them to continue with their conversation.

Ruban gestured to the circle of men. "We were just talking about The Ice Vales, your Grace. I have to say, of all the places you've taken me, this has to be the strangest..."

Vighon smiled with the pipe still in his mouth. "I find that hard to believe."

"We were all born in the north," Ruban continued. "*I* was born in the coldest winter for forty years they said. Yet, I cannot bear this cold." The knight adjusted his scarf to cover more of his neck.

"I think we northerners find the place stranger than most," Vighon opined to a reception of agreeing nods. "Coming south should never be colder. That's magic for you..."

"Magic?" one of the men echoed. The curiosity in his voice was stained by a touch of fear.

Ruban looked to the king and smiled knowingly, aware, perhaps, that they were about to hear a story. Vighon had never been one for reading or learning anything beyond swordplay, but his years on the throne had instilled an appreciation for history and those who ruled before him. The king would rarely admit it, but he enjoyed telling a tale or two from one of the books in his library.

"It's been this way for a thousand years," Vighon began after puffing out more smoke. "Reyna Galfrey herself updated the history books in the keep's library. Have you ever heard of Elethiah?" he asked the men.

They shook their heads and Ruban frowned. "I can't say I have. It sounds elvish."

"Indeed it was," the king replied. "Elethiah was the elven capital of Illian for thousands of years. Its ruins can still be found south of here. It was also the place where their Dark War came to an end, marking the beginning of the Third Age. The elven elders placed a strong curse over the city, ensuring that no one would disturb its only prisoner."

The men leaned forward, falling into the king's tale. "Prisoner?" they questioned.

"Aye, an elf, and a powerful one at that." Vighon paused to swig some of his drink.

"Valanis," Ruban concluded.

The men looked to each other, the name long associated with The War for the Realm, fought before any of them were born.

"The elves wanted to make sure all would be turned away should they try and enter Elethiah's halls. But the spell had far-reaching effects they hadn't anticipated. The land grew to be as cold and life-less as those halls." Vighon stretched his back and savoured his ale. "I could say only the hardiest of people came to call this place home, but I feel *stubborn* would describe them better." The men laughed and, as always, the king struggled to judge whether it was genuine amusement or not.

Ruban surveyed their snowy environment. "Why would anyone choose to live in a land so cursed?" The men muttered agreements into their drinks.

"Because," the king answered, "home is what you make of it, wherever that is." He turned to look at the light emanating from within the city. "And it looks pretty warm in there..."

"What's that?" the soldier beside Ruban asked. "Up there." He pointed to the top of the plateau, where dark silhouettes from the grander buildings blocked out the stars.

Vighon turned and focused his eyes, quickly discovering the cause for his man's alarm. By the very edge of the cliff, men started appearing, visible by the small flames that accompanied them. The king dropped his tankard and pipe, aware of what was about to happen. A second later, those flames were cast away and launched high into the night's sky, outshining the stars.

"SHIELDS!" Vighon bellowed.

The flaming arrows, however, landed at least two-hundred yards short of their camp, creating a line between the Namdhorians and Grey Stone - a warning for any who dared advance on the city.

A great ruckus erupted across the army as they were roused from their slumber. But, through it all, a single arrow found its way between the tents and horses. This arrow had not come from atop the cliffs, but from the east, within the forest behind the Namdhorians. The king realised all of this as he watched the man beside Ruban fall to his knees with an arrow piercing his throat, robbing him of his last words.

Dardaris shoved the king hard away from the small camp and picked up a discarded shield in the same motion. It was an action that saved them both when a salvo of arrows exploded from the trees, two of which impacted the shield.

Those arrows were followed by more and more. The men could be heard falling all through the ranks, crying out as they were brought down by the deadly projectiles. Horses, the largest of targets, fell too, often crushing soldiers or collapsing a tent.

Vighon ducked his head when one arrow careered off a tent post and whipped past his face. All the while, Ruban was hollering for more of the king's guard to rally on his position. One such guard came sprinting between the tents when three arrows caught him in the side and saw him barrel into a stack of supplies.

The king reached for his sword but Ruban gripped his wrist. "Don't!" he instructed over the din. "The arrows will find you!"

Vighon loved the sword of the north - one of the greatest weapons in the realm - but the flames did have their disadvantages.

"We need to move!" one of the king's guard shouted.

Having just seen a spray of arrows pierce the tent in front of them, Vighon and Ruban were inclined to agree. As one, they dashed from cover to cover, pausing only long enough for the king to heft a dead Namdhorian's shield. Two arrows found the shield, their impact spurring the northman on.

General Garrett's voice resounded above it all. "ARCHERS!"

Vighon checked over his shoulder to ensure they weren't about to be flanked from the city itself. Grey Stone was a silent observer of their ambush.

Another king's guard emerged from the chaos in a bid to reach them, but soon met his end by the tip of an arrow, its biting steel buried in the side of his head. Ruban didn't even spare the fallen guard a second thought as he dragged Vighon in the opposite direction and threw them both to the ground. Only the carcass of a fallen horse saved them from the next salvo.

"How could Thaddeus have positioned his men behind us?" Ruban barked. "We would have seen them!"

Vighon berated himself - how could he have been so naive? "They were in position before we arrived!" the king shouted back.

"What?"

"This was Thedomir's plan all along," Vighon unravelled. "He never intended for anything but war..."

Ruban nodded gravely, his understanding catching up. "Then he knew we were coming," he reasoned.

Vighon gritted his teeth. He didn't have time to consider who had betrayed him or even the larger picture that brought a conspiracy to light. Right now, he needed to survive. The king nodded at General Garrett and raised his shield in time with Ruban. The men ran, leaving the cover of the dead horse, and rallied all they could to join them - they needed shields and spears.

"Form up!" Garrett commanded, pushing soldiers into their defensive positions.

One by one, the Namdhorians locked their dwarven-forged shields into place, concealing them inside their armoured shell. Captains up and down the camp were mimicking their general and ordering their men into identical formations. On the wings, the archers were firing blindly into the shadowy forest, but without visible targets, many arrows were wasted.

Safely behind the shield wall, Vighon finally freed the sword of the north from its scabbard, letting loose the flames. It reminded both sides that the king of Illian still drew breath.

The king held the blade high and roared, "ADVANCE!"

The soldiers did their best to move forward, navigating their dead brothers and fallen mounts. The snows were splattered red with blood but they meant to spill more, making their enemy pay for their treachery.

Vighon kept his shield high as he trailed behind the armoured cluster. The spray of arrows narrowed, focusing on the soldiers in front of the king, bouncing and skimming over the shields. He periodically stole a glance over the top of the men but found only arrows to greet him.

Then, without warning, an explosion rocked the forest. It was music to Vighon's ears, however, for he had heard that devastating torrent before and knew well it belonged to a dragon.

Athis!

Searching beyond his shield, there was no sign of the red dragon, but there were indeed great flames tearing at the trees from north to south. The enemy's archers had stopped their relentless assault and piercing screams of agony replaced their deadly arrows. The dragon's wrath also brought the Namdhorians to a halt.

"Steady!" the king yelled, waiting with the others to see what emerged.

Men set alight could be seen through the trees, running wild in their final moments of life. Then the rest came charging, men of Grey Stone with sword, shield, and a war cry on their lips.

"Break!" Vighon barked, ordering the soldiers to break free from their clusters.

The two sides were moments away from crashing into each other when another jet of fire hammered the men of Grey Stone from the sky. The firestorm created an inferno up the enemy's line and replaced the dark of night with the light of day. There never came a clash of swords for there were none who dared to leap through the flames.

Vighon couldn't help but smile at the dragon's timing. Searching for their saviour, the king traced the line of fire to the end and looked up. He froze, mouth agape, and eyes wide.

It wasn't Athis...

CHAPTER 5
TWO WORDS

Having replaced his axe with a mop, Doran Heavybelly did his best to make amends for the terrible mess created by his captured Gobber. The stools and chairs had been righted, the abandoned tankards collected, and most of the monster's blood had been wiped away.

No dwarf was cut out for this kind of work.

The son of Dorain sighed with every third sweep of his mop, grumbling incessantly all the while. His day had started on such a high; his prize bound and unconscious, a decent payday coming his way, and a warm bed at The Pick-Axe awaiting him. How could it all have gone so wrong to the point that he was now mopping floors?

Compounding his bad day, there was still the matter of informing his current employer, Maester Dhask, that he had failed to deliver the Gobber alive. The local maester had needed samples from the monster's mouth glands, samples that apparently were only viable if extracted while the Gobber yet lived.

The bloody water in his bucket spoke volumes of the monster's fate, just as it spoke of the dwarf's misery.

"Gods have mercy!" Russell groaned from the kitchen.

The door swung open and the old wolf stepped into the main tavern with a block of Darkwell cheese. At least that's what it appeared to be beneath all the blood.

"Do you know how much this stuff costs, Heavybelly? I can't sell any of it now!"

Doran could only shrug apologetically. He didn't even have the coin to replace the cheese. Before any argument could be had, and there was one coming, the tavern door opened and the cool night breeze preceded another monster...

At least that's what Russell saw it as. To Doran, it was a Warhog named Pig!

"Oh no!" the old wolf cried warningly. "That beast isn't allowed in here on the best of days! Get rid of it, Heavybelly!"

"A'right, a'right!" Doran waved his hand at Russell before using the mop to discourage Pig from coming any farther. "Go on, be off with ye! Go an' terrorise The King's Inn down the road." The Warhog snorted and tried to find a way around its master. "I said off with ye!" he yelled again, ushering it back with the dripping mop.

With a disgruntled squeal, Pig finally turned around and left The Pick-Axe. It wouldn't be long before the patrons of The King's Inn were fleeing their seats and leaving their drinks in search of somewhere more peaceful. Hopefully, Doran thought, they would find their way to The Axe and start helping with the coin Russell needed for repairs.

With possible customers in mind, Doran went back to mopping. No one wanted to share a drink with Gobber's blood under their boots. The door opened again, however, forcing a long sigh from the dwarf.

"I told ye, Pig, be off with—" Doran caught himself upon seeing the young man standing in the doorway.

"Evening," the young man greeted politely enough, if somewhat exhausted.

"Well met," Doran replied in his bloody apron. "Would ye care for a drink? Russell! The Pick-Axe sells the best mead in the realm!"

"What now?" Russell complained as he entered via the kitchen door. "Oh. Good evening, Sir. What can I do for you?"

The man held up his hands in apology. "I'm sorry for the confusion. I'm not here for a drink. My name is Rik Delaney; I'm a runner from Namdhor."

Russell arched a thick white eyebrow. "A runner? Now who would be sending me post from the capital?"

"I couldn't say, Sir," the runner replied, his chest heaving. "I was given it by my master." Reaching into his satchel, he retrieved the letter in question and handed it to the tavern owner.

"How much do I owe you?" Russell asked without even looking at the envelope.

"It's already been paid in full, Sir."

Doran gave a sharp laugh. "It must be a *good* friend, Rus!"

The old wolf turned the envelope over and frowned. "It isn't addressed to me..."

Doran's surprise increased when it became clear that the letter was addressed to him. "Bah! It must be a mistake, lad. I've called this land me home for over a century now an' I ain' never once received no letter." The dwarf made to break the seal when he recognised the sigil of his clan imprinted in the wax. "Ye say ye don' know who sent this, boy?"

"No, Sir."

Without taking his eyes off the seal, Doran said, "Get the lad a drink will ye, Rus. He's come a long way..."

His hands hesitated before he broke the seal and removed the letter therein. The parchment was of fine quality and thick between his fingers. Such details were quickly lost on Doran when he noted the blood staining the letter and a single thumbprint smeared in the corner. In the centre of the parchment were two dwarvish words and nothing else.

Father's dead.

Doran held his breath, absorbing the news. Dorain, son of Dorryn, had just over a thousand years to his name - a grand old age for any dwarf. Father and son had never seen eye to eye, but that fact did little to soothe his grieving heart.

The writing was definitely Dakmund's, Doran's brother and now Grimwhal's king. It appeared to have been written in haste if the nature of the scrawl was anything to go by. The dried blood gripped Doran in a fearful hold. Was it his father's? Was it Dakmund's? Why had it been written in such haste? It could never be known that the king was contacting his older brother, the exile, but if he was going to risk so much by writing to him, why didn't it say more?

There were too many questions for the son of Dorain's liking. Unfortunately, there was only way he was going to get any answers...

"Thank you for the water, good Sir." The runner was polite enough not to linger and made for the door. "Oh, begging your pardon," he apologised as Asher walked in at the same moment.

The ranger stepped aside and waited for the runner to leave the tavern before checking the streets and closing the door behind him. "Is anyone else here?" Asher asked.

"No," Russell answered. "And he wasn't even a customer, just a runner from Namdhor."

"A runner?" Asher looked at Doran, who was still holding the letter from his brother.

"He's dead," Doran croaked, as if his friends had been aware of his thoughts.

Russell came out from behind the bar. "Who's dead?" he questioned.

"Me father." Doran held out the letter.

The two old rangers made sympathetic expressions and offered their condolences. "Is that blood?" Asher noted.

"Aye. An' I could do with knowin' whose." Doran held the letter out to Russell.

The old wolf accepted the letter and sniffed the parchment. "This is your brother's blood," he announced gravely.

That answered one of Doran's questions and brought up a dozen more. "Ye're sure, lad?"

"It's been a long time since I've been in the presence of Dakmund Heavybelly, but a wolf never forgets a scent."

"You're sure that isn't the scent on the parchment?" Asher checked, taking the letter from Russell.

"I might be getting a little long in the fang but I still know how to use my own nose."

"This was written in a hurry," the ranger observed.

"That was me own thinkin'," Doran agreed. "Why would me brother go to all the effort o' sendin' me a note an' only write two damned words."

"Because that was all he had time for," Asher concluded.

That led Doran to one outcome. "Grimwhal is under attack..."

Russell wasn't convinced. "If that was the case, why would he send you a note at all?"

"He'd want me to know abou' father," Doran explained. "If the clan has been under attack, there's every chance they haven' even given 'im his funeral rites yet."

"Doran..." Russell's tone was full of warning. "You can't be thinking like that. You wouldn't be welcome in Grimwhal, not to mention the position you would be putting your brother in."

Doran whole-heartedly agreed with his friend. "I'm goin'."

"You're going to Dhenaheim?" Asher was clearly on Russell's side of the argument.

"Namdhor first," Doran replied, taking his apron off. "There's Heavybelly dwarves in the city for tradin' an' the like. They should 'ave a better line o' communication with Grimwhal. Hopefully, they'll know what's goin' on up there."

Russell wasn't finished trying to dissuade the dwarf. "I'm truly sorry for the loss of your father, Doran, but you should reconsider getting in the middle of this. Grimwhal's business isn't yours to worry about anymore. Besides, those boys can take care of themselves."

"What if the other clans 'ave finally turned on 'em?" Doran posed, looking for his axe.

PHILIP C. QUAINTRELL

"How many wars have clan Heavybelly fought since you walked away?" Russell countered. "Adding your axe to whatever's going on up there isn't going to solve anything."

Doran whipped his head around. "Me axe has solved plenty o' problems I'll 'ave ye know!"

Russell sighed and let his head hang to his chest. "You stubborn sack of hammers... Fine. I'm coming with you."

The son of Dorain strapped his axe to his back and turned once again on the old wolf. "What are ye abou'? Ye've got a tavern to run. Like ye said, ye've been workin' on this place for years."

"I've got savings to see me through, don't you fret. Besides," Russell continued with a touch of melancholy, "this might be my last real outing in the world before these old bones give up..."

Doran quibbled over his response, his honesty fighting with his desire to bolster his friend. "Nonsense, lad! There's plenty o' life left in those rusty bones o' yers!"

"Either way; I'm coming with you."

Doran could see Russell wasn't to be discouraged. "Then I shall appreciate the company. Will ye be bringin' some o' ye wares?" he added, sliding his eye towards the ales on the shelf behind the bar.

Russell scowled at the dwarf and turned to Asher. "Will you be joining us?"

The ranger appeared to struggle with the question. "I would gladly accompany you, if only to make sure Doran doesn't end up on the sharp end of a dwarven axe. But the contract I have been offered holds the lives of others in the balance."

Doran's eyes lit up for the first time since reading his brother's letter. "Oh aye! I forgot abou' that! What's the coin?"

"What's the job?" Russell asked with a sideways glance at the dwarf.

"It's... *complicated*. More political than I would like, but the job has an appeal beyond the coin." Asher dropped a fist-size bag of coins on the table in front of Doran. "That should be recompense for the job you lost."

Doran opened the sack with an impressed eye. "Ye don' 'ave to do that, lad..."

"It's yours," Asher insisted.

"The Mother an' Father 'ave blessed me with good friends." Doran did his best to say it without getting choked up.

"That isn't even half," Asher replied.

The son of Dorain turned on the ranger in disbelief. "Ye don' say!"

"Are you going far?" Russell enquired.

"No. Lady Gracen would have me journey into the thick of The Evermoore."

The old wolf caught onto a thread. "The Drakes?"

Asher nodded. "Hunters from Wood Vale who need persuading to find a new prey."

Russell nodded along. "The Drakes are quite the topic in Lirian. There's been arguments for years about sharing the land with them."

"A noble job," Doran proclaimed. "One deservin' o' yer blade, Asher. Ye'd be wasted accompanyin' us; there won' be no fightin' for sure... *probably*."

Russell didn't look so convinced. "Let's take a trip down to the locker and stock up on a few things anyway."

"I have all I need," Asher replied, facing the tavern door. "I will see you... when I see you."

Doran understood, as they all did. Whenever the rangers parted ways, they did so with the knowledge that they might never see each other again. Such was the nature of their job. The son of Dorain could be arrogant at times, but he wasn't cocky enough to believe that it would be he who returned and not Asher: the man simply refused to die.

"The last one back 'ere is buyin' the first round," the dwarf told them.

Asher smiled. "Better save some of that coin then." And with his parting words, the ranger left The Pick-Axe.

Doran laughed to himself. "He's the only person I know who would choose to enter The Evermoore at night."

Russell made for the door that led to the basement. "He's also the only person you know who can see in the dark better than he can see in the light."

The dwarf had to agree. "Wait," he demanded with the tone of a sigh. "'ere, this is for ye..." Doran took two coins out of the sack, pocketed them, and then threw the sack to Russell. "For the damage."

Russell had the look of deep appreciation. "You know this doesn't even come close to covering your tab..."

Doran swore.

CHAPTER 6
REUNION

Deep inside The Black Fort, there was but one sound that filled its gloomy halls of ice and flame. Inara Galfrey danced around her enemies, her Vi'tari blade clashing again and again with the steel of Grey Stone.

They were proficient warriors all, likely among Thaddeus's greatest soldiers. But none of them had ever faced a Dragorn. Despite her youthful appearance, Inara had just over forty years behind her, thirty years of which had been spent wielding a Vi'tari scimitar and training daily in the art of the Mag'dereth.

She was naught but fury.

In her wake, a red cloak billowed in every direction, accompanying her spins and jumps. The Dragorn weaved between their strikes and ducked under Thaddeus's cleaver, sweeping her leg out to then knock the would-be king onto his back. A swift backhand battered another's blade away and a boot to his chest sent him flying into the roaring hearth - his screams drowning out the next meeting of swords.

Enraged, another soldier raised his sword and charged her. Inara dashed to the side while simultaneously levelling her blade across his midriff. The collision of man and steel was momentary but mortally devastating for the soldier. Before the Dragorn was once again engaged in combat, her enchanted sword had already rid itself of the blood.

That didn't last very long.

The next attempted, what he believed to be, a complex twist and spin of his sword. Perhaps once, such a strategy had disorientated his enemy and proven an efficient way to find a deadly blow. To Inara, the soldier might as well have announced his actions in time with his swordplay. First he lost his sword - batted away. Then his hand - severed at the wrist. This was quickly followed by his life - a clean swipe across his throat.

Thaddeus was losing men fast. The son of Thedomir growled as he pushed one soldier aside and came at Inara with his bloodless cleaver. The Dragorn side-stepped his obvious attack and spun around to bring the crystal pommel of her hilt into his nose. The bones and cartilage shattered, spreading pain across his face and splattering his mouth with blood. She followed up the encounter with an attack of her own and jammed the palm of her hand into his throat - she wanted him alive.

On the cold floor again, Thaddeus was a bloody mess who was too busy coughing and choking to assist what was left of his ambush. Inara called on her magic and pushed out her hand at the next soldier too stupid to realise he was already dead. The wave of telekinetic energy that scooped him off his feet drove him so hard into the pillar that the ancient stone cracked behind his head.

The second to last soldier hesitated, perhaps a notch smarter than his comrade. Inara wasn't going to wait, however, her body having given in to the flow of form five and the urge of her enchanted scimitar. Her blade flicked up then down, knocking the soldier's sword away, before her free hand shot up and launched an icy spell into his chest. So cold was the magic that the blood flowing in and out of his heart froze instantly, ensuring his death even before he was thrown into the chamber wall.

The last soldier lucky enough to still be in possession of a pulse was luckier yet. Coming for his attack, he had unknowingly matched his strike with the mage outside. A staccato of lightning was hurled at Athis, tearing at his scales and the muscles beneath. Inara cried out as the pain carried across their bond, her vision blinded by agony.

Only the magic within her Vi'tari blade saved her life. The scimitar reacted to the threat and forced her to raise her arm and block the man of Grey Stone. It could do nothing, unfortunately, against the boot that came up and kicked her in the ribs. With a yelp and a roll, the Dragorn took the hit and tumbled away, though she was quickly hounded by the soldier. His newly gained confidence, however, was to be the end of him. Inara had but to point her scimitar in his direction and the fool charged into it, impaling himself.

A shock of pain ran up the Dragorn's spine - another salvo of spells from the mage outside - and she thrust her blade even deeper into the man's gut. Rising slowly to her feet, Inara pushed him over and reclaimed her sword.

Athis?

This mage is tenacious! the dragon growled. *She has mastered a great many defensive spells to resist my fire.*

Facing Thaddeus again, Inara tried to suppress the rage swelling within Athis. If she gave in to the dragon's anger, she would likely add another body to The Black Fort's throne room...

"Explain yourself, Thaddeus," she demanded. "I see fear in your eyes."

The would-be king wiped the blood dripping over his lips away and sneered. "The difference between you and me, is that I know when I'm beaten." He pointed his cleaver at the Dragorn. "It'll make for a slow death..."

Before Inara could ask him anything else, Thaddeus ran at her with his cleaver in both hands. It would have been easy to let the Vi'tari blade assume control of her movements and have it take his head. But a man without a head couldn't answer questions, and Inara had more than a few.

When the distance between them was just right, the Dragorn leaped forward with her leg flexed and aimed at his burly chest. Her speed, and certainly her strength, were magnitudes above that of the young man of Grey Stone and he fell victim to her surprise attack. After being launched in the opposite direction, Thaddeus looked up from his back and discovered Inara to be standing over him. Her fist dropped him into a world of darkness.

Inara yelled in pain again as Athis took another spell from the mage. The mage herself begged many questions but, right now, the Dragorn just wanted Athis to deal with her and save them both the pain.

His temper flaring dangerously out of control, Athis unleashed some of his animal savagery. His spiked tail came down on the mage again and again, hammering her shield relentlessly. Through their bond, Inara could see that the mage was beginning to tire. The dragon ceased his hammering and whipped his tail from left to right, clubbing the mage into the side of the cliff. Her shield blazed and dissipated around her.

Inara could feel what her companion was about to do. *Don't!* she cried.

In his ire, the dragon dashed in and snatched the mage within his jaws. Inara could taste the blood in her mouth, a sensation that threatened to see her vomit over the floor. Athis refrained from eating the woman, however, and let her broken body fall from his razor-sharp teeth. There was no question - the mage was dead.

Athis didn't apologise, nor would he ever for behaving as his nature demanded. Inara looked past it, doing her best to ignore the lingering taste in her mouth, and gripped Thaddeus by the ankle.

I'm coming out, she told her companion. *I don't suppose you could open the doors for me...*

Inara dragged Thaddeus's body through the halls of The Black Fort free of resistance. There wasn't a soldier in sight; a fact that greatly disturbed the Dragorn. When she finally arrived at the sealed doors, the thick slabs were still closed. Inara waited patiently.

The entrance hall soon began to heat up and an orange glow appeared in the join between the doors. Burning bright, this orange glow swelled, expanding across the doors until molten chunks of iron were dropping onto the floor. Sensing her companion's next action, Inara dragged Thaddeus's body to the side and erected a shield in front of them both.

Athis wasted no time in swinging his tail, slamming it into the molten circle. The doors shook, freeing themselves of centuries' worth of dust, but the circle of slag was launched into the entrance, filling the hall with smoke. Next, the dragon exhaled a breath of ice to cool the passage and allow Inara to pass through.

A starry night greeted the Dragorn, along with a graveyard. The snows around the main doors were strewn with bodies and licking flames. To the side, the mage's body lay very still, her black robes flapping in the wind.

Inara dropped Thaddeus's body in front of Athis. ***Bring them both.***

With a body in each claw and Inara on his back, the red dragon took off into the sky before adjusting his angle to take them down towards Vighon's camp. It was impossible to miss the fire. Inara leaned forward to better see the inferno that ran behind the Namdhorian line. A second fire was visible inside the woods, the light from its flames revealing bodies in the snow, many of which were also on fire.

To the north and south, Namdhorian soldiers were rounding up men of Grey Stone and binding their wrists before sorting them into camps. Within the barracks, bodies were being picked up and laid down again in neat rows, each placed under their navy cloaks. Inara's heart sank. They had fallen for Thaddeus's invitation and left the Namdhorians vulnerable to an ambush.

Can you see him?

Athis searched the chaos below. *No,* he replied. *But the king's tent is surrounded by his guard.*

Inara chose to believe that meant Vighon was alive. **Take me to him.**

The closer they got the more ravenous the fire appeared. Inara had seen aggressive fire like that many times, but since Athis had been with her atop Grey Stone, she assumed it was magic in origin. Clearly, the mage hadn't been working alone...

With no space to land within the campsite, Athis touched down in the space between the Namdhorians and the city. He released Thaddeus's unconscious form and the mage's body before bringing his front claws into the snow. Inara signalled a pair of soldiers, calling them away from their duties. She gave them instructions to have her prisoner and the body brought to the king's tent. The Dragorn would have accompanied them herself, but she was anxious to lay eyes on Vighon and know that he was safe.

A pall of death had taken over the camp. Bodies riddled with arrows were littered everywhere and a handful of tents were still alight. More than once, Inara was forced to navigate around the carcass of a horse that looked as if it had been used for target practice.

Standing outside Vighon's tent, his appearance less immaculate than usual, Sir Ruban Dardaris bowed his head upon her approach. Ruban's presence was a good sign that Vighon was alive; the captain of the king's guard would always die before the king came to harm.

"His Grace is inside," he told her, a notable edge of unease about him.

Inara planted a friendly hand on his pauldron as she passed him by, her curiosity battling her fears. Beyond the flaps, the interior was illuminated by a simple array of candles, scattering the tent with shadows. Still, through the low light, Inara easily found Vighon on the other side of the table - not a mark on him, to her relief.

The smile slipped from her face after following his eyes to the corner of the tent. There stood a man in black armour, not dissimilar to a dragon's scales, and a heavy dark cloak lined with scarlet. Chestnut hair framed his face and flowed over his shoulders, braids scattered throughout. Blue eyes, an identical shade to her own, looked back at her.

"Alijah..." she whispered.

"Hello, Inara."

Hearing her brother's voice brought a sense of relief she hadn't realised she needed - it was like honey. Inara's eyes welled and the instinct to launch herself on him and crush him inside her embrace was overwhelming. But there was something about her twin that kept her rooted to the spot, something that gnawed at the warrior within.

Any threat she felt from Alijah began to melt away with his smile. "I've missed you," he said.

Inara glanced at Vighon, searching for any sign of ill intent that she might have missed, any sign of trickery. The king was entirely at ease, judging by the way he was leaning against the table.

"You're really here," Inara replied in disbelief.

Alijah flashed his disarming smile again. "Yes, Sister, I am really here. Now, are you just going to stand there or are you going to give me a hug?"

Inara took a much-needed breath and managed a smile. Only while embracing him did that smile become genuine and she squeezed him tightly. As they both pulled away, her fingers dragged along his arms.

"Are they actually..."

"Dragon scales," Alijah finished proudly. "Most of the armour is made of it."

Inara was taken aback. "It's exquisite," she admired.

"You look good," Alijah complimented, taking in her brown leathers.

Inara wanted to ask a lot more questions about the nature of his armour, but her more pressing question was, "What are you doing here?"

Alijah opened his mouth to answer but instead looked to Vighon. "He's come to help," the king announced.

A knot formed in Inara's brow. "Help?"

"Illian stands on the edge of war again," Alijah explained needlessly. "A civil war will tear the country apart and see thousands die."

Inara didn't need telling, but Alijah's timing and knowledge prevented her from taking joy in his return. "I don't understand," she began. "How could you know all this? Where have you been?"

Alijah put his hands up. "Forgive me; this isn't how I wanted to return. I saw no other choice once I learned of Grey Stone's treachery. As soon as I knew what Thedomir had planned, I left Erador immediately."

"And I'm glad of it," Vighon added. "Because of you and Malliath, there will be many more wives and mothers in Namdhor who will see their husbands and sons again."

"That doesn't really answer my question." Inara didn't mean to sound rude, but she couldn't ignore the icy feeling that lingered in her gut.

"Inara..." Vighon pleaded.

"No, no, it's fine. You would have asked me the same question if I hadn't just come out and told you." Alijah turned to his sister. "I hope you don't think ill of me, but... I have been watching events from afar."

The knot in Inara's brow wasn't going anywhere. "How long have you been in Illian?"

Alijah shook his head. "I haven't been watching you from Illian. In fact, I never left Erador. There is a place, magical in nature, hidden well in the heights of Mount Kaliban, where one can observe all the world. You can even listen to conversations if you know where to be looking."

There was something awfully wrong about that but, again, much like Alijah himself, Inara failed to pinpoint what the issue was. She didn't know what to say, still flustered by his mere presence as well as the facts he was relaying.

"I know it wasn't the decent thing to do," Alijah continued, detecting his sister's unease. "Since leaving Illian, I have feared what darkness might prey upon it in my absence. But, I assured myself that Vighon, and yourself, could keep the realm in one piece. And so you have..."

Inara raised an eyebrow. "But now we're failing?"

Alijah screwed his face into one of apology. "Of course not! You've simply found yourselves in need of allies. This schism goes beyond Thedomir and Grey Stone. I have *seen* those that meet in the shadows and plot Illian's end."

Inara didn't miss the look of justification that flashed across Vighon's face.

"And who are these conspirators?" the Dragorn asked.

Alijah shrugged. "They never used their real names, but they did use powerful magic to conceal their exact location and appearance. The closest I could pin them to was somewhere inside Velia."

"Valatos!" Vighon proclaimed righteously. "I told you it started inside their walls."

Inara wasn't convinced, yet she failed to find the lie behind her brother's words, or his potential reason for doing so. He wasn't as she had last seen him: cold and detached. Now, he was closer to the brother she had known so long ago, his personality shining through once again. So why was she anything but overjoyed to see him?

"Inara?" Alijah was reading her just as she was reading him. "I'm just here to help," he said quietly, his tone thick with earnest. "I realise that *spying* on you all doesn't cast me in the best light but, I promise you, I only want peace. I'm only here now to help you keep that peace."

Inara nodded along, desperate to believe him. "And how will you help us?"

"When I arrived in Erador, they too were amidst a civil war. Entire cities, generations of people, were being swept off the map because of greed. To this day, that civil war still casts a shadow over the realm, one that might take me centuries to get rid of. But I did bring an end to their warring..."

"How?" Vighon asked eagerly.

"I advised their king for some years. Malliath and I travelled around the country with him, flying from city to city. We provided a safe place for the opposing parties to talk out their differences. In some places, we were needed to enforce the king's laws. The people needed bringing back together again. Seeing their king helped with that."

"I bet Malliath's considerable shadow helped too," Inara had to point out.

Alijah didn't shy away from the obvious. "Malliath's presence was nothing if not preventative. Seeing his size and the threat he posed, there were none who dared lift a sword. Instead, words had their day and peace was found."

"There is still peace now?" Vighon checked. "This king still rules?"

"There is peace, but King Horgarn sadly passed away ten years ago. *I* am the king of Erador now..."

A moment of introspection and Inara realised she wasn't as shocked at that as she thought she would be. Her brother's charisma and power made him the obvious choice, especially given his assistance throughout the land. But it still didn't sit right with her.

"You just took the crown?" she asked as evenly as possible.

"King Horgarn bore no heirs. At the time, there was a lord who attempted to assume the throne, but the people of Valgala, Erador's capital that is, refused to allow him. They wanted *me*. I was reluctant at first, but I soon came to see that it was the best thing for the kingdom - they needed stability more than anything."

"Your Grace?" Sir Ruban called.

"Enter."

The captain of the king's guard entered the tent with four soldiers. Between them, they carried Thaddeus, who was beginning to rouse, and the mage's body, which was still leaking blood.

Inara turned to a questioning Vighon. "You weren't the only one to be ambushed."

The king made his way around the table. "Now there's a fight I would have paid to see."

Thaddeus was brought up to his knees and held in place by two soldiers. He was bloodied and bruised, his eyes swollen. He looked around until he settled on Alijah, the only stranger in the tent.

"He was afraid," Inara informed them.

"Why would you do this, Thaddeus?" Vighon demanded. "Why would your father do this?" Thaddeus had no reply, his eyes shifting nervously. "You knew we were coming before we left Namdhor. Who told you?"

Thaddeus looked confused, even through his swollen features. "I don't... I don't understand," he croaked. "I thought—"

His next word was squeezed from his throat when the golden chain around his neck decreased dramatically in size, cutting into his skin. His eyes bulged and veins swelled within his neck, which was quickly becoming a deep red. Inara was the first to react and snatched at the chain. Up close, she could see that the clasp was that of a snake's head, its mouth consuming the chain.

"It's magic!" she cried, slicing her fingers in an effort to pull it away from his throat.

"Move!" Alijah jumped in and held his palm out to the necklace.

Inara could feel the magic coalescing around him, a fact that everyone else in the tent was ignorant of. The chain twitched before a small curve appeared, as if the metal was being drawn to her brother's hand. Alijah was all focus, all his energy poured into his spell. The snake doubled its efforts and continued to consume the chain, wrapping it tightly around Thaddeus's neck again. He gargled and spluttered, clawing at his own neck.

Alijah groaned under the exertion. Then, the chain cut entirely through the would-be king's skin and into the muscle. It didn't stop until there was nothing left but a bloodied clasp in the centre of his throat. Thaddeus's head rolled off his body and added another corpse to the tent floor.

"What in all the hells was that?" Vighon grimaced.

Alijah took a breath and removed the snake's head from the pool of blood. "Insurance," he said.

Inara agreed. "Whoever gifted him that necklace did so to ensure he would never reveal the identities of his allies."

"More magic," Vighon concluded, gesturing for Ruban and the soldiers to leave them.

"You can't keep pointing your finger at Valatos," Inara reminded him. "There are others who command magic in this world."

"True enough," Alijah concurred. "But, perhaps it would be prudent to rule them out first. They might even be able to point us in the right direction. Surely they know of other magic users in Illian."

Inara heard the sense but she still addressed the king. "We shouldn't interrupt my... *our* parents. Leave them—"

"Our parents?" Alijah repeated, his interest piqued.

"Yes," Inara explained, eager to finish her point, "they're in Valatos as we speak. Did you not *see* that?"

Alijah gave a look of genuine innocence. "You might recall I'm running a kingdom. I haven't the time to see *everything...*"

"Well, they're in Valatos right now," Inara continued. "And I don't think it would be wise to interrupt them. If there is anything to uncover, they will do so without us turning up on dragon back, not to mention with half an army. There's also the matter of the mages' independence," she brought up. "Valatos is campaigning for it and our parents might be able to persuade them otherwise."

Vighon was looking tired, reminding Inara that he was older than she often considered him. He had also endured quite the night, from losing many men in an ambush to reacquainting with his oldest friend - who confirmed his worst fears were indeed true.

The king held his hands up. "Why don't you tell us about the other body in my tent."

Inara almost didn't want to tell him. "I fear we will never know her name. She was, however, a mage..."

Another layer to Vighon's argument was compounded. "She was with Thaddeus?"

"I have to assume so," the Dragorn replied. "She fought with Athis. She was powerful; knew her way around magic."

"Not well enough," Alijah commented, crouching down to inspect the teeth marks that had ravaged her body.

Vighon sighed and leaned back against the table. "How could I have been so foolish? How many have died because I walked us into a trap?" The king turned around and gripped the small bear statue that rested over Grey Stone on the map. "Thedomir knew we were coming. He knew our numbers and even those of Lady Gracen's men. Not only do I have separatists and conspirators to deal with, but now it seems clear I have been betrayed."

Inara made to reassure him, to let him know that the kingdom wasn't spiralling out of his control, but her brother spoke first, his words less of a balm and more of an oil to keep the fire burning.

"Those that seek to harm your kingdom have struck the first blow," Alijah said, "but they have failed to kill you. This gives you an opportunity to root them out now. They won't have anticipated my arrival. I'm confident this will give them pause before they strike again. The window is slim but, *together*, perhaps we can quash this evil and keep the peace."

"You would help me do this?" Vighon asked, his eyes flashing with hope in the candlelight.

"I haven't just come to save you from an ambush," Alijah replied with a warm smile. "Maybe it's time for an alliance between Illian and Erador..."

The king almost laughed. "I like the sound of that."

Inara had a lot she wanted to say in that moment, mostly of restraint and the importance of keeping a clear head while in command of an army. In the presence of her brother, however, the Dragorn kept her comments to herself and straightened her back.

"It warms my heart that you have returned, Alijah." She truly meant that, despite her reservations. "And I am grateful for your timely arrival this night. As the Guardian of the Realm, though, I would ask that I might speak with the king alone..."

Alijah looked to understand and offered no protest - something he certainly would have done in another life. "Of course. I will go and find Malliath." Bowing to Vighon, the king of Erador, as he was, made his leave.

A moment of awkward silence passed between Inara and Vighon as they waited and allowed Alijah's sensitive ears to fall prey to the hubbub outside.

"I thought you would be glad of his return," Vighon remarked, stepping away from the two bodies.

Inara didn't know where to begin. "He caught me off guard..."

"Is that all?" the king pressed. "I thought I detected a hint of... *disbelief.*"

"Have you forgotten what happened to him?" The Dragorn moved around the table to mirror Vighon's path. "Have you forgotten *why* it happened to him?"

"Of course I haven't forgotten," the king assured. "What The Crow did to him was an atrocity, but it was fifteen years ago, Inara. He seems every bit the Alijah I remember."

Vighon made fifteen years sound like a very long time, but Inara knew better. An immortal, even one who had yet to live a hundred years, felt the passage of time differently. Still, he wasn't wrong about her brother; there were familiar aspects she had long missed.

"Besides," Vighon continued, "he's a king now. He has his own people, his own land, and responsibilities. Whatever The Black Hand drummed into him about his destiny to rule has surely been fulfilled by his current position."

"I still remember what he was like," Inara replied, "just before he left. He wasn't Alijah then, not the Alijah we knew. I told myself then, and have spent years coming to terms with it, that my brother died in The Bastion. That if he was ever to return he would be someone else."

Hope, wingless one, Athis told her. *There was always hope that he would find his way and free himself of The Crow's torment.*

"He *has* returned as someone else," Vighon agreed. "He's returned a king! He's come as an ally. Yes, he was wrong to have spied on us, but he admitted as much. Had he not come when he did, you would be burying the king of Illian tomorrow."

"You are more than that to me," Inara reminded him.

"Then trust me, as a *friend*," Vighon pleaded. "We now have a powerful ally, one our enemies couldn't have planned for. We should use this gift and bring the kingdom to order. We've fought too hard to lose it..."

Reluctantly, Inara conceded. "What is to be your next step then?"

"First things first: take count of our dead. Lady Gracen will wish to know how many of her own have fallen, and we should help Grey Stone too. This mess aside, the province still resides under my care."

Inara was pleased to hear that Vighon still knew his role was to be a caretaker, not a tyrant. "We can reassess the situation tomorrow," she said. "It would be unwise to make any decisions after tonight's events - violence has a way of clouding our judgment."

"True," the king replied. "But, Inara..." Vighon paused, struggling with his words. "This *will* be met with violence - too many have died."

Athis's voice filled Inara's mind. *That's why we will be there, to ensure he stays true to himself.*

Inara felt both dispirited and uplifted by the two comments. "If there *is* justice to be dealt, Athis and I will be by your side."

With that, the Dragorn left the king to his duties - which were many in the wake of Grey Stone's ambush. Walking back into the bitter cold, Inara shrugged her shoulders to bring her red cloak about her. In front of the soldiers, she kept her chin up and an air of confidence about her. They didn't need to see the tempest of emotions that battled for supremacy.

Having cleared the camp, there was nothing between her and Athis. As always, his red scales and deep blue eyes were a comfort to her. For all the turmoil that threatened to unbalance the world, the dragon would continue to be the centre of her reality, her anchor in stormy seas.

Something in the sky caught Athis's eye and drew Inara's gaze to the stars above. A dark shadow eclipsed the moon and glided over the twinkling heavens before turning around and crossing the cliff face.

Malliath...

The black dragon was menacing in appearance, a characteristic always taken from his gargantuan size. He was too far away to make out his purple eyes, but Inara was sure one of them would be trained on her. Astride his back, Alijah was seated in a saddle that wrapped all the way around Malliath's chest - a highly unusual sight on any dragon.

Do you trust him? Athis asked the obvious question.

Inara watched her brother and his dragon ascend back into the night's sky and disappear. ***I don't know...***

CHAPTER 7
HUNTING GROUNDS

Stepping between the trees and leaving civilisation behind was like taking that first gulp of air for Asher. The farther he left Lirian behind, the farther he penetrated the wilds of the world. The ranger could never feel more free than when he was trekking across the realm with nothing but the land itself for company.

His green cloak scraped the ground behind, but the summer and lack of rain had kept the mud hard, preventing his attire from becoming so dirty as for him to appear as an Outlander of The Wild Moores.

Every few hundred yards, his hands would fall lightly over various parts of his body, checking that he was still in possession of his supplies and weapons. At the base of his back lay a curved dagger from Tregaran, in the southern lands. Resting over the sheath was his quiver and recurve bow - both basic in design but highly efficient in the right hands. Nestled neatly between the two was his silvyr short-sword, easily the most valuable item he owned.

On his left hip rested a two-handed broadsword - his favoured weapon. With a spiked pommel, the sword was deadly at both ends.

Besides the dagger hidden in the back of his right boot, there were concealed knives within his belt, mostly used for cooking if he was being honest with himself. There wasn't much else required when his broadsword was out of its scabbard...

His armour was predominantly leather, a dark brown that often allowed him to blend in with the woods. There was a piece, here and there, that had been gifted to him or simply bought when needed. A pair of tired and scarred pauldrons sat on his shoulders, gifted to him by a captain of Namdhor more than a decade ago, as thanks for saving his life during the reclamation of Velia from the orcs.

The bracers, tight around his forearms, had been a gift from the king himself, an added thanks for his service during the battle on The White Vale. So old were they that the flaming sword sigil was barely visible anymore. Still, much like the pauldrons, they were of the best make and tough against weather and foe alike.

Greying hair fell to his shoulders, though he kept much of it tied back to keep it out of his eyes. On a job like this one, he needed his eyes. Seeing through the density of trees wasn't easy, but knowing he was searching for multiple enemies, all of whom could have fanned out, made it all the harder.

He journeyed through The Evermoore for many hours after leaving Lirian behind. Keeping his bearings was key, but he had more than one lifetime's experience in navigating the world. The ranger was sure to alter his heading to bear west, away from his northerly route. He needed to skirt past Ikirith, the Drakes' woodland city, not actually enter it. The hunters would be coming south, from Wood Vale, giving Asher a narrow band of forest to intercept them.

He moved like a wraith, a creature that could hardly be said to exist in the physical world. His every footstep was calculated but swift, ensuring that he made not a sound while maintaining his speed. Moving unseen and unheard was among his first lessons in Nightfall, a place that served agonising punishment to those who failed to embrace their new life as an assassin.

There were times, such as this, when the ranger would find

himself thinking back, dwelling on his time as a killer. They had been brutal years, nearly three decades of training under the best murderers in the realm until he was good enough to be called an Arakesh. Then he had been unleashed. Being the best among his fellow assassins had once been a source of pride for Asher, before it turned to shame.

How many monsters had he slain? How many people had he saved? All had been in atonement for his previous life, but the number never satiated his guilt. Even now, after playing his own part in keeping the dark at bay in more than one war, the ranger still searched for jobs that offered the most risk, wondering if it was time to pay the ultimate price for the lives he had taken.

Asher shook his head in an effort to rid himself of such dark musings. Working in solitude had been his way for so long that he had forgotten the benefits of journeying with company. At least with Doran by his side, or even the quieter Galanör, he was offered some distraction from his own thoughts. The ranger almost laughed to himself. Once upon a time he would have done anything to avoid travelling with company. The Galfreys had a lot to answer for...

Before Asher could spare a thought for his oldest friends, a foreign sound reached his ears. Without seeing it he couldn't say exactly what it was, but he knew the sound of steel knocking against steel. It wasn't a sword against a sword, for the sound had been fleeting and light. His best guess: one of the hunters was carrying too much and had knocked his weapons together.

It never failed to surprise Asher how easily he slipped back into being the hunter. His muscles carried just as much memory as his mind and they reacted smoothly and always with deadly efficiency. Becoming very still, Asher crouched low and waited, listening for his prey.

They were skilled hunters. He couldn't guess their number by sound alone for none of them made a false step. Not one of them skimmed a bush or stepped on a fallen twig. The only reason he could hear them moving at all was because of their proximity - and they were very close.

Asher carefully lowered himself onto his stomach and crawled in the manner of a cat, his fingers and toes keeping him elevated. His destination was an old log, the remnants of a fallen tree. The ranger froze and held himself in place half a metre away from the cover of the log.

One of the hunters had ascended a nearby collection of rocks, giving the man a lofty view of the landscape. Asher slowly lowered his head and relied on his cloak and leathers to help him blend in under any cursory survey. Ikirith was too far away to expect any Drakes to be in the area, so the hunter was likely in search of something else. Judging by the long shadows, the sun was reaching for the west. There was a good chance the hunter was simply in search of a good place to camp for the night ahead.

A melodic whistle, similar to the calling of a bird, escaped his lips. His signal rallied the other hunters and saw the scout turn away from Asher. It was only for a moment, but it was all the time the ranger needed to reach the shelter of the old log. It was partially hollowed out and he took full advantage of the concealment. If the hunters were indeed about to make camp, they would likely patrol the surrounding area throughout their set up.

A large boot stepped onto the log, raining debris down on Asher's head. The ranger's hand settled instinctively on the hilt of the dagger at his back - the perfect weapon for such close quarters.

"This'll do," the owner of the large boot muttered. "Farley," he rasped, calling to a distant hunter, "scout the area. And keep an arrow nocked. These aren't Drake lands but they're damn close."

After the hunter jumped down from the log, Asher finally got a look at the man. He cared very little for his features, focusing more on his build, the way he carried himself, and the equipment and weapons he hauled. He was tall with wide shoulders on a strong frame. The hunter kept himself in decent shape, likely a result of his profession, indicating proficient skills. His only weapons were a sword, hatchet, and a bow slung over his shoulder. His pack might have supplies inside, but its shape was lost behind the bear traps that had been strapped to the outside.

Turning to look over his shoulder, the hunter revealed a dagger tucked into the front of his belt. It was unusual and immediately caught Asher's eye. An extra moment of inspection revealed the blade to be made of dark bone, ridged and slightly twisted.

A Drake's horn...

This wasn't the first time the hunter had stalked their kind then. Asher was awfully tempted to remove his own dagger, lash out, and sever the tendons in the back of his ankles. It would hurt. A lot. But it would also be very loud and he had no idea how many he was up against yet. His training demanded that he assess first, then plan his attack with a catalogue of his enemies' noted weaknesses.

Remaining inside the old log, Asher waited for the world to pass into starlight. In that time, the hunters set up their makeshift camp and even started a small fire. The ranger inched his way out of the log and edged around their camp, stealing glimpses of the hunters from behind the cover of the foliage and the trees. By the time he had skulked around half of the perimeter, Asher had made a headcount and knew he faced seven men.

Again, he listened.

The men spoke in hushed tones but their words were crystal clear in the sleeping forest. Of all the names bandied around, Farley was never mentioned. Asher had never seen the man referred to as Farley, but there was a very good chance the scout was yet to return. Sense told him to deal with the archer first, making sure he didn't return in the middle of Asher's *argument* for turning home.

Melting farther into the shadows beyond the firelight, the ranger renewed his hunt. Keeping the camp on his left, Asher weaved through the dark forest as if he were a part of it. He had almost come back on himself by the time he came across the silhouette of Farley against the distant fire. The archer was standing very still, giving the ranger pause. Had the scout seen him? It was very possible, given the shadows that enveloped Farley, that he was even aiming his bow at the ranger.

But he didn't so much as twitch.

None but an elf could stand that still. Asher decided to progress with caution, his hand hidden within his cloak as it rested on the curved dagger. He didn't want to kill any of them, if it was possible, but if it came down to him versus an arrow, he would let fly that dagger and bring the hunter down.

Slowly but surely, Asher found himself so close to the archer that he could see all of him in the shadow of the tree. His bow was still slung on his back and his hands hung limply by his sides. The ranger stepped quickly out of the darkness when he realised the truth of the situation.

Farley was dead.

Keeping himself in the shadow of the tree, Asher made a quick inspection of the dead scout. The only reason he was still standing was because the knife in his throat had also impaled the tree.

The ranger abandoned his dagger and, instead, reached over his shoulder for the silvyr short-sword. Whoever had killed Farley had done so with enough stealth that not even Asher had heard a thing, not to mention the strength of such a blow...

The ranger kept very still as his eyes darted between the trees, looking for any threat. He had to entertain the idea that a Drake had done this, regardless of such a violent act being entirely against their nature. They were known for being a physically strong race and this was close to their territory.

Asher couldn't count on both hands the variety of monsters he had slain during his long life, but a Drake wasn't among them. If it came to defending himself, he wasn't so confident that he could survive.

Making his way back towards the hunters' camp, the ranger found his senses were more occupied with his surroundings than the men. There was someone out there, hiding as well as he was - did they know he was here?

This wasn't part of his plan. More troubling for the ranger; he hadn't even considered this scenario. The Evermoore was home to its fair share of monsters and wild animals, but the scout had been killed with a dagger, not claws or teeth. Had Lady Gracen hired someone else to see to the hunters? Asher would have sighed if he wasn't maintaining complete silence.

Sparing a glance at the camp, the ranger did a double take. The hunters weren't sitting around their fire anymore. Asher swore with his lips alone. Pressing his back to the nearest tree, he scanned the forest in every direction, not sure if he should be looking for the hunters or something else entirely.

The fire crackled and spat, drawing his attention back to the camp. Something beside one of the logs caught his eye, a shape the human mind could always find. Leaving the cover of the tree, Asher crept towards the camp, his eyes shifting from the forest to the head that poked out from behind the log. After reaching the log, he discovered the rest of the hunters, all dead and sprawled across the ground.

Asher's experienced eye assessed the scene and came to the conclusion that all seven of them had been killed while still seated. Their cause of death was as obvious as it was gruesome. The ranger turned the jaw of the nearest hunter, examining the gash that opened up his throat - a wound they each shared.

Fresh blood wormed across the ground around the fire, soaking the hunters' prone corpses. How could they all have been killed at the same time, the same way, and without a sound? The worrying conclusion was the number of this mysterious enemy. To have killed them all at the same time and without warning the hunters, there had to be at least seven of them.

The next conclusion Asher found himself arriving at was magnitudes above worrying. There were few, in all the realm, who could take life in this manner. Once upon a time, he had counted himself among that elite group...

Rising to his feet, Asher didn't bother being quiet. They knew he was here. In fact, they had probably been watching him for days to have tracked him this far into The Evermoore.

"Shall we begin?" he asked, his voice gruff.

All around him, the forest seemed to withdraw as the finest killers in Illian emerged from the shadows. In each hand they wielded their infamous short-swords, an hour-glass of steel, similar in shape to Asher's. A strip of red cloth covered their eyes, though none of them were in need of such mundane perception; not when they had Nightseye elixir flowing through their veins.

Asher finally allowed himself that sigh. It was going to be long night...

CHAPTER 8
MAGIC OVER MATTER

The warm glow of dawn shone through the gap in the curtains and settled over Clara's sleeping form. As always, Kassian, who had awoken only moments earlier, took a few precious moments to admire the beautiful woman he was lucky enough to call his wife.

With a delicate finger, he hooked back the auburn hair that covered her cheek and gazed at her face. After losing his parents and sister in The Ash War, the Keeper had convinced himself that he would never again know the love of family.

Clara had taught him otherwise.

She was his family, the keeper of his heart, and the promise of so much more happiness to come. Thoughts of children had started to enter his mind, but the duties of both had kept them from discussing their future of late.

Kassian sighed seeing his Keeper's coat hanging in the corner - he had to go. The Galfreys were still guests in Valatos, wanted or not, and he had to relieve the current Keeper outside their chamber. He took one last look at his wife, already missing her.

"You know it's peculiar when you do that," she said without opening her eyes.

Kassian smiled from ear to ear. "How can it be peculiar to marvel at my wife's beauty?"

Clara groaned before lifting her head to kiss him. "You should definitely be dressed by now. If you're shirking your duties though, I would happily accept some breakfast."

"If only, my love," Kassian complained, making for his uniform. "I should have more free time after the ambassadors have finally left us."

"Are you still harping on about them?" Clara replied mid yawn. "You know they come up in my history classes. They're quite the heroes; you shouldn't complain about being their escort. If anything, you should be boasting about it. Did you know they fought at the battle for West Fellion, atop Syla's Gate, *and* on the walls of this very city during The War for the Realm?"

Kassian did indeed know all of that after his reading. "They have done a great many things," he agreed, shoving his feet into his boots. "But I am more concerned with what they're doing right now. They're here on behalf of the king, Clara. They have been sent to *strong arm* us into giving up our campaign for independence."

Clara got up from their bed and walked around the post to greet him with an affectionate smile and another kiss. "Do not be so quick to judge, my love," she told him, cupping his face in her hands. "They deserve our respect at the very least. And besides, they're here to do nothing but talk; what's the worst that could happen?"

Kassian was taken back to his last conversation with the master and found himself instantly distracted by thoughts of rebellion, not to mention the question of whether he would kill for Valatos. Clara said something else but her words had become nondescript as he considered the act of taking a life on the basis of an order.

"Kassian?" Clara's questioning tone finally brought him back to the present.

"I'm late," he told her, flipping his serious expression to a charming smile. A quick kiss and he was gone, moving so fast he hoped to stay ahead of his dark musings.

It was mid-morning by the time the talks were resumed. One of the masters had left instructions for Kassian to bring the Galfreys to his office in the west wing of the central hall. It was an overly large chamber, especially considering it was only for one man.

Kassian could see, however, that the master had made full use of the space and not wasted an inch. Workstations had been set up almost everywhere, each cluttered with alchemy equipment, various ingredients for spells, and stacks of books from the library. Like all of the Archon, the master was dedicated to the expansion of knowledge where magic was concerned.

As before, there had been no pleasantries between the Galfreys and the master. Of course, the only significant difference was the lack of members from the Archon. A fact not missed by Nathaniel...

"These are supposed to be official talks," the old Graycoat pointed out in his usual rude tone. "The entire Archon should be present. Every word should be noted."

"And so it is, Ambassador," the master replied coolly, gesturing to an open book on the adjacent table. The blank pages were steadily being filled by their conversation, the ink imprinted by magic.

"The Archon's absence is self-explanatory," the master continued. "We see nothing to be gained by further conversation on the topic."

"Then why are we sitting in your office?" Nathaniel demanded.

"You are guests, Ambassador. Though we might disagree on the future of Valatos and perhaps the kingdom as a whole, I would never be so rude as to eject you from the campus."

Reyna placed a soothing hand on her husband's forearm. "I fear we haven't explored all the possible avenues. If Valatos would like to play a more significant role in the workings of the country, I am sure we can find a solution. You spoke with King Vighon a couple of years ago, I believe, concerning the Keepers."

The master nodded pleasantly, though his expression remained concealed behind his mask. "I did, yes. Our Keepers are fine warriors with an exceptional sense of good and evil, right and wrong. The Archon agreed that they would make an excellent replacement for the Dragorn, though they would have been far more similar to the Graycoats. I offered the king our services, patrolling the realm and the like, but he declined."

"Perhaps he wouldn't decline a second time," Reyna suggested with a confident smile, a smile matched by the master's.

"I wouldn't ask a second time. Since then, the Archon has seen a new future for Valatos and our mages. I'm afraid it doesn't include the banner of the flaming sword..."

Their dialogue went on in this fashion for another hour. The Galfreys, to their apparent dismay, found nothing but a wall standing in front of their proposals. Inevitably, the ambassadors grew irritable, if not outright infuriated, and made to leave, promising that a peaceful solution would be discovered before they left Valatos.

Outside the office, Nathaniel turned to Kassian and requested some time in one of their sparring halls. It surprised the Keeper, to be sure, but he could think of no reason they wouldn't be allowed to use one of the halls for an hour. His wanting to deny them their every request was not a good enough reason, he knew.

After the ambassadors had changed into their leathers again, and retrieved their swords, Kassian escorted them across the campus to the Keepers' Sanctorum. It was inside those walls where he had discovered the true strength of his magic, as well as his purpose. Other Keepers, old and young, turned suspicious eyes on the ambassadors, but in the presence of Kassian they moved unchallenged.

The sparring hall was bare of all decoration having been designed with magical combat in mind. A single row of windows ran along the top of one wall, flooding the hall with enough natural light to reveal the clouds of dust that floated lazily on the air.

Nathaniel and Reyna took up their positions opposite each other, their blades in hand. The old Graycoat wielded a straight length of steel with a hand and a half hilt, the pommel a simple disk of gold. It appeared basic from an aesthetic point of view, but Kassian had to assume it was of the very best forging, possibly even elvish given the family he had married into.

Reyna looked to be preparing for a dance, her form elegant and delicate. The scimitar in her hand was certainly of elvish make, the steel's curve and tip so sleek and subtle that it was pleasing to the eye, if deadly to all else. Her blonde hair was tied up in a ponytail to keep her face clear mid-combat.

Husband and wife darted into the centre of the hall and their swords clashed three times before they separated again. Kassian noted that no enchantment had been placed over the blades to ensure that neither could be cut by the sharp steel. The Keeper had to remind himself that these two individuals had been fighting for seventy years.

Kassian couldn't imagine being that age, but he suspected he would struggle to lift a sword, let alone take part in a sparring match. It was easy to see why elves were revered warriors given all the time they had to hone their skills.

Trying not to dwell on the fact that he was past his prime years, Kassian remained against the wall and studied the pair. Reyna was undoubtedly faster, her movements so sharp they often made her husband appear to be moving purposefully slowly.

That wasn't to say that Nathaniel was a poor swordsman. With an experienced mind and a young body, he was technically skilled and even inspiring in the way he was able to blend so many different fighting forms. Though he moved slower, he moved with more purpose, his strikes and footwork deliberately manipulating his wife to constantly reposition her. He also seemed to always know where to find her, though that was likely from decades of sparring with her.

Inevitably, his human stamina failed to stand up to that of an elf's. Worn down, Nathaniel ended the fight on one knee with his wife's scimitar pressed against his neck. Reyna didn't even look tired.

There was a brief pause before they took up their positions again and started the fight anew. After a few strikes, they began talking to each other between blows, only Kassian couldn't understand a word of it. He focused on their pronunciations and individual words and came to the conclusion that they were speaking in Reyna's native tongue.

This troubled him from a security perspective. He had no idea what they were talking about, but Valatos was repeated several times. Instinctively, he reached for the translation spinner in his pocket, but he would have to spin it on the floor since there were no raised surfaces inside the empty hall. Deciding that was too obvious, Kassian resigned himself to his suspicions and paranoia instead.

When Nathaniel's chest was heaving and sweat was dripping down his brow, he finally relented and held up his hand to stop their sparring. Reyna had a touch of fatigue about her now, but she looked ready for the next opponent.

"Kassian," she called. "Would you care to spar?"

The Keeper hesitated. He wondered exactly what the rules were when it came to sparring with guests. Then again, he had been encouraged not to decline the ambassadors anything they might want. And, of course, there was the opportunity to engage an elf in combat; no Keeper could boast of such a thing.

"It would be an honour, Ambassador," he exaggerated.

Most would relieve themselves of their cloak or coat before entering a sparring match but, for Kassian, his coat was part of his form, not to mention a weapon itself. He did, however, shift the bulk of it on his right side to rest behind the holster around his thigh. He had logged more practice hours than he could recall when it came to drawing his wand at speed.

Seeing as his opponent wielded a sword - and he wanted to be gracious - the Keeper freed his own blade. Of a mind to show off,

Kassian dragged his sword across the top of his left vambrace, sparking the magic that bound the armour to the blade. The spell took effect with a blinding show of magic.

"Impressive," Reyna commented, observing the white-hot glow of Kassian's sword. "Perhaps we should continue with steel alone..."

Kassian bowed his head and tapped the blade against the same vambrace. The brilliant white glow died away, leaving wavy lines of heat in the air - given enough time and pressure it would have cut through the steel of any man's sword.

Reyna stepped forward and stopped, her form one of exquisite discipline. Kassian didn't have her patience and he lunged. The elf was cunning, her blade rising to meet his strike before she moved aside with uncanny speed. The Keeper, fearing a swift counterstrike, dropped into a roll and came up with a defensive posture. Reyna was upon him in a blink of steel and precision, her scimitar weaving in at every angle. It was only when her boot found his chest that Kassian realised he had been manipulated.

The kick hurt, but the landing hurt even more when his pride caught up with him. Against his training, Kassian allowed a little of his anger to dictate his next attack. The Keeper flicked his sword up, forcing Reyna back a step, and followed up with a leaping downward strike. It was a foolish thing to do, given the clarity of his actions, and the ambassador reacted as anyone would - another boot to the chest.

Kassian skidded across the floor until he rolled back and came up in a crouch. A deep breath and a stern word to himself later, and the Keeper was ready to bring his foe down with his greatest weapon. He had always wanted to test the magic of an elf...

Reyna darted forward with her scimitar in both hands. She could come at him from any angle, her approach too vague to discern. It didn't matter; the elf would never touch him. Kassian's right hand flickered over his holster and came up with his wand pointed directly at Reyna. In the second that existed before he discharged his spell, the Keeper witnessed a look of fear break across her face. The elf tried to stop her own momentum and her attack melted away, but it all happened as the spell formed in Kassian's mind.

The magic flowed through him, safely harnessed by the Demetrium in his wand, and exploded from the tip with a blue flash. The spell caught Reyna in the chest and flung her backwards at some speed, taking her feet from the floor.

"Reyna!" Nathaniel shouted.

The Keeper had expected the elf to raise a shield using her superior reflexes. As she hit the floor on the other side of the hall, however, a sharp jolt of guilt and shame ran through him. Regardless of his emotions towards the Galfreys, he should never have raised his wand in a sword fight.

Thankfully, Reyna was already sitting up and rubbing her chest by the time her husband made it to her side. Kassian holstered his wand and dashed across the hall with a string of apologies on his lips.

"It's fine," Reyna reassured. "I'm alright. Just caught me by surprise..."

"My deepest apologies—"

Nathaniel's head snapped up at him. "Stay your words, Keeper. Something you might apply to your wand."

Kassian had more to say but he could see his part was only one of offence. Quite awkwardly, the Keeper stepped back, unable to decide on his next course of action.

"Leave us," Nathaniel fumed. "We know our own way back."

Again, Kassian had more to say in response to that - chiefly his responsibility to stay at their side - but his guilt weighed all the more seeing Reyna struggle to breathe deeply. With the bow of his head, the Keeper sheathed his sword and made to leave.

CHAPTER 9
KINGS OF EAST AND WEST

I t was another bleak morning in The Ice Vales. Besides the cold and treacherous landscape, the Namdhorian camp was decorated with the bodies of sons and husbands who would never see home.

Vighon gripped the sword of the north in one hand, moments away from adding to that number. Though they hadn't hailed from the north, the three governors who presided over The Ice Vales would never return to their towns or families.

Brought before the ravine-like entrance of Grey Stone, the traitors had been forced to their knees and their wrists bound behind their backs. A crowd had gathered in the gap between the towering walls and still more packed out the bridges above and lined the zigzagging stairs.

"I take no pleasure in this!" Vighon announced. "However, the governors of these lands have schemed against the realm, spreading discord and seeds of rebellion! Most of you here remember The Ash War! I, myself, fought in the shadow of this great city to see it defended against the orcs! We cannot have another war! There can be no more needless death!" The king looked down at the governors. "Do you have any last words?"

"Please!" Governor Tarwun of Snowfell pleaded, tears streaming down his narrow face. "We only did as Lord Thedomir demanded! We knew nothing of an ambush!"

"Ignorant or not," Vighon replied, "you pledged allegiance to another banner! I cannot have governors running my provinces if they are ruled by greed and tempted by power! We are to be servants to the realm and the people, the same people you would have suffer a war so that you might claim more land and wealth..." The sword of the north came up, its steel alight with righteous flames.

"Please, your Grace!" Governor Palkor sobbed. "I have a family waiting for me in Kelp Town!"

Vighon glanced at the expectant crowd and struggled to gauge their reaction. He reckoned there were some who wished to see the governors lose their heads for such deceit, but he could also see more than a few sympathetic expressions.

Looking over his shoulder, Inara and Alijah stood stoically in the snow beside General Garrett. Alijah gave him a nod, a signal of both approval and encouragement. As a fellow king, his old friend understood the importance of keeping the peace, even if it left a permanent mark on his soul.

Vighon looked back at Governor Palkor. "Do you see the bodies behind me? They all had families! Some of them had families in these very walls! How many men of Grey Stone lost their life fighting for your treachery, Governor?"

There were calls from the crowd from people who had lost their husband or father to Malliath's fiery breath. Vighon could only hope they directed their ire at those who were truly responsible for so much death.

"And you, Governor Viedt?" Vighon asked the oldest of the governors, kneeling at the other end. "Do you have any final words before you meet the King's Justice?"

"I see no king!" he yelled back. "My father never bowed to any king from the north and neither did his father!" Governor Viedt spat at Vighon's feet.

The king clenched his jaw. He hadn't wanted it to come to this. Hours earlier, he had offered the governors exile for information on the ones who had planted this rebellion in Thedomir's mind. All three claimed to know nothing beyond seeing the mage Athis had killed outside The Black Fort. Her name and reason for being in The Ice Vales escaped them.

Vighon took a deep breath. "Then I, Vighon of house Draqaro, King of Illian, and Steward of Namdhor sentence you all to death for crimes against the realm!"

The governors were pushed down by a soldier each, their heads pressed against a log. The sword of the north came down across Governor Tarwun's neck and sank into the wood beneath. His head rolled forward with flames licking at the ragged skin and hair. The crowd was silent.

Governor Palkor continued to sob until Vighon removed his head with one clean cut. His head rolled into the snow beside Tarwun's.

"This won't change a damn thing..." Governor Viedt muttered.

"It will for you," Vighon whispered back. Then his silvyr sword separated the old man's head from his body, bringing an end to the bloody deed.

The sword of the north had never felt heavier...

Half a day later, Vighon was clapping General Garrett on the shoulder. "Good man," he praised. "See to the details and make sure the people know the king's word still comes from The Black Fort."

The king watched Garrett walk away knowing the old warrior had everything in hand. He had already found a suitable, if temporary, replacement for the stewardship of Grey Stone. Now the general just had to install him and see to the orders that would be sent to Snowfell, Bleak, and Kelp Town.

"This mess is far from over," Vighon remarked in Sir Ruban's direction. "But at least we're done with the bloodshed."

"Very good, your Grace. We will be returning to Namdhor?"

Vighon caught sight of Alijah walking towards his tent. "Likely not," he replied, motioning for his old friend to join him. "We're not to be disturbed," he told Ruban.

"What of the Guardian, your Grace?"

Vighon hesitated. "You couldn't stop her if you wanted to..."

A moment later, Vighon was offering Alijah a drink in the privacy of his tent. It was such a common thing to do, but considering the time that had passed between them, the king could scarcely believe he was reunited with the half-elf.

"It's never easy, is it?" Alijah remarked, looking at the sword of the north on Vighon's hip. "The life of a king isn't one of banquets and balls. Your every word carries weight. And your sword must bring justice wherever it goes."

Vighon gripped the hilt of his blade and thumbed the lion head that served as a pommel. "It's a life I could never have dreamt of having. It's also a life I couldn't even have had nightmares about..."

Alijah looked to agree with the statement. "Taking the lives of three men, even three traitors, should always haunt you. It's how you know you're still a good king. A good *man*."

Vighon shook his head in disbelief. "The mere fact that you and I, of all people, are both kings gives me reason to wonder if this isn't all a dream. For all I know, I'm still unconscious inside Paldora's Fall."

"The future has a strange way of unravelling," Alijah commented.

"After you left," Vighon began, "I would look out over The King's Lake every day, *scouring* the peaks of Vengora in search of you."

The half-elf smiled. "How long before you gave up?"

The king matched his friend's warm smile. "I never did..."

Alijah laughed into his drink. "Liar."

Vighon shrugged. "I might have stopped looking for *you*, but not a day went by that I didn't set my gaze to those mountains... I just forgot what I was looking for."

Alijah set his goblet down and walked around the western edge of the map. "I'm sorry I was gone for so long," he said, pressing his finger into the table where Erador would have been, if such a map existed in Illian. "I've had a lot to do. There are just as many people in Erador as there are here, Vighon. All of them in need of guidance, protection, stability. It's a country that's seen war in all its forms, going back more years than you can fathom."

Vighon raised his cup to Alijah. "Then thank the fates you found them. I hope, in turn, that your time among the Eradorans has given you all that you needed. Malliath too..."

The king watched his old friend closely, looking for any sign that he might be hiding something. Alijah, however, was an open book.

"True enough," he replied. "Malliath and I needed to heal after... well, everything. I wouldn't be so bold as to claim we are entirely whole, but our bond has never been stronger. Over the years, we've both found that having a purpose has brought us together better than simply wandering the skies of Verda."

"And your purpose now?" Vighon asked as lightly as he could.

"Unity," Alijah declared. "I know there was a time when you all feared my destiny, as laid out by The Crow, but I've come to see that he was right."

Vighon offered an expression of interest as he placed his cup on the table, freeing both of his hands. "We never feared your destiny," he countered. "You're *Alijah Galfrey*! You were always going to do something worthy of history's note. We feared what lies The Crow put in your head - that he might twist your fate."

Alijah swallowed and tapped the table. "He never lied," he said quietly. "He just didn't tell all the truth," he continued with a more pleasant tone. "He was right: I was to be king, and a *good* king. With Malliath's guidance I have brought Erador under one banner and given them the same purpose that drives me."

"Unity," Vighon concluded.

"Exactly!" Alijah flashed a familiar smile that Vighon had long missed. "The Crow said I was to bring the world together in a way that had never been done before. That's why I'm here. You and I, Vighon, have the power to deliver peace to the people of both our realms."

"If only it were so simple," the king lamented.

"But it is," Alijah stated boldly. "Erador isn't perfect, but peace now exists where there once was only war. With my help, Illian can know that same peace. We just have to rid it of rebellion first," he added with a more serious tone.

Vighon eyed the king of Erador. "You have a plan, then?"

Alijah turned his attention back to the map. "I told you about my travels in Erador, journeying beside the king from one region to the next. This was necessary due to the level of corruption and dissidence that had been allowed to spread in the absence of strong leadership." The half-elf looked up at Vighon. "That is not the case in Illian. You are a capable and worthy king. Those that have risen to challenge you have done so from a place of malice and evil intent."

The king was pleased to hear such words. "You don't think we will have to visit the other provinces?"

Again, Alijah walked around the map until he could reach out and touch The Arid Lands, the southern province of Illian. "There is unrest in Tregaran, but it doesn't stem from a place of rebellion."

Vighon agreed. "A faction has emerged devoted to their ancient ways. They want slavery to return..."

"Barbaric," Alijah sneered. "It certainly requires your attention, but their troubles go no farther than The Arid Lands. Do you trust the lord to keep their struggles contained for now?"

"I do," Vighon replied confidently. "Lord Hasta Hash-Aseem has long been a trusted friend. I know he wishes to put an end to this talk of slavery as much as I do."

"Then we shall leave Lord Hasta to his work... for now. We must concern ourselves with those who target your reign. What of Lirian? I noticed that a number of your men here are from Felgarn."

"The entire province has done nothing but support me," Vighon testified. "From Lirian, Lady Gracen offers her aid in every way."

Alijah responded with a coy smile. "In *every* way?"

Vighon couldn't help but laugh a little. "I doubt Lady Gracen is truly interested in being my wife. I suspect her feelings towards me are insisted upon by her advisors and governors."

Alijah pulled up his bottom lip. "Is she beautiful? Gracen doesn't exactly sound like the name of an old hag."

Vighon considered the lady's beauty, as he had with so many women over the years, and found none of them compared to Inara. He wasn't about to say that to her brother though...

"She's ambitious is what she is," the king decided on. "The people of Felgarn were happy enough for her to replace her father and, since then, she has proven herself quite the leader and most certainly my supporter."

Alijah didn't appear quite as satisfied by his response but he was happy to move on. "So, we need not visit Lirian," he surmised. "Obviously, the north needs no reminding of the banner they live under. I remember when you were crowned. The *roar* of the people... It must have carried all the way to The Undying Mountains."

Vighon dwelled on that day, an eternity past. "That seems like a lifetime ago," he mused. "Seeing you now, unchanged by time, I am convinced it truly was a lifetime ago. Look at me! It won't be long before I forget what colour my hair was!"

Alijah took in his oldest of friends and smiled. "You look just as formidable as you did back then. A little grizzlier perhaps..."

The two shared a laugh, a moment that took Vighon back to the days when they would travel the land side by side in hunt of the next adventure. They had been good times.

"So," Alijah announced, drawing them both back to the map. "Grey Stone is back under your control. The rest of The Ice Vales will fall into line behind it. That only leaves..."

Vighon followed Alijah's gaze to the last province to be mentioned. "Alborn," he concluded. "Palios, Barossh, Galosha... There is unrest in all, including Whistle Town."

"The province has been infected," Alijah stated. "But where is the source of the conspiracy?"

The king pointed to the largest city in the eastern province. "Velia. I was uncertain before, but the mage who attacked Athis has confirmed my suspicions; the source lies within Valatos."

"And it lies within the city walls?" Alijah enquired.

"Very much so. It looks like a city inside a city now."

Alijah chewed over the information. "And what of the lord in the east?"

"Lord Carrington of house Landor. There was a time when I would have counted him as a supporter, but I fear the mages of Valatos have corrupted him. My spies tell me he is in possession of maps with new borders on them, borders that would grant him a lot more land were they enforced."

Alijah folded his arms. "Do you think they have corrupted him with magic?"

"It's possible. Or they could simply have promised him a larger kingdom and a crown if he successfully dissociates from my banner. Greed can be just as powerful as any spell."

"What of the mages themselves?"

"They arose from the ashes of Korkanath," the king explained. "There was talk, years ago, that magic was on the rise due to the return of the dragons. The Archon, as they are now, came to me with a proposal for a new school, one where they could teach these magical people to use their abilities safely. It has grown considerably since then."

Alijah tapped Velia on the map. "That is our destination. Root out this conspiracy. Bring the realm back under one banner. Unite all of Verda."

Hearing it said like that made it all seem so simple, yet Vighon had lost more nights of sleep over the matter than he could count. "You're right. I'm the king. That should still mean something."

Alijah nodded in agreement. "What could possibly stand in our way?"

It was only minutes later that Vighon had left his tent and was issuing commands to his captains, ordering them to muster the soldiers. Two thousand were to remain in Grey Stone and ensure the transition of lords was a smooth process. Half of the force that remained would travel east, across Illian, to face this evil at the gates of Valatos, while the other half returned to Namdhor with the dead. Malliath and Alijah would easily make up for the difference in soldiers.

It felt right.

Then he saw Inara. The Dragorn was striding towards him as Athis took back to the skies in the distance. A pang of guilt struck the king: he should have consulted with her before giving his orders. Why? he asked himself for perhaps the first time. He was the *king*. He had still taken advice from a Dragon Rider, if not a Dragorn.

"I'm hearing orders to march east," Inara said once Vighon was within earshot. "You're going to Lirian?"

The king inhaled a long breath. "Actually, yes."

Inara narrowed her eyes. "By way of Namdhor?" she pressed.

"You *know* I'm not returning home yet..."

Inara fell in beside him while he marched through the camp, his presence rousing for the men. "You're taking half the army across the country *again*? Can you not see the—"

"I *wish* I was taking half of my army, Inara, but too many lives have been lost to say that. Do you know why so many lives have been lost? Because something wicked stirs in the east, an evil that demands my attention. Yours too."

Inara stopped, forcing Vighon to turn back. "I am well aware of the lives that have been lost, *your Grace*. My duty, as Guardian of the Realm, is to ensure that we lose no more. Marching soldiers to the gates of a community who wield magic is a fine way to lose lives."

Vighon took three purposeful strides towards her and lowered his voice. "That's why *you're* coming with me. We will get to the truth of all this."

PHILIP C. QUAINTRELL

"My presence wasn't enough to stop Thedomir from enacting his plan," Inara pointed out. "Why should Velia or Valatos be different?"

Vighon was loath to give her the answer, but it was the only one he had. "I highly doubt the mages have forgotten about Malliath the voiceless."

Inara looked shocked. "So you're using them as a threat."

"A deterrent," the king corrected. "In the absence of violence, words will prevail. I thought that's what you wanted." Vighon didn't wait around to hear Inara's argument. He had made a decision and he wasn't going back on it, not when so much hung in the balance.

With Sir Ruban and the guard trailing behind him, Vighon made his rounds, encouraging the men to pack down their gear and prepare to journey east. He made promises that those responsible for their brothers' deaths would be brought to justice - something he believed himself.

He *had* to believe...

CHAPTER 10
THIS IS GOING TO HURT

Dawn was upon The Evermoore and the trees stretched their branches, reaching for the new light that streaked through the canopy. It should have been the last moment of peace before the creatures of the forest roused from their slumber, but the clashing of steel had disturbed the night and carried on into the day.

Asher had been set upon by seven Arakesh of Nightfall, the best assassins in Illian. Clad in their traditional dark leathers and red blindfolds, the killers had given no warning but for the hunters they had slaughtered in the dead of night. They had been taunting the ranger, no doubt aware of his position at all times thanks to the elixir flowing through their veins.

As deadly as the seven were, Asher now only faced four of them.

The first two to die by his sword had made the fatal error of underestimating him, most likely due to his perceived age. The third, and latest to find his end between the trees of The Evermoore, had been used by Asher as a human shield and taken a mortal blow intended for the ranger.

125

The remaining four had yet to make a mistake that Asher could take advantage of. After the deaths of the first three, they had assumed a more cautious approach to their target, always circling him. With his silvyr blade still inside the head of his second victim, the ranger drew his two-handed broadsword, raised it to shoulder level, and pointed it at the nearest assassin.

"Who's paying for my head?" he spat. "Give me an answer and I'll make your end the swiftest."

The closest assassin smiled, his eyes hidden behind his blindfold. Of course they would never divulge such information - he certainly wouldn't have during his time as a servant of Nightfall. Instead, the Arakesh darted in, feigning a left attack before angling his twin blades from the right. Asher, however, had already detected the slightest of movements and knew the entire attack was a distraction.

The ranger dropped and rolled to the left, narrowly avoiding the blades from the assassin who had been flanking him. Deciding the odds needed shifting in his favour, Asher came up swinging, engaging one of the Arakesh who had been circling to the side. Their swords clashed, ringing out in every direction. Wielding the longer blade, the ranger was able to direct their fight, pushing the assassin towards his comrade.

The scenario was simple in Asher's mind: drive them together and create chaos as their fighting patterns intersected. He knew from experience that the Arakesh were miserable when it came to fighting side by side, always trained to be individual killers. Whoever had paid for his head, however, knew better than to send just the one after him...

The ranger's plan fell apart when a small dagger cut through the air and impaled his arm. He spared a yell for the pain but never stopped fighting - despite his sword's weight in one hand. The Arakesh he had been driving back easily batted the broadsword away, sending it spinning into the grass and dirt. Asher had no choice but to barrel into the younger man and take them both to the ground.

The Arakesh took double punishment when his head bounced off the ground only to find Asher's forehead smashing into his nose. Letting loose an ounce of feral rage now, Asher growled and pulled free the dagger lodged in his arm. The tip was driven straight into the boot of the approaching assassin, halting his inevitable attack.

Leaving the grounded assassin to his head wounds, the ranger shot up and drove his palm into the next Arakesh's throat. He was forced back at such speed that his boot came up with the dagger still piercing his foot. Killing him now was a simple matter of snapping his neck, but there were still two unharmed assassins leaping in to claim their target. Instead of breaking his neck, Asher planted a boot in the chest of the man who could barely breath and launched him into a tree.

There was only half a second to react to the incoming short-swords behind him now. Asher lifted one leg, ducked his head, and shifted his shoulders to evade three edges of steel. That left one sword he couldn't avoid and it went straight into his leg, biting through the muscle of his thigh. The ranger was instantly dropped to one knee, though the cry on his lips was immediately stolen by a second blade plunging into his shoulder, piercing his armour and cloak.

Believing they had won, the two assassins pulled free their weapons and backed off to take in the sight of him. Asher couldn't help but fall to his hands and knees, which became a struggle with an injured leg and shoulder.

"This is it?" the dark-haired assassin remarked with dissatisfaction. "For all my years of training, hardly a day would go by that we didn't hear about the fearsome Asher."

The blonde Arakesh beside him tilted her head in Asher's direction. "Are we sure this is him? He's too young."

"It's him," the other replied confidently. "You're supposed to be a *legend.*"

The blonde assassin smiled wickedly. "A legend is exactly what he'll be in a few minutes."

Now they were making mistakes. They should have cut his throat the moment he fell to all fours. The ranger, on the other hand, was still playing out the various scenarios in his head, each one ending with their blood on his hands. That was just how his mind worked...

With a smile pushing at his cheeks, Asher said, "At least you had the sense to bring numbers..."

The female assassin approached with a sneer. "What was that, hero?" she mocked.

Asher's reply came in the form of a rock to the side of her leg. Using his good arm, he hammered the rock with enough force to shatter the knee, snapping it to the side, and bringing her down to his level. Her scream of pain was cut short when the ranger grabbed her wrist and shoved one of the blades into her heart.

The dark-haired assassin hesitated, succumbing to shock. It was all the time Asher needed to remove the hidden dagger from the back of his boot and throw it underarm into his groin - he had been aiming for his throat. Still, the Arakesh stumbled backwards with a length of steel jammed in a place no one wanted a length of steel. The assassin fell back and over his guild brother who was still nursing his head wounds, only to acquire one himself upon hitting the stump of a tree.

The ranger groaned as he forced himself back onto his feet. "You clearly... don't know... who you're *dealing* with..."

Asher limped towards the Arakesh, each step sending shooting pains through his leg and hip. He grabbed the fallen assassin roughly by the quiver on his back and pushed him down until his face was pressed against the dirt.

"Who sent you?" he demanded, snatching the blindfold from his eyes.

The assassin turned his head as much as he could. "You should know when you're dead," he hissed, his eyes flitting to the side.

More mistakes.

The ranger detached the folded bow from his victim's back and snapped it open with a quick tug. Raising the bow over his head, he blocked the incoming strike using one of the extended limbs, preventing his flanking foe from gaining victory. A twist of the bow disarmed his silent attacker, allowing Asher to spin around on the ball of his foot without the fear of a deadly counterattack. At such close range, there was no opportunity to use the bow as designed, but that didn't stop him from using one of the arrows in his quiver. He plunged the bolt into the Arakesh's eye, through his blindfold, until it was deep enough to ensure his death.

Asher would have marvelled at the bow he had long missed but, instead, he collapsed it with another quick tug and hooked it onto his own quiver. He then turned his attention back to the dark-haired Arakesh who had been stupid enough to open his mouth in the first place.

Falling upon him - for anything else would have taken more effort and finesse than he could handle - Asher pinned him to the ground. Judging by his pained expression, the transition was hard on the assassin's eyes, betraying his inexperience. Asher slipped the curved dagger from his belt and rested it against the Arakesh's throat, the touch of the steel enough to overcome the pain in his eyes.

"Who put a mark on my head?" As the last word left his mouth, Asher could feel his senses drifting away with the blood trickling out of his wounds.

"We but obey the will of the—"

The ranger took a handful of the killer's hair and slammed his head into the hard ground. "Who put a mark on my head?" he growled.

Off to the side, the assassin sporting two head injuries finally managed to stand on both feet. His dark armour was smothered with mud and splattered with blood from his broken nose. It was the short-sword in his hand, however, that stole Asher's immediate attention.

"Wait here," he commanded before rising back to his feet. His right arm was practically numb now, preventing him from doing anything but hold onto the red blindfold still clutched between his cold fingers.

The assassin caught wind of the ranger's approach and spun around with his blade angled to cut across Asher's face, but he half ducked, half staggered under the short-sword and came up with his dagger. It plunged into the Arakesh's ribs once, then twice before the pair fell over and rolled over an awkward rise in the ground.

The assassin groaned, though the sound was gargled by the blood frothing in his lungs. Trained to see things through, Asher climbed over the killer's body and drove his dagger down into the man's heart. The armour was tough, forcing the ranger to slam the hilt with the weight of his chest and hammer it home.

He was exhausted, bleeding out, and in the kind of pain that even his training struggled to deal with. Then, it got worse.

Asher was torn off the dead assassin and pulled back by a hand wrapped around his jaw. With nowhere to look but up, the ranger was met by the bloodied face of the dark-haired assassin. Gone was the stony composure typical of an Arakesh, replaced now with rage and hatred. It was the kind of emotional outburst that Asher could have used to his advantage but, then again, a fresh blade had just been rammed into the side of his chest.

A short gasp escaped the ranger's dry lips. Fatigued as he might be, the old assassin knew a mortal wound when he saw it or, in this case, felt it. At last, he thought, his past had finally caught up with him. In the years since his exile from Nightfall, Asher had always known, deep down, that he would meet his end by the blade of an Arakesh...

He also knew that whoever delivered that final blow would go to hell with him. Asher took what breath he could, gritted his teeth, and threw his arms up with the red blindfold scrunched at each end. The fabric looped over the Arakesh's neck before dragging his head down into the ranger's. It hurt, to say the least, but their collision hurt them both and, combined with the assassin's wounded groin, he crumpled to his knees behind Asher.

A swift elbow to the eyebrow dropped the killer flat to the ground, where he was at the mercy of Asher's weight. The ranger yanked the knife from the side of his chest and clambered over his foe's fallen form with deadly intent. With what was left of their strength, one pushed down with the dagger and the other pushed up, keeping the tip of the steel only an inch from the Arakesh's throat.

Death was coming for one of them and Asher could sense it. The dark claws of fate had finally won out against his stubbornness to die and stay dead. The ranger could do nothing but accept that and make sure death came for them both instead.

The assassin relented one of his hands in the resistance and thumped Asher over the new wound in his ribs again and again. Every blow stung deep inside and he growled with the impacts. In the end, the ranger had no choice but to let all of his weight drop onto the end of the dagger and drive it into his enemy's throat.

Death claimed its next victim.

Asher rolled off the corpse and waited for the same fate. He was bleeding from his arm, shoulder, leg, and a particularly wicked wound to the side of his chest. That didn't take into account the bruises, broken ribs, and gashes he had acquired. It was also possible he had fractured his skull if the blinding pain in his head was anything to go by.

At the end of his very long journey, Asher should have dwelled on his life and the accomplishments he had managed to attain in spite of his earlier career. After all, he had played his part in saving the world a couple of times. But his mind would never cease. Instead, he thought about the circumstances of his death. Who had hired the assassins of Nightfall to murder him? They had long given up their hunt for him - he had died once already since his exile. Who wanted him dead so much that they would get involved with the Arakesh?

Those questions melted away, along with his vision. He could actually see death walking towards him now, a silhouette in the forest. As he expected, it was a demon of the blackest hell. It came to tower over him, its spiralling horns clear to see against the light of the dawning sky above.

It reached down for him and the world fell away to darkness...

CHAPTER II
ON THE ROAD

Entering the province of The Ice Vales was like trekking into the past and leaving summer behind. Only the biting chill of the westerly winds pulled Doran Heavybelly from his dark musings.

The dwarf looked up from astride Pig and realised he had barely spared a moment to look at anything other than the missive from his brother. Stealing one last look at the two words and the blood stain, the son of Dorain folded the letter and tucked it safely inside his long coat.

"I bloody 'ate The Ice Vales," he muttered, retrieving a fur cloak from the back of his saddle and wrapping it around his shoulders.

Beside him, astride his own horse, Russell Maybury frowned. "Look behind us, Heavybelly," he instructed.

"Eh?" Doran looked back over his shoulder and saw the outline of The Carbel Slopes.

"We've been in The Ice Vales for some time," Russell continued.

"Oh aye..." Doran drawled.

Before them now was a flat horizon that ended with the southern tip of the Vengoran mountains. Continuing along The Selk

Road, they would soon reach Gray Stone and then Kelp Town, the last havens before journeying north to Namdhor.

"Your concern for your brother grows," Russell observed.

"If only it were jus' me brother," Doran replied hopelessly. "If Dak had jus' pricked his finger, he would 'ave written a new note. If the clan wasn' in the middle o' somethin' bloody, he would 'ave written more, I'm sure o' it."

"I thought your clan had been exiled by King..."

"King *Uthrad*," Doran supplied. "Aye, he exiled the clan. Bloody fool."

"If clan Heavybelly has been exiled from the hierarchy, why would they be attacked?"

"Exiled or not," Doran explained, "Grimwhal still has plenty o' supplies an' resources the other clans would kill to obtain. Then there's the alliance with Illian to consider. There will be more than a few among me kin who believe such an alliance to be treason against all dwarf-kind, not jus' the sanctity o' the clans."

Russell looked out across the snowy horizon, considering Doran's words. "If the clan is under siege, perhaps Namdhor can be of assistance. The king could send soldiers through The Iron Valley and bolster their ranks."

Doran could see how such a thing made logical sense, but there wasn't a dwarf alive, in any clan, who would call on humans for aid. "Dak would be seen as weak if he were to ask the king for help."

Russell pointed his finger into the air to accompany his look of revelation. "What if that's the reason he sent you that note?"

Doran's brow creased into confusion "What are ye abou'?"

"Hear me out," Russell argued. "What if Dakmund needs help and he can't ask for it. So he sends *you* a note and *you* bring help."

Doran gave it a moment's thought. "No," he replied bluntly. "There are far easier ways to seek aid without sendin' a two-worded note to Namdhor's runners, who then 'ave to go to the trouble o' findin' me. No," he reiterated, "he wanted to tell me that father has died an' nothin' more. It's me *gut* that tells me there's somethin' else goin' on, Rus. Somethin' bad..."

Russell gestured to the plains ahead. "Then let's push through The Ice Vales and get to the truth of it."

They journeyed together for many more miles as the cold tightened its grip on the land. It was easy to believe they had travelled much farther and reached the frozen shores of the north, beyond Vengora's mountainous slopes.

After a fresh covering of snow, the thick clouds that had settled overhead finally dispersed, revealing patches of blue. Doran would have welcomed the sight and the change in weather, but it was the view on the horizon that had captured the dwarf's attention. They were impossible to miss, given their great number, and they only grew closer with every step.

"That's got to be an *army*," Russell remarked.

Black against the white snow, the army in question marched towards them with riders leading from the front. Doran and Russell guided their mounts to the east and up a forested rise, taking them beyond the army's path. It wasn't long before they could see the banners flapping in the wind and the flaming sword of house Draqaro became clear.

"What's this abou'?" the son of Dorain chuntered.

"Look!" Russell nodded his head at the riders leading the army.

Doran raised his bushy eyebrow. "It's not every day ye see a king," he replied, having spotted Vighon astride his horse.

A pair of riders broke away from the formation and rode out to the base of the rise, below the companions. They hadn't drawn their swords, but they both wore a scowl that suggested they weren't too happy about a man and a dwarf watching them from afar.

"State your business in these lands!" one of them called up.

Doran raised his hands. "We're jus' passin' through, fellas! Namdhor's our destination!"

The riders scrutinised them. "You will stay where you are until the king has passed!" the same soldier commanded.

"O' course!" Doran shrugged. "We're actually old friends o' the king! Got history we do!"

The riders broke their frowns and smiled with amusement. "And we're elven princes!" they mocked.

The dwarf's expression fell away and he rolled his only eye. There was nothing he could say that would convince them, especially since history had done little to mention his deeds in the last two wars to rock Illian.

"Idiots," he grizzled to himself.

Thousands of Namdhorian soldiers trailed past, ensuring The Selk Road could always be found. Soon, Vighon was lost to the south and the riders behind him. Doran couldn't even recall the number of years it had been since he last spoke to the king.

"How long's it been then?" he asked aloud.

"What?" Russell replied. "Since we met with the king?" The old wolf scrunched up his weathered face. "It's got to be nine years, maybe ten. We saw him in Tregaran, after we cleared the last of the orcs out."

Doran finally recalled the memory. "That was damned sweaty work," he reminisced. "There's a reason I don' take work in The Arid Lands if I can help it. Too bloody hot for the likes o' a dwarf I tell ye!"

Doran was about to complain about how entrenched those particular orcs had been until his eyes drifted over the sky. The words fell away as he looked upon two dragons soaring over the army. The son of Dorain had been blessed in his lifetime to have seen several dragons grace the sky, but for the last fifteen years there had only been one: Athis. From their vantage, they could make out the red scales of Inara's dragon and his dark slate chest, lending him the name of Athis the ironheart.

It was the other dragon that robbed Doran of speech.

Black of scale and visibly larger than Athis, this second dragon was unmistakable. The last time Doran Heavybelly had clapped eyes on Malliath the voiceless he had lifted a monstrous stonemaw clear of the battlefield and ripped it to shreds. He was the scariest thing the dwarf had ever seen...

As the black dragon glided and banked across the sky, Doran caught a glimpse of a figure resting on what appeared to be some kind of saddle. There was only one person who could ride Malliath.

"He's back..."

"Alijah Galfrey," Russell clarified. "What's he doing back in Illian?"

"An' with the king?" Doran added.

Once the majority of the army had marched past, the two riders took their leave and galloped to reach the front again. The dragons glided effortlessly on the cold winds until they too began to fade from view.

"Well..." Doran let out a long breath. "It doesn' look like I could ask the king for any aid if I wanted to; he's headin' in the wrong direction for a start!"

"What strange times are we living in now?" Russell posed.

"I don' know," Doran replied honestly. "But that bad feelin' I've got ain' goin' anywhere..."

Russell agreed and pulled his hood over his head. "Let us make haste, old friend. I would leave the vales behind as soon as possible."

And so north they continued. The son of Dorain could only hope that, once in the capital, his fears would be abated. It pained him to think that the best scenario he could rely on was attending his father's funeral... in manacles.

CHAPTER 12
BAITED

Still stricken with guilt, Kassian Kantaris made his way to the Galfreys' chambers. Regardless of his feelings towards them and their errand, he should never have hurt Reyna or any guest of Valatos for that matter. He had, however, felt like showing off his power from the moment he drew his sword, making his slight against the ambassador inevitable.

He had truly believed the elf would block his spell in the moment. Otherwise, he wouldn't have had a shield spell ready in his mind to block her counterattack. The Keeper was lucky he hadn't been reported to the Archon and punished already. How would he face Clara?

He ran a hand through his sandy hair before rounding the corner of their hallway. As instructed after leaving the Sanctorum, Jovus, a trusted Keeper only one rank below Kassian, was standing guard outside the Galfreys' door.

Jovus bowed his head. "Kassian..."

Not wanting to make a topic of the lapse in his responsibilities, Kassian simply asked, "What time did they return?"

Jovus glanced at the door. "He returned just before dusk."

Kassian was nodding in acknowledgement when he hesitated. "*He?*"

"Nathaniel Galfrey," Jovus clarified.

Kassian had a sinking feeling in his stomach. He immediately attempted to open the door but the knob wasn't shifting. Stepping back, the Keeper withdrew the wand from his holster and pointed it at the lock. A simple spell and the door swung open in time with his march.

Nathaniel was stripped down to his waist with his hands dipped into a bowl of fresh water. The two men looked at each other expectantly, though Nathaniel was notably absent the wrath he had displayed only hours earlier. If anything, he appeared somewhat amused.

"Can I help you, Keeper?"

Kassian searched what he could see of their luxurious chamber. "Where is the ambassador?" he asked pointedly.

"After having the wind knocked out of her," Nathaniel replied with a look, "she felt like going for a walk in the gardens." The old Graycoat shrugged his toned shoulders. "If you ever lose an elf, always look—"

Kassian stormed out without hearing the rest. He had been baited and it stung. The Keeper closed the door behind him, locked it with his wand, and ordered Jovus to inform him if anyone came or went. Once out of sight, Kassian let some of his stress show and rubbed his forehead with the back of his hand.

How could he have let them manipulate him like this? Reyna was out there somewhere doing something she wasn't supposed to be doing. They had rid themselves of the only eyes watching them with ease, betraying Kassian's inexperience and arrogance. The Keeper knew he should report this and have everyone in Valatos searching for the elf, but to do so would announce his failure. Instead, he went about the task on his own.

It made sense to Kassian that Reyna would stay inside the central hall. If she was in the act of something nefarious then the most damage she could cause was here. This was where the Archon resided, with the ancient library, and, of course, the vaults below. That was still a lot of space to hunt down one person. No, he reminded himself, Reyna Galfrey was an elf, a being far harder to track down than any human.

The vaults were first on his list. Inside were relics brought over from the ruins of Korkanath, some of which, including The Elder Book, were deemed too powerful for even the Archon to fully investigate. The vault door, fortunately, was still in place and the Keepers stationed in front of it reported no unusual activity... besides his presence and questions.

Leaving the Keepers to watch the forbidding circular slab of enchanted iron, Kassian returned to the upper levels and made his way to the library. Every book inside was one of a kind and had been brought to Valatos from all over the realm - they weren't for outsiders.

There was a lot more space to investigate inside the library, including the upper tiers; all of which had multiple rooms attached to them. Kassian stood in the middle of the ground floor, turning on the spot, as his eyes roamed over every detail. Overhead, the books continued in their eternal current, a peaceful sight and sound that did nothing to soothe him.

Something told the Keeper that Reyna Galfrey wasn't here. Valatos boasted an archive unparalleled across Illian, but the elves of Ayda were said to possess libraries ten times this size, each filled with more ancient knowledge. There was no reason the ambassador would be here unless there was a book she genuinely wanted to read.

"You look as if you've lost something," came a startling yet familiar voice from behind.

"Samuel," Kassian greeted the potions instructor with a tight smile. "Yes... a book. I can't seem to find it and it isn't in the library."

"Have you tried using a tracking spell?" Samuel replied quietly, eyeing the only other two people inside the library.

"No," Kassian drawled, "because they're illegal inside Valatos."

The instructor smiled happily. "So they are. Well, good luck finding it, Keeper Kassian."

The Keeper watched Samuel leave the library, but his mind was racing through possibilities. Since he wasn't searching for an inanimate object, he would need more than just Reyna's name. There was only one place he was going to find anything remotely close to what he needed and Kassian had a strong feeling that her husband wasn't about to let him rummage through her personal belongings.

But he did need to find her, urgently. Whatever Reyna Galfrey was up to, it wouldn't be for the betterment of Valatos. What if she was planting false evidence of some kind and setting up the entire school for the King's Justice? And it would be his fault...

The Lexichronan.

Kassian took a breath as he considered this particular path. The Lexichronan was the only thing capable of finding Reyna instantly, if she was still on Valatos soil, but it wasn't meant for Keepers. In fact, it wasn't meant for any but the Archon and it was guarded by a fiend.

But it was the only way...

As casually as possible, Kassian left the library and broke into a run the moment he rounded the corner. As quickly and quietly as he could, the Keeper made his way to the west wing of the central hall. As always, there were very few people around since this wing had been used predominantly by the Archon but, in the evening, there was no one to question the desperate aura that clung to the Keeper.

Up the narrow winding staircase, Kassian was sure to use the enchantment already etched into his boots and remove any sound his feet might make. He had heard plenty of tall tales surrounding the fiend that protected the Lexichronan and, if even one of them was right, he didn't want it to know he was coming.

The wooden door that barred his way was simple, if locked. Wand in hand, he very slowly twisted his wrist until the door was unlocked. There was no reaction from the other side, no roar, no screech, and no unholy wail from a man-eating banshee. Aware that time was running out, the Keeper cautiously made his way to the other side with his wand held out in front of him. The first three destructive spells he brought to mind were powerful enough to tear any beast apart.

There was, surprisingly, no beast to speak of.

Kassian frowned at the sight of another door before unlocking it in an identical fashion. Again, on the other side stood another door, only this one was situated in the left wall. The Keeper used his wand to pull back the lock and pushed through to the next room. Another door awaited. A very bad feeling began to settle over him.

Immediately turning back, he discovered the door he had just used was gone, replaced by more stone. Kassian swore and faced the only route available to him. His wand had no trouble undoing the lock and he made his way through to the next identical room. He was stuck in a loop spell...

The first feeling that fought for supremacy was panic. Standing back from the door, he let loose a fireball into the wood, blasting it from its hinges and launching it into the next chamber. Wafting his way through the smoke, Kassian stepped over the charred debris only to find the looping spell was still very much in effect. Turning back again, a new wall had already replaced the broken door.

Kassian cursed, aware that the only people who could get him out of a loop were those who made it. In this case, that would be the Archon. Explaining why he was trapped in here in the first place was a sure way to find himself demoted at the very least.

The second feeling to emerge was born of experience, experience in getting himself out of tough situations by his wits alone. Thankfully, over the years in Valatos, he could now add education to his wits, even if he was to call upon knowledge he wasn't strictly supposed to have.

In the devastating wake of The Ash War, Kassian relied on many skills considered criminal in order to survive. Among them was the art of breaking and entering, something he had become very proficient at. With magic at his disposal, however, the Keeper had soon learned that old habits die hard, and when the opportunity arose to get his hands on some of the forbidden books, he consumed them. In Valatos, he had never used anything he had learned in those texts, but the younger version of himself had *needed* the knowledge.

Crouching to one knee, Kassian examined the locking mechanism as one particular spell came to mind. In most instances, looping spells could only be disarmed by the one key forged specifically for the door. Placing the tip of his wand just inside the lock, the Keeper muttered the enchantment. He got it wrong and the end of his wand sparked, sending a painful shock up his arm.

He swore again.

After shaking his wrist, the Keeper returned to his spell and swapped two lines of the incantation. He felt the familiar tug on his energy as it strained his connection to the magical realm. His wand, fortunately, was in the process of building a key inside the lock that would fit perfectly to its unique size and shape. One twist and the door opened to an entirely new chamber that thankfully didn't present him with another door.

Kassian wiped the sweat from his brow, closed the door quietly behind him, and took in the Lexichronan. It was the size of a family table and all cogs and gold framework. One foot moved forward to bring him closer when two things forced him to hesitate.

The first was the moonlight shining through the only window in the tall tower. The sun had almost disappeared when he set off to find Reyna, but now the moon was significantly higher than it should be. The looping spell obviously had an effect on the passage of time as well, meaning the ambassador had an even greater lead on him.

The second thing to keep him rooted to the spot was the legendary fiend that apparently protected the Lexichronan. Looking around, there was no sign of any creature and there weren't any doors from which it could appear - the whole room was devoted to holding the device. Perhaps, he pondered, the stories had been started by the Archon to dissuade the mages from coming up here.

Approaching the Lexichronan, Kassian soon learned the truth of it. The shadows that clung to the edges of the room slithered and coalesced until the darkness began to take shape in front of the powerful device. Judging by its flickering ethereal state, the Keeper decided he was confronted by a wraith - a notoriously difficult fiend to banish if one didn't have the correct equipment and spells to hand.

It was at this moment that Kassian realised he had spent too long reading all the wrong books...

The wraith's twitching face protruded from the inky shadows and its clawed fingers came for the Keeper. Since the concept of time had been on his mind, the only useful spell to Kassian wasn't far from the front of it. Assuming the Nifdel Configuration of the Keepers' duelling form, his wand expelled a wave of magic designed to attack the passage of time in both this reality and the magical one. It was magnitudes above the key spell he had used a moment ago and he felt the relentless drain on his muscles.

The wraith, thankfully, was entirely caught up inside the time spell. Its scrawny limbs and nightmarish features slowed to a crawl, allowing Kassian to simply walk around it and finally get his hands on the Lexichronan. Time was even more of a factor now, since his spell would continue to drain him until he freed the wraith.

Despite being a large device, there was only one way to control it and the mechanism was similar to a lock in a door, only the key required was the user's wand. Kassian moved to insert his wand when his whole arm paused. The Lexichronan was more than just a tracking system for Valatos's interior, it was also tied in to the campus's security features.

Right now, the device was tethered to the wands and staffs of the Archon, meaning only the masters had the power to rescind invitations or simply activate the security measures. The moment he inserted his wand, Kassian would override their authority and assume full control without anyone knowing. The only way to return power to the Archon would be to inform them of this and have them reinsert their wands.

Kassian had never been caught between two decisions as hard as this before. Ultimately, and he knew this, as a Keeper, he had to put Valatos's security first; that meant locating Reyna Galfrey.

Before he could overthink it, he inserted his wand into the decorated port and the Lexichronan gripped it firmly. The cogs started spinning, each one setting off another until the whole block was alive with movement. The glass top hummed for only a second before a three-dimensional, real-time map of Valatos was constructed in the air above it. The blue outline of the buildings and grounds was dotted with golden figures, most of which were sleeping in their beds. A handful of Keepers sparred in the Sanctorum and a couple of instructors were still in their classrooms going through lesson plans.

Kassian used both of his hands and spread them apart, focusing the map on the central hall. The golden figures grew in size and he quickly located himself in the west wing. A dark mist floated beside him, the map's recognition of the wraith. The Keeper raised his hand into the air and waved, noting that the smaller, golden representation of himself did exactly the same thing.

His eyes darted to the chamber below and to the side of his own. Inside, seated around a large table, were seven figures - the Archon. What they were discussing was beyond the Lexichronan's ability, nor did Kassian care; he was more concerned by the golden figure standing very still above the masters. Zooming in, he could see that the figure was using the crawl space in the roof and was positioned between the beams, above the vent.

That could only be one person.

The most expedient thing to do was also the most costly. If he barged into the Archon's meeting and exposed the ambassador, he would also be exposing his tampering with the Lexichronan and the fact that he had lost Reyna in the first place. Since time was against him, the Keeper moved forward, the only thing he could do.

Taking back his wand, Kassian opened the grate in the wall and crawled into the dusty space. As soon as he was beyond the Lexichronan's chamber, he released his spell on the wraith and welcomed a portion of his magic back. His progress was deliberately slow so as to avoid detection by both Reyna and the Archon below. Unfortunately, the attic space in which the elf was hiding was also extremely dark. Beams intersected at awkward angles and the roof itself was pointed, creating a cramped environment.

The only illumination was a column of light and dust that shone up through a single grate in the middle of the floor. It was down there where the Archon sat in session, discussing the future of Valatos no doubt. Kassian lingered by the crawl space before half standing in the attic. He couldn't see Reyna anywhere. Drawn to the voices, the Keeper carefully made his way between the beams and over to the central grate. Again, the elf was nowhere to be seen, much to his dismay.

"It would be a great risk," one of the masters voiced from below, distracting Kassian.

"It's beyond a *risk*," another countered. "We have not been *instructed* to remove them from the board."

"They are not only a threat to Valatos but to the entire plan," a third voice opined. "We are expected to act and see that they don't interfere."

"What we are *expected* to do has been made very clear," a female voice replied. "It would be foolish to start acting outside of the plan."

"Think of what we were promised," another female voiced. "The magic of the Jainus belongs in our hands. We should not shy away from making decisions that ensure success."

"We're assuming it can even be done," a deeper voice put forward. "The Galfreys have survived more than most."

The master who had spoken to Kassian said in his familiar voice, "We have a singular advantage they cannot defend against: magic. While the ambassadors were in my chambers today, I was in the process of digesting a Falansium leaf. I should have been able to see the magic that surrounds all elves, but there wasn't so much as a wisp of magic about her. And the only magic in Nathaniel Galfrey lies dormant in his bones, the source of his youth and well beyond his ability to wield."

"How is that possible?" another asked. "Reyna Galfrey is an *elf*."

"The reason remains a mystery," the master answered. Mystery or not, Kassian now understood why the ambassador had failed to protect herself against his spell.

"If we are to do this, we should act quickly, before the king arrives," one of the female masters suggested.

"Agreed. Allowing for any margin of error, we should also remove ourselves from the equation and have another act on our behalf."

"The Keeper?" one of them clarified.

"Kassian Kantaris. He is more than qualified to get the job done."

"He is able," another agreed, "but is he *capable*? The Keepers are sworn to protect Valatos, not murder for it."

"The seeds have already been sown," the previous master replied confidently. "I will hold his hand a while longer to make certain he understands what must be done."

"That hardly removes us from the equation," a young male voice pointed out. "For all his skill, there is still a chance the Galfreys will best him. If he is compelled to reveal his secrets they will be directed back to us..."

"Do you doubt me?" the master asked rhetorically. Something was placed on the table between the masters but Kassian was too high up to see what it was. "As before; steps will be taken to ensure the truth dies with him, should it come to that."

A moment of silence settled over the Archon before one of the female masters spoke again. "Then we are in alignment," she stated.

With that, the masters rose from their high back chairs and left the private chamber. They also left Kassian in shock. His world had just been flipped upside down for the second time in his life and he discovered he couldn't move.

But Reyna could. A shadow in the corner of his eye flitted between the beams and disappeared through a grate on the other side of the attic. The elf had barely made a sound but she had still caught the Keeper's attention, giving life back to his muscles again. Covered in dust and soot, Kassian made chase, following behind Reyna in the narrow spaces.

He lost sight of her until they were both back in the hallways. Left and right he pursued, skidding into statues and bouncing off walls, never quite catching her up.

Finally, he rounded the last corner to find Jovus still standing guard outside the ambassadors' suite. Kassian skidded to a stop, blatantly stunned.

"Is everything alright, Sir?" Jovus asked.

Kassian looked from the door to the Keeper. "Has anyone entered their room?"

Jovus couldn't hide his confusion. "Not a soul."

Kassian took a deep breath and licked his lips. How could she have lost him? A flick of his wand opened their door again and he stormed in with a list of questions for Nathaniel Galfrey.

Reyna met him with a quizzical expression. And a collection of colourful flowers in her hands...

"Is everything alright, Keeper?" she asked innocently, if concerned.

Kassian looked from the elf to the open window behind her, where the light drapes blew lazily in the breeze.

"He does like an entrance this one," Nathaniel remarked, walking out from behind the adjoining wall.

"If this is about the flowers," Reyna continued, "I would beg forgiveness. I couldn't help myself; they're so beautiful and our room was absent—"

"When did you return?" Kassian croaked, his mouth dry and coated with dust.

Reyna looked to her husband with the hint of a shrug. "It was some time ago. Is there a problem?"

Kassian didn't like to be played for a fool. "Jovus told me that no has been to this room since I left it."

"Jovus?" the elf repeated. "There was no one outside our room when I returned from the gardens. Has something happened?"

With no evidence and no witnesses, Kassian knew he was very close to crossing a line he couldn't come back from. "No, Ambassador. I would ask that next time you feel like going for a stroll, you let me or another Keeper escort you."

Reyna shot him her disarming smile. "Apologies, Keeper."

Kassian bid them good night and returned to face Jovus with a face of thunder. "Have you left your post?"

The younger man began to shake his head. "No, Sir."

Kassian took a step closer. "You haven't taken your eyes off this door since I left?"

The Keeper's eyes shifted nervously left and right. "I... I couldn't hold it any longer."

Kassian sighed and clenched his fist. He knew for a fact that Reyna had been in that attic with him, but her alibi matched up seamlessly with Jovus's lapse in duty. More than anything, Kassian wanted to punish the young Keeper, but he himself had broken more rules than anyone in the last few hours.

"Learn to hold it," he growled before stalking away.

With every step, the Archon's conversation came back to him, their words weighing on him. There was a whole web of problems that now clung to Kassian, each one a moral dilemma of the likes he had never faced. Chiefly; there was the murder of two people he was about to be tasked with. During his time living on the streets of Velia and the surrounding towns, he had done some terrible things to stay alive, but killing someone was not one of them.

Sprouting from that terrible insight into the Archon, there was also the added complication that those he was going to be tasked with murdering now knew as much as he did. Should he tell the masters they knew of their plan? Did that mean he was going to go through with it?

Kassian stopped in the quiet passage and pressed his back into

the cold wall. His long breath did nothing to calm him and he soon
found himself sliding down to the floor with his head in his hands.

As his thoughts swirled, a specific comment came back to him
and he lifted his face.

"We have not been instructed to remove them from the board."

Who were they referring to? Besides King Vighon, there was no
other the Archon were said to receive instructions from.

Convinced that he was about to be sick, Kassian pushed himself
up and quick-stepped to the nearest door. A gulp of fresh air calmed
his stomach and he wiped the sweat from his brow.

Murder. Was that to be his future?

Not a day went by that Kassian didn't look around Valatos and
tell himself he would do anything to keep them all safe. Now, he was
to be truly tested...

PART TWO

CHAPTER 13
HALF-HUMAN

Standing in the streets of Lirian, the elven part of Inara should have felt comforted by the surrounding pines of The Evermoore; their gentle rustle in the night breeze and the majesty in their climb for the heavens. The Dragorn, however, felt nothing but deflated.

The Pick-Axe was closed.

Her opportunities to stop by the rangers' tavern were few and far between but, whenever she did, The Axe was alive with music, merriment, and good company. She had hoped to find Doran, Russell or possibly Galanör inside. The way she was feeling right now, Inara would even have been happy to speak with the more elusive Asher.

Am I not enough? Athis asked coyly.

Inara managed a smile as she looked up to the starry sky. Only one with a sharp eye could spot the black silhouette of the dragon as his form passed over the stars.

Of course you are enough, she assured.

Then why do you seek out more wingless ones?

Inara wasn't sure of the best way to reply, though she often didn't need to when talking to her companion. **Maybe it's the** *human part in me,* she posed. *We naturally seek each other out. I remember there being comfort in it...*

Athis didn't speak, his emotions loud enough.

You shouldn't be jealous, Inara told him, making her way back to the palace. *You and I are one, now and forever.* Athis was holding something back but it felt buried beneath layers of memories. *What are you not saying?*

The dragon paused and his mind focused. *You seek them out because of Alijah,* he said.

Inara wasn't convinced that that was what her companion had been thinking about, but she let it go since he was also right. *I suppose his return was always going to be sudden,* she explained. *I just thought we would know before he arrived. I think I assumed there would be a party or a parade or... something. I don't know why. It would be the last thing he would want.*

It's what he wants that concerns me. Athis voiced what they were both really thinking.

You don't trust him, Inara concluded.

I want to, just as you do, Athis replied. *But Malliath has ever been unstable, even before his imprisonment by the mages of Korkanath. I cannot believe he has changed in fifteen years, regardless of his bond with Alijah.*

Did he speak to you? Inara asked, though she could feel the sarcastic response rising in Athis before her last word.

The voiceless one? No, he did not speak to me, just as he has refrained from speaking to every dragon for the last ten thousand years.

Inara gave a friendly nod to a pair of Namdhorian soldiers enjoying their evening's freedom. *Is he up there with you?* she enquired.

Yes, but he is much higher.

Just like a predator, Inara thought. Athis shared that same thought a moment later and they both decided to be on their guard until her brother could prove his motives to be otherwise.

Entering the Ever Hold, Lirian's exquisite palace, Inara's environment took on a more luxurious finish. The beautiful wood aestheticism that ran through the city did not reach as far as the Penrose family home. If the rumours were true, Lady Gracen had begun redecorating the palace the very same day her father passed away. There was too much gold for Inara's taste and it did nothing to represent the people of the Felgarn province.

It wasn't hard to find anyone since the lady's servants were scurrying in and out of the grand hall with trays of food and drink. Then there was the band, or *bands*. Lady Gracen had spread her welcome party across four enormous halls and placed a band in each.

Taking a step into the first hall, Inara remained by the wall, more than happy not to be announced. A roar of laughter erupted on the far side and the Dragorn soon found Vighon in the middle of it all. It was a sight that would perhaps have once made Inara's eyes roll, but she was glad to see the king get out from under the shadow of this conspiracy he feared. Then, the thought of his rotten head in the morning made her smile.

"I haven't seen him like this in a long time," said a voice in her ear.

Inara turned to greet the captain of the king's guard. "Are you not enjoying the comfort of Lady Gracen's walls, Sir Ruban?"

"I like to keep two eyes on the king outside of The Dragon Keep. I find that mead gets in the way of that."

Inara couldn't help but laugh and place a warm hand on his shoulder. "I hope he knows how lucky he is to have you watching his back all the time."

Alijah crossed Inara's path and quietly made his way onto the balcony with a cup of wine in hand. The Dragorn apologised to Ruban and weaved between the party to reach her brother. As she stepped onto the balcony, Alijah casually emptied his cup over the rail and leant on his elbows to take in the city below.

"Did I just see Alijah Galfrey throw away good wine?" she jested, seeing his cheekbones raise into a smile in the torchlight.

"You know as well as I," he remarked, half turning to gesture to the sky, "you shouldn't drink and fly."

Inara laughed silently to herself, imagining Athis struggling to fly because of her intoxication.

"You're not joining in yourself?" Alijah asked.

Inara considered her words carefully. "This isn't exactly my idea of a good time. In fact, I don't think we should be here at all..."

Alijah rolled his eyes. "You disapprove of the king's decision." He scrutinised her a moment longer. "You disapprove of my advice," he corrected.

"We don't know for certain that there is any conspiracy," Inara began. "And taking most of an army across the country just makes Vighon look paranoid and fearful, not to mention somewhat tyrannical."

"He's not marching *most* of an army across the country," Alijah protested with a shrug. "I convinced him, did I not, to keep a couple of thousand soldiers in Grey Stone to maintain peace. And he's not long agreed to leave the Lirian soldiers here before we move on."

"Oh, so he's just going to arrive at Velia's gate with a *thousand* soldiers..."

Alijah sighed. "I see there's still no pleasing you," he jibed.

Inara's back went up. "And what does that mean?" she demanded.

"It means you haven't changed," Alijah retorted. "It has to be *your* idea, executed by *you*, and judged by *you*."

"You think you're any different?" Inara fired.

Surprisingly, Alijah threw his head back and laughed. "No, I suppose I'm not. Look at us, fighting like old times. I've missed this... until just now that is."

Inara let her expression soften and she swallowed the line of argument she had waiting on the end of her tongue. "I might have missed you," she confessed, joining him by the railing. "Once or twice," she added with a wicked smile.

"I thought of you every day," Alijah offered. "It couldn't have been easy for you. First, I left, then Gideon left. You've been holding Illian up by yourself."

"There hasn't been much to hold up," Inara replied modestly. "Vighon has been a great king. You must have had a hard time," she added. "It sounds as if you single-handedly brought a whole country into line."

Alijah stared at the horizon. "Not really. Erador had everything it needed to thrive. I just reminded them of that."

"What's it like? Erador?"

Her brother stood up straight. "It's not unlike Illian. Similar size in population. There's forests and plains and deserts and ice caps... But it's *old*. No matter where you go, you know it's ancient. The history there is so rich you could get lost in it for an eternity."

"The people are the same?" Inara enquired.

"Of course. There are villages, towns, and cities full of families trying to survive just like they are here. They love the same, they fight the same, they even want the same things out of life. I suppose the most notable difference is religion."

"The people of Erador have gods?"

"Just the one," Alijah answered. "And you already know his name."

That name easily returned to Inara. "Kaliban..."

Her brother smiled. "It's amusing really. Everyone in Illian worships Atilan and his pantheon but, in Erador, they're all figures of *history*. There used to be a statue of Atilan in Valgala's main square."

"And what do you make of their Kaliban?"

Alijah frowned. "We both know The Echoes made him up eons ago. I did a little digging actually. It wasn't easy to find, but there are records of Erador's most ancient past. They were a warring people, driven by bloodlust. The first priests of The Echoes made Kaliban up as a way of taking control of the masses and ending the wars. A noble beginning to be sure. But, like so many things, it became rotten, corrupted by the power it wielded." Alijah took a long breath. "I see the religion of both countries being the only factor that will get in the way of any alliance. But, we'll have to cross that bridge when we get to it."

Inara had listened intently, but her eyes had been scrutinising her brother's every facial movement searching for the truth in him. So far, she guessed, he was being entirely honest, if reserved.

"It seems even a crown can't stop you from hunting history down," Inara quipped with a lighter tone.

Alijah softened. "Unlocking our history will give us the key to our future. You should come back with me, to Erador. You wouldn't believe some of the things you'd see. Mount Kaliban is twice the size of Mount Garganafan. The Glimmer Lands will stun your eyes. And The Silver Trees of Akmar..." The half-elf had a look of wonder in his eyes. "There are beings in this world you couldn't imagine in the west."

"It sounds beautiful," Inara agreed.

"It is," Alijah said wistfully. "The hard part is keeping it that way. That's why it's so important that the throne belongs to an immortal, especially one with the wisdom of a dragon behind them. Where mortal kings and queens would forget their ancestors' deeds, good or bad, *I* never will. The mistakes of the past will stay with me forever and I will learn from them."

Inara could hear the logic, but she wasn't as convinced. "Shouldn't the people be ruled by *one* of the people?"

Alijah waved her suggestion away. "An antiquated notion. History is riddled, on both sides of The Hox, with kings and queens who cared for nothing but the size of their statue they left behind. Mortality makes people look inwards, a path that can only lead to greed and selfish acts. Kings and queens are supposed to be servants."

Inara glanced back at the party. "What of Vighon then? *He* is mortal..." Now the Dragorn really watched her brother for any hint of antagonism.

"Vighon is unlike any king that has ruled before him," Alijah replied eloquently. "He hasn't come from a royal family. Aspects of his childhood were privileged thanks to us, but most of his later life was spent trying to survive. He's always enjoyed a good fight but he never went looking for one. Most importantly, he never wanted the crown. He accepted it with a servant's heart. And, of course, he has you by his side," Alijah added with a coy smile.

Inara turned her attention to the distant pines. "Athis and I advise him where we can."

Alijah tilted his head, scrutinising her now. "You're still going to deny that part of yourself? After all these years?"

"What part of myself?" Inara asked with genuine ignorance.

"The part of you that's human," Alijah said as if it was obvious. "The part of you that's been in love with Vighon Draqaro since we were children."

Inara shook her head. "Those feelings died a long time ago. I have Athis now, I'm a Dragorn. I don't need nor do I want those kinds of attachments."

Somewhat exasperated, Alijah pushed back from the railing and looked at his sister in disbelief. "You still think that's what you are? Dragorn? Gideon took the Dragorn and left, Inara; they're gone. You're the *Guardian of the Realm* now; that's something else entirely, isn't it?"

Inara could feel her defences rising again. "I am Dragorn, Alijah. And Gideon and the others aren't gone; they're training. When they're ready, they will return."

"It's been fifteen years," Alijah pointed out. "I think you have to accept that they aren't coming back."

The Dragorn shook her head. "You don't know what you're talking about."

"I know a lot more than you apparently," he countered, his tongue always faster than hers. "I've been to Drakanan, where the first Dragon Riders lived and trained for thousands of years. This life you've embraced is not how it was meant to be, Inara."

"My *life*," Inara intoned, "is that of a Dragorn's, like all those before me."

159

"The Dragorn was an order created by the elves five thousand years ago - a mere speck compared to the age of the Dragon Riders. Their monk-like ways might have worked for elves, but you and I are not elves. There is a part of us, an undeniable part, that is very much human."

Inara opened and closed her mouth, deciding to swallow the snapping reply she had ready. "And how did these Dragon Riders live exactly?"

"Like the people they swore to protect," Alijah answered simply. "They had lovers, wives, husbands, and even children. They weren't afraid of families."

"I'm not afraid of having a family," Inara defended. "I just don't want one. There isn't a part of me that needs one to feel complete when I have Athis."

"Do you really *feel* like that?" Alijah probed. "Or do you just *tell* yourself that? Gideon drummed the Dragorn code into you from the day you met Athis. He cannot be blamed for that; his mentor was an elven Dragorn and it's all he'd ever known. But you're apart from all that now. You have a *choice.*"

"It's not a choice for me," Inara argued. "And it *is* how I feel. You must feel the same. Surely you can't have the need to be with any woman while you're bonded to Malliath."

"And yet I have." He shrugged with that same arrogant smile he had worn in his youth. "There are techniques, never sought after by the Dragorn, that can allow you to... detach from your dragon."

"That sounds *awful.*" Inara couldn't think of anything worse.

"You're still bonded just as you ever were," Alijah went on to explain. "Your minds will still be one, but you can put up a wall of sorts. It allows you to have moments where your focus is just on you, moments where you can embrace your human half. It's the only way to truly live, Inara. Anything else and you're only living half a life. It might seem like the right thing now, but a few decades from now, a few *centuries*, and you might start to wonder why it feels like there's a piece missing."

Inara looked at the stars above, listening for Athis. He said nothing, his feelings unnervingly private.

Movement in the corner of her eye drew Inara back to the balcony doors, where Lady Gracen had paused. She didn't even register the Dragorn, her hungry eyes fixed on Alijah instead. With an alluring smile, she slowly turned around and walked away, making for doors on the far side of the hall.

Alijah, grinning from ear to ear, placed his cup on the stone railing. "If you'll excuse me..."

"*Really?*" Inara managed to intone her disbelief with just enough disappointment as to sound judging.

"It's all in the name of the alliance," he replied, walking backwards towards the party. "Inara," he added more seriously, "there's more to *both* of your lives than just companionship. Don't be afraid to live..."

Inara waited a moment before returning her attention to the sky. *Is there a particular reason you're not saying anything?*

She could feel Athis's position relative to her own and knew he was gliding directly above her. The dragon's mood shifted uncomfortably and in a way Inara had never felt before. There had never been an occasion where Athis didn't know what to say.

Alijah speaks the truth, he finally said. *At least in part.*

Why do you say that?

I do not possess the memories of the Dragon Riders. They remain with Rainael the emerald star and our elders. But I do have knowledge of their time in the skies. I know they had families and relations outside of their bond.

Why did you never share this with me? Inara wasn't upset, but honestly curious.

You embraced the Dragorn and their principles, Athis replied. *You have never shown any inclination towards another of your kind. And... I don't want to share you.*

Inara found it all too easy to empathise with her companion. **Then it's a good thing I don't want that.**

Athis paused. *Don't you?* His question resonated somewhere deep in her soul, robbing her of an immediate answer.

I want all I've ever wanted: to protect the realm with you by my side.

Inara turned back to the party, where the king was still in the midst of an audience which hung on his every word. Vighon's smile had been long missed by the Dragorn and she quickly came to realise the sight of it resonated as deeply as Athis's question. Though she could never truly deny her love for him, she could certainly deny its power over her. Whether Gideon and the rest of the order returned or not, the Guardian of the Realm still had her duty.

And she would see it done.

CHAPTER 14
IT'S IN THE BONES

The world came back to Asher in shades. The light, however fleeting, was always blinding, painful even. Dark shapes moved around him and warm hands pressed into his skin. In between, there was a deep dark nothingness so powerful it was oppressive in manner, restraining the ranger's mind.

More than once, in his brief but lucid moments, he wondered if this was death. It wouldn't be the first time he had departed the world, though the ranger held no such memories of the beyond. As painful and exhausting as his life had been, a deep dark nothingness sounded quite peaceful.

When the light wasn't assaulting his eyes and the hands weren't moving his body, Asher heard voices and unusual noises. The voices were always light and melodic, but the sounds that accompanied them were almost magical in nature. Sometimes, these voices and sounds brought more pain and he heard his own voice cry out into the ether.

Then, without warning or reason, the ranger's eyes snapped open. The haze was gone and the edges of his mind felt clear and sharp for the first time in a long while. He was lying down on a cot made from branches and leaves, his chest bare, though it was patterned in some kind of clay that had been dyed purple and green. He still wore his leather trousers, which bore more than one tear, especially around his left thigh.

The serious wounds he had sustained came flooding back and Asher sat up to inspect his leg. The leather was stained dark with the blood he had lost, but the skin was perfectly intact. As the fight came back to him in more detail, the ranger wiped away a portion of the pattern that swirled around his chest and shoulder. The clay smeared, he could see no evidence of the sword that had impaled him. Similarly, his ribs showed no signs that a dagger had been plunged through them and his breathing was smooth and effortless.

Why wasn't he dead?

Having taken stock of himself, Asher quickly examined his surroundings. It was cramped but, like the bed, the hut was made from branches, the wood twisted into unnatural shapes. If he hadn't been in The Evermoore when he succumbed to his injuries, the ranger would have said he was in the hands of the elves. Since they were a few hundred miles south, in Ilythyra, he had to be in Ikirith. He was among the Drakes...

Unsure what that meant exactly, Asher shot up to check one of the pane-less windows, the source of the hut's warm light. He instantly regretted it. His heart rate increased dramatically and his skin became clammy as the blood drained from his head and raced to his feet. The ranger managed half a curse before he crumpled to the ground and lost himself in the darkness once more.

When next he opened his eyes, the ranger had been returned to his cot and the angle of light streaming through the window had changed significantly.

There was also a Drake seated beside him.

Asher couldn't say that it was fear that rose up in him, but the Drake's formidable yet beautiful appearance made him uneasy.

This particular Drake was a male by the look of him. He had the high cheekbones of an elf that cut across his angular face and led Asher to his pointed ears, both of which stuck out from his flowing black mane of hair. His skin was fair, lighter than a human's but most definitely darker than an orc's. A patch of tiny, paper thin scales caught the light on one side of his face. His hairline was broken in two places where a pair of dark oak horns curved over the back of his head before flicking up to the sky.

It was the eyes, however, that captured the ranger. He had seen eyes such as those before, only much bigger and situated in the skull of a dragon. This Drake had yellow green eyes with a reptilian black slit cutting down the middle. They were the eyes of a predator, ironic considering they were in the head of a passive creature.

"How you feel?" The Drake spoke quickly, though his command of man's language sounded broken in his mouth.

Asher tried to sit up before answering him and soon found the Drake's strong hand pressed into his chest. "Slow," he advised, drawing the word out. "Lost big blood," he told the ranger.

Nodding his understanding, Asher slowly positioned himself on the edge of the cot and rubbed his eyes. The side of his head felt sore where he had crashed into the ground. Still, it was nothing short of a miracle that his bruised head was his only injury - he should be dead.

"How long was I out?" he asked gruffly.

The Drake tilted his head quizzically, unfamiliar with the phrasing.

Asher stumbled over his next words, searching for the elvish equivalent. *"How long have I been here?"*

The Drake corrected his posture, his surprise written all over his face. *"You speak elvish?"*

Asher's mouth curled into half a smile. *"Better than you speak man's tongue."*

Another Drake entered the hut at that moment, pushing through the leathery flaps that hung to the ground. *"Indeed,"* the new Drake said, oozing authority and age, *"you are full of surprises... for a human."*

The ranger didn't miss the submissive body language that overcame the Drake seated in front of him. In comparison, the two males were similarly dressed from the waist down; their clothing made from nature itself. Both bared their chiselled torsos, which had been tattooed with intricate patterns. The new Drake, however, was bald, reminiscent of the orc he had once been, and he walked with a staff of entwined branches.

Asher let his eyes drift to the window. *"This is Ikirith?"*

"This is but a simple dwelling," the older Drake replied. *"Would you like to see Ikirith?"*

Asher nodded. *"It would be an honour."*

"Then we would know your name," the older Drake leveraged.

The ranger stood up and the younger Drake rose with him. *"My name is Asher,"* he said with a slight bow of the head.

The younger Drake turned to his elder with a look of curiosity and concern - at least that's what Asher took from it; he hadn't spent nearly enough time with them to learn their unique facial expressions.

"Asher..." the elder repeated, tasting the name in his mouth. *"An unusual name among your kind, though it has been heard before among my people - by the elves of Ilythyra. They told us a ranger by that name, an* Outlander's *name, was the person responsible for our existence."*

Asher could hear the question in his tone and was too tired to even think about lying. *"I am he,"* the ranger stated boldly.

"The currents of fate are strong around you," the elder observed, his eyes searching the air over Asher's head. *"How intriguing that you, of all your kind, would be brought here."*

"You fought the orcs on The White Vale?" the younger Drake blurted.

"I did. We didn't know the weapon would transform them into... you."

The older Drake raised a hairless eyebrow. *"You thought it would kill them."*

Asher couldn't say he felt ashamed at that. *"We did. The orcs would have ravaged all of Verda given the chance."*

"Of course they would," the elder agreed. *"It is in their nature; something none of us can fight."*

Asher felt the Drake was saying more than the sum of his words but he continued, *"The emergence of your race was unexpected, but welcomed. There had been too much death."*

"However indirectly your part was in our creation," the elder replied, *"you have the gratitude of the Drakes, Ranger. You will always find sanctuary in Ikirith..."*

"We are not welcomed by all," the younger Drake grumbled to himself.

"Adan'Karth," the elder chastised softly. *"His tone is unwarranted but he is correct; there are those who do not welcome the Drakes. Adan'Karth was watching the hunters: that is to say, he was watching you watch the hunters. Your intended intervention has our thanks, but we have been evading the men of The Evermoore since we arrived here, fifteen years ago. What concerns us are those that killed them and nearly killed you."*

Asher put two and two together. *"Thank you for saving me,"* he said, looking from the elder to Adan'Karth. *"I would certainly have died had you left me. As for those who attacked me, they are no threat to you; it was me they came for."*

The elder remained stoical. *"We are a young race by any comparison, but we possess a wisdom shared only with the dragons of this world. We know the difference between men who can kill and men who were born to kill. Sense tells me, Ranger, that should we continue to stand between these killers and yourself, my people will be threatened..."*

Asher made to argue that point but he held his tongue when he realised it was true - nothing would come between the Arakesh and their target.

"With nothing to give you as thanks for my life, I would take my leave

and ensure no such threat reaches your home." The ranger looked around for something to cover his chest when a wave of nausea passed through him and nearly took him from his feet.

Adan'Karth was there to catch him, his hands quick and firm. *"You have been healed, but the blood you lost will take time to replenish. You must rest."*

Asher took a deep breath and resumed his stature. *"I'm not one for resting."*

"Perhaps a walk instead," the elder suggested. *"Adan'Karth and I can keep you on your feet until you feel the need to rest again."*

In truth, the ranger knew he could fall straight to sleep if he lay down, but the need to always be on the move would never let him rest.

"My name is Abun'Sun," the elder introduced himself with his hand raised and palm presented expectantly to Asher.

The ranger hesitantly raised his hand and pressed it to Abun'-Sun's. For less than a second, a bridge was formed between man and Drake, a connection that carried their true intent as well as a portion of their personality. Asher saw Abun'Sun for what he was: a father. Or at least that's how the Drake saw himself among his people. There was a curious nature about him but, more than anything, he was protective and not just of his people, but all life. It was quite the impression for a moment's touch.

Asher jerked his hand away and examined his palm. *"What was that?"*

"We call it transference. It allows us to see into each other and know who they are. And you, Ranger, are unlike anyone I have ever met."

The ranger felt violated, though his only reaction was to shrug the comment off. *"Well, you haven't met a lot of people."*

"There is more than just yourself inside your mind..."

Asher saw flashes of purple eyes in the dark.

"If you saw my intentions," the ranger began, *"you know I don't want your people to come to any harm. The assassins who tried to kill me*

will *try again. Being in Ikirith won't deter them, nor will taking innocent lives. I should leave."*

"*In your current condition,*" Abun'Sun countered, "*you would not make it to Lirian. Our borders are watched; any strangers will be shown a different path should they wander too closely. Come now, see our home. Perhaps after surveying your surroundings, you will find rest.*"

The latter of Abun'Sun's remarks had come straight from their brief yet intimate bond. It was certainly expedient, but Asher couldn't help but feel like his soul had been scrutinised - or what was left of it.

Adan'Karth gestured to the door draped with leathery flaps, suggesting that he would walk behind the ranger. Had Asher not seen inside the elder's mind, he would have considered the younger Adan'Karth to be his guard but, as it was, the Drakes accompanied him out of support should he need it.

What greeted Asher was a world unlike anything he had ever seen. No more than a glance was required to see that the Drakes were beings in total harmony with the magical realm. Everywhere he looked, there was a Drake using magic to reshape the forest around them, giving the trees new structures that nature could never achieve. The grass was thick under foot and it sparkled in the sunlight, as if infused with diamonds.

These details, however, paled when compared to the view, a sight so incomprehensible that it robbed Asher of speech. The ranger believed he had seen everything the world had to offer, from wonders to nightmares, but Ikirith was unlike anything he could even dream of.

The ground, meadows of lush green, rose up and curved high into the sky, shifting the horizon to the position of a midday sun. Trees equal in size to giant cliffs arched out of the vertical ground and rooted themselves into the ground beneath Asher's feet. The Drakes appeared to have made homes inside of them, hollowing the bark out with more magic.

The air was filled with every kind of bird and flying insect. The fields were scattered with deer and woodland creatures. It was a paradise.

"How..." Asher had to fight to reclaim his wits as well as his elvish. *"How is this possible?"*

Abun'Sun wandered into a ray of light with a satisfied smile on his face. *"We are part dragon, part elf. Very different beings, but they have one common trait; their affinity with magic."*

Asher had seen the world be physically reshaped by magic, but nothing on this scale. The ground rose up like a tidal wave, reaching higher than any stone-built structure he had ever seen.

"It's beautiful," he uttered.

Movement caught the ranger's eye and he turned to see more Drakes crowding around. Adan'Karth broke away for a moment to touch hands with his kin, transferring his impression of Asher as well as some knowledge. Judging by the way the Drakes proceeded to look at the ranger, he assumed they had just learned of his part in their creation.

"Lady Ellöria showed us a way to create a world inside the world," Abun'Sun explained. *"I believe they call it a pocket dimension. Clever, and extremely elegant,"* he added.

"That's why you aren't afraid of the hunters," Asher reasoned. *"They can't find the entrance..."*

"Nor do they possess enough magic to force their way through. It keeps us safe and reduces the risk of conflict."

Asher couldn't help noticing the crowd growing in size. There were even Drakes journeying towards them from across the curving plains.

"What's happening?" he asked.

"They want to see you," Abun'Sun told him. *"Until now, you have just been a name."*

Asher instinctively began to step back. He had been trained for decades to remain anonymous and he had never been able to rid himself of the habit. Having so many eyes on him made the ranger feel vulnerable, something Abun'Sun immediately detected. The

Drake flicked his jaw up and made a guttural sound with his throat - a signal to disperse apparently. Within seconds, Asher was once again in the company of Abun'Sun and Adan'Karth.

Asher fell in beside Abun'Sun and the pair walked farther into Ikirith with Adan'Karth trailing closely behind. The Drakes had nothing else to say for a time, allowing the ranger to take in the unique majesty of their home. Asher could see that they were walking up the curve but, looking back, he had already traversed enough distance to see his hut now appeared higher than his current position.

He wasn't even close to understanding it.

"You do not enjoy attention," the elder stated. *"That is something you have in common with the Drakes."*

"I feel our reasons are vastly different," Asher quipped.

Abun'Sun tipped his horned head *"The need to remain hidden is a part of who you are; I felt as much. We choose to hide because our outlook does not blend well with the rest of Illian."*

Asher couldn't disagree with any of it, especially since delving into Abun'Sun's mind. *"Your passive nature would see you crushed,"* he surmised. *"Man's world is full of conflict and violence; it's unavoidable."*

"We are patient," the elder replied. *"We have only walked the earth for fifteen years. We have been led to believe that humans require time to overcome their fears. Our hope, given time, is that our previous forms will be resigned to history."*

Asher had an idea of how long that would take, but he decided against voicing it and spoiling their conversation. There was something so calming about Ikirith that the ranger felt almost protective of it and those who called it home.

"Do you recall anything of your previous life?" he asked, hoping he wasn't offending Abun'Sun in the process.

The elder stroked the head of a deer as it strolled past, unafraid of them. *"Myself no, but there are those among us who speak of... flashes. They see images in their sleep, terrible things that haunt them for days. The life of an orc is tortuous..."*

The ranger shook his head in disbelief. He was talking to a being who only possessed fifteen years of memories and experiences, but Abun'Sun spoke and carried himself as if he was hundreds of years old.

Asher paused by a bush with blue leaves and vibrant fuchsia flowers. As a ranger of the wilds, he made it his business to know every type of plant and he was confident he knew them all, but he had never seen one like this. Looking around, there were more flowers and even small trees that he had never seen anywhere in Illian.

"*It's like a different world...*" he mused.

"*You are the first human to see Ikirith,*" Abun'Sun commented, continuing to wander. "*I am glad, of all your people, that you are the one to see it. I imagine your own connection to the magical realm gives you a greater appreciation for our work...*"

Asher didn't move, his eyes shifting from Adan'Karth to the elder Drake. "*My connection?*" he questioned.

Abun'Sun turned to regard him. "*The magic that resides within,*" he replied, as if that explained his remark. "*I have met very few humans, but none of them resonated with the magical realm as you do. I can see it,*" he pressed, waving his hand across the ranger's body. "*Your bones hum with magic.*"

"*It's like a song,*" Adan'Karth added, his dragon eyes searching Asher's body.

"*I don't know what you're talking about,*" the ranger said, subconsciously looking for somewhere to sit.

"*Our connection was brief,*" Abun'Sun went on, "*but I glimpsed enough to know that your life has been complicated... and long. How many years have you wandered Verda's soil?*"

Had anyone else probed into his life so deeply, Asher would have refused to answer, and not politely. Abun'Sun, however, was not anyone else. They had only just met, but the Drake's mannerisms, body language, and even his tone of voice made him feel like an old friend and a harmless one at that.

"*I was born to an Outlander tribe,*" he answered, "*over a thousand years ago. The elves were at war with each other at the time. They used magic to end the war and... Well, that's all the complicated part. I was trapped in their spell for a thousand years.*" Asher clamped his jaw shut, his natural reaction when talking about himself, especially this particular story.

"*How did you break free?*" Abun'Sun enquired.

"*I was in possession of a powerful gem.*" Asher looked up at the sky. "*It came from the heavens a long time ago. It broke the spell around me, setting me free. What followed was less complicated, but a much harder story to tell...*" The ranger was ashamed to this day of the decades that ensued, his fate sealed when Nasta Nal-Aket found him on the boggy plains surrounding Elethiah.

"*You hurt people,*" Abun'Sun said softly.

Asher glanced at Adan'Karth. "*Those killers in the woods... I was one of them. For the next four decades I kept that gem in secret - it protected me from magic and allowed me to use it at will.*"

The two Drakes met each other's reptilian eyes and conferred with expressions alone. Had they been humans or perhaps elves, Asher might have guessed their thoughts from analysing their faces and body language, but the Drakes were too subtle.

Abun'Sun walked over to a tree and raised his hand to feel the hanging leaves. "*What is the most important thing any living being possesses?*" he asked curiously.

Asher considered his answer, believing he knew the correct response, but unsure if the Drake was referring to something closer to a sense of morality. "*Blood,*" he replied, wondering if that high-lighted his time as an assassin.

"*Correct,*" Abun'Sun said with a smile. "*Do you know where your blood comes from?*"

Again, Asher had only his Nightfall education to fall back on. "*The heart.*"

"*No.*" The Drake shook his horned head. "*Blood is made in the bones. Our bones are important; they do more than simply provide us*

173

with shape. They give blood... and they absorb *magic, clinging to it long after death has eaten away at the body. For all that you have lost in your long life, your bones have survived, the same bones that were trapped with a powerful source of magic for a thousand years."*

Asher shrugged off the dizziness building in his head and examined his hands as if he could see the bones within. *"You're saying that I'm... immortal?"*

Abun'Sun tilted his head and scrutinised the ranger. *"No. You no longer possess the gem; all that is left is the magic you were able to absorb in that time. It might be decades from now, centuries even, but the magic will fade and your body will continue to age."*

Asher couldn't ignore the warnings his body was giving him anymore. "I need to sit down," he said in man's tongue, reaching out for support that wasn't there.

Adan'Karth's superior reflexes had him catching the ranger before he hit the ground. *"You cannot escape rest,"* he said. *"You've lost too much blood."*

Sitting with his back to a tree, Asher let his head drop between his knees in an effort to stay conscious. Abun'Sun's words were swimming around in his mind, searching for purchase so that he might understand. For all his training, however, there was nothing to be done to combat blood loss. The edges of his vision blurred before disappearing altogether. He was getting really sick of passing out...

CHAPTER 15
A STORM IS COMING

A s Doran's hot breath faded before him, the rising city of Namdhor appeared through the vapour. Set into a cliff that angled forty-five degrees from the ground and rose at its peak to just under a thousand feet, the capital of Illian was naturally fortified. Its foundation was that of solid rock, a damned good rock if the northern pillar was anything to judge by. That one column of rock held up the slope, preventing it from falling into The King's Lake.

This was how Doran's dwarven eye took in the view. Perhaps he should have appreciated the way Namdhor looked in the morning, its ancient towers and buildings a warm gold in the rising dawn. He could even have noted the majesty of the lake, the largest in Illian, and full of fishing boats taking advantage of the thawed ice.

The son of Dorain, however, couldn't help but look at the world the way the Mother and Father had made him to. He saw good stone and sturdy architecture. The likes of boats or anything to do with the lake was beyond his interest.

To the east of the city, The White Vale still bore the scars of war fifteen years on. Giant holes, partially filled with snow, potted the land where the orcs and their terrifying stonemaw had breached the surface. Doran could still remember charging out of the ground himself, backed by his clan and his brother.

"Why can't we ever go anywhere that's warm?" Russell grumbled.

Doran also remembered a time when his supernatural friend barely noticed a change in the temperature. He had opened his mouth to state as much when he closed it again. They all knew Russell's curse was waning and his life with it - there was no need to bring it up.

"Come on then," he said instead, spurring Pig on. "Let's find me kin."

The closer they rode to the city the more defined the barracks became. The army of Namdhor was situated farther north, closer to the Vengoran mountains. Within those mountains were the remnants of the orc horde and beyond them the dwarves of Dhenaheim. Doran could see the sense in their position...

Passing through the lower town that sprawled across Namdhor's base, the presence of dwarves was evident. Though neither companion had yet to see a dwarf, shops, trading posts, and taverns had been established with the sigil of clan Heavybelly printed on their signs. By the look of the shops, his kin were primarily dealing with metal works and stonemasonry - their speciality.

"I never thought I'd see the likes o' this," the stout ranger observed. "Dwarves livin' amongst humans, tradin' with 'em, drinkin' with 'em... The price it's cost the clan is a shame," he added offhandedly. "But livin' under the shadow o' Silvyr Hall couldn' 'ave gone on for ever."

Russell peered down at him from his horse. "There's no chance the Heavybellys will be invited back into the hierarchy?"

Doran waved such a notion away. "King Uthrad's every word might as well be etched into stone. Once he's made a decree, that's that."

The son of Dorain hopped off his Warhog and made for the nearest window that apparently belonged to a dwarven locksmith. After wiping the glass, he cupped his eyes and searched inside for any sign of life. The sun was up, after all; there should be dwarves making coin somewhere.

"Must be out," he muttered.

Russell crossed the street and checked a small tavern - the door was locked and the windows boarded. "No one here either," he called.

Perplexed, Doran shook his head. "That ain' right..."

The companions met back up and pulled their mounts along behind them. Now that Doran thought about it, he hadn't actually seen any dwarves since they had arrived.

"Me kin live for the trade," he commented without taking his eyes off the streets and buildings. "If they're 'ere, we should be seein' 'em everywhere!"

As they approached the rise in Namdhor's slope, Russell reached out to get the attention of a young man walking past them. "Excuse me," he said politely.

"Morning," the Namdhorian replied, his attention narrowing on Russell's unusual yellow eyes.

"Where are all the dwarves of clan Heavybelly?" the old wolf enquired.

The man licked his lips, clearly unsure who or what he was talking to. "There looks to be one right beside you, sir."

Russell glanced at Doran and flashed a smile. "Any others?"

The Namdhorian shook his head. "No dwarves round these parts for months now. One day they was here, selling their wares, then they were gone." He stepped forward to make his leave before turning back. "Oh, there's still old Thaggadar, just up the road."

"Thaggadar?" Doran echoed, the name unknown to him.

"He runs the bounty hunters," the young man answered. "There's usually someone shouting about it outside his shop."

Russell thanked the man with a smile, but his eyes were enough to keep any smile from the Namdhorian's face. "Let's see what's going on around here," he suggested.

Together, they ascended the rise, taking the main road that ran straight up to The Dragon Keep. Again, Doran had memories of fighting where he now journeyed. He could still see in his mind where the rows of spikes had been dug into the road and the city separated into tiers. There was no better feeling than wading into a horde of orcs with Pig beneath him and a hefty piece of steel in his hand.

"That must be it," Russell announced, bringing his horse to a stop beside him. "A little on the nose, isn't it?"

Doran looked up at the sign above the door: *Bounty Hunters*. "The children of Grarfath aren' exactly known for their creativity when it comes to words an' such. We do our best talkin' with our hands!"

Russell stepped back to take the shop front in. "It doesn't appear to be open. Maybe this Thaggadar has disappeared with the others."

Doran walked a little farther up the rise to see the building from the alley. "There's smoke comin' out o' the chimney," he pointed out. "I'd say old Thaggadar is still around..."

Russell tethered his horse to a post and walked up the steps to investigate. The rounded doorknob rattled in his grip but the door refused to budge.

"We're closed!" came a barking reprimand from inside.

"Is that right," Doran mumbled, nodding at the doorknob in Russell's hand.

The old wolf grinned and increased his grip around the bronze doorknob. A quick twist of his wrist and the lock succumbed to his supernatural strength.

"Oi!" the voice cried, but Doran and Russell made their way inside all the same.

It was musty and glum inside, the air filled with dust and the windows streaked with grime. The furniture was made with dwarves in mind, lending more height to Russell's broad stature. The wall on the right was covered with wanted posters and descriptions of criminals who had evaded the law. There weren't many with a red X painted over the parchment.

"What's yer game?" The gruff voice and pointed question preceded the appearance of a legless dwarf on a chariot of wheels. It was quite the ingenious design, with smaller wheels at the front and larger wheels at the back for the hands to guide.

"Thaggadar, I take it," Doran concluded.

"Ye'll be payin' for a new lock, ye will!" Thaggadar argued.

Russell put his hands up to calm the air. "Sorry about the door. We're here looking for—"

"We're closed!" Thaggadar repeated, spitting through his scraggy white beard. "There ain' no hunters to be doin' any lookin', so ye wastin' yer time!"

"That's why we're 'ere!" Doran countered.

"Ye want *work*?" Thaggadar replied, arching half of the only eyebrow he possessed. "We ain' never employed a human before but..." The old dwarf shrugged at Russell. "Now, we ain' no Blood Boys, but we're still damn good hunters I'll 'ave ye know—"

"We're not at yer door lookin' for work," Doran complained, already exhausted with the old fool. "We're 'ere because..." The son of Dorain reconsidered his angle. "Where are all the dwarves?" he asked instead. "I thought Namdhor was home to more than a few these days."

Thaggadar narrowed his eyes at the stout ranger, scrutinising his features. "Do I know yer face?"

Doran sighed. "I doubt it."

"Wait a minute." Thaggadar leaned forward in his wheelchair. "Who *are* ye? All Heavybellys 'ave been recalled, so ye're either not o' me clan or ye're a coward! Which is it?"

Doran frowned, bringing his bushy blond brow into his eyepatch. "Recalled? What are ye on abou'? Why would Dak recall 'em all?"

Thaggadar scowled as the words reached his ears. "Why would..." Revelation appeared to strike the old dwarf. "Ye're Doran, son o' Dorain! Ye're the exile!" he accused.

"Aye, that be meself. Now what in all the hells are ye talkin' abou', old dwarf?"

Thaggadar folded his arms and sneered. "I neither see nor hear the likes o' an exile."

The stout ranger wanted to shake the answers out of him. "We're all exiles now," he stated bluntly. "So jus' tell me why me brother would recall every dwarf in Illian?"

Thaggadar remained stubbornly quiet, his dry lips tight together. The son of Dorain growled and started forward, only to find Russell's hands holding him back. Shrugging his friend away, Doran rooted around inside his shirt and brought out the note his brother had sent.

"Has it got anythin' to do with this?" he blurted, shoving the bloody parchment into Thaggadar's face. "King Dakmund sent this to me. This is his blood! I've come a long way to discover the truth, ye old goat, so ye'd better believe I'm goin' to get it!"

Thaggadar cleared his throat and drew his head back to better see the note. There were only two words to read so it didn't take him very long to understand the message.

"Aye," he finally said after much deliberation, "King Dorain passed away a couple o' months ago."

Doran had come to terms with that fact, but it still hurt to hear it from someone who knew for certain. "Did they 'ave a funeral?"

"Aye, ye missed it. They buried 'im in the stone, where we all belong..."

Doran nodded along as his gaze shifted to the side and pierced time and space.

"Why is King Dakmund's blood on the note then?" Russell asked for him, bringing him back to the present.

"That's the king's business," Thaggadar protested. "How am I to know?"

Doran scowled at the old dwarf as he picked apart every twitch of his face. "Ye're lyin'!" he glowered. "Ye know exactly why me brother's blood might be on his note *an'* ye know why he's recalled everyone!"

Thaggadar rose to the ire. "Why do ye care, exile? Business o' the clan is no longer yers to be concerned with!"

Doran was faster this time and managed to snatch Thaggadar's collar with both hands before Russell could grab his shoulders. "He's me blood, ye dolt! I need to know that he's a'right. I need to know that the clan is..." The ranger stopped himself before he sounded any more like a hypocrite.

Thaggadar's eyes roamed over Doran's desperate features as he considered his next words. "Grimwhal is at war," he hissed.

Doran released him and stepped back. "War? With who?" Geographically, he knew that Grimwhal was situated between Bhan Doral and Khaldarim, meaning it could easily be attacked by either the Brightbeards or the Goldhorns.

"I don' know," Thaggadar answered far too quickly. Doran advanced again, forcing the old dwarf to raise his hands. "I told ye, I don' know! I wasn' recalled," he added bitterly. "I gave me legs fightin' the orcs. Now they jus' leave me 'ere..."

Doran allowed some of his anger to fade away. He didn't know Thaggadar, but he had potentially fought shoulder to shoulder with him at the end of The Ash War. In a way, Doran was partly responsible, since he had set events in motion that saw Grimwhal's army march south to face the orcs in the first place.

"What happened?" he asked with a softer tone.

Thaggadar brushed away some dust from his sleeve. "Official messengers were sent from home. The orders were quite clear: return home to fight. The missives they carried said little more than that, but..."

Doran tilted his head to meet Thaggadar's eyes. "But what?"

"The messengers said..." Thaggadar swallowed. "They said death had come."

Doran glanced at Russell, his concern growing. "Death has come? What does that mean?"

Thaggadar looked nervously from one shadowed corner to the next. "A black army, birthed by The Dread Wood itself. They told us the Stormshields were all but gone, the Hammerkegs too."

"Bah!" Doran refused to believe it. "There's no army in all o' Verda capable o' bringin' down the Stormshields! Hyndaern has stood for thousands o' years against more sieges than ye've had hot meals. An' the Hammerkegs? In all me time as War Mason, we never even touched the stone o' Nimdhun - that city is encased by the mountains!"

Thaggadar shrugged and wrinkled his face in offence. "I ain' no liar! An' I won' be called one by no exile either! That's what they told us an' that's all I know!"

Doran huffed and walked away until he was facing the grimy windows. Thaggadar was either wrong or the tale he had been fed was long indeed. This still left the son of Dorain with only one option if he was to discover the truth.

"What's the fastest way to Grimwhal?" he asked, partly to himself.

"That depends on yer definition o' fast," Thaggadar replied. "Go east an' take The Iron Valley. It's a long way round, but it's a clear route so long as ye don' trespass on barbarian territory."

"An' the other route?"

"There's a big hole out there." The old dwarf threw his head back, towards The White Vale. "Same one we travelled through fifteen years ago. If ye can find a way down, the tunnels will take ye straight to Dhenaheim. From there, it's a straight shot to Grimwhal... an' death." Thaggadar rolled his wheelchair forward. "Whatever's goin' on back home, ye won' find a parade waitin' for ye, son o' Dorain."

This wasn't news to Doran and, by the look on Russell's face, it wasn't a surprise to him either. But there was no other way.

"We're going to Dhenaheim, aren't we?" The old wolf puffed out his chest, resigned to accompanying his friend wherever he might go.

"There's no need for ye to get yerself caught up any more in this. Ye've got a life an' a business waitin' for ye, Rus."

"I'd listen to 'im if I were ye," Thaggadar chipped in without invitation. "They'll kill ye jus' for bein' with 'im."

Russell simply looked from Doran to the door rather than reply. The son of Dorain agreed; he had heard about as much as he could stomach from Thaggadar.

"Ye 'ave me thanks for the information," he offered on his way to the door.

"I care nothin' for ye thanks, exile. As far as I'm concerned, I spoke to a man an' a ghost today..."

Doran paused as Russell pulled the shop door open. The stout ranger removed a few coins from his pouch and left them on the windowsill as payment for the broken lock. Outside, they were both able to breathe in the clear northern air, though it would take a lot more than that to rid themselves of the musty scent that now clung to them. Not to mention the memory of Thaggadar himself.

"Seriously, Rus," Doran continued, "we've been through a lot, but that bitter old fool was right. There's a good chance that goin' to Dhenaheim will be the end o' ye, maybe both o' us. I don' want what's left o' yer life to be cut short because o' me."

Russell collected his horse's reins with a quizzical expression for the dwarf. "If you get any softer, Heavybelly, you're going to be good for nothing but dough."

Doran's smile was slow to reach his face but it eventually left its mark there. "So be it. But don' come cryin' to me when ye're too *cold*."

Russell laughed to himself as he climbed into the saddle. "So, what's this Dread Wood he mentioned? I've never heard of such a place."

The son of Dorain found his comfy spot on Pig's saddle. "Aye, ye won' be findin' it on any map o' Illian. It's a forest, an' a damned big one too, much bigger than any forest in this country, maybe Ayda too. It lies on the other side o' The Whisperin' Mountains. No dwarf has ever passed through it to see what's beyond, nor 'ave they gone around it. There's not a tale abou' the place that ends well."

Russell absorbed the dwarf's description. "What's he talking about then? A black army?"

Doran shrugged. "I'd say old Thaggadar lost more than his legs in the war. The Dread Wood is jus' that, a *wood*. There ain' no army inside o' it." A troubled look crossed the son of Dorain's face. "It's likely jus' another war between the clans that's got out o' control. Not that such a thing would see Dhenaheim fare any better. It's been millennia since all-out war between the clans."

The old wolf guided his horse up the rise. "We can set off at dawn and take the tunnels under Vengora."

"No," Doran disagreed. "The tunnels under Vengora might be quicker, but the journey would be too risky - I 'ave to reach Grimwhal, Rus. We take The Iron Valley."

"Are you certain? It *will* take longer."

Doran shrugged hopelessly. "It's more than likely that we'll run into trouble under Vengora; if it's not monsters o' the deep it could be orcs - both will slow us down more than any terrain. We take the pass."

"Well," Russell concluded, "if we're to be journeying even farther north, we'd better purchase fresh supplies and find somewhere to put our heads down for the night."

Doran looked up the rise and back to Russell with a mischievous grin. "The Raucously Ruckus," they both said.

"I'm pretty sure that pig of yours is still barred," Russell quipped.

"That's likely so," Doran replied, patting the Warhog's hide. "Not everyone can love him like you do, Rus..."

Doran's hearty laughter filled the streets of Namdhor, defying the concern that continued to grow in his heart. It was this concern that warned the stout ranger of one thing.

A storm was coming...

CHAPTER 16
DUTY-BOUND

The rousing light of dawn shone through the curtains, only this morning Clara Kantaris was cast in the shadow of her husband. Kassian was seated on the edge of the bed with his back to his wife. He had been positioned like this for many hours, soaked in sweat from the terrors that had haunted his sleep.

His heart pounded in his chest, a rapid drumbeat that filled his ears. The Archon's secret conversation played over and over in his mind. He had been hand-picked by the masters to escort the Galfreys - an honour given the couple's status and celebrated achievements.

Murder...

That's what he had been hand-picked for. He was the wand in the Archon's collective hand. They believed he had but to be aimed and fired to see their will done. There was certainly a compliment in there somewhere, given the pair they wished for him to assassinate. It was impossible to focus on, however, since he had been reduced to naught but an expendable weapon.

Then there was the question that continued to present itself. Shouldn't he serve the Archon as they wished? He was a Keeper after all, a sworn protector of Valatos and its mages. The masters were

185

equally sworn to them all and their choices only served the interest of Valatos. If they told him to kill the Galfreys in cold blood, shouldn't he do it?

Kassian's fingers dug into the mattress, creasing the sheet with white knuckles. He could already picture the blood on his hands, their bodies at his feet. Reyna Galfrey was looking up at him with her impossibly green eyes, now lifeless.

"Kassian?" Clara's tone dragged him back to the present. "Is everything alright?" she asked, stroking a single finger through the sweat on his bare back.

The Keeper swallowed hard as he blinked before turning to flash his wife a beaming smile. "I'm fine," he lied, desperate not to burden her with his troubles. "Bad dream is all. I would make you some tea, my love, but I have to go..."

Clara gripped his wrist as he rose from the bed. "Are you sure?" she pressed, referring to his dream.

The Keeper offered her another smile before kissing the back of her hand. "Of course. Have a good day. I'll see you later..."

Returning to the hall outside the Galfreys' suite, Kassian dismissed the Keeper who had replaced Jovus, and knocked on their door. They were scheduled to meet with three of the Archon today, a response to their complaint that meeting with only one master was an insult.

Had he not heard of the Archon's schemes, he would have rolled his eyes at another day of tedious talks but, since the memory haunted him, he was more than nervous to face the Galfreys. He had no doubt that Reyna had been in that attic space, hearing exactly the same thing he had.

How would they react? Would they confront the Archon? Perhaps they would leave Valatos this very day to avoid the confrontation. To express their knowledge, however, would tip their hand and reveal their true intentions had been to spy on the masters all along.

Kassian took a long breath, hating the politics of it all.

Hearing no response to his knocking, the Keeper began to wonder if the couple had already fled in the night. Relief was beginning to flood Kassian's spirit when the door opened to reveal Nathaniel Galfrey.

"Knocking today, are we?" he remarked with a tight smile.

Kassian couldn't think of any suitable reply but to bow his head and avert his eyes. The old Graycoat moved past him into the hall, closely followed by Reyna. The elven ambassador locked eyes with the Keeper as she glided into the hall. It was all there in her face. She knew there was a plan to murder both herself and Nathaniel, and she also knew that Kassian was in possession of that same information.

"Good morning, Keeper," Reyna greeted pleasantly.

"Ambassador," he replied with a bow. Looking her in the eyes made him feel guilty for an act he hadn't even committed yet.

The word *yet* hung in his mind for the remainder of their journey through the central hall. He could feel them both staring at his back the entire way, drawing more sweat to the surface of his skin.

Sitting with three of the seven masters - still an insulting number if Nathaniel's remarks were anything to go by - the Galfreys started their talks like any other. Kassian had been moments away from allowing his concerns to distract him when the tone changed and a palpable tension overtook the room. Tuning back in with greater focus, he quickly came to realise that the ambassadors were changing their approach.

They were becoming aggressive...

"There are factors you simply aren't taking into account," Reyna said simply. "Valatos exists inside a *kingdom*. It's ruled by one man, not a *council*. There will be no campaign, no vote, and no debates. King Vighon will not tolerate separatism, especially if it poses a threat to the realm as a whole. The people have been through too much to see the landscape of Illian changed again."

Nathaniel leaned forward in his chair and jabbed his finger into the table. "We have presented you with plenty of options in the hope of appeasing your need for independence, *and* you've had enough time to reconsider your position. It's time to lay all of our cards out. You don't have the power to resist an order from Namdhor. If Valatos continues to press for independence or shares such views with other provinces, it will be pulled down brick by brick."

Kassian looked from the ambassadors to the three masters. He had no way of gauging their reactions through the reflective fabric that masked their faces, but their body language suggested they weren't deterred by the proclamation.

The squat female of the three masters gestured to the table between them, as if their plan was laid out. "Is this to be your new line of dialogue? Threats?"

"Call it what you like," Reyna replied. "We're bringing an end to this now, before it gets out of control."

"I would argue that it has already gone beyond your control," the master countered. "As we speak, Grey Stone is enforcing the ancient laws of its land once again. The banner of the bear flies in the west. And Velia, this very city, has whispers of unrest. Lord Carrington would have Alborn returned to a kingdom in itself, as it was for a thousand years. How long before Lirian and Tregaran desire independence from a northern king?"

"The provinces and their lords will be addressed in due time," Reyna responded evenly. "The fact is: the loudest voices are coming from Valatos. The king demands that you submit to his reign and cease and desist your campaign for independence."

The female master interlocked her fingers, pausing before speaking again. "Just so we're clear, Ambassadors, how will King Vighon be enforcing his command?"

"The banner of the flaming sword still holds sway over Velia," Nathaniel replied with a menacing tone. "Even if Lord Carrington has ideas beyond his station, the soldiers of Alborn will be called upon to forcibly disband Valatos. If they aren't enough, soldiers will be called upon from Lirian, Tregaran, and Namdhor itself."

"And what of your daughter?" the master questioned. "Will the Guardian of the Realm bring her dragon to bear?"

"Inara serves the people," Reyna reminded the master. "If she deems your efforts a threat to the realm... Athis will melt the stone."

Kassian couldn't believe what he was hearing. Why were they being so aggressive now? If they knew a plot was being hatched to eliminate them, why weren't they smoothing everything over in Valatos's favour?

The three masters stood up, led by the smaller female. "Tell me, Ambassadors, do you know what happens when an unstoppable object collides with an immovable one?"

Reyna glanced at her husband before answering, "I can't say that I do."

The master shrugged her rounded shoulders. "Nor do I. I suspect, however, we are soon to learn..." With that, the three members of the Archon left the office.

Reyna was the first to rise from her chair and face Kassian. "I don't expect us to be receiving any further invitations from the Archon. Perhaps, Keeper, you would be best escorting us back to our room."

Without a word, the Keeper led the ambassadors back to their suite. He wanted to turn around in the passage and fire one question after another at them. After today, the Archon would be calling for their heads on spikes instead of making them disappear.

Arriving back at their room, Reyna paused in the doorway after Nathaniel had entered. "Kassian." Her voice was soft and melodic, drawing the Keeper in. "For all of the oaths and promises one makes, however just that cause may be, there should be nothing that clouds your judgment. We always have the power of choice. You just have to know what is *right*... and what is *wrong*."

Kassian made to speak but he closed his mouth again. He couldn't decide whether to play ignorant or to accept her advice and acknowledge his awareness of the awkward yet serious situation they found themselves in.

"I would very much enjoy another trip to the gardens this evening," the ambassador spoke for him. "The scent of flowers after sunset is most pleasant. If you could return, I would appreciate the escort."

Kassian straightened up. "Of course, Ambassador Galfrey. I shall return after dinner has been served."

After walking away, Kassian arranged for another Keeper to wait by their door. Every second he spent around them was making his head spin all the more. He could still smell Reyna's sweet scent. Just keep walking, he told himself. He needed every moment he could get to pin down his thoughts and emotions on the matter.

"Keeper?" The voice guided Kassian to a familiar master. "You look distressed. Is everything alright?"

Kassian tugged on his long coat and lifted his chin in the master's presence. "Of course, Master," he lied for the second time that day.

"Glad to hear it," the master purred, stepping closer so that Kassian could see his distorted reflection in the mask. "Would you care to walk with me?"

"It would be an honour," the Keeper replied naturally and without consideration.

The master had set the leisurely pace of a stroll, but he was most definitely steering the pair through the central hall. Kassian soon found himself standing on a balcony, looking out over Valatos, and Velia beyond its high walls.

"Unlike our youngest," the master began, his voice slightly muffled by his mask, "you can recall this sight from the end of The Ash War."

Kassian didn't have to think too hard in order to recall the black smoke that rose up from Velia in thick columns, pluming into the ash clouds above. So many of the buildings were ablaze and torn to pieces. Screams carried across the city from east to west, mixed with the roar of the orcs. It was the darkest of times, fraught with death and despair.

"Live long enough," the master continued, "and you come to see that war is inevitable. Like the seasons, it sweeps across the land again and again, changing everything. Whether the next war is in our lifetime or not, it will return to claim as many lives as possible, especially the innocent ones such as those you see before us. It is our job, yours and mine, to ensure that Valatos remains protected. Our predecessors in Korkanath underestimated the threats posed, both foreign and domestic. They thought a dragon could watch over them. Then, they thought the kingdoms could shelter them. Trusting the Dragorn to keep them safe was their final mistake; one that cost many lives..."

Kassian looked down at the master's hand, embracing the stone railing. The knuckles were flat and the skin from nail bed to wrist was white with old scarring. It had been the worst of burns, leading the Keeper to the likely conclusion that this particular master had been a student at Korkanath when Malliath razed it to the bedrock.

"The only way Valatos will ever be safe is if we are unburdened from the chains of our northern king. We will reside outside of any petty rivalries that arise between provinces. Mark my words, Kassian, at the first sign of a skirmish, our magic will be called upon by Namdhor to enforce the peace. The Archon will not have it!" He beat his fist into the railing. "Without the king's restrictions on our studies of magic, we will learn of new ways to keep ourselves safe, maybe even the entire realm. But we need our freedom first, and before civil war forces us *all* to fight."

Kassian clenched his jaw and felt all of his muscles tense. The master was clearly building up to that fateful order and the Keeper had to appear swept away with his speech.

"You were in the room earlier so I don't have to repeat the ambassadors'... *remarks*. The king sent them here to make such bold statements, as if their threats would be enough to see us heel like *dogs*. The Archon agrees that the ambassadors would make an equally powerful statement in our favour, if certain measures were taken."

Kassian's heart began to beat like thunder in his chest again. "Should I expel them from the grounds, Master?" he suggested innocently.

"Ah, but it would be the *manner* in which they were removed that would send the right message. I would task *you*, a Keeper of Valatos, with taking that last step on behalf of us all and ensuring our independence."

"I live to uphold the oaths of my order," Kassian said, his words hollow in his mouth.

"That is most reassuring to hear," the master replied, his smile evident in his tone, "because the ambassadors have threatened us. Your duty would have you respond accordingly. See to it that the Galfreys never threaten Valatos again and your name will be etched into the history of our people for all time."

There it was. The Archon had given him the command to kill two people in cold blood. He had hoped that when he heard the order, he would feel a sense of duty and know that he was serving for the betterment of Valatos, for his wife and future family. Instead, he heard an order that made him feel like a murderer.

It was just wrong...

The master tilted his head to make contact with Kassian's eyes. "What say you, Keeper? Will you do this and see our defences made stronger? Will you spill blood for our people?"

Kassian took a deep breath to steady his voice. "I serve as the Archon commands. I will see it done."

The master placed a warm hand on the Keeper's shoulder and squeezed affectionately. "Very good, Kassian. Very good. I leave the details to you, but make certain the deed is complete before the arrival of our next guests."

"The king?" Kassian had almost forgotten that the king was apparently coming to Valatos in person.

The master paused, his concealed face directed towards the Keeper. "Have you told anyone of the arrival?"

"No, Master."

"Very good. Your task is singular - stay *focused* and you will not waver." The master held up a finger as if he had just remembered something. "Here, something to keep your mind steadfast." From within his robe, the master produced a fine golden chain with the clasp of a snake's head. "Allow me," he said, wrapping the necklace around Kassian's collar. "Keep that tucked away now. Feel it against your heart, where you hold Valatos so dear."

Kassian pressed the golden chain into his neck as it slipped down his shirt. "An honour, Master."

"A mere token really," the master remarked casually. "Your deeds will see us all rewarded, Kassian."

Only moments later, the Keeper was left alone on the balcony, prey to his own conscience. That fine necklace felt very heavy around his neck. He made to leave until his well-trained eyes spotted the auburn hair of his wife in the grounds below. She was escorting one of the younger classes back to their teaching room - she didn't notice her husband. He thought that was just as well, since his face was likely ashen.

He would avoid Clara for the rest of the day, he decided. She would know something was wrong and press for the answer. Instead, the Keeper spent the afternoon in the Sanctorum, busying himself with wand and sword routines.

As the evening set in and an ocean of stars began to emerge, Kassian remembered his promise to Reyna and put his legs in motion, hoping they would see him returned to the ambassadors' room without thought. His mind was crowded like a battlefield, two sides warring for victory. The fact that he imagined an army of orcs fighting for the Archon was very telling.

The Keeper felt the necklace bouncing against the top of his chest and it brought one word to mind: duty. For all that sounded wrong, the master was right about war. How long would it be before the next one? As the finest magic wielders in the realm, wouldn't Valatos be called upon to fight for one side or the other?

Reyna Galfrey opened the door and Kassian blinked, unable to recall his journey or even knocking. The elf smiled warmly, her cloak already fastened around her shoulders.

"Shall we go?"

Kassian collected himself and looked past her. "Is the ambassador to accompany us?"

"Oh no. Nathaniel would rather read a book than simply wander around some gardens." Closing the door behind her, Reyna hooked her arm inside Kassian's, the action appearing natural but allowing her to guide him away from their suite. He had but a moment to flash the guarding Keeper a look, one which told him to stay at his post and watch the door.

In the south-west corner of Valatos, a series of lush gardens had been maintained by magic for many years. The trees were thick and tall, their branches full of green leaves that currently stretched for the moonlight. Hedges lined the paths, directing visitors from one grove to the next so that they might admire the flowers, many of which changed colour from one moment to the next. It was truly enchanting...

Reyna, graceful in her every movement, retrieved her arm and slipped between the hedges to walk on the grass, between the trees. Kassian subconsciously checked their surroundings, making certain they were alone. It was sheltered here, under the canopy and between the maze of hedges and trunks.

The ambassador strolled and skipped here and there, the elf in her coming alive within the embrace of nature. She cupped flower heads, ran her fingers across the bark, and inhaled the scent of it all carried on the breeze. This was not the same ambassador who had recently threatened the Archon, nor could Kassian envision the warrior history spoken of.

"Do you ever visit here?" she asked.

The Keeper gave the question a second's thought. "It has been some time, I'll admit. My duties keep me busy."

"Isn't that always the way," Reyna mused. "We have a beautiful home on The Shining Coast, just south of here. It has been too long since I tended my gardens there. Duty has a way of tying us down, doesn't it? Or at least it creates the illusion. To have a duty is to simply bind yourself to an ideal or, in most cases, someone else's ideals. *I* am duty-bound to the realm and its people. As a result, I have a duty to the king, so long as he serves the realm. *You* are duty-bound to Valatos and the mages therein. Consequently, you have a duty to the Archon... so long as they serve Valatos."

The elven ambassador looked up from the flowers she had been inspecting to discover Kassian pointing his wand at her. He couldn't recall drawing it from the holster on his thigh, but here he was, aiming it at Reyna. It occurred to him, right then, that he should have come up with a plan before drawing his wand, but if he thought about it any longer he wasn't sure he could go through with it.

Reyna, however, was entirely unfazed by the wand pointed at her face. "*Do* the Archon serve Valatos, Kassian? If you follow their actions through to the end, do you see it averting war or causing it?"

"The Archon only wants what's best for Valatos," he blurted, struggling to unclench his jaw.

"You heard everything I did," she countered smoothly. "We both know the masters are acting on the instructions of another. That sounds like they are serving themselves, though their price remains to be seen."

Kassian's knuckles were white around his wand. "Stop talking." He couldn't think straight. Even his intended spell flittered from one to the next.

Reyna slowly shook her head. "Don't let them make you into a killer, Kassian. I see something far more noble in you. You believe in Valatos, in what it can do for the mages here. You must know there is no future in anything if it is forged with blood."

The Keeper blinked hard, squeezing tears down his cheeks. "This is who I am," he managed. "They took me in. Trained me. Gave me a purpose. Valatos is the *only* future I have."

"I once thought like that," Reyna replied softly. "I first came to Illian under the instruction of my father. I was to take the first step toward conquering the realm and bringing it back under elven control... at the expense of humanity. I was brought up to believe that the elven way was the only future I had." The ambassador stepped closer to that wand tip. "But I saw what was right and what was wrong with my own eyes. And so I made a choice. Because of that choice, your parents survived a war that was never allowed to happen and you were born, along with thousands of others."

Kassian absorbed her words though, through it all, he wondered why he hadn't unleashed his spell and seen his duty through. It would be easy, bloodless even. But Reyna's voice was like honey and her words carried weight, much like the master's.

"Now is your time, Kassian Kantaris," the elf continued. "You'll never get a better chance. Make your choice, but know that you will have to live with it for all of your days."

The Keeper gritted his teeth and twisted his wrist, searching furiously for the will to fire his spell. But he couldn't banish that burning question, the one that burrowed deep into his mind, warning him that without the answer he was making a terrible mistake: Who did the Archon serve?

He lowered his wand.

Reyna nodded her understanding before looking past the Keeper and subtly shaking her head. Alarmed, Kassian whipped his head around to see Nathaniel's sword had been aimed at the back of his neck. How long had the old Graycoat been behind him? That question was obviously plastered across his face.

Nathaniel lowered his sword. "Seventy years of practice, kid."

Kassian believed him, but he turned his attention back to Reyna. "I have to know who the Archon are working for. But I warn you, should I learn that they and Valatos lie on the side of virtue after all, I will see my duty through..."

"Fair enough," Reyna replied.

The keeper took a much-needed breath before holstering his wand. "What now? I've been instructed to kill you both before the king arrives."

"The king?" Nathaniel echoed. "Vighon's coming here?"

Kassian nodded. "That's what the Archon told me. They have hired musicians and stocked up on food for a great feast."

It was obvious that the Galfreys had no idea about the king's imminent arrival. "I fear the Archon mean to take more than just our lives," Reyna voiced.

"Murdering the king wouldn't just grant Valatos independence," Nathaniel reasoned, "it would create a void around the throne. The entire realm could be thrown into civil war over it."

"We need to warn the king." Kassian couldn't quite believe the words had left his mouth. "Until the truth can be uncovered," he added. "I can't get you out of Valatos. The intricacies of opening portals is beyond my skill. And there are too many Keepers guarding the main gates."

Nathaniel put his hand up. "I've been searching for a way out since they closed behind us. I don't think we'll be meeting the king until he arrives."

"Valatos boasts quite the expanse," Reyna pointed out. "We will have to hide until the right moment reveals itself."

"You're going to hide inside Valatos?" Kassian questioned in disbelief.

"We will have to keep moving," Reyna accepted. "But we have no other choice."

"What will *you* do?" Nathaniel asked pointedly.

The question raised a very important factor that had only just occurred to the Keeper. "I will see to it that you cannot be tracked inside the grounds."

"You can do that?" Nathaniel questioned with doubt.

"There is a device," Kassian replied, referring to the Lexichronan, "in the Central Hall, that can reveal everyone's location. I can... disable it."

"What will you do then?" Reyna asked. "You are well known in Valatos."

"I will report your apparent escape and my failure. I will face the punishment that awaits and, hopefully, in the aftermath I might be able to discover the truth behind all of this. I serve Valatos," he announced with conviction. "If it is being led astray then I see it as my duty to correct that, whether I still hold the rank of Keeper or not..."

Reyna walked up to him and placed a hand on his shoulder. "You don't know if this is truly the right path yet. Don't let doubt cloud your judgement, as it tried with me. In time, you will see the path left behind you and know you made the right choice."

Kassian's mouth contorted as he struggled for the right response. "I hope you're right, Ambassador." It was all he could say right now, as his doubts tried to convince him he had jumped from one coup to another. "It needs to look like you caught me by surprise," he asserted. "The Archon are aware you possess no magic. They won't believe me if I don't look—"

Having already come to Kassian's conclusion, Nathaniel drove the pommel of his sword into the side of the Keeper's head ...

CHAPTER 17
WANTED: DEAD

Where before the world had come back to Asher in a clearing haze, the ranger now woke up with a start. In his dreams, his mind had taken him back to the ambush. The Arakesh had been looming over his wounded body with wicked smiles pulling at their cheeks. As was typical, he woke up a second before that final blow could take his life.

Again, Asher ran his hand over the patches of skin where he had been seriously injured. His mind could still recall the bite of their steel and the icy grip of death as it surely claimed its prize. The vivid memory was hard to marry up with his body, which only bore the scars of a violent life.

Looking down at his body, Abun'Sun's explanation came back to him. There was magic in his bones...

Asher wasn't entirely sure what to do with that information. He was glad, however, to finally have an answer to his appearance and lack of ageing. Of course, there was nothing he could do with the knowledge except to keep on going. As the Drake had pointed out, the magic in his bones could fade away in a handful of years or a handful of centuries. In truth, he wasn't sure which one was crueller.

As the ranger perched on the edge of his cot, he took stock of his senses. There was no dizziness, his heart wasn't pounding in his chest, and there wasn't a drop of sweat forming over his skin. The only evidence that he had suffered at all came in the form of a headache.

The leather flaps in the hut's doorway rustled when Adan'Karth entered carrying a wooden tray. Asher was instantly curious about the tray's contents, a result of his growling stomach and dry mouth.

"*I am glad to see you are feeling better,*" the Drake said, placing the tray of fruit and vegetables on the cot. "*I brought you some food and water - you will need both to keep your strength up.*"

Asher took in the tray of food with ravenous eyes and tried not to think about the things he would do for a large steak. "*Thank you.*" The elvish words barely had a chance to leave his mouth before the first apple was between his teeth.

"*You have been the source of many discussions since your arrival,*" Adan'Karth continued, his lightly scaled skin glittering in a ray of light. "*Many of my people would like to meet you, the one who made us.*"

The ranger mixed a mouthful of water with the apple, his eyes never drifting from the Drake. "*I didn't make you,*" he stated, wondering how many times he would have to tell them that before they accepted it. "*And they have nothing to gain by meeting me. I'm just a man,*" he added with a shrug.

"*The only experience we have with your kind is one of predator and prey,*" Adan'Karth explained. "*We have met many elves, but your people have hunted us since we fled The White Vale. Abun'Sun believes it is important for us to meet a human who wants to help us.*"

Asher couldn't help but absorb the Drake's words having heard it said so plainly. He didn't often stop and think of himself as someone who wanted to help. It felt good.

"*Where is Abun'Sun?*" he asked, snapping a carrot in half with his teeth.

Adan'Karth tossed his horns to the window. "*He is tending to the gardens in the north. Would you like to see him?*"

Asher stood up from his cot and walked to the window, where he was given a view of Ikirith in all its glory. He didn't belong here. It was beautiful and serene - a world he had never known.

"*Can you take me back to where you found me?*" he asked, ignoring Adan'Karth's question.

The Drake looked away before replying, "*I can take you there, but you will find nothing but death. Their bodies have entered nature's cycle now.*"

"*They might possess clues as to who sent them,*" Asher responded. "*I need to know who's paying for my head.*"

Adan'Karth looked to the north. "*It has already been decided. Abun'Sun has granted you a place among us. You would be safe in Ikirith.*"

"Not for long," Asher countered. "*And neither would you. The people who are hunting me; they won't stop until the contract is fulfilled. They're trained to infiltrate anything, magic or otherwise.*"

The ranger had a plethora of memories to look back on to affirm his assessment. He had infiltrated everything from fortresses to palaces without ever being caught and he always left with blood on his hands.

"*If you wish to leave, I will show you the way.*"

"*Thank you.*" Asher looked around the hut. "*Now where's all my gear?*"

Adan'Karth gestured to an exquisitely carved wardrobe behind him, the wood decorated with intricate patterns and swirling lines. Opening the doors, Asher looked upon his leathers, cloak, and weapons - all hanging neatly, the weapons stood on end.

"*Where's my bow?*"

Adan'Karth hesitated. "*Ah, the hunter's weapon... The one you possessed was snapped in half. I left it in the woods.*"

The ranger stopped himself from groaning and, instead, went about dressing himself. He was surprised to discover that his green cloak was clean and absent any tears. Similarly, his leathers and armour were free of blood. He strapped the quiver of arrows to his back and slid the silvyr short-sword down beside it. His two-handed broadsword was the only weapon remaining since all of his daggers were still buried in the Arakesh.

Then he saw it, the only thing hanging on the beam.

The ranger reached up to grab the strip of red cloth but his hand paused in the air. Like everything else, it appeared to have been cleaned, the sweat and blood removed likely by the Drakes' magic.

Asher finally took the red cloth in his hand and turned to Adan'Karth. *"Why did you bring this back?"*

The Drake looked from the cloth to the ranger. *"Because you were clenching it in your hand when I found you. I thought it was yours."*

Asher rubbed the material between his finger and thumb. *"No,"* he replied absently, *"I lost mine a long time ago..."*

He should have left it in the hut or given it to Adan'Karth to destroy, but he didn't. The ranger tucked half of it into his belt and let it hang there, as he had done for years before his death in the pools of Naius.

The ranger pocketed the rest of the food and swigged the last of the water. *"Let's go."*

Asher garnered the attention of every Drake between his hut and the fringes of Ikirith. Those he made eye contact with would always look from him to the weapons on his person. They showed no sign of real disgust, but their contempt for the weapons was palpable. During his brief time in their world, he had seen no steel at all, but he was sure that if they were to incorporate it into Ikirith it wouldn't be forged into swords...

The farther away from the plains they journeyed the more familiar the surroundings became. The trees gradually reduced to The Evermoore's natural size and began to close in, hiding any magnificent views. Even the colours seemed to fade, as if there was less life in the world outside of Ikirith.

Seeing the way the Drake moved, as he led through the trees, made it all the easier to see that there was an animal side to his species. He glided through the forest with a level of ease that Asher could never attain - and he had been trained to move unheard in every environment.

It wasn't too long before they came across the first body; the hunter that Asher had discovered pinned to a tree. The ranger waved the flies from his face before pulling the dagger free from the hunter's throat and the tree beyond. It had all the telltale signs of being forged in Nightfall, from the serrated edge to the symbol of Ibilis, the god of shadows, stamped into the flat surface of the hilt.

Leaving the hunter's corpse to slump down the tree, Asher moved on to inspect the camp. Just as he had left it, the cold fire pit was surrounded by more dead hunters, all with their throats slit open. Among them were two dead Arakesh and a third lay a few yards away from the makeshift camp, a red gash connecting his shoulder to his groin.

Adan'Karth remained by the tree line, almost wary of even entering an area where there had been violence. Asher quickly went about searching through the corpses of the three assassins, his hands patting them down for anything concealed. It wasn't often an Arakesh would keep anything that tied them back to Nightfall, their contact or their intended target. But these three had been the least experienced among them, making it at least a possibility.

"*You killed these men?*" Adan'Karth asked quietly.

Asher spared a glance at the massacre. "*Not all of them.*"

The first two assassins possessed nothing but weapons. Stepping over their bodies, and those of the hunters, the ranger moved on to check the third Arakesh, whom he had used as a shield during the fight.

"*These men,*" Adan'Karth continued, "*they are paid to kill others?*"

Asher imagined how that concept must sound to a being as passive as a Drake - it only added to his deep shame. "*They are. In this case, they have been paid to kill me.*"

Adan'Karth dared to tread a step into the clearing so that he might better see the ranger. "*Where do they come from?*"

Asher looked up from the corpse, happy to see that curiosity wasn't a solely human trait. *"They come from all over, but they're trained in a place called Nightfall, in The Arid Lands. At least that's where it used to be,"* he added, his focus shifting to the assassin's pockets. Nothing.

Rising back to his feet, Asher made his way through the trees to another clearing not far away. It was here that he had faced the remaining four Arakesh and almost died himself. He immediately began searching the body of the nearest assassin, pausing to reclaim the dagger in the man's foot. Next, he removed the arrow from his face and replaced it in the quiver on his back.

"This Nightfall can move locations?" Adan'Karth continued to question, trailing Asher to the side.

"They've likely relocated now," Asher replied, his hands rummaging through more pockets. *"Nightfall was in the same place for a thousand years. But, fifteen years ago, it was invaded by The Black Hand - necromancers - and the order was decimated. We thought they were gone for good. I haven't heard a thing about them in all this time. Now they return... Though why they're hunting me again remains to be seen."*

"They have hunted you before?" the Drake asked, familiar with being the prey.

"A long time ago - punishment for abandoning my oaths. I survived the Court of Assassins though. After that, I was just to be eliminated if I ever crossed their path; which I went to great lengths to avoid."

Adan'Karth looked to be absorbing every bit of information, even if he didn't understand it all. *"What is a necromancer?"* he finally asked.

"I suppose it isn't the most common word," Asher conceded. *"They're dark mages; wizards who use forbidden magic to bring back the dead."*

The Drake subtly shook his horned head. *"The world beyond Ikirith is truly unknown to us. I understand all that you say... but I also do not understand any of it."*

Asher shrugged. *"That's not far off the way the world works actually."* He moved on to the next body, this one the blonde female.

She still had her own short-sword impaled in her chest and a displaced kneecap.

It wasn't long before he was checking the next body, dismayed by the lack of clues he was finding. The last two bodies to be checked were down an incline, a bloody ditch to be exact. Neither body had anything but his own daggers to find, all of which he sheathed across his body.

"*If they were decimated as you say,*" Adan'Karth called from the top of the hill, "*how can there be seven of them in The Evermoore?*"

Asher didn't have anything but educated guesses for that question. "*Nightfall was a maze of burrows. There had to be a few who made it out. They must have relocated and started from scratch.*"

Ploughing back up the hill, the ranger made his way to the camp of hunters, dissatisfied with his findings or lack thereof. Stepping over one of the Arakesh's bodies again, he noted the folded bow hooked on to the back of their dark armour. The scavenger in him - a product of his years living as a ranger - picked up the bow and snapped it to life, bringing the limbs out. Nightfall made the best bows in all of Verda, rivalling even those of the elves. He was keeping it. Using his thumb, he flicked the small latch and snapped it back into its folded position.

"*You are attracted to weapons,*" Adan'Karth observed.

Asher considered his whole life, from Outlander to assassin to ranger, and realised it was probably the closest thing he had to a religion. "*They're an unfortunate necessity. Another reason you should stay in Ikirith. Life is violent out here...*"

Adan'Karth shifted nervously and his reptilian eyes scanned the surrounding trees.

"*What is it?*" The ranger looked around, anxiously wondering what his inferior senses were missing.

The Drake held out a hand to quiet Asher. "*The trees are talking. Men are approaching...*"

The ranger didn't have time to contemplate Adan'Karth's unusual ability - the assassin in him had already begun looking for the best place to make himself disappear. As his eyes roamed over the camp, Asher noticed something that he had previously missed and it tugged at his attention, distracting him from the potential danger.

Adan'Karth was turning back towards Ikirith. *"We should leave, now."*

Asher knew there was sense in the Drake's suggestion, but he was already crouching down to examine the parchment half scrunched up in the lead hunter's bloody hand. Prising his cold fingers open, the parchment was now the ranger's to peruse. The script was elegant, written by a high born. The top left corner was stained with blood, the words now illegible.

The sound of boots trampling through the undergrowth reached Asher's ears, but he couldn't take his eyes off the parchment.

"Asher!" Adan'Karth hissed.

The ranger read what he could and quickly discovered that the hunters from Wood Vale had not been stalking Drakes of their own volition - they had been ordered to. At the very bottom was a long signature and a stamp bearing the sigil of a high born house, but it was not the house of Wood Vale's governor...

Asher screwed the parchment up in his hand, the pieces of the puzzle coming together only to form a larger mystery he didn't have time to work through. Voices could now be heard accompanying the many footfalls, both of which informed the ranger that the approaching men in question were not Arakesh.

"Captain Kade!" came an alarmed call from the other clearing. "I've got bodies!"

Asher dashed to the nearest tree before anyone emerged and saw him standing in the middle of the massacre. Stealing a glance, he watched a group of soldiers in Lirian uniforms step out of the forest and into the other clearing. They all drew swords seeing the dead Arakesh littering the ground. A strong Drake hand gripped Asher's shoulder and moved him aside, preventing him from being seen by even more soldiers who now entered the clearing containing the dead hunters.

Another quick glance informed the ranger that at least a dozen Lirian soldiers were now in the vicinity. The odds were mounting against him, but past experience gave him the confidence that he could still walk away if it came to combat.

"More bodies over here, Captain!" The soldier who yelled out was only a few feet away judging by the volume of his voice.

Looking over his shoulder, Adan'Karth was nowhere to be seen, another display of his enviable natural talents. The ranger spared a moment longer to search for the Drake, his own eyes that of a long-time hunter. Amazingly, he discovered Adan'Karth halfway up a tree, only ten feet away. The Drake had almost coiled himself around a branch, making himself blend in with its shape.

Asher judged the height and shape of the tree and decided that he couldn't make that climb without his gear and weaponry making a sound. A twig snapped twenty-feet away, stealing Asher's attention to the south, away from the soldiers and the bodies. A glimpse of yellow and green between the trees told the ranger that more Lirians were approaching...

"These are the hunters," the previous soldier observed, drawing their captain over.

Asher stayed very still with his back pressed against the trunk. Until a few minutes ago, there had been no cause to distrust any soldier from Lirian. Now, unfortunately, he could guess why so many were patrolling The Evermoore.

"Who are the ones in black?" another asked.

There was a creak of leather and a knocking of armour as the captain, presumably, crouched down. "Red blindfolds..." he mused aloud. "By the gods, I think they're *Arakesh*..."

"Assassins?" one of the soldiers said with audible trepidation. "They're just legends, aren't they? Stories from The War for the Realm."

Captain Kade stood up. "Do they look like *stories* to you?"

Their assessment was interrupted as a new group of Lirian soldiers stepped out from the trees. One of them took up a position by the edge of the clearing, putting Asher in his peripheral vision. There had to be closer to twenty men now, possibly more.

"Sir, this is not what we were told. The hunters were to bait him and the trap was to be sprung by mercenaries. These are *not* mercenaries."

"And the hunters are supposed to be alive," another added.

"Easy boys," the captain bade. "We were sent out here because we're the best at what we do. Any man that loses his nerve now is going to find himself in Captain Yarwyn's pitiful garrison. Understood?"

"Aye, Sir," came the soldiers' united reply.

"I'm not seeing the ranger among them, Captain."

"No, you're right," the captain agreed. "None of them match his description. To be honest, boys, I'm not sure what we've come across here. I'd say the hunters were slaughtered - not one of them has a weapon drawn. So the obvious question is: who killed all the assassins? Unfortunately," Kade continued, "the obvious answer is the ranger."

"Agreed, Sir," the trusted soldier replied. "Their wounds were inflicted by a sword."

"Now that *does* match the ranger's description," the captain concluded.

"The ranger's kind might be knowing their way around a sword, Sir, but how could one man kill all of them?"

Asher couldn't see the captain, but he heard the man walking around the camp. "Bale, Harding - you're both quick on your feet. Get back to Lirian and request more men. We're going to need at least another garrison to comb the forest. Oh, and say nothing of the Arakesh; better the stories of such monsters don't spread among the folk or the ranks."

"Aye, Captain!" Bale and Harding sheathed their blades and returned to the forest, heading south.

"Right," the captain announced. "We haven't discovered anything we didn't already know about our quarry. The ranger is a killer and a damned good one. I know our orders were as clear as mud, but what was clear still stands. We are to bring back the ranger's body as proof that he's dead. So if we find him breathing, and it's looking likely that we will, we're to bring him back just as requested: dead."

A sixth sense, developed over many decades, told Asher that he was being watched. Since there was only one obvious person who might have spotted him, the ranger slowly turned his head to the south, where a rather confused soldier was staring at him. Asher only had enough time to think one word, and saying it out loud would do him no good.

"He's there!" the soldier screamed, pointing his sword at the ranger.

Of course, no other among them could actually see Asher as they were directed to the other side of the tree he was pressed against. There was, however, barely any time to consider a plan that didn't involve running away.

He looked up at Adan'Karth and whispered, "Run!"

Before the Drake could react, a soldier advanced from the other side of Asher's tree, leaving the ranger little choice but to draw the curved blade from below his quiver and slam the hilt into the man's face. A quick look revealed the soldier's identity as Captain Kade. It also revealed a broken nose...

"Run!" Asher shouted this time, darting under the Drake's branch and heading west into the forest.

Adan'Karth dropped down with the grace of a panther and sprinted past the ranger. The soldiers of Lirian were on the hunt now, their swords surely being replaced with bows.

"Get him!" the captain barked, nursing his shattered nose.

Both ranger and Drake had covered nearly a hundred yards before the first salvo of arrows began whistling through the air around them. One missile cut through Asher's cloak and sank into the bark of an adjacent tree. Another came so close to killing Adan'Karth that it careered off one of his horns.

"You need to stop them!" Asher yelled ahead.

"I cannot," the Drake replied, his tone short and clipped.

More arrows found their way between the trees and landed around Asher. *"Use magic!"* he snapped.

Adan'Karth kept running and skipping over any obstacle with all the agility of an elf. Asher couldn't match the Drake's agility, but he was well versed in the art of evasion. Cutting left then darting right kept him from fleeing in a straight line and kept his enemies guessing. It also slowed his progress down, bringing the soldiers ever closer.

Then, rounding an outcropping of rocks, the young Drake was gone. Asher had no choice but to keep running and assume Adan'Karth had scaled another tree or slunk into a hiding place no human would think to search.

An arrow skimmed along the edge of the rough stone and curved towards the ranger, grazing his shoulder before meeting its end in the bark of a tree. Flinching from the arrow, Asher misstepped and slipped on the edge of a damp log - a costly mistake, though he told himself the soldiers would suffer the ultimate price for slowing him down.

Rising as fast as he could, one hand gripping his broadsword while the other reached to hold firm the scabbard, Asher prepared himself mentally to take life without conscience. There was a blur to his left and Adan'Karth's hand came down on his own, forcing the sword back into the scabbard. Just as quickly, the Drake's other hand wrapped around the ranger's neck and covered his mouth.

"Don't move," he whispered in his ear.

Seconds later, two soldiers in Lirian's garb came rushing around the rocks with nocked arrows. They stopped only a few yards in front of Asher and Adan'Karth, their eyes boring into the pair. Why weren't they raising their bows? Now that he thought about it, the soldiers weren't actually looking at him but, rather, looking through him.

"Where in all the hells did he go?" one of them fumed.

The other took a step forward and paused. "Don't know," he said absently." Maybe he went that way," he suggested, nodding to the north.

"Let's go," the other soldier agreed. "He went this way!" he cried over his shoulder, directing the rest of them.

Captain Kade was the last to pass by Asher and Adan'Karth, his nose streaming blood across a face raging with anger. "Find him and kill him!"

Adan'Karth waited for the sound of their departure to grow distant before stepping away from Asher. "*We must go,*" he insisted.

The ranger looked from the Drake to the spot where the soldiers had been standing like gormless fools. "*What was that?*"

Adan'Karth ran his finger over an invisible line on the ground. "*We have entered the farthest boundaries of Ikirith. We are back inside the pocket dimension.*"

Asher shook his head. "*They should still be able to see us.*"

"*We have lined the edges with...* suggestive *spells. To step on the boundary uninvited would only lead to disorientation.*"

Asher was impressed. "*That's very clever. And passive...*" he added.

"*There is no need for violence,*" the Drake stated.

If only that were true, Asher thought, dipping into his pocket to retrieve the hunter's parchment. He straightened it out and scrutinised the sigil in the bottom right corner one more time.

"*You found something of note?*" Adan'Karth enquired.

"*I found something of concern,*" Asher corrected, showing the Drake the sigil.

"*What is that?*"

What it was, to Asher's understanding, was a stinging betrayal as well as a failure in judgement on his behalf. "*It's a sigil, specifically the sigil of house Penrose. Lady Gracen ordered those hunters out here, not the governor of Wood Vale.*"

"*Lady Gracen is the stewardess of Lirian,*" Adan'Karth pointed out with some alarm. "*Why would she order those men to hunt my people down?*"

"*That wasn't why they were out here,*" the ranger clarified, recalling the soldiers' conversation. "*The hunters were just the bait, to lure me into the middle of the forest. The Arakesh were the trap.*"

The Drake was taken aback hearing such a devious plot. "*Why are the soldiers here?*"

"*I imagine they were sent because neither the Arakesh nor the hunters reported back to Lady Gracen. The captain mentioned bringing her proof of my death.*"

"*Why would the lady of Lirian want you, of all people, to come to harm. She has shown our people nothing but kindness and patience.*"

"*That's the same question I have,*" Asher replied. "*And, unfortunately, the answer won't likely come until there's been a little more violence...*"

CHAPTER 18
BROTHERHOOD

Having crossed the banks of The Unmar, Vighon Draqaro set his eyes to the east, where the last rays of light revealed Velia's distant spires. From his vantage, the four enormous kings that lined the city's walls were no bigger than his little fingernail. It wasn't far, but when he was marching a thousand soldiers across the land, every mile counted against their morale.

One more night, he told himself, and he would confront the mages of Valatos. Cut off the head - that was the saying. Then, with Alijah and Malliath, he would visit every city in the realm and ensure that peace still reigned.

Maybe then he could sleep...

The king had hoped that some merriment and copious amounts of ale would allow him to rest for an entire night, but even Lady Gracen's generosity had failed to give him the slumber he desired. At least the men had enjoyed their brief stop in Lirian, and the lady's soldiers had been more than happy to be reunited with their families.

"Your Grace?" came General Garrett's familiar voice.

Vighon only half turned to greet the man, his eyes wary of straying from Velia. "Our presence here won't go unnoticed," the king remarked with irritation. "If Lord Carrington has been subverted by the Archon's magic, he may well warn them of our imminent arrival. They could be scurrying away into the night as we speak."

"With respect, your Grace, I have no idea what to expect in Velia. What I do know, is that the city cannot be seized by a thousand men, especially given that Lord Carrington's bannermen count for four thousand."

Vighon could hear the criticism in his general's voice. "You don't approve of my decisions, Garrett."

The general paused. "With respect, your Grace, I wouldn't have left so many men in Grey Stone. Or left the thousands of Lirian soldiers behind."

Vighon couldn't help but smile. "Try saying something *without* respect."

The general glanced at the king before returning to the horizon. "This is foolish."

"I suppose that must make me the fool," Vighon concluded.

Garrett didn't miss a beat. "It would, aye. The evidence has become overwhelming: Valatos is behind the unrest. It might be a school, but there's plenty of mages behind those walls who haven't been students for a long time. I can't fight magic, your Grace. None of these boys can. At least a larger force would have given me more options."

"You're right," Vighon conceded. "But, you're forgetting about them." The king flicked his chin up, directing Garrett to the dragons in the sky. Malliath and Athis glided lazily in circles over the camp, both absent their companions.

Garrett tracked Malliath's flight path, scrutinising the dragon with his old eyes. "I don't like there being two kings in Illian, even a *visiting* one."

Vighon sighed, tired of hearing the caution thrown Alijah's way.

"He's not visiting. *King* Alijah is an ally, *Erador* is an ally. When this Valatos business is dealt with, I will make official announcements and inform the people of such. Though, explaining Erador's existence could prove complicated," he mused. "We may need to consult with the scholars in The All-Tower on the best approach."

"I'd keep it simple, your Grace. Forget the history. Erador is simply a new land with new people. Talk about the trading possibilities and keep Illian thinking about the prospects, not the religion."

Vighon nodded along. He always enjoyed the general's straight and simple way of thinking. He spoke his mind and always told the king the truth of any situation. What more could he ask for in a general?

Patting him on the shoulder with brotherly affection, he said, "Promise me you'll die on the job."

Garrett looked at his king and laughed deep in his gut. "Don't worry, your Grace; I'll still be giving this lot their marching orders from my deathbed."

Vighon let the man have his laugh before he continued, "Don't concern yourself with the magic of Valatos. There's no force in the world that can stand up to a pair of dragons. We'll walk through their gates, find the truth, and rid the kingdom of this *rot*. There won't be a soldier here who needs to draw their sword, I promise you."

"You have a lot of faith in him... *King* Alijah."

Vighon watched Malliath bank from east to west as he put his thoughts in order. "He's always been like a brother to me. For all the evil he faced, there's no doubting he's the same Alijah I once knew. Besides, he's already saved our lives. Perhaps *you* should have a little faith in him."

Garrett grimaced. "It's my job to doubt, your Grace. Keeps me young!" he jested.

General and king continued their conversation until the light had finally gone and the stars reigned supreme. After that, Garrett retired in search of a hot meal while Vighon remained rooted to the outcropping of stone. He just couldn't seem to tear himself away, as if by sight alone he could remove the rebellion that stirred in the east.

"I'm beginning to wonder if you sleep at all."

Vighon looked over his shoulder to see Alijah approaching from within the camp. His dark cloak rippled in the light breeze, revealing glimpses of a red interior. The two king's guards whipped their heads around, caught out by the half-elf's sudden appearance. Vighon gave them both a nod to relax, allowing the king of Erador to reach him on the outcropping.

"I could say the same of you," the northman replied.

Alijah offered his casual yet disarming smile. "I don't need as much sleep as I used to. Malliath lends me his strength and sees me through days at a time."

"I could do with some of that," Vighon remarked, turning back to the dark fields of Alborn. "I feel like the crown ages me years with each passing day."

Alijah cast his blue eyes over Vighon's head. "Is that why you don't wear it?"

The king almost laughed to himself. "If only its absence would undo its work. I only wear it when I have to; ceremonies and such. I wasn't born with one on my head and I don't intend to live with one on my head. The way I see it; a king is made by his deeds, not his appearance."

"I couldn't agree more," Alijah said, folding his arms.

"What about you?" Vighon returned. "Don't kings of Erador wear crowns?"

"They do," the half-elf replied. "But it kept flying off my head," he added with a look to the sky and an amused grin on his face.

Now Vighon laughed, picturing Alijah's crown being carried away into the clouds, never to be seen again.

A serious veil shadowed Alijah's face. "Don't expect this insurrection to be dealt with in a day. Our presence should be enough to dissuade any violence, but if we are to rely on words to bring about peace, we should expect it to take time."

That wasn't what Vighon wanted to hear. He gestured for them to take a walk along the edge of the camp, hoping some exercise would help him to think. "My fear is the extent of the Archon's schemes. I have to suspect Lord Carrington culpable. The mages must be using his resources to stretch their reach across the realm."

Alijah strolled effortlessly beside him. "If it comes to light that the lord of Velia has been aiding your enemies, you have but to speak and he will face justice. Though, given the executions in Grey Stone, the people of The Ice Vales will expect you to deliver equal punishment to others who betray you."

Vighon gripped the hilt of his sword. "I've never been so reluctant to draw my blade."

Alijah chuckled. "I recall all too easily your appetite for a good fight. Do you remember that crypt we discovered in The Iron Valley? You deliberately chose a path that would take us through barbarian territory."

Vighon recalled the event, though likely not with the same clarity as Alijah. "It had been weeks since I had cause to take a swing at anything. Besides, the barbarians love a good fight!" The two men shared a laugh before Vighon was drawn to the sword on Alijah's belt. "I haven't seen that since the day you left," he commented.

Alijah let his hand casually fall onto the black hilt of his elven scimitar, though his lips remained sealed in response. Vighon struggled with the details, but he remembered Alijah's mother, as well as Gideon Thorn, taking offence to his wielding of the blade. What he did recall was the scimitar's colour - a rare steel of green.

"Have you had much cause to use it during your time as king of Erador?"

The half-elf looked off into the night. "There were occasions. But wielding a Vi'tari blade has many benefits; one being its understanding of your will. Where I could, I would disarm my opponents or maim them, sparing their lives."

Vighon considered his flaming sword - anything but a swift

death for his opponent was difficult at best. "You sound like a very good king," he complimented.

Where once Alijah's ego would have fed off such a comment, he now only shrugged with indifference. "Is that ever enough though? Gal Tion was said to be a very good king - for a time. So was Atilan," he added with an incredulous tone. "The people deserve more than just *very good*. I've given it much thought over the years and realised it is impossible to be the greatest of kings... if you try it *alone*. That's why our alliance is so important. Together, I truly believe we can make each other better kings."

Vighon found himself smiling. "I would like that. You know, there are times when you sound just like the Alijah who used to flirt with barmaids and cheat at Galant. Then there are times when you speak with a passion I don't recognise in you."

"My passion for the people grows with every beat of my heart," Alijah replied. "And I'm not averse to flirting with the occasional barmaid," he continued in a lighter tone.

Vighon chuckled. "I bet! I saw you with Lady Gracen. You still work fast I see. You'd only known her a handful of hours."

"Oh..." Alijah smiled. "Yes. The lady of Lirian simply wanted to show me her private collection of blades - she's quite the sword fighter by all accounts."

"I'm sure she is," Vighon replied coyly. "Well, I'm glad you enjoyed her *private* collection." The king frowned as a thought occurred to him. "I thought your type didn't *mix* with others?"

"That's a Dragorn point of view," Alijah explained, unaware that it shattered everything Vighon had been told by Inara. "I like to think of myself as a *Dragon Rider*," he continued.

Whatever he said next was missed by Vighon. He was taken back fifteen years to a conversation with Inara, in which she had told him there could never be anything romantic, as he had desired, as it was impossible even, given the bond that existed between herself and Athis. Vighon wasn't unaccustomed to rejection - he had spent more of his life *not* being a king - but this particular rejection stung the most, even years later.

"— you should come and see it," Alijah said, his words finally breaking through to Vighon.

"See it?" the king repeated, somewhat lost.

"Drakanan."

"Dra—kay-nan?" Vighon was unfamiliar with the word.

"Yes. The home of the ancient Dragon Riders. It's unlike anything you've ever seen, beautiful really, if something of a tomb."

"Perhaps one day," he agreed, unable to see a day when he would be in a position to physically leave Illian. "We should establish ports on our respective coasts. Imagine that! The first to sail across The Hox..."

"That would be something," Alijah admitted, the sound of defeat carrying his words. "The Leviathan that stalks those waters has been on my list of things to deal with for many years now. The problem is the water itself. Dragons can swim, but their effectiveness is diminished. Until it rears its ugly head, Malliath poses no threat to it."

Vighon shook his head, still, after all these years, struggling to wrap his mind around the gigantic beasts of the pre-dawn. "I have a similar problem, though my Leviathan plagues the land instead of the sea," he added.

Alijah lifted his head into the air, his eyes suggesting he was recalling the past. "Ah yes, the Cerbadon. It *is* still dead, I hope."

"Very dead," Vighon clarified. "I believe the realm has yourself to thank for that."

"And Malliath," Alijah was quick to point out. "Why is it still causing problems?"

"Due to its size, the damned thing is still lying on top of that island. We'll never be able to move it, which means we'll never be able to prevent the marrow extraction."

Alijah turned to Vighon with real confusion. "Marrow extraction? What in all the hells is that?"

"Maybe ten years ago, some of the criminal organisations that survived Dragorn's destruction made a discovery. Don't ask me how or why, but they extracted some of the marrow from the Leviathan's bones and experimented with ways of ingesting it. Apparently, the marrow has properties not found in any herb or magic known to man."

Alijah raised a suspicious eyebrow. "What does it do?"

"In small doses it can make a person feel invincible, immune to pain even. Larger doses are damn right evil. I saw it myself a few years back. It can make a man feral, like a beast. They're strong, fast, and *hungry* for anything."

The king of Erador took it all in his stride. "And these criminal organisations? They still exist?"

"Unfortunately," Vighon admitted. "They've proven even harder to root out than the orcs."

Alijah patted the king's shoulder. "One thing at a time. Let's prevent civil war before we eradicate the gangs, eh?"

"You make everything sound so easy; it's refreshing."

A cocky grin, long missed by Vighon, spread across Alijah's face. "That's because everything is easy... for me."

The king laughed again. "Is that why you always cheated at Galant?"

Alijah suppressed his own laugh and displayed a face of mock insult. "I never cheated at Galant..."

The two walked side by side around the camp, covering the distance twice before they returned to the warmth of a fire. Ruban and his drinks were welcomed by both men and the three sat together in front of the king's tent. It reminded Vighon of old times and brought a smile to his face. Garrett, his meal eaten, also joined them by the fire, the lines of his face exaggerated by the flickering light.

The last to emerge from the dark of night was Inara, draped in her red cloak against the chill. She was welcomed by the others, but not the king. Vighon remained silent as she settled down beside Ruban, his eyes fixed on the flames. He had struggled to accept her reasoning for fifteen years - her feelings consumed by a love he could never understand. Now her reasoning was flawed, making her rejection of him a choice, a choice to prevent them both from being happy.

Since he was no longer in his youth, he did what any man from the north would do in this situation: quash it. He needed a distraction to help him ignore the lingering emotions long enough to bury them. A smaller, though more rational, voice whispered in his mind to confront her, hoping that some spark might be ignited between them and their mutual feelings finally be unleashed. But, also like any stubborn northman, he had long learned to replace hope with practicality. Theirs was a union to be doomed by their difference in lifespan.

To the distraction then. "Tell us something of Erador," he spoke up, looking to Alijah. "Such a land must be filled with great stories."

"Yes," Ruban encouraged, "I would love to hear anything of Erador."

"Just so long as it's got a good fight in it," Garrett added. "Lest I fall asleep."

Alijah offered the general an amused smile. "Erador has seen more wars than Illian ever *will*." The half-elf took a moment to consider his tale. "The Red Fields of Dunmar..." he began, apparently satisfied with his choice. "Now there was a battle worthy of note. It should be known, before these events, the land was simply known as Dunmar, a stretch of unremarkable plains. It was only after blood rained from the skies for three days that they changed the name..."

Now Garrett looked very interested. "Go on," he said.

Indeed, Vighon was finding himself already drawn in. He had forgotten how good Alijah was at telling stories.

"In all their years, the Dragon Riders only once fell into civil war. Now, at that time, King Selaghan, third of his name, was seated on the throne of Erador. His reign would have gone entirely unnoticed by history were it not for Lord Kraiden, the leader of the Dragon Riders. Ashamed as the Riders were, there is little to explain why

Kraiden tried to take the crown from Selaghan. Most accounts from the time speak of simple greed or frustration at how the realm was being ruled.

"What was recorded, and in far greater detail, was the schism Lord Kraiden caused within the order. Lya Galastos, another Rider, protested Kraiden's declaration of war on the king and led an uprising against him. The Dragon Riders were split in half, each side opposing the ideals of the other. Before Lord Kraiden could take Valgala, the capital, Lya amassed her force and met the usurpers over the fields of Dunmar."

Ruban paused before taking a sip from his cup. "Imagine that," he said. "Dragons fighting dragons..."

"A spectacle I'm sure," Inara replied dryly.

"For three days they battled," Alijah continued. "For three days they fought in the heavens with fire, steel, and magic. Dragons and their Riders fell in their dozens, littering the plains with corpses. Now, thousands of years later, those same fields are an eden of wonder, with plants and flowers of every colour, never to fade or wilt."

"What happened to Lord Kraiden?" Vighon enquired.

"Kraiden and his dragon, Morgorth, were among the few of the usurpers to survive. It is said, however, that by themselves they significantly reduced what remained of Lya's numbers."

"But he was defeated yes?" Ruban clarified. "This Lya Galastos - she killed him?"

Alijah took a breath. "That would lend the tale an epic ending, would it not? The hero beating the villain in a duel of fates. Alas, Lya Galastos was not the one to bring Lord Kraiden down, though she did survive the battle."

"What became of him then?" Inara asked.

"Seeing that the fight was lost, a Rider under Kraiden's command made a desperate bid to survive. By way of surrender, he stabbed Kraiden in the back..."

Garrett appeared satisfied. "Sounds to me like he had it coming."

"A fascinating tale," Ruban agreed.

"'tis but one," Alijah confessed. "Erador's history is long and wholly unbelievable in places."

"Then we look forward to more," Vighon said, rising to his feet. Ruban and Garrett made to stand with him out of respect but the king waved them away. "Stay a while, enjoy the night. I would rest."

He glanced at Inara before leaving the firelight and was thankful to find his emotions were less turbulent. The king closed his eyes that night, dreaming of ancient dragon wars and adventures in a far-off land.

He was happy to have his brother back.

CHAPTER 19
NEVER TRUST A FART

Keeping the northern face of Vengora to their left, Doran Heavybelly and Russell Maybury had finally reached The Iron Valley not two days past. Since taking the northerly path, into the land of Dhenaheim, they had spent most of that time avoiding the barbarians who claimed much of the valley as their territory.

It wasn't going well.

They had awoken at dawn to find their foraging mounts had wandered farther than they could see - a fact that Russell blamed entirely on Pig. During their search, the duo had been forced to seek shelter as a band of barbarians had emerged from a narrow passage in the western block of mountains.

Their hiding place was discreet enough and the two companies should never have met. There was, however, an extra portion of beans to consider as, the previous night, Doran had insisted on consuming them.

The barbarians, hunters all, were highly attuned to their environment, taking to it like any animal. Catching the dwarf's pungent scent had been inevitable, leading to a conclusion that was just as unavoidable: a lot of running.

"Pick your feet up, Heavybelly!"

Doran was struggling to ignore the burning in his lungs and decided to throw himself down the slope rather than spend precious energy trailing Russell down the path.

Hitting the snow-covered rock had not been part of the plan.

With a sore head and spiralling vision, Doran was yanked to his feet again by Russell's meaty hands. Whatever the old wolf said next was drowned out by the howls and cheers of the pursuing barbarians, who had just reached the top of the slope. Most of them mimicked the son of Dorain and used the slope to shorten their hunt, only none of them collided with the rock.

"Can you see the horse?" Russell called over his shoulder, searching the icy desert for any sign of his cowardly mount.

"I'm not seein' much o' nothin'," Doran complained, blinking as hard as he could to straighten out his vision. That was when a spear, twice the length of his own body, sailed past his ear.

Daring to steal a glance over his shoulder, the band of barbarians weren't in short supply of spears and large cleavers. Covered in leathers and furs, they were a hard people to judge when it came to size and sheer muscle, but if they could throw a spear as far as they did, Doran had to assume they were as strong as man could be.

Of course, Doran had only ever known one barbarian - Bale, son of Hyil, from the Oakbreaker tribe - the Mother and Father rest his soul. If his hulking mass was anything to go by, neither of the old rangers would survive in a fight against a whole band of them.

Even with that argument in mind, the son of Dorain knew there was a very good reason his ancient kin had combined the skill of swinging large axes with their short legs: they weren't made for running away.

"Down there!" Russell yelled, pointing to his horse close to the valley floor.

There was no sign of Pig, who had naturally run away after

Russell's horse had been spooked. Since his friend now had a way of surviving this mess, which Doran refused to admit was his fault, the dwarf saw no choice but to give the old wolf a chance.

"Try not to tense!" he warned.

"What?" Russell spat, a moment before Doran shoved him hard down the last slope, towards his horse.

Doran barely had time to spare a glance at his rolling friend before the next spear came hurtling his way. The dwarf, a warrior to his core, rolled under the spear and came up facing his enemies. The two-handed axe felt like a deadly extension of himself and he intended on sinking it into the gut of the first barbarian to challenge him.

He was about to tell the band that he had no quarrel with them, but he also had no problem reducing the number of their tribe. Those particular words, or any words for that matter, never quite reached his lips. With only seconds before the barbarians crashed into him, a certain Warhog beat them to it, slamming into its rider from the side and carrying them both over the edge of the slope.

A stream of broken curses and expletives could be heard roaring from Doran's mouth every time his face came up from the snow and dirt. His profanities aside, the son of Dorain was more than happy to see his trusted mount - though this particular thought wouldn't occur to him for several hours.

In the chaotic tumble down the slope, the dwarf had become tangled in Pig's straps, specifically around his ankle. Emerging from the fall with a feral squeal, the Warhog made a mad dash, running past Russell and his horse, and across the valley floor. More spears and a few arrows chased them off, each with a promise of death. For Doran, unfortunately, death had yet to be ruled out as he was dragged through The Iron Valley by his ankle.

"Stop ye darned pig!" the dwarf yelled over and over again.

The barbarians were ants on the ridge by the time Doran rolled free of his shackle. His armour had made the escape bearable, protecting the majority of his body from serious injury. Only the backs of his hands were scraped and his ankle in particular wasn't looking forward to taking his considerable weight; but he was *alive*.

The sound of Russell's horse reached him first, its thudding hooves racing to catch them up. "That pig can run when it wants to!"

"Aye," Doran groaned, cracking his back as he rose to his usual stature. "We should press on as well. The barbarians are territorial if nothin' else. They'll hunt us until we're out o' the valley."

"Then let's not dally, Heavybelly." Russell urged his horse onward.

"Dally?" Doran echoed, scrambling to get astride his Warhog. "I'm a dwarf, laddy! We don' dally!"

With a decent lead on any barbarians, the companions pushed on into the northern half of The Iron Valley. Doran had decided to use that time wisely and drink his nerves to sleep. Thanks to some Hobgobbers Ale, the pain in his ankle was barely noticeable and the cuts on his hands didn't hurt half as much when he squeezed the reins.

"Thank you," Russell said, some hours into their journey.

Doran adjusted the pipe in his mouth. "Thank ye? For what?"

The old wolf threw his head over his shoulder. "Back there, on the slopes. You were going to fight them to buy me time."

The son of Dorain frowned, as he so loved to do. "What are ye abou'?"

Russell sighed, expelling a large cloud of vapour. "I'm thanking you, you tiresome dolt!"

Doran straightened his back. "A'right, a'right! Ye could o' jus' said, ye tetchy goat!"

Russell looked down at him in disbelief. "That *is* what I'm saying! I'm saying thank you!"

The dwarf lifted the pipe from his lips. "Ye would o' done the same for me."

Russell's mouth curled into a cheeky grin. "You mean if the size of our legs were reversed?"

Doran turned on his old friend with his pipe clenched hard

between his teeth. "Me height's got nothin' to do with it! I was jus' sure that if it came to a fight - an' it would - they'd whip *ye* up an' down them slopes."

The cantankerous duo continued to bicker and banter for many more miles of their journey, just as they always had. It was only as the valley began to curve round to the west that Doran came across a sight that robbed him of all words. The pipe, which had long been exhausted, fell from his mouth and he stared hopelessly at what greeted them in the valley.

"What is this?" Russell asked.

Doran couldn't comprehend the numbers, but he could see that the thousands of dwarves trudging towards them were a mix of several clans by their various colours and sigils. Most were in a state of undress, missing pieces of armour or weapons, their clothes torn and bloodied. Every one of them carried the weight of defeat on their shoulders.

Taking themselves to the side, Doran and Russell continued on until the trail of dwarves were passing them by though there seemed no end to the convoy. Mixed throughout the warriors of the mountain were hundreds, if not thousands, of families - all with children. Many looked to be hauling hefty sacks and bags as if they had all packed in a hurry.

A young boy walked past, holding his father's hand, at the periphery of the exodus. His eyes, still sparkling with youth, found Doran astride his Warhog. The son of Dorain could feel his heart breaking at the sight.

Desperate for answers, the stout ranger spurred Pig to close the gap between them and his kin. "*Well met!*" he hollered in his native tongue. Doran hesitated when he realised the dwarven soldiers bore the sigil of the Battleborns - the supreme clan within their hierarchy.

"*Well met, yourself,*" a soldier replied miserably.

Doran turned his Warhog to come alongside the soldier. "*What is this? Why are you making for Illian?*"

The Battleborn glanced at Russell behind him and scowled up at the dwarf. *"What rock have you been living under?"*

Deciding his name was better kept to himself, Doran offered a vague response. *"I've been hunting in the valley - bear pelts."*

"Then you've missed the war..." the Battleborn grumbled, his feet determined to keep him heading south.

Doran heard the last word and stopped Pig from going any farther. *"What war?"* he called after the departing soldier.

The Battleborn didn't even look back as he gestured to the thousands of dwarves. *"The one we lost!"* he shouted.

The ranger could feel his heart falling into his gut with the weight of a lead ball. He envisioned Grimwhal being torn down stone by stone and its people slaughtered, including his mother and brother.

After hundreds more slogged through the valley, passing him by, Doran finally turned his Warhog back to the north.

More than one dwarf called out, *"You're going the wrong way!"*

Doran, however, was too busy scanning every sigil he could see, searching in hope for any sign of a Heavybelly among the throng. There were plenty of Brightbeards, their home the closest city to The Iron Valley, as well as Goldhorns scattered throughout. There were notably less Hammerkegs and those he did spot were injured and blood splattered. There wasn't a single Stormshield or, at least, there were no soldiers bearing their sigil.

As the back end of the exodus came into view, so too did the bulk of the Battleborns. Though still possessing the look of a deflated rabble, they were the only ones with soldiers holding to some form of ranks. A close group on Warhogs, surrounded by War Chariots, were in the centre of their cluster. It was hard to say for certain, but Doran was confident that King Uthrad of Silvyr Hall - a king among kings - was riding in the lead.

Any attempt to get his head around what he was seeing only caused Doran's mind to fracture all the more. The dwarves hadn't abandoned their home in such a manner for five thousand years, not since The Great War against the orcs.

The son of Dorain directed Pig to come alongside another lone Warhog, its rider evidently from the Brightbeards clan judging by his blue and green beard and matching hair. *"Where's the rest of the clans?"* he asked urgently. *"This can't be everyone?"*

The Brightbeard frowned, bringing the circled piercings in his eyebrows together. *"Hit your head have you?"*

Exasperated, Doran blurted, *"I've been away for a while. What happened? This can't be everyone!"*

"War, lad. We've been at war for six months." The Brightbeard tutted. *"Six months,"* he repeated incredulously. *"Even the orcs couldn't have boasted of such a feat..."*

"Who are we fighting against?" Doran couldn't be more desperate for answers.

The Brightbeard displayed a subtle shiver. *"They ain't got a name. There's been no talking or demands - just conquest."* The dwarf whipped his head around to face Doran. *"You're not a Stormshield, are you?"*

The ranger hesitated. *"No..."*

The Brightbeard shrugged. *"I can't say if that's a blessing or not. It would have been good to say that at least one son of Hyndaern yet lived. But you'd be the last of your kin I suppose..."*

Doran struggled to comprehend those words. *"The Stormshields... They're all gone?"*

"Aye, they were the first would you believe. Second only to Silvyr Hall - gone in less than a month. You've never seen the clans strike an alliance so fast, let me tell you!"

"What about the Heavybellys?" Doran asked so fast that all four words came out as one. *"Does Grimwhal still stand?"*

The Brightbeard opened his mouth to respond but he paused instead. *"I neither see nor hear the likes of any such name."* The dwarf eyed Doran with suspicion. *"Why would you ask that?"* he hissed quietly.

The son of Dorain was getting tired of his own kin. *"Tell me,"* he growled, grabbing the Brightbeard by the straps on his chest. *"What has happened to my people!"*

Outraged, the dwarf from Bhan Doral shoved Doran back and quickly guided his Warhog away from Pig. *"You're one of them!"* he cried. *"Be on your way, exile! You've no place among us!"*

"Bah!" Doran waved the Brightbeard's ignorance away and turned Pig around to return to Russell.

The old wolf was watching from afar, cautious of the distance between himself and the dwarves of Dhenaheim. "What have you learned?"

In a foul mood, Doran practically sneered at his friend. "What is there to learn from this lot? They've got nothin' but solid stone between their ears!"

"They look broken," Russell observed.

The son of Dorain couldn't argue with that. "They say this is all that's left..."

A look of shock overcame Russell. "That can't be true. There's not a force in all of Verda capable of such a thing."

"Apparently there is," Doran grumbled.

The old wolf turned his yellow eyes down at the dwarf. "The black army Thaggadar spoke of?"

The stout ranger shrugged hopelessly. "We'll learn nothin' more 'ere. We need to reach Grimwhal."

"Then so we shall," Russell replied confidently, directing his horse northward.

Doran was a little slower to do the same. He was convinced that knock to his head was giving him visions and what he saw couldn't be real. If nothing else, Illian was in for a shock when many thousands of dwarves passed between The Watchers.

Continuing the journey in his people's wake, Doran's Warhog was forced to navigate the debris left behind by such a massive group. A child's doll in particular caught his eye, the toy half trampled into the mud. A rogue tear gathered in the corner of his eye as he contemplated all the lives that had been lost in Hyndaern alone - an entire clan eradicated.

The tear ran down his cold cheek and he gritted his teeth. A burning forge of rage was sparking to life inside the son of Dorain. The need to swing his axe was becoming all-consuming; a source of frustration given the desolate land that surrounded the companions.

They travelled in relative silence for the rest of the day and shared nothing but food around their fire that night. Doran could conjure naught but images of himself laying waste to some dark army that dared to extinguish the light of his people.

Before sleep could claim him that night, the dwarf gave himself over to one simple notion - there would be a reckoning...

CHAPTER 20
THE POWER OF CHOICE

K assian waited anxiously for his wife to say something, anything. He had just told her everything he had learned about the Archon, including his aiding the Galfreys. Clara had listened to it all, the weight of the news clearly pressing upon her.

Had she been anyone else, she would have asked the Keeper if he was sure about what he had heard or told him he was simply a fool for believing that he had been tasked with murder. But Clara wasn't anyone else and she knew him better than anyone.

"You're hurt," she pointed out, raising her hand to the bruise beside his eye.

"Their escape had to look real," he replied, taking her hand in his own before she could touch his face.

"Where are they now?" Clara asked.

"They could be anywhere," Kassian stated. "There are numerous places to hide in the grounds and we decided it would be better if I didn't know."

Concern and sympathy pulled Clara's expression in different directions "You should have come to me about this; straight away!"

PHILIP C. QUAINTRELL

"Then I wouldn't be the fool you married," he quipped, attempting to add some levity to their dire situation.

"What will you do now?"

Kassian considered telling his wife of the ill-intent he had towards the Lexichronan, but it would only give her something else to worry about. "I have no choice but to return to the Archon and report my failure," he said. "If I'm not instantly stripped of my rank, I will try to uncover the truth. If the Archon are taking orders from another, Valatos deserves to know."

"And if you *are* punished?"

Kassian held her gaze as he thought through the scenario. "If I am to be punished then so be it. The worst they can do for failing them is take my title away, maybe my sword too. My wand is mine. After that, it would probably be better if we quietly departed Valatos, Velia too. We can start again somewhere else," he suggested wistfully.

"I don't want to start again somewhere else," Clara protested. "Now that we know we must act and discover the truth."

"That might take us down a dangerous path, my love. There is still the danger that the Galfreys will be caught and I will be revealed as a traitor. I fear they would punish you too."

"The principles of Valatos deserve to be upheld," Clara continued righteously. "Archon or not, you are a Keeper and it will always be your duty to preserve what we stand for."

Kassian took his wife's cheek in his hand. "You would make a great master."

Clara smiled. "My name is Kantaris. I'm not giving that up for anything."

A flash of moonlight caught Kassian's eye through the window, reminding him that he didn't have much time left. "Go to sleep as normal. You haven't seen me since yesterday."

Clara gripped his hand and squeezed. "Tread carefully. Whatever happens; make sure you come back to me."

"Always..."

~

Breaking into the Lexichronan's chamber was far easier the second time around. The door opened to the same spell and the single-minded wraith fell prey to the same magic. Navigating the device itself, however, was a learning curve for Kassian.

He inserted his wand into the lock mechanism and the device recognised him. The three-dimensional map of Valatos came to life, along with a number of ethereal keys above the surface of the Lexichronan. There were options available to him that he couldn't say he understood. What he did recognise was the option to lock the ancient device.

His fingers glided over the ethereal words, his touch activating one menu after another. He decided the mage who had built the Lexichronan had an eye for tedious detail. He just wanted there to be one, very obvious, option that allowed him to become the only recognised wielder. Eventually, after pressing more than one wrong key, he discovered the correct sequence that bound his wand, and only his wand, to the device. Now, he alone could open it and allow others the required access.

It felt wrong, but not nearly as wrong as murder.

In the pre-dawn, having pressed his thumb into the cut on the side of his head, Kassian now stood before the Archon with blood slowly trickling down his face. Added to the dirt that stained his clothes and face, he did indeed have the look of a man who had been beaten into the ground.

The master who had given him his task turned to look at the others behind him. Their reflective masks made it impossible to glean their reactions, though it did appear they understood each other's. Without a word, following his disastrous report, all but the master in front of Kassian filed out of the council chamber.

Walking over to the partially stained-glass window that domi-nated one of the walls, the master looked out and clasped his hands behind his back. "I thought you would be more resourceful than this," he remarked.

Kassian swallowed the lump in his throat and made to approach the master. "I beg your forgiveness. I sought to split them up and dispatch them separately. I underestimated their devi-ousness."

"No, Kassian, it is I who have made the mistake of underestimat-ing. I truly believed you were the right man for the job, a Keeper of unparalleled skill, and loyalty to Valatos." The master turned his featureless face towards him. "I was wrong..."

Kassian could feel new beads of sweat forming on his brow. "Master?" he said, choosing to play ignorant.

"Were you all that I had hoped, the Galfreys would now be dead and Valatos's future would be secured. As it is, two agents of the king are now running around the campus unchecked. They could be doing anything from murdering children to planting evidence to ensure the country turns on us."

Sure that he had been ensnared in some trap of his own making, Kassian took a quick breath and continued his charade. "Let me make it right, Master," he pleaded. "I can find them; I know Valatos like the back of my hand."

The master returned his attention to the window and view of the city. "Finding them won't be a problem."

Kassian maintained a blank expression and forced himself to keep his eyes off the ceiling.

"Perhaps a second chance will redeem you," the master contin-ued, oblivious to the blood draining from Kassian's face. "Rally the Keepers. I'm sure you can see to the details, but make sure they are positioned everywhere. As soon as we inform you of the Galfreys' whereabouts, you are to arrest them. Make it look like they resisted," he added.

"It will be done, Master." Kassian turned on his heel and strode towards the door, only to find the way barred by the returning Archon.

"The Lexichronan does not recognise any of our wands," the short female master announced.

"Impossible," the master muttered from beneath his mask.

"It has to be them," another master opined. "The Galfreys have done this."

Kassian did his best to look as small as possible and blend in with the stone, head bowed. He had to look apologetic and nervous if he was going to fool them all.

"Your orders have changed, Keeper," the master called, drawing Kassian from his shell. "This just turned into a hunt. Task the mages of your order as you see fit and find the ambassadors."

"Immediately, Master." Kassian had his hand on the doorknob when the master's voice called to him one last time.

"Kassian. Fail the Archon again and you may find yourself sharing the streets with the beggars of Velia."

The Keeper bowed his head in understanding before making a swift exit. Alone, on the other side of the door, Kassian caught his breath, unsure how he had got away with the last few minutes. He had never been one for lying, often without the need to even do so, but he had found it surprisingly easy when he kept the truth in his heart: everything he did now, was for Valatos.

The starlight had begun to fade by the time every Keeper had been sorted into groups and designated somewhere to begin searching. The hardest part for Kassian had been telling his fellow Keepers that the Galfreys were enemies of Valatos.

Some had appeared reluctant to believe it, while a disturbing few had looked eager to begin the hunt and exercise their magic. Kassian could do nothing, however, but relay the Archon's exact commands and issue them all with kill orders.

Kassian took charge of three other Keepers and led them into the grounds first, starting with the gardens. He explained that the ambassadors had attacked him there, making it a good place to start. In truth, he knew they would be nowhere near the gardens by now.

Pretending to think like the Galfreys, Kassian took his group and began to systematically search nearby buildings, his false assumption being that they would immediately seek shelter. Of course, they were never anywhere to be found. Nathaniel and Reyna had kept their whereabouts from the Keeper, but he was confident they would remain well hidden.

That was until a fellow Keeper came crashing through a second-storey window and became horribly entangled in a thorn bush.

Kassian cursed and ran across the open courtyard with his group in tow. The Keeper had been launched out of the Sanctorum, his scream easily heard over the shattering glass. From inside the building, flashes and explosions blew out more windows and sent debris flying out into the grounds. Then, another Keeper was thrown from a window farther down the hallway. One of Kassian's group was fast on the draw and managed to direct her wand at the falling Keeper, her magic preventing his legs from being broken.

Barrelling through the Sanctorum's main doors, Kassian charged upstairs with his wand in hand. He had no idea what he was about to encounter and, worse still, he had no idea what he was going to do. He was no closer to discovering the truth behind the Archon's schemes and the Galfreys were now in open combat with Valatos.

Rounding the corner, two groups of Keepers lay motionless on the floor, their staffs and wands scattered. A little farther up, Reyna was using hand-to-hand techniques against a male Keeper who was desperately trying to hit her with a spell. Unfortunately for him, the elf was too fast and her hands continuously shifted the position of his arm, redirecting the wand everywhere but at her.

Ridding herself of the opponent, Reyna moved inside his reach and snapped his wrist. His fingers lost interest in gripping the wand

and it fell from his hand into the ambassador's. It only got worse for the Keeper when she stabbed the wand into his leg, dropping him down to one knee. An open palm attack to the side of his head and the man fell into the wall and slumped down to the floor.

Farther up the hallway, Nathaniel was locked in battle against a staff-wielding Keeper. The old Graycoat parried the incoming staff and held it down as the Keeper unleashed a torrent of destructive magic. It was as blinding as it was devastating, but Nathaniel held his nerve and spun the staff up and round, causing damage in a swooping arc. The brick exploded and burst apart before the magic swooped up and splintered the rafters. In one smooth motion, the staff was brought down on the other side where it tore up more of the floor.

Like his wife, Nathaniel sought to be rid of his foe and back-handed the Keeper across the face. The spell was cut short and the fight brought to its conclusion when the old Graycoat brought his pommel down on the back of the Keeper's head. However brief, it was still a comfort to Kassian to see that the ambassador's sword was clean of any blood.

Now there was only a couple of seconds left before Kassian's group rounded the same corner and let loose spells of their own. He shared a look of grave concern with both ambassadors - the hallway behind them was too long for any escape.

That left Kassian with one choice.

His wand flicked sideways through the air and Reyna was shoved through the adjacent door at some speed. This, in fact, saved her life. Had she still been standing there a moment later, Kassian's group would have reduced her body to smaller pieces, just as they did the walls and doorframe.

A variety of sounds and colours then filled the hallway, their wands and staffs flashing with every discharge. Nathaniel covered his face and darted into another room farther up, narrowly avoiding the spells that flew his way.

Kassian held out his hand, gesturing for them to cease their attack. Silently, he signalled for them to fan out across the hallway and slowly advance towards Reyna's room. By the edge of the broken doorframe, Kassian stole a glimpse inside but found no evidence of the elf. He had no choice but to lead his Keepers inside. What he did next, though, was still a mystery to him.

A quick hand signal and all four of them charged into the room; three of them with their wands raised and the fourth with his staff braced in both hands. It was hard to believe that Reyna didn't possess any magic when she had so effectively disappeared from sight in a room with only one door. They were all reminded of her heritage when she dropped down from the corner behind them, her strength alone having kept her braced against the ceiling and walls.

The staff-wielding Keeper was the first to feel her wrath. The haft was forced up into his face - a disorientating blow - before the elf snatched the staff away and whipped the end into his chest, hurling him from the room. The female Keeper beside Kassian pointed her wand only to have her hand knocked aside by Reyna's new weapon. The spell, however, was still unleashed upon the far wall, blowing most of it into the next room along.

It was in that moment that Kassian had to make a split second decision. One of the Keepers stood several feet away, beyond Reyna's reach, and his wand was coming up to strike. If his spell was even half as powerful as the one that had just blown the wall out, the elven ambassador was about to be obliterated.

Kassian flicked his wand at the Keeper's feet and struck the floor with a destructive spell. There was nowhere for the man to go but down into the chamber below, his own spell flying wildly into the ceiling.

His pre-emptive strike distracted the female Keeper engaged with Reyna. The elf landed three successive and surgical hits that knocked the Keeper back in a spluttering mess. Kassian flourished his wand and released a non-lethal spell that threw her back into the wall, robbing her of conscious thought.

All too late did he notice the Keeper who had been relieved of his staff watching from the shattered doorway. His nose was broken and his eyes swollen, but he couldn't have missed Kassian's treachery. Neither elf nor man were able to prevent the Keeper from sprinting away and disappearing down the stairwell.

Nathaniel appeared through the hole blown out of the wall, wafting the cloud of dust and debris away. "That didn't go according to plan," he commented.

"What are you doing here of all places?" Kassian snapped.

"We thought," Reyna offered, "that after all the Keepers left here in search of us, they wouldn't return."

Kassian sighed. "I've either overestimated your intelligence or you have underestimated the Keepers of Valatos..."

"It's definitely the latter," Nathaniel remarked, sheathing his sword. "We need to keep moving."

"You're going to need to come with us," Reyna pointed out.

Kassian paused, hearing half a dozen pairs of boots hammering up the stairwell. "No. I'll hold them off while you put some distance between us." The Keeper held up his hand to silence the elf's protest. "Try and disappear this time. Just hold out until the king arrives."

Nathaniel started away. "You heard him, Reyna. We need to go."

"Thank you," she said earnestly, her emerald eyes meeting Kassian's.

The Keeper didn't even bother to watch them vanish. He gripped his wand and reminded himself to call only on non-lethal magic. After all, they had all been tricked by the Archon; they just didn't know it yet.

The group burst into the room with wands and staffs ready to turn it upside down. They were led by the Keeper with the broken nose, who now wielded his glowing sword. Ripples of heat rose from the blade as he pointed it at Kassian.

"Traitor!" he accused venomously.

Kassian took a deep breath. "I have no argument with any of you,

PHILIP C. QUAINTRELL

but if you don't walk away right now, I can't guarantee the condition in which you'll find yourself when next you wake."

The injured Keeper sneered. "Get 'im!"

Many in Kassian's position would have started blasting away, hoping to shift the odds in his favour, but the first thing he did was erect a specific type of shield. This shield flared a brilliant white when struck by another spell and became a blinding light when struck by multiple spells at once.

All six of the Keepers cried out and covered their eyes but it was too late for them. Kassian's wand shot out again and again until four of the six were strewn around the room with multiple injuries. The fastest amongst them dived to the side and rolled away, giving his eyes precious time to recover. By the time he jumped back up, however, Kassian had a spell waiting for him. As the Keeper bounced off the wall, no longer a threat, the sword-wielder jumped forward with a high swing.

The blade connected with Kassian's wand and sent it spinning away to be lost in the debris. A solid boot was thrust up into his chest, taking Kassian from his feet. By the time he landed, it was hard to say what hurt more: the kick to the chest or the hard floor that had greeted his back. There was no time to dwell on his choices - there was a glowing hot sword bearing down on him.

"Traitor!" he yelled again, striking the floor between Kassian's legs.

The blade was so bright it was hard to look at, but it certainly illuminated the righteous anger that pulled at every muscle in his opponent's face. Kassian rolled to his left and slammed his boot into that same face, changing the expression dramatically. He staggered back and tripped over another Keeper, allowing Kassian more than enough time to find his feet and draw his sword.

He dragged the steel across the surface of his vambrace and ignited the blade. The room's temperature increased with both swords glowing white hot, drawing sweat from both men.

242

"You would betray the order?" the Keeper spat, rising back to his stature. "You would betray Valatos?"

"You know nothing of what you speak!" Kassian retorted.

The Keeper snarled and lunged at Kassian with a two-handed swing. The swords came together with a sparking clash, then again underarm. The Keeper spun away and came back with a flurry of strikes, most of which Kassian parried or evaded. The last thrust, however, cut a burning line across his arm and stung deep into his muscle.

Enthused by his successful blow, the Keeper pressed his attack. Pushing through the pain in his arm, Kassian met every swing and strike with the discipline instilled by his order. Sparks harmlessly impacted their coats and danced across the debris. When locked together, their swords would violently crash into tables and chairs, melting through them with ease.

Being so close during these encounters, Kassian had the opportunity to headbutt the Keeper in his already broken nose - and he took it. The agony that shot through the Keeper's face threw him back, opening him up for a clean knee to the midriff. Now doubled over, Kassian had but to bring his pommel down on the back of his head and the fight would be over.

That was when two members of the Archon entered the room. What followed was an instance of pain and then a lack of air. The golden necklace, gifted to him by the Archon, shrunk in size until he had neither the strength to hold his sword or remain on his feet. The masters walked over to him, but their image blurred all the more upon their approach. Then, there was nothing at all...

~

When next Kassian Kantaris opened his eyes, that instance of pain had developed into a dull ache that stretched around the back of his head. His surroundings had changed, evident by the colourful stained-glass window that painted him in red, pink, and yellow. A circular table dominated the centre of the room - the Archon's table.

Rising to his hands and knees, Kassian paused to see one of the masters walk in front of him, followed by a group of Keepers. One of them presented the master with Kassian's wand and sword before being instructed to leave them on the table, beside his coat.

The master loomed over him. "You have made a grave error in judgment, Kassian." His reflective mask showed the Keeper his own bruised and lacerated face. "You have been taken in by the enemy. And you have betrayed Valatos..."

Kassian stood up in defiance and spat the blood from his split lip. "We both know who has betrayed Valatos, *Master*."

The master whipped his wand out and pointed it up into Kassian's jaw. "You should know when you're beaten," he whispered. "Now," he continued, resuming his elegant stature. "Tell me where the ambassadors are hiding and her punishment will be less severe."

Kassian's mind tripped over that. "*Her* punishment?"

The master gave one of the other Keepers a nod and they quickly moved to open the chamber doors. Kassian's heart sank at the sight of his wife in chains, held in place by the brothers of his order.

"Kassian!" she pleaded.

"Clara!"

The Keeper started forward with renewed energy, but before he could even rise to his feet, manacles shot out from the far wall and snatched at his wrists and ankles. Kassian fell face down on the stone and glimpsed the master manipulating the new chains with his wand. His wrists jerked and Kassian was flung backwards, the chains retreating into the wall as they dragged him with them. The impact was sudden and painful, but he was powerless to do anything, pinned as he now was.

The doors were closed again and Clara vanished from sight. "We have to assume your wife is complicit," the master explained. "She will reside in the cells until you cooperate. Her treatment therein, however, depends on the extent of your compliance."

"I don't know where they are!" he yelled, fighting against his restraints. "I will kill you if you hurt her!" the Keeper promised.

The master tilted his head. "I believe that is the one thing you are incapable of."

The doors opened again and Kassian looked on in desperation. Clara had been taken away. Instead, a new Keeper entered the room at some speed with a missive in hand.

"Master." The Keeper bowed his head. "King Vighon has arrived - his company pass through Velia's main gate as we speak."

The master snatched the parchment. "Why were we not informed sooner?" After scrutinising the note, he continued, "The king arrives with a thousand men... and two *dragons*."

Had Kassian not been so worried about his wife, he would have taken a moment longer to consider that news and question the number of dragons in the king's company. Instead, he let the mystery go and turned his attention to the other Keepers in the room.

"The Archon mean to kill the king! They've been plotting—" Kassian's throat clamped shut at the behest of the master's wand. The necklace tightened as the snake's head consumed the chain bit by bit.

"Inform Lord Carrington that he is to expect the king and his entourage. Tell the lord that *we* will meet the king in person and escort him to the palace. Not a single Namdhorian is to step foot inside Valatos, understood?"

The Keepers nodded their understanding and strode out of the chamber, leaving the master and a suffocating Kassian behind. A flick of the wand and the golden snake released its grip on the chain. The Keeper swallowed as much air as he could, taking it in one massive gulp at a time.

"Why don't you stay here for a while and contemplate your fate... and that of your wife. When all of this ugly business is dealt with, perhaps you can help us with the Galfreys and everything can return to how it was."

Kassian couldn't speak for the pain in his throat. All he could do was watch the master leave the chamber with malevolent intent and dwell on the horrid conditions Clara now resided in. He dropped his head onto his chest, the place where all of his rage was steadily building. His muscles tensed and he fought against his chains to no avail.

How quickly his world had turned to rot...

CHAPTER 21
A FLYING VISIT

Of all the cities to approach on dragon back, Velia was perhaps the most beautiful to behold. With the ocean sparkling to the east and green pastures sprawling for miles in the west, the city was a white gem fixed between the two.

Four of the region's most distinguished kings adorned the walls, their towering forms carved from the white cliffs of The Shining Coast. Of the four, one king - whose name Inara failed to recall - was still in ruins from The War for the Realm, surrounded with scaffolding.

Within its high walls, spires and towers of both human and elven design gave Velia an elegant look that no other city in the realm could boast.

Inara adjusted her position on Athis's back as they flew over the bulk of the city. Centred almost exactly at Velia's heart was Valatos, a city in itself. With walls of dark brick, Valatos stood out against Velia's white landscape - a metaphor Inara decided not to dwell upon...

You are still not convinced there is a conspiracy against the king? Athis asked.

Inara shifted her gaze from the domed building in the centre of Valatos to her companion's horned head. *There is an undeniable connection between the mages and this rebellion - the mage you killed at Grey Stone is proof of that. But I fear Vighon is being sweeping in his accusation. His paranoia has only increased since Alijah returned...*

Athis didn't reply right away, instead waiting until he banked along the shoreline and turned back around to face Vighon and his massive entourage of soldiers. *Are you really thinking about that?* he questioned. *Or are you thinking about what your brother told you?*

Now it was Inara's turn to hold back for a moment. Of course she was thinking about Alijah's revelation. Though the Dragorn couldn't say she was excited by the prospect of embracing her human side again, she was certainly intrigued by it.

You already know my thoughts on the matter, she pointed out.

That I do... Athis responded cryptically.

Seeking to change the topic, Inara looked down at Velia. *Those streets are too crowded for the both of us. Take me down and I will accompany Vighon on foot.*

Without a word, the red dragon altered his flight path and began his descent towards Velia's main gates. Before Athis could touch down, Malliath graced the earth for a handful of seconds before taking off again, leaving Alijah in his stead. Inara was happy to join her brother on the ground, the novelty of his presence having yet to wear off. Vighon and his parade were almost upon them in the west, while an amassing group of Velians gathered to welcome the king at the gates.

"Am I sensing some tension between you two?" Alijah enquired, his blue eyes darting from Athis to Inara. "I hope it's nothing *I've* said."

The Dragorn watched her companion climb higher into the sky, his path taking him away from Malliath. "You're awfully perceptive for one who hasn't been around a lot of dragons."

"True enough. But Malliath has met more dragons than we have humans. I see with his eyes now," he grinned.

That worried and impressed Inara all at once. "Well, there's no tension," she lied. "I've just been thinking about what you said - in Lirian."

"I see," Alijah said knowingly. "As you embrace your human side, so too will Athis embrace his animal side: something he will have neglected since bonding with you. Trust me; he would come to enjoy it."

Inara waited for Athis to speak into her mind but the dragon remained silent. There was no time for her to say anything before Vighon and his soldiers were upon them. The king was wearing his crown now, a circlet of gold and silver with stylised flames forged into some of the points. Every time Inara saw him wear it, she couldn't help but think back to their earlier years, when they had been young and in love. She could never have imagined that that scruffy young man would become the king of the entire country.

"Fetch them horses," the king commanded to no one in particular.

Inara held up her hands. "I'm fine with walking... *Your Grace.*" The Dragorn added, apologising with her eyes for her familiarity with Vighon around others.

"You cross the world on dragon back," Vighon argued. "I will not have you *walk* into Velia beside me."

There was no time to insist before a horse was brought to her, handed over by its rider. Tentatively, the Dragorn assessed the saddle and stirrups, as well as taking in the whole horse - a rather large animal up close.

"Inara?" Vighon looked at her questioningly.

The Dragorn used what grace she possessed and mounted the horse, hoping that her muscle memory would do most of the work for her. "It's been nearly thirty years since I rode a horse," she remarked to the king.

Alijah, whose pointed ears missed nothing, laughed to himself. "Where was that excuse thirty years ago?"

Inara offered his quip a smile that suggested he would pay for the remark at a later time. That's if she didn't fall off the horse and break her neck first...

"Sir Roddik will accompany you," Vighon reassured, giving the knight an instructive nod.

"I'll manage," Inara promised, gesturing for Sir Roddik to leave her be.

She came to regret that at least twice before they reached the main gates. It was there that they were met by several companies of Velian soldiers, all of whom created a path through the growing throng of on-lookers. Waiting ominously in the road was the Archon - the seven mages who governed Valatos. Either side, protecting the mages, were the renowned Keepers, armed with their wands and swords.

As one, adding to their strangeness, the Archon bowed to the king. There was something about their all-encompassing masks that put Inara on edge and she especially disliked seeing her own face in their reflection.

"It is an honour to receive you, your Grace," one of the master's greeted politely enough.

"It is an honour to visit this great city!" Vighon declared to an eager crowd.

It pleased Inara to see the people welcome Vighon with genuine praise. She hoped this would help to soothe the king's worries regarding the state of the realm. It certainly helped her.

The master waited for the cheers to die down and came up beside the king. "Lord Carrington is preparing a welcome, your Grace - in the palace."

Inara watched Vighon closely now. It would be an insult to the people to refuse an invitation from their lord, but the Dragorn knew well that the king wished only to enter Valatos.

"Very good," Vighon said reluctantly. "You received my ambassadors?"

"Yes, your Grace," the same master replied with a curt bow of the head.

"Excellent. Have them meet me in the palace immediately." Before Vighon was able to spur his horse, the master side-stepped in his way.

"Your Grace, the ambassadors left Valatos two days ago. I have it on good authority that they left Velia that same day."

"They left?" Vighon echoed, his disbelief evident in his tone.

"They talked of returning to the capital, your Grace."

The king turned to his left and looked from Inara to Alijah, though neither could offer a comment in such company. Inara wanted to tell him that it was completely reasonable that her parents had left the city. It was likely, in her eyes, that they had found nothing to report and that the mages were still urging for independence. She suspected Alijah thought the opposite...

With no other choice, the king and his entourage followed behind the Archon and their Keepers. The Velians continued to greet them warmly, with a few even attempting to kiss Inara's boot as she rode by. The Dragorn wasn't ignorant to the people's view of her and was often asked by those she met to cradle their babies and offer a blessing. Taking it all in her stride was the only thing Inara could do, though her brother's presence did make her self-conscious of the situation.

You are the only Dragorn in Illian, Athis reminded her, his voice most welcome again. *You are a symbol of hope to them; something you should be proud of.*

Inara held on to that. They were representing an order that had stood guard over Illian for thousands of years and that meant something; even if Alijah had chosen not to be a part of it...

In the palace courtyard, Lord Carrington's servants gave the impression that they were anything but ready to receive the king.

"They must have known we were coming," Inara remarked to her brother.

"I think Lord Carrington expected us to visit Valatos," Alijah reasoned. "Now why would he expect that?" he asked sarcastically.

Inara glanced at the king and made sure he couldn't hear them. "We should not fuel suspicion," she warned. "Lord Carrington hasn't done anything illegal - everything we know is just a rumour."

Alijah paused before dismounting. "You're too smart to believe that. This is Lord Carrington's city; if there's a rebellion stirring here he'll know about it. Since he hasn't come to the king with such information, we have to assume he's complicit."

Inara couldn't oppose her brother's assessment. Growing up, Alijah had always been a poet with words, his arguments succinct and logical. That didn't mean she had to like it.

Lord Carrington stepped away from his family, who had lined up from his wife to his fourth child, and greeted the king with a broad smile and a low bow - or at least as low as his round frame would permit. He was not as Inara recalled him from years earlier. Back then, the lord of Velia had carried a vibrant aura about him, promising a great leader for the people of Alborn. Now, he had a greedy look in his eye that Inara couldn't ignore.

Do not allow Alijah's perspective to affect your own, Athis advised, wise as ever. *Lord Carrington has always been ambitious - that much we saw when the king was choosing the lords of his land. We decided that ambitiousness would be good for the people; that he would always seek to better their lives. There is no reason to suspect he has changed...*

You're absolutely right, Inara agreed, chastising herself for judging the lord so quickly and with no real evidence. **What would I do without you?**

Athis's usual witty reply to such a question was notably absent and Inara sensed the dragon was genuinely pondering upon it. The Dragorn would have told him to stop dwelling on the matter as they would never be separated, but Lord Carrington approached, robbing her of the opportunity.

"An honour to have the Guardian of the Realm in my home," he announced.

Inara was all too happy to hand the reins of the horse back to Sir Roddick and greet the lord instead. "The honour is mine, Lord Carrington. It has been too long since last I visited your fine city."

The lord smiled and his eyes shifted uncomfortably to the right, where Alijah was standing confidently as ever. "This is my brother, Alijah Galfrey. He is..." Inara struggled to find the right explanation as to his being there - Lord Carrington knew nothing of Erador.

"Complicated," Alijah finished, bowing to the lord. "I'm with him," he added, pointing to the sky where Malliath was seen briefly soaring from one side of the city to the other.

Lord Carrington's eyes went wide with surprise. "You're..."

"Here to help," Alijah said quickly. "Perhaps we should accompany the king?" he queried, gesturing to Vighon, who was swiftly entering the palace.

"Of course," Lord Carrington agreed, bowing to Alijah.

Inara raised a questioning eyebrow at Alijah, silently asking him why the lord would bow to him. Alijah shrugged and waited for the lord of Velia to follow behind the king.

Only then did he lean in to his sister and playfully whisper, "Maybe he can just sense that I'm more deserving of respect than you."

Had they not been in the sight of so many, Inara would have thumped her brother on the arm.

Inside the palace, all formality came to an end. There were no more pleasantries to be had, the king waved away any offer of food or drink, and Velia's royal hall was emptied on Vighon's orders. He strode ahead of the party and assumed the throne that would regularly be used by Lord Carrington. Such a thing was the king's right, but the manner in which he took his seat was more aggressive than usual.

He is frustrated and angry, Athis observed through his companion's eyes. *You should stand beside him. Your presence is a balm.*

Inara left Alijah to stand to the side and joined the king on the podium. Vighon barely noticed her approach, his attention fixed on the Archon and Lord Carrington who, besides Sir Ruban and General Garrett, were the only ones the king had permitted to remain.

"This is where you hold court, Lord Carrington?" Vighon enquired innocently enough.

"It is, your Grace."

"Then this is a hall of truth," the king continued, "a place where justice reigns over all." Inara could hear it now, the hostility hiding in his tone. "I have recently delivered justice to The Ice Vales. Perhaps word has already reached you of Lord Thedomir's rebellion?"

Lord Carrington licked his lips nervously. "Indeed, your Grace, such treasonous news has reached my city. It is unthinkable that—"

"Thedomir is dead," Vighon stated bluntly, cutting the lord off. "He wanted to break the realm into pieces... and now he is dead. As are the governors of The Ice Vales." The king let his words hang in the air. "Do you know what happened next, Lord Carrington?"

"No, your Grace."

"His son, Thaddeus, took up arms against me. He even tried to kill the Guardian of the Realm. He's dead as well."

Lord Carrington could be seen to take a hard swallow. "A treasonous line, your Grace."

Without even an attempt at subtlety, Vighon's gaze shifted to the Archon. "They rebelled at the bidding of another, one powerful enough to terrify the Longshadows."

One of the masters clasped his hands behind his back. "Has this *other* individual been identified, your Grace?"

"No," Vighon said. "And we don't know it's an *individual*," he added, forcing Inara to conceal her wince. "What we do know is that Thedomir was in league with a mage."

"His court mage?" the same master posed.

"If only it had been." The king shuffled in his seat, never one to find a throne comfortable. "The mage died fighting Athis the iron-heart. So you see; we have come to this fine city to ensure that any

254

thoughts of separatism are contained to those who now lie in the ground. A schism would lead to civil war. Illian can't afford another war, not now."

Lord Carrington cleared his throat. "I can assure you, your Grace, there is nothing to be concerned with in Velia. We are, as always, loyal to the crown."

"That's not what we're hearing," General Garrett asserted.

Lord Carrington turned on the general with an attitude he would never dare unleash upon the king. "Spying is an unseemly business, General Garrett. Those in the trade are liars by nature and therefore are not be trusted." He looked back at the king with a softer expression and tone. "There is no treason here, your Grace. Velia has thrived under your kingship."

Vighon waved the discussion away, obviously exasperated. "Let's not bandy words; I have travelled too far and shed too much blood."

Inara cleared her throat beside him, hoping that the king would hear the caution therein and calm down. He didn't.

"We all know that Valatos seeks independence from the kingdom. I can only hope, Archon, that you heard my ambassadors loud and clear: there will be no such thing. I have come to Velia to lead an investigation myself. If I find that you or any of your fellow mages have incited this rebellion, Valatos will be dismantled brick by brick and those strange masks of yours will be burnt." Vighon turned on the lord. "If it also comes to light that you have aided them in this endeavour, you will meet the King's Justice and join Thedomir and his ilk. And—"

Inara stepped forward before any farther threats could be issued. "As the king said; we have travelled far and our journey has not been without its perils. Perhaps we should reconvene over a meal, where cooler heads might prevail?"

"Of course," Lord Carrington agreed. "I already have rooms prepared for you all. A feast is being cooked as we speak!"

Vighon leaned forward on his knees, steeping his face in shadow. He offered no words but merely nodded his permission. The lord of

Velia bowed and turned around to leave, along with the seven masters of the Archon.

"Wait," the king commanded. "Lord Carrington, have rooms made up for the Archon. They are not to return to Valatos unaccompanied - a prudent necessity where the investigation is concerned."

Lord Carrington looked hesitantly from the king to the Archon and back. "As you will, your Grace."

One of the masters remained very still, failing to trail the lord of Velia. "We will not be kept from our home, your Grace."

"Your defiance does you no favours," Alijah spoke up, garnering everyone's attention. "This is an order from your *king*. Will you obey?"

The master tilted his head, distorting Alijah's reflection in his mask. "We will obey," he said simply. With that, the entire Archon bowed their heads and followed Lord Carrington from the royal hall.

Vighon looked to Garrett and Ruban. "Leave us," he ordered.

The two soldiers almost looked to argue that command but ultimately bowed their heads and walked away, soon followed by Alijah. Inara had a sinking feeling in her stomach.

"I would have you stay," the king called out, halting Alijah in his tracks.

"I think not," the half-elf replied casually, his tone reminding them that he was a king himself and, therefore, not to be commanded. Inara didn't miss the way he looked from her to the king either.

The Dragorn waited until the tall doors were sealed behind her brother. "I thought we came here so that *words might have their day*. Your choice of words, however, will lead to nothing but violence and—"

"Don't do that again," Vighon interrupted, his tone flat and serious.

Inara was stunned. "What?"

"Don't undermine me!" he snapped, rising from the throne.

Inara scowled. "I didn't realise your ego was so fragile, *your Grace.*"

"They're subjects," Vighon reminded her. "And dangerous ones at that. Carrington commands loyalty from thousands of soldiers and the Archon wield enough magic to challenge even you."

"I only act to keep civility - a much-needed environment where peace is concerned. You want peace, but you court civil war with your actions here. We should not bully the Archon to—"

"I'm preventing war, Inara, not starting it! If I have to be the bully to do that then I will! This is why we need kings," he continued. "There has to be an authority that all obey. Without my word, the realm would fracture and civil war would become a way of life."

"This is being a king?" Inara challenged. "Would you be serving the mages of Valatos if you tore their home down? Of all the people in the realm, they carry the most potential. They need to be nurtured, not threatened."

"If they *are* the threat they will be removed," Vighon said clearly.

"You cannot punish them all, Vighon. If this conspiracy has come from Valatos, it hasn't come from all of them. There are children and teachers behind those walls. Families! If you must bloody your sword to punish the few then do so. But do not threaten the rest - *they* come under *my* protection."

"If only the world was as you see it," Vighon returned. "It's black and white, good and evil. I have to consider more than all of that. I'm responsible for a kingdom that hasn't known unity for a thousand years. I have to think about the past, present, and future with every decision I make. You just see evil and injustice and swing your sword. Everyone praises you when you do. There are far reaching conse-quences every time I draw my sword."

"The same could be said for every time you open your mouth," Inara retorted, immediately regretting her particular choice of words.

Vighon opened and sealed his lips, showing the first moment of consideration he had taken that day. "I will bring an end to these whispers of rebellion. I will do it with minimal loss of life. And I will do it with or without you. Alijah and Malliath are here to help *me*."

That stung the Dragorn. "I am here to help you. Even if you're too pig-headed to see it."

The king shook his head and made for the doors. "Do as you wish, Inara." Vighon swung open the door to find Eatred Mannus, his court mage, standing outside. "Contact your peers in Namdhor," he told the mage. "As soon as the ambassadors arrive, I want to speak with them."

"At once, your Grace."

Vighon paused in the doorway and gave Inara one last look of disappointment before leaving. It infuriated the Dragorn.

I'm the one who is disappointed with him! she complained to Athis.

I fear the king has become lost in his paranoia, the dragon replied from far above. *He is losing sight of allies and sees himself as surrounded by enemies.*

According to Alijah, Inara recalled, *we are surrounded by enemies.*

Even if that proves to be true, we should be here to advise the king as well as protect him.

Inara sighed. *I know,* she admitted. *But I would very much like to leave him and see how he fairs without us.*

For the good of the realm, the dragon replied, *we should ensure that day never comes...*

The sun was setting over The Moonlit Plains when Inara was invited to the dining hall. Through one of the many windows in the palace, she glimpsed Athis's silhouette crossing the orange glow of the western sky.

The Dragorn wasn't looking forward to the next confrontation with Vighon, nor the tension that would arise upon his next accusation. She wished Athis could be with her in the dining hall, his physical presence always an extra comfort.

Inside the hall, Inara found Alijah standing in front of the large fireplace with a goblet in his hand, his gaze lost to the flames. Lord Carrington intercepted her first and welcomed the Dragorn as his servants offered her a drink. Only one of the masters was present to represent the Archon and remained seated at the long table, ignorant or oblivious to her arrival.

The lack of high borns was notable in the room. Inara had to ponder upon the meaning behind their absence and became unsure as to whether it cast Lord Carrington in a guilty light.

Untangling herself from the lord's small talk, Inara made her way over to the fire. "Have you seen Vighon?" she asked her brother.

Alijah stood perfectly still, his eyes unwavering. Inara dipped her head to bring herself into his sight, wondering if that would be enough to break his reverie. His head snapped up and he turned on his sister with a hint of confusion about him.

"Sorry," he said, his usual smile returning. "I was talking to Malliath…"

Inara sniffed her goblet of wine. "That must have been quite the conversation - you looked a hundred miles away."

"He doesn't like being this close to Korkanath," Alijah explained. "We've worked hard since we were last on Illian soil," he continued quietly. "Putting the past behind you can be just as difficult as trying to see a future yet to be revealed. That said, we have made great strides to rebuild ourselves into something new, something wholesome."

"I would say you have succeeded," Inara commended.

Alijah sighed and looked into his untouched goblet. "Being here, in sight of Korkanath… it threatens to undo him."

Inara sympathised. "The mages of Korkanath did terrible things to him, things that shouldn't be done to any creature."

Alijah nodded along before standing up straight - he was shutting their conversation down. "I'm assuming Vighon is angling for the dramatic entrance."

Inara was sure to leave the topic of Malliath alone, aware that prying into the bond of another was considered rude. "Oh yes," she agreed. "He will likely come flying through those doors any second."

Alijah laughed to himself. "Some things will never change."

Inara couldn't say the same. "He's not entirely as you remember."

"He does appear on edge," Alijah commented.

"It's more than that. The weight of the realm is taking its toll and recent events aren't helping."

Alijah shrugged. "I struggle to recall how I ever lived without the mind of a dragon to help me see the world. I can only imagine how hard it is to run a kingdom with the mind of a mortal..."

"It's harder with you fuelling his paranoia." That hadn't sounded so harsh in her head, but her tone was undeniably venomous.

"Not this again," Alijah replied, glancing over his shoulder at their hosts. "I saw what I saw, Inara. There's more than unrest stirring in this city and Vighon should be more than wary of it. Our presence here is necessary."

Inara wanted to argue all of her brother's points but she couldn't. Alijah had seen, through means she couldn't yet fathom, that a plot was unfolding in Velia and their presence was indeed the only thing that could diffuse the situation and bring peace.

"I just want all of this to be over," she said instead.

Alijah's head flicked to the doors as both siblings caught the sound of approaching feet. "I think it's about to be..."

Vighon entered the dining hall, preceded by the master of servants who was determined to announce the king. Before he could utter a syllable, however, the northman stormed ahead with General Garrett and Sir Ruban in tow. All three men appeared concerned.

"Your Grace!" Lord Carrington stood up from his chair and bowed. The master from Valatos was much slower to rise and his bow barely perceptible.

Vighon held up his hand to stop the lord from rabbiting on. "I would have the room," he stated, looking from the lord of Velia to the master.

Lord Carrington hesitated, his eyes shifting from the king to the master. "Of course, your Grace." With that, the two men left the room and the master of servants closed the doors after them.

Satisfied that they were alone, Vighon took a deep breath and placed a diviner on the table. The black orb was inactive and was usually in the possession of the king's court mage.

"What's wrong?" Inara asked.

"Eatred has not long spoken with his council in Namdhor," Vighon explained, somewhat exhausted. "Apparently, every dwarf in Dhenaheim has just passed through The Iron Valley into Illian."

"*Every* dwarf?" Alijah checked.

"Their numbers would suggest so. King Uthrad of Silvyr Hall sent an envoy to The Dragon Keep this very day. He claims that every kingdom in Dhenaheim has been attacked by a foreign invader."

Inara's blue eyes went wide. "A foreign invader? In the north?"

"There weren't many details," Vighon answered. "Whoever they are, they came from something called..." The king looked to his general.

"The Dread Wood, your Grace."

"How could I forget," Vighon quipped wearily.

"I've never heard of it," Inara admitted.

"It's west of Dhenaheim," Alijah said, "Just beyond The Whispering Mountains. It lies on a stretch of northern land that bridges Erador and Illian."

"You've been there, your Grace?" General Garrett enquired of the western king.

"No one goes there," Alijah told him, his tone unmistakably grave. "Eons past, Atilan spent years searching for a way around. So terrible is The Dread Wood, that the most powerful mage to ever live chose to take his army along a narrow and treacherous cliff, south of the forest."

"That's my second problem," Vighon declared. "My first problem is the thousands of dwarves now heading for Namdhor."

"What will you do?" Inara asked, glad to have some eye contact with Vighon for the first time.

"I cannot be in two places at once," the king replied. "The dwarves appear to advance without any signs of hostility - it's even possible King Uthrad will seek an alliance against this new invader. Unfortunately, I must stay here and see this investigation through; I will not risk out-right rebellion."

"You're staying here?" Inara questioned incredulously. "Dhenaheim has been conquered! We should return to the north and investigate *that*, not stay in Velia and interrogate mages!"

"This isn't a debate," Vighon stated, his tone clipped. "The bulk of the army is already in the north and the dwarves are there too. No foreign invader would attack against such an alliance. The most immediate danger lies here."

Inara had reached the end of her patience. "You cannot be so blind! A real threat has just emerged and you will do nothing?"

"We cannot face any threat if we are a country divided, Inara! What stirs in this city could fracture the entire kingdom. I'm staying!"

Inara felt Athis lend her a portion of his control and she managed to hold her tongue. She composed herself, considered her various responses, and decided what she needed to do.

"Very well, your Grace. I hope you resolve the matter to your satisfaction." The Dragorn said nothing more and made for the doors.

"Where are you going?" Vighon demanded.

Inara paused before opening the door. "I'm going north," she answered calmly. "I would see this threat for myself."

Vighon started forward. "I need..." The king hesitated. "Go," he finally said.

Inara did her best to conceal the hurt she felt at that moment.

With a polite bow of her head, the Dragorn turned around and left the dining hall as her mind called out to Athis.

Her keen ears heard Alijah say, "I will speak with her."

"Let her go," Vighon replied.

Whatever their exchange, Alijah was soon behind her in the passage, his black and red cloak flapping behind him. He called out to his sister and she reluctantly halted her stride.

"You shouldn't go alone," Alijah told her. "You said it yourself; Dhenaheim has been conquered. We both know that any force capable of such a feat can best a dragon."

Inara ignored the sneer that Athis passed across their bond. "Someone has to go, Alijah. If it isn't to be the king then it will be Athis and me."

Alijah, rooted to the spot, could do nothing but sigh and watch as his sister walked away.

CHAPTER 22
AN UNEXPECTED WELCOME

Grimwhal, the ancient home of clan Heavybelly, was impossible to miss, regardless of where one was standing on the snowy plains. Its grand entrance was the width of the mountain itself - a hollow supported by one massive pillar of shining gold and dwarven script. It was a captivating sight for all, including those who called it home.

The same should have been said of Doran Heavybelly, who sat astride his Warhog on those familiar northern plains. Before him was that towering pillar - a monument to dwarven architecture - and Grimwhal's portentous doors. The son of Dorain, however, was entirely captured by the view to the west, where the land stretched across an expanse from Vengora to The Whispering Mountains.

He would always be a slave to his instincts, and his instincts told him the gathering storm clouds residing over that expanse were insidious. Everything beneath those ominous dark clouds was smothered with fog and dancing shadows.

"I wouldn't like to get caught up in that," Russell commented.

"Aye," Doran agreed, his sight failing to pierce the approaching mist.

Together, the pair rode their mounts past the pillar and entered the hollow of Grimwhal. Not a step did they take past the pillar before a single ballista bolt impacted the ground in front of them, spraying snow across Pig's snout. The bolt had been fired from within one of the hundred burrows that lined the concave wall surrounding the doors. From left to right, Doran could see that every one of them was currently manned, their ballistas trained on the new arrivals.

"This brings back memories," Russell remarked.

"Ye can' say I don' take ye places," Doran quipped, raising his hands into the air.

In the distance, the doors were slowly opened and a contingent of Heavybelly warriors filed out with spears and shields. When they advanced no farther than the doors, Doran gestured for Russell to follow him on foot with their mounts guided by reins alone.

Ploughing through the snow, Doran let his only eye roam over the burrows whose ballistas turned to track them. Of course, it would only take a single bolt to wipe them from the face of Verda.

Upon reaching his armoured kin, the dwarf heading the group immediately stood out to the son of Dorain. He was the only warrior among them who didn't have his helm on, possibly due to the eccentrically large mohawk of jet black hair. It had been fifteen years since he had seen him, though he hadn't been wearing clan armour at the time.

"*State your business!*" the familiar dwarf barked.

"Is that ye, Revek?" Doran enquired.

The mohawk lowered his spear and scrutinised Doran, then Russell. Revelation smoothed out his features and he relaxed, but he was the only dwarf to do so.

"Doran?" The Blood Boy stood his spear in the snow. "What in all the hells are *ye* doin' 'ere?" The sound of his name sent a ripple of murmurs through their rank.

"I got..." Doran stopped himself from saying any more on the note from his brother. "I got word abou' some war. The clan's been recalled from Illian. I thought I'd..." The ranger shrugged, realising now that he should have thought this part through in at least some detail.

"Oh, there's a war on a'right," Revek replied. "Grarfath knows we could use every axe an' blade goin'." Sparing a glance at the approaching storm, he continued, "We should get inside, *now*."

One of the Heavybellys objected. "*He's an exile!*"

Revek turned on the dwarf. "*Doran, son of Dorain, was leading this army before you were even born you little snot! You'll do well to shut your mouth before I do it for you!*"

This was not the welcome the ranger had expected - having expected to argue his way inside. He wasn't going to protest, however; especially given the storm on their tail. With Russell by his side, the two passed between the warriors and followed Revek into Grimwhal's torch-lit halls.

"The last time I saw ye," Doran commented, "ye weren' wearin' all o' that."

"True enough," Revek agreed. "It wasn' that long ago I were wearin' me Blood Boy gear. For the last five months though, since we joined the war effort, I've been forced to hang up me coat an' join the ranks. It was actually the king 'imself who thought I'd be better suited as a captain, given me history workin' for the guild."

"How goes the war effort?" Doran pressed, eager for information. "We saw the other clans makin' for Illian."

"Ain' that answer enough," Revek shot back. "Dhenaheim's been losin' this war since it began. There were a few battles that could - *should* - 'ave gone our way, but the stubborn fools in the other clans refused to integrate us. We had to insert ourselves where we could."

"'ave we suffered losses?" Doran couldn't help including himself in the question, though he did feel like a hypocrite.

"Heavybellys 'ave been lost," Revek grieved, "but our casualties are nothin' like the others. Ye've heard abou' the Stormshields?"

Doran ignored the pointed looks he garnered from those they

passed. "Aye, though I'm strugglin' to believe it. King Gandalir commanded an army almost equal in size to Silvyr Hall."

Revek shook his head, steering them down the next passage. "Hyndaern is a ghost city now. Then again, so are the rest. Ye said ye saw the other clans. Once the Hammerkegs abandoned Nimduhn, King Uthrad took 'em in an' bolstered his ranks, but even Silvyr Hall was left to the enemy. The Goldhorns offered 'em all a place in Khaldarim an' it was from there that the Brightbeards an' ourselves helped to stage a defence." Revek went silent for a moment, his thoughts his own.

"By the time the clans had no choice but to flee, the white walls o' Khaldarim were red with the blood o' our kin. After that, the Brightbeards emptied their own halls, hopin' to save as many lives as possible before this evil could befall them. All but Grimwhal are tombs now..."

Doran was robbed of words; even his emotions were numb after hearing such bleak news. "What in all the hells are we facin'?" he muttered, tying Pig to a post beside Russell's horse.

Revek paused before the doors of the throne room. "I'd say there's nothin' left to fear in *any* hell - the demons are 'ere now..."

The doors were opened for them, revealing the majestic throne room filled with wounded dwarves. Blood spilled out across the polished marble and cries of pain echoed off the walls. Nurses and healers moved from dwarf to dwarf, tending to whatever they could. Scattered throughout were white sheets covering the dead.

"This is overflow," Revek explained with dismay.

Doran's already broken heart shattered into a thousand more pieces for his people. "Where's me brother?"

"This way." Revek weaved through the injured and the healers, begging apologies where he could. Before they could reach their destination, however, they were confronted by none other than the queen-mother.

Doran swallowed. Hard.

"You may return to your duties, Captain Revek."

Revek bowed to Queen Drelda and offered Doran nothing but a look before disappearing the way they had come. Russell remained standing to the side, though his broad shoulders and stature made it impossible to fade into the background.

"Hello, Mother."

Queen Drelda's stoical expression broke as she pounced on her son with open arms. Stronger than she looked, the queen-mother squeezed the air out of the ranger. Taken aback, Doran could think of nothing to do but embrace her.

"Thank Yamnomora you're here," she declared, surprising Doran all the more.

"I think you're supposed to be threatening me," he corrected.

Drelda cupped his face. *"Not this time."* Her thumb ran over the edge of his eye-patch - a new wound as far as she was concerned.

"I know about Father," he told her sympathetically. *"I'm so sorry..."*

His mother smiled faintly. *"He had his time. Now he resides in Grarfath's Hall - consider him the lucky one."*

"Have I missed the funeral?"

"Only by a few months," the queen-mother replied as if it was no bother. *"His tomb was ten times bigger than it needed to be... But what else would the son of Dorryn have demanded?"* Drelda's eyes flitted over Russell. *"Now come. And bring your human."*

Following his mother now, Doran gestured for Russell to follow. Even the old wolf appeared confused at the love his mother had so openly displayed. To the son of Dorain, it was only further proof that the world was ending.

The queen-mother pushed her way through the opposing double doors and stood defiantly before King Dakmund and two of his generals, all of whom had been pouring over maps of Grimwhal.

"Not now, Mother," Dakmund growled, putting Doran on edge.

"It's time for a new perspective," Drelda stated, her tone not one to be argued with.

Dakmund looked to reply until he saw Doran and Russell enter behind his mother. The generals looked from Doran to their king expectantly.

"*The exile is forbidden from—*"

"*Out,*" Drelda commanded, cutting them off with her quick tongue.

Dakmund gave them both a nod and they exited the room with a glare reserved for Doran. The queen-mother ordered them to seal the doors behind them, the mundane task an added insult.

"*Why are you here?*" Dakmund snapped, continuing to appear out of character.

Doran held up his hands before thumbing at Russell over his shoulder. "He doesn' speak a lick o' dwarvish. This would be easier if we—"

"Answer the damned question," Dakmund interjected using man's tongue.

Doran straightened up. "I'm 'ere because o' yer *damned* note!"

Dakmund frowned his solid brow. "Note? Abou' Father? Ye've come because o' that?"

"O' course I 'ave! The note had yer blood on it! Then I heard abou' ye recallin' all the dwarves from Namdhor."

Dakmund threw his hands up. "O' course it had me blood on it!" He pointed to the scar that cut a red line vertically down his cheek. "I was in the middle o' fightin' a war! Ye weren' supposed to actually come 'ere!"

"Well, I am 'ere. An' it looks like there's still a war to fight."

"Not for ye." Dakmund waved him away. "There's not a dwarf that'll fight beside ye."

"They did on The White Vale! They didn' mind cuttin' down orcs with me at their backs then!"

Dakmund sighed and pressed his clenched fist into the table. "Ye shouldn' o' come, Doran. Death has laid claim to these lands..."

Doran reigned in his rising anger, seeing now that his little brother hadn't wanted him to get caught up in all this. He would have been exactly the same were he the one burdened with the crown of Grimwhal.

"Why're ye still 'ere?" he asked. "The other clans 'ave fled to Illian."

"Grimwhal has never been taken, not in five thousand years. We 'ave the best defences in Dhenaheim. I even offered King Uthrad an' the others safe haven, but the fools rejected it because o' *hierarchy!*"

Doran walked up to the table and leaned over it. "Ye're mad!" he accused, noting his mother's approving nod. "Grimwhal doesn' boast better defences than Silvyr Hall. Ye need to get everyone out, *now!*"

Dakmund shook his head. "Let the rest o' 'em run! Dhenaheim will be left for the Heavybellys! We could plunder every city, even Silvyr Hall!"

Doran noted the wild look in his brother's eyes. "Ye've seen too much fightin', little brother. Ye're not thinkin' straight. Grimwhal can' stand up to anythin' that can bring down all o' the clans combined."

Dakmund shut his eyes. "I'm not goin' to be the king that abandons Grimwhal."

"Then ye'll be the king that sees Grimwhal to its end." Doran jabbed his finger into the map. "This is just stone. Grimwhal is its *people*. Get them into Illian. King Vighon can help; an' that's somethin' even Uthrad can' argue with."

Dakmund lifted his head and looked at his mother. Just as she had with Doran, Drelda offered her youngest son an approving nod. It seemed this was an argument she had already made but it had found nothing but deaf ears.

"It's taken me fifteen years to earn their respect," Dakmund groaned, "to get the lords in line an' on me side. If I order 'em all to leave, I will be seen as *weak*. History will remember me as *weak*."

Doran looked his brother in the eyes. "If ye don' get everybody out, lad, there won' be anyone to even record history, let alone look back on it. It's leave an' survive or stay an' die. Don' be a fool..."

Dakmund opened his mouth but his words were buried under the horns that rang out, penetrating every chamber in Grimwhal. The king assumed his full stature, though his defeated expression failed to match his confident demeanour.

"It's too late..." he said.

Beyond the chamber, the sound of rushing feet, clanging armour, and calls to arms created a cacophony of noise. Dakmund turned to the wall and picked up Andaljor, the legendary weapon of clan Heavybelly. With a hammer at one end and an axe at the other, it was a formidable killing tool in any dwarf's hands.

"Ye shouldn' o' come," Dakmund repeated. "But I'm glad we will go to Grarfath's Hall together, Brother."

Doran hadn't taken his eye off the maps. Pressed for time, his mind worked fast. It had been decades, maybe longer, since he had analysed these maps, but it was all coming back to him; specifically a certain tale their father had told them when he was only a child.

"We can still get everybody out!" he exclaimed, stopping Dakmund in his tracks.

"I've seen what we're up against, Doran. There will be no pushin' through 'em to escape now that they're at our doors." Dakmund shut his eyes again. "I've doomed us all..."

"When Father was a boy," Doran said frantically, "the city was under siege: it was the Hammerkegs, I think. Grandfather wasn' sure the defences would hold at the time - that's why we overhauled them - so he sent everybody into the tunnels."

"He's right," Drelda added. "I was among them."

Doran hammered his finger into the map. "Those tunnels still exist; last I heard we were jus' usin' 'em for storage. We can get everybody through there!"

Dakmund had the spark of hope in his eyes. "Where do these tunnels lead?"

Doran moved the maps around until he found one of Dhenaheim. "Right there!" He was pointing to the western banks of the Largo River. "It's a trek an' a half, but we can seal the tunnel behind us - they couldn' follow!"

Another horn blew while Dakmund considered the new course of action. "The tunnels," he agreed.

What followed was chaos. Doran and Russell did their best to follow in Dakmund's wake, but his stream of orders only created more chaos in every direction. Heavybelly warriors began pushing to the main entrance, ready to repel their enemy and give the people as much time as possible to flood the tunnels, led by the queen-mother.

The wounded would all need more time to be evacuated, with at least two dwarves required to move every one. Doran got that all too familiar feeling when he was on the precipice of a battle. The hairs on the back of his neck stood strong against his collar. His heart thundered in his chest. His mind began to quieten, ready to analyse his environment and his enemies.

Passing back through the throne room, the stout ranger paused briefly behind his brother to retrieve a fallen helm. It had been a long time since he had last worn anything with the sigil of his clan on it.

It felt good.

"Ye're not exactly dressed for battle, Rus."

The old wolf hefted his trusty pick-axe in both hands. "I haven't needed it yet," he replied.

Along with the king and several hundred soldiers, Doran and Russell entered the long, wide passage that led to Grimwhal's thick doors. The son of Dorain couldn't count how many times he had led the Heavybelly army down this passage and out into war. This felt very different. He had yet to even face this new enemy and he was sure the war was already over, his people defeated. They just had to hold the line...

"Where's ye shield guard?" Doran asked, searching for any sign of the loyal warriors entrusted with the king's safety.

Dakmund pointed his mouth over his pauldron. "I lost 'em in Khaldarim," he lamented.

Doran had to concentrate then to keep one foot marching in front of the other. "All o' 'em?"

"Aye," his brother replied.

Doran didn't know what to say and was thankful to be passing Pig at the time. He untied the Warhog and gave it strict instructions to follow the flow of Heavybellys into the tunnels. His orders were likely misunderstood by the old animal, but when pushed in the right direction Pig followed his nose - specifically the food being carted down into the tunnels.

The warriors of Grimwhal moved aside, allowing their king to the front line. There were already teams of Heavybellys there heaving the mighty bolts across the sealed threshold - no battering ram was getting through them any time soon.

Dakmund walked out in front of the line and turned back to face his kin. The king had the look of a dwarf who had only just returned from battle, his armour marred and his face beaten. Dakmund still held himself like a warrior though; still a strange sight for Doran. Andaljor suited his broad frame, appearing to be wielded with ease despite its considerable weight.

"*Who fancies a drink in Grarfath's Hall tonight?*" the king bellowed to a resounding cheer. "*Right now, our families are escaping into the old tunnels! This will take time! It is our job to make sure they get it, even if we have to pay for it with our lives!*" The Heavybellys roared, a sound so fierce Doran wouldn't be surprised if their enemy retreated.

"*We will hold them here for as long as possible!*" Dakmund continued. "*But this is not the day clan Heavybelly falls into ruin! We will survive so that no citizen of Grimwhal suffers the same fate as the Stormshields! If you hear my horn, we...*" The king caught himself and shared a look with his older brother. "*We will retreat to the tunnels ourselves! This wretched menace that plagues our land will never stop, and I will not see our people left defenceless! This isn't about dying in our home! This is about preserving our clan!*"

Doran shifted his good eye to inspect the warriors surrounding him. They weren't entirely moved by the king's final words - no dwarf wanted to contemplate retreat, for dying in the process would jeopardise their place in the Father's Hall. Unlike those around him, the stout ranger could see the sense in Dakmund's words and, perhaps, even see something of his old brother again.

But the clan needed to be picked up.

"What are we?" Doran yelled in his gruff voice, just as he had done many decades earlier.

"HEAVYBELLYS!" came the deafening reply, unaware that the exile had been the one to speak.

Doran repeated his question and the clan shouted their answer again. *"No son of Grarfath dies today!"* he yelled back before receiving an appreciative nod from his younger brother.

The clan beat their weapons into their armoured chests again and again until another sound silenced them all.

The ballistas were firing...

Bolts, two and a half times the length of the average dwarf, were being unleashed across the plains. It was raining death that none could withstand given the silvyr tips that headed every bolt. There was an agonising pause as the ballistas were reloaded.

Doran turned to the doors and braced himself. "What *exactly* are we up against 'ere?" he asked Dakmund.

"They walk like men," the king replied, his eyes locked on the doors. "They even fight like men. But they are not o' such ilk. None 'ave seen what lies beneath their dark armour. Jus' make sure ye aim for the head."

Doran cocked an eyebrow. "The head?"

"Anythin' else an' they'll jus' get back up..."

Doran lost his focus and turned to face his brother. "They get back up?" he clarified, sure that Dakmund had lost his mind.

Another salvo of ballista bolts were let loose beyond the doors.

The king spared him a glance. "I told ye they're not men. They're unnatural. Monsters o' The Dread Wood."

Doran looked the other way and met Russell's eyes. "The head," the old wolf said boldly.

There was another pause as the giant ballistas were reloaded, only this time the silence that followed was interrupted by a shrieking roar. The stout ranger couldn't say he had ever heard a sound like it, though to be heard so clearly from behind the doors it had be a very large beast. He looked up at Russell who appeared just as quizzical - a bad sign considering the two had made a career of hunting down every known monster.

The ballistas never fired again following that roar, though the entire mountain shook and debris rained down from the ceiling. Doran waited anxiously for another wave of ballista bolts to cut through the icy air, but there came nothing but an eerie silence. So confused was he that the ranger failed to even ask the question aloud. In all his years, he had never known anything that could wipe out all of the ballistas in one attack.

Then, there was nothing at all - not a sound.

Despite the quiet that settled over the passage, the dwarves were so tense that their collective breath was barely audible. Doran reminded himself to breathe, a key strategy in any fight if there was a chance it would go on and on.

Then it began to get hot.

The son of Dorain could feel sweat gathering in his eyebrow and saw it dripping down Russell's temple. It was uncomfortable and disturbing: this particular passage had never been anything but freezing.

"What foul magic is *this*?" he mumbled to himself.

A murmur broke out among the clan until one dwarf pointed at the doors. "*Look!*" he cried.

Waves of heat were rippling off the surface of the doors. This was soon followed by loud *pangs* as the metal was battling with two very different temperatures. Then, on the inside, large patches began to melt, and slowly oozed towards the floor. The clan's murmurs quickly became audible questions, many of which were edged with a tone of fear.

It would have been easy to give into that same fear, but Doran, son of Dorain, of clan Heavybelly was nothing if not stubborn. *"Come on then!"* he growled in his native tongue. *"My axe is hungry!"* His rant set off a few close by, who shouted their own war cries, before it spread throughout the clan. Only Russell was quiet, his feral, yellow eyes fixed on the doors.

The heat intensified and even the overlapping bolts began to melt in their stirrups. Very soon, the doors were unrecognisable, their patterns and shape reduced to dripping slag.

BOOM!

Doran flinched with everyone else. The impact echoed down the passage, assaulting their ears. The doors were physically out of place now, their shape becoming convex. Another earth-shattering impact knocked the doors farther still, bending the heated bolts all the more. The third, thundering *boom* revealed a crack of light between the doors. It wasn't the light of the sun, however, but orange flames.

The fourth impact was also the last. The weakened bolts snapped and the doors flung open with dramatic effect. A wave of fiery heat washed over the clan, followed by the cold breeze of Dhenaheim's plains. Whatever had wrought the doors was naught but a shadow beyond the dancing flames and clouds of smoke.

Doran gripped his double-headed axe with white knuckles. He told himself that whatever came at them, it would still succumb to the silvyr that made his weapon so deadly.

But then he saw what marched through the ragged flames and knew he looked upon death. His nerves were frayed instantly, robbing him of thought or prayer. Numbed as he was, one feeling rose to the surface and demanded his belief.

This was the end...

CHAPTER 23
A TIME TO ACT

Seated on Velia's throne, the king of Illian fell deeper and deeper into thought and concern. The sound of Lord Carrington's voice had become a drone in the background, his words lost on Vighon. Even the Archon's presence, beside the lord, was barely noted by the northman, whose focus was held by the parchment in his hand.

General Garrett had given him the missive only seconds before he assumed the throne. The writing was that of Eatred's, his court mage, who had spoken again with his council in Namdhor. The report was dire, to say the least...

Having read the report from the capital three times, Vighon now knew that the dwarves of Dhenaheim had been savaged by this new invader; a fact that was only just starting to sink in. The various clans had arrived at Namdhor and what was left of them had set up their camp on The White Vale.

According to King Uthrad of Silvyr Hall, only himself and King Gaerhard of the Brightbeards had survived the invasion. King Torgan of the Hammerkegs was dead, along with King Thole of the Goldhorns. King Gandalir and the Stormshields had been wiped out from their youngest to their oldest. It was impossible for Vighon to comprehend the magnitude of that statement. Hundreds of thousands of dwarves had been slaughtered and apparently in as little time as six months.

There had been no mention at all of the Heavybellys...

The report went on, adding to the weight pressing down on Vighon's shoulders. According to King Uthrad, this enemy was moving ever eastward, towards The Iron Valley and into Illian.

What in all the hells was coming for them?

There was one person who was going to discover the truth of that question and he had practically ordered her to go. Right now, as he resided on a throne, Inara was flying towards these invaders on her own. What had he done?

"Your Grace?" Lord Carrington's voice finally broke through to the king.

Vighon looked up from the parchment in a daze, as if he was only just beginning to wonder what he was doing there. His fist gripped the hilt of the sword of the north. Even without drawing it from the scabbard, the blade felt heavy. He knew this couldn't be the case since silvyr was notoriously light. But, to the king, it was heavy...

It reminded him of the oaths he had taken, to the people, to the realm... to himself.

"An opportunity has arisen for you to prove your loyalty, Lord Carrington." The king stood up and descended from the podium. "Rally your bannermen at once and have them march to the mouth of The Iron Valley."

Lord Carrington's face went through a multitude of expressions before landing on confused. "Your Grace?"

Vighon held up the parchment. "Dhenaheim has been invaded and Illian is to follow." There were clearly more questions waiting on the end of the lord's lips, but the king continued, "We will meet this threat as a unified country. Every man fighting under one banner is easily our greatest advantage."

Lord Carrington stumbled over his words. "Invaded, your Grace? By who?"

Vighon didn't answer straight away, curious as to why the Archon showed no similar distress. "We don't know," the king admitted. "But they have bested the dwarves and driven them into our lands. Send word ahead to Palios: inform them we will be passing through and any soldiers there are to join me. Have Galosha and Barossh send as many as they can and meet us in the north."

The lord of Velia cleared his throat. "At once, your Grace."

"General, choose a small company of your best to travel with us. Inform the rest that they are to stay in Velia until my return."

The general appeared conflicted. "Your Grace?"

"I want men here that I can trust," Vighon explained.

"What of our force in the north?" the general questioned.

The king turned to Lord Carrington. "Send word to Grey Stone and have the soldiers there return home at once. Send a similar message to Lady Gracen of Lirian - I want every man she can spare."

The lord bowed his head and left the chamber, soon followed by General Garrett. Vighon crossed the open space to stand before the seven mages of the Archon. All of them remained silent, their masks reflecting the king's derisive expression.

"My business in this city is far from concluded," he told them. "I *will* return and I *will* root out any who seek to harm this kingdom. In my absence, it is in your interest to find those who conspire and have them turned over to the custody of my men upon my next arrival." The king nodded at Alijah and the pair made their leave.

One of the masters, however, called out, halting their exit. "It would be easy to find the culprits, if there are any, were we able to use more powerful magic. If we could consult the books you confiscated from Korkanath, your Grace, we might even deal with this conspiracy ourselves..."

"You have all the magic you need, Master. The books of which you speak can help no one - I told you that many years ago." Vighon didn't wait around for a reply; he had a journey to begin.

Everything felt rushed after that, but at least they were moving forward. Every second that passed was a second this new enemy drew closer to Illian and Inara flew into danger. Sir Ruban and the king's guard surrounded him as they made their way through the streets - Vighon was already thinking about reaching The Selk Road and removing his crown.

General Garrett had the men forming up outside the city, preparing to ride and march north. It would be another day before Lord Carrington's own forces were ready to join them on the road. Vighon had decided that was time Illian didn't have.

Passing by the dark walls of Valatos filled the king with an urgent sense of anxiety that he had to fight to keep down. The issues surrounding the mages and their conspiracy to fracture the kingdom would have to be left unresolved - a guaranteed thorn in Vighon's side that would pain him every day.

Seeing Alijah by his side, it felt natural to voice his thoughts, just as he had done when they were younger men. "Am I doing the right thing?" he asked, his eyes scaling Valatos's high walls.

"You are king," Alijah pointed out. "It is your duty to prioritise the needs of the realm. I would say an invading force is more worthy of your attention, though the separatists here will need seeing to."

"Has Erador ever faced a threat of this magnitude before?"

"You mean a threat from inside *and* outside?" Alijah shook his head. "It's endured its fair share of wars, but never with a foreign invader. And given what's happened to the dwarves, we have to assume these invaders pose a greater threat than the orcs ever did."

Vighon didn't even want to imagine such a foe. "I shouldn't have sent Inara..."

"You didn't," Alijah said firmly. "From memory, no one has ever told Inara what to do."

"She's alone up there," Vighon continued, his concern spiralling. "By the time we reach the north she will have already faced the enemy."

The half-elf turned to look at his old friend. "I will go," he

280

insisted. "I will fly north, ahead of you. Malliath is faster than Athis; we might even reach her before she crosses Vengora."

Since they were abandoning their investigation into Valatos, the king could think of no reason they would need Malliath's might on the road. "I cannot ask you to do that," Vighon replied as they passed through Velia's main gates. "You are the king of Erador; you shouldn't be fighting our battles and I wouldn't risk another kingdom losing their ruler."

Alijah flashed his signature smile. "You can neither ask me nor command me, good king. I go as a brother seeking his sister."

Vighon stopped before reaching his horse and turned to his oldest friend. "Then I would pray that you make all haste. Make sure she doesn't do anything too... *rash*."

Alijah tilted his head. "Upon our safe return, and there will be such a thing, I urge you to finally act on these feelings. I have a feeling they will be reciprocated this time."

Vighon frowned, imitating confusion. "I don't know what you mean."

Alijah's smile broadened as he parted from the king. "I mean act while you're still young enough to do so." The half-elf spun on his heel and walked backwards. "You old fool!" he added in jest. At that moment, Malliath's majestic form dropped out of the sky and landed in the field beside the road.

Vighon mounted his horse, an entirely different animal, and watched in awe as the black dragon leaped back into the sky. His awesome wings flapped hard and blew the king's dark hair over his shoulders. Fate was truly smiling on him to have delivered such a powerful ally in this time of great need. More than that, however, it was good to have his friend back.

CHAPTER 24
MARKED BY THE PAST

Asher's oldest memories washed over him, taking him back to his years under Nightfall's shadow. He stood motionless in the forest, face to face with his foe. To be looked upon but never seen was the way of the Arakesh.

The soldier from Lirian moved his torch left and right, his eyes searching the darkness. It felt entirely foreign to Asher to be caught in that firelight and remain hidden, a product of the Drakes' magic.

Seeing nothing, the man continued his search for the ranger. He was accompanied by three others, all of which passed by without concern. They were followed by more groups, all equally fooled by the mirage of the Drakes' making.

Like the soldiers of Lirian, Asher was in company. Along with Adan'Karth, dozens of Drakes had volunteered to man the boundary and keep watch for any stray soldiers who might discover a weak point in the barrier. Since being attacked at the hunters' camp, The Evermoore had been flooded with more soldiers, all sent on the orders of Lady Gracen.

They were all hunting Asher.

There had been several times the ranger believed the moment

was upon him to make his leave and find his way back to Lirian. Every time, Adan'Karth had held him back, pointing into the depths of the dark forest. It might have been moments or minutes later, but more soldiers always emerged from the place the Drake had pointed to. Trusting their eyes, Asher remained by their side... for now.

As the night stretched on, the ranger only became more agitated with his lack of action. His days of waiting patiently for targets to be in the right place at the right time were long behind him now. He wanted to be moving. He wanted to be pressing Lady Gracen for answers. It had been a long time since anyone wanted him dead, but to go to the extent of hiring assassins of Nightfall spoke of more than wanting. The lady of Lirian *needed* him dead.

Putting the ranger's skills to shame, the Drakes moved about the forest unheard. After more hours of waiting for his opportunity, Asher came to realise he was seated on a log with Adan'Karth alone. Bare chested, the young Drake appeared more in tune with the animal world than any other. A closer inspection showed that his right horn had a deep chip in the middle - the mark of a sword. It was so easy to forget that he and his entire species had lived many years as orcs.

"*What will you do when you reach Lirian?*" Adan'Karth asked quietly.

Asher considered his reply carefully, aware that the Drakes might attempt to foil him should they learn of the violence he had in mind. "*I'm going to talk to Lady Gracen,*" he said simply.

Adan'Karth turned to look at the ranger. "*You will hurt her?*"

"*Often the threat of harm is enough to yield answers.*" Asher knew his statement to be true, even if it didn't entirely answer the Drake's question.

"*You are sure the lady is behind this hunt? That she sent the assassins?*"

Asher produced the parchment bearing her sigil. "*I don't know for certain that she paid for the assassins, but I know she sent those hunters to bait me.*"

"*This proves it?*" Adan'Karth scrutinised the parchment.

Asher pointed to the mark at the bottom. "*That sigil belongs to her family.*"

The Drake manipulated the parchment to better see every aspect of the design. "*A sigil...*" he muttered.

Seeing his confusion, Asher elaborated, "*It's the mark of her family name. Since they're all dead, only Lady Gracen can use it.*" The ranger gestured to the faded tattoo on Adan'Karth's arm. "*Like that,*" he said.

The Drake's confusion only increased as he looked at his own arm. "*That is a sigil?*" he questioned. "*We have often wondered what they mean.*"

Asher raised an eyebrow. "*None of you know what they are?*"

Adan'Karth shook his head. "*We all possess one, though they differ in size and pattern. They were distorted after our transformation.*"

The ranger nodded his understanding. "*And none of you remember your old lives.*"

The Drake brushed his fingertips against the faded sigil. "*Do you know what this means?*"

Asher squinted at the mark. "*It's too dark to make out.*"

Without pause, Adan'Karth opened up his free hand and produced a small orb of pure light. Asher instinctively sheltered his eyes from the soft glow before looking to the edge of the magical barrier.

"*They cannot see the light,*" Adan'Karth reassured. "*Only loud noises can penetrate the shield.*"

After blinking a few times, the ranger became accustomed to the light and turned his attention back to the faded sigil on the Drake's arm. The faint scales that layered his skin had indeed taken much of the colour and pattern out of it. During his time clearing out the cities and towns, however, Asher had come across every tribe of orcs and even interrogated a few of them, learning what he could.

"*That sigil belongs to the Born Horde,*" he explained.

Judging by Adan'Karth's reaction, that meant nothing to the Drake - though he was clearly interested.

"*They were at the top of the orcish hierarchy. Karakulak, their king, was from that tribe. They're all gone now, the Born Horde. After their defeat in the north, Karakulak's tribe took the brunt of the punishment from the surviving tribes. The last I heard, and this was years ago, was that a new tribe had assumed control: the Sons of Gordomo.*"

"*The orcs are few,*" Adan'Karth commented with a hint of sadness.

"*There are a few tribes still left,*" Asher recalled, though the years following the war had been violent and bloody. "*They hide in Vengora, like their ancestors.*"

Adan'Karth probed the faded sigil. "*I remember none of it. To capture even a single memory is to grasp smoke with your bare hands.*"

"*Take that as a blessing,*" Asher remarked. "*The life of an orc is... not worth reliving.*"

The Drake went quiet, his contemplation his own for the moment. "*Is that a sigil?*" he asked, looking at the black fang tattoo under Asher's left eye.

Asher was naturally self-conscious of any detail pertaining to his appearance. "*Of sorts,*" he answered cryptically. "*I was marked as a child... a long time ago.*"

"*What does it mean?*"

"*It's a fang,*" the ranger replied, "*if a crude one. You've heard of the Outlanders in The Wild Moores?*"

"*The elves have told us of them. They warned us to stay out of The Wild Moores.*"

"*Good advice,*" Asher concluded. "*The humans who live in there are savage. They live in war-like tribes akin to the orcs.*" The ranger pointed to the tattoo under his eye. "*This means I was to be a hunter in my tribe.*"

Adan'Karth's reptilian eyes settled on Asher with a touch of revelation in them. "*You come from The Wild Moores?*"

"*Apparently. I don't really remember any of it.*" Whenever Asher tried to surface any memories from that time of his life, he found only a blank spot that was quickly filled by a violent upbringing in the depths of Nightfall.

"Abun'Sun was right: you are unlike anyone we have ever met..."

"I could say the same of you, Adan'Karth. Your people seem content to stay within their borders. I get the sense that you're more curious than the rest of your kin."

The Drake set his eyes to the dark forest again, the light from his orb slowly fading. *"I would very much like to see this world,"* he admitted.

Before Asher could comment, another group of Lirian soldiers came by, the rustle of their attire impossible to miss. Like all the others, they approached the unseen barrier and paused to share quizzical expressions. They were about to move off when another soldier emerged from the south with a torch in his hand.

"Oi!" he called out. "I've been looking for you lot for ages!" The soldier approached the group, careful not to fall over the forest debris. "I only stopped to have a—"

"We know what you stopped for, Wendel," one of the group interrupted. "We haven't got time to stop. You heard Captain Kade: no one goes home until the ranger is caught. I, for one, would very much like to feel the softness of my own bed again."

"Haven't you heard?" The new soldier continued, "The captain's just sent Byron's group back."

"What?"

"Apparently," the new soldier explained, "Lady Gracen is going north, to the capital. The captain has sent Byron's group to join the escort."

The group of soldiers collectively cursed their luck. "And we have to stay here? Searching in the dark!"

Asher sat back and let his muscles ease as they chose a diverting path. They were terrible hunters. Had the ranger possessed only a fraction of his skill, he would still have evaded the noisy morons. He did, however, have his own path to consider now.

"She's going to Namdhor," he mused.

"*Namdhor?*" Adan'Karth questioned in elvish.

"*Lady Gracen, she's heading to Namdhor.*" The ranger looked over his shoulder. "*I need to reach the north...*"

"*We have waited here a long time,*" the Drake pointed out. "*You should return with me to Ikirith and rest; the north will still be there when you rise.*"

Asher opened his mouth to argue but he couldn't deny the fatigue he was still experiencing after his recovery. Fleeing the Lirian soldiers had shown him that he had yet to return to fitness - something he would need to make the trek north.

"*As you say,*" he conceded.

Together, they melted into the shadows and journeyed into the depths of Ikirith, where a world of colour and tranquillity awaited. It was all too easy to imagine himself living out what was left of his life in such a place.

If only he wasn't so maligned by fate...

PART THREE

CHAPTER 25
HOLDING THE LINE

Coated in sweat and blood, Doran Heavybelly knew nothing but the swing of his axe. There were times his vision was clouded, be it by the blood of another dwarf or blind rage, yet still he heaved that axe and aimed high. His foe were relentless in their advance, adhering to no form of conventional warfare or invasion tactics.

It seemed that neither was a necessity when the attacking army had no fear of pain or death.

The son of Dorain ploughed his axe into the neck of one, burying it so deep that whatever foul magic kept the creature on its feet lost its hold. As it dropped to the floor, motionless, he got a good view of the horde that waited patiently behind it.

They were the manifestation of pure menace. To simply look upon them gave every dwarf pause. Shrouded in their black armour and cloaks, a design of which Doran had never come across, the dark knights appeared as wraiths sent from the pits of the deepest, darkest hell. Though sleek in shape, their helmets revealed nothing of what creatures occupied them.

How many had Doran introduced to his axe only to watch in

horror as they rose from the ground without so much as a sound, oblivious to their mortal injury? Taking off their heads wasn't easy given their elevated stature and the sheer number of them assaulting the clan. The ranger had lost and regained sight of Russell two or three times in the melee. From what he could glean, however, the old wolf was ripping off heads with a dwarven sword in one hand and his pick-axe in the other.

It wasn't long before the dark knights pierced the dwarven line and cleaved their way into the ranks. Soon after, Doran was slowly retreating while simultaneously navigating the bodies of his fallen kin behind him. There were far too few of the enemy littering the floor...

Every now and then, Dakmund would come into view with Andaljor chopping down around him. The king severed all manner of limbs, reducing the dark knights to crawling or writhing monsters that still refused to halt their advance. His axe would slice through necks and heads before Andaljor was twisted in his grip and the hammer thundered into helmets and chests. He was a worthy king of Grimwhal.

Doran barrelled into one of the knights that had found an opening across his brother's back. The armoured fiend went down under his weight and felt the bite of the ranger's axe as it split its head in two. Rising back to his feet, he took out the legs of another and beat its head in with the pommel of his weapon. It wasn't enough to stop the knight, but it gave Doran just enough time to prepare for the next three who came for his life.

It was packed from wall to wall with constant fighting, but Russell's supernatural senses gifted him a degree of accuracy very few could boast. Using his curse to his advantage, the old wolf launched his pick-axe at the three knights pressing down on Doran and caught one in the head, slamming it into another. Two clan warriors burst forth from the chaos and tackled the third, bringing it down under their swords.

This left Doran with a clear view of one particular dark knight.

Like the others, it was satisfied to simply walk into battle with its jagged sword held casually by its side. Setting it apart, however, was the crown that had been blended into its helm - a circlet of five tall spikes. A silhouette against the low flames that licked the doors, this knight spoke of an evil that surpassed the others, sending a shiver up Doran's spine.

Challenged by a group of Heavybelly warriors, this crowned knight exploded into action, spinning and skidding around the dwarves. His sword lashed out in every direction, parrying and attacking, until, one by one, the warriors were felled by his blade. Dakmund also witnessed the feat and roared in defiance with Andaljor in his hands.

Doran leapt forward and gripped his brother with all the strength his fingers had left in them. *"Don't,"* he warned in their native tongue. *"We need to retreat!"*

With every word, they were already stepping backwards from the oppressive knights. Doran's heels felt for bodies and discarded weapons - to fall over now would spell his doom.

Dakmund used the haft of Andaljor to block an incoming attack. *"We can't retreat yet!"* he shouted. He followed his parry with a mighty swing of the hammer end and knocked the dark knight onto its back. *"They need more time!"* the king added before bringing the axe end down into his opponent's head.

The stout ranger dared to look through the throng of fighters and spy the crowned knight again. It killed dwarves with greater efficiency than its peers and sped up their advance.

Before he could renew his argument to retreat, a devastating cry echoed through the passage. It came from the hall on the left that led to the eastern ballistas. Doran cut a swath until he could see the hall in question. His jaw dropped. Three dwarves came running out of the hall on fire with dying screams on their lips. They rammed into the dark knights crossing the threshold and brought them down under their heavy weight.

Within the hall, the bend in the corner glowed a warm orange and Doran knew immediately what was coming for them all. "*SEAL THE DOOR!*" he bellowed, barging his way towards the thick wooden posts that propped the slab of stone above the threshold.

The ranger repeated his order again until those nearby caught on. As two of his clan knocked one of the posts out with their hammers, Doran had no choice but to throw himself into the second one. His momentum was enough to shove the post out of place, but it was also enough to launch him into the eastern hall, where that glow was swiftly revealing itself as a torrent of fire.

His fate appeared to be sealed in that moment: if the falling slab of stone didn't cut him in half, the jet of fire now consuming the entire eastern hall would roast him alive. To die saving the lives of his brothers was a good way to die; possibly even enough to redeem him and have a place in Grarfath's Hall.

It paid, surprisingly, to have a werewolf for a friend.

Russell's meaty hand grabbed Doran by the ankle and dragged him to safety with only a second to spare before the slab fell into place and the fire reached its end. "Get up, Heavybelly!" the old wolf commanded, retrieving his pick-axe from the corpse of a knight.

Doran couldn't believe he was actually still breathing. He also didn't have the time to dwell on it. On the other side of the passage, the doorway to the western halls was aglow with approaching fire. This time, it was Doran's turn to save Russell. Wrestling him around the waist, the son of Dorain threw them both farther down the passage, away from the main entrance. They narrowly escaped the flames that burst into the passage and set a dozen dwarves and a group of dark knights alight.

The chaos was tenfold by the time Doran and Russell found their feet again. Dwarves were on fire and screaming as they ran wildly in every direction. The dark knights caught in the blaze simply fell to the ground, dead. The crowned knight strode through it all, his blade whipping out here and there to dispatch any who sought to bring him down.

"What's causing the fire?" Russell wiped the sweat and blood from his brow.

Doran didn't have time to think about it. "Dak!" he yelled over the fighting, searching frantically for his little brother, and fearing the worst.

"There!" Russell pointed to the west wall, where the king of Grimwhal was crushing a dark knight's head between the stone and his hammer.

Doran fought his way through until Dakmund could hear him. *"We need to retreat!"* he barked. *"Order them back, now!"*

Dakmund nodded this time - there were too many of their kin lying on the floor. One deep breath and he blew into his horn, filling the chamber with his coded message. The horn blared out several times while Russell and Doran protected the king.

"To the tunnels!" Doran pushed another dwarf away, forcing him back.

For the most part, they had to back out due to the sheer number of dwarves that occupied the passage and the larger number of enemies that funnelled through. Doran was only too happy to keep swinging. He pictured the fall of Hyndaern and all the people that had been murdered by these foul creatures. He thought of the children...

"Come on!" he growled, hacking with abandon.

Time became increasingly hard to measure, but the ranger was sure at least an hour or two had gone by before they cleared the throne room and entered the city proper. From there, Grimwhal opened up, offering the warriors multiple passages and chambers to flood.

It was tempting for Doran to order a group of Heavybellys to surround his brother and escort him to the tunnels, but Dakmund was now more than just his little brother; he was their king. He also wielded Andaljor. Those two facts alone meant he had to lead from the front and head their defence, not their retreat.

Looking around the streets of Grimwhal, it was comforting to discover that none but soldiers remained. Hopefully, he thought, the ancient tunnels were crammed with the city's inhabitants and they were fleeing east with all haste. Doran didn't even want to entertain the number of Heavybellys that had been slain between the main doors and his current position. Seeing his brothers all around him, however, only fuelled his rage and kept his muscles pumping.

They continued their relentless defence just as the enemy continued their merciless advance. Mile by mile, Grimwhal was invaded. It became apparent that the dark knights cared little for the city itself, displaying restraint where its destruction was concerned - typically in these situations, the opposing foe would see to it that their enemy's home was utterly destroyed in their wake. This army, dredged from the hells, had come only for them, it seemed. They wanted life, not stone...

Finally, after losing every inch of ground, the company of dwarves fought before the open doors of the ancient tunnel system. Sundry items were scattered across the floor where the people had moved as one giant rabble to escape certain death. The warriors at the back turned on their heels and dashed into the tunnels, while Doran and those at the front continued to repel the knights.

As always, the crowned knight made himself known. One dwarf after another fell at its feet until Dakmund himself was the only one left to confront it. The king didn't have the energy to let loose a war cry; his reserves the only thing keeping Andaljor in motion. The crowned knight moved as swiftly as ever and evaded every blow of both axe and hammer. For Doran, it was all happening too fast and his little brother was too far to reach.

Another Heavybelly got in the ranger's way and he missed the crowned knight's strike - but he heard Dakmund's pain. The king roared and fell to one knee with the edge of a sword biting deep into his thigh. The wicked knight pulled free its weapon and angled the tip to drive it home into Dakmund's heart.

Doran was naturally opposed to this and burst through the battle to kick his brother in the shoulder, shoving him aside just enough that the sword plunged into that same shoulder and missed his heart. Dakmund cried out as he was stabbed, kicked, and dropped to the floor: but he was alive. Fortunately for Doran, the king also took the knight's sword with him.

"Now ye're goin' to get it!" he promised.

The silvyr axe cut through the air left then right, each strike forcing the crowned knight to dance away. His fury, however, robbed Doran of some precious energy. A downward strike buried the axe in the floor and he failed to find the immediate strength to retrieve it. The crowned knight jumped forwards and slammed a boot into the ranger's face, taking him from his feet.

The malevolent knight looked down on the son of Dorain, his spiked crown glistening with blood. Slowly and deliberately, it yanked Doran's axe out of the floor and spun it around in one hand. The ranger moved his hand to pull free the sword strapped to his hip, but he knew there was no way he could move fast enough to stop his own axe from killing him.

As the crowned knight lifted the weapon, a familiar voice shouted, *"You dropped this!"* From the side, a badly wounded king launched himself at the fiend and returned the creature's sword, driving it deep into its gut. Like the others, it would survive such a blow, but Dakmund's attack was heavy enough to barrel the knight over and drop Doran's axe.

As the weapon hit the floor, so too did the king, his wounds too much to bear.

"*Brother!*" Doran yelled, struggling to his feet.

Russell skidded in on his knees and helped Dakmund to rise as much as he could. Doran found Andaljor in his sights, abandoned on the floor, but the legendary weapon was soon behind the advancing enemy. The prince of Grimwhal that lived deep inside of him wanted to fight through hell to retrieve that weapon, but the brother in him wanted to get Dakmund out of this alive.

The crowned knight stood up with no assistance and calmly removed the sword from its midriff.

"Run!" Russell turned Dakmund around and half carried him into the tunnel.

Doran wanted to take the fight to the crowned knight, but how much more did he really have to give? He was sporting his own injuries and his muscles felt starved. The ranger yanked on the arms of any dwarf still consumed with the battle, tugging them towards the tunnel. The doors were too large and certainly too heavy to close in a hurry, but this was a factor taken into account by Doran's grandfather.

The passage sloped down and round, taking them deeper into the mountains. After a few hundred yards, past stacks of crates and barrels, the hewn stone came to an end and the natural rock surrounded the dwarves. Torches lined the walls, showing them all the way. In the distance, Doran could just make out the back of the exodus, but he was looking for something in particular.

The ranger skidded to a stop when he came across one of the iron pins sticking out of the wall. It was the size of his arm and twice as thick, its length half buried in the rock. He quickly caught another dwarf charging past and directed him to the identical pin on the other side of the tunnel. This had never been done before, but dwarven architects were just as good at bringing things down as they were at building things up.

The pins had been hammered into the tunnel walls at specific places and pushed in to a predetermined length. The mathematics behind it all was beyond Doran's expertise, but he had faith in his people, especially where destruction was concerned. Using the flat of his axe, the son of Dorain slammed the end of the iron pin, hitting it with all that he had left.

The dark knights were passing beyond the hewn stone now and steadily advancing into the tunnels. There was something eerie about the way they walked - it would have been less intimidating if they had charged. It spoke of a confidence in their victory.

By the fourth beat of his axe, the rock began to crack up the wall. The dwarf on the other side of the tunnel had made better progress

298

and had nearly made the pin flush with the tunnel. Deep fissures were opening across the ceiling now, dropping chunks of stone. Doran roared with every hammering blow, determined to save what was left of his people.

Finally, after nearly a dozen blows, the tunnel could hold no more. Doran and his fellow dwarf dashed to catch up with their kin and avoid the collapsing ceiling behind them. Smaller rocks dropped and bounced off their armour, but the slabs of immovable rock thundered into the ground behind them, filling the tunnel.

Deciding that he had escaped the most dangerous area of the collapse, Doran stopped and looked back - the crowned knight was staring at him. The creature's black mask and tall spikes were visible but for a second before the last rock fell into place and sealed the tunnel shut.

～

What followed was arduous, a taxing trek through the oldest of tunnels beneath the mountains. For all of his injuries and exhaustion, Doran made sure to accompany his brother at all times. The king of Grimwhal had been laid down in the back of a cart and covered with blankets.

The clan's healers had descended upon him with haste and seen to his wounds, ensuring the crowned knight would fail in its endeavour to kill the strong dwarf. Doran still hated seeing his brother so weak when all of his memories of Dakmund had him so full of life.

Their mother, Queen Drelda, was never more than a few feet away from the cart. Astride Pig, the queen-mother was making a statement to the rest of the clan. Though she said not a word, the rest of the Heavybellys made no protest where Doran was concerned and tolerated his presence.

Russell walked beside the eldest son of Dorain, pulling his horse by the reins. The ceilings were so low that riding his mount was out of the question.

After the first day and night of trekking, the old wolf began to appear agitated.

"What's with ye?" Doran asked, noting the old ranger's clenched fist.

Russell shrugged off the dwarf's concern. "I'm fine. I could just do with some fresh air is all..."

His answer didn't sit right with Doran. He took an extra moment to consider the possibilities, aware that little shook his friend so visibly. Fighting that dread horde was new for all of them, but Russell was a fighter through and through, whatever the foe. Then it came to the stout ranger and he knew exactly what the issue was.

The revelation brought with it no lack of trepidation.

"It's a full moon tonight!" Doran hissed.

Russell didn't take his yellow eyes off the tunnel ahead. "Tomorrow night," he corrected. "But the wolf knows it's coming..."

The son of Dorain took in their surroundings, dire as they were. The tunnels were filled to bursting with dwarves of every age. He could think of no worse conditions for Russell to transform into a killing machine of claws and fangs.

"How close to the surface are we?" the old wolf asked, struggling to unclamp his jaw.

"At this pace?" Doran calculated as best he could. "I'd say the next dawn, maybe later."

Russell nodded. "When we breach, I'll have to go my own way; get as far from the clan as possible."

Such an occasion had only arisen a handful of times during their friendship and Doran knew better than to try and offer his help. There was nothing to be done in the face of such a powerful curse. The wolf will out, as Russell had always said.

"Jus' don' go west," Doran advised. "You'll run straight into these fiends an' they'll 'ave no problem cuttin' down a werewolf."

"Don't worry about me," Russell insisted. "I've been doing this for a long time now."

And so they continued their trek in silence in a bid to give Russell a chance to control the beast raging within. Doran desperately wanted to take charge of the exodus and have every dwarf running for the surface. If he told a single one of his kin that they were accompanied by a werewolf, Russell would lose his head before they caught the first breeze of the outside world.

As expected, the clan stopped and rested for a portion of the night. Russell didn't sleep a wink. Neither did Doran. The stout ranger had laid down and kept his eye on him. Though the full moon was his trigger, he had seen Russell turn violent in the hours leading up to its arrival. Credit to him, he sat perfectly still with white knuckles clenched around his knees.

Doran kept one hand on his axe...

The last few hours of their journey felt like a lifetime. Doran would have busied himself by making conversation with his mother or his weary brother, but the son of Dorain was sure to keep his only eye on Russell. If he went feral, Doran would have none but himself be the one to put him down.

Proving he still had all the innate senses of a true dwarf, Doran finally emerged from the tunnels and looked upon the cresting sunrise he had predicted, a golden light he had surprisingly missed. There were cheers from many that they had survived the invasion as well as the long trek. It was much colder on the surface, a fact that was lost on Russell, who was visibly sweating.

"*We need to move south!*" one of the generals yelled over the rabble. "*Follow the Largo River and cross The Old Bridge! From there, we can make for The Iron Valley!*"

Dakmund waved his hand lazily in the air to signal his agreement. Doran turned to translate the general's words for Russell, but the old ranger - absent his pick-axe - was already steering his horse east, towards a shallow and rocky portion of the river.

"Rus!" he called, breaking away from the clan.

"You shouldn't be following me, Doran."

The son of Dorain stopped by the bank of the river. "Jus'... Jus' be careful, ye hear? Come an' find me in Namdhor!" Russell gave no reply but continued his way across the freezing river. "I can take yer horse!" Doran offered, sure that it would be torn apart come sunset.

Russell halted in the middle of the shallows and looked back at the dwarf. "I'm hoping the horse will satiate the wolf. It might be the only thing that stops it from tracking you..."

"Trackin' me?"

Russell looked almost apologetic. "I've known you a long time, Doran. The wolf has your scent..."

It was a grotesque thought, but undeniably logical when he put it like that. It wouldn't have been the first time the werewolf had tracked Russell's scent back to civilisation or a person and wreaked havoc. Doran tried not to dwell on the horse's fate and nodded his friend on with a quick prayer to Grarfath and Yamnomora.

Returning to the clan, Doran hurried to catch up with his brother's cart. They still had many miles of the Largo River to trace before they came to The Old Bridge and the icy air would do Dakmund no good at all. His integration, back into the trail of dwarves, was met with a mix of responses. There were those who wouldn't even look at him, choosing to accept that as an exile, he simply didn't exist. Others didn't mind looking at him, their expressions scornful. Here and there, however, the occasional soldier would pat him on the arm as he walked past; a thanks for his aid in the battle.

Though they were among the few, it was more than the son of Dorain could ever have hoped for.

As summer's midday sun reached its apex, The Old Bridge was just coming into view. It didn't feel right to be crossing it without Russell by his side, but Doran had to put such feelings aside and remind himself that the old wolf would be just fine without him. After all, wasn't it Doran who often put Russell in danger in the first place?

As the first half of the clan crossed over to the eastern plains,

Doran found his head lifted by the outcries that erupted from all around. For just a moment, the son of Dorain gripped his axe as he himself was gripped by fear. It was only when he observed the direction of everyone's gaze that he realised their calls had not been one of dread.

Athis the ironheart was soaring above them!

His red scales cut a line through the blue sky. From the ground, they could all see his slate-coloured chest that ran down and into his long, spiky tail. Like all dragons, he was magnificent to look upon, whatever the vantage.

And, of course, wherever Athis could be seen, Inara Galfrey was close by. As the dragon glided and banked, Doran caught sight of the Dragorn's red cloak flying out behind her in the rushing wind. He wanted to yell her name and call her down to help his brother - not that any dwarf would ever allow a half-elf to use magic on them.

Any thought of a joyous reunion with the Dragorn was quickly replaced by a rising sense of panic. Inara was heading west, farther into Dhenaheim and undoubtedly towards the dark army and their shrouding mist.

"No," he whispered. "No, no, no!"

"Doran?" his mother enquired.

The son of Dorain spun around to see his mother guiding Pig away from the procession. She looked as tired as everyone else, but still maintained that core of strength that had served as a supporting pillar for Grimwhal.

"*She doesn't know what she's flying into!*"

Drelda raised a bushy eyebrow and looked from her son to the departing dragon. "*You know the rider?*"

"*Aye, she's a friend. She's also the most powerful weapon the realm has got. I have to warn her!*"

"*You would go after her, back into Dhenaheim?*" Judging by her tone, the queen-mother considered such a thing to be beyond foolish.

Seeing his brother's cart roll by, Doran was instantly torn. His clan might not want him around, but they were travelling into Illian, a place they didn't understand - they needed him. But Inara was perhaps the best chance they had of defeating this new foe and she was blindly flying into their midst.

"*I'm sorry...*" he said, giving his answer.

Disappointed and now very concerned, his mother sighed. "*It seems you are destined to leave me.*" With that, the queen-mother climbed down from Pig and handed the reins over to her elder son. "*May Yamnomora give you the speed and Grarfath the strength to see you returned to me. The Heavybelly clan needs the sons of Dorain...*"

Doran was unaccustomed to hearing such sweet words but for in his dreams. He would have held his mother then had she not turned around and walked back into the waiting embrace of her guard. Since no one else appeared bothered by his departure, the stout ranger mounted his Warhog and made for the west, into certain peril...

CHAPTER 26
AN ORPHAN OF TWO WORLDS

There was but one place in all of Illian that felt like home to an elf. In The Moonlit Plains, south of The Evermoore, a small forest had become something of a large forest. At its heart, beyond the view of travellers, lay Ilythyra. It was a place where the trees grew impossibly tall and impossibly thick with as little as decades behind them.

Such was the magic of the elves...

In the soft orange glow of floating orbs and organic lights, formed from tree roots, any of the fair folk of old should be content. But there was one elf who was never content, for all his endeavour.

High above the ground, perched on the end of the decking that stretched out from his cosy hovel, Galanör, of house Reveeri, looked down on the elven paradise and sighed. For the last three years he had taken up residence inside Ilythyra, in a hollowed bower carved out of an enormous tree. For the last three years, he had tried to embrace the ways of his ancient kin and live in harmony with nature - a peaceful existence.

For three years, his hands had itched to pick up his swords...

Today, like every day behind it, was a struggle. He had already sprinted through the forest, taking the highest and most dangerous path across the thick branches. Hours had been spent sitting with others, practising his magic; something he had long neglected in favour of his swords. Using the patience his ancestors were renowned for, Galanör had sat through another of Lady Ellöria's history lessons.

He had spent almost all of that time fantasising about his days as a ranger of the wilds.

Now, perched above the peace and tranquillity, the elf realised he had stopped wondering what tomorrow would bring. For most of his four centuries, he had never given much thought to what would come next; everything had been about training and bringing glory to his house, to his father above all. Then, forty-five years ago, he met a young mage, a human by the name of Gideon Thorn. After that, everything had changed for Galanör.

Every day brought with it a new adventure and a chance to be someone else. He had relished the life of a ranger, putting his skills to good use for a change.

"You're thinking about it again, aren't you?"

Galanör whipped his head around to see Lady Ellöria standing on the end of the decking. Her blue gown flew out into the breeze, along with her silky blonde hair. Her skin was smooth and pale, a contrast to her vibrant green eyes. The lady of Ilythyra was the only elf who could sneak up on Galanör. After three years of contemplation, he had decided she used magic to float...

"I can see it on your face," she continued in their native tongue. *"Your mind is cast back into the past."* Ellöria turned to look at the chest that resided in the corner. *"Something you cannot let go of,"* she observed.

Galanör didn't dare lay eyes on the chest. If he looked at it for too long, he knew the swords therein would be in his hands within seconds. Guardian and Stormweaver, gifts from Queen Adilandra herself. He battled with the urge to retrieve them.

"I'm trying," he said.

"I see you try every day," Ellöria replied. *"But you hold on to that which lies behind you. Remember, Galanör; it was you who came to us. Killing is killing - your words. How many years did you fill with slaying orcs after the war? You spilled enough blood to fill a dragon. Again - your words. You wanted a new start to—"*

"I know," Galanör cut in. *"I'm sorry,"* he immediately apologised. *"I forget my place."*

"You are tightly wound," the lady remarked.

Galanör shrugged in a very human way. *"I'm trying to find a better path."*

"You are a product of your upbringing. Four hundred years of fighting lie behind you; you can't expect three small years in Ilythyra to undo all of that."

"I want... I want to be more than I am. I just don't know how to exist without a sword in my hand."

Lady Ellöria smiled at the elven ranger. *"To seek growth in one's self is no bad thing. And it doesn't mean you have to become someone you aren't. You remind me of an elf I once knew..."*

Galanör turned away from the sprawling view to face the lady. *"Who?"* he asked, sure that there had never been another elf like him.

"Lady Syla, of house Arinör," she said casually, despite the legend that she had just named.

"You knew Lady Syla?" Galanör stood up as Ellöria entered his hovel behind him.

"Oh yes; she instructed the queen and myself in the art of the bow. Syla was a warrior. She only bore the title of lady because of her family's position. She was never happier than outside the city, facing Valanis and his hordes. She struggled to find the balance between her own nature and that of her people."

Galanör couldn't believe he was being compared to one of the greatest warriors who had ever lived. Growing up, he had read all that there was on Lady Syla, even to the extent of studying her tactics.

Ellöria extended her hand to smell a flower beside his bed and it opened up to her. *"She fought with herself for centuries, often vowing to her family that she would leave the warrior's life behind after the war."*

"How did she find a balance?"

"She didn't," Ellöria said bluntly, her tone absent its usual melody. *"As history notes, Lady Syla rode into every battle she could. Then, Valanis killed her."*

Galanör took a breath and let that sink in. *"You're saying if I don't find a different way of living, it will be the end of me?"*

"No," Ellöria replied softly. *"You came here because you were lost. An elf stuck between two worlds. If you remain in man's world, apart from your kin, you will witness their cycle of birth and decay for eternity. If you return to Ayda, and the ways of our ancestors, you will have to reject the very skills your kin ladened you with. I did not pledge to help you find a better way to live or to embrace the ways of old. I pledged to help you find yourself. If that is to be the warrior then so be it. But you will leave here sure of yourself."*

Galanör's lips formed to say thank you, but the word never found life in the world. Another elf had appeared by the edge of his decking - Aenwyn. He had grown particularly fond of her since his arrival in Ilythyra and enjoyed more than a few conversations with the hand-maiden. Her duty to Ellöria, however, had kept her at arm's length, preventing him from making anything more of their budding friendship.

"My Lady," she greeted with a bow.

"Aenwyn," Ellöria replied pleasantly.

"Word from the north, my Lady," Aenwyn reported, her tone grave. *"The lands of Dhenaheim have been emptied of dwarves."*

"Emptied?"

"There is talk of an invader," Aenwyn shared, glancing at Galanör. *"Every surviving dwarf has taken refuge in Namdhor."*

Galanör frowned. *"What could possibly force the clans out of their own lands?"*

Lady Ellöria moved to the edge of the decking, concern creasing her smooth features. *"Nothing good for Illian,"* she said absently. *"Where is the king?"* she asked Aenwyn.

"Hopefully not chopping another lord's head off," Galanör commented, still struggling to comprehend Vighon doing such a thing.

"He decapitated the governors," Aenwyn corrected, *"not Lord Thedomir."*

Ellöria appeared entirely unamused by the exchange. *"The king?"* she reminded.

Aenwyn bowed again in apology. *"He travels north, back to Namdhor in the company of a few hundred men. They left four days ago."*

"And the dragon?" Ellöria queried.

"There have been no further reports since leaving the king," Aenwyn replied curtly. *"There is nothing to suggest they have deviated from their northerly heading."*

"Inara?" Galanör had to enquire given the serious demeanour of the lady.

Ellöria paused as if assessing Galanör. *"Inara and Athis were seen leaving Velia days ago, travelling north. But there are sightings from Grey Stone to Velia of another dragon... a black dragon."*

Dragons came in many colours, but Galanör knew of only one with black scales. *"Malliath?"*

"We believe so," Ellöria confirmed.

"And Alijah Galfrey? Has he been seen?"

"We have eyes and ears in many places, but none that can attest to identifying him."

This was something of a revelation to Galanör. *"How long have you known Malliath was in Illian?"* His pointed question was proof alone that he didn't truly consider himself a part of the elven hierarchy.

"Since he first arrived in Grey Stone and saved the king's life from an ambush," Ellöria said plainly.

"*Why wasn't I told?*" he demanded.

The lady of Ilythyra had but to look at Aenwyn and the elf quickly disappeared. "*There are few who know what really happened to my nephew, but I am among them, like you. I am aware of the importance his return might spell for the realm, and I am taking the necessary actions.*"

"*What actions?*" he enquired.

Ellöria raised her hand to quiet him. "*I did not inform you, Galanör of house Reveeri, because his presence bears no consequence for you.*"

Galanör opened and closed his mouth. He might not be in the elven hierarchy anymore, but Lady Ellöria was over a thousand years old - a fact that demanded his respect.

"*I should have been told,*" he said calmly.

Ellöria raised an immaculate eyebrow. "*Why?*"

"*Because I know him... knew him. I know his parents. I was there when...*" He finally closed his mouth and kept it closed. He couldn't settle on the exact reason why he should have been informed.

The lady approached, her movements graceful, even by elven standards. "*You have played your part in more than one event that has shaped the realm,*" she complimented. "*Perhaps you should stay away from matters surrounding the king, including this threat from beyond Dhenaheim. You need time to introspect; something you cannot do when you're dragged into current events.*"

Galanör's argument was rising to the surface but he quashed it and, instead, bowed his head. "*You're right, of course, my Lady. I came here for a reason...*"

Lady Ellöria began to walk away before stopping in front of the ranger. "*You are not a prisoner here, Galanör. This is not Dragons' Reach and I am not Adriel. You made it clear at the end of The War for the Realm that you were not to be commanded by my family anymore. If you wish to go, then do so. Should you choose to stay, however, I expect you to continue your efforts of self-discovery without distraction.*"

Galanör bowed again. "*Thank you for your patience, my Lady.*"

Raising his head, Ellöria was already across the decking and disappearing around the girth of the mighty tree. He had just received a lot of information that needed digesting. In the past, he would have picked up his swords and begun his routines to help him think. In Ilythyra, they encouraged him to sit and meditate.

He settled for a second run...

CHAPTER 27
A DARK KNIGHT IN DHENAHEIM

At the top of the world, Vengora's snow-capped tips welcomed Inara and Athis to a land of inescapable beauty and never-ending cold. Beyond Illian's northern border, the white plains stretched in every direction, halted only by Vengora's twin sister: The Whispering Mountains. Between the two ranges lay the vast and mesmerising valley that was Dhenaheim.

Inara cast her eyes to the north and the end of any map she had ever seen. The Whispering Mountains sprawled to the west and curved south, mirroring Vengora. They were distant and small from the Dragorn's vantage in the sky. It was in those distant mountains, however, that the dwarves had carved out their majestic halls of stone and left their mark on Verda for all time.

They were all empty now...

They had both witnessed the last of the clans following the Largo River, heading for Illian soil. With no dwarf to call it home, Dhenaheim was once again an untamed and desolate realm. The ability to traverse the barren land was a testament to this invader's tenacity and strength.

Having cleared the Vengoran mountains, Athis glided through

the centre of Dhenaheim. So immense was the valley that they could see everything and anything that might cross the snows. What they failed to see, given that they weren't looking, was anything crossing the snows via the sky.

Inara instinctively ducked as Malliath's hulking form descended from the heavens, narrowly missing Athis's head. The black dragon displayed his enviable speed and cut through the air, quickly putting distance between them. Athis huffed and beat his wings with all the force he could muster. No dragon enjoyed being shown up.

What are **they** *doing here?* Inara asked.

Getting in my way, Athis replied with obvious irritation.

When the two dragons were finally side by side, Inara reached out through her bond with Athis to connect with Malliath and therefore Alijah. They were well aware that the black dragon would say nothing while they were all bonded, a fact that only made their interaction an awkward affair.

Alijah turned in his saddle to look at his sister. His black cloak whipped about behind him, flashing the red interior. He looked so confident astride Malliath, a contrast to fifteen years ago when they had both been new to flying together. The saddle was still an odd sight to Inara, who had been trained in the ways of a Dragorn, an order which believed that dragons were not to be ridden, as a saddle would suggest. It certainly looked comfortable though...

What are you doing in Dhenaheim? I thought you were with the king...

Alijah would have replied straight away if he wasn't laughing to himself. *Hello Inara,* he finally said, his tone suggesting there was sarcasm to come. *We're fine in case you were wondering, despite the fact that we haven't stopped since leaving Velia. How are you? It must be nice to see a familiar face.*

Inara caught herself and let her brother feel some of her embarrassment. *Sorry. I am glad to see you. Sometimes, when you don't see anyone else for a while, you can forget how to talk to other people.*

I'm the same, Alijah confessed. *Malliath and I have been known to carry on private conversations for days at a time. It's usually followed by an equal amount of days apologising to the palace servants for my rude behaviour.*

You speak so easily of your kingship, Inara observed. *I can't imagine my brother with a crown on his head. Or servants for that matter!*

Alijah grinned. *That's funny. Growing up, that's all I ever imagined!*

Athis mentally nudged Inara to focus, a reminder that she so easily fell into old ways around Alijah. Regardless of all that had transpired and all the time they had spent apart, she still enjoyed his company. There weren't many in her life she could so naturally talk to.

You have left the king? she enquired, approaching the topic from a different angle.

At his behest, Alijah explained. *The reports coming out of the capital are only getting worse. Like Vighon, my concern for this new threat was growing.*

We can handle ourselves, Athis felt the need to say.

No doubt, Alijah quickly recovered. *But even astride Athis the ironheart, I couldn't let my twin sister fly into the unknown,* he added with genuine warmth.

Inara gave an appreciative nod while simultaneously instructing Athis to calm down. Of course, the root of the dragon's discomfort was Malliath beside him. The older dragon unsettled them both, regardless of Alijah's demeanour.

Well your company is most welcome, Inara said. *How goes the king's investigation?*

There is no investigation, Alijah replied surprisingly. *Vighon has called on Lord Carrington's bannermen to join him on his return to the north.*

That was the first good decision Vighon had made in a while, though Inara kept that thought between herself and Athis. *I haven't seen anything but fleeing dwarves,* she said instead.

Alijah surveyed the land. *Well, nothing can pass through here without us seeing them. Malliath and I would appreciate some rest before that happens...*

Of course! Inara replied, intoning some of her gratitude. *You must be exhausted.* In truth, Malliath appeared to have more than enough strength to keep flying until the land ran out.

The dragons searched for a high outcropping, somewhere they could maintain the advantage over anything that crossed the flat valley. Between the four of them, starting a fire was easy, though dragons had a tendency to create larger fires than any camp required. Alijah was the one to usher in the first flame, sparking a cosy fire for the two riders, both nestled within the lying forms of their dragons.

"I'm not accustomed to seeing you use magic," Inara commented over the fire. "You always preferred the bow..."

"I'm still better than anyone you know with a bow," Alijah replied with his amusing arrogance. "But some things have changed - I'm not the boy you grew up with."

"Well," Inara quipped with a broad grin, "you're still cocky, so that hasn't changed." The pair fell into laughter, a sound the Dragorn had long missed, even if she hadn't realised it until this very moment.

"I will concede that some things have changed," Inara continued. "You were always confident, but I could always see through it to the young boy desperate to prove himself. *Now...* Now, you carry yourself with such surety, as if your every action has already been calculated."

Alijah smiled as he stoked the flames. "It has," he said with the same surety Inara was speaking of. "Besides my work in Erador, I've spent a great deal of time studying the Dragon Riders. *They* were a confident order. They knew themselves, a truth they shared with their dragons. It only made them stronger."

"And you know yourself?" Inara couldn't help the suspicion that crept into her voice.

"You mean because of what The Crow did to me?" Alijah laid it out plainly. "I know myself," he reiterated. "Better than you know yourself at least."

The latter naturally began to stir Inara's feelings, just as it did to Athis. "I know myself," she stated as a fact.

"What does your sanctuary look like?" Alijah asked.

Taken aback, Inara glanced at Athis, feeling vulnerable at the idea of sharing such details.

"You have a sanctuary yes?" Alijah pressed. "A place out of time and reality where only you and Athis can exist?"

"I know what a sanctuary is," Inara replied with the perfect eye roll. "It's all very personal and not a question you ask."

"That sounds like something a Dragorn would say..."

"Well, I *am* a Dragorn," she protested.

Alijah tilted his head as if he were assessing his sister. "I would wager it's somewhere high, your sanctuary that is. As close to the sky as you can get with your feet on the ground."

For just a moment, Inara wondered if the dragons were still connecting their minds together. "It is, as it happens," she admitted reluctantly. "It's a beautiful range of mountains, unlike anything you'll find in all of Verda."

Alijah appeared to be very proud of himself. "Somewhere in those mountains, there will be a cave or a lake or a valley... *something*. It will be too small for Athis to fit. In there, you will find the path to yourself."

Inara didn't say anything at first, her mind quietly eager to seek out such a place.

"It's that easy?"

"Stepping inside is easy," he answered. "Living with the changes takes time. And it can be hard, at first."

Inara was moved, excited almost, to think of a place inside her own sanctuary she had never come across before.

Athis did not share her feelings...

The sun was reaching for the western tips of The Whispering Mountains by the time Alijah and Malliath were ready to scour Dhenaheim. The snowy plains were painted in the burnt orange of the dying light - soon, they wouldn't be able to see the mountains in the north.

"We should go," Inara said, doing her best to disguise her frustration with urgency.

"We would be better waiting until true dark," Alijah countered. "They see better at night than they do at twilight," he added, gesturing to the dragons.

Inara looked out from the plateau, her red cloak flapping about her legs in the northern wind. She wanted to be out there, hunting this new enemy. Staying still disagreed with her.

"Come," Alijah bade, seated by the fire. "Eat. You will need your strength if we meet these invaders."

"I don't want to eat," she replied, deliberately slowing her speech so as not to be heard snapping at him. "I want to find whatever threatens Illian and—"

"And what?" her brother cut in. "What will you do when you come across a force so powerful it beat the dwarves?"

Inara knew her reply before Alijah had even finished his question though, upon reflection, the Dragorn could see that *deterring* the invaders from advancing any farther was folly.

"We will show them these lands are guarded by dragons," she settled on. "And then we will report our findings to the king so that defences might be put in place."

Alijah nodded along as if he was only casually listening. "Why?" he asked, his expression perplexed.

"Why?" Inara echoed, equally perplexed by his strange question.

"Why do you do it? Any of it? They call you the Guardian of the Realm, but why are you guarding it? Gideon left and the Dragorn with him - I remember the speech. You're free of your order; you could go anywhere. There's more to Verda than Illian or Dhenaheim. You could go east and see where the sun truly rises. Or west and leave Erador behind in search of land evergreen. And this certainly isn't the top of the world, as much as everyone would like to believe it is."

"I..." Inara couldn't quite put her sense of duty into words; it was simply a state of existence she had long accepted. "From the time of the elves, the Dragorn have watched over—"

"Those aren't your words," Alijah interrupted. "I can practically hear Gideon's voice. Why are you spending your eternal days alone, watching over a kingdom that isn't your own?"

"This is our home," Inara answered, taking the words from Athis's mind. "Our parents are here, we were raised here..."

"You're immortal, Inara. The world is yours!"

"Why are you asking me this?" she demanded, tired of his argument.

"Because we're about to face an army that threatens our long lives. You could leave all this and come back in a few hundred years. It won't matter who wins now - everyone currently alive will be dust one way or another."

"You cannot be serious?" Inara stepped closer to the fire, the flames mirroring those that ignited in her heart. "You would suggest leaving everyone to this enemy just because they're all destined to die anyway?"

"I could never do such a thing," Alijah replied calmly. "I am a king and a man who knows what he was put on this earth for. But you are free, bound only by your sense of responsibility, a responsibility put upon you by an order that abandoned you, I might add."

"Why are you speaking like this?"

"Because I want you to live, Inara. I want you to be free, to enjoy your life and the wonders this world has to offer. But, if you keep travelling down this path you will be throwing yourself in front of danger time and time again. And for what? A kingdom you can never

THE KNIGHTS OF ERADOR

connect to? You would bear witness to an endless cycle of death - I do not want that for you..."

Inara sighed - her exasperation knew no bounds when it came to her brother. "What you want for me is irrelevant. You chose a different path, one that took you away from me, from our home." She shook her head and moved closer to Athis, seeking comfort from him instead.

It was in the crook of his front leg that she waited for nightfall to assume its dominance over the land. The stars became veiled by thick rolling clouds that came in from the north-west.

"Inara..." Alijah's voice carried on the breeze, his tone laden with apology.

The Dragorn wasn't interested in talking anymore. "Let's go," she said, climbing onto Athis's back.

The red dragon stretched his wings and dropped off the side of the cliff while Malliath and Alijah shot up into the air. With as brief a discussion as possible, they decided to fly farther north, reasoning that any invading force would be following The Whispering Mountains in order to root out the dwarven kingdoms.

The bond between Athis and Inara was constantly probed by Alijah, perhaps searching for a way of apologising. Neither of the companions intended on letting him in to do so - further conversation would likely just irritate them.

Hours went by as the hidden moon undoubtedly shifted across the sky. Athis reported signs on the ground, evidence of a massive force marching over the plains, as well as debris from the fleeing dwarves.

Again, Alijah made it clear that he would like them all to bond via the dragons. This time, however, he didn't have the feel of someone who wished to apologise.

What is it? Inara wasn't even bothering to hide her annoyance.

Something doesn't feel right, he said. *I can feel it in the air... magic.*

Inara put her feelings towards her brother to one side and

focused on their surroundings. Athis too could feel the hum in the air, a resonance that only those attuned to the realm of magic could understand.

Dhenaheim is the last place I would expect to feel magic in the air, Inara replied. *The dwarves don't practice it and they've ruled these lands for thousands of years.*

Alijah half stood up in his saddle and pointed ahead. *There! That fog... it's unnatural.*

He's right, Athis agreed. *It isn't moving with the wind.*

The dragons closed the gap and brought the wall of fog within feet of them. It reached from the ground to the clouds above, offering a view of nothing between the two.

Can you see anything on the ground? Inara asked her companion.

No. Athis banked away from the fog and glided back again. *There is no sign of any life on the ground.*

We're going to have to go in, Alijah concluded.

Before Inara could suggest otherwise, her brother disappeared beyond the mist. Malliath's hulking form was lost to them immediately, as if the black dragon had been swallowed by a Leviathan.

Fools! Inara cursed.

Athis had no choice but to follow them in and use what senses he could to track them. The world was instantly robbed from Inara's eyes and they were both plunged into a realm of mist. It was eerie for the eyes and ears. Every now and then, Inara would hear another set of beating wings, but they didn't always come from up ahead.

Alijah! she called across the bond. It became apparent, however, that Athis and Malliath were no longer connected.

Dragon and rider continued to fly through the fog, relying entirely on Athis's acute sense of direction to avoid the mountainside. That same sense, unfortunately, would do nothing to stop them from flying directly into Malliath.

We should get out of this mist, Athis warned.

Agreed. Turn us around.

Beating wings flapped over their heads and vanished into the fog again. Athis changed direction for a second time and followed Malliath, but for all his speed there was no catching up with the larger dragon. Then, from behind them, another set of beating wings raced by.

How did they get behind us? Inara looked back over her shoulder but struggled to even see beyond Athis's tail.

Again, Athis altered his flight path in a bid to reach Malliath. A dark and massive shape glided past them at great speed, the tip of a black wing visible as it cut through the mist.

What are they doing? Inara fumed. "Alijah!" her audible yell was quickly absorbed by the fog.

Another dark shape angled up right in front of Athis's face and disappeared into the mist above. This would only have served to anger the Dragorn all the more, except she also heard beating wings behind them at that same moment. Looking back, Inara caught sight of a pointed tail diving down before vanishing altogether.

Athis...

The red dragon shared her dread. *We are not alone,* he replied gravely.

Inara searched in every direction. *What are—*

A deafening shriek-like roar bombarded the pair before a nightmarish dragon hurtled out of the mist and rammed into Athis. Inara didn't even have time to scream, thrown as she was from her companion's back.

The fog enveloped her, blinding the Dragorn to everything. She could feel the pain in her ribs where Athis had been slammed, but her concerns were focused on the sudden stop that was coming her way. She had no idea how high they had been, but the ground was no doubt waiting for her with its definitive embrace.

It was only her connection to Athis that told her not to panic. As always, they could sense each other's presence, allowing them to home in and find one another.

Now! Athis cried.

Inara twisted her body round and reached out. Athis's spinal horns came into view below her and rose up until she was able to grab a hold. Her grip firm, the red dragon beat his wings and took off, avoiding the ground and certain death for them both.

What was that thing?

A dragon! Athis shouted his response as he was forced to bank and dive under another surprise attack.

Inara caught only a glimpse of the beast that flew over them, its ragged maw wide with serrated teeth. *A dragon?* she echoed incredulously.

There was no time for anything else before a second dragon emerged from the mist and grappled with Athis in a tangle of raking claws and gnashing teeth. Inara held on with white knuckles and a touch of magic, but it was still a jarring experience, not to mention the pain from the slashing claws.

Through their bond, she acquired an impression of the dragon they were fighting, though she couldn't believe what Athis was relaying. Proving the nightmare to be real, the dragon arched its neck to bring a mouth of fangs around Athis's head. The face that came at them was not of any dragon Inara had ever seen before.

It wasn't sight, however, that revealed the truth of this creature. Athis's nostrils inhaled the dragon's scent and found it to be a familiar one, if a foul one. There was no question that the monster attacking them was, for all its appearance and animation, very dead...

It's a Reaver! Inara exclaimed.

Athis manoeuvred himself to evade the clamping jaw, which came together with a vicious *snap*. Now, the entire head was visible, revealing a pair of milky white eyes inside skeletal eye sockets. The skin and muscles were in various states of decay and its rough scales were scattered in patches along its angular body. Ragged wings, torn throughout, flapped furiously to keep it level with Athis.

Inara had no choice but to crawl around Athis's back and spikes to avoid the gnashing head. Its beastly jaw was top heavy, rising to a point from a ridged and curving chunk of bone. One successful ram would see that horn easily pierce Athis's scales and thick hide.

We need to get away from this thing! she warned.

I'm trying! Athis roared and clubbed the undead dragon with his front claw.

The Reaver shrieked and clawed all the more at Athis's body to keep level. Then, showing itself to be agile in the air, the undead dragon brought its wings in and dropped to curl around Athis before spreading its wings to bring it up again. A devastating tail whipped across Athis's ribcage, the pain passing through to Inara, who almost slid right off his hide.

Scaling back to her usual position, the Dragorn just caught the last glimpse of the Reaver before it vanished back into the mist. Athis continued his flight through the fog, his jaw clamped in a bid to shut out the pain. There was no time to take stock of any injuries, of which there were now many, before the Reaver returned.

This time, the hellish fiend emerged from the haze with a blast of fire shooting from its mouth. So decayed was it that the fire could be seen through jagged holes in its jaw. Inara ignored the monster's details and focused on the jet of fire tearing through the mist towards her. With an outstretched hand, the Dragorn expelled her magic and erected a shield of hardened air to meet the blaze.

It was blinding. The flames spread across the shield, testing Inara's strength, and illuminated the cloud that engulfed them. There were more shadows dancing around them, their bat-like wings flapping through the fog. Dealing with one dragon Reaver was unthinkable, but to be surrounded by them was implausible. How could there be any dragon Reavers at all?

The dragon with the pointed snout finally relented its attack and continued along its path into the fog once more. No sooner did it disappear than another Reaver shot out with all four of its claws diving down on them. Inara immediately sensed Athis's intended reaction and used another spell to keep her pressed against his neck. The red dragon twirled in the air, bringing his tail with him. The spiky ended clubbed the incoming Reaver across the face and sent it sprawling into the clouds.

His orientation corrected, Athis made for the edge of the mist with all haste. More Reavers made themselves known, determined to dog them through the sky and bring them down. Inara hurled spells in every direction with nothing but hope that one of them might strike true.

"Alijah!" she screamed, desperate to see her brother in the chaos.

The horn-snout reappeared, this time right in front of them. Its oppressive wingspan opened up, blocking their way and forcing Athis to dive. A shrieking roar told Inara that it was chasing them down, though how *far* down actually was remained a mystery. Thankfully, Athis had a better idea.

His red wings unfolded and their direction was altered with enough speed to apply pressure along Inara's spine. What they discovered on the ground, however, was bone-chilling. Through the wisps of fog they could make out the dark outline of numerous ranks - armour-clad soldiers marching over the plains of Dhenaheim. The sudden appearance of Athis didn't seem to bother the soldiers, who simply continued their march.

Behind Athis, the horn-snout Reaver was catching up. Their chase saw both dragons zig-zag over the top of the army, disorientating Inara all the more.

We need to get out! she reiterated.

We're close! Athis replied.

As close as they were, both dragon and rider would not be leaving the mist together. Without warning, another dragon rushed them, launching out of the fog from directly ahead. The Reaver angled up, avoiding any collision, but its powerful tail curled up and pummelled Athis under the jaw. It was a fierce attack with enough strength behind it to knock the red dragon from his flight and hurl him into a backwards somersault.

Inara was flung away with what felt like a broken jaw and a brief moment of unconsciousness. When the blackout abated, the

Dragorn was sliding down a snowy slope, her path clear of soldiers. When at last her momentum came to an end, her red cloak was wrapped around her head and her Vi'tari blade was twisted on her belt.

Everything hurt.

Even to groan sent a sharp spike of pain through her jaw. Inara reached out for Athis and found him to be some distance away in a similar state with damaged wings.

The snow crunched around her - the enemy closing in. Inara pulled back her cloak and rolled onto her hands and knees. More pain attempted to make itself known but the Dragorn gritted her teeth and focused what attention she could - there were soldiers everywhere. Clad in dark armour and black cloaks, the enemy approached from all sides.

A grunt of pain escaped her lips as she rose unsteadily to her feet. Her cloak fell back into place behind her and she drew her enchanted scimitar. There had to be thousands of them, all moving in on her perfectly in time with each other. They had to be Reavers all, but such a thought was hard to comprehend at this terrible moment.

A portion of the mist retreated, as if reined in by some supernatural master.

Death approached...

The horn-snout Reaver shrieked upon its appearance, its wings outstretched as it came to land. The soldiers moved aside, welcoming the undead dragon with seemingly choreographed movements. The hulking Reaver stalked towards Inara with its head dipping low and a flicker of flame sparking in its mouth.

She had reached the end then. A plethora of spells were at her disposal, but the strength to wield any of them sufficiently to withstand a dragon's breath escaped her.

But those flames never came. Instead, the nightmarish dragon closed its mouth and the soldiers came to a halt. It was only then, in the calm that followed, that Inara noticed the figure astride the dragon's back. Attired in the same dark fashion as the soldiers, this figure dropped down to the trodden snow with a black cloak flowing behind it and a tall crown of spikes. Before it passed the dragon's head, a devilish blade was pulled from a scabbard, its length ridged with sharp points of steel.

There were but moments before this crowned knight was upon her. Inara's fingers drifted over her belt in search of the pouch that contained her elixirs. Her hand, instead, paused over the pouch that housed the diviner, given to her by Gideon Thorn. Perhaps she should have contacted him before now, but her hubris had won out, damning her...

The Dragorn shook her head, ridding herself of such concerns. All that mattered right now was the foe walking towards her. By the shape of the glass vial between her fingers, Inara knew she was holding *Allidai's Voronum,* an elixir designed to put some fight back into her bones.

The vibrant yellow liquid was vile to the tongue and even worse on the muscles, but she had no time to contemplate. The liquid went down in one gulp and she embraced the pain and burning sensation that was ignited inside of her. Inara gasped, her injuries felt all the more now that she was fully alert.

The Vi'tari blade connected with her will and responded to the incoming strike from the crowned knight. Inara fell into the flow and worked with the scimitar, gripping it in both hands to put her strength behind the parry. She came face to armoured face with the dark knight and found nothing but malice emanating from the Reaver.

The combatants pushed each other away by the edge of their blades, only to come back together with a clash of swords again and again. The crowned knight was swift, his movements agile and his attacks incredibly precise. Inara had to work to hit anything but air while simultaneously blocking the sword that always came for her head. *Allidai's Voronum* kept her limbs moving and her scimitar swinging, but the elixir could only give her so much - she needed to end this.

To what end?

It was a disheartening question, but a valid one. If she bested this foe there were thousands to take its place and an unknown number of undead dragons hiding in the mist.

Since the elixir was unable to cross their bond, Athis could but whisper in her mind, though even his words felt faded, leaving the Dragorn with nothing but an impression of his feelings.

Make them hurt.

Inara embraced Athis's feelings as her own and lunged at the crowned knight with everything she had. On the attack, her Vi'tari blade danced through the air, pushing the dark figure back. For just a second, Inara actually saw herself ridding the world of the supernatural fiend. But, unlike any other kind of foe, the crowned knight had no fear of walking into her blade.

The scimitar ran him through with ease, piercing his back and cloak. An armoured glove wrapped around Inara's wrist and squeezed until her grip relinquished the Vi'tari blade. The pommel of the Reaver's hilt hammered her in the face, cutting a line through her eyebrow. Inara cried out and staggered backward, the pain blinding. Her cry was cut short when the air was kicked from her lungs by a boot in her chest. The next thing she knew, her feet were flying through the air and the snow rose up to greet her with the hard and unforgiving ground.

Allidai's Voronum was fading fast, a reminder that she should have studied alchemy just as much as her swordplay. There was nothing she could do now but cough and splutter as the crowned knight stalked towards her, a Vi'tari blade lodged in its chest.

With one hand, the Reaver removed the scimitar and tossed it aside. Inara tried to crawl backwards through the snow and icy sludge, her eyes fixed on the jagged blade being raised by the crowned knight. She had seconds remaining of her life before that sword came down and sent her to the next world. She thought briefly of her parents and then Vighon, discovering a tremendous amount of regret where the king was concerned.

The jagged blade was lifted above the Reaver's head in both hands. Inara stopped crawling, her fate sealed.

I love you, she told Athis, her heart aching to see him in all his majesty one last time.

The crowned knight took one last step and made to bring his blade across Inara's head. But the mortal blow never fell. Instead, the Reaver froze mid-stroke, his blade hanging in the air above her. Without explanation, it sheathed the jagged sword and took a step back before genuflecting with a bowed head.

Looking around, Inara could see that the surrounding Reavers, and even the dragon, had bowed their heads. There was no answer for what she was seeing, but Inara had no intention of staying on the ground. The Dragorn rolled over in a bid to pick her broken self up and froze, just as the crowned knight had done moments earlier.

"Alijah?" The name barely left her lips.

Her brother stood in the clearing, his cloak still in the quiet air. His suit of dragon armour was pristine, displaying no signs of a fight. Gone was his casual arrogance or even his air of confidence. What stood before her now was a man of sorrow.

"Why did you have to come here?" he asked. "I offered you a way out. A new life filled with love. You had but to take it and you would have been free, Vighon too."

Tears began to well in Inara's blue eyes. "Alijah?"

"You could have gone anywhere and been happy," he continued, becoming increasingly frustrated. "All you had to do was take those steps."

"What's happening?" Inara staggered to her feet as her gaze roamed over the bowing soldiers. "Why are they..."

"You're not strong enough to see this through," Alijah told her. "Only I can do what needs to be done," he added aggressively, thumping his chest.

"Alijah..." Inara's heart was breaking as the truth sank in.

"This is what I was born to do," he said with a half-hearted shrug of his shoulders, as if he had no other choice. "I'm going to unite all of Verda. But there has to be pain before there can be peace. I didn't want you to be here for that."

"What have you done, Alijah?"

He raised his arms to encompass the army around them. "I have done what no other could, even The Crow. The knights of Erador! They will help me bring order to the chaos."

"They're Reavers!" Inara spat.

Alijah remained calm. "The perfect army. When they fall, no one else suffers. There are no grieving wives or mothers. No children absent their father. They all died eons past. I have given them purpose again."

"You've made monsters of them," Inara accused.

Alijah's frustration was morphing into exasperation. "Sometimes, the world needs monsters. At least I have control of these ones."

"You lied to us," Inara continued, the sting of his betrayal stirring rage within her. "You said you came to help, to form an alliance. But you're just another invader..."

"I *have* come to help. And the alliance I'm going to create will bring about a kingdom that even Atilan couldn't have dreamt of. Imagine it, Inara - humans, elves, and dwarves all living under one banner. Erador, Illian, and Ayda united by a common cause: peace."

Inara shook her head in despair. "The world is more complicated than that."

"It doesn't need to be!" Alijah yelled, his calm demeanour evaporating. "You couldn't... You... You don't have the vision!" He began to pace, a process that worked to calm him down. "That's not your fault," he said quietly. "You weren't chosen. This is my burden, not yours."

"You have lost your mind," Inara glowered. "How could you do this? Look around you, Alijah. This is wrong. The dark magic you have harnessed to create these fiends is evil."

"You know nothing of magic!" Alijah snarled. "There is no light or dark. Magic just... *is*. The problem lies in the wielder. In the wrong hands magic can be used to tip the scales, be that for a good cause or an insidious one."

Inara felt like throttling sense into him. "You have allowed The Crow to poison your mind."

The mist beyond Alijah was battered away by Malliath's enormous wings. His dark bulk settled on the ground, shaking the earth beneath their feet. His purple eyes locked onto Inara with predatory intent.

"You're supposed to be wise!" Inara barked at the dragon. "You're the oldest dragon alive!" She gestured to the army of Reavers. "You should know better!"

Malliath created a rumble deep in his throat and bared his fangs. "I wouldn't talk to him like that," Alijah advised.

"I see now," Inara said, her veins igniting. "The Crow had a far simpler task than I thought. He had but to put you together. Malliath's mind has bent yours to his will. This isn't you—"

"You know as well as I that there is no him and me... There is only *us*. Seeing through Malliath's eyes has opened my mind, given me a picture so big it spans millennia. I have seen history unfold through him in a way you couldn't fathom. I see now what needs to be done..."

Inara frowned. "And what is that?"

Alijah took a breath and assessed his sister. "I'm going to change everything. But you won't survive it if you don't find your humanity. You need to take those steps, Inara, just as I told you. If you don't, I can't save you."

"What are you talking about?"

Alijah flashed the palm of his hand and expelled a staccato of lightning across the snow and into Inara. It was a short burst but powerful enough to knock the Dragorn off her feet with a clipped scream. It was hard to move after that. Her muscles spasmed beneath stinging skin, most of which was now covered in smoking leathers.

Alijah came to stand over her. "I'm going to break the scales," he finally answered, crouching down. "I offer you this one last chance. Flee Illian, flee the entire continent. There will only be suffering if you stay."

Inara strained to say something, anything. Her jaw, however, failed to move as she commanded, leaving her mute at her brother's feet. Seeing him now, she wasn't sure what she would say to him anyway. There was no doubt that she was many years too late to help him see sense.

"Monsters only beget monsters..."

Those words, The Crow's words, came back to her then. There was so much more to that statement, but her mind and body were in too much pain to fully comprehend it. All she knew was the person standing over her wasn't the brother she had loved. It shattered what remained of her broken heart and left her lying helplessly in the snow.

Alijah resumed his stature and positioned his open palm over Inara's body. "Don't come back." There was a blinding flash, an instance of pain, and then nothing at all...

CHAPTER 28
THE COMING OF THE TIDE

Namdhor, the jewel of the north, was always a sight to behold when returning home. Rising high above the ground, the city was surrounded by the splendour of the Vengoran mountains, white sheets of clean snow, and the sprawling King's Lake.

Seeing it now, crowded with dwarven refugees, Vighon was taken back more than a decade to when the land was similarly filled with human refugees from the southern regions. The dwarves of Dhenaheim, however, were far more self-reliant. Their camp was colossal in size and well established by the look of the markets in place.

General Garrett observed, "Even in the face of extinction, dwarves will always find time to trade."

Trading they were, but Vighon didn't miss those on the fringes, grieving their losses. So many of them appeared wounded, their clothes torn to rags in the desperate escape from their homeland. So many were in need of aid and they had arrived at his gates.

"See to it that the wounded are treated," the king commanded. "Every healer in Namdhor is to offer their help - the crown will pay. And get word to King Uthrad; I would welcome him in my hall."

Garrett refrained from any further comments and relayed Vighon's orders without delay. In the days since leaving Velia, the king had lost sleep wondering if he should return to Namdhor or not; after all, there was a disease in his kingdom and its source was Valatos. But, seeing the defeated clans of Dhenaheim, beaten and injured, on his land, Vighon knew he was exactly where he was supposed to be.

"I have been a fool," he muttered to himself.

Ruban, ever close, heard his king. "Your Grace?" he questioned.

"I lost my focus," Vighon said, urging his horse towards the city. "We have open communication between Namdhor and Grimwhal - I knew the clan's numbers were beginning to dwindle here. I should have been looking to the north, not south."

"To be fair to your Grace," the king's guard replied, "no one could have predicted a force so powerful it would defeat the dwarves."

"Predict it: no," Vighon agreed, "but we could have fought beside them."

Ruban turned to his king. "And died beside them?"

Vighon continued to look out across the camp. "If we had to..."

After breaking away from the small force he had travelled with from Palios, Vighon and his even smaller escort made their way up through the main street of Namdhor. They were met with cheers and hollers from the crowd that had gathered to welcome their king. But there were more than a few shouting for answers - apparently, the welcome some had for their king did not extend to the dwarven camp.

The Dragon Keep soon loomed at the top of the rise. Vighon had once hated the very sight of those dark walls, but he had done his best to undo his father's mark on the place. Long gone were The Ironsworn, as well as any relics of Namdhor's first ruler, King Gal Tion, the dragon-slayer.

Having spent days on the road, the king's bed called to his aching muscles. His days of lounging whenever he liked, however, had ended the day he was crowned. Instead of rest, Vighon walked past his bed and stepped onto his balcony, which afforded him a view of the eastern plains and the dwarven camp.

From this vantage, he could see that many thousands currently called The White Vale their home. It was a daunting sight that only added to the weight of responsibility he already carried. Dotted on all sides of the camp, were dwarven regiments from their surviving kingdoms, their improvised tents lined into neat rows. They enclosed the camp, but the opposing clans were sure to complicate such close living quarters.

To the north of their camp, closer to the mountains, lay the Namdhorian force. Stone barracks and a collection of forts had been built since The Ash War, giving the army a permanent base on the plains. Their presence, along with the dwarves, littered The White Vale with black dots - a messy blot on a previously pristine landscape.

Dragging himself away from the view, the king made his way to the war room. Over the last fifteen years, it had predominantly been used as a strategy room for planning the post-war rebuilding projects. Now, walking into the large chamber, the map carved into the length of the floor was decorated with small statues representing various forces across Illian. Dhenaheim was notably absent any statues...

A handful of captains used long sticks to push and pull the statues across the map as they reviewed various reports from across the realm. General Garrett liaised with two of the northern governors who had journeyed from their respective towns and cities, each bringing with them a large contingent of soldiers.

Upon sighting the king, the entire chamber ceased their activity and bowed their heads. Vighon waved the formality away and gestured to the map as he walked around the edge.

"Where are the Galfreys?"

General Garrett's mouth hung open for a second. "We have been unable to locate them since arriving, your Grace. Their usual guest quarters are empty and no one in the keep reports of seeing them for some time..."

Vighon sighed and rubbed his eyebrow. The Archon had either blatantly lied to them or the Galfreys had been set upon during their return. If it was the latter, chances were still high that they would have made it back to Namdhor by now. It boiled his blood to think of why the Archon would lie. He was powerless to act, however, given the state of the map before him.

"Ruban," he called to his side. "Choose four of your best king's guard and go with them back to Velia."

"Your Grace?"

"You are to enter Valatos. Do so with any of the soldiers I held back. Search every inch of Valatos until you find the ambassadors. You aren't to be denied."

Sir Ruban looked distressed. "Your Grace, the king's guard are to stay by your side."

"They are my most loyal soldiers," Vighon explained. "You above all. Return to Valatos and make certain Reyna and Nathaniel are safe."

The captain of the king's guard was not convinced. "I cannot leave you *now*. Not when the city is under threat."

"You can and you will," Vighon told him.

Ruban cast his eyes briefly over the room before resting back on his king. "As you command, your Grace," he relented miserably.

Vighon watched him leave the war room and wondered if he had just saved his friend's life. "Report, General."

Garrett nodded his thanks to the governors and addressed his king. "Lord Carrington has rallied men from Barossh and Galosha - they're heading north as we speak."

"How many?" Vighon enquired.

"A reported two thousand," the general answered with disap-pointment. "The six hundred that accompanied us from Palios have—"

Vighon shook his head and cut in. "Carrington the swine! There must be double those numbers between Galosha and Barossh. What of The Arid Lands? Any word from Lord Hasta Hash-Aseem?"

"Only one of apology," Garrett reported. "Apparently, this high born revolt for the return of slavery has turned violent. He states that his forces are needed in the south right now."

Vighon thought of all the dwarves who had lost their lives and the thousands who remained without a home. "Send word back to Lord Hasta and tell him there is no need for apology. His *king* commands forces to be moved north immediately. If there is a realm left after we have dealt with these invaders, he can be assured the high borns will be given my full attention."

General Garrett nodded his understanding and delegated the task to one of his underlings. "We've heard nothing from The Ice Vales, your Grace" he continued gravely.

"What?" Vighon snapped. "What of the men I stationed there?"

"There has been no reply from Grey Stone," Garrett reiterated. "At last report, not a single soldier had been rallied to journey north."

The king clenched his fist. "If I discover that my orders never found those soldiers, Lord Carrington will lose more than just his position."

Vighon pinched the bridge of his nose in despair. What kind of king fails to rally his own bannermen? He kept that question to himself, concerned that others might begin to wonder the same thing.

The king examined the map and discovered a statue of a stag on The Selk Road, heading north. "Lady Gracen?"

Garrett scrutinised the report in his hand and instructed one of the captains to move the stag a few inches farther north. "We have received word from her court mage," he said, looking to Eatred Mannus, the king's mage.

Easily the eldest person in the room, Eatred's reactions weren't as quick as the others and the mage was practically startled by the eyes on him. Vighon had no doubt the man was next to useless in a fight, but that wasn't why he kept Eatred around. Thanks to his age, he had been trained in Korkanath, before its demise, leaving him free of any influences Valatos might otherwise hold over him. What he lacked in his knowledge of destruction spells he made up for with his expertise around healing magic - it was never a bad thing to keep a healer close.

Eatred straightened his heavy robes and lightly touched the diviner on his belt. "Yes, your Grace, I spoke with Lady Gracen's man not long ago. They have left Lirian with nearly four thousand men and should arrive just after sunset."

A horrible twitch in Vighon's gut told him that would be too late. "Very good," he lied. "We should reach out to the elves. Send word to Lady Ellöria. If Ilythyra can spare any of her kin we will be forever in their debt."

That was if they survived to pay any debt, Vighon thought. He had left too many men across the country, spreading his force too thin. An easy gamble to make when he had not one but two dragons in his company...

His spiralling thoughts were broken when the doors behind the general were opened by a pair of servants. A soldier, ragged in appearance and breath, staggered into the chamber with barely enough energy to bow his head. His expression was harrowing, adding to the ill feeling in Vighon's gut. The young soldier spoke quietly to General Garrett on the other side of the map.

Garrett's face dropped.

Without a word, the general took a stick from one of the captains, stepped onto the map, and moved a collection of plain black statues from Dhenaheim through The Iron Valley and into Illian. Then, he requested five more black statues and added them to the rest.

"They're here," he stated gravely. "They've passed The Watchers," he added, gesturing to the soldier who had clearly been manning the outpost.

"Then death is upon us!" came a gravelly voice from the doorway.

In the finest armour Vighon had ever seen, King Uthrad of Silvyr Hall strode into the room. He was the very definition of burly, with broad shoulders made all the wider by the thick cloak of dark fur draped over his silvyr pauldrons. A golden helm encased much of his head and rose up into a geometric crown that looked too heavy to rest on any head. A thick grey beard burst out from between the edges of his helm and hung over his chest.

Six armoured dwarves brought up the rear, their golden sheen a contrast to the silver coloured silvyr. Their features were hidden behind plated masks that had been forged into the approximate shape of a dwarf's face. They were nothing if not menacing.

"King Uthrad!" Vighon welcomed. "You have my deepest condolences—"

"Let's save the pleasantries, northman." The dwarven king made his way around the map, ignorant of those in his way or the rudeness with which he had addressed Vighon. "Whatever yer estimates are," he continued, "they're wrong. These devils move with more speed than ye can imagine. They don' rest, they jus' march." Uthrad stepped onto the map and looked down on the black statues. "It's taken yer man, what? Two days since sightin' them in the valley?" The dwarf used his hefty boot to push the statues closer to Namdhor. "They'll be 'ere by tomorrow, maybe even tonight..."

There seemed no point getting stuck on the dwarf's lack of respect after hearing such dire news. "I have more soldiers on their way as we speak," Vighon confirmed. "We also have—"

"Where's yer dragon?" Uthrad asked, his breath not to be wasted.

The king of Illian stumbled over the answer, though not because of the dwarf's directness. "Inara and Athis travelled into *your* realm, good king, searching for this invader. They have not—"

"Returned," King Uthrad finished, shaking his head. "Aye, an' nor will they. This is not a foe to be challenged alone. Though, the dragon would 'ave certainly helped against theirs..."

Vighon felt his gut twist into knots at the thought of Inara and Athis never to return from Dhenaheim. He imagined them smashing into an army twenty-thousand deep and falling to their might. Then, he caught up with Uthrad's words and an entirely new kind of terror crept into the king's bones.

"Their *dragons*?"

"Unnatural beasts," the dwarf described. "Full o' holes they are, an' wounds said to be mortal even for a dragon, yet still they fly. They are to be seen to be believed. But trust me, northman, they breathe fire so foul it rooted us out o' our homes and into yers." Uthrad paused. "Do ye 'ave catapults?"

Vighon was still trying to comprehend the dwarf's description. "Yes," he replied with obvious distraction.

"Let me boys see to 'em," Uthrad suggested. "There's not much time, but if they can be improved then we'll see it done."

Vighon gave the nod to General Garrett. "Your engineers are welcome, King Uthrad. We will move our forces north of here and have them take up position beside your own. Together, our combined strength may be enough to—"

"We're not stayin'." The king of Silvyr Hall brought silence to the war room.

Vighon glanced at Garrett before settling back on the dwarf. "You're fleeing?"

Uthrad huffed. "A dwarf never flees! We make strategic retreats, but only if it serves a strong counter attack."

"Where will you go?" General Garrett asked.

Uthrad walked south-west across The White Vale, past Namdhor, until he was presented with the three-dimensional mountains of Vengora's southern curve. "If there's a way through the mountains an' back into the far reaches o' Dhenaheim, me people will find it. Or we'll make one. Navigatin' the mountains is in our blood. An', as an added precaution, we can collapse any tunnels behind us."

"You would return to Dhenaheim?" Vighon clarified, seeing no future in that plan.

"We weren' prepared for 'em the first time. Now we know what we face. Measures will be taken, our homes rebuilt. Should they return from yer lands we will be waitin' for 'em. With any luck," he added callously, "yer various armies will 'ave whittled their numbers down."

Now Vighon did take offence. "You brought them to my gates to slow them down?" He took a threatening step towards Uthrad and the dwarf's masked entourage mirrored his action. "You would sacrifice all of Illian to return to your home? We were going to fight beside you!"

Uthrad scoffed. "That romanticised notion would see both our people fall into ruin. I pray that Grarfath sees ye through these dark days, as He has for us, but I am not so foolish as to stay in an open field with naught but hope for comfort. The mountains are where me people belong an' it is to the mountains we shall return." With his final word, the dwarven king turned to leave.

"That's to be it then?" Vighon called after him. "The alliance of man and dwarf is to begin and end in the same day?"

Uthrad stopped in the doorway. "Ye 'ave an alliance," he corrected. "Though I shall not be sayin' their name. Perhaps *they* will die beside you."

"Heavybelly," Vighon announced proudly. "Their name is clan Heavybelly. And they have more honour than the rest of you combined."

Uthrad kept his gaze lowered and his hands clenched. "They did not travel with us, which means they're on the other side o' this scourge. Ye're on yer own, northman." Now, the dwarven king turned just enough to lay his eyes on Vighon. "Destroy the brain or jus' take their heads. Failin' that - burn 'em. Nothin' else will stop 'em." Leaving Vighon more confused and no less terrified for his people, Uthrad and his warriors left The Dragon Keep.

A palpable tension rested over the war room. Half of Uthrad's words spoke of their inevitable end, brought upon them by the dwarves themselves. The other half spoke of a dark army the likes of which had never been seen before.

"Dragons?" General Garrett echoed incredulously. "I thought all the dragons were in the south of Ayda, with Gideon Thorn."

Vighon considered the dwarf's description and wondered if they were indeed dragons. "That remains to be seen. We must hope that Inara and Alijah return to us soon. Until then, mobilise what few we have in the barracks. Keep them in the north for now; let the dwarves leave first lest we add to the chaos."

The war room returned to its buzz of activity, allowing General Garrett to make his way over to the king. "What did Uthrad mean? Take their head or burn them..."

Vighon turned his attention to the black statues. "I've seen all manner of evil in this world. There's only one creature I know of that requires such a death."

Garrett raised a white eyebrow. "What would that be?"

The king met his general's eyes. "Reavers."

What remained of the day was spent making preparations for battle. To the north, the barracks had become a knot of preparation with what few soldiers there were readying for battle. The dwarves themselves were slow to pack up, still sprawled across the snows even as the sun began to wane.

For the king of Illian, the remainder of the day had been spent contemplating what was surely an impossible nightmare. He thought back to his earliest days on the road with Alijah, when they had been on the hunt for any relics connected to The First Kingdom. Almost every run-in with The Black Hand had seen them encounter the undead.

He recalled the Darklings with frightening clarity. The lowest form of resurrection created nothing more than monsters that responded only to their insatiable hunger.

"What in all the hells are Reavers?" the general had asked him.

"They are the combination of black magic and ill-intent. The dead brought back to life with all their worldly knowledge but none of their will. They don't eat, drink, sleep or even breathe. They simply obey the one who resurrected them."

General Garrett had been the epitome of disbelief. "There's an army of dead men marching towards us?"

Vighon had shrugged. "Have you ever known a dwarf to exaggerate?"

"So who's controlling them?" Garrett had asked.

That question had kept Vighon's mind occupied ever since. His thought led him to the possibility of a Black Hand remnant, but given The Crow's last act of slaughtering them all on the shores of Dragorn, it seemed unlikely.

In his study, the king stared at his considerable library of books. Lessons from history were in those books, lessons that could teach a man the very best strategy and tactics in war or, indeed, the finest art of conversation.

None of them told of a way to beat an army of the undead...

Vighon was tempted to visit the more extensive archive beneath the keep, where the forbidden books had been stored. He knew he wouldn't understand much in them, but he would read anything right now if it made mention of Reavers. Alijah would know more from his studies under Hadavad, years earlier. But like Inara, Alijah had yet to return from beyond the mountains.

The king slammed his fist into the table and leant over it, fuming. Why now? he asked himself. He needed more time to rebuild the realm after the war - Illian couldn't survive another one. How many wars was one man supposed to see during his lifetime?

Before he could collect himself, a distant sound caught his attention, freezing him in place over the desk. It came again, and by the third time he recognised the noise to be that of a horn. Since Namdhor used a system of bells, it had to belong to the dwarves which could only mean...

Vighon rushed to the small balcony off his study and threw open the doors. As he stepped out into the chilling air, the bells of his city rang out and his people began to scatter below. All of this, however, was taken in from his periphery, for his gaze was firmly set across The White Vale, beyond the camp of dwarves. It was there that the king discovered the meaning of dread.

The army that approached was so vast that Vighon was sure his own would fit neatly inside their ranks. Their distant march rolled over the land, setting a beat to Namdhor's inevitable demise. How could they best such a force? That question tried to steal the heart of Vighon Draqaro, but he gripped the hilt of his sword and clamped his jaw shut.

He would fight to his last breath.

If needed, he alone would stand against this dark army and draw a line they would be foolish to cross. Vighon reminded himself that in all recorded history, Namdhor had never been taken. He himself had ensured that during the orc invasion.

Descending from the thick, grey clouds came a dark dragon, quickly followed by four more. Even from a distance they were clearly skeletal in comparison to a dragon such as Athis or Malliath. Their shrieking, unnatural roars broke over the marching soldier beneath them, proving all the more that these dragons were different. It occurred to the king, at that terrifying moment, that the dragons were Reavers too.

General Garrett rushed into the room but Vighon's attention was captured by the dwarves mobilising below.

"What are they doing?" Garrett frowned.

"There's no time to leave now," Vighon replied gravely. "They must fight or die..."

Their armoured forces moved up, away from the camp, and towards the dark army. The dwarves offered a roar of their own, followed by a rhythmic beating of sword against shield. There was no question as to who possessed the larger army, but the dwarves of

Dhenaheim were the fiercest warriors Verda had to offer and every one of them was encased in silvyr.

Looking north, to Vighon's left, his own Namdhorian soldiers were forming up and marching south to join the dwarves, regardless of orders to stay and wait for them to leave. The distance between the two forces, unfortunately, was vast - the Namdhorians would never reach the dwarves before the dark army was upon them. Not that their limited numbers would offer much aid in the face of such a sizeable army.

Vighon cursed but his words were drowned out by the crashing of his own door. A group of king's guards burst into the study and surrounded the northman, their guiding hands pushing him towards the door.

"To the throne room!" one of them barked.

Vighon was aware of this scenario - a strategy devised by Ruban Dardaris. The throne room was the most fortified chamber in the keep, with the thickest walls, only two doors, a balcony that offered a view of The King's Lake, and it was located in the heart of the fortress.

"Stop!" Vighon bellowed as he was forced from passage to passage. "We need to face them, not hide!" He was finally able to shove away those holding him and stand his ground. "A king must be the first to shed blood for his realm. If you want to protect me, bring me my armour and prepare yourselves for battle."

The king's guard would have looked to Ruban at this point, the captain the only person, beside the general, who would dare question the king. Vighon didn't wait for them to make up their minds but, instead, made for the nearest door that would take him out onto the ramparts of the keep.

The biting northern air didn't even register as he crossed the rampart, towards the cacophony of chanting dwarves. By the edge, he once again looked out on the armies that would soon collide in a wave of violence and blood.

The dwarves had formed into an arrow, with King Uthrad at the very front, astride his humungous Warhog. That's what a king was supposed to do.

"Your Grace!" General Garrett strode across the rampart to join him. "The horses are ready, but we should wait to ride with our men. Fighting beside the dwarves now is suicide." Garrett looked at the king in his leathers before turning to one of his underlings. "Fetch his bloody armour already!" he growled.

"We take whatever men we have and join the dwarves," Vighon corrected, much to the general's dismay.

"Vighon," he said quietly, his tone full of urgency. "This isn't like the old days. We never faced a force this size."

The king turned to look at his old friend. "I will not stand here and wait for our men while dwarves die on my land."

Garrett opened his mouth to reply when the five dragons shrieked again, an oppressive sound that hurt the ears. They scattered across the sky, dramatically altering their flight paths.

Malliath dropped out of the cloud bank with a roar so powerful it was sure to break the sky. For the first time, hope swelled in Vighon's heart.

The black dragon glided lower and lower, coming down directly over the dark army. Vighon dared not take his eyes off Malliath. He waited anxiously for his deadly breath to be unleashed upon their enemy, splitting them right down the middle. Then, the king had no doubt, Athis would emerge from somewhere else and tear another fiery line through their ranks.

They could actually win this...

Vighon clapped Garrett on the shoulder. "I think the tide is about to turn."

What happened next hollowed Vighon out, leaving him numb to his core. Malliath did indeed unleash his devastating breath, but not upon the hordes of Reavers. The dragon cleared their dark army, crossed the strip of snow, and let loose a torrent of blazing orange fire into the dwarven ranks. Where King Uthrad had made his stand was now an inferno that expanded through the lines of his kin, burning them within their silvyr.

Malliath peeled off, banking south, only to bring his tail to bear, dragging it through hundreds of dwarves who had avoided the flames. Their broken bodies were flung high into the air with dirt, snow, and blood. Their formation was in disarray, leaving them vulnerable to another attack. Malliath was swift in the air, proving his hulking size was no obstacle.

Garrett was shouting something beside Vighon, but to the king all was distant. He saw only the death that unfolded before his eyes. The black dragon dived down and cut another line of flames through the heart of the dwarves. His flight, however, continued north, away from the children of the mountain and towards the Namdhorian forces charging south.

"No..." Vighon whispered, his protest stolen by the wind.

Malliath advanced on the Namdhorian soldiers but stopped short of attacking them. Instead, the ancient dragon banked to the east and exhaled a jet of fire across the vale. The heat distorted the air and the smoke masked the riders beyond, but their progress had been halted without a doubt. They would be forced to go around the wall of flames, slowing them down.

What Malliath did next was lost on Vighon, the king snatched away by several hands. Once again, his personal guard were practically dragging him over the rampart and back into the keep. The king did nothing more than make certain his legs kept up, for his mind was far too preoccupied.

He had been betrayed...

His ally, his friend, his brother had betrayed him. Vighon was bombarded with so many emotions he didn't know what to do with them. Still numb from the bloodshed, he found himself sitting on the steps of his throne, wondering how he had come to be there. General Garrett was barking orders at everyone and the main doors were being closed and sealed. The dragon door, built soon after Vighon's crowning, was sealed shut by a massive portcullis.

THE KNIGHTS OF ERADOR

"Protect the king!" Garrett yelled. "You - give him your armour!"

Vighon could do nothing but stare at the floor. How could he have let this happen? How could Alijah betray him like this? He had all the questions and no answers. It infuriated him, filling him with an anger that demanded action.

A king's guard attempted to man-handle him into a plate of armour. Vighon gripped him by the collar and shoved him back.

"You're going to need it," he told the guard, his eyes flashing over the far wall. "I have all the armour I need..."

The king walked over to the wall and removed the rounded shield from its mount. It was simple in design; perfect for a rogue living on the road. Fortunately for Vighon, the shield had been enchanted many years earlier by the mage Hadavad, making it resilient to magical attacks. He hefted it on one arm, feeling its familiar weight.

He had used that very shield to protect Alijah once. Everything had made sense back then.

Now, the world was on fire...

CHAPTER 29
QUIET AS A TOMB

Alone, Doran Heavybelly had watched several suns rise and set over the blanketing snows of Dhenaheim. Ensuring that Pig didn't collapse on him, the dwarf had alternated between walking and riding in his saddle. What rest he and his Warhog had found was always brief.

The exhaustion was better than sleep, which was always accompanied by the horrific images that flashed beneath his eyelid. He saw blood splatter up the stone of Grimwhal, painting the city red with his kin. The smell of dwarves burning was stuck in his nose and refused to vacate. Their dying screams echoed in his mind.

Doran had known many a bloody battle - the dwarven wars too numerous to count - but what had taken place inside his ancient home had been no battle. It had been a slaughter. Those nightmarish creatures, masquerading as men in armour, had swept through Grimwhal without mercy and taken no prisoners.

To make matters worse, Dakmund had been seriously wounded and Russell had taken himself off into the mountains so he wouldn't be inclined to eat any of them. Doran had grumbled about this to Pig for most of their journey, repeating himself over and over, but the Warhog seemed to care very little.

Miserable and cold, the son of Dorain could only pray to Grarfath and Yamnomora that his friend was safe and his brother would recover. If the Mother and Father were smiling on them, the clan would have reached Namdhor and bolstered Uthrad's forces before smashing the invaders to pieces with an army of humans behind them.

The stout ranger had become too single-minded to feel the guilt of leaving his clan anymore. He was ploughing back through Dhenaheim to find Inara Galfrey and that's all there was. The Guardian of the Realm wasn't just Illian's most valuable warrior, she was also Doran's friend and the daughter of Reyna and Nathaniel, who were among his oldest and dearest friends.

His concern for the Dragorn had increased tenfold after the dark army had passed him by, ignorant of his hiding spot amongst a cluster of rocks. Thousands of them had marched through the snow towards The Iron Valley, absent the mist that had previously accompanied them.

To Doran, their numbers were most alarming because it seemed they had taken no losses from a dragon. Athis was a powerful dragon, powerful enough to have reduced this dark army using his breath alone. Yet they had trekked past the dwarf, with significant numbers, without so much as a singed cloak between them.

Then there were the shadows that had danced in and out of the thick clouds. Doran had not dared move at the time, his hand pressed against Pig to keep the animal still. Every now and then, he had glimpsed the end of a wing pierce the clouds or the end of a tail dip into the sky below. None of them had belonged to Athis the ironheart...

So where was Inara?

The Dragorn had flown towards them and apparently made no difference to their relentless advance. Now, with the dark army having long disappeared from view, Doran journeyed in their foot-steps, retracing their path back towards Grimwhal.

Towards ruin...

~

The sun was yet again in search of its resting place by the time Grimwhal's golden pillar came into view. The shining beacon drew Doran in, as it had done many times during his life.

"She's got be 'ere somewhere, Pig," he remarked, if only to hear something other than the rising wind. "Unless we've missed her..." he mused; though he was confident they would have found the Dragorn on the trail.

Walking beside the Warhog, in the midst of a brewing gale, Doran crossed the plains with a roaming eye. He only had the one, but a dwarf's eye, made by Yamnomora, was designed to find the detail in all things. They could spot imperfections and anomalies with naught but a glance.

Unfortunately, that didn't stop the son of Dorain from tripping over a rock. Tired from his journey, the dwarf had little strength to resist the fall which saw him slam face down into the snow with a curse on his lips. Picking himself up, the wind was whipping snow across his face now, enraging the dwarf all the more.

Muttering to himself, the son of Dorain looked down at the rock that had deemed to undo him. He squinted his good eye and shielded his face from the blowing snow, only to discover that the rock was much larger than he initially imagined. Coated in white powder, he followed the end of the rock until it rose up into what he had assumed was a hill - though he could recall no such hill so close to Grimwhal's entrance.

Walking around the supposed *hill*, the dwarf found the truth of what had tripped him up...

"Athis!" he exclaimed.

THE KNIGHTS OF ERADOR

Doran ran to the other end, away from the tail that had got in his way. He brushed the snow down and off the dragon's face to reveal his red scales and a closed eye.

"How long 'ave ye been 'ere then?" he asked aloud, examining the dragon's bulk for any sign of Inara.

The would-be hill moved, displacing heaps of snow from his wings. At this point, Pig made a quick dash for the main doors, Doran be damned.

"Get back 'ere ye coward! It's jus' Athis!"

When next Doran turned around, the dragon had one of his blue eyes gazing out at the world. It took a moment to focus on the dwarf and the lid itself spasmed in its attempt to fully open. The son of Dorain reached out and placed a hand against the scales beside his eye.

"What 'ave they done to ye?" He looked around again. "Where's Inara?" he asked, his heart swelling to know that she too must be alive.

Athis lifted his head just enough to motion towards the main doors, in the distance. To Doran's eye, it was just a black rectangle against the mountainside. If that's where Inara was, however, then that was where he would go.

"I'll find her," he promised.

Finishing his journey to the main doors, Doran found himself back where it had all begun only days earlier. The doors themselves were flat on the ground, scorched and bent out of shape. If this dark army did indeed travel with dragons, their attack on the city made a lot more sense to the dwarf now.

Clambering over the doors, he came across a massacre - what else could he have found? Having fought for his life and his people in this very passage, he recalled many of these dwarves falling to the enemy's blades. Their bodies were partially covered in the snow that had encroached on Grimwhal's interior.

It was their faces that haunted Doran, frozen in their final moments. It was scenes such as this that had made the son of Dorain leave Dhenaheim in the first place. Between them were bodies not of Grarfath's making.

The enemy...

Doran weaved his way through the passage, careful to avoid standing on his deceased kin. He paused and crouched at the body of a dark knight, absent its head. Rummaging through the debris, the dwarf came across the missing head, still encased inside its helmet. The mask plate was stiff, but it couldn't resist Doran's grip.

"What in all the hells..."

The stout ranger looked upon the face of a dead man, only he had been dead a lot longer than a few days. The face was mostly intact, but the nose and lips were notably missing, along with any eyelids. The skin was putrid and poked with ragged holes that revealed teeth inside a closed jaw.

"Reavers," he said with disgust.

His eye caught something move in the periphery and he turned down the passage with one hand gripping the hilt on his belt. Pig came trotting by, his nose pointed down into the filth. Doran let out a sigh of relief and scolded the Warhog as it passed him by without recognition.

Then he saw her, curled up against the wall.

"Inara!" he hissed, rushing to the Dragorn's side.

His hands paused in the air above her, hesitant to make contact with the distortion that cocooned her. The air rippled around her in different colours, always moving.

"Inara?" he whispered, his hands hovering. "Damn it, girl..." Doran dared to push his hands through to grip her arm. The air was warm!

The son of Dorain reached in with all his strength and pulled the Dragorn up, sitting her against the wall. She wasn't in the best shape, much like Athis outside. Her left eye was swollen and her bottom lip was cut. A nasty bruise spread out across her jaw and up her cheek. The leathers that protected her body were scorched in places and lacerated in others.

An icy wind filled the passage and slammed into Doran. He needed to get her food, water, and better shelter, regardless of her fancy spell. Taking her in his arms, the dwarf carried Inara farther into the dark and empty halls of Grimwhal.

Bodies decorated every floor in the city, friend and foe alike. Doran avoided the grander rooms, where the bodies were piled, and located a more intimate room where he could start a fire and not lose the heat to lofty ceilings. Using one of his thick shoulders, he barged open the pantry door just off from the royal kitchen.

"'ere ye go," he said softly, placing her on the ground with all the gentleness he was capable of.

Pig's exploration was cut short when Doran forced the Warhog into the pantry as well, hoping to capitalise on body heat if not smell. Over the next couple of hours, he scavenged the nearby halls and rooms for any supplies he could use and started a small fire inside the pantry. His first instinct was to keep the door closed and trap as much heat as possible, but the smoke needed somewhere to go other than his lungs.

The next hour was spent trying to rouse Inara. Only when her eyes flickered open did he attempt to get some water down her. He pressed the cup to her dry lips, happy to see that not all of it ran down her chin. He spoke to her often, hoping to get something back or at least remind the Dragorn that she wasn't dead.

Eventually, after many hours of trying, Doran sat back on the floor and let her rest without interruption. "What do ye reckon that is then?" he asked Pig, gesturing to the cocoon.

The Warhog snorted.

"Aye, ye right," Doran replied. "It's likely some kind o' Dragorn magic." The dwarf continued to talk aloud for some time before his eye finally shut and his jaw hung open.

He belonged to a world of dreams now. Given all that he had

seen, those dreams couldn't help but morph into nightmares. Restless was his slumber. It was his own words that roused him, spoken against his will into a small room.

When he opened his eye, an ancient part of his dwarven mind told him the night had passed outside the mountain. His face possessed a sheen of sweat and his hand felt numb from gripping the haft of his axe so tightly.

"I have to admit," said a croaky voice, "yours was the last face... I expected to see... If any."

At last, a smile cracked across Doran's face. "Inara!"

The Dragorn looked from the Warhog to the dwarf. "Where are we?" she asked wearily.

Doran crawled forwards and rested on his knees. "Grimwhal," he answered. "This is where I found ye." The ranger handed her some bread and a water-skin. "'ere, ye need to get yer strength up."

Inara accepted the water alone. "I don't... I don't remember..."

"Athis is outside," Doran explained. "He looks pretty banged up, like yerself. I came lookin' for ye."

Again, Inara could only offer a quizzical expression as she sipped at the water. Doran settled himself down again and took the Dragorn through recent events, detailing his battle in these very halls and their miraculous escape.

One detail had stood out to Inara. "They're still moving," she groaned.

"Aye, they are. Headin' for Illian I'd say."

Inara made to move but something painful in her midriff stopped her. "We need... to go." Her words broke through the obvious pain, but her body was less enthusiastic.

"Easy, easy," Doran bade. "I don' think ye're gonna jump' to ye feet right now. Ye need more rest."

Inara tried to stand again but succeeded only in wobbling and sliding back down the wall, her face white as a sheet. "We need to help," she continued.

Doran helped her into a more comfortable position. "Ye're as stubborn as yer mother," he observed. "Ye've been seriously injured!"

"I heal quickly," she replied through gritted teeth.

"Not *that* quickly," the dwarf quipped.

Inara examined her hand. "My spell... It's faded."

"Aye, ye were nice an' toastie in there."

"It wasn't just keeping me warm." Inara let her head slump back. "It was a very old... healing spell. You broke it."

Doran stopped stoking the fire. "I broke it? How's that?"

"You disturbed me," she said flatly.

The dwarf huffed. "Well excuse me for tryin' to save yer life!"

Inara brought her head back and blinked hard to focus on Doran. "I'm sorry. I'm just..." Her words died away.

"It's a'right, lass," Doran reassured. "There's no offence 'ere. Ye're hurtin' I can see."

The Dragorn took a breath. "I can handle the pain. That's not what hurts..."

The ranger took an extra moment to consider her words and scrutinise the pain on her face. "Who did this to ye?" he asked softly. "From what I saw, those fiends don' take no prisoners."

Inara swallowed before resting her gaze on Doran. "Alijah," she uttered.

Hearing that one name robbed Doran of all speech. His insides felt cold, a result of the bottomless void that opened up inside his gut. Alijah's reappearance in Illian had been quite the surprise to the dwarf, but this was a revelation that tied his mind into knots.

"Yer brother?" he finally managed, his expression as startled as his tone. "I don' understand..."

"Neither do I," Inara admitted. "It was as if..." She stared at the wall, seeing something that escaped Doran. "It was like a mask. He just took it off and..." Her words trailed off and she closed her eyes.

"Alijah, he's in league with these monsters?"

"Reavers," she breathed, a hint of disgust on her face. "He's not in league with them. He *commands* them."

Again, Doran was speechless, though his face begged for answers. Through the pain, Inara unravelled events for the dwarf, detailing everything from Lord Thedomir's betrayal in Grey Stone to Alijah's wicked magic. It was quite the tale and it took a lot out of the Dragorn to do it justice. By the time she was finished, her breathing sounded laboured and her eyes appeared heavy.

"Rest," Doran urged, helping her to lie down. Alijah's betrayal stung the dwarf, and not just because of the price his people had paid for it, but for Inara the betrayal was much deeper.

"My sword," she groaned, fighting sleep.

Doran hovered over her, thinking back to the passage in which he had found her. "It wasn' with ye. Don' fret, lass, we'll get it back."

Inara's blue eyes finally disappeared behind swollen lids and her breathing slowly returned to normal. Doran walked around the fire, cupping his mouth in distress. It was all just so... unthinkable. If he had been given another two centuries he would still never have guessed Alijah Galfrey to be at the heart of it all.

Inara's last concern turned Doran's mind to another weapon of great renown. Andaljor was still in Grimwhal's halls, dropped by Dakmund during his fight with the crowned knight. It had been such a pity to have lost the legendary weapon, the emblem of their clan. But what if he could reclaim it? It would certainly give him something to do while Inara recovered. If he remained by the fire he would likely stew over Alijah, an all-round miserable affair.

"Right," he declared to Pig, "I'm off. I won' be back for a little while, so ye're in charge. Got it?"

The Warhog continued to snore.

"Good." Doran slung his axe over his back, grabbed a water-skin, and lifted a torch from the fire.

Beyond the pantry, the dwarf paused, wondering if leaving the Dragorn unguarded by himself was so wise. Looking left and right, however, the passage was devoid of life, as was, unfortunately, the rest of Grimwhal. They were like ghosts, haunting an empty city.

Walking through the streets of his old home, without manacles to bind his wrists, was both a nostalgic experience as well as melancholic. He knew the roads and alleys like the back of his hand, even recalling the construction of certain areas. But it was filled with death in many places and evidence of total abandonment in others. It was a shell of its former self, stained by evil.

Everywhere he went, the buildings were very much intact and the supporting pillars stretched high into the mountain roof without any sign of damage. The Reavers had simply swept through and cleared the inhabitants out, as if their main goal had been to herd the dwarves.

Crossing the heart of the city, Doran found himself standing in the middle of one of the central squares. So busy had it always been that only now did he realise there were rectangular patterns on the ground. He crouched down and placed the palm of his hand against the cold stone, feeling for the pulse of the mountain. His hand should have reported a hum of activity from all around.

There was nothing.

Grimwhal was still, reflecting the silence of a tomb rather than a city. Doran's heartbreak and rage began to stir once more, threatening to rise to the surface and explode forth.

A subtle vibration rippled through his hand, detectable only to a dwarf. He looked one way, then the other. There was nothing but dead bodies, scattered debris, and empty buildings. But *something* had just moved.

"Who's there?" he asked, surprised by the sound of his own voice.

There was no reply so he repeated his question in dwarvish. After hearing his own voice echo through the streets, the dwarf rested one hand on the haft of his axe. He couldn't deny the hope that now sparked in his chest - he could do with burying his axe into something big and nasty. To his dismay, there was naught but the sound of his own breathing to answer his question.

In a huff, the son of Dorain continued his trek through the city. There were less and less bodies the closer he approached to the tunnels. Many of the warriors fighting to hold the line had lowered their weapons and run for the tunnels. This turned the Reavers' intended victims into survivors - a fact Doran was all too happy to acknowledge, regardless of any images he might conjure of dwarves fleeing their enemies.

At last, he was standing before the ancient tunnels. Using his torch, Doran lowered the flames to the floor and searched for the double-sided weapon amongst the bodies. The Reaver bodies were in pieces - the quickest way to put them down for good.

To assist his memory, Doran stood with his back to the tunnel entrance and recalled his position from the fight. In his mind, he could see where Dakmund and Russell had been, as well as the crowned knight. He used this knowledge to narrow down the area where the weapon had been dropped.

A broad grin revealed every one of Doran's teeth. "Andaljor!" he exclaimed.

The weapon demanded a wielder of great strength. At one end was a rectangular slab of iron, engraved with the most ancient of dwarven script. The other end possessed a double-headed axe of biting steel. It was as legendary to the dwarves as Mournblade was to the elves, only prettier in Doran's eye.

The moment of reclamation was ruined by the sharp scraping of armour over the ground. Doran's head whipped around and his jaw clamped together in a growl. It took his eye a few seconds to adjust to the gloom beyond his torch and discover the Reaver, clawing its way over the dead. Its head was hanging on by a few strands of gore, its only lifeline. With one arm and no legs, however, the monster was slow.

Doran smirked and dropped his torch. He was going to enjoy this. Hefting Andaljor in both hands now, he toyed with which end to bring down on the Reaver's body. Either way, he was going to pummel it for a while before he finally ended its miserable existence.

The hammer came up first, but its bloody end never fell. Instead,

Doran jumped back with his heart pounding in his chest from the surprise that leaped out of the shadows.

A Clacker...

The monster's hooked claw came down on the Reaver's head, ridding the creature of whatever spell had given it purpose. All six of the Clacker's legs danced on the floor with excitement, its meal an easy catch. Doran remained perfectly still with Andaljor still raised over his head. If he made any sound, the Clacker would know he was there and leap on him with several rows of sharp teeth and four front claws that had been known to pierce steel.

Two flat nostrils inhaled the Reaver's scent as the Clacker's bald head twitched from side to side. Small holes opened and closed across that grotesque head, all of which were highly sensitive to sound. It was their unique ears that normally kept them away from Grimwhal, for the city's constant din was too painful to bear.

Doran scanned the streets for more of its ilk. Where there was one Clacker, more always followed. Its head shot up in the dwarf's direction, but with no eyes to speak of it could do nothing but wait and listen. Andaljor's weight brought a sting to Doran's muscles, though he dared not lower the weapon. There was a chance his armour would scrape together or the axe on the bottom would catch his belt.

It wasn't the first time he had seen a Clacker up close, but he had forgotten the stench that accompanied their hideous form. To any surface-dweller, a Clacker would be described as having its insides on its outside, revealing the monster's tendons and muscles.

Shaped in the manner of a centipede, the monster's clawed feet stepped forwards, placing its head only inches from Doran's chest-plate. Killing the beast would be as easy as letting Andaljor drop onto its head, crushing whatever brain it claimed to possess. Slaying the Clacker, however, would be a noisy affair and killing one of them by surprise was very different to facing a swarm of them.

Proving its name to be apt, the monster lifted its head and made a clacking sound from within its shuddering throat. As one, more

Clackers slunk out of the dark, their claws tapping against the floor. Doran stopped counting after he reached ten. There wasn't much calculation required to inform the dwarf that he was too far away from the pantry to seek help from Pig. Of course, returning to their makeshift camp would bring the monsters down on Inara. That wasn't an option.

That only left him with one path to take...

Andaljor came down with the might of Doran's arms behind it. The hammer didn't stop until it was buried in the Clacker's skull and its jaw was shattered against the floor. The rest of them had a variety of sounds to home in on, but Doran gave them something extra.

"This is *my* home," he fumed.

The Clackers rushed in, scurrying towards the dwarf on their many legs. Doran swung Andaljor at the first to reach him and sliced its head in half. Then he ran. His immediate dash saw him take the nearest alleyway. The Clackers crashed into the wall behind him, climbing over each other to be the first to claim their meal. He could hear them rising up the side of the building, aiming to come down on him from all sides.

His legs ran as fast as they could, but the Clackers were naturally faster, forcing Doran to barrel into the first door he came across. The narrow spaces inside would make their hunt a lot harder and give the dwarf an opportunity to face them one at a time. The door splintered under his weight and the hinges were wrenched from the frame on his way down to the floor. He scrambled to his feet just in time to turn and challenge the Clacker behind him. Its legs encroached at different angles to ensure it fitted through the door, but its gnashing jaws came directly for Doran's face.

Five rows of teeth clamped down on the end of Andaljor's waiting hammer. Doran drove his fist into the haft between the axe blades and pushed the hammer farther still, dislocating the monster's jaw before finally breaking it. Using both hands, he yanked the weapon back and finished the job with another blow to its head.

Unfortunately, there were at least four more of the fiends waiting to replace it. One of them forced its head through the adjacent window while two others tried to scale the Clacker lying dead in the doorway. Once again, Doran ran for it. He kicked in the back door and started up the next street in search of another place to dig in.

Then he caught sight of more, rising over the top of distant buildings and crawling around thick pillars. Running and fighting wasn't going to work. The dwarf changed his direction while simultaneously throwing his sword across the street and through a tanner's window. He deliberately slowed down, taking lighter steps, before coming to a complete stop in the narrow avenue. The Clackers descended on the tanner's shop, following the sound of the shattered glass and loud clatter from his sword. They mauled at the door until it was in pieces.

Doran held his breath.

Sweat matted his hair and dripped off the end of his nose. He watched as the Clackers tore the tanner's shop apart, hunting their prey. And so he remained, rooted to that spot for what felt like hours. His hands ached from holding Andaljor and his arms told him many times that they were ready to detach and leave him forever. But he was damned if he was going to fill the belly of some beast. He imagined those teeth biting into him and it kept his grip firm and his legs strong.

But there was only so long he could remain there. The Clackers stalked the area for much of his time in that alleyway, only leaving when their hungry stomachs demanded they hunt elsewhere for their elusive prey. Doran took his most cautious footstep and looked out on the empty street. Every little noise his attire made felt magnified to him.

Giving his hands and arms a break, he very carefully entered the tanner's shop and found a strap of leather for Andaljor. It weighed on his back, beside his silvyr axe, but it was better than holding onto it for a moment longer.

His trek back to the pantry was slow and arduous. He often

paused mid-stride, sure that he had heard something. The abandoned city provided the Clackers with no end of hiding places.

Drenched in sweat, the pantry door, still half open, was at last in sight. He could see the smoke drifting out but he began to fear that the noise created by the crackling fire would attract the Clackers. It was tempting to rush those remaining steps and reach Inara and Pig as quickly as possible. But he continued to imagine those teeth plunging through his armour and reducing him to food.

After an agonising last stretch, the son of Dorain eased the door further open. Inara was still asleep, right where he had left her. Pig was missing. Doran cursed the stupid animal, wandering off at the fancy of its nose.

The dwarf took a step inside only to hear the door creak. He winced at the sound as it echoed through the stony halls. It wasn't particularly loud but, after moving in near-silence for several hours, it might as well have been a dinner-bell for the Clackers.

He waited, listening for any sign of them.

Even his sigh of relief was silent. Now his only trouble lay with Pig, who would likely reappear with a clatter. They just needed to get out of Grimwhal. The city had become a hunting ground now.

Doran froze beside the fire.

His heart pounded in his chest.

There was no mistaking the distant sound of guttural clacking. He gave Inara one last look - no beast would touch her so long as he had anything to say about it.

Back in the hall, he closed the door and prepared for the fight of his life. Three passages converged on the pantry and, right now, all three of them were steadily filling with Clackers. Doran growled and slammed his silvyr axe into the ground beside him. The blade cut through the stone and remained partially upright, ready for him to grab it when needed.

Taking Andaljor from his back, he untied the strap and held the haft with both hands. His thumb rotated the mechanism in the centre of the haft and he gave both sides a quick tug in opposite direction. This separated the axe and hammer, offering him a weapon in each hand. By the time he looked up again, the Clackers had advanced halfway down their respective passages. If there was anything to make them hesitate, it would be the blood of their own kind staining both ends of Andaljor.

"Right," Doran grizzled, "which one o' ye is gonna get it first?"

CHAPTER 30
FIRE AND ICE

The bells had stopped ringing. From within the throne room of The Dragon Keep, Namdhor was quiet. Malliath's fires couldn't be heard nor the dying dwarves being consumed by it. The people weren't even screaming as an army of Reavers marched up the city's slope.

It wasn't even the calm before the storm - there had been no storm... yet.

The lack of a battle aside, Vighon was standing in what would be any invader's final destination. When that storm finally arrived at his door, it would come for his crown. Then, there would be nothing to do but meet it with fire and steel.

Spread across the chamber were six of his guard, all of whom were braced for battle. General Garrett stood in front of them, his sword drawn and his cloak discarded on the floor behind him. This wasn't the first time the veteran had stood before an overwhelming force and it showed in his calm demeanour.

With the doors sealed, there was only one other way out of the throne room and that was through the dragon door, just off from the throne. There, beyond a towering portcullis, a balcony large enough to hold Athis had been built. Of course, it was only a way out if Vighon didn't mind diving into The King's Lake; a death sentence to all.

Then the wait was over. The storm arrived to the sound of marching feet and the clatter of armour. There came a ruckus from beyond the doors as Namdhorian soldiers met the invaders. Swords clashed and men screamed, their violent collision sharp and sudden. Bodies hit the floor and silence once again resumed its reign over the keep.

Vighon drew the sword of the north in one dramatic sweep. Elven magic brought the flames to life, dancing across the silvyr blade. It was a Reaver's worst nightmare.

"You've never faced what's about to come through those doors," Vighon warned. "But make no mistake, these monsters need their heads just as much as we do. Swing high and watch each other's backs. Don't waste energy on anything that isn't going to part them from their rotten skulls."

The doors shook, startling them all. Something hit them again and the thick, wooden beam barring the way began to splinter.

"It has to be magic," Garrett remarked.

Again and again the doors were subjected to a battering, yet they refused to yield. Then, without explanation, the assault came to an end. Vighon knew it would be naive, however, to consider the enemy's silence a retreat in the face of a stubborn door. They had come too far for that.

The king listened to his instincts and raised his shield. The only sound was that of his sword, its flames licking the air.

That same air popped in his ears a moment later, a result of the portal that tore through the fabric of reality. Sparks and streaks of lightning erupted from all around the gateway, creating a chaotic atmosphere. The dark void concealed the doors but opened another entrance, allowing the enemy to enter the throne room with naught but a step.

A single figure emerged, clad in black armour and a helm topped with a crown of tall spikes. The portal collapsed on itself in a compression of air that blew the figure's dark cloak out to the side. Death, as it was, walked towards them with a jagged sword in its gloved hand.

Garrett raised his blade with both hands and pointed it at the Reaver's faceplate. "You will not touch him," he promised.

"Surround it!" Vighon barked.

The king's guard moved to challenge the crowned knight from all sides, but the general wasn't waiting for them. He lashed out with his sword, bringing the steel to bear across the Reaver's neck. It was wickedly fast, intercepting his attack and countering with a hard elbow to Garrett's chestplate. Before the veteran had even hit the floor, the armoured fiend was turning to parry the king's guard.

Vighon darted past Garrett and threw himself into the melee with sword and shield. Any hopes of landing a blow were dashed when a member of his guard staggered into his path with a slashed throat. His momentum gone, the king paused, searching for the best angle of attack. The crowned knight presented him with very few, and those openings to be seen were often lures to bring its opponents in for the kill.

Two more of the king's guard fell to the Reaver's tactics, its movements fluid from one attack to the next. Whoever this creature had been in life, he had to have been one of the greatest warriors of his Age.

But this wasn't the Reaver's Age...

The king moved in with his fiery sword and came down hard on the crowned knight. Their blades locked together over their heads and the Reaver retreated a step. One of the remaining guards swept in with his blade and cut though the creature's midriff with one clean swipe. Of course, it did nothing but drive the crowned knight back another step.

"Take its head!" Vighon reminded them.

The Reaver drove Vighon's sword into an arc, freeing it to plunge its jagged blade into the neck of an approaching king's guard. That was four dead in less than a minute. The king roared in anger, all rational thought suspended, and charged at his opponent's back before it could murder another northman. The silvyr found no resistance as it speared the creature through and through.

It was a killing blow to all but a Reaver. Vighon, however, had more than just a blade at his disposal. The flames caught the dark cloak and quickly spread in every direction. The creature thrashed, knocking Vighon back, until it was able to tear the cloak from its shoulders. Through the smoke, the crowned knight leaped at the king, ignoring the guards now.

"Come on!" Vighon bellowed, bringing his shield up.

The impact was hard, but no harder than that of any other man. The king pushed the blade away and came back with his fiery silvyr. Their swords clashed high and low, each searching for the right angle of attack. The crowned knight was swift, best displayed in its ability to parry both Vighon and the incoming guards while simultaneously lashing out to put them on the defensive.

With a roar on his lips, General Garrett rejoined the fight. His sword came down again and again, driving the Reaver towards the doors. The three remaining king's guard followed the melee and sought to attack their foe from all sides. But this foe was unlike any other.

The crowned knight tilted its head to the left and Garrett's blade chopped down into its shoulder instead, lodging the blade in dark plate. In one move, the creature thrust Garrett into one of the guards, parried another, and hacked through the head of the third. A boot to the chest launched Garrett back to the ground and pushed the king's guard back.

Vighon jumped in with the only guard still in the fight, but the crowned knight was prepared for multiple combatants. It yanked Garrett's sword from its shoulder and met the northmen with a blade in each hand. The king used his shield to keep one sword at bay while his own scorched a line down the Reaver's chest, hoping to at least knock it back and give the guard a chance to strike true. The armoured killer, however, spun inside the reaching arm and delivered a hammering backhand that whipped across the guard's face. There was a flash of jagged steel before it ran him through.

Again, the king's burning blade met that of the Reaver's and they danced across the chamber, between the bodies and through the pools of blood. Fighting an opponent wielding two swords was often easy, since the majority of fools to attack with a pair of blades had no idea how to coordinate them both at the same time.

Unfortunately, the crowned knight came at him with an efficiency that reminded the king of Galanör, easily one of the best, if not *the* best, sword fighter in the realm. His sword and shield came up one after the other, then both at once, each time always to defend and never attack. The steps of his throne proved to be his ultimate unmaking. The king tripped backwards and fell across the steps. His shield came up just in time to prevent the Reaver from taking his head.

Over the lip of the shield, Vighon glimpsed the crowned knight raising both of its swords again. The shield would hold up, but how long could his own strength resist the approach of death? Ensuring he didn't have to find out, Garrett and the surviving king's guard tackled the creature from behind, locking its arms in theirs. Together, all three staggered away from the steps in a contest of brute strength that saw both of its blades dropped to the floor.

"Hold it!" Vighon yelled, rising to his feet absent his shield - he was going to cut off its ugly head.

The Reaver ceased its struggling and turned to the king's guard. That malevolent helm came down on the man's nose with a terrible crunch, robbing him of his grip on the crowned knight. The creature then snatched at the guard's head and pulled it into the tall spikes atop its helm, killing him instantly.

Outraged, Vighon swung the sword of the north. Only years of discipline allowed him to halt the weapon's momentum before it killed Garrett, who had been forced into the blade's path at the last second. A dark gauntlet smashed into the general's face and sent him reeling with a bloody mouth, leaving the king to swing again. The Reaver ducked and weaved between Vighon's every strike, avoiding the flames and silvyr by inches. Frustrated, the northman levelled his sword and thrust forwards, his aim intended to spear the crowned knight's head.

Proving its lack of fear, as well as pain, the undead fiend raised its arms and allowed the blade to pass through the narrow gap between its armoured vambraces. The silvyr sliced through the steel and the flames sparked as the sword was rammed towards its head, but the Reaver continued to turn its body, thereby twisting the sword from Vighon's grip.

The sword of the north spun away and clattered across the chamber floor. The king's first instinct was to charge the crowned knight and tackle it to the floor, but pommelling an armoured opponent with your bare hands was a sure way to break bones.

"Oi!" Garrett snarled from behind the Reaver. The grizzled general was a battered sight, with blood streaming from his nose, dripping over his lips, and down his chin. His expression conveyed none of his exhaustion, only that of his true grit; something to fear when his king was threatened.

"If you want him," he growled, "you're going to have to go through me first." The general raised his sword in both hands.

Whether Garrett meant to distract the deadly Reaver or not, Vighon wasn't going to waste the opportunity. He retrieved his shield from the steps behind him and pounced towards the crowned knight. The iron rim of the shield connected with the back of the creature's neck, propelling it forwards and into Garrett's waiting swing.

Unencumbered by what should have been a tremendous amount of pain, the Reaver simply gave into its momentum and dropped into a roll that carried it over a fallen sword.

Vighon foresaw what was about to happen, but he was powerless to prevent it...

Garrett's mighty swing cut through the air, taking his sword far to the side and exposing his body. That was when the crowned knight jumped up from its roll and drove its blade into the general, burying it to the hilt. Garrett's eyes flashed with horror, his bloody mouth ajar in shock.

Vighon cried out for his old friend but there was nothing to be done. He could only watch the life leave Garrett's eyes before the crowned knight let him fall to the floor and join the others in their eternal rest.

There was no longer a word to describe the fury that was ignited in Vighon's veins. He didn't even remember picking up his fiery sword again, but it was in his hand now and he wanted to make this Reaver suffer before he sent it back to hell. The crowned knight kicked out and flicked its jagged blade up, where it easily snatched it from the air.

"I wouldn't do that, Vighon."

The king whipped his head around to see Alijah through the portcullis, standing on the other side of the dragon door. Behind him, the sun was just disappearing behind the western peaks of Vengora.

"Look around you," Alijah warned. "Lord Kraiden wasn't known for taking prisoners..."

"Kraiden?" Vighon spat, recalling the treacherous Dragon Rider from Alijah's ancient tale.

"A shadow of his former self," the half-elf explained. "As a Reaver, he no longer possesses the magic he once claimed. His history is far bloodier than either of ours - I know *I* wouldn't want to fight him."

"I don't care what this monster has done!" Vighon snapped. "I care about what *you're* going to do... the monster I should have seen coming."

"Monster?" he echoed. "I am no monster, Vighon."

Alijah's hand moved in an arc over the portcullis and melted the iron with magic. Bright orange and *sizzling*, a man-sized entrance was burnt out of the massive gate. A flick of his fingers pulled that section of portcullis away and he entered the throne room.

"How many of your people have died?" he asked the king. "This is the most bloodless invasion in *any* history!"

"Bloodless?" Vighon fumed, pointing his sword at Alijah now. "Tell that to the dwarves you just murdered. How many of their kingdoms have you left a graveyard in your wake?"

The hint of a wince crossed Alijah's face. "Clashing with Dhenaheim was unfortunate, but inevitable. Besides their stubbornness, they held the only strip of land that connects Erador to Illian."

"You killed so many because they were in your way?" Vighon didn't know the person standing before him.

"I'm here to bring the world *together*, Vighon - that's always been my destiny. The dwarves, like the elves, are part of that world. At present, however, they are too strong-willed to accept my rule. They need breaking down first, so that they might rise again with a sense of belonging in my kingdom. Can you imagine that? A realm where we all live together in harmony, with no borders to divide us."

Tears welled in the king's eyes. "How could you do this, Alijah? You have lost your mind!" he raged. "You have betrayed me! You have betrayed everything you ever stood for! You always wanted to save the realm, not set it on fire!"

Alijah sighed and walked around Vighon as if he didn't have a flaming sword pointed at him. "You are blinded by your anger, old friend. Understandable," he conceded. "I know you and Garrett had a history and I'm sorry it came to this. The men who perished at Grey Stone were supposed to be the sum of your losses."

"Grey Stone..." Vighon uttered. "You, you were behind... You are the one who started this?"

Alijah gave him a patronising smile. "You don't really believe there's such a place that allows one to see and hear across the world, do you? I thought it was a gamble telling you as much, but even Inara believed me."

"Why didn't you just kill me?" Vighon demanded. "You've had more than enough chances."

Alijah glanced at Lord Kraiden and the Reaver immediately responded without a word passing between them. The ancient Dragon Rider removed the bolt barring the doors and opened them for the knights of Erador to pour in.

"I didn't come here to kill everyone," Alijah claimed. "I could have marched my army from Dhenaheim to Syla's Pass and wiped every living thing off the face of Verda. But I didn't. Instead, I ensured there would be no war. With words alone I kept Thedomir in line—"

"With threats!" Vighon corrected.

"The sight of Malliath is threat enough," Alijah replied. "But your reaction to their separatism was more important. I knew exactly what you would do, and you left The Ice Vales in disarray, without direction; something *I* will correct."

Vighon's breathing grew increasingly ragged as his temper continued to rise. "And the mages? You set Valatos against me?"

"I made the Archon a few promises, nothing more. They, in turn, whispered in Lord Carrington's ear and made certain that Velia would offer you no support. Those soldiers you're expecting aren't coming, I'm afraid, nor the ones I convinced you to leave behind in Grey Stone. But don't worry, I will personally deal with both the Archon and Lord Carrington. This kingdom *will* be brought back into line."

The king shook his head. "You will still have to face my men and those of Lirian. Our alliance alone will spoil your plans."

Alijah couldn't have looked less concerned. "Your men, north of here, dare not take a step towards the city - Malliath is seeing to that. And as for your alliance with Lirian..." The half-elf stood back and gestured at the open door.

The dark knights parted, clearing a path for Lady Gracen to enter the throne room. Gone was her pretty and expensive clothing, all replaced with tough leathers and a pair of short-swords crossed over her back. Behind her, six others trailed her entrance in similar attire and short-swords.

Bar Lady Gracen, they all wore red blindfolds over their eyes.

Vighon's anger was momentarily tempered by utter confusion. "Lady Gracen?"

"My title is *Mother*," she corrected, stunning Vighon all the more.

"This is to be the beginning of your reign then," he reasoned. "In league with the Arakesh? The commander of an undead army? You really have lost your damn mind!"

The Mother, as she had apparently always been, stepped towards the king and removed one of her short-swords. "Would you like his death to be quick or slow, your Grace?"

Alijah ignored the question. "They're not evil," he told the north-man. "They're just tools. And I'm going to use them to re-shape this world."

Vighon gripped his sword all the tighter. "I won't let you," he promised.

Alijah could only be described as disappointed. "This isn't what I wanted for you. But you had to step forward and take the crown, didn't you? If you had stayed by my side that day, we could have dealt with your father together and this burden would never have fallen on your shoulders."

"I brought peace to Illian!" Vighon shot back. "The unrest was caused by you!"

"And look how easy it was," Alijah retorted. "I used words, not steel. In a handful of years I was able to turn your kingdom upside down. Illian needs to be stronger than that. *Verda* needs to be stronger than that."

His words made Vighon think of Inara. "Where is she?" he demanded.

Alijah chewed over his response. "Inara can't help you now," he said ominously. "I tried to show you both a better way, a way that would see you free from all of this. I see now that such a thing could never happen. Whatever love you have for each other is buried beneath your sense of duty - it's admirable, but the root of your demise."

"Is she alive?" The king asked his question with as much control as he could muster.

"You have a choice now, Vighon. Help the people to see this transition of power as a good thing. Or don't. The latter won't end well for—"

"IS SHE ALIVE?" he bellowed, his blade shaking in his hand.

Alijah looked round, still perfectly calm. "If she were, where do you think she would be right now?"

Something primal snapped in Vighon Draqaro.

The king's feral roar preceded his charge. The Mother moved to intercept him but was immediately thrown aside by Alijah's magic. With nothing between them, Vighon leaped into the air and came down with his sword thrusting forward. The half-elf made Lord Kraiden appear sluggish by comparison. He shifted his shoulders, evading the point of the silvyr by no more than the width of a finger.

Again, Vighon came at Alijah with a mighty swing and found nothing but air to greet his sword. After three more unsuccessful swipes, he attempted to spear the half-elf in the chest only to find his opponent was no longer standing there. In a blur of motion, Alijah was suddenly by the king's side and an icy hand was snatching at the sword of the north.

That frozen hand gripped the blade, extinguishing the flames along the length of the sword. Vighon didn't even know that was possible. The distraction was utilised by Alijah and he dislodged the hilt from the king's hand and shoved an elbow of dragon scales into his jaw, hurling him to the stone.

Alijah held up the sword of the north and inspected it, free of the elven fire. "A fine weapon," he complimented before tossing it to the floor. A moment later, his spell faded and the silvyr was once again set alight.

Vighon did not recover as fast.

A pained groan escaped his lips and he managed to crawl away from Alijah and roll onto his back. His head felt like it had lost perspective on what was up and what was down.

A shadow fell over him and he looked up at his oldest friend. "Don't make me do this, Vighon. Were I not a king I would beg this of you. As it is, I am asking you as a brother: *help me*. To do anything else would make you my enemy."

Vighon blinked hard to focus on Alijah's face. "You... You don't get to call me that anymore."

The half-elf looked down on him with glassy eyes. "Then you leave me with no choice." A scimitar was drawn from his belt, its blade a deep shade of green.

Of all the ends he could have imagined, Vighon would never have believed this to be the one. Slain by his friend, his crown taken, and his people left to suffer because of it. At least Inara hadn't lived to see him fail so spectacularly.

Alijah raised the Vi'tari blade over his head, ready to come down. Like the half-elf, Vighon wasn't going to beg. He looked up, meeting the eyes of his murderer with defiance and all the courage he had left.

But the green blade remained over Alijah's head, failing to strike him down. The muscles around his eyes twitched, as if he were arguing with himself. Vighon could see Alijah's arm had the slightest of trembles to it.

"Your Grace?" The Mother had recovered and dared to approach.

Her questioning tone broke whatever turmoil was stirring inside Alijah's mind and he lowered his sword. "He may yet prove useful," he claimed, his blue eyes still locked with Vighon's dark orbs. "Put him in the cells."

The northman had no idea what he had just seen, but the bloodshed that still surrounded him quashed any hope that might have arisen from Alijah's change of heart. The Mother gestured to them and two Arakesh broke away to heave Vighon up from the floor. He was sure to give the half-elf the most venomous and wicked look possible on his way past.

"What now, your Grace?" the Mother asked in Vighon's wake.

"Now," Alijah replied, "I finish what you couldn't."

That was all Vighon heard before he was escorted beyond the throne room and into the hall. The passages between there and the dungeons were littered with Namdhorians who had attempted to repel the Reavers, the same creatures who now manned the keep at multiple stations. This led the king to one inescapable truth.

The monsters were in charge now...

CHAPTER 31
RISE AGAIN

Inara's face was embraced by a cool, yet pleasant breeze. Her eyes opened lazily to settle on her surroundings; a sight that always made her smile.

Sanctuary...

The Dragorn sat up in the comfort of a small cave where even the ground was pleasing to lie on. Beyond the entrance, she could see a stretch of blue sky that knew no end, a welcoming ocean to all who knew how to swim in it.

Rising to her feet, Inara walked onto the small plateau outside and took in the sanctuary. It was as glorious as ever. So high was she that the clouds appeared as a fluffy, white forest below, filling the gaps between the mountainous landscape.

Dotted among the mountains, here and there, were larger plateaus with fields of lush wheat and green pastures. It was an environment not to be found anywhere in the real world and that was just how she liked it.

Something moved against the blue sky, drawing her eye to Athis. The red dragon was flying high but his head was dipped, angling his body towards her. Inara loved this part.

Leaving the cave behind, she ran along the path to her left and then out over the bottomless expanse below, following a narrow outcropping of rock. Only when Athis was in line with her altitude did she let herself go, tipping forward off the edge. Her red cloak flapped behind her and the wind rushed into her face as she plummeted towards those fluffy, white clouds.

And then, as always, Athis glided in below her and steadily matched her descent until they came together. A powerful flap of his wings reversed Inara's momentum and the two shot up into the sky, where the faintest of stars could be seen twinkling in the heavens.

The outstanding view was complemented by Athis's magnificent form. Inara sat back and held her arms out, enjoying every second of their flight. The dragon didn't stay in the air for very long, his chosen path taking them towards a golden field of shallow wheat. He gave the impression that he wished for Inara to climb down and so she obliged, though undeniably curious.

"Is something wrong?" she asked, using her voice, the manifestation of her mind.

Athis looked down at her with his piercing blue eyes. There was a sadness in them that weighed on Inara, bringing her closer. She cupped what little she could of his jaw and found it to be icy cold instead of its usual warmth.

"I don't understand," the Dragorn continued. "Why are you so..." Her words trailed away, drowned out by surfacing memories.

Flashes of reality brought forth recent events, reminding her of the Reaver she had fought and the undead dragons that had hounded them.

Alijah...

It all came flooding back in a wave of pain and heartbreak. The last she recalled, Doran had found her in the passages of Grimwhal.

She looked up at her companion. "You're hurt."

As are you, wingless one.

In their sanctuary, Inara felt only the pain in her heart. "You're cold," she fretted.

It will take more than a chill to bring Athis the ironheart down, he promised.

The dragon's confidence brought a smile to her face, breaking through the emotional agony that threatened to consume her. Inara looked around. "What's happening right now?"

More energy is required to heal, Athis explained. *We had to come here to give our bodies more time. If we wake now the process will slow down again.*

Inara turned away from him and walked farther into the wheat field, her mind racing. She had to remind herself that time passed differently inside the sanctuary. They could spend weeks inside here whereas the real world would only know days. That rationale didn't stop her from wanting to fly to Namdhor with all haste and confront her brother.

"He has to be stopped," she said, turning back to Athis. "He's on a dark path, but we can bring him back, I know it."

Athis sighed. *What if it isn't a path? What if the darkness is all he knows now?*

"I can't believe that. The Crow did this to him." Inara fumed, "I should never have let him go! If he had stayed with us we could have helped him, Malliath too!"

Inara... Athis lowered his head. *What he has done, what he is going to do... Alijah may be beyond redemption now. The Crow unmade him. He is not your brother anymore.*

"What are you saying?

Waves of sorrow emanated from the dragon. *We have a duty to the realm, to the king...*

Inara scowled at her companion. "I will not kill him!"

Yet he must be stopped.

"Then we will find another way!" she argued, irritated by the lack of harmony between them.

Equally stubborn, Athis arched his neck to look down on Inara. *You heard The Crow. Monsters only beget monsters. Everything the wizard did was calculated, including his choice of words. He told you, Inara...*

The Dragorn shook her head. "I have no idea why he said that or why he said it to me."

Athis huffed with frustration. *Think!* he implored. *The Crow knew he was a monster for all of his deeds and he knew he had only the power to create more monsters. We have to accept that Alijah has become the very thing we have sworn to stand against.*

"But that doesn't make sense," Inara countered. "The Crow wanted to bring the realm together in peace, with a *good* king. He thought Alijah was *everything!*"

We cannot begin to fully understand the workings of The Crow's mind, but we do have to accept the fact that he was corrupted by magic he should never have touched.

Inara groaned, as her frustration reached for its crescendo, and turned towards the mountainside. There, against the snowy rocks, lay the mouth of a cave she had never seen before. The Dragorn looked back at Athis with a question on her face.

Our discord prevents me from concealing it, the dragon admitted with a hint of shame.

"Conceal?" Inara repeated incredulously. "What are you talking about?"

I have kept this from you, he confessed. *As have all my kind since the days of Elandril.*

Inara stepped back, stunned by her companion's words. "You keep nothing from me," she pointed out. "We share everything..."

This secret is older than me; it was passed down with the memories of my parents and theirs before them.

Inara scrutinised the cave but could see nothing beyond the dark. "That's it, isn't it? That's the place Alijah told me about."

Yes, Athis confirmed. *In there, you will emerge back into the world with a part of yourself you haven't felt since before we bonded.*

Inara struggled to find the right question. "I don't understand. Why would you... Why would your kind keep this from us?"

Athis glanced at the cave. *To protect ourselves,* he replied cryptically. *Right now,* he continued, *you are influenced by me, my wisdom your own. Your thoughts and feelings are guided by me, a fact that keeps you virtuous. Were you to enter that cave and return to the world,* you *would begin to influence* me.

"Why would that be something worth hiding?"

The emotions of humans and elves are not as tempered as our own. We carry the wisdom and experiences of our ancestors - you do not. Should a rider influence their dragon, there is a chance that dragon could be corrupted and their bond used against the realm.

Inara couldn't help but think of her brother. "Is that what's happened to Alijah and Malliath?"

Impossible to say, Athis answered honestly. *They are a complex pairing, with each being equally broken by their experiences. Given The Crow's work, however, I would say it is likely...*

A rogue tear ran down her cheek. "You hid this from me?"

The dragon took a deep breath, pulling at the scales around his chest. *Not for fear of you. I saw the virtue in you the moment we met. I have only done what is in my blood to do - listen to my ancestors. Though I have no memories of the Dragon Riders, I have to assume their history describes dragons who fell from grace because of their Riders.*

This was all so much to take in. On top of her brother's betrayal, Inara didn't know what to think anymore. She began to question every thought and feeling she had ever had, wondering how much of herself had been suppressed.

It was never to that extent, Athis said, reading her mind. *Your thoughts and feelings have always been your own, they were just... influenced by our connection, by our love for each other.*

Inara met his eyes and said one word. "Vighon..."

Athis had a look of shame about him. *Yes. Though your feelings for him are the only things that have been truly affected.*

The Dragorn turned once again to stare at the mysterious cave. "What would happen to our bond?"

I do not know. It would be different, but I could not say how.

Without warning, Inara strode towards the cave. She could feel the pull of Athis, desperate to keep their bond as it was. It felt like a long walk across the wheat field, a time in which her mind went to battle with itself. Would she be undoing herself? Would their bond be damaged? Angry or not, Athis was her life and she knew those were her true feelings. Weren't they?

There was only one way to find out...

Only feet from the mouth of the cave, Inara paused. Could she really do this? Athis's influence on her had done nothing but steer her to do good. He had made her a better person, a better warrior. Fate had bonded them for a reason...

But she had to know. There was no fighting that itch now that it existed.

There's no coming back, Athis declared. *Once you make that choice, our bond will forever be changed.*

The Dragorn looked down at her feet, struggling to take the next step. Too many revelations plagued her mind now.

A crack of thunder interrupted her thoughts. The blue sky was quickly turning to night with stormy clouds coming in from all directions. Flashes of lightning sparked inside those dark clouds and the wind picked up, blowing Inara's hair about her face.

"What is this?"

Athis's body language showed great concern. *You are threatened,* he told her. *You must return to your surroundings!*

In all their time together, Inara had never entered their sanctuary without being somewhere secure in the real world. "What about our injuries?"

Athis looked away for a moment. *Wounds to the flesh remain, but our deeper wounds have healed. You must return, quickly!*

Inara could feel that her companion's urgency came from a place of real concern for her life, rather than of her entering the cave as she initially suspected.

I cannot help you inside Grimwhal, the dragon reminded her. *Go, Inara!*

With one last look at the cave, Inara closed her eyes and let herself drift back to the real world.

"Right," Doran grizzled, "which one o' ye is gonna get it first?"

The Clackers closed in from three sides, their movements cautious with the blood of their own on Doran's weapons. With Andaljor separated into two halves, the dwarf banged the hammer and axe together. The harsh sound hit the sensitive ears of the Clackers, causing them all to wince as one. Unfortunately, there was no sound Doran was capable of that would banish the creatures for good. Eventually, one of them would be bold enough to endure the pain and attack him.

"What are ye waiting' for?" he demanded, crashing the weapons together again with a manic laugh. "If I'm to 'ave me last breath this day, ye can bet that none o' ye will be slinkin' back into the shadows!"

Collectively, the Clackers raised their nightmarish heads and revealed their vibrating throats. It wasn't the last sound the son of Dorain had hoped he would hear, but it wasn't going to stop him from swinging his hammer and axe.

The passage directly ahead exploded with activity as the Clackers burst into a charge. A moment later, the passages to the left and right became a blur of monsters, all rushing towards the dwarf.

Seconds away from certain death, the door behind him was wrenched open to reveal Inara Galfrey. Her expression was reminiscent of a dragon before it exhaled its fiery breath.

"Get down," she instructed before leaping to his side.

Having seen the power of a Dragorn before, Doran wasted no time in dropping to one knee. Crouched beside him, Inara gripped his pauldron with one hand and held the other over their heads, her fist locked into a ball. The Clackers fell upon them, wave after wave of plunging claws and gnashing teeth. Not one succeeded in penetrating Inara's shield.

Doran looked around them, sure that no one had ever experienced this particular view and lived to tell of it. The shield flared and rippled all around them, each strike taking its toll on Inara. The Dragorn's face was pinched together in concentration and her closed fist began to tremble. It quickly became a battle of wills between the Dragorn and the ferocious Clackers.

"The dagger," she said through gritted teeth.

"The what?"

"The dagger... on my belt."

Doran moved her cloak aside and discovered the dagger in question. He instantly recognised the hilt, made from human bone, as well as the blade's curved shape. Of course, how could he forget such a weapon when it had been he who forged it?

The son of Dorain removed the Moonblade from its sheath and admired its opal-like material. It glowed softly with the magic that Inara's mother, Reyna, had infused it with, transforming the original steel into something else altogether. So powerful was it, that any spell cast by man or elf would be instantly broken.

Since that unique property wouldn't help them in this situation, Doran had to wonder what Inara planned to do with what was effectively just a dagger.

The Dragorn's hand slid from atop his pauldron and accepted the Moonblade. She placed the tip of the blade to the floor between them and took a deep breath.

"Cover your ears," she warned.

Doran dropped Andaljor's separate parts and clapped his hands over his ears. Then, Inara hammered the Moonblade into the stone with all her might. Had it been made from steel, the tip would certainly have snapped, if not the entire weapon. Forged from magic, however, the Moonblade slammed into the floor and released a high-pitched sound that resonated throughout Grimwhal's passages.

The Clackers recoiled in pain, relieving Inara of their oppressive attack. The closest fell to the floor, motionless, as blood trickled out of their many ear holes. Those farther back, scrambled to their feet and staggered around, bumping into each other and the walls around them. It was only seconds later that they abandoned their hunt altogether and fled the area, leaving their dead behind.

Doran carefully removed his hands and took in the graveyard that surrounded them. As a dwarf, a natural warrior, he was immensely impressed by the Dragorn.

"Ye seemed to 'ave perked up," he commented by way of thanks.

Inara exhaled a long breath and assumed her full height. The Moonblade was noticeably still on the floor, glowing as usual. Doran raised a bushy eyebrow and looked to the Dragorn, who was now massaging her hand.

"Are ye a'right?" he asked.

"It's just gone into spasm," she explained. "It'll be fine in a minute." Using her good hand, Inara retrieved the Moonblade and sheathed it at the base of her back again. "What happened?"

Doran scratched his head. "Well, ye seemed like ye were down for a while, so I went in search o' Andaljor. Dakmund left it 'ere when we were attacked. Unfortunately, it wasn' the only thing I found. They must o' tracked me back 'ere, I guess."

"Perhaps we should keep our excursions to a minimum," Inara suggested.

"I couldn' 'ave left Andaljor behind," he expressed with more passion than he reserved for actual people. "This weapon *is* clan Heavybelly. Grimwhal might 'ave fallen, but the clan lives on. An'," he continued, picking the weapons up, "with this in the hands o' the king, the clan will always rally around. They need that now more than ever," he added with a low note.

"Then we should take it to them," Inara announced. "We fly to Namdhor."

Doran frowned. "Whoa, whoa, whoa! Are ye in any fit state to fly? Athis didn' look too good out there."

Inara rubbed the back of her neck. "We're fine," she replied.

The dwarf wasn't convinced. "It wasn' that long ago ye couldn' put a sentence together. I'm not sure ye should—"

"We heal fast," she cut in, making for the left passage.

Her face begged to differ. "Well, ye won' get very far goin' that way," he called after her. The Dragorn turned around and he thumbed over his shoulder to the right passage.

Rather awkwardly, Inara reversed her momentum and made for the opposite passage. It was at that moment when Pig decided to return. The Warhog trotted down the central hall, weaving happily between the Clackers. The animal stopped in front of the one who considered himself its master and looked from him to Inara's departing form. Then it followed *her*.

Doran tutted and rolled his eyes at the beast. "Bloody pig..."

Together, they left the halls of Grimwhal behind and walked out into a bright and freezing world of snow. Athis rose from the ground and shook great heaps of snow from his body before flexing his wings. They were magnificent, even to one such as Doran, though they were pocketed with small tears and jagged holes.

"He says thank you," Inara relayed.

Doran wasn't accustomed to being addressed by a dragon and stumbled over his response. "Oh, well, ye know..." He settled on a shrug and whispered, "It was no bother."

A moment of silence passed between Inara and Athis, their conversation private yet brief. It apparently came to an end after the dragon nodded his horned head to the west. Inara walked away from them all and stopped thirty feet later. The Dragorn crouched down and came back up with her Vi'tari blade in hand, its crystal pommel shimmering as it caught the light.

"We will fly in from the east," she said upon her approach. "If we head directly south from here, we will emerge right on top of Namdhor."

"I thought that was where we wanted to be," Doran remarked.

"We have to assume Malliath is there," Inara explained. "They've had more than enough time to take the capital and there's no reason to hope that any kind of resistance has succeeded. If we come in from the east, Athis can take cover and we can make the rest of the journey on foot."

"Ah, ye want to get the lay o' the land first - good idea! Though, for what it's worth, I think we're goin' to come across quite the battle. I reckon those Reavers 'ave bitten off more than they can chew!"

Inara did not look convinced. "Keep your hope, Doran. Keep it for both of us..."

The Dragorn walked towards Athis's neck and made to climb up. It was only then that the dwarf realised he was supposed to follow her. Something heavy apparently dropped into his stomach and, despite the cold air, he felt sweat collecting in the creases of his face.

"Hang on a second!" he protested. "Ye don' mean for me to... ye know... I mean I can' go up." Doran swallowed hard. "Dwarves are called children o' the mountain for a reason! We weren' made to fly."

Inara looked down at him from Athis's back. "How many days will it take you to reach Namdhor from here?"

The son of Dorain didn't need to work it out to know the answer was *too long*. "I might *never* make it if I go up there! What if I fall off?"

"You won't fall, I promise."

Doran eyed Athis from head to tail and felt the palms of his hands becoming clammy. "Ye had better promise! If I enter Grarfath's Hall because I fell off the back o' a dragon, me ancestors will laugh me back out!"

Scaling Athis proved even more difficult than the dwarf expected, but he eventually found himself astride a dragon. It was terrifying.

"So what do ye do?" he asked, searching Athis's back. "Do ye give him a kick?"

The dragon exhaled a sharp breath through his nostrils.

"I wouldn't kick him," Inara advised.

"Wait! What about Pig?"

Athis turned around to face the south. His movements startled the Warhog and it shot off, heading across the white plains. The dragon braced, his wings extended. Doran was sure that heavy feeling in his stomach was going to continue on its journey until it left his body altogether.

"Hold on!" Inara warned.

The son of Dorain gripped Athis's spikes just in time before the dragon took to flight. Staying low, he glided over the land, covering the distance between them and Pig in mere seconds. One deadly claw reached out and snatched the Warhog from the ground.

Then they rose higher... and higher...

Doran watched the world fall away from their dizzying height. It would have been beautiful and awe-inspiring, but the dwarf was now gripping Inara's waist with his eye tightly shut. After a minute of being in the air, he was certain of only one thing: he wasn't going to reach Illian before being sick...

CHAPTER 32
HEROES DIE

Under the canopy of The Evermoore, Asher came to a stop on his journey with one foot resting on a fallen log. The ranger looked around, taking in the trees, the roots in the ground, the sound of the forest. There was no mistaking it: he had been here before.

"*Stop,*" he commanded, halting Adan'Karth up ahead.

The Drake turned his horned head to see Asher. "*Is there a problem?*"

Asher stepped over the log to meet his escort. "*We've been here before,*" he replied with an accusatory tone. "*I've seen these trees before. Last time you brought us through here from over there.*"

Adan'Karth looked to retreat into himself. "*You are mistaken—*"

The ranger growled deep in his throat. "*I knew this was taking too long. You said we were avoiding the Lirian patrols, but they're not even north of Ikirith are they?*"

The Drake slowly shook his head. "*Forgive me, Asher. I was—*"

"*Days! We've been trekking for days, Adan!*" Asher began searching the area in a bid to gain his bearings.

"*You mean to do harm,*" the Drake explained. "*We had hoped to show you... a better way.*"

"*Taking me in circles is not a better way,*" he retorted. "*Where in all the hells are we?*"

Adan'Karth walked back the way they had come and veered off to the left, bringing them to a thicket. The Drake eased his way through and Asher followed behind, a sinking feeling in his gut. At last, Adan'Karth moved the last of the hanging vines from their path and revealed a green meadow.

They were back in Ikirith.

Asher swore in man's tongue and stepped into the field. He could see dozens of Drakes going about their day, enjoying the life they had forged. To his right, the meadow stretched up and curved into the sky, just as it did in the distance.

"*We have been walking in and out of the barrier to disorientate you,*" Adan'Karth told him apologetically. "*You are most welcome here, to live amongst us. You do not have to return to violence.*"

The ranger shook his head. "It tends to be the other way around," he commented to himself. "*Adan,*" he began. "*I need to reach Namdhor. I can't just stay here and bury my head. Lady Gracen wants me dead and I have to know why. Depending on her reason, staying here might put everyone in danger.*"

"*We are safe in Ikirith,*" came the voice of Abun'Sun. The Drake crossed what was left of the meadow and greeted them with a warm smile. "*You have seen our barrier for yourself. You can live in here... if you want.*"

There was a part of Asher that wanted it, to taste that life at least. But not now. Now, the Arakesh were back in his life and he needed to know he was rid of them.

"*I hope to return some day,*" he said. "*And I hope to be welcomed.*"

"*You will always be welcome,*" Abun'Sun quickly responded.

Asher nodded along. "*But I am leaving. And yes, I will likely see more violence before I return, but that's my future and I've more than earned the right to decide it for myself.*"

THE KNIGHTS OF ERADOR

Abun'Sun bowed his head in respect. *"You have earned the right to decide your future many times over. But we cannot have any part in your violence. For that reason, we cannot show you the way to Namdhor."*

"Don't worry, once I get through the barrier I just need to find north and I can get there myself." As frustrating as the entire scenario was, Asher found it almost impossible to be mad at the Drakes. As if their aura wasn't calming enough, they spoke sense. If all of Verda lived like Ikirith, there would be eternal peace.

Peace, however, was a dream for kings. Asher's life was simply placing one foot in front of the other and seeing what scrap it got him into. With a lasting look at Adan'Karth, Abun'Sun, and their enchanted world, the ranger turned to make for the rest of his life and some answers.

Then the sky fell.

The white clouds were expelled in every direction and a deafening *crack* ripped open the ocean of blue. Lightning hammered the meadow, blinding them all in a series of brilliant flashes. What was left in their wake was a different sky, filled with dark clouds that very quickly unleashed a torrent of rain. Things became far worse after that.

The pocket dimension began to collapse on itself, imploding Ikirith from the edges. The meadow shrank, yanking Drakes from their feet and tearing trees from their roots. The curved land that reached for the heavens was sucked back into the earth, tearing the land up like an earthquake. The unique plants and flowers were flattened by debris and falling trees, as were unsuspecting Drakes.

Asher shoved Adan'Karth out of the way but failed to reach Abun'Sun before a tree thundered into the ground between them. The Drake disappeared beneath the trunk, his death guaranteed in an instant. The ranger himself had the ground taken from under his feet and he was swept away with the contracting land. He bounced off logs and rocks along his journey and even collided with more than one screaming Drake.

After striking the end of a fallen tree at an awkward angle, Asher spun in a circle and skidded to a stop in what was now the middle of Ikirith. He groaned in pain and rolled from side to side until his joints felt up to the task of taking his weight again. The rain poured down on him, adding to the chaos and stinging the fresh cut above his eye and those over his hands.

Rising to his feet, he gripped his sore ribs and examined his new environment. Drakes were calling out for help, stuck beneath The Evermoore's debris. There must have been many more who were now buried under the land itself. Asher relived the previous seconds and saw Abun'Sun die again, crushed by the tree.

Their beautiful world was gone in an instant. Ikirith was now exposed to the outside world, where stormy rainclouds awaited. The ranger couldn't be sure if he had hit his head, but he was certainly struggling to make sense of it all.

A wild and terrible roar reached Asher's ears. He knew that roar, intimately. For a time, he had been bonded to its owner and forced to do the worst of things. It was also the very same creature who had haunted his dreams for the last fifteen years.

The ranger ascended a heap of fallen logs and shattered rocks to better see the devastation. There, standing in the middle of the ruin, was a black dragon...

Malliath the voiceless.

Deep was the dragon's mind and deeper still was his wickedness, a darkness that only Asher had seen. Malliath, however, was not the only thing to rule his nightmares, for the dragon had a rider, a rider who had been forged by dark magic.

Above, through the rain, Asher could just make out the flying forms of another five dragons. They were a mystery in themselves, but the ranger decided to keep his focus on the one that had landed, for that dragon was opening his mouth.

The heat of Malliath's fiery breath rushed towards Asher like a wave. The black dragon swung his mighty head from left to right, igniting what was left of the once magnificent Ikirith. The ranger dived into a muddy hole where the roots of a tree had been ripped out. It was hard to say if Malliath had seen him or if the dragon was just expressing the rage that swelled within him.

Asher sat in the wet mud, his gaze distant and lost to thought. If Malliath had returned to Illian, then so had Alijah. There was only one reason they would come back and it was for the same reason that Asher had threatened the half-elf on the eve of his departure. He had seen it in their minds long ago, a twisted sense of purpose and destiny put there by the necromancer.

They had come to conquer...

"Are you out there, Ranger?" Alijah's voice tensed every muscle in Asher's body. "You're nothing if not the survivor!"

Asher ignored his new injuries and navigated his way around the debris. The sound of the rain made it harder to locate Alijah's exact location. He peered between the piled logs and over the mounds of upturned earth, searching for the half-elf. All the while, he had to keep one eye on Malliath, who surveyed the destruction with his purple eyes.

Movement to his left turned the ranger. Drakes, terrified and wounded, were creeping through the devastation. Asher gestured for them to head in the opposite direction and flee. He waited for them to disappear from sight before renewing his search for Alijah. Of course, the question of what he would do when he found him was very much on the ranger's mind. He had told the half-elf that he would be ready for his return, but was he prepared to kill him?

There was little Asher could say he truly loved, but Reyna and Nathaniel were held above all. How could he ever look them in the eye with their son's blood on his hands?

He closed his eyes and rested his head back against a log, searching for his conviction. It was in the darkness, behind his eyelids, that he saw the pure rage and violence that lived within Malliath. Thousands upon thousands of years lay behind the dragon, and every one of them was filled with bloodshed, anger, and suffering.

Asher knew in that moment that he was the only one who could kill Alijah. No other had seen the depths of Malliath's mind. No other could understand the all-consuming nature of his mind over Alijah's. The half-elf was lost to him.

A distant yell of pain snapped Asher's eyes open. Lowered to a crouch, he weaved through the damp logs and soggy mud until he homed in on the source of the cry. As he had feared, the yell belonged to Adan'Karth. The Drake was on his knees, helpless in Alijah's grip around his throat.

"Where is he?" Alijah demanded.

Adan'Karth squirmed and clawed at Alijah's belt as the air was squeezed from his lungs. Passive as he was, the Drake made no attempt to use his magic to free himself. Asher was on the verge of stepping out and revealing himself but his legs locked into place. There was an old voice in his head warning him of such a foolish advance. The shadows were his ally. If he stepped out now he would be forced to face both Alijah and Malliath - a certain death.

But he wasn't that man anymore. Stepping into the light had seen him risen from that murderous abyss. Ignoring the assassin's voice, Asher drew his two-handed broadsword and stepped into the clearing.

"I warned you!" he called, turning Alijah's head. "You shouldn't have come back!"

The half-elf smirked, pushing his cheeks up his face. "I collapse an entire pocket dimension," he said, releasing Adan'Karth, "and you still have the audacity to survive *and* threaten me. Bold, Ranger, *very* bold."

Malliath closed in, stomping over the debris towards them. Coated in rain, the dragon's black scales were glossy in appearance, though his bared fangs were not dripping with water...

"I didn't believe her when she told me," Alijah continued, his gaze roaming over Asher's features. "You haven't aged a day."

Asher sidestepped in a bid to place Alijah between him and Malliath - his only hope of avoiding a fiery death. "So, *you're* the one who wants my head." His eyes flickered to Adan'Karth, who was steadily crawling behind the ranger.

"It should have been easy," Alijah complained. "Especially for the Mother of the Arakesh..."

Asher failed to hide his confusion, but it was quickly mixed with chastising emotions. It had been a long time since anyone had fooled him so easily, yet here he was... the *fool*.

"I'm afraid things haven't been quite as they seem," Alijah told him arrogantly. "And while you've been enjoying the delights of Ikirith, the balance of power has shifted in Illian. Beyond these woods, the realm is not as you left it."

The ranger lifted his sword in both hands and pointed it at Alijah. "What have you done?"

"That's just it, Asher; I've already done it. There's nothing left for you to do now but return to the embrace of death." There was a flash of green as Alijah drew his scimitar. "I will help you with this," he added menacingly.

Asher flexed his fingers to ensure the tightest grip around his hilt. "You think you're the one to bring me down? You wouldn't be the first..."

Alijah tapped his temple. "I am well aware of your history. You have stood against hordes of Darkakin, slain countless orcs, and cut down more assassins of Nightfall than any other. You even bested Alidyr Yalathanil and defeated the mighty Valanis! You are surely a warrior of great renown, worthy of history's note." Alijah's tone dropped. "But I am none of them."

Asher sneered. "I'm not seeing anything special."

The half-elf grinned. "That's your problem; you haven't seen anything. I've been coming here for years, planning for this while you've been hunting monsters in the dark. You've shaped yourself into quite the hero." Now his grin dropped away. "Heroes *die*," he added with conviction.

"I tried that," Asher reminded him. "It didn't stick. And as far as your *plans* go; you haven't won anything yet."

Alijah frowned. "I took Illian in a single day. I fail to see how I haven't won."

The ranger tilted his head and looked at Alijah down the length of his sword. "As long as I draw breath, your end is assured."

That frown turned into a sigh. "Yes," Alijah conceded, "you're right. Of all the thorns, I have long considered you among the worst. I had hoped Lady Gracen would see you were dealt with, but sometimes you just have to do it yourself."

"Is this doing it yourself, *good* king?" Asher spat. "How many Drakes have died today just so you could kill me?"

Alijah glanced at their surroundings. "This was inevitable, regardless of your presence here. But don't worry; I will bring them together again."

Asher narrowed his eyes. "Why doesn't that sound good for them?"

"Your concern for the Drakes is noble, but misplaced. I value their lives far more than your own."

The ranger maintained his battle stance, ready to burst into action. "Is this the part where you kill me? Or were you planning on talking me to death?"

Alijah twisted his wrist to see both sides of his Vi'tari blade in the rain. "*This* would be the part where I offer you a quick and painless death. But we both know you're not going to get on your knees and bow your head. You've always been destined to be torn from this world swinging that sword of yours."

"On that we agree." Asher dived forwards and dropped into a roll, bringing him up within swinging distance of Alijah.

The Vi'tari blade snapped up to meet Asher's broadsword in a ringing of steel. From there, the combatants fell into a duel that few others could survive. Asher struck high then low before coming around the other side swinging left and right. Alijah was there every time, his defences coming up to parry blow after blow.

The ranger growled, allowing his emotions to drive him. He charged forwards and thrust his sword only to have it batted away.

Two successive strikes were landed against him. First the pommel of Alijah's blade knocked the back of his head and the second came in the form of a boot to the back. Asher felt the ground disappear from beneath his feet before it rushed up to greet his entire body.

Soaked and caked in mud, the ranger pushed up from the ground with blood trickling down his neck. A portion of his back felt numb, the pain sure to make itself known in time.

"How disappointing," Alijah said, circling him. "I heard what you did to those assassins. I expected a real fight. Is it possible I've got into your head? Do my words assault you, Ranger? Perhaps you're just tired... *old*."

Asher roared and came up swinging again. Alijah stepped back and arched his back to evade every swipe of the broadsword. The half-elf only tolerated three attempted attacks before he stood his ground and blocked the fourth strike with his blade. Then he went on the attack. Unlike Alijah, Asher didn't have the speed to step back in time with the sword. Instead, he dropped beneath it and rolled to the side, leaving death to linger on the periphery a while longer.

By the time he had risen to his feet again, Alijah was in the air and coming down on him with the tip of his scimitar. Again, Asher was put on the defensive, his blade working furiously to undo Alijah's attacks. A particularly strong blow from the half-elf brought them together, their swords locked against each other.

"I know why you fear me," Asher hissed before kicking Alijah away. "I'm the only one who's seen inside your head. *I'm* the only one who knows what kind of monster you really are."

Alijah's lip curled and he lunged at the ranger with fury in his eyes. Asher didn't evade this time. The two collided in a display of elven techniques interlinked with the fighting forms of the Arakesh. Their battle was fast and precise, leaving no margin for error. But Asher had something Alijah didn't: a second blade.

The ranger dragged his broadsword down the length of Alijah's scimitar, pushing down towards the hilt, and quickly introduced his silvyr short-sword to the melee. With a weapon on each side of the half-elf's Vi'tari blade, Asher had but to push and pull and Alijah was freed of his scimitar. A sudden elbow to his face and the would-be conqueror was thrown back with a cut lip.

Malliath roared and shook his large head, the injury shared. Thankfully, the dragon remained where he stood or Asher's part in the fight would have been over.

"I fought the last person to wield that sword," Asher managed between breaths. "It didn't end well for him either."

Alijah wiped the blood from his lip. "Like I said; I am none of them." His hands came up beside him, one conjuring a ball of fire while the other froze over with ice and vapour. "Fire or ice? I leave the choice to you, out of respect for your service to the realm."

Asher's shoulders sagged. "How gracious," he quipped before spitting blood from a cut inside his mouth.

The fighter in him worked through every scenario that would see him get past Alijah's spells to deliver that mortal blow. Given the half-elf's speed and reactions, however, the ranger had no choice but to accept these as his final moments.

He assumed the last fighting stance of his life - knees bent, swords braced. If he was about to die, he was going to die a warrior.

Teeth bared, Asher wore his rage on the outside. He took a single step forward, preparing to charge one last time. Fate, as ever, was determined to come between the ranger and death, prolonging the pains that came with a life such as his.

Asher fell straight down, as if the ground was swallowing him up. Before he plummeted through the abyss, the ranger glimpsed the sparks and flashes of lightning that traditionally encircled a portal. He also saw the surprise on Alijah's face.

A short drop and a sudden stop buried Asher in a pile of snow. Then, a hard weight fell on top of him and rolled away into more snow. Above, the portal imploded, leaving a grey sky in its place.

The ranger sat up, his senses fighting to gain some kind of orientation. To his left, Adan'Karth lay half-naked in the snow, his face ashen and skin marred with mud. Since there was no snow in The Evermoore, Asher guessed they had travelled north. This was confirmed when he turned around to see Namdhor, partially concealed behind a veil of black smoke that rose from a large patch between them and the capital.

"*I am sorry,*" Adan'Karth whispered. "*This is the only other place I have ever been.*"

Asher continued to look around, though he was struggling to adapt to the brand new environment in his beaten state. They were on The White Vale, the very place the Drakes had been brought into being when he activated Atilan's relic.

"*You can create portals?*" he finally managed.

"*No,*" the Drake replied, obviously wary of their surroundings. "*I stole a crystal from the man. He had a pouch full of them.*"

Asher sighed heavily. "*That was no man...*" He stood up and sheathed both of his swords. Replacing the silvyr blade on his back pulled at something in his shoulder, eliciting a wince from the ranger. There were, no doubt, more wounds just waiting to rise to the surface.

"*Thank you,*" he said to Adan'Karth. "*You saved my life.*" The ranger would have thanked him sooner had their escape not been so dizzying.

"*You saved mine,*" the Drake replied, his reptilian eyes cast to the ground in sadness.

Asher looked to the south, where The Evermoore lay beyond sight. "*I'm sorry for...*" He caught himself, unsure how to address the destruction of the Drakes' home.

"*He came for you,*" Adan'Karth stated, his tone absent the expected resentment.

Death had come for him, as it always did. Alijah was just the new weapon of choice. Still, Asher didn't correct the Drake; he was still reliving their fight in his mind. He shouldn't have entered the fight as if it was a battlefield. The foe he had just survived possessed advantages he should have taken into consideration.

It was possible Alijah Galfrey wasn't an opponent to be killed by a mere ranger. Perhaps it would take an assassin...

He took a breath and recalled what he could from Alijah. He turned on the spot, taking in the realm that had apparently changed since he entered Ikirith. It was only then that he began to take in the details that surrounded them.

There were dwarves everywhere outside the city, their camp decimated by the look of it. Closer to the ranger was that smoking, charred patch of land. Within its borders were hundreds of dwarven bodies, their flesh a crisp black against their shining silvyr armour. Amongst them were Warhogs who had met the same death as their masters.

Between the camp of dwarves and the city, a long row of Namd-horian soldiers were being filed from their barracks in the north to the lower town at the base of Namdhor's rise. They had been stripped of their weapons and armour and looked to be freezing along their slow procession.

What really captured Asher's attention were those that kept them in line. Soldiers, clad in black, and absent any sigil. There were thousands of them, some even visible in the rising streets of the city. They patrolled through the dwarven camp, scrutinising the clans. To the west, they appeared to be sending scouting parties out on horse-back, their numbers in the dozens.

Asher despaired. The north was indeed occupied. If this army had come with Alijah, they had to be knights of Erador; a faction he knew nothing about. Their tactics, fighting style, even their preferred weapon of choice were unknown to the ranger. He didn't like the unknown.

"*We're too exposed here,*" he said, his sight tracking the riders heading south. "*We should get lost in their camp and—*" Movement in the corner of his eye drew him to the north-east, where a pair of foreign soldiers approached on horseback. They were only just emerging from the distance but, on mounts, they would likely catch up with them before they could disappear inside the camp.

Asher cursed. *"Stay behind me,"* he warned, resting one hand on his broadsword. A glance over his shoulder told the ranger his Drake companion was in a state of shock by his absent stare.

It wasn't long before the two riders crossed the plain and met them. Up close, he was able to gain nothing more about this new enemy. Shrouded in armour, even their faces were hidden, though they each wielded a sword.

"Well met," Asher began politely enough. "We're just hunters, from Wood Vale. What happened here? I see no flaming sword," he added, referring to King Vighon's banner.

Indeed, the soldiers displayed nothing that could tie them to Alijah, or any other for that matter. Another noticeable feature was the condition of their armour. Without much examination, Asher discovered battle damage on both of them, including, most curiously, a few gouges where a sword had been plunged.

When the soldiers offered no reply, Asher continued, "We've come to trade..." He stopped, realising the absurdness of his statement considering they had no supplies with which to trade. "That is, we've come to buy goods to trade in Wood Vale."

Again, his words were met with silence. The soldiers, having dismounted, remained where they stood, staring out from their dark helmets. Asher had dealt with many soldiers in his time and he could confidently say that none had ever unnerved him as they did.

"We'll take our leave," the ranger said, filling the void.

Be it his movement or his words, the two soldiers took umbrage and drew their swords. Without a word, they both advanced on Asher with an outstretched hand, meaning to seize him. That meant they didn't know who he was.

Under threat, Asher's body relinquished its aches and pains and gave in to the warrior. His heart sped up, his muscles tensed, and his mind worked through the appropriate strategy to rid him of his opponents in as few moves as possible. Given the amount of armour they wore, he also opted to use his silvyr.

Once the soldiers had stepped into striking distance, Asher held up his hands as if surrendering - a tactic that brought his right hand within inches of the short sword poking over his shoulder. The first to reach for him attempted to grab his right arm.

The ranger exploded into action.

The silvyr's satisfying sound was still rising in his ears by the time he had broken the soldier's wrist, cut open his midriff, and plunged it into the chest of his partner. Both soldiers were knocked to the ground by the sheer force of his attack, but they wouldn't be getting back up if his well-placed strikes were anything to go by.

"We need to go, *now.*" Asher sheathed his short-sword and moved to pick Adan'Karth up. There was no telling who had seen their fight from a distance and they still needed to reach the sprawling camp before they could disappear.

The ranger froze when he saw the Drake's face, his eyes locked in terror. It wasn't terror born of the violence that had just unfolded, however. Plates of armour grated against each other and a pair of swords were dragged up through the snow. Had he not had a lifetime of witnessing the unbelievable, Asher would have claimed the noise behind him to be impossible. Given that he had seen more than most, he turned around with one word on his lips.

"Reavers..."

The soldiers came at him with their swords raised in both hands this time. Asher left his short-sword where it was and dived into the melee with his broadsword coming free. He batted the first blade aside and swung across the neck, removing the first soldier's head before the fight had even got started. The second struck at his exposed back, but the ranger had anticipated such an attack.

"*Look out!*" Adan'Karth yelled, unaware of the extent of Asher's prowess.

The ranger whipped his sword over his head, keeping the broadsword in line with his spine, and parried the incoming attack. Following through with his momentum, he swung around and put all of his strength into one mortal blow. Still encased in its helmet, the Reaver's head flew away from its foul body.

His breath laboured once more, Asher looked from the Drake to the camp. "*We need to go,*" he reiterated.

Picking the Drake up by the arm, the ranger guided him westward. He looked back at the bodies he was leaving in the snow before turning his attention to the thousands of Eradoran soldiers - Reavers all.

Alijah had been right: the balance of power had shifted; the realm was not as Asher had left it...

CHAPTER 33
WRATH AND RUIN

Kassian Kantaris opened his eyes to the sound of a slamming door. They didn't open with a snap, but more a lazy blink, accompanied by hazy vision. First there was confusion. There was always confusion. Then, inevitably, the pain followed.

The master who had volunteered to extract the Galfreys' whereabouts from him had inflicted severe damage to his body, over and over again. Then, she would heal him, leave him to rest, and begin the torture anew.

In truth, she had asked very few questions pertaining to the ambassadors' location within Valatos. Her main focus was the destructive spells she claimed to have invented herself. Apparently, Kassian was her test subject...

The pain brought him to a level of alertness that made him take stock of his surroundings. He was still chained to the wall inside the Archon's council chamber. He hadn't seen Clara since she had been dragged away for her own kind of questioning. Kassian had vowed to himself that he would slowly murder anyone who harmed her.

He would also kill the man who he saw as being responsible for all of this. That man had just entered the chamber in his ordinary robes and his extraordinary mask. Kassian didn't need to see his face or hear his voice to know it was him anymore. He could tell by his walk, the way he carried himself.

"Any progress, Master?" he asked Kassian's torturer.

"No, Master," she replied, her silvery mask flecked with the Keeper's blood. "He offers naught but threats."

The master walked over, his presence dismissing the smaller female. "You still have some fight in you, Keeper. It's such a pity. You could have helped us make Valatos strong. Instead, you, and your wife, will suffer a traitor's death."

Kassian collected the blood pooling in his mouth and spat it across the master's mask. "You don't have the right... to order my death. Only the king—"

The master whipped out his wand and shoved the tip under Kassian's jaw, activating the chain around the Keeper's neck. His airway was quickly sealed shut by the snake eating its own chain. The female master had an air of concern about her, worried, no doubt, that her test subject was about to expire before her work was completed.

"She is tormented daily," he hissed. "Your wife... I fear she will not last as long as you."

Kassian raged, deepening the shade of red that had already taken over his face. As always, he could do nothing but look at his wand and sword, discarded on the table and out of his reach. He only needed one to take his revenge.

The master removed his wand and the chain returned to its normal size around his neck. Kassian coughed and spluttered over the curse he blurted, his words lost on the master. As he gained control back over his breathing, the room quietened and they all heard the same thing, coming from beyond the stained-glass window.

Wings...

PHILIP C. QUAINTRELL

The master's mask stretched into a smile. "The king returns..." Using his wand, he removed any trace of blood from his mask.

Kassian strained his eyes to see through the stained-glass - he had never seen a dragon up close before. The sound of its wings told him it was very close... and impossibly large. It was as if a giant bat was flying over the central hall.

"I told you he was coming," the master continued. "Now we can have our feast! What better way to bring in a new era than with a cup of wine and royal company!" He made to leave and paused upon noticing the female master, who remained diligently beside her *work*. "Are you not to join us, Master?"

"I will be along shortly, Master," she assured. "I have a few more lines of questioning I would like to explore."

The master held out his hands. "Your efforts are tireless! Just make certain you aren't drenched in so much blood when you meet the king."

The door closed behind him, leaving Kassian with the sadistic mage. She removed a glass vial of black liquid from a small chest and presented it in front of him.

"A new elixir I have been brewing for some time," she explained. "A mouthful of this and you will spill all of your secrets, little Keeper."

Kassian considered the torture he had been through. "Why didn't you use that first?"

The master shrugged and casually replied, "It needed more time to brew." She popped the cork and held it towards his lips. "You *will* drink it."

"I don't need to drink it to tell the truth," Kassian growled, pulling on his manacles. "When I am free of this wretched wall, I am going to kill you with your own wand. Then, I'm going to expose the truth of the Archon to the rest of—"

"You're a dead man," the master announced, silencing him. "Your chains are tied to the master's will, and he wishes for you to remain on this wall until death. The *manner* in which you are to greet

406

death, however, is in my hands. Tell me where the Galfreys are hiding and your end will be painless. Lie to me or refuse and you will watch your wife die first."

Kassian slowly leaned forwards, pushing his chains to the limit. "I-will-*kill*-you."

Her mask stretched over her plump cheeks. "I was hoping you would say that."

Kassian braced himself for the next round of pain. Torture was so much harder to endure when magic was the implement of choice. Using her wand, the master could revive him at will or simply keep him awake, pushing him through the pain and robbing him of sweet oblivion.

The master brought her wand up, ready to force the truth elixir down his throat. Then came a loud scream, though it didn't come from Kassian. The wicked mage faltered, her wand poised. The Keeper looked to the stained-glass, where the sound had originated. Then there was another before a chorus of horrified screams resounded across the campus.

"What in all the hells..." The master walked over to the large window and immediately jumped back, startled by the ear-splitting roar that drowned out the screams.

The colours of the stained-glass were brought to life, back-lit by a great blaze. The screaming continued in earnest after that, only to be silenced by successive bursts of dragon's fire. The central hall shook and another almighty roar exploded across all of Velia. A fiery glow lay beyond the stained-glass - Valatos was being set alight!

The female master backed up and rounded the table until she rejoined Kassian by the wall. She was visibly shaken. This was compounded when the doors flew open and the previous master scurried in with singed robes. He slammed the doors shut behind him and locked them with his wand.

"What's happening?" the torturer demanded, her voice strained.

The master staggered into the chamber, barely aware that he

shared it with anyone. His mask was torn on one side, revealing half of an old man's face and a pale eye.

"He ate them," the master uttered.

"What did you say?"

The master turned a petrified expression on them. "The dragon... he ate the Archon."

Now the female mage was truly on edge, gripping her wand in both hands. "Why... Why would he do that?"

Kassian couldn't help but chuckle to himself. "Is this not the feast you had in mind?"

The master who had first tasked him with assassinating the ambassadors was too shocked to even retaliate. He wandered over to the window in a daze and looked out on Valatos.

"He's burning everything," he whispered.

"We need to leave," the other master insisted. "We can take the tunnels and—"

The doors were blown to splinters in a deafening *boom*, showering the chamber in debris and smoke. A dark figure entered the room, his features masked by the smoke. Whoever he was, the masters knew enough about him to panic. The torturer reacted like a cornered animal and flicked her wand at the figure. His arm came up and deflected the destructive spell in a flash of magic, illuminating his angular face.

"It looks like Malliath will have dessert after all," he said cheerily.

The female master backed up to the wall, trembling with fear. Being eaten alive had to be at the top of anyone's worst fears. She fired another spell, then another and another. The so-called king shielded every one with little effort, as if the mage was hurling no more than snowballs at him.

Kassian got a good look at him now. He had never seen him before but assumed him to be an elf due to his pointed ears. That would certainly explain his apparent affinity for magic. It didn't, however, explain why he was attacking Valatos.

"Will you offer yourself to him?" he continued. "Or do I have to throw you into his maw myself?"

Proving that a rider was always in communication with their dragon, Malliath's hulking body slammed into the side of the building. His enormous head, styled with curving horns, violently burst through the stained-glass window. The male master dropped to the floor, cowering in a mess, bloodied by shards of colourful glass.

The dragon's hot breath rolled over the room and he licked his blood-soaked fangs. The female mage, Kassian's personal torturer, was flat against the wall and standing in a puddle of her own making.

Then, she placed the tip of her wand into the soft palate under her jaw. There were no last words, just a stifled cry before her spell blew the top of her head off, spraying blood and gore across one half of Kassian's body.

"Pity," the dark figure mused. "However, there is still one morsel left," he observed, eyeing the surviving master on the floor. "Perhaps *you* will satiate his hunger..."

"Why have you done this?" the master cried. "You gave us your word! We did everything you asked!"

"And in doing so you only showed your true colours," the man replied. "There is no place for your kind in my new world. In truth; there never was." Without explanation, Malliath pushed off from the building and continued his rampage of Valatos.

"You... You.... You promised us the knowledge of the Jainus," the master whimpered. "That... That was all we wanted. We would never have sought independence from *your* kingdom." He swallowed hard and tried his best to offer the man a pleasing smile. "The realm of King Alijah..."

The man known as Alijah laughed to himself. "Your hunger for knowledge and power has betrayed you, blinded you even. I could never trust the knowledge of the Jainus to you. You're corrupt, greedy, dishonourable - all the things that brought the Jainus down to begin with. It's time the power in this world was wielded by those who know what to use it for."

The master was sobbing now. "But... We did what you asked. Have mercy!"

Alijah crouched down and reached out like a parent caressing their child's face. "Mercy will have its day. But it is not *this day*." In a feat of incredible strength, he dragged the master up from the floor and threw him out of the open window. His scream was cut short when Malliath flew by and caught him in his jaws, snatching the mage from sight.

Kassian stayed very still, hopeful that he would remain a spectator. His chains, however, were reduced to smoke in the wake of the master's death, drawing Alijah's attention to him. Having fallen to his hands and knees, the clasp on his necklace broke and the golden chain dropped to the floor. Despite his freedom, the Keeper's heart picked up the beat in anticipation of his death.

Surprisingly, Alijah glanced at the fiery vista beyond the shattered window and simply said, "Enjoy the view." Then he was gone, out of the window himself.

Most would have remained where they fell, frozen with shock or terror at what they had just witnessed, but Kassian didn't have time to contemplate it all.

"Clara," he breathed with some urgency.

In his mad scramble out of the room, the Keeper's haste battled with his limbs to get his coat on, his wand strapped to his thigh, and his sword sheathed on his hip. There was a good chance he was going to need all three if he was going to get out of this alive with Clara.

Running through the central hall, it was clear to see that chaos had erupted everywhere. Malliath had pockmarked the building with jagged holes and exhaled his fiery breath therein. Scorched bodies were strewn throughout the passages while others lay still beneath crushing debris. Then there were those still running for their lives, searching for somewhere to hide from the dragon's spreading fire.

His wand was required to blast through the debris blocking the main doors. Once outside, he was presented with a vision of hell. Everything was on fire. There wasn't a single building that hadn't been damaged or set alight by the dragon. Mages and Keepers were doing their best to put the fires out, their wands and staffs producing jets of water, but the flames were stubborn. Others were hurriedly escorting the younger students to the main gates, their eyes darting across the sky in fear.

Malliath's roar preceded him. The black dragon came round from the east and exhaled a line of fire that reduced the gardens to ash. Dozens of mages hiding there were forced to flee before being consumed. Gaining height once more, Malliath curled his tail down and dragged it through the corner of the alchemy building. Tons of stone were flung across the campus with enough speed and force behind them to kill anyone unlucky enough to get in their way.

Higher still, five more dragons danced in and out of the clouds. For just a moment, Kassian dared to hope that the Dragorn had returned and with the best of timing. His hope, however, was dashed when he realised they were content to stay away from Valatos.

A woman's scream snapped Kassian from the nightmare. He couldn't find the owner of the scream, but it reminded him that time was against them all now - Valatos was being transformed into a giant forge. The Keeper sprinted across the grounds, leaping over bodies and debris to reach the tower block that housed the cells. He was desperate to reach Clara, to hold her again, and tell her everything was going to be alright.

Rounding the potions building, Kassian came across a group of Keepers who had banded together to challenge Malliath. Their collective wands and staffs were aimed at the sky, but the black dragon blended into the fading light and smoke. When he cut through the smoke to face his challengers, they were wholly unprepared for his wrath and quickly concealed within the raging inferno that engulfed them.

Kassian altered his direction and took an alternative route to the tower block. After rushing past more horrors, some of which would have caused him to vomit if he had stopped to consider them, the cells were finally in view beyond the circular fountain in the courtyard. Parts of it were smoking where Malliath had expelled his deadly breath. Other parts were crumbling, threatening to destabilise the entire block.

Barely stopping to catch his breath, Kassian pushed himself to reach that single gate at the tower's base. That same gate flew open a moment later and a handful of Keepers fled the building. In their midst was Clara!

"Clara!" he yelled, trying to direct her attention towards him.

The Keepers outpaced her, but he could still see her shock of red hair between them. Kassian called out her name again and again, running as fast as his legs would take him. He had almost reached the fountain, half way, when he saw Malliath, descending from the stars behind his wife.

Kassian's world dropped out from under him, just as it had during The Ash War. Like then, he was too far away to help the ones he loved. Back then, it had been the orcs who murdered his family. Now, it was to be a dragon...

"NO!" he screamed, waving his hand to the side. "RUN!"

There was nothing to be done. Kassian could only watch as Malliath unleashed a torrent of fire. He found Clara's face in the middle of it all, her desperation turning to hope as she met her husband's eyes. There was nothing in Kassian's eyes but the reflection of the flames. Malliath's wrath consumed the group, even those who broke away.

Clara was gone.

Kassian kept running towards her with tears streaking down the ash coating his face. At his current pace, he would sprint into the jet of fire in moments, there to join his wife. His trajectory, however, was knocked wildly off course without any warning. The thing that slammed into him came from nowhere and launched him off his feet and into the shallow fountain.

It was all a shock. The heat of the fire. Clara's death. A violent collision. The cold of the water. Everything happened at once for the Keeper. Lifting his head from the water, he discovered Nathaniel Galfrey rising beside him. Beyond the edge of the fountain, Reyna was standing in the light of the fire that had just taken Clara's life. The elf was staring into the flames with a sadness that almost mirrored the Keeper's.

Kassian dragged himself up and then dropped to his knees again. His wife's body was charred black and edged with dragon's fire. She was lost to him. He cried out into the fiery night with an almost feral roar.

A strong hand rested on his shoulder. "I'm so sorry, Kassian."

Nathaniel's words meant nothing to the Keeper. How could any words hold meaning ever again? This was a world of violence and death, a fact proven time and time again to Kassian. Everything and everyone he had ever loved had been taken from him.

Now he wanted blood.

"Mother, Father..." Alijah's startling voice came from behind them all. He was standing in the courtyard as if they weren't surrounded by death.

The fact that he had referred to the Galfreys as his parents was entirely lost on Kassian. His loss had hollowed the Keeper out and filled him back up with rage. Before either of them could reply to their son, Kassian charged across the fountain, determined to kill the animal who had brought his world to ruin.

Nathaniel reached out but failed to secure a hold. "Kassian!" he warned.

The Keeper leaped out of the fountain without even bothering to draw his sword or wand - he was going to take the murderer's life with his bare hands!

Mid-air, Kassian's momentum was suddenly reversed, changing

with the wave of Alijah's hand. One moment he was flying towards his wife's killer, the next moment he was being hurled into the stone feature at the centre of the fountain. His head took a knock before he finally fell back into the shallow pool.

His vision felt fractured for a second and he had no recollection of the fall itself. A thumping pain pushed out from the back of his head in waves. Instinctively, his hand investigated the source of the pain and came back to him with blood painted over his fingers. The disorientation soon succumbed to his rage, which was ready to see him rip Alijah apart. Rising to his feet, however, became an immediate problem and he splashed back into the fountain water, struggling to correct his sight.

"This is how you return?" Nathaniel yelled at his son. "Alijah, you're killing people!"

Alijah's eyes shifted from his father to his mother for a second. Had Kassian blinked, he would have missed the sadness that flickered briefly across Alijah's face.

"I wanted to tell you," he said, taking a step closer to his parents. "I wanted to do this with you both by my side. But I knew you wouldn't see as I do. I knew you would try to stop me..."

Nathaniel looked bewildered. "And then what? Would you kill us too? Would you kill your parents for disagreeing with genocide?"

"This isn't..." Alijah stopped himself from protesting any further. "You can't see what needs to be done."

"You have seen nothing," Reyna said, speaking for the first time. "This is what *he* saw, isn't it? This is The Crow's vision for the world. Burn it down and start again, is that it?"

With teary eyes, Alijah shook his head. "I'm not just another monster threatening the world, Mother. My entire reason for existing is to save lives, even the ones that haven't been born yet. I'm here to change everything, to break the scales!"

"You're not saving anyone here," Nathaniel countered with steel in his voice. "Look around you, Son. This is just murder."

Alijah tore his eyes away from his mother. "You don't understand yet," he told them. "But you will. Even if it takes several lifetimes, you will come to see that there was no other way. I'm going to succeed where all those before me have failed. I'm going to bring peace to Verda."

"These aren't your words," Reyna pressed. "They can't be. The boy I raised knew the difference between good and evil, and this *is* evil, Alijah."

"Sacrifice without hesitation," Alijah declared. "This is what a good king must do. You can't see it yet but that's exactly what I'm doing. Until then, I think it would be best if you remained in The Dragon Keep, as my guests."

"The Dragon Keep?" Nathaniel repeated with concern.

"Namdhor is mine," Alijah confirmed. "All of Illian is mine now. And I did it without bringing war to the country," he added, as if that would make all the difference. "It's been the quietest invasion in history. Why? Because I orchestrated it that way. I told you," he continued, looking to his mother, "I've come back to save lives, not take them."

"Unless you deem their sacrifice is necessary," Nathaniel pointed out. "Tell me, how many sacrifices will there be before you're satisfied with your *peace*?"

Alijah's expression turned hard. "As many as there have to be."

His last word was punctuated by Malliath's arrival. The black dragon came down behind his rider with thunderous claws and a mouth brimming with blood-soaked fangs. His purple eyes roamed over the ambassadors, ignoring Kassian completely.

The Keeper clenched his jaw and every muscle in his body did the same. That beast had robbed the world of its most precious and beautiful gem. He had pierced Kassian's heart and left him ravaged, barely a man anymore.

Naturally, his hand dipped into the water and gripped the wand holstered to his leg. He knew of no spell that could slay a dragon, nor one as powerful as Alijah, but he knew a spell that could turn one of Malliath's exquisite eyes to mush in his eye socket. That would hurt like hell. Maybe then, in their combined agony, he could strike Alijah with a more deadly spell, weakening them enough to give him time, time enough to draw his sword and take his head.

He wanted it to be bloody.

As the wand came free under the water, something clicked into place, illuminating Kassian's mind with an idea and a memory all at once.

The Lexichronan!

"Please," Alijah pleaded, "don't fight this. Go to Namdhor and just—"

"*You*," Kassian growled, stealing everyone's attention. "You're not welcome here..." With that, the Keeper hammered the tip of his wand into the base of the fountain, activating the magic granted solely to him by the Lexichronan.

At first, nothing happened, causing confusion among the Galfreys. Then, Valatos's defences came to life all around them in the form of elemental monstrosities. The debris that littered the campus swirled together in a violent tornado, bringing rock and stone into the shape of a giant. Every drop of water rose into the air around Kassian, emptying the fountain. As one, the rock elemental clubbed Malliath across the face and the water swirled into a column and speared Alijah across the campus.

The dragon roared in defiance, revealing his cracked scales and bloody face. His tail whipped around and smashed the rock elemental to pieces, only to discover that those same pieces were quickly pulled back together.

Alijah was slammed into the base of the nearest building and nearly drowned by the water elemental. His drenched cloak clung to his suit of armour, hindering his limbs. Valatos, however, wasn't finished flushing its unwelcome guests out. Malliath's fires were dragged from their victims and blown over the half-elf by what could either have been a fire elemental or possibly one of air.

Unfortunately, he was able to shield himself before the conflagration could set him alight. What he failed to do, however, was shield himself from the next blow, delivered by the rock elemental into Malliath's ribs.

"Come on!" Nathaniel yelled, yanking Kassian to his feet as both Alijah and Malliath howled in pain.

The Keeper tried to fight the old Graycoat off. "No! We need to finish this!"

"Trust me, this isn't going to stop either of them and neither will we."

Malliath attempted to take flight but was battered by a powerful air elemental into the building behind him. The walls came down on top of the dragon in a cascade of bricks, partially burying his hind legs.

Alijah suffered equally and collapsed to his knees as the water elemental rose over him in a tidal wave. Kassian fought through the pain in his head and gripped the hilt of his sword.

Nathaniel's hand came down on top of his. "Don't be a fool! Survive today and fight tomorrow!"

What little remained of Kassian's rational mind heard the sense in Nathaniel's words. He looked to Reyna, who was still standing in the same place. She watched her son take the elementals' wrath with tears running down her face, though she made no attempt to help him, her feet firmly rooted to the spot.

"We need to leave!" Nathaniel shouted at them both.

Kassian took one last look at his wife's body before he allowed Nathaniel to drag him away beside Reyna. Behind them, Alijah fired spell after spell at the rock elemental while Malliath unleashed his fiery breath on the water elemental. Even if the pair survived Valatos's defences, at least they would be distracted long enough for the mages to flee and take shelter in the city.

Numb, Kassian ran beside the Galfreys because all he could do was keep moving. They fell in with other mages and Keepers trying to escape the campus. It was a chaotic free for all. No one understood why this cataclysm had befallen their home but all looked to have lost something more than bricks and mortar.

Outside Valatos's walls, the streets were packed with terrified mages and Velians, many of whom had generously opened their doors to the families who had nowhere but the alleys to flee to.

Kassian pushed his way through beside Nathaniel, who was still guiding Reyna with both hands. As the mob began to thin out, Velian soldiers quickly filled the gaps, maintaining an air of chaos to it all. None of them was interested in being herded or organised by the soldiers and continued along their path, heading for the city's main gate.

"Where are we going?" the Keeper demanded, shoving past a group of curious onlookers.

Nathaniel looked at his wife, huddled in his arms, before boldly replying, "We're going exactly where he told us to. We're going to Namdhor..."

CHAPTER 34
DIVERGENCE

Several miles east of Namdhor, where tall pines marked the base of Vengora, Athis the ironheart touched down in the snow. It wasn't his most graceful landing, but the dragon was hindered by the Warhog in one claw and a general level of exhaustion that Inara shared with him.

The very second Pig was offered enough room to move within Athis's claws, the Warhog shot away at full speed, kicking up snow in its wake. Doran attempted to holler at his stubborn mount, but the dwarf had problems of his own.

"How in Grarfath's name are ye supposed to get down from—" The end of his question was answered by the dwarf himself. He combined sliding with falling until he hit the ground face-first.

Inara winced. "Are you hurt?" she called down.

Doran's face came up laughing. "I'm never leavin' ye again!" he proclaimed, kissing the ground.

The Dragorn would have laughed herself but she was far from a jovial mood. Despite her fatigue, Inara employed her inherent grace and descended to the ground. She deliberately avoided Athis's eyes, still struggling to find any harmony between them.

419

We should talk about it, the dragon suggested, just as he had many times on their journey over the tops of Vengora. *You didn't enter the cave,* he reminded her.

Would that be your influence? Inara retorted.

It has never worked that way, Athis tried to explain. *Our bond has affected your feelings, not your direct thoughts. Your choices and actions have always been your own. My influence has never gone further than ensuring your distinction of good and evil.*

You suggest that your own distinction is superior, Inara countered. **Yet Malliath resides at the heart of my brother's misdeeds. Is my humanity such a threat to you, to the realm? Is it threat enough that you would keep this from me?**

I was wrong to withhold this from you, Athis conceded. *Your heart has always been pure; I saw that the moment we met. But this has been the way of things since Elandril bonded with Nylla, five thousand years ago. Malliath and Alijah are an example of what happens when a dragon's mind is influenced by a human.*

You can't possibly believe that Alijah is the root of this?

In all Malliath's long life, he has never pitted himself against the realm as he now does. Alijah's mind has been spoiled by The Crow and now he shares that mind with a dragon. He told you himself; he has entered that part of his sanctuary, exposing Malliath to—

"You're wrong!" Inara blurted aloud, startling the son of Dorain.

The dwarf was poised to reply but his only eye simply shifted from Inara to Athis and back. "Right..." he said, straightening himself up. "We should probably get goin'. If me clan has flanked the Reavers, ye can bet I want to add Andaljor to the battle!"

Inara quashed her frustration and looked Athis in the eyes. **We will finish this another time,** she told him.

Leaving Athis behind, dwarf and Dragorn set off along the tree line, heading west. It would take them most of the day to reach Namdhor on foot, but at least they would avoid Malliath's detection. They trekked in silence until Athis was out of sight and Pig was found, snuffling in the foliage between the trees.

It took Doran some time to settle the Warhog after a traumatic journey in the clutches of a dragon. The dwarf had to drag him by the reins for a quarter of a mile before the mount felt safe enough to trot beside Inara.

"So..." Doran dragged the word out. "Is everythin' a'right between ye an' Athis?"

It wasn't a topic she wanted to discuss with the dwarf, especially given the fact that Athis would be privy to every word. "Everything's fine," she lied, though her tone did her no favours.

"If ye say so," Doran replied, clearly unconvinced.

Inara had nothing to say. Her mind was consumed by a tumultuous storm that denied her peace. She felt betrayed by those closest to her heart and she feared for the rest. The knights of Erador had most certainly fallen upon the capital. What had become of Vighon? Her parents?

Answers would only come if she continued to put one foot in front of the other. And so she did. The summer sun passed through the sky, overtaking them to reach the west.

When, at last, Namdhor was in sight, the clear, blue sky was just beginning to change colour, casting the capital city in orange hues.

Quite shocking, if not horrifying, was the ruined field of charred corpses, possessing both dwarven and Warhog alike. It was a black stain on the white landscape, just as it was a stain on any hope Doran had harboured. The son of Dorain choked on his words and staggered towards the massacre.

As shocking as it was, Inara took an extra moment to assess *all* of their surroundings. A strip of dragon's fire parted the northern barracks from the city. She couldn't make out any Namdhorian soldiers, but she could easily see the Reavers, clad in their black armour. They were everywhere, throughout the outer lands as well as the city. Spread out beyond the charred bodies lay a campsite of dwarves, their numbers in the thousands.

"We're too late," Doran lamented.

Inara's right hand curled up to her belt where her fingers crept around to the diviner on her hip. She had been tempted to use it many times over the last fifteen years but had always refrained. Whatever the situation, the Dragorn had never failed to find her own way of dealing with the problem. But now, seeing Namdhor in the grip of such evil, she needed Gideon Thorn.

Her hand gripped the spherical object and hesitated to remove it. For just a moment, Inara was seized by shame. Under her watch, Illian had been invaded, both herself and the king had been manipulated and tricked, and thousands of dwarves had already died. How could she tell her old mentor of this?

Athis made his presence known in her mind and washed away her hubris, reminding her that their feelings were trivial. Inara would never say so but, in that moment, she was glad of the dragon's influence. With finger and thumb, she untied the knot and dipped her hand into the pouch, feeling the diviner's glassy surface.

Her hand froze. A twig had snapped not far from their position. Her instincts immediately told her danger was close. Releasing her grip on the diviner, she instead grabbed Pig by the reins and pulled hard, guiding the mount and its rider into the trees. Doran's state of shock kept any protests at bay and his eyes firmly on the landscape. As they disappeared behind the trees, a pair of riders emerged farther up, missing them by moments. The Dragorn held a finger to her lips, signalling the dwarf to be quiet while she acquired a closer look.

Two Reavers on horseback were making their way towards the city, thankfully oblivious to Inara and Doran. The Dragorn looked about, wary of any other patrols in the area.

"Scouts," Doran whispered from behind. "I say we cleave their heads an' be done with 'em," he added with hatred.

Inara placed a hand on his shoulder, calming the dwarf. "Let's leave the cleaving for later, shall we? Right now, we need to learn the state of things."

Doran huffed. "State o' things? The state is bloody obvious!"

"Then where is Malliath?" Inara countered. "He could be anywhere out there and we need to get eyes on him before we make our next move."

The dwarf looked in need of convincing. "An' what exactly is to be our next move?"

Inara poured all of her determination into her next words. "We kill them all."

Satisfied with the plan, Doran and Pig fell in behind Inara as they made their way closer to the city from within the trees. The Dragorn kept her eyes moving, always surveying the land ahead, behind, and above. They were well and truly behind enemy lines now, a statement that Inara struggled to consider given the city in question.

After spending some time watching patrols, noting their repeating patterns, Inara and Doran made a dash from the trees and headed north-west, towards the sprawling camp. They were vulnerable in that open stretch, a feeling that Athis shared from miles away. Were Malliath to descend on them now, their time in Verda would be at an end and any hope of rebellion with them.

It was a moment of great relief when they passed beyond the outer edges of the camp and into the hubbub. That relief, sadly, was quashed by dismay. All around them, the dwarves were grieving, pained by their loss. Children were crying in the arms of their weeping mothers while others cried out from wounds new and old. Adding to the chaos, it was cramped and busy with activity, all of which was underpinned with a general sense of anger and mistrust.

Inara ignored the looks shot her way and ploughed through the narrow passages, towards the base of Namdhor. Every few steps, the Dragorn was forced to stop as dwarves crossed her path, paying her no heed. It was infuriatingly slow progress, but it was better than walking in the open, exposed to the Reavers.

Just as the lower town was coming into view, a tall stranger blocked her path, cloaked and hooded in green. Initially, Inara objected to the man standing in her way, but a moment's pause revealed his identity, gleaned from his weapons if not the cut of his grizzled jaw.

"Asher!"

The ranger flicked his head to the side. "Follow me," he instructed simply.

"What in all the hells are *ye* doin' 'ere?" Doran asked, trailing closely behind Inara. "I left ye in Lirian!"

Asher offered no response but to continue leading them through the camp, away from the city. They passed through a large makeshift tent filled with steam and banging pots as dwarves cooked great vats of beef stew and other dishes that made Inara's stomach growl. Outside was a smaller tent, capable of fitting no more than four dwarves and their gear.

The ranger held back the flap and gestured for them to get inside. "Quickly," he urged, scanning the paths that led off from the tent.

Inside, Inara discovered the last thing she had thought to find. "A Drake," she said without meaning to.

Doran was the last to enter, behind Asher, after tying his Warhog to a post - though there was no telling how long it would remain secure. The dwarf gave the Drake a long hard stare before turning to Asher.

"Somethin' tells me ye've acquired another extraordinary tale, as if ye didn' 'ave enough!"

Asher pushed back his hood, revealing features far too youthful for a man of his age. "I could say the same of you, travelling in such company."

Doran looked at Inara. "Our tale is not a light one..."

"Nor mine," Asher replied.

"Does yours end with my brother trying to kill you," Inara quipped, unsure if she was able to speak about his betrayal with any serious tone.

Asher stared at her, his answer horribly clear.

"Ye've had a run in with Alijah too?"

"Of course you have," Inara uttered, thinking like Alijah. "He would see you as a threat..."

"He came for me in Ikirith," Asher explained, glancing at the Drake. "That's where I met Adan'Karth here." The half-elf, half-dragon gave them a polite nod and a smile. "Adan'Karth saved my life, but Alijah and Malliath still razed Ikirith to the ground."

Inara should have been shocked and hurt, but the Dragorn had endured enough heartbreak to harden her against such news. "Are they here? In Namdhor?"

Asher shook his head. "We've been here for a few days and seen no dragon."

I'm coming to you, Athis said into her mind.

Hug the mountains and find somewhere by the lake, out of sight. He could return at any time.

"A few days?" Doran echoed. "Whose tent *is* this?"

"Battleborns, soldiers of King Uthrad who died with him out there."

Doran's face dropped. "Uthrad is... The king o' Silvyr Hall is *dead?*"

"So they tell me." The ranger elaborated, "Your kin witnessed me slaying a couple of Reavers, a feat that granted us favour among them. They showed us to this tent. Since then, I've been gathering what information I could."

Doran wiped his hand over his face. "Uthrad is dead," he said to himself. "I can' believe it."

"They've tried to reclaim his body," Asher continued, "but the Reavers always stop them. I think Alijah wants the dead to stay right where they are."

"For all to see," Inara concluded.

"Wait," Doran commanded, holding up a hand. "Where's me own clan? Where're the Heavybellys?"

"They're not here," Asher told them. "I've looked for them myself. There isn't one in this camp, save for yourself."

The dwarf furrowed his hairy brow. "I don' understand," he stammered. "They should o' been 'ere days ago, before ye even got 'ere."

"Somebody would have noticed an entire clan arriving," Asher reasoned. "They're not here, Doran."

Now the son of Dorain looked concerned. "Well, I need to find 'em!" he declared, rising to his feet. "Me brother was wounded bad. An' me mother was among 'em. I need—"

"Doran." Inara said his name with authority. "We need to think clearly. Look at where we are. Our every move must be calculated lest we attract the Reavers."

"I can handle a few Reavers," Doran argued.

"Can you handle ten thousand Reavers?" Asher queried. "I've seen hundreds march south yet thousands still remain in Namdhor."

Despite their words, the dwarf's rage continued to flow. "I will kill every single Reaver who gets between me an' mine, ye hear, Ranger?"

Asher remained calm in the face of the angry dwarf. "From what I can tell, the Reavers are very particular about keeping your kin confined to this place. I've seen some make it as far as half a mile, but the Reavers always pursue. Your departure wouldn't go unnoticed."

"Why are they keeping the dwarves here?" Inara picked up.

Asher shrugged. "Your guess is as good as mine. From observation, they aren't stopping people coming in and out of the city, but no dwarf has been allowed to travel much farther than the camp boundary."

"Brilliant," Doran remarked sarcastically. "Ye've walked me right into a damned prison, girl!"

"Call me *girl* again and you'll walk right into Grarfath's Hall," Inara snapped. The unusually sharp retort silenced the dwarf immediately, sobering his ire. The Dragorn shrugged off the looks she received and waited for Doran to sit down again. "What have you heard of Vighon?" she asked.

Asher spared a glance for Doran before he answered. "I've ventured into the city only once, but what I heard isn't good."

"Is he alive?"

"Apparently," Asher replied, hesitant, it seemed, to grasp a strand of hope. "Rumour is he's in the dungeons of the keep. He didn't have many soldiers up here, but those he did have can no longer fight. The Reavers have stripped them all of armour and rank, dismissing them to their homes."

"Why didn' he kill the king?" Doran questioned. "It wouldn' be his first, eh," he added bitterly.

"At this point," Asher assumed, "I can only imagine he has something worse in mind."

Inara shook her head. "If Vighon is inside that keep I'm getting him out. Whatever is to come, we will need him if we are to fight back." Her mind began to run through the layout of The Dragon Keep. "There's only one way in and out of the dungeons, but we might be able to get inside the keep via the—"

"There's no *we*, Inara." Asher's response cut right through her.

"What do you mean?"

Curiously, Asher looked at the Drake before replying. "I agree that Vighon should be rescued, but I'm not here for that."

Inara was struggling to guess at his reasons for being in Namdhor if not to help her save the king. How many times had the ranger stepped in to keep the realm from falling into darkness?

"Then why *are* you here?"

Asher remained silent, his eyes averted.

"I know why he's 'ere," Doran said, capturing the ranger's attention. "Ye're meanin' to kill 'im, aren' ye? Ye're 'ere to kill Alijah."

Inara was instantly conflicted, aware that if anyone could get close enough to her brother and actually murder him, it would be one trained in the art of the Arakesh. "I thought your assassin days were behind you," she commented.

"I thought so too, but then he returned - in just the manner I warned he would - and forced me to re-evaluate my position on it."

"You can't be serious?" Inara argued.

"I told all of you what he really was, *years* ago. I warned you of the things I saw inside his mind, inside Malliath's mind. I fought him, Inara. Trust me, there's only one way to stop him and it isn't in combat and it isn't with an army at my back. I'm going to come at him sideways. He won't even know he's dead."

"We can't kill him," Inara stated flatly.

"The hell I can't. I've been killing people since before you were born; I've got pretty good at it."

"Aren' ye gettin' too old for that kind o' work, lad?" Doran insisted. "Ye're not a killer anymore. If ye go back down that path ye might not come back..."

"We can't kill him because this isn't his fault," Inara said, renewing her argument. "That is to say; this isn't his doing. It can't be. It must be Malliath—"

"Of course it's Malliath," Asher agreed, surprising the Dragorn. "The Crow emptied your brother out and allowed Malliath to pour in, filling him with over ten thousand years of rage and bitterness. This might not be Alijah, at least not the Alijah you knew, but you know as well as I do that there's no separating them now. And since I can't kill a dragon, I'm going to kill its rider."

Inara had nothing to counter his point - he was right in every regard. "But he's still my brother," she managed, aware that it wasn't enough of an argument to dissuade the ranger.

Asher didn't miss a beat. "That's why *I'm* going to kill him."

"Ye're not thinkin' straight," Doran maintained. "Don' get me wrong; I'm o' a mind to kill the lad meself! But think abou' Reyna! An' Nathaniel! Ye're gonna kill their boy?"

Exasperated, Asher replied, "He's not their boy anymore! Just as he's not your brother! Or your friend! Alijah Galfrey died fifteen years ago, the very moment he and Malliath laid eyes on each other. Trust me, I know better than most when fate deals you its worst hand..."

Inara was only too eager to match his ire, desperate for a fight.

"What do you know of such hands? I'd say you look awfully good for a man maligned of fate."

Displaying a measure of control and discipline that Inara knew *she* should be the one to exhibit, Asher relaxed his shoulders and glanced at Adan'Karth. "There's magic in my bones," he declared with little enthusiasm.

Doran raised a bushy eyebrow. "There's what?"

"The Drakes - they told me there's residual magic lingering in my bones, from Paldora's gem. *That's* why I'm not ageing." Asher leaned forward and looked directly at Inara. "*That's* why I'm still here. *That's* why I'm still fighting and bleeding. *That's* the hand fate has dealt me - to endure. It also imparted me with a set of skills," he added, removing a red strip of cloth from his belt. "So I'm going to use what I have and set things right."

Inara was taken back to the end of The Ash War, before those final days of violence. Lady Ellöria had offered them all encouraging speeches, words for each that would resonate with them and set them on their chosen path. They were powerful words for all, though the Dragorn still recalled her great aunt's words for the ranger.

"*Prove to us now that you still live to unbalance the scales of fate...*"

Those same scales had once again been tipped against the realm, surely sealing Verda's fate in the grip of Alijah and Malliath. And here was Asher once again, placed in the middle of it all with undeniable, if deplorable, skills to unbalance the scales of fate. Inara had to ask herself if she even *should* get between the ranger and his intended goal.

She resisted the urge to seek Athis's counsel.

"Then we are on separate paths, Ranger," she said instead, "regardless of our convergence. I assume you will attempt your assassination in The Dragon Keep, where Malliath can't help him."

Asher had a suspicious look about him. "Most likely," he replied in his gruff voice.

"Vighon is inside those same walls. I suggest we combine our talents and knowledge of the keep and achieve both our aims at once."

"If *I* succeed," Asher pointed out, "Vighon won't need rescuing. Perhaps you should simply aid *me* instead."

Inara paused. "I'm not killing him," she said slowly. "I'm also planning as if you're going to fail," she added in a lighter, yet practical, tone.

Asher thumbed the red cloth in his hand. "That was my problem; I never failed..."

Doran finally removed Andaljor from his back and placed it between himself and the Drake. "This all seems rather redundant given that Alijah ain' even in the north right now."

"He'll be back," Asher guaranteed. "We use this time to plan our way inside - from there we can go our separate ways."

The dwarf sighed, halting any further conversation. "As ye said, Asher: there is no *we*, I'm afraid."

Inara turned on the son of Dorain, fearful that her list of allies was dwindling by the second. "Do I even need to ask where you're going?"

Doran looked pained to answer. "If I had a choice, I'd fight by yer side until Vighon was freed or death claimed me. But me clan is out there somewhere. They're on Illian soil, a land they know nothin' abou', surrounded by enemies who want to pen 'em in. I walked away from 'em once an' me brother suffered for it. I won' walk away again."

Though his mission was not to be the same as her own, Doran's need to help his people was just as righteous as her need to help Vighon. "I hope you find them," she offered. "What will you do should you cross their path?"

Doran repeated his sigh. "Steer 'em well clear o' this place for starters. I don' know why Alijah would want to be keepin' dwarves for pets but I know it ain' for nothin' good. In time, though, I'd like to find a way to help 'em all."

"You've got to get out of here first," Asher reminded the dwarf.

"Don' go worryin' abou' that, lad," Doran said with a mischievous grin. "I've got out o' far worse than this. Besides, with ol' Andaljor 'ere there ain' none abou' that can stop me. Not yet anyway," he added. "The way I see it, I'm better makin' me way out now before Alijah an' Malliath return."

The three sat in silence for a moment, contemplating the very different paths that lay before them. Inara was sorry to be seeing the back of Doran and conflicted about Asher's mission to kill her brother. Somewhere in all that mess she had to rescue the king of Illian and that was without taking a moment to figure out what they did next. If she focused on the hopelessness of it all, however, the Dragorn was sure to lose all heart.

"And where does he fit in to all of this?" she asked, looking to the silent Drake.

Asher regarded Adan'Karth as if he were more of a nuisance than anything else. "He doesn't fit into any of this. Drakes abhor violence; they would rather die than kill to survive."

"So we just leave him here? With the *dwarves*?"

"I stay with you," Adan'Karth stated quickly, his accent almost too thick to understand.

The ranger scrutinised the Drake. "You pick up languages pretty quick."

Adan'Karth gestured to one of his pointed ears. "I see."

Asher grumbled. "Still a way to go though. *You can't come with me*," he added in elvish, much to Doran's dismay. "*I'm going to hurt people.*"

Inara could see that the Drake was conflicted by this. "*Athis, my dragon, is on his way. You can stay with him. We will find you... when we're done.*" Adan'Karth appeared hesitant to leave Asher's side, but he eventually nodded in agreement.

Doran looked from one to the other expectantly. "Is that it? Are we done speakin' in singalong? Good! I suggest we all get out there an' start gatherin' as much information as possible. I'll comb the camp since I can' leave. Ye two check out the city an' this keep ye're both determined to break into. An' *ye*..." The dwarf eyeballed the Drake. "Ye jus'... stay 'ere I suppose."

Inara was more than happy to leave the tent and stretch her legs elsewhere. Her emotions were frayed, leaving her teetering on the edge between wanting to cry and needing a good fight.

"Oh an' whatever ye do," Doran called after them, "don' come back 'ere without somethin' for us all to eat!"

CHAPTER 35
A RESISTANCE BORN

Under Ilythyra's thick canopy, only slivers of starlight could be seen from the forest floor. The evening was like any other the warm summer had offered, bringing with it a tranquil atmosphere. The surrounding bird song was steadily being replaced by the chatter of crickets, all background to the running stream that weaved between the enormous trees.

Seated amongst it all, with his legs crossed, was Galanör, the eldest son of house Reveeri. Unlike the rest of his kin who shared Ilythyra, Galanör chose to meditate on his own. The isolation was calming, allowing the warrior in him to rest. Around others, especially with his eyes closed, his other senses would heighten to compensate, feeding him information counter-productive to meditation.

He had been in the same position for several hours now and his mind was yet to find its serenity. His muscles ached to explode with energy, propelling him through the world like a storm. How many monsters had claimed victims because he had put down his blades?

That question haunted him.

"I can feel your unease from here," came a pleasant voice.

Galanör's eyes snapped open and he turned to see Aenwyn standing between the trees. "How long have *you* been watching me?" he asked with the hint of a smile.

"You flatter yourself," Aenwyn replied, padding over the soft moss. "Lady Ellöria has tasked me with the impossible."

"I'm assuming that would be to help me."

"Indeed," Aenwyn agreed. "Quite the impossible," she repeated.

"You speak in man's tongue," he observed. "You've never spoken in their language to me before."

"Nor have you," Aenwyn quipped in return. "We each have centuries of life that neither can know of. As for the language of man... I enjoy the way it feels in my mouth. It's *different*. A bit like you."

Galanör tried to absorb this new piece of information about her, just like he did with everything she had ever told him. "The Lady herself has taken me through the various rituals to enter meditation," he explained. "I fail to see what you can do to further my progress, regardless of which language you prefer."

Aenwyn gave the slightest shrug of her shoulders. "Since you're just sitting with your eyes closed and your brow furrowed, I would say you have yet to make *any* progress."

Galanör opened his mouth to reply but found he could do nothing but agree with her.

"Meditation isn't for everyone," Aenwyn continued, coming to sit in front of him. "For the majority of our people it serves them well, allowing for memories to be sorted and emotions to be managed. For others, they simply need someone to talk to... like me."

The elven ranger narrowed his eyes with suspicion. "You don't meditate?"

Aenwyn shook her head of lustrous dark hair. "I have always found that putting thought into words is the best way to understand myself and the world around me. Lady Ellöria believes the same of you."

Galanör had never considered it. "I've always held my words in reserve," he admitted. "I was raised to speak when spoken to and instructed to say only what needed to be said." He looked away wistfully. "My time with the humans, however, has done nothing if not undo my father's work."

Aenwyn smiled. "You have come to enjoy talking," she concluded.

"I have found one or two among the humans who bring that side out in me," he reasoned, thinking of Vighon, Gideon, even Alijah for a time.

"Then why have you only spoken with a handful of people since arriving here?" she questioned.

Galanör didn't answer right away but, instead, looked down at his hands. "Because..." He paused to lick his lips, considering his words carefully. "Because they can see the blood on my hands."

Aenwyn scrutinised his hands with a raised eyebrow. "I see no blood."

"You all know my history. You know what I did for King Elym, at Korkanath. I tried to help him start a war that would have consumed Illian. My efforts ensured the deaths of too many humans."

"That is in the past," Aenwyn insisted. "You are not that person anymore, Galanör. You do not have to let it haunt you."

"But that's just it, the reason I'm here in the first place. It's my past that..." He caught himself and swallowed down his next words. "Why is it so easy to talk to you?" he asked.

Aenwyn smiled again, disarming him. "It's always easier to talk to someone when you're attracted to them..."

Galanör had been around for five hundred years and had yet to discover a way to overcome blushing.

"Why are you here, Galanör of house Reveeri? What surfaces from your past that could have made you lay down your swords?"

That same question had gone round and round in Galanör's head for three years. He couldn't escape the answer.

"You know exactly why you're here," Aenwyn continued, her voice a melodic path that guided him onwards.

"My father had lofty ambitions for our house," he began. "He saw me as a tool, a way of elevating us onto the council."

"He did this by placing a sword in your hand?"

"Two swords actually. He wished for me to become the greatest sword master in all Elandril. I was trained to kill with an art form..."

Aenwyn pursued his line. "An art form you turned into a calling that helps people," she reminded him. "So, I ask again; why are you here?"

"Because I was starting to enjoy it again." Just saying it aloud was a burden lifted from his shoulders. "After we beat the orcs, the king tasked a few of us with rooting out those that still plagued the other cities and towns. I spilled more blood in those years than I did during the war itself."

Aenwyn appeared confused. "Orcs are no better than beasts. You are troubled by the lives you took?"

"I care nothing for the orcs," he admitted. "It was what I unleashed that troubles me - a monster of my own that awoke from its slumber."

"I see nothing monstrous about you," she said softly, her words having a direct effect on Galanör's heart rate.

"Have you ever been to Shalaria?" he asked, referring to the island crown of Ayda.

"Of course not," Aenwyn replied, as most elves would. "Those forests are a nest of predators large and small."

He nodded in agreement. "My father left me there with nothing but my swords and the clothes on my back."

Aenwyn failed to hide her disbelief. "Why would he do that?"

Galanör thought back to his father's explanation. "He wanted me to learn how to survive among predators before introducing me to the world of the royal family. He thought it would make me strong... and fast."

"You would have to be both to survive," Aenwyn reasoned.

"Those years were among the worst in my life," he continued. "But worse still, I brought something back with me, a feral nature that lurks just beneath the surface. It made me hungry for a fight. I soon found pleasure in the hunt and the kill, eliminating my competition for King Elym's favour."

"You cannot blame yourself for this behaviour," Aenwyn insisted. "Anyone would develop this nature if they were forced to survive amongst monsters."

Galanör shrugged off the sympathy. "Centuries of subsequent training allowed me to harness that nature and keep it caged when I needed to." He sighed and looked away in shame. "But killing all those orcs, city after city, town after town... I lost control of it."

Aenwyn's vibrant blue eyes pulled him in. "What happened?"

"When we were finished dealing with the orcs, I returned to the life of a ranger. But I was still hungry for the fight. I took every contract I could, always looking for the most dangerous job. But, eventually, even they began to diminish. That was when I..." Galanör looked away, unable to say it.

Aenwyn tilted her head to find him. "That's when you turned on the humans," she surmised.

The ranger nodded, collecting himself to speak again. "At first, I went in search of fights wherever I could find them; mostly tavern brawls and the like. But when that didn't satiate me, I turned to the gangs."

"I have heard of these gangs," she replied. "They survived the Leviathan's attack on Dragorn."

"I found there to be little difference between them and the orcs," Galanör said. "They just blend in better."

"You were paid to deal with them?"

"I wasn't interested in coin," he stated. "I just needed a target. I became something of a scourge to them, but all the while I was drowning in blood, losing myself to that beast."

"How did you get from there to here?"

"I was in Ameeraska, in The Arid Lands. A branch of the Fenrig syndicate had established roots there. They were importing the marrow drug from the dead Leviathan and selling it to *children*," he added with disgust.

"They sound like monsters to me," Aenwyn commented.

"That's what I kept telling myself." Galanör could still see his blades, coated in blood and not an inch of the steel to be seen. "And then he found me."

"Who?" she enquired, more curious than ever.

"Asher," he answered simply.

Aenwyn's eyes lit up with understanding. "The ranger," she said. "I have heard much of him."

Galanör managed a brief smile. "Most of it is hard to believe, but it's all true. He had heard what I was doing or, more specifically, what I had become. He has his own history when it comes to the hunting and killing of men."

"He stopped you?"

The elven ranger subconsciously rubbed his jaw where Asher had clubbed him, tearing him away from his instincts. "It wasn't without its pain, but he made me look at myself, what I had done. He even came with me to Ilythyra's border."

"He sounds like a good friend to have."

"Travelling with Asher can be a double-edged sword. In a fight, you want him by your side. But," he added with a caveat, "you often find yourself in that fight *because* you're by his side. Trouble has a way of finding him."

Aenwyn was looking at him intently, as if she wasn't really listening to his description of the legendary ranger. "And where do we find you? On your own, sitting amongst the trees searching for answers. Who are you? What is your purpose? Where should you be?"

Galanör shook his head. "I can't answer any of them if I don't have control."

"Then perhaps you need to stop doing this by yourself," Aenwyn countered.

The elven ranger felt a smile force its way out. "Maybe you're right. Will... Will you help me?"

Aenwyn mirrored his smile. "That depends on you."

Both of them heard the approaching footfalls beyond the small clearing. Another member of Ellöria's personal entourage emerged from the trees. Her name, as Aenwyn's had once done, escaped Galanör and he chastised himself for having been such a hermit since his arrival.

With a sense of urgency, the handmaiden said, *"The Lady wishes to see you both immediately."*

Galanör and Aenwyn looked at each other, equally disturbed, before accompanying the handmaiden to the Lady's private garden, where she held many of her councils.

Ellöria was in the midst of giving out instructions upon their arrival. The Lady of Ilythyra sent elves about their business with haste, leaving the oval garden to the three of them.

"My Lady?" Aenwyn was the first to reach her side.

Galanör bowed his head. *"What is the calamity?"* he asked having seen more than a few elves running around on their journey.

There was a shadow about Ellöria, as if something dared to dampen her ethereal beauty. *"Smoke rises in the east. The heart of Velia burns."*

That was the last thing Galanör had expected to hear. *"Orcs?"*

"No," Ellöria replied with a hard tone. *"Valatos burns to dragon's fire..."*

The elven ranger made to speak but no words came out. His mind raced through the potential culprits, but there was only one dragon in Illian and Athis would never...

"Malliath," he breathed.

"There's no doubt," Ellöria confirmed.

"When did this happen?" Aenwyn asked with concern.

"Two days ago. His motivations—"

"Alijah's motivations," Galanör added. *"If Malliath torched Valatos, then so did Alijah."*

Ellöria's stern expression softened with despair. "*Indeed*," she accepted.

Galanör was taken back fifteen years, when certain revelations had come to light regarding the ancient prophecy. The Echoes of Fate had been created by none other than The Crow, a necromancer who had his sights set on Alijah Galfrey ten thousand years before he was even born. A silent, yet menacing, question had surrounded the half-elf since his rescue from The Bastion, high in The Vrost Mountains.

It seemed that question had been answered...

"*That's not all,*" Ellöria continued. "*Our connection with Ikirith has been severed and smoke has been seen rising over The Evermoore.*"

"*The Drakes?*" Aenwyn questioned.

"*There has been no word from them. I have tasked agents with locating as many as they can.*"

That was the first time Galanör had heard Ellöria speak about the elves she had planted throughout the kingdom. He knew better than to comment on such secret activities.

"*It would take some powerful magic to burst through a pocket dimension,*" he said instead.

"*We have to assume he possesses such magic,*" Ellöria reasoned. "*We also have to acknowledge the pattern of their attacks.*"

Aenwyn frowned. "*Pattern, my Lady?*"

"*Of course...*" Galanör looked away briefly as he put it together. "*The Drakes, the mages... They're the biggest threats.*"

"*Not the* biggest," Ellöria corrected, leading the ranger to the obvious conclusion.

"We're *the biggest threat,*" he whispered mostly to himself.

Ellöria nodded gravely. "*I have issued commands to evacuate Ilythyra.*"

"*We're leaving?*" Aenwyn glanced at Galanör. "*Where will we go?*"

"*North,*" was the Lady's only reply.

"*Why north?*" Galanör, like many elves, preferred warmer climates.

Ellöria's shoulders sagged and she looked him in the eyes. *"Because I haven't told you the worst of it yet..."*

Rather absently, Galanör was guiding the children among them to Ilythyra's northern pass. Every now and then he would encourage them to make haste or retrieve an item they had dropped. His mind, it seemed, was mostly consumed by Lady Ellöria's last words.

Namdhor had been taken.

The capital, Vighon's home, was now under the command of a foreign army, the same army that had driven all the dwarves into Illian. It was dire news but it lacked the details Galanör craved.

Was the king alive? Despite their years apart, he counted Vighon as a good friend and, above all, a good man. If the north had been taken did that mean he was dead? He would never give over the crown while he still drew breath.

Why had there been no response from the other provinces? If the realm was under attack, why hadn't Vighon's bannermen come to Namdhor's aid and held the line? It felt like a quiet war had broken out and passed them by.

Through the procession of his kin, the ranger spotted Aenwyn coming towards him. Like him, she was outfitted in her travelling leathers and cloak, but she also held something in her hand.

"You might want these," she suggested, passing him Guardian and Stormweaver, both concealed inside their scabbards.

Somewhat reluctantly, he took them in hand. Their weight was familiar and all-too comforting.

"They're a part of you," Aenwyn told him. "Running from them won't help."

"Thank you," he replied quietly. Strapping them either side of his hips made the ranger feel like he was ready for anything.

Aenwyn stepped closer and squeezed his hand. "I must join Lady

Ellöria now. She has contacted Queen Adilandra to inform her of current events."

"Good," he said, struggling to focus beyond the news that she was about to leave him. "I was hoping that we might journey north *together*."

"Alas, my place is beside the Lady. Though, I am sure she will welcome your company." Aenwyn's added comment came with a reassuring smile.

"I would like that. And thank you... *again*."

Aenwyn made to leave. "It's nice to know you're not one of a kind, isn't it?"

Before Galanör could answer, a distant sound reached his sensitive ears and set the hairs on the back of his neck on end. He stepped away from Aenwyn and the procession and turned his gaze upwards, to those slivers of starlight.

Wings... He could hear wings.

What happened next was heard by all. There was a crashing of trees as the canopy gave way to the largest dragon in all of Verda. Branches snapped and fell to earth, splintering into deadly shards on impact. Orbs of light winked out of existence under Malliath's bulk. And, finally, the ground shook as all four of his claws came down in the middle of Ilythyra.

The black dragon raised his head into the air and unleashed an ear-piercing roar that set every elf to a sprint.

"Run!" he shouted at Aenwyn, directing her north with the others.

Astride Malliath, Alijah stood tall between the dragon's spikes. "Elves of Ilythyra!" His voice boomed with magical enhancement. "Your time on Illian's shores has once again come to an end! Return to Ayda!"

Chaos had erupted across the forest floor. Galanör weaved between his fleeing kin, working his way towards Alijah.

"On foot or by sail, you will return to Elandril!" he continued. "Any elf found on Illian soil will be executed!"

442

Galanör helped a fallen boy to his feet, all the while in disbelief at what he was hearing. This wasn't the Alijah he had known and it certainly wasn't the son of Reyna and Nathaniel. Yet there he was, standing tall with a stern expression. Beneath him, Malliath's purple's eyes roamed over the scattered elves with a hint of hunger in them.

The threat of them both, however, had incensed a group of Ellöria's warriors. With scimitars and bows, they placed themselves between Malliath's head and the rest of their people. Galanör shouted ahead, warning them not to fire on the dragon - the ranger had seen him take lives by the hundreds.

It was too late. Malliath had turned his head to track a family running past him and one of the archers reacted. Having witnessed unfolding events from above, Alijah dropped down in front of the arrow and erected a shield with the back of his closed fist. The missile struck his shield in a flash of blue light and bounced away harmlessly.

Galanör descended from his elevated position and moved silently across the forest floor. As he came up, he saw the first of the elven warriors fall to the ground in a splash of blood. Alijah's green scimitar, his cursed Vi'tari blade, danced around the remaining warriors, parrying and lashing out with deadly accuracy. By the time Galanör had crossed the small pasture, the last of the elves was impaled on Alijah's ancient weapon.

"Galanör?" The half-elf almost smiled. "I was wondering when you might turn up in all of this."

The ranger's expression reflected his horror, watching his kin slide off Alijah's blade, dead. Every one of them had been an exquisite fighter with centuries behind them. Together, they should have beaten him regardless of his Vi'tari blade.

Yet, somehow, Alijah had killed them all...

The half-elf turned to regard Malliath. Though their conversation was private, it must have gone something like: *burn it all*, because the dragon immediately opened his mouth and engulfed the nearest tree in an inferno. The blaze spread quickly to the adjacent tree and the next.

"This is madness!" Galanör yelled over Malliath's torrents of fire. "Why are you doing this? We are your kin!"

Alijah stepped over the dead, towards him. "I have to be more than the sum of my parts, Galanör. I can cling to neither heritage; not if I am to rule justly."

"Rule?" the elf echoed, his hands braced to the hilts on his belt. "Illian has a king. You were there for his coronation!"

"And he will be there for mine," Alijah countered casually.

"So he lives? Vighon is alive?"

"Focus, Galanör. You might be losing perspective here," he added, taking in their fiery surroundings. "I'm going to re-shape the realm but, right now, elves pose a complication. Integration will happen in time. Until then, I need Illian to be a blank slate."

"I heard what you did to Ikirith. Valatos too. Is this how you make a blank slate?"

"Fire has long been used as a tool for... *purging*. Malliath and I were destined to bring the world together, but we're not so naive as to think it will be handed over to us. People are stubborn. They don't always know what's best for them."

"And you do?" Galanör spat.

"We don't claim to be perfect," the half-elf countered, "but we *are* better than all those who came before us, from Atilan to Vighon!"

"History will remember you as a monster!"

"*History* is yet to be written," Alijah pointed out. "And, generations from now, when Verda is enjoying an everlasting peace, we will ask for no thanks, no praise, no statues that reach for the heavens. We will continue to do our duty..."

Galanör flinched as Malliath let loose another jet of fire, igniting a strip that eventually ran up another tree. Ilythyra was quickly beginning to fill with smoke and collapsing branches fell to the ground with enough weight behind them to crush a house.

"You're a Galfrey!" the ranger berated. "You should know better!"

"I won't be lectured by an elf who's taken more lives than I have. Just leave, Galanör. Do the smart thing and lead your people back to Ayda."

Galanör's grip tightened around Guardian and Stormweaver. *Just leave...* That would be the easy thing. Walk away and let others stand up for the realm. That path would see him abandon his blades and submerge himself back into elven society in Elandril.

But he wasn't an elf of Ayda nor a citizen of Elandril. He was a ranger of Illian...

Gleaming scimitars, long missed, flowed out of their scabbards. Galanör was whole again, a fact he wasn't sure how to feel about. What was certain, however, was the dark pit from which Alijah drew his beliefs.

"You should have stayed away."

The half-elf became very still. "And you should have left when I gave you the chance."

Both combatants exploded with energy, colliding in a flurry of sparks and clashing steel. It quickly became apparent to Galanör that Alijah was a student of multiple fighting forms. He initially met the ranger with identical elven techniques, likely instilled in the half-elf by his mother. But he flowed elegantly into a style that reflected the efficiency of the Arakesh. It was this particular form that won him more than a couple of strikes that left Galanör staggering back.

His third technique was of a more brutal style, often found in mercenaries who had honed their skills fighting in random encounters. They were survivors, happy to use anything that would help them claim victory. It was this particular form that encouraged Alijah - with their swords locked - to headbutt Galanör, pushing him back. A swift kick to the inside of his leg then dropped the ranger to one knee, bringing him to the mercy of an overhead strike.

Crossing his scimitars into an X, Galanör prevented Alijah's Vi'tari blade from cutting him in two. His strength was another issue. Being a child of both races, he should be stronger than the average man, but being bonded to a dragon increased his abilities to that of a full-blooded elf. Right now, seeing the edge of that green blade inches away from his face, Galanör knew they were evenly matched in their struggle.

Alijah looked down at him, his head and arms trembling with exertion. "You're said to be the greatest sword fighter alive. I've wanted to test myself against you for a long time."

Galanör knew better than to waste time with words - his blades would talk for him. A growl rumbled from his throat as he put all of his strength into one arm, an effort that allowed him to free Stormweaver. The scimitar thrust forward and Alijah jumped back to avoid the tip. Galanör was in no mood, however, to give the half-elf an inch.

The elf sprang up and came down with both blades, putting Alijah on the defensive. He spared a glance to check on Malliath, aware that the dragon could intervene any time he pleased and end the fight. Alijah, it seemed, had something to prove. Galanör decided that would be his opponent's error, an error he would make him pay for.

Employing every technique he had picked up over the last five centuries, the ranger laid into Alijah's defences, wearing him down until he found that opportune moment. He only needed one strike to end this madness and bring both Alijah and Malliath down. And, with two blades against one, it was inevitable.

The warrior in Galanör saw his moment arriving three moves from his current position. Guardian, tip to the ground, parried Alijah's counterattack. The elf spun on his heel, disorientating his foe. Stormweaver came up to block the second attack, just as predicted. Then, to finish what it started, Guardian swung around with his momentum and cut the half-elf from shoulder to hip.

Alijah cried out and fell backwards, his dark cloak covering him. Galanör remained where he stood, his chest heaving. It was a mortal blow for anyone, a thought that made him consider Reyna and Nathaniel - he could never look them in the eye again.

It was only a second later that it dawned on Galanör: Malliath was still standing, his nostrils flaring with smoke. The ranger examined Guardian's edge and was dismayed to find a clean length of steel. If anything, the scimitar looked blunted in areas.

A brief groan escaped Alijah's lips as he found his feet again. The half-elf rotated his shoulders and cracked his neck before turning around to face Galanör once more. A faint line marred the black scales of his armour but no more.

"That's going to bruise," he complained, touching the scar with his fingers. "Still, there's a reason you can't kill a dragon with a sword..."

Galanör had no time to respond before he was looking at the back of Malliath's throat. A pair of glands, either side of his thick tongue, exhaled two streams of fire that combined to jet a single column of dragon's fire. The heat slammed into Galanör before the flames were even close enough to burn, blowing his chestnut hair out behind him.

In that brief moment - his only moment - the elf pushed out with his magic and erected a shield between him and Malliath. The fire was all-consuming but the power behind it was intense, testing the strength of his magic. It was only a matter of time before the dragon wore him down...

This wasn't the first or even second time the ranger had faced Malliath's wrath but, like he had then, he considered this to be his final breath. It wasn't, however, as so many tales would tell. He didn't see all five hundred years of his life flash before his eyes. He didn't even think of any particular individuals. There was simply no time for any of it.

Blinded by the fire, he only caught glimpses of the inferno curving around his body, scorching all but him. The magic bit into his muscles, draining him. The heat from the flames began to penetrate his shield, promising an agonising death. The elf cried out, putting everything he had into the spell.

Then it was gone, his magic over-extended. Yet, somehow, the fire continued to curve around him, kept at bay by the shield of another. When, at last, Malliath shut his powerful jaws, the world around Galanör was hot and the air rippled in waves, distorting his saviour.

"Ellöria!" Alijah said his great aunt's name as if he was genuinely pleased to see her. "Your magic is a testament to our bloodline! I'm sure—"

"You are not welcome here, *nephew*." Ellöria's interruption soured Alijah's expression but she continued to approach with Aenwyn by her side.

"I'm afraid it's the other way around," Alijah corrected, Galanör long forgotten. "Illian is mine. I don't want to spill more blood than I already have, so don't make me."

Ellöria's open palms crackled and sparked with flickers of lightning. "No elf shall suffer the likes of your reign."

Ice began to collect around Alijah's clenched fist. "I *will* break you."

The lady of Ilythyra frowned at her nephew. "I wasn't talking to you, boy."

Confused, Alijah followed her gaze to Malliath. "If only it was that—"

Ellöria whipped up her hands and released the lightning that had been steadily building. A staccato of agonising bolts tore across the ground and ripped through the air with elven fury behind them. Alijah caught the brunt of the spell and was launched off his feet and sent hurtling towards the blaze of Malliath's making. The dragon himself shared the pain of his rider and reared back with a terrible roar. So pained was Malliath that he collapsed onto his front, his legs unable to support him.

"Get everybody out of the forest!" Ellöria commanded of her entourage.

Galanör ran to her side and that of Aenwyn's. "You can't stay!" he warned the Lady.

Everything about Ellöria was unyielding. "He will hunt us across the land and force us to depart The Shining Coast."

Galanör shook his head. "If you stay, they will kill you and still burn Ilythyra to the ground!"

"Elves have ever been the light in Illian," the lady replied softly, catching the ranger off guard. "When the dark rises we resist it to our dying breath. It's time for you to see your place in all this." Her hand came to rest on his chest. "Keep the dark at bay. *Resist.*"

Ellöria gave Galanör no chance to reply, nor any of her entourage. The hand touching his chest produced a spell that threw all of them back towards the interior tree line. The ranger felt his limbs roll over more limbs before his momentum came to an abrupt end at the foot of a wide tree.

Despite the distance that had been forced between them, Ellöria's whisper resounded with perfect clarity.

"Resist..."

Beside the ranger, Aenwyn and the rest of Ellöria's handmaidens had tears streaming down their faces. There was no mistaking that the next few minutes would be her last. Beyond the lady, Alijah and Malliath were picking themselves up. Smoke drifted off Alijah's scaled armour and a patch of his exposed neck was clearly burnt, adding to his older injuries.

Galanör picked up his fallen scimitars and prepared to fight by Ellöria's side when Aenwyn gripped his arm. "We have to go!" she urged with glassy eyes.

The ranger took his arm back. "We can't let her—"

"Someone has to survive to fight back," she spoke over him. "Ellöria is giving us that chance..."

Alijah had sheathed his cursed blade now and resorted to magic. He approached the ancient elf with flaring hands and Malliath at his back. Ellöria stood her ground, unflinching in the face of death. The air around her began to swirl, picking up debris. Bolts of lightning spilled out of her hands. She wasn't leaving this world without a fight.

"Quickly!" Aenwyn hissed, yanking Galanör to his feet.

It felt wrong to leave her fighting alone. Ellöria was among the oldest of elves and royalty too - her passing should be observed out of respect, especially given the nature of her sacrifice. But to stay would negate that sacrifice and then the light would go out for good...

The pain in Galanör's heart was almost physical, but he forced one foot to race in front of the other, whisking him away from the heart of Ilythyra. Behind them, they heard all manner of explosions and the trees were brought to life in an array of flashing colours. They heard trees snap and the air being sucked away more than once. The atmosphere around them was thick with all the magical discharge.

Through it all, Malliath's terrifying roar gave them swift flight through the forest.

Resist. The word echoed over and over inside Galanör's mind. He had entered Ilythyra unsure of himself, what he had become, and what he should do next. Now he knew. Now, he left Ilythyra knowing exactly what fate had been training him for all his long life.

He was going to stand against the dark. He was going to resist...

CHAPTER 36
BROKEN PEOPLE

K assian's feet beat against the dry Selk Road without thought of rest. The Keeper had found something new to fuel his life, something to replace the love that had pumped through his heart: rage.

No longer was there darkness when he closed his eyes; only fire. Malliath's flames consumed his wife over and over again, filling his every muscle with explosive tension. More than anything, he wished to kill Alijah Galfrey and slay his dragon.

And that's exactly what he was going to do.

A little ahead of him, the murderer's parents, Reyna and Nathaniel, were walking side by side. The old Graycoat had a strong arm around his wife, holding her close. The elf had yet to speak since reuniting with her son.

Kassian didn't mind the silence. He had nothing to say anyway. The ambassadors were showing him to the capital, a place he had never visited, and was content for them to lead him. Beyond that, he intended to part from them and kill their son at his earliest opportunity. He would find the right way to do it too. Alijah would suffer before he was granted the mercy of death.

The Keeper looked over his shoulder, hoping to see the rising smoke from Valatos. They had travelled too far, however, and the city's burning heart was three days beyond the horizon now. Kassian had wanted to see the destruction. He wanted to see nothing but Alijah's wicked deeds so that his resolve would see no end.

How many mages had been killed in Valatos? How many children and families had been burnt like Clara? Kassian would remind the half-elf of every one of them before the end, even if he had to cut the number into the murderer's skin.

Nathaniel turned to Kassian over his shoulder. "We should rest here a while," he suggested, nodding to a small forest near to the base of The Vrost Mountains.

Kassian was in no mood to rest. "We stopped at Palios," he reminded the old knight. "Then we stopped at Darkwell. We've rested enough, at least until we reach Dunwich."

Nathaniel came to a stop. "It's only going to get colder from here on. You said it yourself; you've never been farther north than Palios before. Trust me; we should rest before ploughing into the snows."

The Keeper wasn't going to let his sheltered life stop him from advancing. "*You* said Alijah would return to Namdhor, so that's where I'm going."

The old Graycoat settled Reyna down on a boulder not far from the road. "We have no idea what we're walking into, Kassian. You heard Alijah - he's taken the capital. We have to assume there are others helping him."

Kassian didn't halt his march. "Then it sounds like I'd find better luck sneaking into the city alone."

"And then what?" Nathaniel questioned. "You saw him back there, both of them! Do you really think you can just walk up to Alijah and kill him?"

Kassian finally stopped and spun around to face the old knight. "I saw him bleed. He's powerful, but he's not *all* powerful. If magic can hurt him, it can kill him."

"Don't be foolish," Nathaniel warned. "You can't wage a one-man war against him."

The Keeper threw his arms up. "Shouldn't you be protecting him? He is your son after all!"

"Did he look like he needs protecting?" Nathaniel fired back, the truth of his question dampening some of Kassian's fury. "And I wasn't blind to what he did. You won't be the only one seeking revenge against my son. But you're a good man, Kassian. If you give into this madness now you'll—"

"I'll what? Never come back? Find only death? Do I look like I give a damn?" Kassian shook his head in despair and took in their surroundings. "I'm going on. And I'm going to kill the man and his beast responsible for Clara's death. That's all there is now."

The Keeper turned his back on the old knight and made to continue his arduous trek into the cold depths of the north. Reyna's soft voice, however, caught in his ear and brought his feet to a stop. It was absent her usual melody, a tone typical of the elves that always worked to bring a man to a stop. Now she sounded flat, much like himself.

"You need his guard to lower," she had said, bringing him back around. "There is a greater chance of that happening around us."

There wasn't much capable of breaking through his burning anger, but there was some strategic sense in Reyna's words. Alijah had stopped the carnage in Valatos to speak with them, leaving him vulnerable to surprise attack. But sticking with the Galfreys meant slowing his progress, not to mention any interventions to his future plans when it came time to act.

Frustrated, the Keeper groaned and clenched his fists. "I should have stayed in Valatos and finished the job when I had the chance! He was injured! The elementals were beating him! I should have... I should have..."

Kassian's subconscious wall cracked and a drop of heart-breaking emotion spilled into his rage. Tears welled in his eyes and he paced in every direction, pulling at his sandy hair. When the dam finally broke he dropped to his knees, his shoulders shaking with sobs.

"I should have saved her," he wept, saliva collecting between his lips.

Nathaniel placed a heavy hand on his shoulder and squeezed hard. Having let some of his exhaustion in, Kassian silently followed them to the small forest and gave no protest to the fire Nathaniel started. The Keeper hadn't realised until the warmth washed over him that the air had indeed taken on a chill not known in a Velian summer.

In the silence that sat between them, the old knight stoked the flames, looking from his wife to the Keeper. "Once we get around The Vrost Mountains, it's going to be damn cold in the day and freezing at night."

Kassian simply nodded his understanding. They still had several hours of daylight, given summer's longer days, and he was becoming eager once more to set off. He wasn't of a mind to sit idly - Clara deserved action. But the Galfreys *would* provide the potential window he needed to avenge her. It was an infuriating position to be in.

"Would you like to tell us about her?" Nathaniel offered.

Any mention of Clara got Kassian's back up. "Of course. She was the most beautiful, intelligent, and caring person to ever walk Verda's green earth. And your son and his pet murdered her without a second thought."

Nathaniel winced and focused on the fire instead. Reyna didn't so much as blink, her attention lost to the flames that danced between them all.

"Would you like to tell me about *him*?" Kassian asked venomously. "Perhaps you could start by telling me how the son of two renowned heroes became a mass-murdering monster..."

The old Graycoat took an audibly deep breath, likely to gain some measure of control. "The things done to Alijah are beyond your comprehension, Keeper," he said with a hint of aggression. "There have been forces at work behind every great moment in history, turning the wheels, guiding events, amassing a death toll so high it makes Valatos just another drop in the ocean."

"It wasn't a drop in the ocean to me," Kassian retorted.

"But that's just it," Nathaniel replied. "You're nobody. Fate doesn't care about you or Clara for that matter."

"Don't you say her name!" Kassian spat, rising to his feet.

"Clara's death was assured ten thousand years ago," Nathaniel continued ignorantly, "just as your death is assured if you try to kill my son."

Kassian snapped and leaped at the old Graycoat, kicking up dry dirt as he reached for the man's neck. Nathaniel didn't even rise to meet him but, instead, waited until the Keeper was almost on top of him before rolling backwards with Kassian's collar snatched between his fingers. The two men tumbled away from the fire and came to a sudden stop with the old knight straddled over the Keeper's chest and a slender dagger pointed down at his face.

Throughout it all, Reyna remained perfectly still.

Nathaniel held his dagger steady, the tip only an inch from Kassian's eye. "You're only just entering a battle we've been fighting for a very long time. I'm so sorry that you've lost your wife. We've lost people too. And now... it seems we have lost a son as well."

Kassian looked past the dagger and saw the father, not the hero or the knight or even the man. He saw the father that grieved.

"What do you mean?" the Keeper managed beneath Nathaniel's crushing weight. "You said Clara's death was assured."

With an uneasy truce, the two men untangled and wandered back to the fire. Nathaniel didn't say anything for a moment. He looked at his wife, his thoughts his own. This was either something they didn't like talking about or it was something neither had voiced in a long time.

"Have you heard of The Black Hand?" he asked.

Kassian frowned, surprised by the question. "They were a cult, a group of dark mages devoted to forbidden magic. I heard they were behind that monster that razed Dragorn to the ground."

"That was just the last thing they did," Nathaniel continued. "Their cult was started by a man named Sarkas. He also went by another name: The Crow. Ten thousand years ago, he used the darkest of magic to see into the future. He saw Alijah sitting on a throne over Illian..."

Kassian had heard more than a few rumours regarding Illian's secret history, a history that spoke of humans coming before the elves. "So it's true then. There was a kingdom of man long *before* Gal Tion."

"There was a lot more before that fool named himself a king. The history of our people goes back more than just a thousand years, possibly even more than twenty thousand years."

Kassian took the news in his stride; it wasn't the past that greatly concerned him so much as it was the future, a future that had become a darker place of late, where he might bloody his hands. "So how does this Crow have anything to do with Alijah? Ten thousand years is a long time."

Nathaniel paused to glance at his wife again. "He wrote a prophecy, a cryptic account of what he saw. Then he wrote another prophecy, one which he had foreseen would cause a cascade of events that would ultimately lead to... Lead to Alijah's birth."

Kassian put all of that together. "You're saying Alijah is the product of dark magic."

"No," the old knight snapped. "Reyna and I fell in love and had two beautiful children. That evil wretch just made certain he was able to return to spoil all that."

"Return?" Kassian picked up.

"Necromancy," he answered in a word. "He died not long after man fled the dragons, into The Wild Moores. Then, twenty years ago, his cult of death worshippers resurrected him as instructed. He ripped our family apart. He knew Alijah was destined to bond with Malliath, so he put them together and tormented them both with his magic. He did *cruel* things to my son. Turned him inside out, made him forget who he really was."

Before Clara died, Kassian would have empathised with Nathaniel, sharing in some of his heartbreak. Now, however, he had nothing left to give. But such information he could use, so he tempered his anger, held back his wicked retorts and engaged.

"Why would The Black Hand want Alijah to be king?" he asked.

Nathaniel stoked the fire some more. "Sarkas was twisted - his masters saw to that before either of us were born. More than that, the magic he used broke his mind. I suppose that's why it's forbidden. He thought he saw Alijah ruling over Verda, bringing in an age of peace for *all* the races."

"Of course," Kassian quipped, "this is about *peace*."

Nathaniel nodded in agreement. "If there's one thing I've learned over the last eighty years: it's that peace was usually there before we started killing people for it."

The Keeper kept any reply to himself for the moment, letting the knight's words hang between them. "Where is The Crow now? Does he still control Alijah?" Learning of a powerful necromancer was vital should he be connected to the man he intended to kill.

"He's dead," Reyna said, speaking for the first time since they left the road. "Our daughter ran him through."

"Your daughter," Kassian considered. "As if your family wasn't complicated enough, the Guardian of the Realm is your daughter."

"Inara killed The Crow," Reyna explained, her eyes looking into the past, "but no one, it seems, could undo his life's work. Alijah's mind has been poisoned by the same dark magic that stained Sarkas's mind."

"You're talking like he can be saved." Kassian's remark garnered looks from both Galfreys.

"Everyone can be saved," Reyna replied softly.

Kassian tried not to sneer. "Tell that to my wife."

"Easy," Nathaniel warned.

"I'm so sorry Clara didn't survive Valatos," Reyna persisted. "If I had the power to change that I would. What I can do, however, is help my son to find himself again."

"Dead men have no need of redemption," he said, making his intentions more than clear. Before either of the Galfreys could reply, the Keeper rose from his log and walked away, tired of their conversation. They were a means to an end, nothing more.

He wandered for a while, slowly making his way towards the tree line. He was called to the road where he might return to his journey north. There would never be any peace for him again, but killing Alijah would at least take some of the fire out of his veins.

There was a growing sound beyond the trees, setting Kassian's heart to a quick-step. With caution now, he crept behind the nearest tree and peered out across the clearing, to The Selk Road. Hundreds of soldiers, clad in black armour and dark cloaks, were marching south, towards Velia. He scrutinised them all the more, failing to recognise anything about them.

There was no sound to announce Reyna and Nathaniel's approach, only their appearance behind the adjacent tree.

"They don't look like Namdhorian soldiers," Kassian whispered.

"That's because they're not," Nathaniel answered. "I've never seen soldiers like these before."

Reyna narrowed her eyes. "Something isn't right about them. I can't explain it. The way they move..."

Kassian couldn't say he was experiencing a similar feeling, but if they weren't Namdhorians - and they were marching out of the north - there was a good chance these soldiers were under Alijah's command.

"It's them, isn't it? These must be the soldiers who helped him take the capital."

"We don't know that," Nathaniel reminded him.

"Well, who else could they be?" the Keeper countered, reaching for his wand.

"What are you doing?" the old knight scowled.

"Making him hurt," Kassian replied through gritted teeth.

Nathaniel dared to cross the gap between the trees and grip Kassian's shoulder. "Have you lost all sense? What are you going to do? Take on a few hundred armoured soldiers with your wand?"

Kassian pulled his shoulder away. "Magic always beats steel."

"Not that much steel," Nathaniel hissed.

"What does it matter to you?" the Keeper snapped back. "You want to save your son and I want him dead. If I go out there and die you have a far greater chance of succeeding."

"Maybe I don't want another death on my son's conscience."

Exasperated, Kassian sighed. "You can't save him. He's invaded our country with an army. He's murdered innocent people. Do you think he did that on a whim? This takes *years* of planning. You're the deluded ones if you think words alone will change him."

Nathaniel looked to lose some heart and stepped back from the Keeper. "As you will," he said.

Kassian withdrew his wand and turned back to the marching soldiers. About half of their procession had passed them by now. He already had a spell in mind that would kill at least three of them and seriously injure half a dozen more. The Keeper closed his eyes to consider a few more spells from the destructive branch of magic. If he was going to challenge so many, he would need a plethora of spells.

Behind his eyes, he saw Clara running towards him. Then there was only fire.

He opened his eyes again, unable to bear the sight for too long. Killing these men wouldn't bring her back and it wouldn't even avenge her death. How long could he really keep up his barrage before the magic drained him, leaving him at their mercy. No, he thought. His revenge would be precise and lasting. Clara's death would soon become Alijah's greatest regret.

The wand slid back into its holster. "We go north," Kassian insisted. "There, I *will* kill your son. If you get in my way, you'll share the same fate..."

The Keeper didn't wait for a reply before he quietly slunk back into the forest. He stepped behind a tree, out of sight, and closed his eyes tightly. There he saw Clara dying over and over again. He deserved to see it. He should have saved her. Kassian slid down the trunk, his mind caught somewhere between wanting to disappear down a dark hole and wanting to set the whole world on fire.

This would be where he lived now...

CHAPTER 37
RIDE HARD

By the eastern edge of the dwarven camp, Doran Heavybelly looked out on the smouldering remains of clan Battleborn's greatest warriors. Among them was King Uthrad, son of Koddun, the lord of Silvyr Hall. What an Age he was living in to have seen Dhenaheim's most powerful clan brought to its knees...

So baffling was the sight that this was Doran's second time visiting the graveyard. They had been gathering what information they could for two days now, yet the dwarf always found himself standing in the same place. How could he be living in a realm where King Uthrad was dead, his clan ravaged, and King Gaerhard of the Brightbeards - the lowliest clan - still lived? The hierarchy had been turned on its head.

It would only be a matter of time before someone stepped forward from each of the surviving clans and proclaimed themselves the new king. Without the appropriate bloodlines, however, this would be brought into question. No one would bow to a Brightbeard king - a clan that had achieved very little in all their history. And so the in-fighting would begin and they would lose all sight of who their real enemy was.

It deeply saddened Doran to consider that these might well be the last days of the dwarf. It saddened him even more to think that they would be the ones to diminish their own numbers. If the children of the mountain were going to leave Verda for good, it should be on the battlefield, united against their foe.

It didn't seem that long ago that the very ground he now stood on had been a battlefield. The Heavybellys had reminded the orcs that the dwarves would always be there to grind them back into the earth. Heavybellys were warriors to the bone, a clan of fighters with a rich history when it came to war.

Doran needed their mettle now...

The son of Dorain looked out, beyond the corpses, to the distant white plains of the vale. They were out there, somewhere. Why they hadn't reached Namdhor was a question that Doran very much needed answering, if only to settle his stomach.

His train of thought was quickly ruined in the shadow of a Reaver. The knight from Erador stepped in front of Doran, blocking his view of the dead Battleborns. The creature gave him no verbal command but simply flicked its head at the camp, ushering him back. The son of Dorain felt his hand creeping up the scabbard on the back of his belt, searching for the hilt of his dagger. First, he'd chop its legs out, bringing the beastie to its rotten knees. Then, he'd draw his axe and drive it through the faceplate, burying the silvyr deep.

Doran gripped his belt instead and offered the undead knight a sneer. Turning away, he re-entered the oppressive sights, sounds, and smells of the dwarven camp. It wasn't as loud and busy as the kingdoms had been in Dhenaheim, but what it lacked in activity it made up for with its cramped environment.

Passing through, the stout ranger became aware of the territories that had been carved out of the camp. Bar the Stormshields, forever lost to the hierarchy, the sigils of every clan had been carved, drawn or painted on various posts and objects, letting everybody know where they were. The two largest areas - in the centre of the camp - were occupied by the surviving Battleborns and King Gaerhard's Brightbeards. The Hammerkegs and the Goldhorns surrounded them, leaderless and fearful.

Doran kept to himself as he moved through, his eye focused on the intended path. It was impossible to identify him as a Heavybelly, though there were going to be more than a few of his kin who found his absence of any sigil suspicious in itself. He gave friendly nods where he could and simply waved away any attempts made to sell him wares or supplies.

It was the groups of warriors that bothered him the most. They lingered generally around the established borders, watching for any foreign dwarf looking to cause trouble in their area. To them, Doran knew he must appear threatening, given the dagger on his hip, the silvyr battle-axe slung over his shoulder, and the two halves of Andaljor, separated and resting in an X pattern at the base of his back.

Keeping his head down, the son of Dorain made his way into the heart of the camp, until every dwarf around him was sporting a brightly coloured beard. He hadn't been looking forward to this but, having discussed it with Asher and Inara, he could see that it was his best option for escaping the camp.

The tent he was looking for was easy to find, being the largest and most guarded. Groups of Brightbeard warriors sat huddled around fires, dotting the surroundings with extra protection. Seeing the royal guard, however, Doran was sure they were all surplus to requirement. Ten of the guards in question barred the entrance to the tent with long pikes, a great weapon for keeping unwanted guests at bay.

Unfortunately, that's exactly what Doran was...

"*State your business!*" the captain barked in dwarvish.

Doran was sure to keep a calm demeanour about him. "*I need to speak with the king.*"

"*Do I look like I'm troubled by your needs?*" the Brightbeard retorted. "*Get lost.*"

Doran sighed. "*I really need to speak with King Gaerhard,*" he emphasised.

The captain gave him a cursory inspection. "*And who are you to speak with the king of Bhan Doral? I see no clan about you.*"

Answering that truthfully carried a certain amount of risk - but his name and heritage were all he had left. "*My name,*" he announced so loudly it would be heard inside the tent, "*Is Doran, son of King Dorain, prince of Grimwhal, and bearer of Andaljor!*" In one smooth motion, he retrieved both sides of the legendary weapon and connected them at the haft.

The royal guard fell into a battle stance and aimed their pikes at Doran. He was very quickly beginning to wonder if his gamble would prove the end of him.

Then a voice bellowed from inside the tent. "*You are Doran, son of a dead dwarf, exile of Grimwhal, and unworthy of Andaljor!*"

Doran moved on from his wondering and knew for certain that his gamble would be the last thing he ever did. He prepared himself to surrender, staying true to his vow to never again take the life of another dwarf.

"*Now that your title has been corrected... you may enter!*"

King Gaerhard's invitation surprised the son of Dorain just as much as it did the royal guard. They hesitated, slow to raise their pikes, but the word of their king was law. Doran passed between their ranks and entered the tent, more than pleased to forego the camp's pungent odour in favour of the mead and cooked meats that lined the king's tent.

Seated at the back of the tent, King Gaerhard adorned his makeshift throne with all the regality he could muster since being forced to flee his kingdom. His mane of hair was a shocking red to match his fulsome beard, collected in places by golden rings. His silvyr armour was polished but clearly absent all of the pieces, abandoned perhaps in his haste to outrun the knights of Erador. His golden cloak was torn and muddied, much like his large boots. His puffy face was flushed pink across his cheeks and nose, a feature that made his blue eyes stand out.

It had been fifteen years since Doran had seen the king of the Brightbeards. Then, of course, he had been an ethereal image at his father's table, his details and features obscured by the magic that projected him. At the time, Gaerhard had sided with Uthrad - or he at least offered no protest - when the king of Silvyr Hall exiled clan Heavybelly and refused to ally with Illian against the orcs.

"*Let it be known,*" the king announced, "*the only reason you are permitted in my presence is because you wield a weapon I have long wished to see with my own eyes. You are still an exile even among exiles, making you the lowliest of the low.*"

Doran knew better than to try and correct the king, let alone argue with him. "*I have come before you, good king, because——*"

Gaerhard thrust his open hand out expectantly, silencing the son of Dorain. A servant accepted Andaljor from Doran and carried it to the red-bearded king. He licked his lips as his eyes took in every inch of the ancient weapon. His thumb ran delicately along the axe's blade and his knuckles rapped against the flat of the hammer. He appeared satisfied with every aspect of it, even the battle scars from previous wars.

"*There isn't a dwarf who didn't grow up on the stories of this weapon,*" he admired. "*You know the tale, I trust?*" he asked with a glance at Doran.

Of course he knew the tale - he was a Heavybelly, not to mention a direct descendant of Thorgen, Andaljor's original owner. Sensing the king hadn't finished, however, he kept his mouth shut for now.

"*Thousands of years ago,*" Gaerhard began, "*when the orcs had forced our ancestors from Vengora, a handful of heroes emerged, dwarves of great renown who had slain orcs by the hundreds. It was they who formed the new kingdoms, dividing us into clans.*" The king hefted the weapon in both hands. "*Andaljor - the orcsbane! Thorgen Heavybelly was said to be the best of them, as long as you don't ask any Battleborns,*" he added with a chortle. "*Had Thorgen emerged from the war a dwarf of*" *riches, as others had, it would have been your clan, son of Dorain, who presided over Silvyr Hall and not the Battleborns."*

Doran had often heard his great grandfather say something very similar. *"Heavybellys are just proud to have come from such stock,"* he said. *"The Battleborns can keep their riches."*

"Were there any to keep," Gaerhard remarked. *"And the Battleborns sit beneath us now, as do all the clans."* He added the latter with an air of superiority to him.

Time for another gamble. *"With all respect,"* Doran said, *"you're the king of nothing."*

Gaerhard scowled at the stout ranger and his grip tightened around Andaljor. *"Not too fond of your tongue, are you, boy?"*

Doran ignored the threat. *"The dirt beneath us belongs to King Vighon - you've neither the claim nor the numbers to say otherwise. Bhan Doral, like every other kingdom in Dhenaheim, has become a tomb in your absence. What's left of our people, all of our people, are huddled on The White Vale, surrounded by thousands of enemies."*

King Gaerhard leaned forward in his throne. *"Come to point out the obvious, have you? Typical Heavybelly!"*

"I've come to speak to the only dwarf who can do something," Doran countered, weighing his words with a compliment fit for an egotistical king. *"With Uthrad dining in Grarfath's Hall, you're the only one left with any claim to authority."*

Gaerhard eyed him suspiciously. *"And what would you have me do with said authority, lowly prince?"*

Doran thanked the Mother and Father - so far, every response from the king of Bhan Doral had been just as the dwarf had planned with Asher and Inara. *"I would have you free our people,"* he said boldly, inflating Gaerhard's ego all the more. *"Nobody knows why we're being kept here, but we can all agree it isn't going to be for anything good. If we don't fight back and get out of the north soon, every child of the mountain may suffer."*

The king placed Andaljor vertically between his legs. *"We've tried fighting back, several times. If we gather in too great a number the black knights draw their swords. If a few of us make a run for it, they hunt us down on horseback. We are outnumbered five to one at every turn.”*

“*There* are *others,*” Doran insisted. “*Those who would rally to the call of a king such as yourself. If you could unite what's left of the clans, there's a chance we might all see home.*”

King Gaerhard sat back with a frown that brought his red eyebrows together. “*You're talking about Heavybellys,*” he deduced.

“*They aren't among us,*” Doran said, ready to take his argument to the next stage.

“*That's because they don't* belong *among us!*” the Brightbeard snapped with a hammering fist. “*Exiles, the lot of them! They turned their backs on the hierarchy, on King Uthrad himself!*”

“*To fight orcs!*” Doran contested. “*They did what no other clan dared. And in doing so, they claimed another victory against our most ancient enemy. We're warriors, King Gaerhard. Right now, you are sorely in need of warriors...*”

The king tilted his head, taking the measure of the stout ranger. “*Thorgen's blood certainly flows through your veins, Doran, son of Dorain. But you speak of the Heavybellys as if you are one of them. You are a rogue. In fact, Illian has long been your home. What do you have to gain from all this?*”

It was hard to explain to a fellow dwarf that he had nothing to gain but the saving of lives - a ranger's calling. In many ways, it would be less suspicious to claim that his brother would reward him with coin and title or simply ask Gaerhard himself for reward. But, as he had for so long, Doran could rely on naught but his words alone. At least that's what Inara had told him, should the argument escalate as it was.

“*I just want...*” Doran caught himself. Right here, in the moment, he could see that telling Gaerhard the truth regarding his virtuous cause would increase the risk that his plan would fail. He needed to say something convincing, something that would sway the king to trust him. He also just needed to say anything before the king had him thrown out of his tent.

"What I propose, good king, is simple. You create a distraction - draw as many of the black knights as you can to the west. I will then escape to the east and find clan Heavybelly. Once I've reunited with them, I'll lead the charge myself if I have to and see every dwarf in this camp set free."

King Gaerhard narrowed his eyes. *"My question still stands, exile."*

"What do I have to gain?" Doran repeated the question, giving him a few extra seconds to think. *"Let them back in,"* he blurted. *"Open trade with them again, acknowledge their existence. Things will be different after this. The Brightbeards will emerge the most powerful clan. I would ask that the Heavybellys be given the second seat, just as the Stormshields were to the Battleborns."*

The king of Bhan Doral remained quiet, his free hand combing through his beard. *"An interesting proposal,"* he replied at last. *"And I suppose they would welcome you back with open arms to have brokered such an arrangement. Though your plan would rest a lot on the Heavybellys responding to my call to war. Why would they listen to you? Why would they risk their lives to save ours? I can see my people dying in this distraction, all so that you might run away, never to be seen again..."*

Doran had asked himself that same question and found the answer to be somewhat vague. Even Inara and Asher had seemed sceptical about his ability to convince the Heavybellys - should he even find them - to aid the clans that had shunned them for more than a decade now.

That was, however, a problem for another time. Right now, he just needed to convince King Gaerhard that he was the dwarf for the job. Luckily, he had been convincing people he was the dwarf for the job for nearly a century now.

"They'll listen to me because I have that," he said, pointing to Andaljor. *"I retrieved it from Grimwhal, after the invasion. It will be seen as a loyal feat for the clan. And they would risk their lives because of your generous offer, good king. To not only be welcomed back into the fold, but to also be appointed the second seat... What dwarf wouldn't risk everything for such an honour?"*

The red-bearded king looked from Doran to his closest advisors who shared his tent. They discussed nothing openly, but their silence spoke of no protest. The son of Dorain dared to hope...

"*I find your terms agreeable,*" Gaerhard announced. "*But I tell you, prince; them Heavybellys had better crash into these black knights with the fury of Grarfath Himself. Anything else will see us all at the Father's door.*"

"*You have my word, King Gaerhard.*"

"*Your word means next to nothing,*" the king replied casually. "*I am entertaining this risk because we have nothing left to give... and yet still so much to fight for.*"

The sun was firmly situated in the western sky when it came time to say farewell. Doran was close to the eastern edge of the camp, but not too far out from the camp that he might be spotted by any patrols. Asher and Inara were hooded and seated on a couple of crates, concealing their height and identities.

"What exactly are they going to do?" Inara enquired.

Doran looked to the west, where Namdhor rose high above the ground. "Gaerhard's War Mason, Gimmel, is handlin' it apparently. From what I could gather, he's amassin' a pretty decent force to push the camp's border closer to the lower town."

"That should do it," Asher commented.

"Where will you go?" Inara was looking out across the vale's flat horizon.

Doran had given this some thought already. "They 'ave to 'ave taken The Iron Valley," he reasoned. "There were more than a few among 'em who knew Namdhor was west out o' the valley, so somethin' must 'ave driven 'em away."

"That still leaves you with west or south," Asher observed.

"Or north even," Inara pointed out. "They could have followed The Guardian Cliffs to the west before turning back on themselves, towards Longdale."

"The cliffs are exactly where I'm goin'," Doran replied, checking over Pig's saddle. "They're pocketed like a giant slice o' Calmardran cheese. In trouble or not, me clan will naturally look to put some stone over their heads."

Asher nodded in agreement. "It's as good a place as any to start."

Doran eyed the ranger, scrutinising him. "Aye, but I bet ye won' be missin' me, will ye? I suppose there's not much room for a dwarf when it comes to killin' from the shadows..." The son of Dorain was sure to let the old assassin hear his disappointment.

Ashamed of his decision or not, Asher still averted his eyes, focusing on the ground instead. Taking that dark path was the last thing Doran wanted for his oldest friend, even if he agreed it was likely to yield the result they wanted.

"We'll find a way," Inara reassured. "Just as you must find a way to free these dwarves."

It was the first time in several days that Doran had heard any positivity in the Dragorn's voice. Unfortunately, he couldn't say he knew her well enough to know how forced her tone was. He decided to give her the benefit of the doubt; she was the Guardian of the Realm after all.

"I hope ye free the lad - the king that is!" he quickly corrected. "Come find us when ye do. Together, we'll find a way to undo all o' this."

"I see you're both still assuming I'm going to fail," Asher said from within his hood.

"I'm *hoping* you will," Inara replied.

"*I'm* assumin'," Doran nodded.

"Though, I hope you won't die in the process," Inara added.

Asher nodded some semblance of a thank you for the afterthought.

"Look on the bright side, lad. If ye die up there, ye finally get to 'ave a little break." Doran couldn't help but laugh to himself.

A distant chorus found them from the west, an uproar that was unmistakably dwarven in origin. It grew louder by the second until the sound of ringing steel caught up to them. Doran moved closer to the eastern edge and looked both ways, searching for the patrols. The Reavers were mobilising around the circumference and heading towards the ruckus.

"Are you ready?" Asher checked.

"As I'll ever be, old man." Doran held out his hand and the two rangers clasped forearms. "If ye die up there, I'll 'ave someone bring ye back again an' then I'll kill ye meself."

Asher smiled. "Understood." Before he let go of the dwarf's arm, he added, "With or without your clan, make sure you come back to us, you stubborn fool."

Doran gave a sharp laugh. "Ye don' think I'd let ye fight a war without me, do ye?"

Inara waited for a patrol of knights to rush past before standing up. "When Athis and I were heading into certain danger, you came after us, master dwarf, regardless of your own life. For that, you will always have a Dragorn in your debt."

Doran sniffed hard and loud in an attempt to keep his only eye free of tears. "Don' mention it, lass. The realm *needs* its Guardian. Besides, neither yerself nor that fierce dragon o' yers needs the likes o' my help."

Inara gave him a warm smile. "I hope you find your clan."

"I hope ye can put yers back together..." With that, Doran mounted Pig, adjusted Andaljor on the saddle, and guided the Warhog towards the farthest edge of the camp.

There was no sign of any patrols to the north since all of the Reavers had moved around the southern curve of the camp, to his right. There were still a pair on horseback south-east of his position, a little farther out across the vale, though their attention seemed to be on the growing tension in the west. They didn't look to be moving and his window of opportunity was slipping away with every second, not to mention the casualties the Brightbeards were potentially suffering.

"Right, Pig," he whispered in the Warhog's ear. "Ye need to get us over that horizon an' fast, ye hear. Don' stop for nothin' an' there'll be a big fat juicy steak in it for ye," he lied.

Though Pig's intelligence and understanding were often under scrutiny, there was no question as to whether the Warhog understood the word steak. Its slimy tongue ran over its top lip and snout in anticipation of the meal to come. Doran knew he would have little choice but to ply it with his Strider Cider in order to calm the disgruntled Warhog, cheated of its meal.

"Doran," Asher called. "Ride hard..."

The son of Dorain grinned. "Is there any other way to ride?"

Seeing that it was now or never, Doran knocked his heels into Pig and set the animal at an immediate sprint. Within seconds they were putting a good amount of distance between themselves and Namdhor and Pig didn't look to be slowing down any time soon. The son of Dorain felt the pull of his friends all the more. He wanted to stay and help them both, despite the stark differences between their errands.

But his clan were out there somewhere. And if the dwarves behind him stood any chance of surviving Alijah's machinations, they would need the Heavybellys to come to their aid. The stout ranger questioned how he had ended up, once again, in the middle of dwarven affairs. He had walked away from that life and been shunned by his kin ever since, yet here he was, working to unite the clans and save as many of them as he could.

He decided this must be how Asher felt all the time...

There was movement to his right, from the south-east. Doran cursed. The two outriders he had seen earlier were galloping towards him. He began assessing his options and came to the conclusion that their horses' stamina would see them ultimately gain on him when Pig lost some of his energy. His next conclusion was simple: he could take two of them. His Warhog made him nimble and hard to catch in mounted combat.

Then there was movement from the north, to his left. Another pair of outriders were emerging from the trees at Vengora's base and cutting a diagonal line across the snows to reach him. Damn - they clearly wanted all the dwarves confined to the camp! What could they possibly want from his kind that they would hunt a single fleeing dwarf down?

Doran ducked his body down and hastened Pig with some encouraging words, promising the Warhog all the meat and mead in Illian. And so their escape continued with all the speed his mount could muster. Stealing regular glances over his shoulders, however, the dwarf could see that a fight was inevitable - they were getting closer.

It wasn't long before he could hear the sound of thundering hooves behind him. The dark rider on his left had drawn its sword and was lining up its approach to swing down on the Warhog. To his right, the second rider was braced in its stirrups with two hands gripping the reins and closing fast.

It was the horse that caught Doran's eye.

The mount was haggard with strips of flesh hanging from visible ribs and its coat was a ghastly colour - more Reavers.

The revelation that the knights of Erador were riding undead horses made Doran's decisions much easier. From his hip, he pulled free his one-handed sword - gifted to him on King Gaerhard's command. It was a length of steel far wider than any human would choose to wield and certainly of superior crafting.

Without warning to his enemies, the dwarf brought his Warhog to a sudden stop, yanking hard on Pig's reins. The rider to his left shot past, hurtling into Doran's outstretched blade, positioned to take out the horse's legs.

At such speed, it was a spectacular crash. The knight from Erador collided with the ground at an angle that would have guaranteed death for any ordinary person, its body bending backwards over itself again and again before the weight of its undead horse skidded into it.

Doran laughed heartily.

The rider to his right continued past him unharmed before

quickly turning around. The dwarf sneered and set his Warhog to the task of meeting the Reaver head on. Both at full speed, they were on a collision course that would certainly be the end of Doran, if not the knight. Unlike the undead horse, fortunately, Pig was able to change direction in the blink of an eye with barely any loss in speed. At the last moment, Doran directed the Warhog to the right, crossing in front of the horse's path to take them over to the other side.

Then his sword lashed out again. The sound of both rider and mount violently meeting the unforgiving ground was both satisfying and amusing to the ranger. Laughing some more, he turned to admire the devastation and saw the other two riders. They each stopped, surprisingly, to assist the fallen Reavers from under their horses. The fact that there was anything to recover sent shivers up Doran's spine.

Still, their decision to take on an extra rider each only slowed them down, allowing Doran to gain a great advantage. And so he rode east with fire in his veins, all too aware that thousands of dwarves were relying on him.

He just had to stay ahead of his hunters...

PART FOUR

CHAPTER 38

REGRESSION

Meticulous. Methodical. Controlled. These were the traits typical of an Arakesh in the midst of their work. To be an assassin of Nightfall was to be a servant of death, a being of singular purpose. Planning the final moments of any man required studious preparations and forethought, always designed to leverage the target into a position of inferiority. Such a thing was all the more difficult when the target was, perhaps, the most powerful man in the realm...

Inside the privacy of his dwarven tent, Asher embraced his *work*. It had been two days since Doran's departure from the camp and the ranger had only fallen deeper into his old ways.

Planning his breach of the keep had taken some time, given that the Reavers never had the need to patrol in shifts or even take a break to relieve themselves. Then there was the layout of the keep to consider: which passages to take, what shadows to utilise, and which room he would take advantage of to kill Alijah in.

Though an unlikely scenario, he had also taken some time to figure out an escape route should it become clear that he wasn't going to win the fight. The assassin in him was ever practical, forcing him to accept that he might be better escaping and returning at another time to try again. It would be foolhardy to believe he had but one attempt and that he should give his all or die.

Nightfall had expected results, not heroes. The Mother or Father didn't care if an Arakesh made more than one attempt to take a designated life, only that they succeeded in the end and in a timely manner suiting the client. In this case, Asher was both the client and the assassin - the target one of his own choosing.

He *would* kill Alijah Galfrey tomorrow. Or the next day. Or the day after that. Nothing would stop him, not even his own hubris.

In the event that he did indeed kill Alijah, the ranger had little need of an escape route, given that every Reaver under his command would return to a heap of bones on the ground. For most, at this stage, there would be a quiet voice in their mind telling them that the chances of this were slim, their own death far more likely. But Asher had never been considered among the *most*.

And now, submerged back into the mind of the killer, there was but one voice, confident and calm, if frighteningly cold. He hadn't heard that particular voice in a long time and, though it sounded like his own, he had long believed it to be that of death itself, guiding him when it wasn't, instead, trying to claim him. He would succeed. Alijah would die.

That's all there was.

Continuing his preparations, Asher focused on the task in front of him. When he hadn't been gathering information, he had been gathering ingredients and supplies to ensure his victory. Now, inside the cover of the tent, under the stars, he brewed his elixir. Using a small bowl, he ground the herbs and granules into a fine powder, ready to add them to the pot of boiling water.

"This looks interesting," Inara commented as she entered the tent. The Dragorn crossed her legs and sat on the ground opposite the ranger, her shoulders tucked within her red cloak.

"Adan'Karth?" Asher enquired.

"I saw him safely to Athis," Inara answered, her eyes examining all that Asher was preparing. "Hiding his horns wasn't easy but, since he's clearly not a dwarf, the Reavers showed no interest."

"Good," he replied absently, adding another expensive ingredient. "What of the Brightbeards? It's been quiet around here."

"From what I've heard," Inara replied, "they suffered a few casualties. No deaths thankfully. The Reavers didn't give them an inch though."

Asher offered a grunt in recognition of her words.

"What *is* all this?" she continued.

"I told you," Asher said, "the keep is crawling with Arakesh."

"Ah, yes, Lady Gracen..." Inara stopped to sniff a small cup of unusual paste he had made earlier. "That's foul," she remarked, placing it back down again. "How is this going to help you with the Arakesh? I know their senses are heightened in the dark, but I don't think they'll be subdued by a bad smell."

Asher kept his eyes on his work. "Heightened doesn't cover it. When submerged in total darkness, they tune into their surroundings as if they were a part of it, like the roots of a tree spreading underground. They can feel the air moving against their skin, informing them exactly of where you're about to be. They can taste your sweat on their tongue and gauge your fear, using it against you. If you're bleeding, they'll sniff you out through stone. And," he said, pouring the powder into the pot, "they can hear your heart beating in your chest..."

"You forgot to mention their legendary skills in combat," Inara quipped.

"One problem at a time," he replied, stirring the liquid.

Inara peered over the lip. "What will this do to you?"

"It should slow my heartbeat down. It won't conceal me, but it might give me enough of an edge to gain the upper hand."

"*Should*? You've never made this potion before?"

"Once, but it didn't work as intended." Asher recalled the experience as one of the few times he had had luck on his side.

"What happened?" Inara asked.

Asher gestured to the paste. "I forgot to add in the Nefalyn. Without it, your heart slows down and so, naturally, do you. I damn near passed out last time - not a good thing when you're climbing up a cliff."

"This horrid stuff keeps you on your feet?" Inara's nose wrinkled as she scowled at the Nefalyn paste.

"After stripping your tongue, yes."

"How did you survive last time?" Inara placed the cup of paste much farther away this time.

"I had a rope and harness. I was hanging from that cliff for hours..."

Inara rested back against a small chest. "Struggle as I might to understand how my brother could be in league with the Arakesh, I still don't understand how they survived the war. I thought The Black Hand wiped them out in Nightfall."

Asher had asked himself that same question since learning that Lady Gracen had tricked him. "Escape and evasion are among the earliest of lessons in Nightfall," he explained. "Some must have survived to continue the order."

"Well they haven't been using Nightfall," Inara pointed out. "We searched that wretched place twice after the war and found naught but corpses."

"They've adapted," the old assassin reasoned. "That's what we've always been best at..."

"That's what *they've* always been best at," Inara corrected.

He could feel her gaze on him after that, her interest lingering on his facial features. It made him uncomfortable, a natural response for one taught in his trade. When he finally looked up at her he realised her gaze wasn't on him but, rather, through him. It seemed her thoughts had quickly run away with themselves, though he could see a hint of concern pulling at her brow.

The ranger hoped to take advantage of her distraction and to continue with his work. But he kept glancing at her, his own concern growing by the second. Once upon a time, he would have happily ignored the Dragorn's quiet distress, but she was a Galfrey and, apparently, he had a weakness for them.

"Spit it out," he said, sure that there was a better way he could have approached the subject.

Inara, snapped out of her daze, focused on Asher. "What are you talking about?"

"What's on your mind?" he tried again, convinced, irritatingly, that he was becoming more empathetic by the day - some would simply say he was going soft.

Inara reached around her belt and pulled out a small black orb with a polished surface. Asher examined it and saw a distorted version of himself looking back at him. Though he had never used one, the ranger knew it to be a diviner. They were always paired with another, and the list of people Inara would have contact with was undoubtedly short.

"Who has the other one?" he asked immediately.

"Gideon," she uttered.

Asher couldn't help but notice her lack of enthusiasm. "Have you spoken with him?"

Inara dropped the diviner on the ground between her crossed feet. "I've tried several times since we arrived here. He's not there..."

"Maybe he lost it," the ranger suggested.

Inara shook her head. "Unlikely."

"Then what?" Asher posed, "He's dead?"

"Even more unlikely," Inara replied.

"Then you fear the worst," Asher concluded. "He doesn't care..."

"You don't know Gideon Thorn like I do," she countered. "The only reason he moved the order to Dragons' Reach is because he cared. Possibly too much," she added. "He wanted them to be strong enough to protect the realm as well as themselves."

"Then maybe they're just busy training." Asher was beginning to regret opening the conversation.

Absent a reply, Inara went quiet again, offering the ranger an opportunity to return to his preparations. As usual, the emotions he had found later in life rose to the surface in a bid to control his thoughts and actions.

Irritating indeed...

"Keep trying," he encouraged. "We need your order now more than ever. And I'm sure that after fifteen years of training, Gideon will arrive with quite the force at his back."

Inara held another moment's thought before scooping up the diviner and replacing it in her belt. "What need will we have of my order when you're going to solve everything with a blade in the dark?"

The ranger flashed his eyes. "You'd be surprised how many problems have been solved by a blade in the dark."

"I grew up hearing stories about you," Inara began, an edge of disappointment in her voice. "Stories of how you faced an army of Arakesh at the gates of West Fellion. How you stared down the army of Karath with no one at your back. My mother tells of the hero who fought by her side atop Syla's Gate, standing his ground against hordes of Darkakin. My father told us again and again of the giant you brought down from Velia's walls. How can you be that same man?"

"It wasn't an army," he simply replied.

"What?" Inara frowned.

"It wasn't an army of Arakesh, at West Fellion. There were maybe five hundred and I didn't face them all." It was a guarded response but, when Asher felt defensive, he either shut down or drew his sword.

Clearly frustrated, the Dragorn tilted her head and scrutinised the ranger. He gave nothing away, his focus returned to his preparations.

"I can't read you like she can."

Asher dared to meet her eyes again. "Who?"

"My mother. She says she can tell what you're thinking just by looking at you."

Asher was able to recall many a time that Reyna had proven such a thing. In the beginning, it had made him even more uncomfortable than being observed by someone. The ranger had soon come to love that about the princess though, realising that her insights made everything easier. The elf had told him it was quite a common thing among friends. He missed her, Nathaniel too.

"Do you believe they're here, as the Archon claimed?" The art of manipulating conversations was another of Nightfall's earliest lessons and, in this instance, he was grateful for the skill.

"No," the Dragorn replied confidently. "Given everything that's happened here, I am sure we would have seen some evidence of their presence."

Asher had to agree. "Then where are they?"

Inara appeared troubled by that same question. "I don't know. Knowing them, they're probably heading *into* trouble rather than *away* from it. You have that much in common with my parents," she added.

"Speaking of heading into trouble, *Galfrey*; have you planned your way into the keep?" Asher kept himself busy with the potion.

Inara looked to the tent's entrance, as if she could see Namdhor. "The dungeons are located towards the back of the keep, closer to the lake—"

"They're also several hundred feet *above* the lake," Asher cut in sarcastically.

"I had noticed, *thank you*. That's why I'm going to climb up the King's Hollow and enter the keep from behind."

Asher stopped what he was doing. "You're going to climb to the top?"

"Yes."

"And then break Vighon out of the dungeons?" His increasing disbelief was evident in his tone.

"Yes."

The ranger put himself in her position and knew well that he would need a night's sleep to recover from such a climb, never mind breaking someone out of a cell. "You should definitely think about helping me instead."

Inara rolled her eyes. "It's a big climb, yes, but I'm as strong as an elf and a Dragorn to boot - it's doable. Besides, I thought you preferred to *work alone*," she added in a gravelly voice.

Asher took the mockery in his stride. "I do far better alone," he agreed. "But I've never tried to kill a Dragon Rider with Arakesh bodyguards before. I could do with some of that elven strength..."

"Maybe I don't want you to have my strength," Inara posed. "*Maybe* I want you to fail."

Satisfied with his elixir, Asher poured the liquid into a small vial and corked it. "If you wanted me to fail," he countered, "you would have stopped me by now."

The ranger let that hang between them, a shared knowledge that Inara was one of the few people in all of Verda who could stop Asher in his tracks. He could see it dawning on her, the quiet revelation enough to silence the Dragorn, be it shame or ignorance. Asher couldn't blame her for either. In fact, he would rather commit the gruesome act in her stead.

They didn't speak again that night...

The next day was one of yet more preparation, including the whetstone he took to his silvyr short-sword. The wait for his prey, however, was finally over. Not long after sunset, the stars came out with the company of a thunderous roar, quickly followed by a chorus of terrified screams. Asher, it seemed, would never escape that roar. He rose from the ground with one hand locked around the hilt of his broadsword.

Inara was lighter on her feet and the first to leave the tent. Asher was close behind, his eyes turned skyward. There was no missing Malliath, nor the escort of dragons flying behind him. They were terrible beasts, unnatural and fiendish in appearance as they cut across the northern sky. Beside Malliath, their undead forms were all the more obvious and hideous.

It was the black dragon himself that pulled at the ranger's attention. His flight path continuously veered to the left, forcing Malliath to correct himself every few hundred feet. Asher had been astride the fierce dragon, while enthralled to The Crow, and experienced first-hand such an unusual flight.

Malliath was injured...

Observation and memory told him the dragon's left wing was wounded. That meant Alijah was similarly wounded. Asher was overcome with a hunger not dissimilar to that of a predator's when it caught sight of its prey, the kill a certainty.

Malliath cast his considerable shadow across the city before coming to rest on the ramparts of the keep, his long neck hanging low. The remaining dragons, Reavers all, ascended higher into the sky and scattered in every direction.

"There aren't many who could injure either of them," Inara contemplated. "I fear for those in his wake..."

Asher was holding the red blindfold in his hand, though when he had grasped it escaped the ranger. "Tomorrow night," he asserted, turning to Inara. "Get Vighon and get out. Don't get in my way."

The Dragorn looked to protest when a much louder protest was made not far from their tent. Dwarves, angry by the sound of them, were shouting and cursing in the tongues of both man and dwarf. Together, Asher and Inara raised their hoods and moved to investigate, bringing them to the eastern edge of the camp. Several rows of dwarves were lined up on the boundary, yelling at the black knights trampling through the scorched field of Battleborn corpses.

"What are they doing?" Inara questioned.

Asher kept most of himself concealed behind a post as he observed the knights of Erador. Dozens of them were spreading out amongst the charred remains, their helmeted heads searching the ground. Then, as one, they began yanking and tearing the silvyr armour away from the dead. This angered the dwarves all the more, increasing the size and volume of their protest. A dozen extra Reavers broke away from the vale and placed themselves in front of the dwarves, deterring them from taking action.

Asher weaved through the camp and found a better vantage farther down. The knights were removing every scrap of silvyr and piling it up on carts. When the carts were full, they were guided away by undead horses and led to The Selk Road. Curiously, they were heading south.

Inara came up behind the ranger. "What's this about then? What could Reavers want with silvyr?"

Asher shook his head. "The question is: what does your *brother* want with silvyr?"

Inara had no answer to that, but she gripped his arm before he could walk away. "I know what you mean to do. But there comes a time when we have to make a choice. That choice has the power to—"

"Really?" Asher interrupted. "Look at me, Inara. Do I look like someone you give *that* speech to? I've lived long enough to know what my choices are and I've lived long enough to know what the consequences are. After I've put this on," he said, showing her the blindfold, "if you get in my way, you too will come to understand those same consequences."

The ranger walked away from the Dragorn, determined to finish his preparations. Tomorrow night, he would kill a king...

CHAPTER 39
THE PROMISE OF BLOOD

Vighon's eyes snapped open to the sound of a heavy bolt shifting out of its lock. Chained to the wall and on his knees, the northman kept his head hung low, keeping his face concealed behind a curtain of hair. He knew who was about to enter the cell and he didn't care to receive them.

The iron door *creaked* open on its old hinges and a rattle of keys resounded from the passage. Then he walked in, the betrayer, the fiend who wore his friend's face. Alijah's steps were light as he crossed the short distance to take the only chair in the cell.

The door *creaked* once more and slammed shut, sealing them in together.

"There isn't much that can make this keep shudder," Vighon croaked, his throat dry. "I do hope that wretched dragon of yours isn't damaging my home."

"I had hoped this would remain your home," Alijah replied, his own voice out of sorts.

Vighon finally looked up, curious. Alijah was slumped in the chair, his head resting back against the stone. His left arm hung by his side with streaks of dried blood running from his wrist down to his fingertips. His right arm was wrapped around his chest, gripping his ribs. Around that area, the northman could see that the scales of his armour had taken damage and were chipped and scratched in places.

He was certainly injured and his complexion, pale and clammy, told of deeper injuries. A nasty bruise spread out from beneath his collar and over his jaw, where it met a patchwork of cuts and more dried blood.

The northman smirked. "So, you're not invincible then."

Alijah's expression didn't change. "No one is invincible, Vighon. Even Verda's most powerful can be killed..."

Vighon's brow pinched as he put the pieces behind Alijah's words together. "What have you done?" he asked, horrified by his suspicions.

"What needed to be done." The half-elf winced as he adjusted his posture. "In time, there will be balance. But until then, I need Illian to be free of... *complications*."

Vighon pulled hard against his manacles. "Who have you *killed*, Alijah?"

The new king of Illian took a deep breath and groaned with the effort. "She gave me no choice," he began. "I told them to leave and she refused."

"The elves?" Vighon said with despair. "You've attacked the elves?"

"I *defended* myself," Alijah corrected. "Against family, I might add."

"Family? No..." Vighon couldn't believe the logical conclusion. "You've killed Lady Ellöria."

Alijah didn't say anything. His gaze was distant, piercing Vighon and the stone behind him. Was it guilt that robbed him of words? Or was he so consumed by darkness that he felt nothing at all? Vighon was inclined to believe it was the latter.

"She was your blood!" The northman sighed, his shoulders sagging under the disbelief. "I suppose if you have it in you to kill your sister," he said, his tone dripping with venom, "your grandmother's sister is barely a consideration."

Alijah's eyes refocused and found Vighon. "Sacrifice without hesitation," he stated. "To you those are just words but, to me, they mean *everything*. Blood is important, but nothing can come before the realm, before the *people*."

"Don't talk to me about absolutes," Vighon spat. "I gave up everything for this country! I've done nothing *but* put the realm first!"

"I'm not disputing you were a good king, Vighon. I haven't supplanted you because you were wicked. You simply don't have the vision or the power to give Illian what it really needs. Stability. Unity. Peace. Equality. And I wasn't lying when I said this was still to be your home. I've spent years dreaming of the world I would forge. I always envisioned you and Inara living beside me, here, in The Dragon Keep. My parents too. You would all help me to maintain a—"

Vighon spat on the floor at Alijah's feet. "I forgot how much you enjoy the sound of your own voice. Is there a reason I'm still alive?"

"Impatient as ever," Alijah remarked mostly to himself. "Are you so eager for death?"

"I would just prefer a quick death to whatever *this* is." Vighon inspected his cell. "Can I expect this to be my fate? A dank cell and your voice droning on until my heart gives out."

Alijah attempted to sit forward. "You don't have to treat me like the enemy. I've relieved you of a great burden. You never really wanted any of this. The politics of the crown, the rebellions, the sheer weight of the people. When I'm finished, there won't even be war."

Vighon almost laughed. "You can't be foolish enough to believe that's even possible. How much history is in that thick head of yours?

There have been wars for as long as there have been people to fight them."

The half-elf smiled, pulling at his bruises. "There can't be war if there's only one side."

The northman briefly closed his eyes and let his head fall back. "You're deluded if you think bringing Verda under one banner will free the realm of all war."

Alijah narrowed his eyes, pulling Vighon in. "You see," he whispered, "you lack the vision to fully grasp what needs to be done. And the power," he added, gesturing to the northman's chains.

"Maybe," Vighon retorted, "if I had been the one who was stupid enough to *walk* into The Bastion, The Black Hand would have given *me* the vision and power you're so fond of."

Alijah snapped and shot forward as if all his ailments were forgotten. Vighon matched his ferocity and jumped up to meet him, only to have his manacles stunt his advance. The two came face to face.

"You have no idea what happened inside that place," Alijah told him. "You can't even wrap your mind around the thousands of tiny events that had to take place in order for me to arrive at The Bastion's doors. You're just a leaf caught in a storm, Vighon Draqaro."

"Is that right?" Vighon could feel the iron digging into his wrists. "Then why is the king of the world wasting his time talking to someone so insignificant?"

Alijah deflated somewhat and took a step back, his pain clearly returning with a vengeance. "For a moment, you almost took a hold of your own destiny. You rose from nothing to a king, the first king of Illian in a thousand years! You could have spent what's left of your life in happiness with the woman you've always loved. I would have liked to have seen that. But you let it all go right when it mattered most. Now, your fate is in my hands. You will either do as I wish and live, or *refuse* and you will still do as I command, and die painfully."

Vighon let some of the tension out of his muscles and allowed the chains to gain some slack. "You want me to make a few speeches, is that it? You think a few words from me will convince the realm that we haven't been invaded, we've just joined a larger kingdom that none of them knew existed in the first place?" The northman laughed.

"You've no idea of the size of the task you've taken on," he continued. "Most of Illian still worship Atilan and the rest of his twisted lot. They have no idea he was just a man, or that he came from a place called Erador. You're about to upturn a thousand years of religion and you think you're heralding peace. Not to mention the army of monsters that marched into Illian on your orders!"

"You're right," Alijah conceded, surprising Vighon. "There will be great upset, maybe even a revolt or two. But another generation from now and everything will be different again. Then there's the generation after that to consider. Eventually, the current state of things will be consigned to history and the new order of things, *my* order, will be all there is. That's always been the problem with you mortal kings - you think too small."

Vighon had little left to throw at his old friend. "The Dragorn will return!" he promised, pouring as much conviction into his statement as possible. "Gideon Thorn won't let you get away with this."

Alijah looked around the cell expectantly. "I see no Dragorn. I have been planning this for years. I've been in open war with the dwarves for six months. Illian has been under my banner for several *days*. I don't think Gideon Thorn is coming..."

"Then *I* will stop you," Vighon insisted. "That's the only speech you're going to get from me. I will rally any and all to the flaming sword and we will make you *bleed*. Do you hear me, Alijah Galfrey? I am going to make you hurt!"

"Look around you, Vighon. You're not going to do anything unless I want you to." Gripping his ribs again, the half-elf turned towards the door. "I was trapped in a cell like this once. I hope, like me, you will come to see the truth of things... in *time*. You can still be of value to this kingdom. Think on that."

The door was opened for him and the new king walked away without a second glance. Vighon wanted to break his chain from the wall and strangle Alijah with it. Giving him time was the biggest mistake the half-elf could make. With time, the northman would find a way out of his own dungeon. And then, he would find a way to take back his throne.

CHAPTER 40
ALLIES ON THE ROAD

The town of Dunwich was wholly uninspiring, even more so on a wet and dreary morning in the north. Through the lashing rain, Kassian took in the flat town. Bar one decrepit-looking tower, there wasn't a single building higher than two storeys. Everything was a shade of brown.

The Keeper had always wondered if he was missing the world by staying inside Valatos's walls but, since leaving Velia altogether, he had come to the conclusion that the rest of Illian had little to offer.

All across the town, chimneys exhaled plumes of smoke into the rainy air. The people were already going about their daily routines taking no care of the rain nor of the biting cold that gripped the north. At first glance, most appeared to be fishermen taking advantage of the lake east of the town.

Of course, Dunwich's main advantage was its location. Travelling north or south, everyone from traders to soldiers had no choice but to journey through the town as it sat atop The Selk Road.

What had been a passing thought triggered a question for the Keeper. What was he now? He was neither a trader nor a soldier. Most, he assumed, would simply consider him a mage. Any who knew anything of Valatos would recognise him specifically as a Keeper thanks to his attire, but who in Dunwich would know anything of Valatos?

As an appointed Keeper, it had been his sworn duty to protect the mages of Valatos, though he had long considered his duty to extend to mages everywhere. Now, it seemed, he was just a man. No, he thought - not *just* a man. He was a man with significant power at his fingertips and no one to tell him what to do with it. That was just as well, he decided, since he was hell bent on using his magic to kill Alijah Galfrey.

Kassian's fist repeatedly clenched and unclenched as he entered Dunwich's southern gate. He was itching to whip out his wand and cause some destruction. He just wanted to lash out at the world and make them feel his pain. It burned inside of him, demanding constant management.

"Focus," Nathaniel warned from his left.

Kassian snapped out of his spiral. "I am focused," he lied, returning to his scan of their surroundings.

The Galfreys walked beside him, their hoods raised to hide their faces and Reyna's ears. They appeared well versed in the art of blending in, moving naturally from stall to stall, group to group, always feigning interest. This wasn't Kassian's world. He had been trained to deliberately stand out so that his authority might be recognised around Valatos's grounds.

His sandy hair was plastered to his battered face, but it did nothing to hide his features. And there was no hiding the sword on his belt or the fine craftsmanship of his vambraces. Then again; what did it matter if he stuck out like a sore thumb? He doubted there was anyone in Dunwich who posed a threat.

"Something isn't right," Nathaniel observed.

Kassian looked around and found nothing out of the ordinary. "Are you seeing something I'm not?"

"Actually, it's what I'm not seeing." The old Graycoat stepped away from the nearest stall and scrutinised the crossing streets.

"Where are the town watch? I haven't seen a single soldier since we arrived."

"They aren't the only thing that is missing," Reyna pointed out. "Where is the flaming sword? I see none of Vighon's banners."

Through the patter of rain, Kassian heard the distinct clamour of armour marching down the street. The three companions moved deeper into the market but kept their eyes on the soldiers advancing in their direction. Clad in black, their identities sealed, Alijah's soldiers made themselves known to the people of Dunwich, only there weren't many who paid them much attention.

"They must have been here for a few days," Nathaniel reasoned. "Those we saw south of the mountains must have left some behind to replace the watch."

The soldiers turned away from the market stalls and entered another street. Kassian looked around and noted the subtle apprehension among the northerners. They were determined, it seemed, to continue with the business of their daily lives, but they had likely witnessed something that kept them quiet.

Heading in the opposite direction to the dark soldiers, Kassian and the Galfreys soon came across the scene that, no doubt, was the cause of the people's submission. Hanging from a beam, in the middle of the town square, were four men bearing the sigil of King Vighon. Crows squawked from above as they sidled along the beam, oblivious to the rain. At the base of the scaffolding, flowers had been laid down, most likely by family members.

It was a gruesome sight, though not the worst Kassian could conjure from recent memory.

"I think we should put Dunwich behind us," Nathaniel suggested ominously.

"Agreed." Kassian was only too happy to move on.

"We haven't much coin," the old knight said, fingering the pouch on his belt. "Maybe enough to buy a couple of furs."

The Keeper pulled on the collar of his long coat. "Get your furs. I'll be fine."

Kassian waited outside while the Galfreys purchased their new cloaks. He kept to himself, leaning against a wooden post, under a lip to keep as dry as possible. The people of Dunwich were passing him by, going about their day as if Clara hadn't died. How could the whole realm possibly get on with their lives when the sun had been taken from them?

Children ran past, giggling. Merchants convinced people to buy their wares. Couples walked by hand in hand. There wasn't even talk of the soldiers who had invaded their home or the fact that a dragon had torched Valatos!

It infuriated him.

Without realising it, he had his hand on his wand, his fingers fidgeting around the handle. Unfortunately, there was someone who had noticed what he was doing. By the corner of the next road up, standing perfectly still in the rain, was a dark soldier. The narrow slit in his helmet made it impossible to see his eyes from this distance, but he was definitely looking in Kassian's direction. Then he started walking towards him.

The Keeper pushed away from the post, bracing himself. He wasn't sure what he had done to gain the soldier's attention. Were wands forbidden in Dunwich? There was no time to ponder on his slight before the soldier was upon him.

"Is there a problem?" Kassian asked, seeing a pair of armoured gloves moving to seize his arms. "I said is there a problem?" he repeated.

Only one hand gripped his arm. The other was too slow, missing the opportunity to prevent Kassian from drawing his wand. A flash of light and a physical pulse erupted between the tip of the wand and the soldier, throwing him clear across the street and through a butcher's window. It was an awfully loud crash, eliciting screams from people in and out of the ruined shop. In hindsight, the Keeper wondered if he had poured a little too much power into his spell...

Ignoring the looks he was now receiving, Kassian turned to see the Galfreys bursting out of the tailors. It didn't take them long to discover the destruction on the other side of the street.

Nathaniel looked from the wand to its owner. "You don't know any quiet magic?"

"He tried to seize me," Kassian explained.

"Why?" Reyna enquired, her elven eyes scanning the streets.

"I was just holding my wand," the Keeper shrugged. "We should probably..." His words died away as his attention was pulled back to what was left of the butcher's shop.

The dark soldier was clambering over the meats and shattered glass. Once free of the debris, he stepped back onto the street and drew his sword.

"Impossible," Kassian breathed.

Reyna and Nathaniel braced themselves and pulled free their own swords. "What did you hit him with?" the elf asked.

"A kinketik spell. His bones should be no better than jelly."

The dark soldier stopped in the middle of the street without a word. "He doesn't seem to be having that problem," Nathaniel commented, falling into a fighting stance.

At this point, the townspeople decided that they were better off somewhere else. Their reaction was quite the opposite to the half dozen soldiers that rounded the corner to join their comrade.

"I count seven," Nathaniel stated.

"Make that ten," Reyna corrected, noting three more approaching from the other end of the street.

Kassian brandished his wand. "I think I can do something about that."

"Destruction magic is taxing," Reyna warned. "There are too many."

"Then I had better use the right spell," the Keeper replied with a wicked grin.

Eager to fight, Kassian pointed his wand at the largest cluster of soldiers, approaching from his right. There was naught but a green flash for the spell itself moved too fast to be seen. It was, however, felt by the soldiers marching towards them.

The leader took the full force of the spell and was hurled backwards off his feet. Before he could be launched out of their cluster, his entire body exploded with the charged magic. Windows on both sides of the street were blown in and the surrounding soldiers were violently propelled in every direction. Shrapnel from the black armour buried itself in the buildings and bounced harmlessly off Kassian's waiting shield.

It had been a powerful spell and he could already feel the dull ache in his arm. He would do it again though if it meant seeing so many of Alijah's men meet their end. Returning his attention to the first soldier he had thrown through the butcher's window, Kassian flicked his wand and hit the man with a spell specifically designed to damage armour. It was, technically, a harmless spell, unless the armour in question was encased around a man's chest.

The soldier's progress towards Nathaniel was halted by the spell and his life was subsequently halted by the armour that imploded into his chest. The man's body was twisted and distorted out of shape, dropping him to his knees where he became very still.

Reyna had already moved into the middle of the street to face the three soldiers approaching from the north. Rain drops ran down the length of her elven scimitar but for a second before she whipped the blade across the leg of the closest foe. A backhanded lash cut across his armoured chest and threw him back. The elf was fast. Her scimitar danced around her, parrying and striking all at once until she was surrounded by fallen bodies.

Kassian rotated his shoulder in a bid to soothe it. "*Now* we should leave Dunwich."

That was when the truly impossible happened.

On its knees before Nathaniel, the soldier, killed by his own crushing armour, leaped up with a sweeping arc of its sword. Only years of experience kept the old Graycoat alive in that moment, as his own sword flew up to block the attack. Kassian was frozen in disbelief. No man could survive that kind of devastation...

Nathaniel kicked the dead soldier back and pursued it with his sword. At the same time, Reyna cried out down the street when she was pulled to the ground by one of her own kills. Kassian made to help her when he heard movement to his right. Except for the leader, reduced to small chunks, all of the soldiers who had been tossed around like rag dolls were rising to their feet without so much as a groan.

"Help Reyna!" Nathaniel barked. The old knight severed one of his opponent's hands but it troubled the dead soldier no more than the armour embedded in its chest.

Kassian holstered his wand and drew his sword. "There's more coming on your right," he warned Nathaniel before moving to aid Reyna.

"I can handle them!" Nathaniel assured, running steel through his enemy's gut.

The Keeper dragged the length of his sword across his left vambrace, activating the spell that bound both items together. The blade ignited from within as if it contained the sun itself. From guard to tip, the steel burned a bright white, turning every drop of rain into *sizzling* steam.

Of the three soldiers brought down by Reyna, two of them rose from the ground and moved to intercept Kassian. Unfortunately for them, the Keeper was naught but fury given life.

He dashed to the left and swung his sword through the first soldier's hip, almost chopping the dead man in half. The second soldier failed to land its blow, missing Kassian by an inch, only to have the top half of its head cleaved off by the hottest sword in the realm.

With no one between him and the soldier on top of Reyna, Kassian raised his weapon to finish the assault. The elf was faster and clearly angered by the dead man trying to strangle her. Using both hands, Reyna twisted his helmeted head, snapping the neck with an audible *crack*. The ambassador rolled the body aside and jumped to her feet before ramming her scimitar down into its head.

"Nathaniel!" she cried.

Turning back, the old Graycoat had successfully dispatched the soldier with a crushed torso - the body was lying several feet away from its head. But now he was quickly being surrounded by the remaining five. Kassian was only too happy to jump into the fray, his sword keen to melt iron and flesh alike.

Halting their charge, the adjacent alley exploded with activity as five men, hooded and cloaked in navy, collided with the soldiers in a clash of steel. Their form betrayed years of training and their brutal efficiency demonstrated a level of skill reserved only for the realm's elite fighters. Assisted by Nathaniel, the six men quickly overcame the dark soldiers. The battle ended with all five of the soldiers losing their heads...

Somewhat exhausted, Nathaniel staggered away from the scene. "They're Reavers!" he declared.

Kassian had a lot of questions given what he had just witnessed and Nathaniel's announcement wasn't an answer the Keeper understood.

One of the men from the alley pulled back his hood to reveal a grizzled square jaw and a short mane of dark hair. "That they are, Ambassador," he agreed.

"Sir Ruban?" The old knight frowned.

"What are the king's guard doing here?" Reyna asked.

"The king charged us with finding you in Velia," Ruban replied, sheathing his sword. "Alas, we never made it farther than Dunwich before *they* arrived."

"What in all the hells are they?" Kassian demanded.

Sir Ruban looked him up and down. "A Keeper?" His assessment was followed by a hand reaching for his sword again.

"He's with us," Nathaniel vouched, holding a hand over Ruban's.

Reyna turned to face the three soldiers who had attacked her. "*They* are Reavers."

Kassian followed her gaze to discover, quite horrifyingly, that the soldier he had damn near sliced in half was slowly crawling towards them. "What's a Reaver?" he asked absently.

"The undead," Reyna said bluntly.

That explained why Kassian had never heard of a Reaver before - necromancy was the most forbidden of magics. "Of course," he said as if it was obvious. "He couldn't just be a tyrant. He's a necromancer too..."

Neither of the Galfreys had a response. Ruban gave one of his men the nod and they intercepted the crawling Reaver without delay. A quick chop and its head was parted in the middle of the street.

"Decapitation or fire," Sir Ruban stated. "Nothing else will kill them."

"Good to know." Kassian touched his blade to the enchanted vambrace on his left wrist, retiring the weapon to its previous state.

"Who is this tyrant you speak of?" the king's guard enquired.

The awkward silence that rose between Kassian and the Galfreys was short-lived. Along with the king's guard, they all heard the sound of more clamouring armour coming towards them.

One townsman poked his head out of a second storey window and hissed, "Run!" He was looking down the intersecting street in terror.

"Follow us," Sir Ruban insisted. "We have rented rooms not far from here."

The king's guard took the lead and retraced their steps down the alley. Kassian couldn't help but look back at the massacre they were leaving behind. The street was littered with severed heads, butcher's meat, and shattered glass.

"Keep up, Kassian." Nathaniel's call reminded the Keeper that there were more undead soldiers hunting them down and he picked up the pace.

They were led through a maze of alleys and streets, disorientating Kassian. His time in Valatos had done him no favours when it came to navigating the world. They paused by every corner, checking the way was clear of Reavers. Here and there, the dark soldiers patrolled in pairs. It was unnerving to see two corpses walking like men.

At last, Sir Ruban and his men brought them to The Wayfarer, a cosy-looking inn. The owner gave them a knowing nod as they passed through and ascended to their rooms. Once inside, Nathaniel positioned himself by the window and peered through the crack in the curtains. Kassian had to wonder how many times the Galfreys had been in a similar position.

"It is a gift that our paths should meet like this," Sir Ruban said. "King Vighon has been most concerned for you both. We would have reached Velia by now were it not for these fiends. After they arrived in town, we were immediately targeted." He gestured to a neat row of armour lined up against the far wall. "We were forced to remove anything that connected us to the king."

"Did they kill the entire watch?" Nathaniel asked.

"No. After the four in the courtyard were executed, the rest surrendered their plate and weapons. We have managed to meet with a few, but most have families here - they don't want to risk anything."

Reyna joined her husband by the window. "Have they hurt anyone else?"

"Not that we know of," Sir Ruban replied. "Are they in Velia too? Is that why you left?"

The Galfreys looked at each other but neither offered the king's guard an answer. "Should I tell them?" Kassian had no qualms about telling everyone how evil Alijah Galfrey was.

Reyna reached out and squeezed her husband's wrist, ushering him forward a step. "I'm afraid, Sir Ruban, things are worse than you think..."

Kassian remained leaning against the wall while the old Gray-coat told of their tale, detailing everything from their arrival in Valatos to their son's betrayal. Reyna had turned away for the latter, her face hidden from the room. News of Alijah's part in the invasion hadn't just hit the Galfreys, but the king's guard too, especially their captain. Sir Ruban had slumped into a chair, his expression a mix of confusion, horror, and disbelief.

"He was travelling with us for weeks," the captain uttered. "He fooled us all..." Sir Ruban held a moment of silence as he put his thoughts together. Then he jumped up. "The king! We must return to the capital at once." He nodded at the armour across the room and his men immediately began preparing it all for travel.

Nathaniel raised his hand. "We're going to Namdhor," he told them. "But if Dunwich is proof of anything it's that the realm is crawling with Reavers. We would be best waiting for nightfall before leaving the town."

Sir Ruban wasn't satisfied. "King Vighon is in danger. He needs the best of the king's guard around him."

Kassian pushed off from the wall. "The Reavers are already south of here. There's a good chance they've taken Namdhor. Your king is likely dead and buried."

The captain started forward threateningly but Nathaniel got in his way and shoved him back.

Kassian raised his hands. "That said, I'm ready to go now."

Nathaniel rolled his eyes at the Keeper. "You're lucky to have made it this far with that rage of yours."

Kassian narrowed his eyes. "My *rage* will be the last thing Alijah Galfrey ever sees." He looked to the captain. "Help me get inside that keep and I promise I'll avenge your king."

"He's *your* king too!" Sir Ruban spat.

"Enough," Reyna declared, her eyes glassy. "We will wait for the cover of night, lest we never reach the capital at all." The elven princess carried a manner that wasn't to be argued with.

Kassian, of a sour mood, made for the door.

"Where are *you* going?' Nathaniel called after him.

"Anywhere but here." The Keeper paused as he opened the door.

"Just be ready to leave. I'm not waiting a minute longer than sundown..."

$\sim$

Having seethed in a quiet booth for the rest of the day, Kassian returned to the room as the sun's last rays of light were burning the sky orange. He returned to a room of confusion.

Nathaniel was trying to see past him, into the corridor. "Where's Reyna?" he asked in a concerned tone.

The Keeper's eyes shifted from one part of the room to another before glancing over his shoulder. "I saw her last in here," he replied.

The old Graycoat shook his head. "She said she was going after you, to *talk*."

Kassian shrugged. "Well, she never found me. I haven't left the inn."

Nathaniel was becoming increasingly frustrated. "Did you see her leave?" he demanded.

"I told you," he repeated, "I haven't seen her since I left this room."

Now the king's guard appeared just as concerned as Nathaniel, who quickly dashed to the window and scanned the streets below.

"The sun is setting," Kassian pointed out. "I'm sure she will return soon."

Nathaniel ran his hand through his hair, his stress mounting. "You don't know Reyna. If you were downstairs, she would have found you." He held up his left hand and pinched his wedding ring between finger and thumb.

"Well, what would Reyna do if she didn't find me?"

"If she didn't find you it's because she wasn't really looking for you." The knight's fingers fluttered to the window and his shoulders sagged. "She's gone."

"Gone?" Kassian echoed. "Gone where?"

Nathaniel raised his arm and watched his hand intently as the fingers twitched, steering him to the left. "She's gone north," he said. "She's going to Namdhor…"

"Are you sure?" Sir Ruban asked, as he gestured for his men to grab their gear.

Nathaniel held up his left hand. "Our bands are enchanted, paired to each other." He rubbed his eyes in frustration. "She wants to confront Alijah. That's where she's gone…"

Kassian groaned. "There goes my element of surprise."

Nathaniel turned dark eyes on the Keeper. "Your inevitable death at Alijah's hands is not my concern right now." He faced the captain. "We need to leave, now."

Sir Ruban nodded his agreement. "With any luck we'll catch her up on the road."

Nathaniel didn't share his optimism. "She's an elf. She only has to run for an hour and there'll be days between us."

Kassian was still fuming, lingering on his *inevitable* death. "Whether Reyna tells him I'm coming or not, Alijah Galfrey *will* die by my hand."

Nathaniel exploded with energy on his way past the Keeper. A strong arm slammed into Kassian's chest and shoved him hard into the wall, bringing the men face to face.

"When are you going to see past your grief and see sense?" he growled. "I've fought against odds like these more than once. Trust me, Kassian Kantaris, they cannot be fought alone. You don't beat your enemy with might. You outmanoeuvre them. You outthink them. You wait for the opportune moment to strike and when you do, you make sure you've got swords at your back."

Nathaniel released Kassian's shirt and backed off. They held the other's gaze for a moment as the Keeper took in what he could of Nathaniel's speech.

"We're leaving," the old Graycoat announced at last, making for the door.

Kassian was the last to leave. He waited with his back to the wall and a stare that could pierce time itself. He had heard Nathaniel's words and even seen the logic in his strategy. But, the truth was, he had no one *to* help him. The Keeper was alone in his crusade for none had suffered as he had.

Besides, where would he find an army to give him swords at his back?

CHAPTER 41
ORDERS FROM ON HIGH

By The Evermoore's most northern edge, where the tree line met the blanketing snows of The White Vale, Galanör Reveeri looked out on a cold and uninviting horizon. Such was the land of the northerners, a hardened people. He couldn't imagine Namdhor being taken from them, just as he couldn't imagine Dhenaheim being taken from the dwarves.

But then he recalled Alijah and Malliath, laying waste to Ilythyra. Seeing their power and ferocity had taken his imagination to nightmarish heights where anything was possible. The fact that Lady Ellöria no longer walked the earth was still shocking, a feeling that swelled amongst the other elves.

Save for Queen Adilandra and perhaps Gideon Thorn, there wasn't any in all the realm that Galanör would have believed capable of defeating Ellöria. Yet defeated she was...

In the wake of her sacrifice, the elves of Ilythyra had raced across the land with admirable speed. With help from the centaurs of The Moonlit Plains, they had cut across those ancient fields, avoiding The Selk Road, and made their way into the dense embrace of The Evermoore. Steering clear of Vangarth and Lirian, they had travelled north through the forest, pausing only to investigate the ruin of Ikirith.

There they had found nothing but a handful of dead Drakes.

Maintaining their speed, the elves continued, circumnavigating the town of Wood Vale, until they were faced with the bitter north.

The warrior in Galanör was eager to move on again and finish his hunt. Alijah was likely on the other side of The White Vale, cosy and warm inside his new keep. All the while, Ellöria's body lay cold and stiff on Ilythyra's hard ground.

"Speak your mind, Ranger."

Galanör turned from the view to see Aenwyn standing between the trees, her approach unheard. There were others within the hierarchy whose voice carried above her own, but Aenwyn's long-time position by Ellöria's side gave her words more weight than other's. She had rallied the elves more than once, giving them encouragement to keep going in light of their loss. She had also proven quite the hunter on their journey, displaying skills from a life before she sailed to Illian.

With her white bow slung over her back, Aenwyn crossed a fallen log and joined Galanör. "Speak your mind," she repeated. "You will discover that when your words reach my ears, your burden will be lighter."

"We're close," he replied, his eyes set on the horizon once more. "Namdhor lies just beyond sight. There we will find our quarry."

"And you are eager to free your swords and see the matter dealt with," Aenwyn stated.

Galanör paused and gave the elf a sideways glance. "Ellöria's death must be answered for."

Aenwyn turned to face him. "Is that why you think we have travelled all this way? To invade Namdhor and slay an elven prince and his dragon?"

The ranger frowned. "Alijah's days as a prince are over. He sits on

508

the throne as a king now. And why else would we have come all this way?"

Aenwyn put a hand flat against his chest. "Balance, Galanör. You must find your balance. You're falling off the edge again - do not give in to the hunter. Instead, make it work for you."

"Speak plainly," Galanör replied in frustration. "Why have we journeyed to the north if not to challenge Alijah?"

"You have spent too long fighting alone in the wilds, Ranger. You must think like a soldier again. We must learn all that we can before revealing ourselves. This terrain is new to most of us and our enemy's reach is unknown."

"We came to observe?" Galanör clarified incredulously. "No," he said shaking his head. "The terrain isn't new to me. And our enemy's reach grows with every second we waste *watching* them."

"Were you blinded by Malliath's fire?" Aenwyn asked. "Did you fail to witness the power of our foe? If Alijah can kill Lady Ellöria then he can certainly kill you. This is not a cause to be fought alone."

Galanör took a much-needed breath. Aenwyn's voice was among a very short list of things that calmed the ranger. He could still feel the heat of Malliath's fire on his skin. When he closed his eyes, he saw the blinding light of Alijah's magic colliding with Ellöria's.

"Perhaps," he drew out, "an element of strategy wouldn't hurt."

Aenwyn smiled, an infectious thing. "And I was beginning to fear that there was nothing but empty space between your ears..."

Galanör quietly laughed to himself. "You speak of strategy and thinking like a soldier," he observed. "Is this from experience or from others?"

Aenwyn's smile turned coy. "I wasn't always a handmaiden. I was once an archer in the army, when it was King Elym's army. I was even among those who set sail for Illian, at the end of The War for the Realm."

"You were there?" Galanör recalled seeing the hundreds of elven warships from astride a dragon as they added their numbers to the battle of Velia.

"I was," Aenwyn confirmed. "I saw you *fly* into battle. I never got any farther than Velia's walls."

Galanör was shocked. "I never knew this about you."

Aenwyn held his gaze. "You still have a lot to learn..."

It was then, at that moment, that Galanör realised how important it was to survive Alijah's invasion. "When did you return to Illian?"

"I never left. Queen Adilandra commanded us to help the humans rebuild Velia and aid the wounded. Like you, I found a new part of myself among them, a part that didn't want to fight. I volunteered to stay and join Lady Ellöria in Ilythyra."

"How do you feel about fighting now?" Galanör asked.

Aenwyn glanced over her shoulder before meeting his eyes. "That's why I've sought you out."

Galanör quickly put it together. "You have used the diviners?"

Aenwyn nodded. "We have spoken to our agents in Namdhor."

"Why wasn't I..." Galanör took a breath. "Is there a reason I'm being left out of these meetings?"

Aenwyn raised an immaculate eyebrow. "You have made it very clear, on a number of occasions, that you no longer live by our hierarchy. Using the diviners and speaking with Ilythyra's agents does not concern you."

"I know Alijah better than any of them," Galanör argued. "The lands too. I can advise on what we do next."

"You still think with your swords before you think with your head. And you're committed, are you not, to the life of a ranger? The elves of Elandril do not heed the words of a ranger..."

"Well they should," Galanör huffed in a characteristically human way.

Despite his sullen demeanour, Aenwyn maintained her calm and melodic tone. "Would you care to return to your original question?"

For just a moment, the ranger glimpsed his impetuous behaviour and felt somewhat ridiculous. "How do you feel about fighting now?" he asked again.

"I am not naive enough to believe this can be resolved without a fight," Aenwyn replied. "But I do not wish to see my kin fall to an army of Reavers."

"Reavers!" Galanör turned on her with wide eyes.

"Our agents in Namdhor claim as much. Further proof that Alijah has taken a dark and corrupting path."

Galanör walked away from the tree line, battling his disbelief. "What has he done?" he uttered.

"It has been agreed that he must be stopped," Aenwyn continued. "But Alijah Galfrey is nothing if not complicated. His grandmother is our queen, his mother and father are considered heroes of the realm, as is his sister. Then, of course, there's his dragon to consider. Killing Alijah will mean killing Malliath, the oldest dragon in recorded history. Such a thing would seem unthinkable, regardless of his malice."

Galanör didn't like the number of points against stopping Alijah. "What has been decided in my absence then?"

"Any direct course of action against Alijah is to be decided by Queen Adilandra herself," Aenwyn reported as a matter of fact. "In the meantime, as I said, we are to observe and gather information."

The ranger dropped his head in despair. "I am not... *accustomed* to inaction," he admitted. "How long before Adilandra makes her decision? How many more will suffer while we watch? How many of us will be executed just for breathing Illian air? Ellöria told us to resist. You don't do that by sitting on your hands!"

"I knew you would struggle with this decision." Aenwyn stepped out to join him under the stars. "That's why I volunteered both of us to relieve the agents in Namdhor." The elf nodded to the north. "I believe you know the way..."

Galanör eyed her suspiciously. "We're going to Namdhor? Just you and I?"

"If you would accompany me," she replied, setting off across the snow.

The ranger was still a little surprised by the turn in events. "Where we will *observe*."

Aenwyn paused on her journey to look back at him. "Where we will *resist*..."

CHAPTER 42
TOGETHER AGAIN

Doran Heavybelly had been woken up in a variety of ways over the course of his three centuries but, of them all, the most familiar was a slimy wet tongue bathing his face from jaw to brow. He groaned, as always, then cursed the Warhog's affection.

"Get away with ye!" He used one of the tusks to push the animal back.

The smell of smoke breached his disorientation, alerting him to a grave mistake. The dwarf chastised himself for falling asleep with the fire still burning. He scanned the surroundings while his boot shovelled snow onto the embers, dousing any smoke.

"Ye dolt," he muttered, looking to the morning sky. There was still some smoke rising high before being caught by the breeze and dispersed.

Tall and jagged boulders encompassed his makeshift camp, with the narrow passages between being the only way in and out. He would have preferred a wall at his back and one entrance, but there was little shelter to choose from on The White Vale.

"Let's be off," he told the Warhog. "Those that hunt us 'ave no need o' shelter nor sleep."

Doran hadn't seen the dark riders from Alijah's army since getting ahead of them in Namdhor, though he wasn't foolish enough to doubt their pursuit. They certainly had the numbers to spare and they were keen to keep as many dwarves in captivity as possible.

Ascending out of the shallow pit, the son of Dorain led Pig to the rise at the edge of the rocky outcropping. To his right, The White Vale stretched on with a seemingly endless plain of snow. The mountains of Vengora were at his back, The Iron Valley long passed. His attention was to the left, where The Selk Road cut through the land from north to south.

Were he to take the southern path, the dwarf would soon come to the town of Dunwich, but he could think of no business to be had there. Instead, he considered the northern route. Once The Black Wood was behind him, The Guardian Cliffs would come to dominate the view. It was in there, he believed, that clan Heavybelly had taken refuge.

"Right," he said, pulling on Pig's reins. "This ain' the time for dilly dallyin'." He stepped forward, an act that saved his life.

The arrow that would have speared his shoulder embedded itself in the thick leather of his saddle, aggravating Pig to the point of bolting out of the rocks. Unfortunately for the dwarf, he was still holding on to the Warhog's reins when this happened. At some speed, Doran was yanked away from the outcropping and dragged through the snow for several feet before he relinquished his grip.

He came up with an aching shoulder and a mouthful of snow. Ignoring both, he removed the silvyr battle-axe from his back and turned to face the one who had fired upon him. He had no one to blame but himself when he saw the four knights from Erador, each atop a different boulder. Had he remained a few minutes longer inside the depression, they would have ambushed him from all sides.

"Ye're gonna regret comin' after me, lads!" he yelled, twisting his axe round and round.

The archer took aim again as the remaining three Reavers drew their swords. Besides being downhill of the archer, there was nothing but air between Doran and the nocked arrow - he was an easy target. In truth, the dwarf wondered what he was going to do to survive the next few seconds. He had seen Asher bat arrows away with his sword, but it wasn't a skill the son of Dorain had ever boasted of.

"Ye'd better not miss," he growled, as if his threatening tone made any difference to the undead creature.

Doran blinked, giving him only a brief glimpse of the dark blur that flittered across the boulder's surface. Whatever it was, it collided violently with the archer and carried the Reaver down into the depression, out of sight. The three knights still atop the rocks discarded their dwarven quarry and dropped down after their comrade.

A multitude of noises resounded from between the boulders. Doran recognised the sound of crashing armour and swords clattering against rocks. There was the sound of bones breaking and, perhaps, even limbs being torn away from their bodies. One of the Reavers was tossed high enough that it managed to get a grip on the boulder. A clawed hand reached up and raked it back down into the depression, scraping the armoured suit across the rock.

Then, from the silence that followed, came a feral roar that the dwarf hadn't heard in a long time...

Doran gripped his axe all the tighter, though it couldn't possibly be the monster he suspected. It was a summer's morning after all.

Emerging from the rocks, hunched over on all fours, came a terrible and ferocious beast. With a hide of dark brown and a black mane that ran over its head and spine, the monster approached the dwarf. Its snout was long and thick, perfect for housing so many fangs. Long, clawed fingers dug into the snow, bringing it closer and closer until its hot breath could no longer mask its yellow eyes.

To the dwarves of Dhenaheim, such a creature was known as a Lycan, but to the world of man, they were werewolves...

Like all monsters, there were a plethora of opposing tales and laws assigned to the werewolf. Some stated that they could only be killed by silver, while others believed it had to be gold. To that effect, they believed that such a weapon had to be plunged into their heart. Some said that a man bitten by a werewolf would take on that hideous form for all time, doomed to an eternity of never-ending starvation.

Doran knew the truth of them. Silver, gold, steel - it didn't matter as long as the weapon was sharp. A werewolf could survive a great deal of injury, but losing too much blood was a death sentence for all creatures. Those that believed werewolves were stuck in their form forever were just wrong. Their transformations were ruled by the full moon and nothing else.

That said, Doran was currently looking a Lycan in the eyes under the glorious morning sun. He then had to wonder how rotten his luck could be that not only had he been tracked down by the knights of Erador, but also by a werewolf. The Reavers had been following him since Namdhor and had likely seen the smoke - again, his fault. But where had the werewolf come from?

The dwarf looked long and hard into those eyes as the gap closed between them. There had been one werewolf in this part of the world not long ago, an old friend who had walked off into the mountains...

Doran glanced back at the west, to The Iron Valley. "Mother an' Father... Is that ye Rus?"

The werewolf stopped in its tracks and snarled. There wasn't any part of the beast that resembled Russell Maybury, except for those yellow eyes.

"Russell?" Doran was sure to keep his axe in front of him. "If ye're in there ye need to—"

The werewolf howled before bursting into a short sprint. The son of Dorain was confident he faced his friend, but he could do nothing except defend himself. Unlike humans, if a dwarf was bitten by a Lycan, they would die from the toxins in the saliva. It had long been considered a better conclusion than to be cursed and become a werewolf.

Doran raised his battle-axe, ready to bring the silvyr blade down on the Lycan's head. Most hunters and rangers made the mistake of running away from a werewolf; a foolish endeavour given their speed. The dwarf had learned some decades ago that a well timed swing could end the fight before it had a chance to begin. He just wished it wasn't his friend.

The silvyr cut through the air, perfectly timed and positioned to cleave the beast's head in two. The axe, however, continued through nothing but air - there was nothing to hit. Pig had rammed into the side of the Lycan, catching its ribs with a pair of hardened tusks. The two animals tumbled over each other through the snow and Doran wasted no time pursuing them.

As their struggle came to an end, the momentum lost, the werewolf brought up a razored hand of claws to tear Pig to shreds - the Warhog was a prize meal as far as any monster was concerned. Doran was far from ready to part with his faithful companion and so delivered the haft of his axe into the Lycan's face, bloodying its brow. Pig scrambled to all four hooves and ran from the scene, happy to get out of the way of Doran's axe.

He raised it again, preparing to deliver another blow to the head, when the werewolf whimpered and rolled away. In all his encounters with their kind, he had never seen one do that before. Up close now, he scrutinised the animal in detail. It was scrawny for a Lycan and patches of white hair were visible throughout its dark mane.

It twitched and he readied himself to hammer the beast. Holding himself back, he witnessed what few ever did. The brown hide began to pale and the muscles beneath contracted until bones could be heard reconfiguring. All at once, the body went into spasm. The mane of hair broke at the roots and dropped away. The hands reduced in size and the claws were sucked back into the fingers. The entire process only took a minute and left behind a naked man curled up in the snow.

Cautiously, Doran approached the naked back. He crouched down and rolled the man over - it was Russell alright. He had a cut above his eye where the dwarf had struck his blow and a pair of gashes across his ribs courtesy of Pig.

Doran sighed with sympathy for his old friend. "Oh Rus..."

Midday was upon the north by the time the old wolf began to stir. Doran had dragged him back into the shelter of the rocks, where he had discovered four mangled Reavers, their heads ripped off by claw and tooth. After piling them up - and stabbing each of them in the head for good measure - the dwarf had restarted the fire and done his best to dress Russell's unconscious form in what remained of the Reavers' tattered clothes, hidden beneath their armour. He had taken special care to cover him in their cloaks and a fur blanket from his saddle.

"Easy, lad," Doran bade.

Russell appeared dazed to say the least. He took in his surroundings again and again, looking from the fire, to the Reavers, to Doran in confusion. He pulled at the black clothes and heavy cloaks, struggling to put his world together.

"It's a'right," the dwarf reassured, slowly rising to his feet.

"Doran?" the old wolf croaked.

"Aye, it's me, lad. Ye took quite the knockin'." Doran touched his own head, directing Russell to his new injury.

Russell rubbed his eyes. "I don't... I don't understand." He looked at the Reavers again. "The last time I saw you, we parted at the River Largo."

"That we did," Doran agreed. "Ye went yer way, an' I went mine."

A look of revelation crossed Russell's face. "You were heading to Namdhor!" he recalled. "Where are we?"

"East o' The Iron Valley. Dunwich is jus' a few miles south o' 'ere."

THE KNIGHTS OF ERADOR

Russell winced as he found his feet and gripped his ribs. The cloaks dropped to the ground by his feet and he stepped over them to stretch his legs. He didn't look good. Doran had seen his friend many times in the hours after his transformation and never had he seen him look so weak. A Lycan's bite was undoubtedly a curse, but it provided the man or woman a degree of strength unknown in humans. Russell didn't even seem to possess that anymore...

"What are you doing out here?" the old wolf asked. "What am *I* doing out here?" he added, scratching his head.

"My story is probably longer than yer own," Doran reasoned. "But I've not long crossed The Iron Valley from west to east. Me best guess is ye were in the valley an' caught me scent. Truth be told, the wolf saved me life." He gestured to the pile of Reavers.

Russell touched the cut above his eye. "It feels like you had to save your own life..."

"Aye, with some help from Pig. He's given ye a couple nasty grazes."

The old wolf tentatively lifted the dark leather under jacket away from his chest. "They're already healing." He looked up at the cloudless sky. "How long was I out?"

Doran shrugged, eyeing his friend with curiosity. "I'd say an hour, maybe two."

Russell's confusion returned tenfold. "Is it not midday?"

"Aye it is," Doran confirmed. "It's midday around a *week* after ye became the wolf..."

Russell's confusion was quickly replaced by shock, as evidenced by his blank expression.

Doran sat down by the fire. "I've got a theory," he posed. "I've been thinkin' while ye've been sleepin'."

Russell gathered a cloak around his shoulders and joined his friend by the fire. "It's my age, isn't it?"

The dwarf nodded slowly. "I'd say so. I've never met a Lycan that's survived as long as ye have. I reckon this curse is gonna run ye to yer end." Doran sighed, struggling to voice the next part. "I hate to say it, but I think the wolf is gonna be all that's left."

Russell leaned forward on his knees, his yellow eyes lost in the flames. "There was never any outrunning this. I just thought I'd have longer. *He* did."

The son of Dorain cocked a bushy blond eyebrow. "Ye knew abou' this?"

"The same thing happened to the one who bit me," he explained. "This is going back fifty years."

"I heard ye *killed* the one that cursed ye."

"With some help from Asher," Russell admitted. "He claimed to be over two hundred years old. Every time he became the wolf it lasted longer and longer. Days, then weeks, even a month once. He was building a pack; I was just another recruit."

"How long have ye got?" Doran had to ask the question, despite not wanting the answer.

"Impossible to say. I'm almost a hundred years old, not even half the age of my maker. I could have years before I'm stuck as the beast, but it could easily be months instead."

Doran clenched his jaw, wishing more than anything that he could have bumped into Russell's maker a few decades earlier and saved his friend from ever being cursed in the first place. "I'm so sorry, Rus. This isn' the end I'd want for ye."

Russell harrumphed. "I don't plan on letting the wolf determine my end."

Doran couldn't say he liked the sound of that, but who was he to say how another man should meet his death? "It seemed weak to me," he observed, shifting the subject. "The wolf, it didn' put up much o' a fight after I tapped it."

Russell nodded in understanding. "The wolf will be weaker during the day - for a time. Eventually, it'll adapt."

A palpable silence filled the void between them. It was clear to both - hunter and monster - that they were heading towards the only reasonable conclusion. Russell wasn't asking the dwarf to kill him, however, and Doran wasn't looking to end his friend's life with a swing of his axe.

Russell straightened his back and looked at the dwarf, signalling the end of such bleak talk. "So why *are* you out here?"

Unfortunately, Doran had nothing but bad news and worse news. "It's a tale an' a half an' I don' 'ave time to tell it sittin' cosy round a fire." He stood up and roused Pig before dousing the fire for the second time that day.

Russell stood with him. "Well, where are we going?"

"The Guardian Cliffs. Me clan never made it to Namdhor an' I mean to find 'em an' find out why. Then, I'm leadin' 'em back to Namdhor to free the rest o' the clans from the Reavers."

Russell stared at the pile of bodies. "They've taken Namdhor?"

"That's not even half o' it, lad. Come on, I'll tell ye on the way."

Together, they set off from the outcropping of rocks and crossed the snows to The Selk Road. Doran guided Pig to the north, a route that would take them to the most eastern range of Vengora's mountains and from there The Guardian Cliffs.

Russell, curiously, was still standing in the middle of the road with his back to the dwarf. His newly acquired cloak blew about him, revealing trousers with claw marks torn through them. Doran, quite impatiently, remained seated astride his Warhog.

"What are ye abou'?" he called down the road.

"You say you lost the tracks," Russell replied.

"Aye, abou' a mile back," Doran confirmed. "Storm blew in an' removed any trace o' 'em."

The old wolf lifted his head and sniffed the air. "They didn't go north," he stated.

The dwarf frowned. "What are ye talkin' abou? O' course they did! They'd hug the mountains searchin' for shelter. They wouldn' stray from Vengora!"

Again, Russell sniffed the air before crouching down to sniff the ground. "I'm telling you, Doran: they didn't go north. We're talking about thousands of dwarves, huddled close. The wolf can't miss their scent."

Doran sighed and turned Pig around. "So, what? They journeyed south instead? There's probably not a dwarf in the clan who knows abou' The Vrost Mountains! An' I'm tellin' ye, they wouldn' go within a mile o' Dunwich."

Russell assumed his full height and turned to the east. "They didn't go north *or* south..."

The son of Dorain followed his friend's gaze to the distant wall of trees. "Ye must be jokin', lad. Ye reckon me kin 'ave taken refuge inside a forest? Have ye never met a dwarf?"

"That's The Black Wood," Russell continued. "It's not the biggest forest but it could easily hide a few thousand dwarves."

"That may be the case," Doran conceded, "but there ain' no dwarves in there. It might not be The Dread Wood, but The Black Wood is still a damned *forest*!"

"My nose doesn't lie," Russell maintained. "The dwarves of Grimwhal crossed this road and entered that forest."

It made no sense to Doran, but disagreeing with Russell's sharp nose made even less sense. "Fine. Let's see where this goes..."

Russell stepped off the road and made for The Black Wood. "Let's hear this tale and a half of yours, Heavybelly."

Doran could think of no better way to begin a tale than with a hero, and there was no better hero in all of Illian than Inara Galfrey...

CHAPTER 43
END OF THE ROAD

For the first time since setting out from Velia, Kassian Kantaris didn't feel that burning drive to beat his feet into the road with all haste. He still wanted to reach Namdhor and confront the one who had destroyed his world, but now, for the first time, he was considering his approach.

For all his rage, Alijah Galfrey's death was imperative. Anything else would be failing Clara. To that end, he had to put aside some of his impulsive emotions and contemplate all that Nathaniel had said to him before they sneaked out of Dunwich.

How *was* he going to challenge Alijah? It was more than likely that he would be surrounded by guards, not to mention the dragons who had accompanied him. And, for all of Kassian's power and magical knowledge, his chances were slim when it came to beating a Dragon Rider in a duel. With all that in mind, the Keeper had trekked The Selk Road with his eyes on the ground and his mind deep in re-evaluation.

He needed to be smart. He needed to be cunning. He needed allies...

Surrounding him were six impressive warriors, five of which he was confident would rebel against this new king. Nathaniel remained a wild card, his attachment to Alijah muddying the waters. It was a start at least, but he wasn't going to get within striking distance of his enemy, even with five good fighters.

Then there was the added complication of King Vighon. Had he survived Alijah's invasion, these men, and most others, would rally to him rather than Kassian. Of course, if the king's sole ambition was to make Alijah Galfrey suffer and die, Kassian would be happy to take his commands. It was likely, however, that King Vighon's head now resided on a spike outside The Dragon Keep.

His strategising was shattered over and over again every time he closed his eyes and saw Clara's end. In those moments, he wanted to break into a run and reach Alijah as soon as possible. Then, he would unleash his anger upon the half-elf and have his revenge.

And so his mind repeatedly tipped from one extreme to the other, each an opposing strategy. Kassian looked to Nathaniel and considered talking to the old Graycoat about it, absurd as it was. Nathaniel, however, had been the only one to speak sense to him since the world had been turned upside down. That counted for something.

The Keeper kept to himself, however, unsure how to broach the subject with his enemy's father. Also, Nathaniel didn't look to be in the mood for congenial company, even with the king's guard, since Reyna had gone missing. Much like Kassian, he had become very single-minded in the pursuit of his wife. The Keeper couldn't blame him. If Clara was still alive he would move the mountains to reach her...

"What's that up ahead?" Sir Ruban asked, bringing them all to a stop.

Kassian was gripping his wand before his eyes even found the horizon. Between the king's guard, he discovered the distant outline of a horse and carriage coming towards them. Either side of the carriage were more horses bearing riders in black...

"Get off the road!" Sir Ruban hissed, gesturing to the forest on their right. "Into The Black Wood! Quickly!"

It wasn't long ago that Kassian would have ignored such an urgent suggestion and, instead, met the riders with magic and steel. Now, the Keeper decided to try a different approach, one that included a level of restraint. He ran across the snowy grass, trailing Nathaniel, to the tree line of The Black Wood. They could only hope that at such distance, in the twilight, they weren't as easily seen as such a large caravan.

"Stay down," one of the king's guard cautioned.

Remaining fairly close to the edge of the forest, the men hunkered down in the foliage. They didn't take their eyes off the road. There was quite the wait before the caravan caught up with their position. With one finger, Kassian carefully pushed a large leaf out of his eye line to get a better look at those passing by.

Reavers...

Alijah's dark militia made no attempt to deviate from the road and come looking for them. They continued on their southerly heading with nearly twenty carriages in total, all covered in tarpaulins and escorted by at least a hundred soldiers on horseback.

"What are they doing?" Sir Ruban whispered.

"Supplies maybe," Nathaniel mused. "Let them pass. Getting into a fight now will only slow us down."

Kassian couldn't help but look at the old Graycoat. He sounded confident that they could indeed beat such a force between the seven of them. The Keeper had expected him to speak of certain death were they to challenge the riders. He couldn't help but think of Clara's description of the Galfreys and wondered if such confidence came from surviving odds more dire than this. It was still difficult to look upon his youthful appearance and see the experience and skill he possessed.

And so they waited, hidden in The Black Wood. The sun was almost set by the time the Reavers had passed them and were well on their way to Dunwich.

"Alijah seems to be in no short supply of those creatures," Kassian remarked, rising into a crouch.

Sir Ruban nodded in grave agreement. "The reports we received before we left the capital suggested they numbered close to twenty thousand."

Kassian glanced around at the forest as he contemplated that terrifying number. Without at first realising it, the Keeper had just seen something equally terrifying in the forest.

A pair of eyes no farther away than the length of his arm...

He did a double take to find those stark eyes once more, but it was too late. The foliage around the men came alive, bringing axes and spears to the throats of them all. The surprise slowed Kassian's mind, forcing him to require an extra moment to see that they had taken refuge inside a dwarven ambush. The dwarves were large beings and covered in debris from the forest - even their skin had been muddied to hide their complexion.

He had believed them to be naught but boulders...

The dwarf with an axe to Nathaniel's throat brought his face in to loom over the crouching men. "If any o' ye opens yer mouth to speak a single word o' yer stupid man's tongue, ye'll lose somethin' too precious to live without." He had spoken quietly and with no lack of menace, leading Kassian to believe that they would follow through with their threat.

"On ye feet," another dwarf commanded. "Hands on ye head!"

Kassian complied with the others and they were all disarmed of their weapons and wand. Next came the binding tied around their wrists, behind their backs. The Keeper sighed - they were never going to reach Namdhor. His frustration was mirrored on Nathaniel's face.

"Ye're to follow 'im." One of them pointed to the dwarf who held an axe to Nathaniel's throat. "If any o' ye decide to run, Porckus 'ere will put a bolt in ye back."

Off to the side was Porckus, easily the largest of the dwarves. He brandished his crossbow and smiled from ear to ear.

With that, they were led farther into The Black Wood on a meandering trek likely taken to confuse the prisoners. Before the last of the light gave way to night, they came across the last thing Kassian expected to find in the heart of a forest.

A settlement of dwarves...

The Keeper had gone from having never seen a dwarf before to being taken as their prisoner and brought into their camp. It would have been more of a shock were his emotions not so generally numb to everything.

The activity among the dwarves came to a stop as they stood to watch the human prisoners paraded through the heart of their woodland home. From what he knew of their kind, being ambushed in a forest seemed a rather extraordinary piece of bad luck. He had heard them be called the children of the mountain by some of the teachers in Valatos, just as elves were commonly known as the woodland folk.

They were forced to a halt outside a large makeshift tent in the centre of their settlement. It was surrounded by hardened dwarves, much like those that had captured Kassian and the others. The one who had threatened them began talking to one of the guards in their abrupt language, every word lost on the Keeper. Their brief conversation came to an end when a female dwarf emerged from the large tent.

Kassian didn't miss the reverence shown to her by the surrounding dwarves. She clearly spoke with authority given all the nodding heads her words received. The female's tone, however, was flat, matching her saddened expression. To Kassian, it looked akin to grief. He was led to wonder what had happened inside the tent.

The female flicked her wrist, ushering them away, and retired to the large tent once more. Kassian received the blunt end of an axe in the side of his hip, directing him away from the tent. They were taken to a small ditch and each dropped to their knees before being surrounded by a new group of dwarven warriors, relieving the scouts of their burden.

Kassian let his shoulders sag and his head fall onto his chest. After a long sigh, he looked up and turned to find Nathaniel, his expression one of quiet determination. Not that such determination would do any of them much good. The old Graycoat could offer any look he preferred, but it wouldn't get them out of the ditch and it wouldn't put their weapons back in their hands.

With all that in mind, Kassian swore without any restraint on his volume. This was quickly rewarded with the blunt end of an axe again, only this time it struck him a great deal harder... in the head. There wasn't much to get frustrated about after that.

CHAPTER 44
HOPE IS NOT ENOUGH

The last cords of sunlight silhouetted Namdhor in a golden haze while the city itself cast the dwarven camp in shadow. Pensively, looking up from the vale, Inara Galfrey stood with her arms folded inside her red cloak. Everything about The Dragon Keep was designed to keep out unwanted guests - it was a fortress at the top of a great rise.

Climbing up the sheer pillar of rock, at the back of the city, was the best way to infiltrate the keep, given that no invader would be so foolish as to attempt it. The rear ramparts would be the least patrolled, an opportunity not to be missed. The rock face, however, was certainly taller than anything else she had ever climbed before. It would be icy in parts and jagged in others. Asher was right: by the time she reached the keep exhaustion would have set in.

But Vighon was inside that keep...

That fact alone meant the Dragorn would never rest until she freed him. The king had become something of an ass of late, but it was all forgotten in the face of a betrayal they were both reeling from.

The sun continued to set in the west. It wouldn't be long before

Asher covered his eyes and the assassin assumed control. How long would it be before her brother was dead? For all his power and skill, she couldn't fault Asher's record when it came to results, not to mention his experience when it came to killing people.

But, then again, Alijah wasn't *people*. He had become something so much more... terrifying. Gone was the reckless boy who lived for the present. Now, her brother had a greater knowledge of the past than any other, and his forethought wasn't just strategic, it was foretold. Then there was Malliath to consider, as well as his army of Reavers and the Arakesh surrounding him.

There was only one conclusion to the night: Asher would be dead by dawn.

The ranger is on his path, Athis began, *and we are on our path. We can only do what we feel is right.*

Inara was immediately irritated by a niggling question. **Do we feel this is right? Or do you feel this is right?**

Athis was hurt by her response, that much she could feel. *Saving the king is more in line with your feelings than my own. In truth, I think you should be assisting Asher.*

You think I should kill my own brother?

I think you should save the realm, Athis countered. *Right now, Illian is relying on Asher's success, not yours. But I also know you couldn't live with Alijah's blood on your hands.*

Inara couldn't help but think Alijah's blood would still be on her hands. Ultimately, to do nothing to stop Asher was as good as helping him...

It doesn't matter, she replied, somewhat defeated. **We both know Asher isn't coming out of that keep; his fate is sealed.**

Adding your blade to his would tip the scales. Alijah couldn't hope to beat you both.

We don't know what Alijah's truly capable of, Inara was quick to reply. **Besides, the king should be our priority - the people will always rally to him.**

Inara, we cannot ignore the facts. Asher's actions have changed the face of the realm twice over. Aligning ourselves with him might be the only way we—

I will not align myself with an assassin, Inara snapped. **You've seen him through my eyes. You know what he's becoming, the path he's taking.**

He is letting go of himself to do what must be done, Athis insisted. *Is there a greater sacrifice than to lose oneself in the cause for good?*

The Dragorn closed her eyes, feeling a headache brewing. **I'm saving Vighon. That's all there is. If you want to help Asher you can fly him up to the throne room yourself.**

A great deal of apprehension flooded their bond, originating from Athis. *I don't think I will be able to help either of you...*

Inara opened her eyes and returned her attention to the sky, where all five of Alijah's nightmarish Dragon Riders were descending from the thick clouds. Their roaring shrieks cracked the sky and scratched at the ears.

One by one, the undead dragons found their perch on and around the ramparts of the keep. The monstrous gargoyles dipped their heads and unleashed their unnatural screams upon the city, causing more than a few to seek shelter inside their homes. From Inara's angle, she couldn't make out any of the individual Riders, though she guessed they intended to enter the keep itself.

That complicated everything...

If you take the cliff face now you will be exposed for too long, Athis told her with great concern. *If they saw you, I wouldn't be able to reach you in time.*

Inara swore aloud and began to steadily fall back into the hubbub of the dwarven camp. Her mind was racing as she attempted to recall any and all memories that might give her a new idea. The only person she had ever freed from an elevated fortress was Alijah. The Bastion, however, hadn't been covered with dragons.

From nowhere, Asher was suddenly walking beside her. "This is a problem," he said in his usual gravelly voice.

"I take it you hadn't factored dragons into your approach," Inara replied.

"Including Malliath," Asher continued, "there are now six of them guarding the keep. That reduces my odds."

"I didn't know assassins dealt in odds," she remarked, navigating a dwarven merchant.

"I need a distraction," Asher said, ignoring her comment altogether. "Something that will give *all* the dragons a reason to leave the keep..."

Inara gave the ranger a sideways look. "You want me and Athis to lure them away? What were you saying about reduced odds?"

"The numbers are against you, but I only need enough time to get in and find Alijah. There won't be a fight this time..."

Inara stopped at an intersection to allow a small cart to wheel by. "Let's skip to the part where you've heard my answer and suggest something else."

Asher groaned. "We need to—"

"*We?*" Inara echoed. "I thought there was no *we.*"

Asher gripped her arm and pulled her to the side. "You're supposed to be a Dragorn. That means you have to make the hard decisions. That means you have to plan for everything. Gideon isn't here, the rest of your order isn't here - there's just you, and these people are *relying* on you. The king needs freeing and your brother needs to be stopped. Neither of us can do both."

Inara listened to every word and then waited for Athis to add his agreement, but the dragon remained silent. "You're right; I am a Dragorn, the only Dragorn. That's why it's up to me to carry what the order stands for. It's my duty to give the people—"

"If you say *hope*," Asher interjected, "I promise I'm going to—"

"Hope!" Inara boldly declared. "It is the current of life itself. For five thousand years, my order has kept the realm up on its shoulders. I won't abandon that ideal."

The ranger sighed. "Hope isn't going to change a damn thing. You're the *only* Dragorn - you need to give *more* than hope. You need to fight and you need to make a *difference*. With words or sword, Vighon Draqaro isn't going to change what's happened here. But *you* can. You want people to have hope, give them a future without Reavers for guardians."

Inara turned her head to look at anything other than Asher. The ranger had struck a chord that the Dragorn couldn't ignore.

"Fine. I will help you get inside the keep. I won't stop you from challenging my brother, but I won't help you either. And you're wrong about Vighon. He's the king; he might be the only one who can make a difference. Once we're inside, we go our separate ways."

Asher narrowed his eyes, assessing the Dragorn. "You know of a way inside," he stated.

"I might have thought of something while you've been making your speeches…" Inara subconsciously felt the outline of a pouch on her belt. "But not here. Come."

With Asher by her side, Inara led them out of the camp and north, towards the shore of The King's Lake. They followed the shoreline farther still until Namdhor was no bigger than a hand and the moon had replaced the sun. It was here that the base of the mountains stretched around the lake in a jagged wave, offering a multitude of hiding places out of the city's eye line.

Perfect for a large red dragon.

Athis was snuggled round the curve of a rock face with his wings tucked in and his tail curled. Despite the current state of their relationship, Inara found the sight of her companion to be a joyous one - it always would be. Dragons were magnificent by nature and Inara had a biased opinion when it came to Athis's specific shade of red scales. Also, she loved him with all her heart…

Inara had to believe they were her feelings, free of influence.

Adan'Karth emerged from the other side of Athis's claw. The Drake appeared happy to see them, though he clearly carried a great deal of sorrow about him. So far, his people had endured a short existence dogged by prejudice and unwarranted violence.

"We're here," Asher announced impatiently. "What's your idea?"

Inara reached around her belt and removed the only item inside that particular pouch. It was no bigger than her thumb nail and it shone with the magic that had formed it.

"You have a crystal!" Asher strode towards her, examining the powerful artefact. "Why have we been considering infiltration when you had a crystal all this time?"

"It takes many hours of meditation to produce one of these," Inara explained. "And even that isn't half as draining as actually using one to open a portal. If I use this to get us inside, I'm going to have to fight my way out. Given the presence of the Dragon Riders, I would rather be at full strength." She threw the crystal up and caught it again. "I *had* planned on using it to get Vighon out of the keep..."

Asher, quick as ever, looked from Inara to Adan'Karth and back. "You want him to open it."

The Drake looked confused. "I do not know... all words," he said.

"She wants you to—"

Inara held up her hand, cutting the ranger's elvish off mid-flow. *"Adan'Karth,"* she began in a gentle elvish tone. *"We need to free the king. He's imprisoned inside the keep, a dark and horrible place. Those that guard him are naught but monsters, as you've seen. I have a crystal."* The Dragorn opened her hand to bask the Drake's face in its glow. *"We need you to use it and open a portal inside the keep. Can you do that?"*

Adan'Karth's reptilian eyes blinked once. *"There will be violence. You may come to harm."*

"We just want to—"

Asher pulled her away from the Drake and quickly returned to man's tongue. "This is against his nature," he warned.

Inara frowned. "I thought you wanted to get inside the keep."

"He might as well be a child, Inara. You're asking him to do something he believes is wrong. Neither of us know what will happen to a Drake if you set them on a path separate to their beliefs."

"You wanted *more* than hope," Inara reminded him. "You wanted me to make the *hard* choices." The Dragorn stared at the ranger until he conceded and stepped back.

"*I can have no part in violence,*" Adan'Karth said, drawing Inara back.

She glanced at Athis before starting her argument. "*You are part elf and part dragon - an enviable bloodline. For thousands of years, both races have strived for peace in their lives and that of others. Like your ancestors, you have the power to reshape the realm. It is noble that you would shape it with peace. But neither elf nor dragon have ever changed the world for the better by doing nothing. Sometimes, you have to fight for good, and those who can't fight for themselves.*"

The Drake looked at the ground before walking away to take in the stars. His kind were too young and new for Inara to understand his expressions and body language. Inara watched him closely, wondering if she had chosen the right narrative to persuade him.

Adan'Karth finally turned back to speak, his mouth partly ajar. Then he closed his mouth and looked out at the lake, contemplating. Inara shared a brief glance with Asher, the pair equally curious and anxious for the Drake's response.

If he declines, Athis said, *we should not push him.*

Reluctantly, Inara agreed.

At last, Adan'Karth turned to face them and spoke in man's tongue. "I... will help you."

The Dragorn smiled. "Thank you, Adan'Karth."

"*Though,*" he added in elvish, "*I have never seen inside the keep. I cannot open a portal to the unknown...*"

"I can show you," Asher replied, touching the side of his head. "*I've had the pleasure of spending some time inside those cells myself.*"

"*I do not possess Abun'Sun's skill,*" Adan'Karth confessed to the ranger. "*It will take me some time to find the memory you speak of.*"

"*How much time?*" Inara asked.

The Drake scrutinised the night's sky. "*I will have it before the stars pass,*" he answered unhelpfully.

Asher cracked his neck. "*Better get started then...*"

CHAPTER 45
FULL CIRCLE

Using the firelight from his torch, Doran crouched down to examine The Black Wood's forest floor. A ranger's skills were not required to find the tracks left by so many of his people. The dwarf shook his head in disbelief.

"What in the name o' Grarfath are they doin' 'ere?" he muttered to himself.

From the darkness ahead, Russell Maybury emerged, his unnatural eyes shining in the light. Those same eyes were shifting in every direction, ignoring the son of Dorain altogether.

Doran pulled Pig's reins, bringing the Warhog a little closer. "What's got up ye nose?" he asked, searching the darkness himself now.

"Dwarves," the old wolf warned him. He turned his head sharply to the right. "We're being surrounded."

"Good," Doran concluded. "This should speed things up..."

The stout ranger placed his torch firmly in the ground before removing Andaljor from Pig's saddle. He reattached both ends of the legendary weapon and stepped away from the Warhog in the manner of an actor preparing to address his audience.

"Let's be gettin' on with it then!" he said at the top of his voice. *"We are friend not foe!"* Doran declared in dwarvish. *"You know us both! We fought in the halls of Grimwhal! I am Doran, son of Dorain! This is Russell Maybury! I come bearing Andaljor!"*

There was no response from the forest, surprising Doran. His people were better at navigating the realm of trees than he would have given them credit for.

Impatient, Doran looked at Russell. "What are they doin'?"

The old wolf narrowed his eyes, turning his head left and right. "Whispering..."

Doran rolled his eye. *"We haven't got time for this!"* he shouted. *"I need to speak with the king!"*

Finally. A twig snapped and a branch of leaves rustled to their left. The edge of the firelight gave way to the broad outline of a Heavybelly wrapped in the forest itself. Then the rest emerged, closing in on them from all sides.

Doran hefted Andaljor. *"I return this to my brother, the king."*

The first to have arrived said nothing, though Doran could hear the whispers that passed between a few of the others. One or two recognised Russell as helping them when the Reavers invaded Grimwhal. A couple of others called Doran a traitor and toyed with the idea of leaving him naked in the forest. He did, on the other hand, hear one of his kin speak of the heroism he had displayed in holding the line. It was refreshing to hear one of his own speak so highly of him.

"Come," the burly Heavybelly said.

Doran offered Russell a shrug and fell in behind those of his clan. They journeyed deeper into The Black Wood under a canopy of stars and tall trees. Eventually, they caught the flicker of torchlight between the trunks. A series of makeshift camps had been set up across a number of clearings dotted between the trees. Here and there, Doran made out the silhouettes of more dwarves stationed on the edge of the light, keeping their eyes from the torches.

They passed through two of these clearings before they were

brought before a large tent surrounded by guards. The Heavybellys stepped aside, seeing Andaljor in Doran's hand, but the stout ranger received a tap on the shoulder, turning him to Russell. The old wolf purposely sniffed the air and nodded his head to the right, directing the dwarf to another cluster of young-looking Heavybellys. They were sitting around a small ditch lined with torches - an unusual sight made all the more unusual by the seven men partially visible above the top of the ditch.

Doran squinted his good eye. "Is that..."

"It's Nathaniel Galfrey," Russell confirmed.

The son of Dorain scowled. "Bah! What are ye fools doin'?" he barked in man's tongue. Seeing the confused faces of their escort, he said in dwarvish, "*Why have you got Nathaniel Galfrey in a bloody ditch?*"

The leading Heavybelly frowned. "*Who?*"

"*Who?*" Doran repeated incredulously. "*He's only a hero of the sodding realm, an ambassador of King Vighon, married to the princess of Elandril, and a knight of the old Graycoats to boot!*"

Again, the Heavybelly frowned. "*Who?*"

Exasperated already, Doran sighed and broke away, making for his imprisoned friend. Those of his clan shouted out, ordering him to halt. The dwarves guarding the humans took note of the argument and jumped to their feet, ready to stop the stout ranger in his tracks.

"Nathaniel!" he called, drawing the knight to his voice.

"Doran?" Nathaniel tilted his head to see past the guards. "Is that you, Doran?"

"Aye. Don' worry, lad, I'll 'ave ye—" Doran was cut short when the shaft of a spear was shoved into his chest by one of the guards. "*Best be moving now, boy,*" the ranger warned.

The young dwarf hesitated for just a moment before finding his resolve. "*They're prisoners of the king,*" he told Doran, standing his ground.

By now, their escort had caught up with him placing Heavybellys on all sides, cutting him off from Russell. He couldn't count their number, but there were enough to call it more than a brawl should it come to violence.

"*I've taken an oath, fellas,*" Doran said, tightening his grip around Andaljor. "*Not a drop of dwarven blood will be spilled by these hands. But,*" he articulated, "*if you don't release my friend here, I will shatter that oath in much the same manner I'm going to shatter your skulls with this here hammer. Take heed and step aside.*"

There were more than a few of them taking his warning seriously, their feet shuffling away. Those who didn't get out of his way were likely too young to have witnessed his brutality on the battlefield. That was about to change...

"*Have it your way,*" he grumbled. His knuckles whitened around Andaljor, a weapon his grip had become accustomed to since retrieving it in Grimwhal.

"*Enough of this!*" came a familiar voice.

The dwarves surrounding Doran slowly backed off, their attention turned to the large tent. The son of Dorain, however, remained exactly where he stood, frozen by the same voice that had snared him in its grip as a child. Footsteps preceded his mother's arrival and the surrounding dwarves dispersed all the more to give the queen-mother room.

It appeared their long journey had taken its toll on Drelda Heavybelly. Her eyes were sunken and her skin pale. Every item of her clothing was frayed or muddied, a change to the pristine clothes befitting of a queen. There was something in her eyes that Doran had never seen before and he required an extra moment to learn the truth of it.

She was defeated...

All his life, his mother had been the epitome of victory. She had ruled his earlier years and even continued to shape him long after the battle masters had delivered his training. But, now, Drelda looked to be carrying a burden that weighed her down further with every breath.

"*You know these men?*" she enquired bluntly.

Doran cleared his throat. *"I know that one. He's something of a hero in these parts. If he vouches for the rest, they're to be trusted."*

"Very well," his mother replied, absent her usual words of argument or caution. *"Release them,"* she commanded, already turning away.

Doran held the same expression of surprise as the dwarves guarding them. One by one, the humans were freed of their bonds and allowed to climb out of the ditch.

"Our weapons?" one of the men questioned with a demanding tone.

Doran threw a questioning look at Nathaniel who replied, "He's a Keeper, from Valatos. Long story."

The stout ranger turned to the Keeper. "One thing at a time, mage. For now, enjoy the use o' yer hands."

Nathaniel nodded at the royal tent. "What's going on?"

Doran eyed his retreating mother with an icy pit in his stomach. "I'm not entirely sure, lad. I'll find out." He turned to Russell. "Stay with 'em for now."

"Doran," Nathaniel called before he could pursue his mother. "We *really* need to get out of here. We were heading to Namdhor when they ambushed us."

Doran narrowed his eyes as he cast them over the men in Nathaniel's company. He recognised none of them, but it was Reyna's absence that caught his attention. Connecting that to Nathaniel's urgency didn't do wonders for that icy pit in his stomach.

"They won' let ye leave yet," he told the old knight. "They look to be hidin' an' as far as they're concerned: humans aren' to be trusted. Leave it with me, lad. I'll get ye out in no time, I swear." Nathaniel didn't look pleased with Doran's response, but he was powerless to do anything else.

As he approached the entrance to the royal tent, a couple of things dawned on the son of Dorain. He had yet to see his brother, the king, despite causing trouble since entering the camp. Dakmund had been injured during the battle in Grimwhal, but the crowned knight had only wounded his leg and shoulder - Doran would barely have called it a wound were he the one to have been struck. Then there was his mother's flat demeanour to consider.

He couldn't help but put it all together and fear for his brother's life...

No one stopped him from entering the tent, though the smell therein was nearly enough to see him turn away. Inside were a variety of dwarves, sullen one and all. He recognised the healers by their robes and belts, laden with medicines. Three priests of Grarfath and two priestesses of Yamnomora were also present and all deep in prayer to the Mother and Father.

Standing apart from them all was the cleric of clan Heavybelly. He was the only dwarf permitted to practise magic and even then it was very limited in comparison to that of a human or an elf. It was a statement in itself though that the cleric had been invited into the royal tent.

There was no missing the two generals who commanded the Heavybelly forces. Somewhere between Doran's age and that of his late father, they were white of beard and hair. Encased in their fine armour, the pair looked upon Doran with stoical expressions.

The stout ranger followed his mother until she led his gaze to a low bed at one end of the tent. Dakmund was lying very still on that bed.

"No..." Doran rushed past the healers and his mother to reach his brother's side.

"*He yet lives,*" Drelda told him in the same tone she had greeted him with.

Doran watched carefully to see his brother's chest slowly rise and fall with each laboured breath. "*What's happened to him?*" he demanded.

The queen-mother crouched down and peeled back a portion of the king's cover to reveal the source of his ailment and, indeed, the smell that permeated the tent. His leg was wrapped in a bloody bandage and smeared with green paste, likely applied by one of the healers. His shoulder was similarly dressed and appeared just as bad. Dakmund himself was sweating and horribly pale.

"*The wretch!*" Doran cursed. "*The blade must have been soaked in some kind of poison.*"

"*Whatever it is,*" his mother said, "*the healers have never seen anything like it. When the poison is unknown, so too is the cure, but we have to assume it's deadly. And unfortunately,*" she added with a hint of anger creeping into her tone, "*Grarfath and Yamnomora are taking their time deliberating over my son's life.*" One of the priests attempted to soothe her but the queen-mother silenced him with a wave of the hand.

"*Why are you in The Black Wood?*" Doran asked, changing the subject.

"*Is that what this place is called?*" his mother replied with apathy.

"*I thought you would be hiding in The Guardian Cliffs.*"

Continuing in her apathetic vein, she replied, "*We were heading south in The Iron Valley when our rear scouts saw the fiends on the horizon - they need nothing of rest it seems. We assumed they would go west, to the capital, so we went east instead. We decided to take refuge in the last place any would seek to find a dwarf.*"

Doran was impressed. "*Good thinking,*" he complimented.

Drelda looked back at her younger son, lying on the bed. "*The woods is the last place a dwarven king should meet his end...*"

Doran squeezed his mother's hand. "*He's not going anywhere,*" he promised.

The queen-mother met his eye. "*How did you find us?*"

Doran stopped himself from saying anything about a werewolf. "*I'm a good tracker, Russell too. This is what I've been doing since I left Dhenaheim.*"

Drelda squeezed his hand in return. "*I am glad you are here.*"

"*Brother,*" Dakmund croaked, surprising them all. "*Is that... you?*"

Doran crouched to the king's eye line. "*I'm here, Dak. Everything's going to be alright, you hear.*" He brought Andaljor to bear and placed it in Dakmund's weakened grip. "*Can you feel that, brother? You wield Thorgen's weapon once more. Feel its power.*"

Dakmund's fingers investigated the haft. "*I feel... nothing.*"

Doran arched back, wondering if his brother could even feel the weapon in his hand. "*It's alright. Give it time.*" He took Andaljor back and laid it down beside the bed.

"*Why is the exile here?*" one of the generals asked.

The queen-mother looked to reprimand the old dwarf but Doran answered for himself. "*You're in my land now,*" he said fiercely. "*Don't be forgetting that here is Illian. I've journeyed its length and breadth more times than you've found occasion to lift your sword.*"

The general took offence and gripped the sword on his hip. "*I might just find the occasion right now,*" he growled.

"*Silence,*" Dakmund rasped from behind Doran. "*You will listen to my brother... He gave blood to ensure the clan's survival... He has earned your time...*"

Drelda placed a gentle hand on Dakmund's chest. "*You should rest—*"

"*A king does not... rest,*" Dakmund insisted. "*Speak, brother.*"

"*I have come from Namdhor,*" Doran began. "*There, the unspeakable has happened. The dark army fell upon our people there with dragon fire. King Uthrad is dead.*" He let that hang between them for a moment, and it was a moment they all needed.

"*Dead?*" his mother echoed.

"*Impossible,*" one of the priests uttered.

"*King Gaerhard of the Brightbeards is all that remains of their hierarchy,*" Doran continued. "*Our kin are in disarray. Our numbers diminished. Now, they remain in the capture of this dark army, as does all of Illian.*"

"*Then perhaps this is our time,*" one of the priests spoke up. "*We should return to our home.*"

"*I agree with the priest,*" the general said. "*If this dark army is occupied in the west, we should take the opportunity to return to Grimwhal. We can go back through The Iron Valley and—*"

"*We can't retreat!*" Doran admonished.

"*Who said anything about we?*" the general retorted. "*There is still no place for you in Grimwhal, exile.*"

"*Don't let your fear take a hold,*" Doran argued. "*There's a fight to be had and there's no running away from it.*"

The general gripped his sword again. "*How dare you—*"

"*Silence!*" the king choked before falling into a coughing fit.

Doran took the advantage. "*I have spoken directly with King Gaerhard.*" This seemed enough to quieten the tent's occupants. "*I have come to an agreement with him on behalf of clan Heavybelly.*"

"*With what authority do you speak for us?*" the second general bellowed, to which he received a wicked glare from the queen-mother.

"*The dwarves in Namdhor are in peril. We don't know what this dark army intends to do with them, but it will not end well for our kind. We all know the Brightbeards lack the gumption to get themselves, and what's left of the clans, out of this trouble - they've been on the bottom rung for millennia.*

"*But they aren't just Brightbeards or Goldhorns or Battleborns. They're dwarves, children of the mountain. Even the Hammerkegs are of our blood. They cannot be left to this fate.*"

"*Why not?*" one of the generals asked in a calmer tone. "*They banished our clan and left us to trade with the humans.*"

"*King Gaerhard is willing to let go of our old feuds and embrace a new future,*" Doran explained. "*A future that sees Brightbeards and Heavy-bellys at the top of a new hierarchy.*" This caused more than a few looks to pass between them all.

"*But... we must fight,*" Dakmund concluded from his bed.

"*Yes,*" Doran confirmed. "*We must free them, the humans too if we can.*"

"*Humans?*" a priestess scowled.

"*We allied with them for trade alone,*" the general told him. "*Human lives are not our concern.*"

"*This scourge won't be satisfied until it's consumed us all,*" Doran persisted. *"They will keep coming for us. Our only hope is to ally with the humans and beat this dark army. Only then will we be free to return to our lives."*

"My brother speaks the truth," Dakmund managed. *"It was only together... that we defeated the orcs, be it five thousand years ago... or this very century."*

"My king," the general pleaded. *"Even our attempt to free the other clans comes with great risk, but to continue fighting for the humans is—"*

"My decree," the king finished. *"I want the monsters... who ran us from our home... to hurt. I want them to find defeat... at every turn. I want them to fear dwarven steel... before we grant them their end. I don't care... if we have to fight side by side... with the elves to accomplish that end."*

Despite his brother's illness, Doran couldn't help but smile at him.

"My king." The other general lowered his head. *"I fear your fever has taken your senses."*

Dakmund attempted to laugh but fell into another coughing fit. *"If you disagree with me already... General, you're going to loathe... my next command."*

The king exerted what energy he had left and sat up to perch on the edge of his bed. Servants dashed to his side, helping to steady him, before Dakmund ushered them away. He picked up Andaljor, groaning as he did.

"I, Dakmund, second son of Dorain... King of Grimwhal... Battle Lord of Dhenaheim... hereby decree that Doran, son of Dorain, be raised to the title of prince... an exile no more." The king flicked his head at his older brother and let Andaljor fall from his grasp. Doran caught it before the mighty weapon created an ear-splitting clamour.

"My king!" the generals protested as one.

Dakmund held up his hand, silencing them. *"What's more,"* he added, *"I grant him the title of War Mason."* He looked directly at Doran. *"You will... wield Andaljor in my stead. And you will lead my army into battle... in my stead. Do you accept this duty?"*

Doran was stunned, speechless, and from one ear to the other, utterly numb. His brother had positioned him perfectly to force him back into the fold. If he refused, a great insult, they would likely side with the generals' view and retreat to Dhenaheim. If he accepted, they stood a chance of repelling Alijah's invasion and creating a brand new hierarchy that could unite thousands of dwarves.

But it would come at a price for the son of Dorain...

The title of War Mason would once again belong to him, as it had during his father's reign. Under this title, he had committed terrible acts against his own kind, all in the name of war and advancement. It placed certain expectations on his shoulders that the rest of his clan would enforce. There would be blood on his hands before too long.

"*We have no War Mason!*" the general spat. "*The title was stained by this very dwarf!*"

"*I accept,*" Doran announced.

On the verge of collapse, Dakmund nodded. "*Very good...*" His closest servants caught the king before his body could slump off the bed and onto the hard ground.

The queen-mother barked orders to fetch fresh water and new towels, all between urging the priests to do better.

One of the generals stepped closer to Doran. "*The king is suffering, delusional even. I see no reason why I should accept his command.*"

Drelda whirled on the old dwarf before Doran had a chance to defend himself. "*The king spoke, did he not? Words poured out of his mouth and found your thick heads.*" She clipped the general around the head, embarrassing him. "*Prince Doran is clan Heavybelly's War Mason, second only to the king himself. He has done what no other has and found a way to bring us back into the hierarchy. You will inform the soldiers as much and you will have them prepare to march on Namdhor. After that, return here so that the War Mason can help you strategise.*"

The generals simply nodded their heads and shuffled out of the royal tent. The queen-mother thumbed over her shoulder and the cleric followed them out without a word. After he left, she turned to her son and began straightening him out.

"*Try not to look like you've stumbled across a Dweller,*" she advised, forcing Doran to take some control of his features. "*You're one of us again. Our War Mason...*"

Doran took a breath. "*I have sworn to never again command dwarves to kill dwarves. Whatever comes of this, I will uphold that oath.*"

Drelda held his gaze. "*Good,*" she said. "*Now, I suggest you find your* friends...*"

He watched his mother return to Dakmund's side, leaving him with Andaljor in hand. For all the good he was trying to accomplish - and he had succeeded this day - he still found himself in the same position he had been in before he exiled himself. Somewhere in the Great Hall, Grarfath was laughing at Doran.

After leaving the royal tent, the stout ranger rallied his friends and their companions. His newly reinstated title spread quickly among his kin, whether they liked it or not, and he was given one of the tents.

Doran managed to convince them to stay awhile and eat something, though they were clearly eager to move on. The dwarf took the opportunity to tell them of his journey thus far, including his interactions with Inara and Asher.

Nathaniel had listened intently upon hearing his daughter's name, Asher's too. Apparently they hadn't seen the old ranger for several years. The king's guard almost dropped their cups when they heard of Vighon's imprisonment. Sir Ruban looked ready there and then to draw his sword and sprint to Namdhor.

In turn, they each filled Doran and Russell in on their own exploits, all quite the tale when put together. The son of Dorain could imagine all too easily the sight of Valatos burning in the heart of Velia's walls. Ultimately, they were left in a dejected mood thanks to Alijah's betrayal, a sting felt more so by Nathaniel than any other. Reyna's absence was also a worry for them all, including Doran who had always thought fondly of the princess.

"I don' understand," the dwarf began. "Why would she jus' leave like that? An' without yerself!"

Nathaniel was twisting the ring on his finger. "She thinks she's doing the right thing."

Doran shrugged in an agreeable manner. "If there's anyone he's gonna listen to I suppose it's gonna be his mother. But she's still walkin' into trouble. There's a lot o' danger between Dunwich an' Namdhor, not to mention the monsters Alijah's surroundin' 'imself with these days."

"I know how she's feeling," Nathaniel replied. "Reyna needs to confront him before..."

Doran tilted his head to try and catch the knight's eyes. "Before what?"

"Before everyone else does," the Keeper spoke up for the first time. He had remained quiet throughout everyone's recounting, even the parts where he was mentioned, if briefly. Doran could see there was a lot going on inside the man - he looked capable of exploding at any moment.

Doran looked back at his old friend. "Oh aye," he said quietly. "That I understand..."

If there was a chance Alijah could be stopped without force, there was likely less than a handful of people who could talk sense to him. But their window of opportunity was closing fast.

"So what's yer story, lad?" Doran asked eventually.

Kassian kept his eyes on the bowl of broth in his hands. "My story has already ended," he answered miserably. "I'm part of Alijah's story now. Specifically the end of his story."

Doran glanced at Nathaniel, who had no reaction to the Keeper's obvious threat. Theirs was a complicated relationship that the dwarf decided he would keep his nose out of. He couldn't, however, stop himself from taking advantage of the man's magical knowledge.

"Ye any good with that thing?" he asked, nodding at the Keeper's wand.

"When we reach Namdhor, I will show you, master dwarf."

"You will journey with the clan?" Nathaniel spoke up, preventing

Doran from continuing his intended proposal. "They will be slower," he continued, "given their numbers."

Kassian shrugged. "It's like you said: I need swords at my back. The dwarves of clan Heavybelly will create quite the chaos upon their arrival, I'm sure."

"You've never seen two armies collide in battle before," Nathaniel pointed out. "You'll quickly discover the chaos consumes you."

"I'll find a way," Kassian assured. "If it takes me years, I *will* find a way."

"Years?" the old Graycoat questioned. "No man should let his rage burn so bright for so long."

Kassian half-dropped his bowl of broth onto the ground. "It'll burn until *I'm* dead or *he's* dead." He stood up to leave.

"Wait," Doran bade. "I need ye help."

Kassian frowned. "*My* help?"

"It's me brother, the king. His wound ain' healin' - there's somethin' foul abou' it. Perhaps magic can change that..."

The Keeper was clearly torn, his internal debate likely one of energy reserves. Doran had never used magic, but he wasn't uneducated on the subject; he knew that certain types of magic or spells drained the user more than others.

"Ye want to fight with us, eh? Help the king an' ye'll get all the aid ye need." Doran caught Nathaniel's eyes flicker over him, but the knight said nothing.

"I promise to try," Kassian replied. "My magic has always been used for quite the opposite."

"I appreciate it, lad." Doran stood up and straightened his shoulders. "It'll take some convincin' to let ye at him, but I can get ye in." He looked at Nathaniel and the king's guard. "I know ye're all eager to reach the capital, for Reyna an' Vighon. Me advice would be to travel with us - the land between here and Namdhor is crawlin' with Reavers."

"We are eager," Nathaniel agreed, twisting his wedding ring, "but getting killed on the way isn't an option. It would be an honour to join the Heavybellys."

A smile tried to creep up one side of Doran's face but failed to settle. "Ye an' I both know there ain' no honour to be found on a battlefield. Just blood." He clapped the old knight on the shoulder and left to convince his mother of Kassian's potential aid.

The night, it seemed, would have no end...

CHAPTER 46
WHOLE AGAIN

Inara was seated cross-legged on a small boulder within the shelter of a mountain inlet. The lapping water of The King's Lake found her ears and the cold air washed over her skin. The Dragorn, however, could neither hear nor feel the environment around her.

Instead, she was standing in a yellow pasture under the rich blue sky of her sanctuary. As before, Inara was confronted by the cave. It was still very odd to see something new in their private space and it only reminded her of Athis's deceit.

I know you are deeply upset with me, he said, towering over her. *Just as you are angry that such a lie has stretched from the time of Elandril to Gideon. But I can also sense your understanding. There is a part of you that agrees with this state of being.*

"I am not naive enough to believe that we don't pose a threat to the realm. Alijah is proof enough of that. Though this lie has existed between Dragorn and dragon for five thousand years, it has kept the order a noble one, a force for good. And I do not wish to become something even close to my brother, just as I do not wish to stain your own thoughts."

Athis's hot breath came down on her. *There is more,* he reasoned.

Inara turned from the cave. "Regardless of the good that has come from this, I want to be..."

Whole, Athis finished.

The Dragorn looked up at her companion. "Yes," she agreed. "I have no idea how the Dragon Riders existed alongside their dragons, but I know that they did. If they can, then so can we." She could sense the dragon's agreement despite his lack of words.

Inara returned her attention to the cave and began to walk towards it. Her hands felt hot and her stomach felt bottomless. Both excitement and fear collided in a maelstrom inside her mind.

Athis spoke as she stepped onto the threshold. *More than anything, Inara, whatever our bond, I just want you to live...*

Inara gave the dragon her first smile in days. "Whatever happens next," she said, "we will always be together."

One foot after the other, the Dragorn journeyed deeper and deeper into the darkness. She walked until she could no longer feel or hear the ground beneath her steps. The light behind her died away and the silhouette of Athis with it.

"Inara?"

The Dragorn looked around or, at least, she thought she was looking around. It was impossible to tell in the depths of the darkness. The male voice was familiar but she couldn't hold onto it.

"Inara?" he called again.

A strong hand gripped her arm and her blue eyes snapped open to the world. The King's Lake was before her and thick clouds were gathering overhead, promising rain. Asher, the owner of the voice, was standing beside her.

The ranger was looking down at her. "It's time," he said.

Battling her disorientation, Inara untangled her legs and stepped away from the boulder. She turned around to find Athis - the dragon was still curled around the rising mountain.

Can you hear me? she asked anxiously.

Athis continued to stare at her, dragging out the moment. *Yes,* he finally replied, relieving the Dragorn.

Inara visibly relaxed. ***Do you feel any different?***

No. Do you?

Inara looked around, sifting through a variety of thoughts and emotions. There was no way of telling if anything had changed, a fact that pleased them both.

"Inara?" Asher drew her to him. "It's *time*," he reiterated impatiently.

She offered Athis a warm smile and turned to Adan'Karth, who willingly accepted the crystal from her. It was almost uncomfortable to give the crystal to another, as if she was giving a part of herself to someone.

"You have the memory you require?" she asked the Drake.

He frowned having only picked up on a few of her words. She repeated the question in elvish and he answered positively. Asher, thankfully, displayed no signs of distress given the intrusion into his mind. Truthfully, Inara was more concerned for the Drake after delving into the ranger's mind for so long...

Inara made a cursory inspection of her person, ensuring she possessed all that would be required. In truth, her mind was somewhat distracted by her very recent change in being. She wanted to explore her own mind in greater detail, searching for any differences. As always, unfortunately, there were others to consider.

Asher withdrew his two-handed broadsword and drove it into the ground beside Adan'Karth. "*Look after this,*" he told him. Next, he removed his green cloak, folded it up, and placed it on the ground in front of the sword. "*And this,*" he added.

Attired in brown leathers alone, with his short-sword, quiver, and folded bow on his back, Asher looked more the assassin than the ranger now. Inara tried not to think about what he was going to attempt, nor the inevitable and bloody outcome for himself. Instead, she focused on the king. Getting Vighon out of The Dragon Keep was all that mattered.

She joined Asher in the middle of the inlet, behind Adan'Karth. "Are you ready?"

Asher took the red blindfold from his belt and tied it around his eyes. "Now I am."

Between them and the lake, Adan'Karth threw the crystal and unleashed the magic within. The crystal shattered and, from its core, sprang a hole in reality itself. Inara spared a last look at Athis, taking in his beauty and power.

Be ready.

Always... wingless one.

Together, Asher and Inara walked past Adan'Karth and entered the void. In a single step, they left the lake behind and found themselves encased in stone.

Specifically, the stone of a prison cell...

The portal quickly collapsed behind them, dropping them in semi-darkness. The only light came between the bars of the square port in the door. A brief examination of the cell was enough to discern its lack of occupants, but a careful push on the door proved it to be locked from the outside.

Quite frustrated, Inara turned to Asher. "This is a great start."

Asher remained very still. His only reply came in the form of a grunt, which only frustrated Inara all the more.

"Why are we inside a cell?"

"This was my cell," he told her. "This is where Vighon's father put me, after you stabbed Malliath with the Moonblade."

None of this was new to the Dragorn. "But why are we inside a locked cell? You must have seen the passage."

"I told you, the Drakes don't think like we do. He probably didn't see any difference between this memory and one on the other side of that door." Asher moved to scrutinise the door and its lock. "Can't you use a spell?"

Inara shook her head and wondered if Asher perceived such an action with his blindfold on. "Vighon had his mage secure all the locks against magic. I could blow the whole thing off its hinges, but we might as well have used the front gate if I do."

Again, Asher grunted his acknowledgment and stepped back from the door. He paused with his head tilted to the side.

"What are you doing?"

Asher's answer came in the form of what Inara considered to be a rather brash action - he knocked loudly on the door.

"I thought assassins were supposed to be quiet!" Inara hissed.

Asher stepped to the side of the door and raised a hand to grip the silvyr short-sword over his shoulder. "We're adaptive," he corrected.

A few seconds later and the lock was being attended by a rattling set of keys. The door swung inwards, concealing Asher all the more, as an armoured Reaver entered the cell. His silvyr short-sword was out of its scabbard in a flash and, before the Reaver knew what it had walked into, that silvyr blade was through its helmet, head, and out the other side. Asher caught the body and lowered it to the floor.

Inara drew her Vi'tari blade and kept her eyes on the open door. It didn't take elven ears to hear the approaching armour.

"More are coming," she warned. Looking over her shoulder, Asher was already waiting.

The first Reaver to step in front of Inara received a blast of magic that slammed it into the adjacent wall. The Dragorn dashed out of the cell and thrust her scimitar up into the creature's jaw and through its skull, killing it for good.

To her left, two more of the undead fiends made themselves known. One was running towards her while the second was running away.

"It's trying to raise the alarm!" Inara called.

Asher exited the cell as he was transitioning from blade to bow. The weapon snapped open in his hand and he nocked an arrow with swift precision. Inara jumped in front of him, careful to stay out of his aim, and met the first Reaver in a clash of steel. The Ranger's arrow whistled through a wisp of her hair and continued down the passage until it became lodged in the fleeing Reaver's head. As it dropped to the floor, so too did Inara's opponent... absent everything above the neck.

Asher turned his head to the other end of the passage. "The king. Second cell from the end."

Inara looked to the door in question. "You can tell that from here?"

"He's sweating." The ranger threw her the keys taken from the dead Reaver.

Inara stopped in front of Vighon's door and looked through the square port. Indeed, he was sweating. The king was desperately pulling against the restraints that fastened his wrists to the wall. She quickly unlocked the door and rushed inside. A swell of hope rose in her upon seeing him, though her relief was doused somewhat by concern - he looked to have endured quite the fight.

"Inara?" Vighon held an expression of great confusion. It slowly melted away, replaced by a relief and joy that brought fresh tears to his eyes. "I thought... He told me you were..."

Inara crouched in front of the king and embraced him. He would have done the same if it weren't for the manacles.

"We came to get you out," she said, scrutinising the chains.

Vighon frowned. "We?"

Inara looked over her shoulder and saw nothing but stone. Of course, he was gone...

"I came with Asher," she explained.

"Asher? He's *here*?"

"I thought he was." Inara stepped back from the king. "Hold out your arms."

Both of her strikes were true and remarkably accurate, slicing through the iron manacles themselves to give him the freedom to move his wrists. He rose to his feet and wrapped his arms around her before she could say any more.

"I thought you were dead," he whispered.

"Never," she replied. "Who else would get you out of trouble?"

Inara stepped back from their embrace. "Come. We need to get out of The Dragon Keep."

Vighon gripped her hand, rooting her to the cell. "What about Asher? Where's he gone?"

Inara didn't have time to struggle with the words. "He's gone to kill Alijah."

Vighon looked away, his thoughts his own. "And how exactly are *we* getting out of here?"

Inara possessed the hint of a smile. "The same way I got Asher out of here, fifteen years ago."

The northman took a moment to recall. "Oh no," he groaned. "We're not—"

"Jumping off the cliff," Inara finished. "Athis will catch us," she reassured, checking the passage was clear.

Vighon followed her out of the cell. "It's still damn... *terrifying*. Some of us aren't accustomed to being caught by a dragon. Or jumping off cliffs," he added, pausing to pick up one of the Reaver's swords.

Once out of the dungeon, the pair began to make their way to the back of the keep on a north-westerly heading. There they would find the pointed cliff that topped Namdhor's rise. They ducked in and out of rooms and corners, avoiding all confrontation. Inara was very aware that there were worse things than Reaver foot-soldiers inside the keep. Somewhere, inside these ancient halls, were five Dragon Riders...

As Asher had pointed out, there were also assassins of Nightfall lurking about. They had yet to come across any of their foul order, leading the Dragorn to believe they were protecting Alijah. This was lucky for Inara and Vighon, but it only confirmed Asher's fate in her eyes.

Their progress was slow, but eventually the pair came to the door that led out onto the rampart at the back of the keep. Inara was dreading this part.

"Once we're through that door," she whispered, "we're going to have to move fast. I think Malliath is in the courtyard and all five of the Reaver dragons are on the walls. Between them, we *will* be seen." Inara thought about the subsequent and inevitable chase but decided Vighon didn't need to consider that right now.

There came no reply from the northman...

Looking over her shoulder, the king was pressed against the adjacent wall, his attention focused on an entirely different passage, one that led farther into the keep.

"Vighon!" she hissed, concerned that an Arakesh might hear her through the walls.

The northman looked at her apologetically. "I'm sorry," he breathed. "He has to be stopped."

Inara sagged against the stone. "I... I don't think I can kill..."

"I know," Vighon replied. "Go," he urged, nodding at the door.

Inara's frustration was returning now. "Neither of you can defeat him, even together. He's too powerful and too well guarded."

"I have to try, Inara."

The Dragorn huffed. "Don't be a fool, Vighon. If you really want to undo all of this you need to at least live until tomorrow. If you go now you will..." Her words trailed off in despair as the king moved down the next hall.

Inara reached out to Athis. **We have a problem.**

What's wrong? the dragon asked.

Inara was taken aback. **You don't know already?**

I lost you after you warned the king of the Dragon Riders.

She hadn't had a thought or a conversation in twenty-five years that Athis didn't know about. That small piece of information was suddenly too much for Inara to understand at this very moment.

The Dragorn remained focused and ploughed through. **Vighon's gone after Alijah too.**

I see... Change of plan?

Inara sighed as she set off from the wall in pursuit of the northman. **Change of plan...**

CHAPTER 47
THE ASSASSIN

The first potion to run down Asher's gullet was offensive to every inch of his tongue. The second mixed with the taste of the first and threatened to make him gag, an action that would come with grave consequences. By the time he was downing the third and last potion, his tongue was incapable of tasting anything.

He replaced each of the vials on his belt, sure to leave no trace of his presence. The ranger stumbled into the wall of the private alcove as the various elixirs took effect, battling against his body's natural state.

The first altered his heart rate, bringing it dangerously low. The Nefalyn ingredient, however, kicked in soon enough and gifted him his senses back and removed the growing dizziness.

The second concoction spread through his body and targeted his nerves, specifically those that informed him he was in pain. This was, he knew, a particularly dangerous and stupid thing to do since pain had long guided him through battle. It was a prudent step to take, unfortunately, since he would likely lose all manner of body parts before Alijah lay dead at his feet - he couldn't afford to be slowed down by such losses.

The third and last potion was one created to trick the mind. When his body told him he had used all of his energy, a fact that would see him lose heart, the elixir would push him. The fight would be long over before his brain realised he was exhausted. Again, this particular concoction was dangerous since he could push himself to the point of death.

None of it mattered to the ranger. Thinking like an Arakesh again, there was only the kill. If slaying his target resulted in his own death, so be it.

He set off from the alcove and moved like a wraith through the passages of the keep. In the darkness behind his blindfold, he could see, hear, feel, smell, and taste the world around him. It had been years since he had embraced the Nightseye elixir that had flowed through his veins, as it had from his earliest years in Nightfall. It made him feel powerful again.

Placing his bare hand to the stone, he could feel the vibrations from the room on the other side. There were six people therein, deep in quiet conversation. Servants, he surmised by the fear in their voices. Asher moved on, distancing himself from the noise they were making. He paused at every corner, absorbing the information his senses fed back to him.

The knights of Erador were patrolling in pairs on this floor, but above him they were moving around in groups of five or more. He stopped by the wall of one passage as his nose caught the scent of human sweat, something the Reavers didn't produce. He opened his mouth and tasted worn leather on the air, leather stained with old blood.

Arakesh...

Asher waited a moment longer and shifted his head. He could hear their leather creaking now, though their footsteps were imperceptible. The assassins were closing in on his position, but their consistent speed told the ranger he hadn't been detected. Feeling the air pressure around him, he knew the ceiling was punctuated with arching elevations, a fact he had taken advantage of years ago, during his escape.

As the Arakesh rounded the corner, Asher was nestled between the narrow grooves that lined the elevated arches. He didn't move a muscle, remaining as still as the stone itself. The potions proved their worth as he maintained his unorthodox position without discomfort. Only when they passed directly beneath him did he pull his limbs in and drop down.

Immediately, they detected the displacement of air above them, but Asher was too close for them to react defensively. With a freshly honed dwarven dagger in each hand, he buried steel into flesh and killed them both instantly. Crouched between their bodies, he waited, ensuring there were no others closing in on him, before he removed the blades.

Next, he completed his arsenal by relieving one of the assassins of a short-sword. He strapped its scabbard to his back, crossing it over his silvyr blade. Rising to his feet now, he felt just as he had sixty years ago - an Arakesh.

The ranger considered moving the bodies, but any other assassin would smell and taste the blood in the air. If anything, leaving them there might draw more Arakesh to this location, allowing him to reach his target unhindered.

Avoiding the Reavers was child's play given the racket they made. Only once was he forced to engage with them, a pair of knights who guarded access to a stairwell. He could have slipped out of a window and climbed up to the next floor, but he could hear the patter of rain outside and feel the pressure change in the air. If he got wet, he would leave a trail for any to follow.

Those same dwarven daggers flew from his hands with uncanny accuracy and drove deep into each of the Reaver's heads. There was nothing he could do about the clatter they made as they hit the floor, but he was swift in his ascension and quick to leave the entire area behind. His presence hadn't gone unnoticed if the padding feet were anything to go by. The ranger ducked into the shadows as he perceived three Arakesh running down the hall, heading towards the stairwell.

They ran past, missing the beat of his heart by seconds. Asher slipped out of hiding and continued on his hunt. The keep was massive, easily noted by its dominance of Namdhor's rise. Every hall and passage was connected to another, leading to the various wings of the ancient fortress. Still, he knew where the royal bedchamber was located.

More than once, however, he was forced to take longer routes to avoid large clusters of Reavers or patrolling assassins. He was running out of time. Dawn would be upon the land soon and Alijah was most certainly the type of man to wake with the sun. He was met, unfortunately, with disappointment as he reached the half-elf's quarters. It wasn't the four Reavers standing guard that made him rethink his attack but, rather, the fact that the royal chamber was devoid of life.

Without rounding the corner, and into the Reavers' sights, he pressed his hand to the stone wall, checking with all his senses that Alijah was, indeed, absent his bed. There was nothing inside. Asher recalled then that Dragon Riders and Dragorn alike didn't need as much sleep.

The ranger mouthed an unsavoury word and began working on a new plan. It started with figuring out where his target was. The king, as he was now considered, would likely be in the throne room or the war room since he could coordinate his efforts from either.

In the old days, Asher would have stalked his target for days, weeks even, gathering information about habits and rituals. With this, he could choose the most opportune moment to turn the target's lifestyle against them. As much as he knew about Alijah and Malliath, they had built upon their personalities since last they encountered the ranger, making them somewhat unpredictable.

Frustrating as it was, he moved on to the next location. Every second of the night he wasted was another second he would lose the shadows.

First, he investigated the throne room - empty. The interior had changed since he had dined in the chamber, years previously. Gone was the dragon skull that Vighon's predecessors had called a throne. In its place was a slender, but tall throne, simple in its design. In the centre lay a large hearth, its flames battling to keep the warmth against the exposed portcullis just off from the throne. The iron had an unusual smell to it, suggesting the bars of the portcullis had been burned.

Asher crouched down and wiped his fingers against the floor. It was bone dry, but he could still taste the blood that had been cleaned from the marble. He tilted his head, allowing all of his senses to fill the chamber. Seven men had died in here, though there was blood from more than seven, some of which still spotted the pillars, missed by the servants.

A dead end, the ranger turned away from the throne room and moved on. The war room wasn't far, located on the same floor and off the same hall. Unlike the throne room, however, the war room was tiered, offering a surrounding balcony that lined the rectangular map built into the ground floor. With this in mind, he ascended the next stairwell to an empty floor, hoping to gain the advantage of height. A set of double doors on his left led onto the balcony but he didn't dare enter.

Lady Gracen was inside...

With one hand on the door, Asher crouched down and focused his senses on the war room. He knew her voice, not to mention the faint aroma of her perfume. Including the Mother, there were eight beings inside the chamber, though only three of them possessed heart beats. The other five were only notable by the stench of death that clung to them. Unlike the other Reavers, their odour was subtly different. Dragon Riders then.

Asher was starting to wonder if he had made enough potions to see him through.

Returning his full attention to the room, he picked out the Arakesh standing beside Lady Gracen. There was nothing unique about the assassin, turning Asher to Alijah himself. He was walking over the map, but there was a subtle limp in every step, displaying a weakness in his left leg. Beside that injury, he could hear the bones grinding in his left shoulder where the surrounding muscles and tendons had been damaged.

Good, he thought - the target was in pain.

"I can reach out to them," Lady Gracen was saying, "and I can certainly be persuasive. But I would caution employing even one member from the crime families, your Grace. They cannot be trusted."

Alijah stopped moving. "The gangs are ruled by greed and power. I have the coin to keep them invested and I can give them the perception of power until I deem to take it away."

More perfume wafted off Lady Gracen's neck as she turned her head to follow the king. "Granted, but, I have to ask, why reach out to them at all? Their type seems ill-suited to the kingdom you have envisioned, your Grace."

"In time, their kind will become relics. But, for now, I need people, not Reavers: who can actually communicate with the dwarves and the people as well as oversee particular aspects that require some level of intelligence... however *limited* it might be. Not to mention the unsavoury nature of what must be done if the realm is to be corrected. The gangs won't question me so long as I fill their coffers."

Asher didn't have time to dwell on Alijah's ominous words before the Mother spoke again.

"Then I will see it done, your Grace." Lady Gracen stepped onto the map and her heart rate and temperature both increased. "Given the realm's ultimate purification, your Grace, one has to wonder what will come of *my* order...?"

Alijah moved to stand in front of the Mother, his hand gently caressing her cheek. "I will honour our arrangement, *gladly*. You will become Queen Gracen of Verda. The Arakesh will be our blade by which we strike down our enemies, a force for good. You will have title, security, power, and... *me*."

Asher detected her attempt to reach up and kiss Alijah, but the king placed a finger to her lips. "First, we must make things right." The half-elf stepped away from the assassins and paraded the enormous map. "The silvyr?" he enquired.

Lady Gracen composed herself. "Every scrap taken from those on the vale has been collected and is in transit as we speak, your Grace. It should reach Qamnaran by week's end - there are boats waiting."

Curious, Asher considered where they were speaking of. Qamnaran was an island just off the west coast, in The Hox. It was almost as large as The Evermoore, but it wasn't the island's size that mattered so much as its depth. Though Asher had never been given cause to visit, he knew Qamnaran was the largest source of Demetrium in all of Illian, with deep mines nearly a thousand years old.

What were they doing with Demetrium - a mage's requirement? And why would they be transporting silvyr to the mines?

"Very good," Alijah said, "but it won't be enough. What of Silvyr Hall's deposits?"

The Mother shifted on her feet. "The silvyr mine is being plundered, but it will be some time before the Reavers can transport it all from Dhenaheim to Qamnaran. It would be faster if a dragon or two could assist..."

"No," Alijah answered bluntly. "I need them in Illian. Unrest is to be expected and I want as many deterrents at my disposal as possible." He moved across the map but Asher couldn't tell what he was looking at. "I will send word back to Erador and have them position ships here, in the break between The Whispering Mountains and Vengora. From there, they can sail down to Qamnaran."

"I thought The Hox was inhospitable for the likes of ships, your Grace. Does the Leviathan you speak of not pose a threat - it would be an awful lot of silvyr to lose."

Alijah waved his hand. "They can hug the coast, where the Leviathan can't swim." He moved again, this time down to the other end of the map. "I think we've delayed our work in The Moonlit Plains long enough. Begin moving the dwarves there at once. Make sure, Lady Gracen, that the gangs can provide all the equipment they will need."

The Mother bowed her head. "We will begin moving them south at once, your Grace. What of the Drakes? After your... *arrival*, in Ikirith, they have scattered."

"They are pivotal," Alijah told her, his tone serious. "Let all in the land know that a great reward awaits any who can bring me a Drake, *alive*. If any are harmed, that person will suffer the King's Justice."

Lady Gracen bowed again. "I will..." Her words faded and her shoulder shifted in Asher's direction.

His heart resounded with a definitive beat...

The time between beats was decreasing, steadily bringing his rhythm back to normal as the elixir wore off. It was never going to last as long with the other potions coursing through his veins, but he had prioritised his ability to take a beating over being detected.

"What is it?" Alijah asked.

"We are being observed," the Mother replied.

"Is that right?" Alijah's tone suggested he was smiling. "There's not many who could get this close to me without alarm. Is that you, Asher? Have you come to deliver on your threat?"

Asher's head rested back against the stone. "Maybe I *am* getting too old for this..."

With that, he resigned himself to death, promising that he would come willingly into its embrace, if only Alijah preceded him.

Both steel and silvyr were unleashed from their scabbards across his back. Speed and ferocity were all that remained in his arsenal now. He barged through the doors and maintained his momentum across the balcony. He knew exactly where Alijah was standing on the map below, his position relative to the others. There were none close enough to the king to get in his way.

First came the distraction, a means of preventing Alijah from hurling any spells before the ranger could strike. He leaped over the railing, twisting his body as he did. A back-hand throw launched the steel short-sword down at the half-elf, giving him something to immediately think about. Credit to his reflexes, Alijah shifted his shoulders at the last second and narrowly avoided the flying blade that went on to impale The Moonlit Plains.

Then came Asher.

The ranger crashed down onto the king, bearing him to the ground in a violent collision. They tumbled over each other before crushing The Undying Mountains beneath their struggle. Asher came up on top, his silvyr stained with royal blood. The tip of the short-sword had pierced the dragon scales of Alijah's armour and plunged under his clavicle bone, above his heart. Only a strong hand kept Asher from pushing the blade through and killing his target.

Alijah gritted his teeth and attempted to worm free his other hand. From those fingers could come a number of devastating spells and so Asher kept it pinned beneath his leg. Their tussle, however, was going nowhere and he was running out of—

His sword arm was yanked away from Alijah by Lady Gracen, freeing the king of the biting silvyr. A swift kick was immediately delivered to the ranger's face, hurling Asher across the map with what felt like a broken nose, though he managed to roll over the steel short-sword impaled in The Moonlit Plains. He jumped to his feet, numb to any pain, and brandished both of his weapons. The potions were in full effect now and he knew, without a doubt, that he was going to kill everyone in this room.

Lady Gracen and her pet assassin put themselves between the ranger and the king. "Get him out of here!" she yelled at the Dragon Riders.

They surrounded Alijah and partially dragged him from the war room. The pragmatist in Asher, first instilled by his old teacher, Nasta Nal-Aket, told him his opportunity had gone. He couldn't hope to kill Alijah now, not tonight. But the elixirs urged him on,

567

convincing him that he possessed the energy and resilience to at least kill the Mother. He would settle for that...

Lady Gracen tasted the air. "What *is* that on your lips?" Her face soured beneath her blindfold. "It's foul whatever it is."

"Let me show you," he growled.

Whether his muscles were tired or his body was in pain, Asher burst forward, ignorant of it all. The lowly Arakesh jumped in front of his master and met the ranger in a dance Asher hadn't partaken in for many years. Their forms were similar, though Asher had developed his over more years than the assassin had even lived. Short-swords collided, limbs lashed out, and their bodies flowed through every conceivable shape to attack and evade.

Inevitably, as Asher knew, it ended with his silvyr blade chopping straight through his opponent's steel blade and into his shoulder, bringing him down to one knee - his every action having been planned before he even rose to his feet. It was then that he brought his own steel weapon to bear and impaled his chest, killing him.

"Impressive," Lady Gracen purred, "for a *relic*..."

Asher kicked the dead body off the end of his sword. "This relic's about to burn down your whole world."

The Mother cocked an eyebrow. "Have you forgotten our ways? Kill me and another shall take my place."

"Then I'll kill them all," Asher spat.

Lady Gracen began walking around him in a lazy circle, her guard down. "You have no idea what we've become, Ranger. Things have changed since the war," she added, gesturing to her blindfold.

Asher shrugged. "Eyes or no eyes; you're still going to bleed out."

"That's your problem," she replied. "That was your entire *generation's* problem and all those before you. Everything starts and ends with a blade in the dark and blood on your hands. After The Black Hand decimated our numbers and left Nightfall a bloody ruin, we knew we had to change, adapt. Keeping my eyes came in handy - I think it would have been a lot harder to convince Lord Penrose to adopt me were I to have shown up at his door that night with ravaged eye-sockets."

Asher remained poised as she circled him. "You must be the youngest Mother in Nightfall's history," he remarked, aware that more assassins were taking up positions in the shadows beyond the map. This, he decided, was a good thing, since he was of a mood to kill anything that moved right now.

"Oh yes," she purred. "It was only the youngest of Nightfall who survived the Darklings. We could fit through all the little cracks. After that, we decided Nightfall was, in itself, one of our weaknesses. It was a place where our numbers came together - perfect for a single devastating strike.

"So we hid in plain sight. Met and trained in secret. The best thing I could have done was claim a title within one of the great families. I had all the resources, heard all the whispers, and there was never-ending opportunity. Now, I will elevate the Arakesh to new heights the likes of which no Mother or Father ever dreamed of. No longer will we live in the dark like monsters."

"Light or dark," Asher observed, "you're still monsters, and I'm going to kill every one of you like monsters."

Lady Gracen laughed. "You're not even going to make it out of this keep, *old man*. Can't you hear them? The Reavers are coming for your head." She gave the subtlest of nods. "They'll just have to settle for your corpse..."

The Mother stepped back as six Arakesh jumped onto the map. Many against one, they charged into the ranger in a flurry of steel and silvyr but, more importantly, Asher brought his rage.

Outside The Dragon Keep, it seemed the approaching dawn was to be marred by dark clouds and rain. For now, however, there was still enough darkness for a couple of elves to move about the capital unseen.

Since arriving in Namdhor, Galanör's attention had been captured by the five hideous dragons resting on and around the keep. Until seeing them, he had truly believed there was nothing more unnatural and hideous than a human Reaver. The elf didn't appreciate being corrected.

In the last few minutes, the ramparts had become busy with activity, stealing Galanör's focus away from the undead dragons. Reavers, clad in black armour, were dispersing, with some entering the halls of the keep, leaving only a handful to guard the walls and gate.

"What could rattle the dead?" Aenwyn mused beside him.

"The call of their master..." Galanör reasoned.

A group of Reavers came running up the main street, towards the keep, causing the elves to dip their heads, concealing them within their hoods. The main portcullis was opened and the armoured creatures disappeared inside the courtyard. Galanör narrowed his eyes, sure that he had glimpsed a portion of Malliath's body.

"It might have been a mistake to send Ellöria's agents to The Evermoore," he said. "Between your bow and my blades, I'm not sure we have enough to survive here."

Aenwyn's eyes flashed from within her hood. "We're not here to survive, remember?"

Galanör smiled and wondered where Aenwyn had been all his long life. "Resist."

"Resist," she affirmed with a nod. "Though, given those that watch over the keep, might I suggest a modicum of caution. Perhaps we should commit ourselves to at least some observation, so that we might find a way in that doesn't see us going *through* a dragon..."

There was still a part of Galanör that just wanted to mount an assault on the keep and find Alijah. But he found himself fearful for Aenwyn. He had fought beside many warriors, some of whom had since been deemed heroes. He had feared for their survival as dear friends and companions but what he was beginning to feel for Aenwyn was something else altogether.

"The tavern across the street has an outdoor balcony. It's cold, but we would have a decent vantage of the keep from there."

Aenwyn eyed him suspiciously. "I expected to wrestle you down this path."

Galanör shrugged. "I've slain a lot in my time, but never a dragon, undead or otherwise." He made to leave the alley and enter the tavern when Aenwyn gripped his shoulder and pressed him to the wall.

"What we are fighting for is worth more than both of us," she stated "You will not treat me differently. Nor will you take the path that ensures my life." Her grip eased and the elf stepped back. "Even if you are falling in love with me..."

Galanör failed to produce a single word that possessed all of its syllables. Tugging on his hood, he could do nothing but follow her across the street and hope his red cheeks had cooled by the time they reached the door.

CHAPTER 48
ALL THAT REMAINS

In the pre-dawn, The Dragon Keep should have been a quiet and tranquil place, its lofty vantage so close to the heavens. And, indeed, it had been as silent as a tomb only a few minutes ago, as Vighon Draqaro crept through his own home. Now, however, the halls were filled with the rushing feet of armoured Reavers.

Asher, he assumed...

The ranger had a talent for drawing such fiends. The king jogged lightly on the balls of his feet, trailing the various clusters only a few feet behind. As they intersected with new groups of undead knights, he would dash to the side and hide in an alcove or through a door.

More than once, he found himself face to face with his own servants, terrified to step out into the hall. He instructed them all to remain calm before reassuring them that he would see to the invaders.

The closer he approached the throne room, the harder it became to advance. The Reavers who had flooded the keep were now beginning to take up positions, barring the passages. Vighon hefted the sword in his hand - a foreign blade. He wasn't used to its grip nor its weight.

Still, Vighon would dispatch the Reavers who got in his way with a spoon if that was all he had. He took a breath, preparing himself to round the corner and challenge the monsters in his path. Once the fight began, his time would be short, the noise drawing more to his location.

Kill them fast and move on, he told himself.

Rounding the corner, he immediately regretted his course of action. There were three Arakesh standing in front of the Reavers now, their presence previously unseen and unheard. They likely knew he was there anyway, given the speed of his beating heart.

Leaving the Reavers behind, the three assassins walked towards him with faint smiles on their faces. Vighon took his sword in both hands and reminded himself that he had fought and beaten worse things than a few Arakesh. He couldn't actually think of any of them right then, but he had to believe it...

They stopped with ten feet between them and their prey as their smiles dropped away. There was just a hint of hesitation in their body language, with one of them even taking a cautious step backwards.

Vighon grinned. "You know who I am then?"

A figure was suddenly standing beside the king where only a second ago there had been nothing at all. Startled, Vighon turned to look upon the Guardian of the Realm, draped in her red cloak, attired in brown leathers, and wielding a deadly Vi'tari scimitar.

Somewhat disheartened by the revelation, Vighon managed a quiet, "Oh..."

Finding their courage, the three assassins came at them both, six short-swords between them. Inara strode forward, her actions hard to follow. Firstly, and most unusually, she tossed her scimitar up into the air, ignoring its flight completely.

The second thing she did would have been impossible to understand if Vighon didn't know of the magic she possessed. Her left hand whipped out and her fist clenched. The spell was entirely unknown to the king, but the window beside the assassins exploded violently into the passage, cutting the nearest Arakesh to bloody ribbons.

Her left hand came back into her body and joined her right hand, where the two conjured a burning spell of pure flames. So close was the middle assassin that he had no hope of evading the fireball that swept him off his feet and launched him down towards the Reavers.

The third and last Arakesh collided with Inara as her Vi'tari blade landed neatly back into her waiting hand. The clash of steel was brief and the blood splattered up the stone was fatally generous.

The Guardian stepped over the three bodies and glanced at Vighon over her shoulder. "Shall we?"

Together, they easily cut down the undead monstrosities blocking their way and moved on. "I thought you couldn't do this," Vighon whispered.

"If by *this* you mean get ourselves killed fighting a superior force then *yes*, I can do this. What I can't do is let you go alone, Vighon Draqaro."

Despite the playfulness between them, Vighon stopped her from rounding the last corner. "I'll do it," he said, hoping to spare her from the act of killing her own brother.

Inara looked him in the eyes. "I'm not sure either of us can do it..."

Vighon had no reply, neither witty nor serious. She was right, of course; there was a good chance that they didn't have the skills or even the gumption to kill Alijah, family to them both. As it happened, any reply he may have offered would have been drowned out by the shattering doors round the corner.

Next came the ringing of swords and the dying cry of a young man. There was no assuming now - Asher was doing what he did best. The ranger, blindfolded and bloody, was in the midst of fighting four Arakesh. One of their dark order was dead at his feet, while another was slumped against the far wall where he had presumably landed after being hurled through the doors of the war room.

The melee was furious, causing Asher to turn in every direction to meet his foe. Every few strikes they landed successful blows against the ranger, slicing his legs and arms, but he never faltered. The same leg they cut would come right back up and shove one of them down the hall. His blades worked to find every opening and if they couldn't find one they made one.

Another Arakesh emerged from the war room, only this one sauntered out as if she wasn't in any danger. Lady Gracen. She ignored the fight altogether and continued down the hall to the throne room.

"Come on," Vighon urged.

With Inara at his side, they ran down the hall to assist Asher - together, they would provide Alijah with quite the formidable force. The ranger, it seemed, was in no need of their assistance. The passage wasn't long but, by the time they reached the fight, he had slain three of the four remaining. The last one began to back off, stumbling down the hall with unmistakable fear about him. His blindfold had been cut, along with his face, and he had apparently decided that Asher couldn't be taken without it.

The ranger sheathed both of his short-swords in one smooth motion and brought his bow to bear. It snapped to life and greeted the waiting arrow with a taut string. Without his heightened reflexes, the assassin had only his skill to thwart the incoming arrow.

He was found lacking...

Asher was already tucking the bow away before the assassin's body hit the floor. "What are you two doing here?" he growled.

"Helping you," Vighon explained.

Asher grunted and turned to the throne room.

Inara tugged at his arm. "We should have a plan before going in there."

"I tried planning," Asher replied. "It didn't work out." He gestured to the bodies at his feet before continuing on.

As they reached the ornate doors of the throne room, the entire keep shuddered. Next came an almighty shriek.

"We really *should* have a plan," Inara reiterated.

Asher retrieved the short-swords with a grunt and shoved the doors open.

Vighon flooded in behind the ranger and discovered the throne room was not as he had left it. Garrett and his king's guard had been removed and their blood mopped up. The banners of house Draqaro had already been taken down, replaced with a black stencilled dragon against a red background - the house of Galfrey...

At the base of the throne's podium, all five of Alijah's Dragon Riders stood motionless, staring at the three intruders. Seeing them up close, they were clearly unique compared to the rest of the resurrected army. Their armour was as individual as they were malevolent. They each possessed a different weapon, all of which were stained with blood.

Lady Gracen, attired in assassin's leathers and a red blindfold, was standing behind them, beside the throne. She was the only one smiling at their appearance, despite those of her order they had stepped over to reach the chamber.

Alijah resided on the throne, slumped lazily to one side with his head resting in his hand. It would have been easy to assume he was bored by their antics, but having seen him in the dungeon, Vighon knew the usurper was wounded. Once upon a time, he would have bled in Alijah's place but, today, he was eager to finish what Lady Ellöria had started.

Standing upright against the side of the throne was the sword of the north, easily recognised by its owner. Vighon's enchanted shield had been placed back on the wall, seen between the pillars.

Behind the three companions, the doorway filled with line after line of armoured Reavers. There would be no going back now...

"What a fine entrance," Alijah remarked. "The heroes three! Bold is your entrance, but I insist you tread softly. Standing before you, I'm afraid, are five heroes of an older and far more *violent* Age. I believe you have already been introduced to Lord Kraiden..."

The crowned knight stepped in front of his fellow Dragon Riders and drew his jagged sword. Vighon had not long seen that same blade take the life of his general and friend.

"I'm sure Lord Kraiden is skilled enough to challenge all of you," Alijah continued, "but he doesn't stand alone. Vilyra of Freygard, heir to Carstane..."

Her armour was sleek and bound only to the larger muscle groups, allowing for swift movements in combat. She drew two twin swords from her hips, the blades a charred black.

"With her dragon, Godrad, she slew the last giant in The Gold Rise."

Alijah's finger flicked to the Dragon Rider beside her, a beast of a thing hidden within a horned helm and armed with a hammer and shield. "Gondrith the *just* and hammer of the north. Yillir, his dragon, was once a rare breed of white scales."

After Gondrith, another stepped forward wielding a spear. "Colvok," Alijah announced, "prince of The Dawning Isles. His dragon, Nersandi, was said to have battled the great Leviathan of The Hox and lived."

The last to join the band of Dragon Riders hefted a fearsome battle-axe. The Reaver's helm bore a single horn that extended from the forehead and curved upwards. It looked similar to a dragon's claw, but Vighon's attention was mostly captured by the formidable axe.

"Rengyr, the beast of Qalanqath! Erador's history notes that his dragon, Karsak, was born of Mount Kaliban itself. A myth to be sure," Alijah added, "but it does make for a good story."

"I don't care for your puppets," Asher growled. "And I didn't come here for a story."

Alijah sat up and sighed, though Vighon detected the hint of a wince flash across his face. "A good story, dear ranger, is all that will remain. Years from now, be it centuries or millennia, your actions here will be naught but a tale."

"Then I suppose it's time we wrote the end," Inara replied.

Alijah focused on his sister. "It is to be an epic then..."

PHILIP C. QUAINTRELL

Tension filled the air, disturbed only by Vighon when he stepped ahead of his companions. "You're sitting in my chair," he stated. "And that sword is mine."

Alijah ran his fingers along the arm rest. "I didn't come here for a chair. I've done nothing if not collect thrones over the last fifteen years. And you can have the sword." A nod of the head and Lady Gracen tossed the sheathed blade across the chamber, into Vighon's waiting hand. "It would leave a bad taste in my mouth to destroy a weapon of such quality. I promise to bury it with you..."

Vighon turned scornful eyes on the half-elf. "You're going to have to kill me first... *brother*."

Alijah puffed out his chest. "Like you said: you don't get to call me that anymore. I gave you a chance, I gave both of you a chance!" The half-elf was on his feet now. "I was going to free you of your burdens. Now, I will have to live with your blood on my hands for eternity." Forlorn, he drew a green scimitar from his hip. "Kill them quick," he commanded.

"Finally." Asher burst into a sprint, hurtling towards the Dragon Riders with a short-sword in each hand.

Before Vighon could even draw his flaming sword, the ranger was skidding low across the marble, evading Rengyr's swinging axe by a hair's breadth. He jumped to his feet and performed an exotic flip into the air, over Gondrith's incoming hammer. Landing back on his feet, Asher was now at the base of the podium with nothing but air between him and Alijah. He took all three steps in one and came at the half-elf with his silvyr blade.

Alijah's sharp reaction held the silvyr at bay, an inch away from his head. It seemed Asher's attack was likely intentional, distracting the half-elf from the steel blade he was bringing up to spear his chest. The steel sword, however, never found its intended destination, batted aside by Lady Gracen. The ranger was treated to a backhand by Alijah and swift kick to the gut by the Mother, throwing him across the podium.

As his momentum came to an end, Vighon's sword was free of its

578

prison and alight with flame. Inara by his side, they charged into the Dragon Riders. Steel clashed and sparks flew from the king's sword as he met Vilyra and her twin blades. Inara ended her charge with a leap, slamming her knee into Col-vok's chest. Her Vi'tari blade reacted to the threat of Lord Kraiden's sword and parried his blow before her feet even touched down.

Now they were in it.

Surrounded on all sides, Inara and Vighon naturally came back to back and faced the Dragon Riders of old. Their actions mirrored a dance as they moved around each other, their swords lashing out in every direction. It wasn't long before the Dragon Riders used their number against the duo and separated them. Vighon was forced to dive away, taking him to the left of the chamber, between the pillars. Inara held her ground, intertwining her swordplay with magic to keep the fiends at bay.

Pursuing him were Col-vok, spear in hand, and Gondrith with the hammer and shield. The northman wasted no time knocking his own shield off the wall - he was going to need it. He side-stepped the incoming spear, noting the extensive damage it did to the stone wall. He considered raising his shield to block the hammer, but decided it would likely weaken his arm and rolled away instead.

As he corrected his orientation, another foe entered the melee...

A dragon, ravaged by death millennia ago, landed on the extended balcony on the other side of the chamber. It unleashed a sharp shriek and pushed its head and neck into the room, searching for fresh prey.

Col-vok, paused and turned to the dragon. "Nersandi..." The Reaver's voice was a terrifying rasp.

The fight was over. Though the dragon was too large to fit its entire body beneath the portcullis, its neck was long enough to bring its reptilian head into the chamber, between the pillars. One breath and they would be reduced to ash.

Gondrith barged into Vighon, shield to shield, and shoved him back into the centre of the room, where Inara was a blur of motion.

She fought with fury, matching the three Dragon Riders in their tenacity.

Then Nersandi opened her mouth of fangs, her putrid glands pulsing as she prepared to exhale a torrent of flames. Inara spun away from Lord Kraiden's attack and paused to briefly face the dragon. Her free hand reached high before clenching and coming back down. There was an audible snap of chains and the portcullis dropped.

The gate didn't stop until it had landed in the grooves of the threshold. It now separated Nersandi's body from her neck and head, which dropped down onto the lit hearth with a loud *thud* and an explosion of sparks.

Interestingly - if alarmingly - Col-vok, Nersandi's Rider, didn't perish in the same manner, nor at all. Instead, the spear-wielding Reaver continued to charge Vighon as if his dragon hadn't just been decapitated. The northman deflected the spear with his shield and cut a burning line across the Reaver's chest, pushing it back.

"I thought they were supposed to die together!" he yelled as Inara fell in beside him once more.

With no time to answer, Inara simply shouted, "Duck!"

Vighon knew better than to question the Dragorn. He ducked as Inara kicked off Vilyra, rolled over the northman's back, and came down on Col-vok with her whipping scimitar. The Vi'tari blade cut through most of the spear-wielder's neck, staggering him. Vighon came back up swinging. The sword of the north finished the job and parted Col-vok's head from his shoulders.

Despite the loss, there was no emotional response from the other Dragon Riders. Enthralled to Alijah's will, they continued their efforts to deliver a quick kill. Inara and Vighon fell back into the rhythm of the battle, interweaving their skills, however imbalanced they were.

On the podium, Asher was facing his past. Lady Gracen, a student and master of the same order, was proving that youth did have its advantages. She had an edge to her, seen in her precise movements, all of which allowed her to evade the ranger's tactics. Their duel was a phenomenal fight to witness, displaying ancient techniques that very few possessed.

Alijah watched it all, standing before the throne. If losing one of his precious Dragon Riders had phased him, he didn't show it. Vighon longed to face him instead of these undead creatures.

There came another shriek, this time from beyond the walls of the keep. There was no time to make sense of it before an entire corner of the throne room was caved in by a dragon. Everything shook, knocking all but Alijah from their feet. The nearest pillar was broken by the dragon's wing, sending the column across the chamber in the form of deadly debris. Every piece of decoration fell from the walls in a clatter and the stonework across the chamber began to crack.

Vighon was able to raise his shield before a chunk of marble flew into his head. Gondrith failed to do the same and was knocked farther across the floor. That left nothing between the northman and the undead dragon bearing down on him.

"Inara?" His only hope was magic, a gift he didn't possess.

The Dragorn, who was already back on her feet, was entangled with Lord Kraiden and Rengyr. Asher could be of no help, though he was pummelling Lady Gracen, blow after blow, with the end of his pommel.

The dragon's head came down on the northman, the stench of it filling his nostrils. He was certain that undead dragons had no need of food, but that wasn't going to stop this one from devouring him.

Without warning, the dragon was pulled backwards, bringing its jaw to the floor in a mighty *crack*. It was then unceremoniously dragged out of the hole of its own making and set upon by Athis the ironheart! The red dragon gripped the Reaver's neck in his maw and thrashed left and right before the two fell away, out of sight.

In their wake, the outer wall crumbled at its base and fell backwards, creating a ramp that now led up onto the keep's external ramparts. A light pouring of rain now spilled into the throne room with the dawn behind it.

There was a gap between Gondrith and Vilyra, both yet to fully rise after being knocked over. Through the gap, Vighon could see Alijah. It was now or never, he told himself. To fight any longer would only wear him down, leaving him too exhausted to face the half-elf.

The northman pushed up from the dusty floor and ran at Alijah. Vilyra tried to reach out and stop him from challenging her master, but the Dragon Rider was hit by a concussive blast. Vighon offered Inara no thanks, his focus sharpening - he was about to kill his oldest friend.

Of course, Alijah saw him coming and was ready for the sword of the north when it came down on him. They were brought face to face, illuminated by flames.

With a strong hand, Alijah reached out, grabbed Vighon's shield, and threw it aside. "You should have let one of them face me," he sneered, glancing at Asher and Inara.

Vighon had no response but to roar and bring his sword back for another swing. They fought across the podium, leaving the others behind. Their blades clashed one way then another until they were both at the base of the fallen wall. Alijah dashed to the top and quickly gripped his thigh in pain, proving his injured leg was yet to heal. By the edge of the rampart, he baited Vighon, bidding him to follow. The northman obliged and trekked up the damaged wall where the north greeted him with a cold and wet summer morning.

Behind Alijah, the light of the sun was beginning to grace the day with a red dawn, an omen of things to come. Overhead, a different kind of battle was taking place. Athis, alone, was fighting the undead dragons, leading them through the sky before turning on them with fang and claw. Theirs was a brutal struggle of speed and ferocity, but it was the only thing keeping the dragons at bay.

There was, notably, one dragon missing from the fray. Vighon walked across the ramparts and looked down at Malliath, curled up in the courtyard. His purple eyes tracked the northman, despite the dragon's inaction.

Caught in the rain, steam rose from Vighon's flaming sword as he met Alijah before all of Namdhor. "This ends, now."

"This isn't the end," Alijah corrected. "This is where my real journey begins. Everything I've done has been in preparation for what comes next. I would have shared it with you, Inara too. But I won't let you get in the way. If the people have to see you fall, then so be it."

Vighon raised the sword of the north in both hands. There was but one thing that remained, and he would see it through...

In the frigid cold, typical of Namdhor, Galanör and Aenwyn appeared to have been forgotten by the owner and patrons of the tavern. Alone, seated outside on the long balcony, they sipped their Ameeraskan tea and committed themselves to what their kin were renowned for: watching.

The discipline and patience required to actually watch and observe the goings on around oneself was hard to achieve for a mortal, their world so small and temporary. For an elf, an immortal, it was as easy as breathing.

Galanör's keen eyes hadn't missed a thing, though, admittedly, it was difficult to miss the dragon that had flown directly into the keep, caving the wall in. Nor was it hard to miss the red scales of Athis as he clawed the undead dragon out of the hole, taking their fight into the sky.

It wasn't long before they caught sight of two figures fighting on the ramparts. Even with elven eyes, they were moving too quickly and too far away to make out their identity, but one of them was wielding a flaming sword.

"Vighon!" he exclaimed, dropping his tea.

"The king?" Aenwyn leaned out from the railing to see beyond the tavern roof.

"He's fighting Alijah," the ranger assumed. "We have to help him," he insisted.

His insistence, it seemed, wasn't needed. Before he had finished speaking, Aenwyn was over the railing and climbing up onto the roof. Galanör smiled and followed her up.

There were three buildings between them and the walls of the keep, each one requiring them to jump and climb with the rising city. The last building had a pointed roof, forcing them to run one behind the other, reminding Galanör of his time running through the canopy of Ilythyra's trees. The edge was set back enough from the ramparts that any human would fall to their death should they attempt the final jump.

It was a different matter for an elf...

CHAPTER 49
A RED DAWN

For Inara, every swing of her Vi'tari blade was followed by a spell from her hand. The blows she deflected with her sword had begun to numb her forearm and the magic she wielded had begun to numb her fingers. Were her foe any other, the fight would be long over by now.

Hounded by Lord Kraiden and three other Riders, Inara had been forced to alter her tactics and begin searching for space. She needed to take the measure of all her enemies and think, she just needed *room* to think.

The Dragon Riders always found her, however, never giving an inch. They came at the Dragorn with sword, hammer, and axe, each utilising a slightly different fighting technique that ground her down.

In truth, she was distracted. Seeing Vighon pursue Alijah onto the ramparts had split her attention and she wanted nothing more than to join him before her brother killed him.

Then, she heard their swords in the distance, urging her all the more. She needed to reach them. Vilyra and her twin swords were in her way, blocking the view of the broken wall. Inara parried both

585

blades over her head and pushed out with her free hand, unleashing a blast of air that launched Vilyra into one of the pillars. Before she could hit the floor, Inara hit her with another spell, impaling her with a spear of ice. It wouldn't put the Dragon Rider down for good, but it would stop her temporarily getting in her way.

With Kraiden, Gondrith, and Rengyr closing in, Inara made the hard decision to use up the last of the magic in her pommel. The crystal held a significant portion of magic, gifted to her from her grandmother, Adilandra. Unlike most crystals, it could only work in tandem with the scimitar to which it was encrusted. Until now, she had been drawing on it to keep her fighting interspersed with spells, but Inara knew of one last spell that would buy her the time she needed to reach Vighon.

Allowing them to surround her, the Dragorn dropped to one knee and hammered the ground with the crystal. The resultant expulsion of energy washed through her and hardened before the wave slammed into the three Dragon Riders. They were immediately scattered across the chamber, violently bouncing off the pillars and walls.

Outside the blast, Vilyra was already in the process of pulling herself off the icicle.

With time running out, Inara made for the broken wall and dashed up onto the ramparts. She had no idea what she was going to do...

Asher had lost count of how many times Lady Gracen had struck true with her short-swords. He was certainly bleeding, that much he could see, both on himself and on her blades.

She was decidedly quicker than him, her movements akin to a snake. The Mother would coil and spring, the points of her weapons always finding a way past his guard.

He felt none of it.

The ranger's body was numb to the pain and his mind was yet to register how long he had been fighting for, pushing him on. He took every slash and blow and kept fighting back, reminding himself that she was just another Arakesh.

That fact was challenged, constantly, with every second Lady Gracen maintained her half of the battle, refusing to die. He could hear her heartbeat, a rapid drum in her chest. The smell of her blood was on both of his blades and her sweat had permeated the air, mixing with her perfume. She was tiring...

Proving her training to be of the highest quality, she pushed through her exhaustion and continued to offer him a worthy fight. The Mother leaped into the air, twisted her body, and kicked Asher in the chest, throwing him from the elevated podium and onto the chamber floor.

From his back, he observed the four remaining Dragon Riders give chase to Inara, out onto the ramparts. On the other end of the chamber, beyond the decapitated dragon, there remained several lines of Reavers guarding the doorway as watchful sentinels.

Lady Gracen wasn't done with him, likely eager to finish the task originally given to her by Alijah. She jumped from the edge of the podium and came down on the ranger with both short-swords. Her time in the air was more than enough for Asher's senses to detect her, and so he rolled aside, happy to bring a knee up into the Mother's head for her efforts.

When they both rose to their feet they paused, taking the measure of the other. Their breath was ragged, their chests heaving beneath their leather armour. The Mother's dark hair was matted to her face with sweat, as was Asher's.

"How much have you got left, old man?" she taunted with a lick of her lips. "Those elixirs are fading fast by the smell of you."

"You'll be dead first," he promised.

The Mother gritted her teeth. "We shall see..."

Once again, they were joined in the only union in which an Arakesh truly thrived. Their blades met high and low and their limbs kicked out at every opportunity. More cuts. More bruises. The punishment continued across the chamber floor, taking them closer to the throne.

Hatred coursed through the ranger's veins, a far more potent elixir. He hated everything Lady Gracen stood for, though he hated her especially for reviving the order. Because of her, the past refused to die, determined as it was to always seek him out.

It was time to end this, to end them all.

Though Arakesh were often pitted against each other in Nightfall - all in the name of training - they weren't expressly taught *how* to best each other, given that they all belonged to the same order. Since exiling himself from their dark ways, however, Asher had become acquainted with the most efficient way to always come out on top: remove their greatest advantage.

It wasn't easy - Arakesh who lost their blindfolds were severely beaten. But Lady Gracen was sufficiently exhausted now, her focus on attack instead of defence.

With no other options available, Asher gave himself over to his plan. With careful swordplay, he positioned himself so that the Mother was in front of him and the throne behind her. His shoulders sagged and he sighed, feigning fatigue as he dropped his silvyr short-sword. It clattered against the floor and Lady Gracen smiled, sure that her kill was imminent.

Asher was careful to keep his movements sluggish until the precise moment he needed to snap. As predicted, given his stature, Lady Gracen dashed forward, thrusting her blade towards his face. It was only an inch, but the shift in his shoulders ensured her blade glided past his nose, bringing her into his body.

He almost left the floor with the force he put into his knee, driving it into her gut. Doubled over, his free hand snatched the back of her blindfold and threw it away, his elbow prepared for her inevitable rise. Her stature resumed and, her senses wholly human again, he broke her nose with his elbow and kicked her hard in the chest. As planned, she caught the bottom steps of the podium and fell into the throne itself.

Asher was already in the air, covering the distance between them. Her reactions were slow, too slow. There was nothing she could do but watch as he came down and buried the short-sword into her heart, pinning her to the throne.

Gone was the drum. Silent was her breath. Still was her body.

Blood began to trickle down and over the seat of the throne. Asher backed up, taking the steps down to the floor again. Lady Gracen was the first Mother of Nightfall he had ever killed and there were no Fathers to add to that list. It was a significant event, but there was no time to dwell on it - he could hear more than one battle raging outside.

The ranger retrieved his silvyr blade and sheathed it over his back. Instead, he flicked his toes and brought Col-vok's spear to his waiting hand. With the broken wall to his side, he paused, allowing his senses to take everything in. Vighon and Alijah were fighting on the far side of the ramparts - too far. Inara was trying to reach them but had been pressed upon by the Dragon Riders again.

Asher raised the spear and waited for the perfect moment. Then he hurled it.

Inara's Vi'tari blade did what it could, reacting to and anticipating her foes, but there were only so many places one scimitar could be. More than once Vilyra's twin blades had explored an opening and taken their bite.

It was Lord Kraiden's sword she feared. Once, the jagged blade had run a finger's width past her face, granting her the briefest moment to inhale a foul odour that lay upon the steel. It was poisoned. In a bid to avoid the edge of his sword, she had frequently dived and willingly accepted a blow from one of the others.

Gondrith's shield was something of a problem, always there to get in her way. This time, her Vi'tari blade connected with his raised shield and Rengyr moved in to kick her wrist, knocking the scimitar from her grasp. Next came a disorientating blow from Gondrith's fist, throwing her onto her back.

Rengyr stood over her, his two-handed axe raised to cut the Dragorn in half. There was nothing she could do. What magic she could still feel in her fingers was faint. She dared not call on Athis's strength - he was in the fight of his life above her.

But this was not to be her end...

She heard the whistling spear a fraction of a second before it impaled Rengyr in the back and launched him over the top of her. Where it had come from was unknown, but she wasn't going to lie there and ponder. Lifting her knees, Inara flipped forwards onto her feet, ducked under Gondrith's hammer, and rolled over her Vi'tari blade.

Emerging from her roll, the enchanted scimitar rang out as it locked against Lord Kraiden's wicked blade. They fought across the ramparts, trailed by Vilyra and Gondrith. Rengyr was already on his feet again and in the process of extracting the spear from his torso.

Kicking Lord Kraiden back, Inara gained some distance and looked down at Malliath in the courtyard. His attention was farther down the rampart, fixed on Alijah and Vighon's duel. She followed his gaze, stealing what glimpse she had time for. Vighon's flaming sword was easy to spot, despite the rising light from the east. He swung wide, always coming at her brother with heavy attacks.

Alijah was notably reserved, defending more than attacking. There had to be injuries at play, causing her brother to alter his fighting style. What was more curious was Malliath's inaction. The black dragon was content to sit back and watch his companion from afar, as if testing him somehow.

Her observations were over as quickly as they began. As per Alijah's orders, the Dragon Riders were to grant her a quick death. So far, they were failing.

Their attack was paused, however, by an earth-shattering quake that rocked the walls of the keep. Athis had grappled one of the Reaver dragons, bearing it down to the city itself. The main street was buried beneath their tussling bulk and their tails whipped out, cleaving entire buildings. The remaining dragons were quickly descending to sink their claws into Athis's back.

Keep moving! Inara warned.

None of us will survive if we don't get out of here! the red dragon countered.

Indeed, Inara agreed, their chances of surviving this now was extremely low. Everything had gone from bad to worse and she could only envision one conclusion for them all.

Taking her advice, Athis raked the head of another dragon and beat his wings, taking him clear of the city. For Inara, there was no escaping her enemies. With firm footing again, Lord Kraiden led the Dragon Riders towards her. She backed up until her heels met the edge of the rampart - to go any farther would see her fall into the courtyard, Malliath's domain.

Aid came in the form of a man possessed. Asher, wild by his look, used the wall of the rampart to gain height and came down on the Dragon Riders with fury. With the ranger attacking them from the back, Inara entered the fight from the front and worked to separate Vilyra and Kraiden from Gondrith and Rengyr. That still left them with two opponents each, two opponents who didn't tire and knew no fear.

How much time did Vighon have left? Alijah's victory was assured before the northman drew his legendary sword. Then again, she thought, how long did any of them have? Reavers were amassing around the keep and could be seen marching up Namdhor's rise, they faced Dragon Riders and their hideous mounts, and Malliath had yet to make his move. All that against three of them...

What hope did they have?

Removed from his companions, Vighon Draqaro had but one single focus. There was nothing but his flaming sword, an extension of himself, and his enemy, the usurper who had stolen his crown and kingdom.

Their fight had crossed the ramparts and continued over the main gate of the keep. Scattered throughout the debris, created by the dragons, the people of Namdhor watched anxiously from their homes and broken streets.

The victor would emerge their king...

Vighon ignored them all, even Inara's plight. She only needed to hold on until he could kill Alijah, an act that would terminate the Dragon Riders. If only killing him wasn't proving so difficult. The half-elf was visibly wounded, along with his dragon, yet he parried and countered every time, never giving the northman an inch.

"You have already lost, Vighon!" Alijah spat, his emerald blade meeting the sword of the north. "Make this easier on them," he continued, gesturing to the city. "Bow to me and this madness stops right now."

Vighon came at him with a two-handed swing, bringing the flaming sword down on Alijah's waiting block. "Never!" he yelled, shoving the half-elf back.

Alijah spun on the ball of his heel, allowing Vighon to rush past him. A quick elbow to the back of the head sent the northman sprawling across the rampart. He quickly flipped onto his back and raised his sword but Alijah knocked it aside, sending it over the edge and down into the courtyard. His sword lost, the northman was exposed to a mortal blow. There was no hesitation on Alijah's part now.

The Vi'tari blade went up, its edge of green steel ready to end Vighon once and for all. The scimitar came down only to find the steel of another in its path, saving the northman's life.

"Galanör?" The elf's name barely left Vighon's lips before the deadly ranger was pushing Alijah back, his dual scimitars flashing.

Injured or not, it became apparent that Alijah had been toying with Vighon. Facing a superior swordsman, the half-elf came alive, his technique now sharp and swift to keep up with Galanör. Another elf appeared by Vighon's side, though he couldn't say he recognised her. She drew an elven scimitar from her scabbard and dropped it by his side.

"Get up, your Grace!" Her bow unleashed arrow after arrow, but they weren't aimed at Alijah.

With her blade in his hand, Vighon found his feet and turned around to see more Reavers than he could count approaching along the rampart. Every one of her arrows flew true and dropped one of the undead soldiers, but they were nocking arrows themselves.

The first salvo to come their way was deflected by the elf's shield, a flaring wall of magic that curved around them. "Help *him!*" she said, nodding her head at Galanör.

Trusting the elf, he turned around and searched for the best place to insert himself into the duel - no easy task...

To Inara's eyes, the situation had actually become worse, despite Galanör's perfectly timed arrival. Beyond his fight with Alijah, a few hundred Reavers were approaching on foot, many of whom were armed with bows and were letting loose with abandon.

Whatever they had all hoped to achieve this day, they had to leave, and they had to leave right now.

Athis! she called.

Her eternal companion collided with the dragon Morgorth and used all four of his claws to ram the undead beast into the main wall of the keep. It would have been spectacular to witness, but Inara was too busy fighting back to back with Asher. They felt the quake that rippled under their feet, but all combatants remained standing this time.

Athis! she called again.

The red dragon extracted himself from the debris and immediately flew north before disappearing altogether. *I will retrieve Adan'Karth,* he told her. *Be ready for my return - I will not be stopping.*

Inara shoulder barged Asher, pushing him beyond the reach of Lord Kraiden's poisoned blade. "Athis is coming!" she told him. "We need to leave!"

Her last words were drowned out by the Reaver dragons, all of which flew over their heads in pursuit of Athis, to the north.

Movement to her left caught Inara's eye: Malliath was taking more of an interest in Alijah's new opponent. Galanör, one of the realm's greatest fighters, possessed one more blade than Alijah and commanded a degree of magic that made him significantly more dangerous than Vighon. If the black dragon decided to take more than an interest in his companion's battle, this would all be over very soon.

Beyond them, Galanör's friend was alternating between her shield and volleying arrows into the approaching Reavers. More than a few got past her and nearly hit Vighon, who was doing his best to join Galanör's efforts.

"We need to get closer to them!"

Asher managed to grip the haft of Gondrith's hammer and reverse its direction into the Dragon Rider's face. A boot to the chest put the fiend on his back, offering them a momentary opening.

"Then run!" the ranger suggested, making a break for the others.

Inara dashed out of the melee and followed Asher along the ramparts, her Vi'tari blade flicking out at regular intervals to deflect stray arrows. Asher, blindfolded as he was, could detect the incoming missiles and simply ran between them.

Malliath's head had turned. He was tracking them.

Inara reached out in search of Athis and discovered he was already on his way back. "Get ready!" she warned.

Galanör released a concussive wave, his spell directed at Alijah. The half-elf staggered back, his own defensive spell repelling the majority of the blow. He gripped his ribs, however, and winced in pain. Inara was impressed by her brother's prowess, if a little terrified. His skills had increased dramatically during his time in Erador.

Vighon jumped in, curving his borrowed scimitar in a wide attack. Alijah pushed through his obvious pain and parried the blow with his cursed blade. Continuing his defence, the half-elf turned on his heel in one smooth motion and kicked Galanör away.

With his back to Vighon, this would have been the northman's opportune moment to strike, but he was just as dumbstruck as Inara was. Having climbed over the wall, there was now another person standing on the rampart, beside Vighon. Her shock of blonde hair caught the dawn and the rain gave her angular face a glistening sheen.

"Mother!" Inara's tone was full of concern.

Reyna leaned in and said something to Vighon that Inara couldn't hear. Then she put something in the northman's hand and flashed her daughter with a warm smile that the Dragorn couldn't understand. Stepping in front of Vighon, she faced her son.

"Mother!" Inara called again, closing the gap between them.

Alijah turned from Galanör and looked upon his mother. The sight of her softened his features.

Athis crested the top of the keep and angled his flight to take him along the outside wall, along the rampart. He was closely hounded by the Reaver dragons, who snapped at the air and shrieked in their terrible cry.

What happened next was hard to comprehend, given that everything happened at once and, to Inara, it was both slow and fast.

Galanör shouted something to his companion, who ceased her defence against the incoming arrows. Together, the elves made for the edge of the outer wall.

Vighon stepped back from Alijah and Reyna, looking at the object in his hand.

The sound of Athis's beating wings came to an end as he tucked in his wings with one powerful push to bring him as close to the wall as possible.

The Dragon Riders were almost upon Inara again, their task unfulfilled.

Asher bellowed Vighon's name and pointed to the edge of the wall.

Though not entirely an elf, Inara's eyes had inherited their extraordinary sight. It was these extraordinary eyes, a rich shade of blue, that saw the approaching arrow. It curved over Alijah's right shoulder, skimming his armour, before arching into her mother's chest.

Together, the twins cried, "NO!"

Asher's arm came around the back of Inara and his hand gripped her shoulder. She was powerless against his forceful shove that took her with him over the outer wall. Just ahead of them, Vighon jumped over the edge, shortly followed by Galanör and his companion. The elves mirrored Inara's grace and adjusted to Athis passing speed with incredible dexterity. Asher tumbled back, towards the tail, but managed to hold on and even snatch Vighon's hand, pulling him with them.

Clearing the keep and even Namdhor's rise, Athis beat his wings again, giving them height. Inara used Athis's spikes to stand up and hold her position - her gaze was cast back at the keep.

Reyna was caught by Alijah before she could hit the floor and he crouched down with her in his hands. He turned around with an outstretched arm and a wave of magic washed over the first few lines of Reavers, reducing them to nothing more than scattered limbs.

Then everything stopped. The Reaver dragons almost fell out of the sky and the legion of soldiers on the ramparts staggered to a stop, with some even crumpling to the stone. It was as if the north had held its breath.

"Why are they not pursuing?" Galanör questioned, his chestnut hair whipping about his face - he hadn't seen Reyna take the arrow.

Inara's vision blurred with the tears welling in her eyes. Farther down Athis's back, Asher roared as his grief and rage collided

THE KNIGHTS OF ERADOR

together. Vighon was clinging to the dragon for dear life, his expression devoid of anything readable.

With Adan'Karth in his claws, Athis flew east, away from Namdhor and across The White Vale, a baron, yet beautiful landscape of snowy plains and mountains. They were unhindered in their escape, a remarkable turn of events.

It had taken a little time, but Asher and Vighon had been assisted to reach the base of Athis's neck. The ranger had removed his blindfold to reveal glassy eyes. His chest was heaving and his leathers stained with blood - when his potions wore off completely, he would need to rest for days, if not weeks.

Vighon had informed Galanör and his companion, Aenwyn, of the wretched arrow. A great depression settled over them all, Athis included, who shared Inara's emotions in this.

"What happened back there?" Galanör asked after some time. "We should not have escaped that?"

"He lost control," Inara answered absently.

Aenwyn frowned. "Control?"

"His will controls the Reavers," Asher growled.

His answer and tone were sufficient enough to bring about another time of silence. Then Inara looked through the mess of images and sounds in her mind and recalled the events prior to her mother being shot.

"What did she give you?"

Vighon patted his belt until he retrieved a small object between his finger and thumb. He placed it carefully in Inara's palm, revealing the item to be a small golden ring - Reyna's wedding ring.

"Why would she give it to me?" the northman asked.

Inara knew why. She put the ring on her own finger and held out her hand. Her finger twitched and guided her arm to the right, a south-easterly heading.

Athis...

I know. The dragon altered his flight path and followed the ring's guidance.

"It's paired with my father's," she told them.

Thanks to the magic of Galanör and Aenwyn, they were kept warm on their journey to find Nathaniel. Inara hated the silence. Her mind relived the moment over and over again. She should have done more. She should have saved her mother. If only there had been enough magic left in her reserves she could have turned the arrow to ash mid-flight.

As her thoughts spiralled to dark places, her gaze drifted out across Athis's beating wing. Her focus sharpened just enough to make her realise how hurt he was. The dragon had suffered in his own fight, losing scales, flesh, and even muscles in places. His wings appeared damaged, both across the membranes and the bone. One of his horns had been broken too, an irritation more than pain. Looking over the side, the leg that carried Adan'Karth was torn in several places by razor-sharp claws.

It was all very alarming, but what alarmed the Dragorn all the more was her *lack* of injury. Inara gave herself a quick check over, making certain that shock wasn't to blame, but Athis's wounds were not mirrored anywhere on her body...

I told you, the dragon said into her mind. *Our bond is forever changed.*

In that moment, his words only saddened Inara all the more. She lay as flat as she could against his warm scales and rubbed him with the palm of her hand.

The world she knew no longer existed...

CHAPTER 50

AFTERMATH

Having followed the ring's constant directions, Athis was eventually flying over The Black Wood, north of Dunwich. Inara had to wonder what her father was doing in the forest. Why hadn't he been with her mother?

The answer came soon enough. From their lofty vantage, they could all see the dwarven camp that sprawled across the clearings in the heart of the forest. There seemed some alarm on the forest floor. Inara noted multiple crossbows and spears aimed up at them.

Slowly, Athis descended into the only space that could accommodate his bulk. Perhaps it was his colour that convinced the dwarves of clan Heavybelly to hold off any attack, or maybe it was because he didn't share the same skeletal and ragged appearance as the Reavers.

Inara was just glad there was to be no more violence. The dawn had brought enough for one day...

Their arrival was somewhat chaotic and even tense as they all wearily climbed down from Athis's back. It didn't help that the dwarves, a species notorious for shunning outsiders, were confronted by two elves, a Drake, two humans, *and* a Dragorn.

It was all resolved when Doran Heavybelly, Russell Maybury, and her father pushed through the cautious dwarves, followed by Sir Ruban and a handful of the king's guard. There were greetings made and embraces had between them. For Inara and her father, however, there was nothing but a telling look.

They came face to face. "You saw her?"

Inara nodded, her eyes tearing up again, just as her father's were. "Is she... Is she..."

"I don't know," Inara had to admit. "I didn't see... We had to leave. She took an arrow to the..." Her words died away and her father pulled her in to a tight embrace.

After a grieving reunion, they parted to see Asher standing close by. Nathaniel held out his arm and the two men gripped each other's forearms before succumbing to a hug.

"She was alive," the ranger whispered, causing Nathaniel to step back. "At least... her heart was beating."

Nathaniel nodded his understanding and clapped his old friend on the shoulder. He had no words for either of them. Inara removed the band from her finger and offered it to her father. He took it in his hand and clenched it, his grief palpable.

Beside them, Doran was motionless, his mouth ajar, and an expression of deep sorrow. He looked to all three of them, seemingly speechless.

"Low is the day when the dawn brin's dark tidin's," he lamented. "Ye should all follow me..."

Trailing the son of Dorain, they were brought to the largest tent in the camp. Upon entering the gloomy abode, they were hit by the strong scent of lavender. Inara was quick to take in the surroundings and those present. Logic told her that the dwarf lying in the only bed was King Dakmund, Doran's younger brother. The older dwarf beside him was most likely their mother, Queen Drelda. Besides a few servants, there was only one person she couldn't explain.

A Keeper of Valatos...

Sandy haired and grubby from head to toe, he stood up from the king's bedside with his wand in hand. "I'm trying everything I know, Doran. The only thing I've been able to affect is the smell in here. The poison that troubles his wound is... *aggressive*, for lack of a better word. It doesn't respond to magic very well."

Doran wiped a hand over his forehead. "Please, lad, keep tryin'." The queen-mother said something in dwarvish and Doran replied, "They're allies. More than that... they're friends." This satisfied Queen Drelda, who remained silent thereafter. "Oh!" The stout ranger appeared flustered for a moment and turned to the side. "This is King Vighon o', ye know, *Illian*."

The northman didn't look much like a king but, then again, that had always been part of Vighon's charm.

Doran cleared his throat, signalling for the tent's occupants to pay some kind of respect. "Ye're supposed to bow," he hissed.

Vighon waved the notion away. "Perhaps we should allow King Dakmund to rest. Is there somewhere we can all talk?"

That somewhere was far more crowded than Inara had expected. The tent wasn't quite as large as the king's, but it was so full of dwarves that it wouldn't have mattered either way. Most looked to be high ranking soldiers in the Heavybelly army with a lot of white beards and frowning faces. It appeared, though Inara couldn't fathom how it had happened, that Doran was now the highest-ranking dwarf in the clan. It also appeared that not everyone was happy about it...

And so began a series of accounts from a number of people, herself included, that helped them to put the larger picture together. None of it was good. The Heavybellys especially were displeased with Asher's news that the rest of the clans were being moved south at that very moment, halting any battle plans they had previously drawn up.

What was more disturbing was the ominous reason they were being moved in the first place. The Moonlit Plains was an odd place to deliberately situate thousands of dwarves. The ranger had also made mention of silvyr being transported to Qamnaran, an island known only for its Demetrium deposits. It all gave Inara an uneasy feeling.

Galanör gave them hope and despair in the same breath. It was uplifting to hear that so many elves were now safe and hiding in The Evermoore, especially given the illegal nature of their presence on Illian soil now. But the elven ranger had also told of Lady Ellöria's death battling Alijah and Malliath - which explained their injuries. For Inara, it was another member of her family to be claimed by this invasion.

No, she told herself. Her mother may yet live; there were none stronger than Reyna Galfrey, that much she knew.

There was unrest amongst the dwarves, though most humans and elves would call it a raging argument. There emerged a camp who believed Grarfath would richly reward them if they continued with their plan and marched on Namdhor. They were decidedly against Doran in every way.

The War Mason, as he was now referred to, explained to them that such a battle would only result in the annihilation of clan Heavybelly. They had to adjust their tactics now, being the minority and many miles within enemy territory. Every non-dwarf agreed with him, including the Keeper, Kassian, who had expressed an almost desperate urge to kill Alijah and Malliath.

"Why should we care what he has to offer?" one dwarf challenged, wagging his finger at Vighon. "He's the king o' nothin' now! He's got, what? Five soldiers still bearin' his sigil?"

Sir Ruban looked to challenge him but Vighon held his hand out, calming the captain. "I still have two thousand loyal soldiers stationed in Grey Stone. Another thousand await my command in Velia. Tregaran, in The Arid Lands, has remained untouched as far as I know. Any man who can wield a sword in the desert owes his allegiance to me."

"For how long?" another dwarf spoke up. "There's a new king on yer throne now. What man will refuse to bend the knee when he is confronted by the black dragon?"

Vighon had no answer to that. "Tregaran or not, we can do a lot with three thousand men."

"*We?*" one of the generals echoed. "Our alliance ended with trade, *your Grace...*"

Doran hammered his fist onto the only table in the middle of the tent. "Enough! Forget all that has ever been - this is a different kind o' war. We're outnumbered ten to one by an enemy that doesn' feel *pain*, that doesn' fear our *mettle*, that never even *tires!* Gone are the days o' marchin' gloriously into battle. We're goin' to 'ave to fight on more than one front. We're goin to 'ave to fight in foreign territory. From now on, there are only two sides: Reavers an' everyone else. Is that clear?"

There was no protest given, a sign of their compliance if not their agreement. Galanör gave them a rough idea on elven numbers to add to this growing allegiance, as well as confirmation that Inara's grandmother, Queen Adilandra, had been contacted. It was hard to see, but a small spark of hope was rising amongst them.

The Dragorn subconsciously touched the diviner on her belt, wishing she too could inform them that more help was coming. She vowed to try again and again until she contacted Gideon - he needed to know what was happening.

The conference went on for many hours, taking them into the night. Inara was very aware that her father had yet to say a word. She wanted to comfort him more than anything, but her attention was required during such an important meeting of the races.

Arguments naturally arose as to who was in charge. The dwarves made a point of stating that they would never take orders from an elven queen or a human king. Vighon put forward a good case for his leadership, given that Illian was his kingdom and he knew the land better than most in the tent. Inara supported this and was disheartened to find that the dwarves cared very little for the words of a Dragorn.

Since there was to be no battle in the north and the dwarves had no march to begin, Doran brought the meeting to an end and sent everyone back to their tents for rest. They could only hope that calmer heads would prevail after a night's sleep.

Leaving the large tent behind, Inara naturally moved to follow her father, who was walking side by side with Asher. They weren't talking, though Adan'Karth's close proximity might have been a factor. The Drake had remained at the ranger's side since Athis touched down and he didn't look to be leaving him any time soon.

"Inara." Despite the several dozen dwarves filing out of the tent and dispersing across the camp, Vighon was easily found being two feet taller than all of them. He looked exhausted, reminding the Dragorn that he was only human - a fact easily forgotten.

What could never be forgotten, especially by the king, was his flaming sword - a symbol in itself. It was notably absent from his belt as he approached, lost to their enemy.

He signalled for his royal guard to hang back while he and Inara walked through the camp, under the stars.

"You did well in there," she told him. "Dwarves aren't easy."

Vighon nodded along, clearly wanting to talk to her about something else. "I'm so..." He closed his mouth and swallowed, grappling with his words. "I'm so sorry. If I hadn't gone after Alijah, things might have been different. Your mother wouldn't have been on the rampart and... I'm so sorry, Inara."

It would have been easy to give into her grief there and then, crumple into his arms, and seek some kind of comfort that would help her through it all. But she held on to what strength remained and reminded herself that her mother was alive. She had to be.

"What happened wasn't your fault, Vighon," the Dragorn reassured. "The truth is... Alijah needs to be stopped. I'm coming round to the variety of ways that deed can be accomplished." Inara looked back at the tent, where she had heard dozens of dwarves and an especially angry Keeper speak of a hundred ways to kill her brother.

The northman sighed. "We've all lost so much. Everyone here, human, dwarf, elf... they're all grieving for someone."

Inara stopped and turned to him. She looked into his eyes and still saw that young boy she had fallen in love with so many years ago. Without realising, she was holding his hand. For the first time in a long time, she felt an attraction that quickened her heart. It was all dampened, however, by the day's events and the loss of which he spoke.

"You were in that tent," she said. "*Together.* That's how we're going to get through this. Whatever happens..."

The northman looked away and attempted to smile. "Still holding that torch of hope, I see."

Inara was incapable of smiling right now, though she did squeeze his hand. Then it came to her, a flash of memory from their fight on Namdhor's walls. With everything that had happened since, it was a detail that had slipped her mind.

"What did she say to you?" Inara asked to a confused Vighon. "My mother. She said something to you before giving you her ring."

Vighon took a long breath, his dark eyes never drifting from Inara. "Rebel."

EPILOGUE

Alijah's mind was a storm few could weather. The arrow that struck his mother brought all of his rage to the surface, wiping away the discipline that held his emotions in check.

Without thinking, he caught Reyna and dropped to one knee with her resting in his arms. Her green eyes looked up at him, taking him back to the best years of his life, when the only thing that mattered was how much fun he could have with Inara and Vighon.

Then they closed.

His rage exploded forth and he turned around to unleash his wrath upon the Reavers who had hurt his mother. A single spell swept across the rampart and obliterated the first few rows.

Sensing his mother's doom, he quickly turned his attention back to her. Tentatively, he gripped the arrow just above her breast. In one smooth motion, he pulled it out and cast it aside. The wound gushed, staining her clothes and warming his hand.

To cover the wound was instinct, but there were few who possessed the power to actually do something about it. The half-elf reached out, making contact with the magical realm that overlapped reality. He, like many others, was a conduit for that other realm and he drew on the power it offered.

Malliath's overwhelming presence filled every space inside his mind. *Leave her.*

No! He poured his magic into the wound, commanding it to bend to his will.

Such magic will drain you, the dragon warned. *Our enemies are fleeing. Now is the time to crush them!*

No! Alijah yelled across their bond. He couldn't remember the last time he had disagreed with his companion.

Her heart was slowing...

Alijah intensified his efforts and the surrounding Reavers began to fade from his will. He didn't care in that moment; he just needed to save her.

Sacrifice without hesitation, Malliath said. *Reyna Galfrey came here to stop us - she is our enemy. You are allowing your emotions to control you.*

Alijah heard his words and knew they were that of The Crow's. But the half-elf held on to another lesson the necromancer had taught him.

"Love gives you the strength to transform pain into power..." The Crow had said.

Right now, that's exactly what Alijah was doing.

Your love is for me, Malliath reminded him. *Your love is for the people. Leave her.*

Alijah could feel his mother's body knitting back together, the damage undone. He couldn't tell, however, whether his face was wet from the rain or the exertion. It was impossible to tune Malliath's voice out, powerful as it was, but he concentrated on the wound for a while longer, until he was satisfied it was healed.

Regaining control of his forces again, he commanded Lord Kraiden to take Reyna from his arms and have her placed inside a secure room in the keep.

He staggered to his feet in the rain and turned to watch the sunrise. There was no sight of Athis or those he carried. Looking over the edge of the rampart, into the courtyard, he could see Vighon's flaming sword lying on the ground. The Crow had warned him, years ago, that those he loved, his closest friends and family, would try to stop him from fulfilling his destiny.

You failed today...

Alijah briefly closed his eyes before turning to the black dragon. **Is that why you did nothing?** he spat. **Were you testing me?**

I am always testing you. I wanted to see if you had the strength to take their lives. A part of you still holds Vighon Draqaro as brother, and Inara Galfrey as your sister. You must let that go if we are to see this through. The scales must be broken... or there will never be peace.

Alijah knew Malliath was right - he was always right. **Nothing will stop us,** he promised.

Finding some resolve, the half-elf walked back along the rampart and down the fallen wall, into his new throne room. It was a mess. Col-vok and his dragon, Nersandi, lay between the pillars, both returned to true death.

Moving to the throne, there was another dead body littering the grand chamber. Lady Gracen, the disappointment that she was, had been slain by Asher if the short-sword in her chest was anything to go by. Alijah removed the blade, unpinning the Mother, and threw her onto Col-vok's body.

Exhausted, he cared little for the blood on his throne - there would be more before the end. He sat down and let out a long breath, sure that rest would never find him, at least not for a century or two. But there were none who could shoulder such a burden, such a destiny as his.

Alijah Galfrey had been fated to change the world for ten thousand years, though *change* was perhaps too soft a word.

He was going to *break* it...

THE SAGA CONTINUES...

PHILIP C. QUAINTRELL

THE ECHOES SAGA

LAST of THE DRAGORN

BOOK VIII

PHILIP C. QUAINTRELL

Hear more from Philip C. Quaintrell including book releases and exclusive content:

 PHILIPCQUAINTRELL.COM

 FACEBOOK.COM/PHILIPCQUAINTRELL

 @PHILIPCQUAINTRELL.AUTHOR

 @PCQUAINTRELL

AUTHOR NOTES

The beginning of the end! Book seven marks the beginning of The Echoes Saga's final story arc.

Well, if you've come this far I'm assuming you're a fan of the series. If you're not a fan, you should really stop punishing yourself seven books in! For those of you who count yourselves as Quaintrellians (I'm making that happen!), thank you so much for sticking with the saga. I know there must be some of you who picked up Rise of the Ranger in May 2017 and have been following my releases for a few years now.

While writing this book something amazing happened. As I posted on social media, the Saga has been optioned by a production company with the view to create an epic fantasy TV series. Wahoo! Though, realistically, there are so many hoops to jump through that there is still a chance it either won't get made or it's several years away. There's a great team working on it though and they're very passionate about the project.

There's not much more I can say than that I'm afraid. That whole industry is very hush hush and like to play things close to the chest until they have something solid to announce. I'm very excited though. Just to have this on the table was something I only ever dreamed about and spoke of with an air of humour, believing it would never be an option.

Watch this space!

So, 'The Knights of Erador'! The cover, another Chris Mcgrath masterpiece, was dedicated to none other than Doran Heavybelly. So far, I've managed to showcase a different character on every cover - it helps to have a diverse cast. I already know who is going to be on the next cover, but the last one is still up in the air. We'll see...

Funny side note regarding Doran in this book. I kept forgetting he had lost an eye in 'Age of the King'. I had to instruct my editor to look for any mentions of Doran using his 'eyes' rather than his 'eye'. It made me laugh.

And, speaking off Doran, he's back in the fold! I might have said it before, but I know what's coming story-wise in the form of beats, like particular scenes that will play out and move character arcs forward. I don't know everything until it happens, such as King Dakmund's proclamation that Doran would hold his old title as War Mason. It's going to be exciting to see what happens next for the son of Dorain now that he has a new level of responsibility.

Overall, I'd say this book took me a little while to get stuck into. Being so focused on the very end as I was, my thoughts had all gone to just that, the end (it's a good'un!). The first challenge to this book was figuring out how all that kicks off, the final spark in the story.

The second challenge was finding the characters' voices having moved forward by fifteen years. The gap in the books is over a decade, but for me it was only a couple of weeks. I had to almost reimagine these characters by inserting fifteen years of events and experiences to see them evolve appropriately.

Interestingly, the prologue you read at the beginning of this book was in fact a second and completely different draft. As it turns out, the first prologue I wrote is going to be the prologue of the last book (the title is a secret for now). Adding to this, I know exactly what the epilogue is to the final book (unless something drastic happens along the way).

The newest character is obviously Kassian Kantaris. He's going to be very different in the next book to how he's been portrayed in this one. I wanted, however, for the reader to see the life he had lost to better understand what makes him tick. Tauren was similar in 'Empire of Dirt', but his history was told to the reader, whereas Kassian's unfolds from beginning to end.

The Arakesh are back! We last saw them being devastated by orc Darklings, but I couldn't let them go. I love the idea that a younger generation survived and decided to change everything, even if they're still evil at heart. More than that, they play a huge part of Asher's story and he has yet to get any closure on that part of his life, so you can expect more from the assassins of Nightfall before the end!

Thinking of Asher, I really loved his regression towards the latter half of the book. We've never seen him this close, psychologically, to his old self (things will be very different in his prequel series). Also, he has magic in his bones! This was one of the 'beats' I had planned out back when I was writing 'Relic of the Gods', so it was immensely satisfying to actually write it four books later. In some ways, it almost feels cruel to prolong his life when fate has nothing but pain and more fighting in store for him!

As far as POV's go, this book is the first time in the Saga that the villains have no chapters from their perspective (except for the epilogue). It was weird writing it this way but, even if it was clear that Alijah was the bad guy, I wanted the reader to constantly see through the eyes of those who felt the betrayal. Going forward, this will be different now that the cat's out of the bag. I'm looking forward to diving into the messed up companionship between Alijah and Malliath!

Another deviation from the previous books is the ending. Due to the nature of the story I'm telling, they have all led to a big battle at the end of each book. The numbers and location was always different, as was the reason for the battle, but that's just the apex every book led to. In book 7, the 'big battle' was far more intimate with only a handful of the heroes squaring off against a handful of villains. It was refreshing but also a challenge for me as a writer since it was a new kind of ending. Still, I was thrilled with the way things came together in the end and you can bet there's going to be some more battles to come.

I have to talk about Inara Galfrey. Her story only began in book 4 and though she had quite the arc from there to book 6, I think we have yet to scratch the surface there. Also - side note - her front cover (Kingdom of Bones) is my favourite so far!

Oooo, I almost forgot to mention the new map! There's a new map! If you haven't seen it yet, it's in the front of the book. We haven't been there yet, but Erador is coming and you can now see the whole map in all its glory, which is more than most people in Illian can say. I love working on the map and I especially love seeing all the places that inspire new stories in me. I will be posting it on my social media at some point too. Oh, and on my website, which is still being built.

My plan for the rest of 2020 is to get my head down and complete book 8 and make a good start on book 9. That's my aim. It's still three times faster than any traditionally published book, but life has its ways of slowing us down. If I am slowed down for any reason, I can't foresee book 9 being released any later than summer 2021.

If you've enjoyed this book please do me a huge a favour and leave a review, long or short, on Amazon and/or Goodreads. Being a self-publisher, your support in this regard helps me to get the word out that these very cheap books are worth the time and money. Apart from that - feel free to tell EVERYONE! I don't mind mega phones being used in the streets.

If you want to get in touch, my email is philipcquaintrell@ gmail.com and I answer every one. Or, you can find me on Instagram and on my Facebook page just by searching for my name. I post updates of all kinds whenever I can.

So, I hope you've enjoyed my ramblings but, more importantly, I hope you've enjoyed the latest book and the Saga so far!

Until the next time...

APPENDICES

Provinces of Illian:

1. ***Alborn*** (eastern province) - Ruled by Lord Carrington of house Landor, the steward of Velia, Alborn's capital. Other Towns and Cities: Palios, Galosha, and Barossh.

2. ***The Arid Lands*** (southern province) - Ruled by Lord Hasta Hash-Aseem, the steward of Tregaran, the southern capital. Other Towns and Cities: Ameeraska and Calmardra.

3. ***The Ice Vales*** (western province) - Ruled by Lord Thedomir Longshadow, steward of Grey Stone, the capital of the western vales. Other Towns and Cities: Bleak, Kelp Town, and Snowfell.

4. ***Orith*** (northern province) - Ruled by King Vighon of house Draqaro from the city of Namdhor, the capital of Illian. Other towns and cities: Skystead, Dunwich, Darkwell, and Longdale.

5. *Felgarn* (central province) - Ruled by Lady Gracen of house Penrose, stewardess of Lirian, the heart of The Evermoore. Other Towns and Cities: Vangarth, Wood Vale, and Whistle Town.

Dwarven Hierarchy:

1. *Battleborns* - Ruled by King Uthrad, son of Koddun. Domain: *Silvyr Hall.*

2. *Stormshields* - Ruled by King Gandalir, son of Bairn. Domain: *Hyndaern.*

3. *Hammerkegs* - Ruled by King Torgan, son of Dorald. Domain: *Nimduhn.*

4. *Goldhorns* - Ruled by King Thole, son of Thaldun. Domain: *Khaldarim.*

5. *Brightbeards* - Ruled by King Gaerhard, son of Hermon. Domain: *Bhan Doral.*

Heavybellys (exiled) - Ruled by King Dakmund, son of Dorain. Domain: *Grimwhal.*

Dragon Riders and their mounts

Lord Kraiden, bonded with the dragon *Morgorth.*

Vilyra, bonded with the dragon *Godrad.*

Gondrith, bonded with the dragon *Yillir*.

Col-vok, bonded with the dragon *Nersandi*. (Deceased)

Rengyr, bonded with the dragon *Karsak*.

Orcish Tribes:

1. *The Sons of Gordomo* - Ruled by Chieftain Targ.

2. *The Berserkers* - Ruled by Chieftain Wuglaf.

3. *The Big Bastards* - Ruled by Chieftain Gargandor.

4. *The Mountain Fist* - Ruled by Chieftain Mezeg.

Other significant locations:

Valatos (within the city of Velia) - School for magic.

Ikirith (inside The Evermoore) - forest home of the Drakes.

Elandril (northern Ayda) - Ruled by Queen Adilandra of house Sevari. The heart of the elven nation.

The Lifeless Isles - An archipelago in The Adean and home to the Dragorn.

Korkanath (on an island east of Velia) - The ruins of the once prestigious school for magic.

Stowhold (an island north of Korkanath) - The headquarters of Illian's largest bank.

Syla's Pass (south of The Arid Lands) - Entrance to The Undying Mountains.

The Tower of Dragons' Reach (south of Velia) - The abandoned tower where once the rulers of the realm would meet with Gideon Thorn and the Dragorn.

Ilythyra (in The Moonlit Plains) - Governed by Lady Ellöria of house Sevari. Home to a small population of elves from Elandril.

Paldora's Fall (inside The Undying Mountains) - The impact site of Paldora's Star, a well of powerful magic.

~

Significant Wars: Chronologically

The First War - Fought during The Pre-Dawn (before elvish-recorded history). King Atilan started a war with the first Dragon Riders in the hopes of uncovering their source of immortality. The war brought an end to Atilan's reign and his entire kingdom.

The Great War - Fought during the First Age, around 5,000 years ago. The only recorded time in history that elves and dwarves have united. They fought against the orcs with the help of the Dragorn, the first elvish dragon riders. This war ended the First Age.

The Dark War - Fought during the Second Age, around 1,000 years ago. Considered the elvish civil war. Valanis, the dark elf, tried to take over Illian in the name of the gods. This war ended the Second Age.

The Dragon War - Fought in the beginning of the Third Age, only a few years after The Dark War. The surviving elves left Illian for Ayda's shores, fleeing any more violence. Having emerged from The Wild Moores, the humans, under King Gal Tion's rule, went to war with the dragons over their treasure. This saw the exile of the surviving dragons and the beginning of human dominance over Illian.

The War for the Realm - Fought 45 years ago. The return of Valanis saw the world plunged back into war and the re-emergence of the Dragorn. Gideon Thorn became the first human to bond with a dragon in recorded history. Valanis was killed by the ranger, Asher, who died in their final battle.

The Northern Civil War - In the wake of The War for the Realm, the north, under the ruling city of Namdhor, was left without its king, Merkaris Tion. In the vacuum that followed, the lords and great families fell into civil war over the throne. The war lasted nearly twenty years and ended with Yelifer, of house Skalaf, seated on the throne.

The Ash War - Fought 15 years ago. The last war of the Third Age saw Illian transition into the Fourth Age. The orcs return to the surface brought with them war and blood on a scale Verda hadn't seen in ten thousand years. Resulted in the destruction of the Dragornian population and island, as well as the restructuring of Illian's kingdoms. The orcs were defeated and from the ashes rose a new species: Drakes - half-dragon, half-elf.